PRAISE FOR SCOTT WESTERFELD'S

UGLIES

"With a beginning and ending that pack hefty punches, this introduction to a dystopic future promises an exciting series." —*Kirkus Reviews*, starred review

"The longing for fairy-tale beauty has never looked so sinister" —Amanda Craig, THE TIMES

"Fast paced, exciting and thought-provoking." —*The Bookseller's Choice*

"Superb sci-fi." —Amanda Craig, *The Times Supplement*

"Westerfeld introduces thought-provoking issues" —PUBLISHERS WEEKLY

"Highly readable . . . The cliff-hanger ending promises a sequel." —*School Library Journal*, starred review

"Teens will sink their teeth into the provocative questions about invasive technology, image-obsessed society, and the ethical quandaries of a mole-turned-ally . . . Ingenious." —*Booklist*, starred review

"Asks engaging questions about the meaning of beauty, individuality and betrayal. Highly recommended for SF fans or anyone who likes a good, thoughtful adventure." —*KLIATT*, starred review

ALA 2006 Best Books for Young Adults
ALA 2006 Popular Paperback for Young Adults
Kirkus Editor's Choice
SLJ Best Book of the Year

ALSO BY SCOTT WESTERFELD

Specials

Extras

Leviathan

Behemoth

Goliath

The Manual of Aeronautics:
An Illustrated Guide to the Leviathan Series

Afterworlds

Zeroes

SCOTT WESTERFELD

UGLIES & PRETTIES

SIMON & SCHUSTER

This paperback edition first published in the UK in 2015 by Simon & Schuster UK Ltd
A CBS COMPANY

Published in the USA in 2015 by Simon Pulse,
an imprint of Simon & Schuster Children's Division, New York.

1 3 5 7 9 10 8 6 4 2

Simon & Schuster UK Ltd
1st Floor, 222 Gray's Inn Road
London WC1X 8HB

www.simonandschuster.co.uk

Simon & Schuster Australia, Sydney
Simon & Schuster India, New Delhi

A CIP catalogue record for this book
is available from the British Library

ISBN 978-1-4711-4492-9

These titles were originally published individually by Simon & Schuster UK

A Letter to Readers

Ten years ago I began to write about Tally Youngblood, a teenage girl defined by her shifting identities. Across the Uglies trilogy, Tally takes on the roles of vandal, outcast, government informer, runaway, prisoner, hedonist, enforcer, and full-throated revolutionary. Several times her memories are erased, her personality reprogrammed, and her face and body remade.

And yet the most common line in my fan mail is simply "I *am* Tally."

It seems *Uglies* readers recognize themselves in this ever-changing character. They know what it's like to switch sides, to try on new selves, to be a little schizophrenic. Of course, these are all perfectly sensible responses to being a teenager—pushing back against expectations and fixed identities on the way to finding yourself.

So this tenth-anniversary edition is dedicated to those of you who were Tally for a while. And to those who still are Tally in some way, refusing to be defined by your tribe, by the body you were born with, or even by the face you woke up with this morning.

Thanks for all the fan mail, and for staying true to the uncertainty of who you are.

—Scott Westerfeld

UGLIES

This novel was shaped by a series of e-mail exchanges between myself and Ted Chiang about his story "Liking What You See: A Documentary." His input on the manuscript was also invaluable.

Part I
TURNING PRETTY

Is it not good to make society full
of beautiful people?
—Yang Yuan, quoted in the *New York Times*

NEW PRETTY TOWN

The early summer sky was the color of cat vomit.

Of course, Tally thought, you'd have to feed your cat only salmon-flavored cat food for a while, to get the pinks right. The scudding clouds did look a bit fishy, rippled into scales by a high-altitude wind. As the light faded, deep blue gaps of night peered through like an upside-down ocean, bottomless and cold.

Any other summer, a sunset like this would have been beautiful. But nothing had been beautiful since Peris turned pretty. Losing your best friend sucks, even if it's only for three months and two days.

Tally Youngblood was waiting for darkness.

She could see New Pretty Town through her open window. The

party towers were already lit up, and snakes of burning torches marked flickering pathways through the pleasure gardens. A few hot-air balloons pulled at their tethers against the darkening pink sky, their passengers shooting safety fireworks at other balloons and passing parasailers. Laughter and music skipped across the water like rocks thrown with just the right spin, their edges just as sharp against Tally's nerves.

Around the outskirts of the city, cut off from town by the black oval of the river, everything was in darkness. Everyone ugly was in bed by now.

Tally took off her interface ring and said, "Good night."

"Sweet dreams, Tally," said the room.

She chewed up a toothbrush pill, punched her pillows, and shoved an old portable heater—one that produced about as much warmth as a sleeping, Tally-size human being—under the covers.

Then she crawled out the window.

Outside, with the night finally turning coal black above her head, Tally instantly felt better. Maybe this was a stupid plan, but anything was better than another night awake in bed feeling sorry for herself. On the familiar leafy path down to the water's edge, it was easy to imagine Peris stealing silently behind her, stifling laughter, ready for a night of spying on the new pretties. Together. She and Peris had figured out how to trick the house minder back when they were twelve, when the three-month difference in their ages seemed like it would never matter.

"Best friends for life," Tally muttered, fingering the tiny scar on her right palm.

The water glistened through the trees, and she could hear the wavelets of a passing river skimmer's wake slapping at the shore. She ducked, hiding in the reeds. Summer was always the best time for spying expeditions. The grass was high, it was never cold, and you didn't have to stay awake through school the next day.

Of course, Peris could sleep as late as he wanted now. Just one of the advantages of being pretty.

The old bridge stretched massively across the water, its huge iron frame as black as the sky. It had been built so long ago that it held up its own weight, without any support from hoverstruts. A million years from now, when the rest of the city had crumbled, the bridge would probably remain like a fossilized bone.

Unlike the other bridges into New Pretty Town, the old bridge couldn't talk—or report trespassers, more importantly. But even silent, the bridge had always seemed very wise to Tally, as quietly knowing as some ancient tree.

Her eyes were fully adjusted to the darkness now, and it took only seconds to find the fishing line tied to its usual rock. She yanked it, and heard the splash of the rope tumbling from where it had been hidden among the bridge supports. She kept pulling until the invisible fishing line turned into wet, knotted cord. The other end was still tied to the iron framework of the bridge. Tally pulled the rope taut and lashed it to the usual tree.

She had to duck into the grass once more as another river skimmer passed. The people dancing on its deck didn't spot the rope stretched from bridge to shore. They never did. New pretties were always having too much fun to notice little things out of place.

When the skimmer's lights had faded, Tally tested the rope with her whole weight. One time it had pulled loose from the tree, and both she and Peris had swung downward, then up and out over the middle of the river before falling off, tumbling into the cold water. She smiled at the memory, realizing she would rather be on that expedition—soaking wet in the cold with Peris—than dry and warm tonight, but alone.

Hanging upside down, hands and knees clutching the knots along the rope, Tally pulled herself up into the dark framework of the bridge, then stole through its iron skeleton and across to New Pretty Town.

She knew where Peris lived from the one message he had bothered to send since turning pretty. Peris hadn't given an address, but Tally knew the trick for decoding the random-looking numbers at the bottom of a ping. They led to someplace called Garbo Mansion in the hilly part of town.

Getting there was going to be tricky. In their expeditions, Tally and Peris had always stuck to the waterfront, where vegetation and the dark backdrop of Uglyville made it easy to hide. But now Tally was headed into the center of the island, where floats and revelers populated the bright streets all night. Brand-new pretties like Peris always lived where the fun was most frantic.

Tally had memorized the map, but if she made one wrong turn, she was toast. Without her interface ring, she was invisible to vehicles. They'd just run her down like she was nothing.

Of course, Tally *was* nothing here.

Worse, she was ugly. But she hoped Peris wouldn't see it that way. Wouldn't see *her* that way.

Tally had no idea what would happen if she got caught. This wasn't like being busted for "forgetting" her ring, skipping classes, or tricking the house into playing her music louder than allowed. Everyone did that kind of stuff, and everyone got busted for it. But she and Peris had always been very careful about not getting caught on these expeditions. Crossing the river was serious business.

It was too late to worry now, though. What could they do to her, anyway? In three months she'd be a pretty herself.

Tally crept along the river until she reached a pleasure garden, and slipped into the darkness beneath a row of weeping willows. Under their cover she made her way alongside a path lit by little guttering flames.

A pretty couple wandered down the path. Tally froze, but they were clueless, too busy staring into each other's eyes to see her crouching in the darkness. Tally silently watched them pass, getting that warm feeling she always got from looking at a pretty face. Even when she and Peris used to spy on them from the shadows, giggling at all the stupid things the pretties said and did, they couldn't resist staring. There was something magic in their large and perfect eyes, something that made you want to pay attention to whatever they said, to protect them from any danger, to make them happy. They were so . . . pretty.

The two disappeared around the next bend, and Tally shook her head to clear the mushy thoughts away. She wasn't here to gawk. She was an infiltrator, a sneak, an ugly. And she had a mission.

The garden stretched up into town, winding like a black river through the bright party towers and houses. After a few more minutes of creeping, she startled a couple hidden among the trees (it was a *pleasure* garden, after all), but in the darkness they couldn't see her face, and only teased her as she mumbled an apology and slipped away. She hadn't seen too much of them, either, just a tangle of perfect legs and arms.

Finally, the garden ended, a few blocks from where Peris lived.

Tally peered out from behind a curtain of hanging vines. This was farther than she and Peris had ever been together, and as far as her planning had taken her. There was no way to hide herself in the busy, well-lit streets. She put her fingers up to her face, felt the wide nose and thin lips, the too-high forehead and tangled mass of frizzy hair. One step out of the underbrush and she'd be spotted. Her face seemed to burn as the light touched it. What was she doing here? She should be back in the darkness of Uglyville, awaiting her turn.

But she had to see Peris, had to talk to him. She wasn't quite sure why, exactly, except that she was sick of imagining a thousand conversations with him every night before she fell asleep. They'd spent every day together since they were littlies, and now . . . nothing. Maybe if they could just talk for a few minutes, her brain would stop talking to imaginary Peris. Three minutes might be enough to hold her for three months.

Tally looked up and down the street, checking for side yards to slink through, dark doorways to hide in. She felt like a rock climber facing a sheer cliff, searching for cracks and handholds.

The traffic began to clear a little, and she waited, rubbing the scar on her right palm. Finally, Tally sighed and whispered, "Best friends forever," and took a step forward into the light.

An explosion of sound came from her right, and she leaped back into the darkness, stumbling among the vines, coming down hard on her knees in the soft earth, certain for a few seconds that she'd been caught.

But the cacophony organized itself into a throbbing rhythm. It was a drum machine making its lumbering way down the street. Wide as a house, it shimmered with the movement of its dozens of mechanical arms, bashing away at every size of drum. Behind it trailed a growing bunch of revelers, dancing along with the beat, drinking and throwing their empty bottles to shatter against the huge, impervious machine.

Tally smiled. The revelers were wearing masks.

The machine was lobbing the masks out the back, trying to coax more followers into the impromptu parade: devil faces and horrible clowns, green monsters and gray aliens with big oval eyes, cats and dogs and cows, faces with crooked smiles or huge noses.

The procession passed slowly, and Tally pulled herself back into the vegetation. A few of the revelers passed close enough that the sickly sweetness from their bottles filled her nose. A minute later, when the machine had trundled half a block farther, Tally jumped out and snatched up a discarded mask from the street. The plastic was soft in her hand, still warm from having been stamped into shape inside the machine a few seconds before.

Before she pressed it against her face, Tally realized that it was the same color as the cat-vomit pink of the sunset, with a long snout and two pink little ears. Smart adhesive flexed against her skin as the mask settled onto her face.

Tally pushed her way through the drunken dancers, out the other side of the procession, and ran down a side street toward Garbo Mansion, wearing the face of a pig.

BEST FRIENDS FOREVER

Garbo Mansion was fat, bright, and loud.

It filled the space between a pair of party towers, a squat teapot between two slender glasses of champagne. Each of the towers rested on a single column no wider than an elevator. Higher up they swelled to five stories of circular balconies, crowded with new pretties. Tally climbed the hill toward the trio of buildings, trying to take in the view through the eyeholes of her mask.

Someone jumped, or was thrown, from one of the towers, screaming and flailing his arms. Tally gulped, forcing herself to watch all the way down, until the guy was caught by his bungee jacket a few seconds before splatting. He hover-bounced in the harness a few times, laughing, before being deposited softly on the ground, close enough to Tally that she could hear nervous hiccups breaking up his giggles. He'd been as scared as Tally.

She shivered, though jumping was hardly any more dangerous than standing here beneath the looming towers. The bungee jacket used the same lifters as the hoverstruts that held the spindly structures up. If all the pretty toys somehow stopped working, just about everything in New Pretty Town would come tumbling down.

The mansion was full of brand-new pretties—the worst kind, Peris always used to say. They lived like uglies, a hundred or so together in a big dorm. But this dorm didn't have any rules. Unless the rules were Act Stupid, Have Fun, and Make Noise.

A bunch of girls in ball gowns were on the roof, screaming at the top of their lungs, balancing on the edge and shooting safety fireworks at people on the ground. A ball of orange flame bounced next to Tally, cool as an autumn wind, driving away the darkness around her.

"Hey, there's a pig down there!" someone screamed from above. They all laughed, and Tally quickened her stride toward the wide-open door of the mansion. She pushed inside, ignoring the surprised looks of two pretties on their way out.

It was all one big party, just like they always promised it would be. People were dressed up tonight, in gowns and in black suits with long coattails. Everyone seemed to find her pig mask pretty funny. They pointed and laughed, and Tally kept moving, not giving them time to do anything else. Of course, everyone was always laughing here. Unlike an ugly party, there'd never be any fights, or even arguments.

She pushed from room to room, trying to distinguish faces without being distracted by those big pretty eyes, or overwhelmed by the feeling that she didn't belong. Tally felt uglier every second she spent there. Being laughed at by everyone she met wasn't helping much. But it was better than what they'd do if they saw her real face.

Tally wondered if she would even recognize Peris. She'd only seen him once since the operation, and that was coming out of the hospital, before the swelling had subsided. But she knew his face so well. Despite what Peris always used to say, pretties didn't really all look *exactly* the same. On their expeditions, she and Peris had sometimes spotted pretties who looked familiar, like uglies they'd known. Sort of like a brother or sister—an older, more confident, *much* prettier brother or sister. One you'd be jealous of your whole life, if you'd been born a hundred years ago.

Peris couldn't have changed that much.

"Have you seen the piggy?"

"The what?"

"There's a piggy on the loose!"

The giggling voices were from the floor below. Tally paused and listened. She was all alone here on the stairs. Apparently, pretties preferred the elevators.

"How dare she come to our party dressed like a piggy! This is white tie!"

"She's got the wrong party."

"She's got no manners, looking that way!"

Tally swallowed. The mask wasn't much better than her own face. The joke was wearing thin.

She bounded up the stairs, leaving the voices behind. Maybe they'd forget about her if she just kept moving. There were only two more floors of Garbo Mansion to go, and then the roof. Peris had to be here somewhere.

Unless he was out on the back lawn, or up in a balloon, or a party tower. Or in a pleasure garden somewhere, with someone. Tally shook away that last image and ran down the hall, ignoring the same jokes about her mask, risking glances into the rooms one by one.

Nothing but surprised looks and pointed fingers, and pretty faces. But none of them rang a bell. Peris wasn't anywhere.

"Here, piggy, piggy! Hey, there she is!"

Tally bolted up to the top floor, taking two stairs at a time. Her hard breathing had heated up the inside of the mask, her forehead sweating, the adhesive crawling as it tried to stay attached. They were following her now, a group of them, laughing and stumbling over one another up the stairs.

There wasn't any time to search this floor. Tally glanced up and down the hall. No one up here, anyway. The doors were all closed. Maybe a few pretties were actually getting their beauty sleep.

If she went up to the roof to check for Peris, she'd be trapped.

"Here, piggy, piggy!"

Time to run. Tally dashed toward the elevator, skidding to a halt inside. "Ground floor!" she ordered.

She waited, peering down the hall anxiously, panting into the hot plastic of her mask. "Ground floor!" she repeated. "Close door!"

Nothing happened.

She sighed, closing her eyes. Without an interface ring, she was nobody. The elevator wouldn't listen.

Tally knew how to trick an elevator, but it took time and a penknife. She had neither. The first of her pursuers emerged from the stairway, stumbling into the hall.

She threw herself backward against the elevator's side wall, standing on tiptoe and trying to flatten herself so they couldn't see her. More came up, huffing and puffing like typical out-of-shape pretties. Tally could watch them in the mirror at the back of the elevator.

Which meant they could also see *her* if they thought to look this way.

"Where'd the piggy go?"

"Here, piggy!"

"The roof, maybe?"

Someone stepped quietly into the elevator, looking back at the search party in bemusement. When he saw her, he jumped. "Goodness, you scared me!" He blinked his long lashes, regarding her masked face, then looked down at his own tailcoat. "Oh, dear. Wasn't this party white tie?"

Tally's breath caught, her mouth went dry. "Peris?" she whispered.

He looked at her closely. "Do I . . ."

She started to reach out, but remembered to press back flat

…muscles were screaming from standing on … eris."

… piggy, piggy!"

…e turned toward the voice down the hall, raised his eyebrows, …hen looked back at her. "Close door. Hold," he said quickly.

The door slid shut, and Tally stumbled forward. She pulled off her mask to see him better. It was Peris: his voice, his brown eyes, the way his forehead crinkled when he was confused.

But he was so *pretty* now.

At school, they explained how it affected you. It didn't matter if you knew about evolution or not—it worked anyway. On everyone.

There was a certain kind of beauty, a prettiness that everyone could see. Big eyes and full lips like a kid's; smooth, clear skin; symmetrical features; and a thousand other little clues. Somewhere in the backs of their minds, people were always looking for these markers. No one could help seeing them, no matter how they were brought up. A million years of evolution had made it part of the human brain.

The big eyes and lips said: I'm young and vulnerable, I can't hurt you, and you want to protect me. And the rest said: I'm healthy, I won't make you sick. And no matter how you felt about a pretty, there was a part of you that thought: *If we had kids, they'd be healthy too. I* want *this pretty person. . . .*

It was biology, they said at school. Like your heart beating, you couldn't help believing all these things, not when you saw a face like this. A pretty face.

A face like Peris's.

"It's me," Tally said.

Peris took a step back, his eyebrows rising. He looked down at her clothes.

Tally realized she was wearing her baggy black expedition outfit, muddy from crawling up ropes and through gardens, from falling among the vines. Peris's suit was deep black velvet, his shirt, vest, and tie all glowing white.

She pulled away. "Oh, sorry. I won't get you muddy."

"What are you *doing* here, Tally?"

"I just—," she sputtered. Now that she was facing him, she didn't know what to say. All the imagined conversations had melted away into his big, sweet eyes. "I had to know if we were still . . ."

Tally held out her right hand, the scarred palm facing up, sweaty dirt tracing the lines on it.

Peris sighed. He wasn't looking at her hand, or into her eyes. Not into her squinty, narrow-set, indifferently brown eyes. Nobody eyes. "Yeah," he said. "But, I mean—couldn't you have waited, Squint?"

Her ugly nickname sounded strange coming from a pretty. Of course, it would be even weirder to call him Nose, as she used to about a hundred times a day. She swallowed. "Why didn't you write me?"

"I tried. But it just felt bogus. I'm so different now."

"But we're . . ." She pointed at her scar.

"Take a look, Tally." He held out his own hand.

The skin of his palm was smooth and unblemished. It was a hand that said: *I don't have to work very hard, and I'm too clever to have accidents.*

The scar that they had made together was gone.

"They took it away."

"Of course they did, Squint. All my skin's new."

Tally blinked. She hadn't thought of that.

He shook his head. "You're such a kid still."

"Elevator requested," said the elevator. "Up or down?"

Tally jumped at the machine voice.

"Hold, please," Peris said calmly.

Tally swallowed and closed her hand into a fist. "But they didn't change your blood. We shared that, no matter what."

Peris finally looked directly at her face, not flinching as she had feared he would. He smiled beautifully. "No, they didn't. New skin, big deal. And in three months we can laugh about this. Unless . . ."

"Unless what?" She looked up into his big brown eyes, so full of concern.

"Just promise me that you won't do any more stupid tricks," Peris said. "Like coming here. Something that'll get you into trouble. I want to see you pretty."

"Of course."

"So promise me."

Peris was only three months older than Tally, but, dropping her eyes to the floor, she felt like a littlie again. "All right, I promise. Nothing stupid. And they won't catch me tonight, either."

"Okay, get your mask and . . ." His voice trailed off.

She turned her gaze to where it had fallen. Discarded, the

plastic mask had recycled itself, turning into pink dust, which the carpet in the elevator was already filtering away.

The two stared at each other in silence.

"Elevator requested," the machine insisted. "Up or down?"

"Peris, I promise they won't catch me. No pretty can run as fast as me. Just take me down to the—"

Peris shook his head. "Up, please. Roof."

The elevator moved.

"Up? Peris, how am I going to—"

"Straight out the door, in a big rack—bungee jackets. There's a whole bunch in case of a fire."

"You mean jump?" Tally swallowed. Her stomach did a backflip as the elevator came to a halt.

Peris shrugged. "I do it all the time, Squint." He winked. "You'll love it."

His expression made his pretty face glow even more, and Tally leaped forward to wrap her arms around him. He still felt the same, at least, maybe a bit taller and thinner. But he was warm and solid, and still Peris.

"Tally!"

She stumbled back as the doors opened. She'd left mud all over his white vest. "Oh, no! I'm—"

"Just go!"

His distress just made Tally want to hug him again. She wanted to stay and clean Peris up, make sure he looked perfect for the party. She reached out a hand. "I—"

"Go!"

"But we're best friends, right?"

He sighed, dabbing at a brown stain. "Sure, forever. In three months."

She turned and ran, the doors closing behind her.

At first no one noticed her on the roof. They were all looking down. It was dark except for the occasional flare of a safety sparkler.

Tally found the rack of bungee jackets and pulled at one. It was clipped to the rack. Her fingers fumbled, looking for a clasp. She wished she had her interface ring to give her instructions.

Then she saw the button: PRESS IN CASE OF FIRE.

"Oh, crap," she said.

Her shadow jumped and jittered. Two pretties were coming toward her, carrying sparklers.

"Who's that? What's she wearing?"

"Hey, you! This party is white tie!"

"Look at her face. . . ."

"Oh, crap," Tally repeated.

And pressed the button.

An ear-shattering siren split the air, and the bungee jacket seemed to jump from the rack into her hand. She slid into the harness, turning to face the two pretties. They leaped back as if she'd transformed into a werewolf. One dropped the sparkler, and it extinguished itself instantly.

"Fire drill," Tally said, and ran toward the edge of the roof.

Once she had the jacket around her shoulders, the strap and

zippers seemed to wind around her like snakes until the plastic was snug around her waist and thighs. A green light flashed on the collar, right where she couldn't help but see it.

"Good jacket," she said.

It wasn't smart enough to answer, apparently.

The pretties playing on the roof had all gone silent and were milling around, wondering if there really was a fire. They pointed at her, and Tally heard the word "ugly" on their lips.

What was worse in New Pretty Town, she wondered? Your mansion burning down, or an ugly crashing your party?

Tally reached the edge of the roof, vaulted up onto the rail, and teetered for a moment. Below her, pretties were starting to spill out of Garbo Mansion onto the lawn and down the hill. They were looking back up, searching for smoke or flames. All they saw was her.

It was a long way down, and Tally's stomach already seemed to be in free fall. But she was thrilled, too. The shrieking siren, the crowd gazing up at her, the lights of New Pretty Town all spread out below like a million candles.

Tally took a deep breath and bent her knees, readying herself to jump.

For a split second, she wondered if the jacket would work since she wasn't wearing an interface ring. Would it hover-bounce for a nobody? Or would she just splat?

But she had promised Peris she wouldn't get caught. And the jacket was for emergencies, and there *was* a green light on. . . .

"Heads up!" Tally shouted.

And jumped.

SHAY

The siren faded behind her. It seemed like forever—or only seconds—that Tally fell, the gaping faces below becoming larger and larger.

The ground hurtled toward her, a space opening in the panicking crowd where she was going to hit. For a few moments it was just like a flying dream, silent and wonderful.

Then reality jerked at her shoulders and thighs, the webbing of the jacket cutting viciously into her. She was taller than pretty standard, she knew; the jacket probably wasn't expecting this much weight.

Tally somersaulted in the air, turning headfirst for a few terrifying moments, her face passing low enough to spot a discarded bottle cap in the grass. Then she found herself shooting upward again, completing the circle, so that the sky wheeled above her, then over and downward again, more crowd parting in front.

Perfect. She had pushed off hard enough that she was bouncing down the hill away from Garbo Mansion, the jacket carrying her toward the darkness and safety of the gardens.

Tally spun head over heels twice more, and then the jacket lowered her to the grass. She pulled randomly at straps until the garment made a hissing sound and dropped to the ground.

Her dizziness took a moment to clear as she tried to sort up from down.

"Isn't she . . . ugly?" someone asked from the edge of the crowd.

The black shapes of two firefighting hovercars zoomed past overhead, red lights flashing and sirens piercing her ears.

"Great idea, Peris," she muttered. "A false alarm." She would really be in trouble if they caught her now. She'd never even *heard* of anyone doing anything this bad.

Tally ran toward the garden.

The darkness below the willows was comforting.

Down here, halfway to the river, Tally could barely tell there was a full-scale fire alert in the middle of town. But she could see that a search was underway. More hovercars were in the air than usual, and the river seemed to be lit up extra bright. Maybe that was just a coincidence.

But probably not.

Tally made her way carefully through the trees. It was later than she and Peris had ever stayed over in New Pretty Town. The pleasure gardens were more crowded, especially the dark parts. And now that the excitement of her escape had worn off, Tally was beginning to realize how stupid the whole idea had been.

Of course Peris didn't have the scar anymore. The two of them had only used a penknife when they'd cut themselves and held hands. The doctors used much sharper and bigger knives in the operation. They rubbed you raw, and you grew all new skin, perfect and clear. The old marks of accidents and bad food and childhood illnesses all washed away. A clean start.

But Tally had ruined Peris's starting over—showing up like some pesky littlie who's not wanted, and leaving him with the bad taste of ugly in his mouth, not to mention covered with mud. She hoped he had another vest to change into.

At least Peris hadn't seemed too angry. He'd said they'd be best friends again, once she was pretty. But the way he'd looked at her face . . . maybe that was why they separated uglies from pretties. It must be horrible to see an ugly face when you're surrounded by such beautiful people all the time. What if she'd ruined everything tonight, and Peris would always see her like this—squinty eyes and frizzy hair—even after she had the operation?

A hovercar passed overhead, and Tally ducked. She was probably going to get caught tonight, and never be turned pretty at all.

She deserved it for being so stupid.

Tally reminded herself of her promise to Peris. She was *not* going to get caught; she had to become pretty for him.

A light flashed in the corner of her vision. Tally crouched and peered through the hanging willow leaves.

A safety warden was in the park. She was a middle pretty, not a new one. In the firelight, the handsome features of the second operation were obvious: broad shoulders and a firm jaw, a sharp nose and high cheekbones. The woman carried the same unquestionable authority as Tally's teachers back in Uglyville.

Tally swallowed. New pretties had their own wardens. There was only one reason why a middle pretty would be here in New Pretty Town: The wardens were looking for someone, and they were serious about finding him or her.

The woman flashed her light at a couple on a bench, illuminating them for the split second it took to confirm that they were pretty. The couple jumped, but the warden chuckled and apologized. Tally could hear her low, sure voice, and saw the new pretties relax. Everything had to be okay if she said it was.

Tally felt herself wanting to give up, to throw herself on the wise mercy of the warden. If she just explained, the warden would understand and fix everything. Middle pretties always knew what to do.

But she had promised Peris.

Tally pulled back into the darkness, trying to ignore the horrible feeling that she was a spy, a sneak, for not surrendering to the woman's authority. She moved through the brush as fast as she could.

Close to the river, Tally heard a noise in front of her. A dark form was outlined in river lights before her. Not a couple, a lone figure in the dark.

It had to be a warden, waiting for her in the brush.

Tally hardly dared breathe. She had frozen in midcrawl, her weight all poised on one knee and one muddy hand. The warden hadn't seen her yet. If Tally waited long enough, maybe the warden would move on.

She waited, motionless, for endless minutes. The figure didn't budge. They must know that the gardens were the only dark way in and out of New Pretty Town.

Tally's arm started to shake, the muscles complaining about staying frozen for so long. But she didn't dare let her weight settle onto the other arm. The snap of a single twig would give her away.

She held herself still, until all her muscles were screaming. Maybe the warden was just a trick of the light. Maybe this was all in her imagination.

Tally blinked, trying to make the figure disappear.

But it was still there, clearly outlined by the rippling lights of the river.

A twig popped under her knee—Tally's aching muscles had finally betrayed her. But the figure *still* didn't move. He or she must have heard. . . .

The warden was being kind, waiting for her to give herself up. Letting her surrender. The teachers did that at school, sometimes. Made you realize that you couldn't escape, until you confessed everything.

Tally cleared her throat. A small, pathetic sound. "I'm sorry," she said.

The figure let out a sigh. "Oh, phew. Hey, that's okay. I must have scared you, too." The girl leaned forward, grimacing as if she was also sore from remaining still so long. Her face caught the light.

She was ugly too.

Her name was Shay. She had long dark hair in pigtails, and her eyes were too wide apart. Her lips were full enough, but she was even skinnier than a new pretty. She'd come over to New Pretty Town on her own expedition, and had been hiding here by the river for an hour. "I've never seen anything like this," she whispered. "There's wardens and hovercars everywhere!"

Tally cleared her throat. "I think it's my fault."

Shay looked dubious. "How'd you manage that?"

"Well, I was up in the middle of town, at a party."

"You crashed a party? That's crazy!" Shay said, then lowered her voice back to a whisper. "Crazy, but awesome. How'd you get in?"

"I was wearing a mask."

"Wow. A pretty mask?"

"Uh, more like a pig mask. It's a long story."

Shay blinked. "A pig mask. Okay. So let me guess, someone blew your house down?"

"Huh? No. I was about to get caught, so I kind of . . . set off a fire alarm."

"Nice trick!"

Tally smiled. It was actually a pretty good story, now that she had someone to tell it to. "And I was trapped up on the roof, so I grabbed a bungee jacket and jumped off. I hover-bounced halfway here."

"No way!"

"Well, part of the way here, anyhow."

"Pretty awesome." Shay smiled, then her face went serious. She bit at one of her fingernails, which was one of those bad habits that the operation cured. "So, Tally, were you at this party . . . to see someone?"

It was Tally's turn to be impressed. "How'd you figure that out?"

Shay sighed, looking down at her ragged nails. "I've got friends too, over here. I mean, they *were* friends. Sometimes I spy on them." She looked up. "I was always the youngest, you know? And now—"

"You're all alone."

Shay nodded. "It's sounds like you did more than spy, though."

"Yeah. I kind of said hello."

"Wow, that's crazy. Your boyfriend or something?"

Tally shook her head. Peris had gone with other girls, and Tally had dealt with it and tried to do the same, but their friendship had always been the main thing in both their lives. Not anymore, apparently.

"If he'd been my boyfriend, I don't think I could have done it, you know? I wouldn't have wanted him to see my face. But because we're friends, I thought maybe . . ."

"Yeah. So how'd it go?"

Tally thought for a second, looking out at the rippling water. Peris had been so pretty, and grown-up looking, and he'd said they'd be friends again. Once Tally was pretty too . . . "Basically, it sucked," she said.

"Thought so."

"Except getting away. That part was very cool."

"Sounds like it." Tally heard the smile in Shay's voice. "Very tricky."

They were silent for a moment as a hovercar went over.

"But you know, we haven't totally gotten away yet," Shay said. "Next time you're going to pull a fire alarm, let me know ahead of time."

"Sorry about getting you trapped here."

Shay looked at her and frowned. "Not that. I just meant if I'm going to have to do the running-away part, I might as well get in on the fun."

Tally laughed softly. "Okay. Next time, I'll let you know."

"Please do." Shay scanned the river. "Looks a little clearer now. Where's your board?"

"My what?"

Shay pulled a hoverboard from under a bush. "You've got a board, right? What'd you do, swim over?"

"No, I . . . hey, wait. How'd you get a hoverboard to take you across the river?" Anything that flew had minders all over it.

Shay laughed. "That's the oldest trick in the book. I figured you'd know all about it."

Tally shrugged. "I don't board much."

"Well, this one'll take both of us."

"Wait, shhh."

Another hovercar had come into view, cruising down the river just above the height of the bridges.

Tally waited for a count of ten after it had passed before she spoke. "I don't think it's a good idea, flying back."

"So how *did* you get over?"

"Follow me." Tally rose from her crouch onto hands and knees, and crawled a bit ahead. She looked back. "Can you carry that thing?"

"Sure. It doesn't weigh much." Shay snapped her fingers, and the hoverboard drifted upward. "Actually, it doesn't weigh *anything*, unless I tell it to."

"That's handy."

Shay started to crawl, the board bouncing along behind her like a littlie's balloon. Tally couldn't see any string, though. "So, where're we going?" Shay asked.

"I know a bridge."

"But it'll tattle."

"Not this one. It's an old friend."

WIPE OUT

Tally fell off. Again.

The spill didn't hurt so much, this time. The moment her feet slipped off the hoverboard, she'd relaxed, the way Shay kept telling her to. Spinning out wasn't much worse than having your dad swing you around by the wrists when you were little.

If your dad happened to be a superhuman freak and was trying to pull your arms out of their sockets.

But the momentum had to go somewhere, Shay had explained. And around in circles was better than into a tree. Here in Cleopatra Park there were plenty of those.

After a few rotations, Tally found herself being lowered to the grass by her wrists, dizzy but in one piece.

Shay cruised up, banking her hoverboard to an elegant stop as if she'd been born on one.

"That looked a little better."

"It didn't *feel* any better." Tally pulled off one crash bracelet and rubbed her wrist. It was turning red, and her fingers felt weak.

The bracelet was heavy and solid in her hand. Crash bracelets had to have metal inside, because they worked on magnets, the way the boards did. Whenever Tally's feet slipped, the bracelets got all hovery and caught her fall, like some friendly giant plucking her from danger and swinging her to a halt.

By her wrists. Again.

Tally pulled the other bracelet off and rubbed.

"Don't give up. You almost made it!"

Tally's board cruised back on its own, nuzzling at her ankles like an apologetic dog. She crossed her arms and rubbed her shoulders. "I almost got snapped in two, you mean."

"Never happens. I've spilled more times than a glass of milk on a roller coaster."

"On a *what*?"

"Never mind. Come on, one more try."

Tally sighed. It wasn't just her wrists. Her knees ached from banking hard, whipping through turns so quickly that her body seemed to weigh a ton. Shay called that "high gravity," which happened every time a fast-moving object changed direction.

"Hoverboarding *looks* so fun, like being a bird. But actually doing it is hard work."

Shay shrugged. “Being a bird’s probably hard work too. Flapping your wings all day, you know?”

“Maybe. Does it get any better?”

“For birds? I don’t know. On a board? Definitely.”

“I hope so.” Tally pulled her bracelets on and stepped onto the hoverboard. It bobbed a little as it adjusted to her weight, like the bounce of a diving board.

“Check your belly sensor.”

Tally touched her belly ring, where Shay had clipped the little sensor. It told the board where Tally’s center of gravity was, and which way she was facing. The sensor even read her stomach muscles, which, it turned out, hoverboarders always clenched in anticipation of turns. The board was smart enough to gradually learn how her body moved. The more Tally rode, the more it would keep itself under her feet.

Of course, Tally had to learn too. Shay kept saying that if your feet weren’t in the right place, the smartest board in the world couldn’t keep you on. The riding surface was all knobbly for traction, but it was amazing how easy it was to slip off.

The board was oval-shaped, about half as long as Tally was tall, and black with the silver spots of a cheetah—the only animal in the world that could run faster than a hoverboard could fly. It was Shay’s first board, and she’d never recycyled it. Until today, it had hung on the wall above her bed.

Tally snapped her fingers, bent her knees as she rose into the air, then leaned forward to pick up speed.

Shay cruised along just above her, staying a little behind.

The trees started to rush by, whipping Tally's arms with the sharp stings of evergreen needles. The board wouldn't let her crash into anything solid, but it didn't get too concerned about twigs.

"Extend your arms. Keep your feet apart!" Shay yelled for the thousandth time. Tally nervously scooted her left foot forward.

At the end of the park, Tally leaned to her right, and the board pulled into a long, steep turn. She bent her knees, growing heavy as she cut back toward where they'd started.

Now Tally was rushing toward the slalom flags, crouching as she drew closer. She could feel the wind drying her lips, lifting her ponytail up.

"Oh, boy," she whispered.

The board raced past the first flag, and she leaned hard right, her arms all the way out now for balance.

"Switch!" cried Shay. Tally twisted her body to bring the board under her and across, cutting around the next flag. Once it was past, she twisted again.

But her feet were too close together. Not again! Her shoes slipped across the surface of the board. "No!" she cried, clenching her toes, cupping the air with her palms, anything to keep herself on board. Her right shoe slid toward the board's edge until her toes were silhouetted against the trees.

The trees! She was almost sideways, her body parallel with the ground.

The slalom flag zoomed past, and suddenly, it was over. The board swung back under Tally as her course straightened out again.

She'd made the turn!

Tally spun to face Shay. "I did it!" she cried.

And fell.

Confused by her spin, the board had tried to execute a turn, and dumped her. Tally relaxed as her arms jerked straight and the world spun around her. She was laughing as she descended to the grass, dangling by her bracelets.

Shay was also laughing. "*Almost* did it."

"No! I got around the flags. You saw!"

"Okay, okay. You made it." Shay laughed, stepping off onto the grass. "But don't dance around like that afterward. It's not cool, Squint."

Tally stuck out her tongue. In the last week, Tally had learned that Shay only used her ugly nickname as a put-down. Shay insisted they call each other by their real names most of the time, which Tally had quickly gotten used to. She liked it, actually. Nobody but Sol and Ellie—her parents—and a few stuck-up teachers had ever called her "Tally" before.

"Whatever you say, Skinny. That was great."

Tally collapsed on the grass. Her whole body ached, every muscle exhausted. "Thanks for the lesson. Flying's the best."

Shay sat down close by. "Never bored on a hoverboard."

"This is the best I've felt since . . ." Tally didn't say his name. She looked up into the sky, which was a glorious blue. A perfect sky. They hadn't gotten started until late afternoon. Above, a few high clouds were already showing hints of pink, even though sunset was hours off.

"Yeah," Shay agreed. "Me too. I was getting sick of hanging out alone."

"So how long you got?"

Shay answered instantly. "Two months and twenty-six days."

Tally was stunned for a moment. "Are you sure?"

"'Course I'm sure."

Tally felt a big, slow smile roll across her face, and she fell back onto the grass, laughing. "You've got to be kidding. We've got the same birthday!"

"No way."

"Yeah, way. It's perfect. We'll both turn pretty together!"

Shay was silent for a moment. "Yeah, I guess."

"September ninth, right?"

Shay nodded.

"That is so cool. I mean, I don't think I could stand to lose another friend. You know? We don't have to worry about one of us abandoning the other. Not for a single day."

Shay sat up straight, her smile gone. "I wouldn't do that, anyway."

Tally blinked. "I didn't say you would, but . . ."

"But what?"

"But when you turn, you go over to New Pretty Town."

"So? Pretties are allowed to come back over here, you know. Or write."

Tally snorted. "But they don't."

"I would." Shay looked out over the river at the spires of the party towers, placing a thumbnail firmly between her teeth.

"So would I, Shay. I'd come see you."

"Are you sure?"

"Yeah. Really."

Shay shrugged, and lay back down to stare up at the clouds. "Okay. But you're not the first person to make that promise, you know."

"Yeah, I do know."

They were silent for a moment. Clouds rolled slowly across the sun, and the air grew cool. Tally thought of Peris, and tried to remember the way he used to look back when he was Nose. Somehow, she couldn't recall his ugly face anymore. As if those few minutes of seeing him pretty had wiped out a lifetime of memories. All she could see now was pretty Peris, those eyes, that smile.

"I wonder why they never come back," Shay said. "Just to visit."

Tally swallowed. "Because we're so ugly, Skinny, that's why."

FACING THE FUTURE

"Here's option two." Tally touched her interface ring, and the wallscreen changed.

This Tally was sleek, with ultrahigh cheekbones, deep green catlike eyes, and a wide mouth that curled into a knowing smile.

"That's, uh, pretty different."

"Yeah. I doubt it's even legal." Tally tweaked the eye-shape parameters, pulling the arch of the eyebrows down almost to normal. Some cities allowed exotic operations—for new pretties only—but the authorities here were notoriously conservative. She doubted a doctor would give this morpho a second glance, but it was fun to push the software to its limits. "You think I look too scary?"

"No. You look like a real pussycat." Shay giggled. "Unfortunately, I mean that in the literal, dead-mouse-eating sense."

"Okay, moving right along."

The next Tally was a much more standard morphological model, with almond-shaped brown eyes, straight black hair with long bangs, the dark lips set to maximum fullness.

"Pretty generic, Tally."

"Oh, come on! I worked on this one for a long time. I think I'd look great this way. There's a whole Cleopatra thing going on."

"You know," Shay said, "I read that the real Cleopatra wasn't even that great-looking. She seduced everyone with how clever she was."

"Yeah, right. And you've seen a picture of her?"

"They didn't have cameras back then, Squint."

"Duh. So how do you know she was ugly?"

"Because that's what historians wrote at the time."

Tally shrugged. "She was probably a classic pretty and they didn't even know it. Back then, they had weird ideas about beauty. They didn't know about biology."

"Lucky them." Shay stared out the window.

"So, if you think all my faces are so crappy, why don't you show me some of yours?" Tally cleared the wallscreen and leaned back on the bed.

"I can't."

"You can dish it out, but you can't take it, huh?"

"No, I mean I just can't. I never made one."

Tally's jaw dropped. Everyone made morphos, even littlies, too young for their facial structure to have set. It was a great waste of a day, figuring out all the different ways you could look when you finally became pretty.

"Not even one?"

"Maybe when I was little. But my friends and I stopped doing that kind of stuff a long time ago."

"Well." Tally sat up. "We should fix that right now."

"I'd rather go hoverboarding." Shay tugged anxiously under her shirt. Tally figured that Shay slept with her belly sensor on, hoverboarding in her dreams.

"Later, Shay. I can't believe you don't have a single morph. *Please.*"

"It's stupid. The doctors pretty much do what they want, no matter what you tell them."

"I know, but it's *fun.*"

Shay made a big point of rolling her eyes, but finally nodded. She dragged herself off the bed and plopped down in front of the wallscreen, pulling her hair back from her face.

Tally snorted. "So you *have* done this before."

"Like I said, when I was a littlie."

"Sure." Tally turned her interface ring to bring up a menu on the wallscreen, and blinked her way through a set of eyemouse choices. The screen's camera flickered with laser light, and a green grid sprang up on Shay's face, a field of tiny squares imposed across the shape of her cheekbones, nose, lips, and forehead.

Seconds later, two faces appeared on the screen. Both of them were Shay, but there were obvious differences: One looked wild, slightly angry; the other had a slightly distant expression, like someone having a daydream.

"It's weird how that works, isn't it?" Tally said. "Like two different people."

Shay nodded. "Creepy."

Ugly faces were always asymmetrical; neither half looked exactly like the other. So the first thing the morpho software did was take each side of your face and double it, like holding a mirror right down the middle, creating two examples of perfect symmetry. Already, both of the symmetrical Shays looked better than the original.

"So, Shay, which do you think is your good side?"

"Why do I have to be symmetrical? I'd rather have a face with two different sides."

Tally groaned. "That's a sign of childhood stress. No one wants to look at that."

"Gee, I wouldn't want to look stressed," Shay snorted, and pointed at the wilder-looking face. "Okay, whatever. The right one's better, don't you think?"

"I *hate* my right side. I always start with the left."

"Yeah, well, I happen to like my right side. Looks tougher."

"Okay. You're the boss."

Tally blinked, and the right-side face filled the screen.

"First, the basics." The software took over: The eyes gradually grew, reducing the size of the nose between them, Shay's cheekbones moved upward, and her lips became a tiny bit fuller (they were already almost pretty-sized). Every blemish disappeared, her skin turning flawlessly smooth. The skull moved subtly under the features, the angle of her forehead tilting back, her chin becoming more defined, her jaw stronger.

When it was done, Tally whistled. "Wow, that's pretty good already."

"Great," Shay groaned. "I totally look like every other new pretty in the world."

"Well, sure, we just got started. How about some hair on you?" Tally blinked through menus quickly, picking a style at random.

When the wallscreen changed, Shay fell over on the floor in a fit of giggles. The high hairdo towered over her thin face like dunce cap, the white-blond hair utterly incongruous with her olive skin.

Tally could hardly manage to speak through her own laughter. "Okay, maybe not that." She flipped through more styles, settling on basic hair, dark and short. "Let's get the face right first."

She tweaked the eyebrows, making their arch more dramatic, and added roundness to the cheeks. Shay was still too skinny, even after the morpho software had pulled her toward the average.

"And maybe a bit lighter?" Tally took the shade of the skin closer to baseline.

"Hey, Squint," Shay said. "Whose face is this, anyway?"

"Just playing," Tally said. "You want to take a shot?"

"No, I want to go hoverboarding."

"Sure, great. But first let's get this right."

"What do you mean 'get it right,' Tally? Maybe I think my face is already right!"

"Yeah, it's great." Tally rolled her eyes. "For an ugly."

Shay scowled. "What, can't you stand me? Do you need to get some picture into your head so you can imagine it instead of my face?"

"Shay! Come on. It's just for fun."

"Making ourselves feel ugly is not fun."

"We *are* ugly!"

"This whole game is just designed to make us hate ourselves."

Tally groaned and flopped back onto her bed, glaring up at the ceiling. Shay could be so weird sometimes. She always had a chip on her shoulder about the operation, like someone was *making* her turn sixteen. "Right, and things were so great back when everyone was ugly. Or did you miss that day in school?"

"Yeah, yeah, I know," Shay recited. "Everyone judged everyone else based on their appearance. People who were taller got better jobs, and people even voted for some politicians just because they weren't quite as ugly as everybody else. Blah, blah, blah."

"Yeah, and people killed one another over stuff like having different skin color." Tally shook her head. No matter how many times they repeated it at school, she'd never really quite believed that one. "So what if people look more alike now? It's the only way to make people equal."

"How about making them smarter?"

Tally laughed. "Fat chance. Anyway, it's just to see what you and I will look like in only . . . two months and fifteen days."

"Can't we just wait until then?"

Tally closed her eyes, sighing. "Sometimes I don't think I can."

"Well, tough luck." She felt Shay's weight on the bed and a light punch on her arm. "Hey, might as well make the best of it. Can we go hoverboarding now? Please?"

Tally opened her eyes and saw that her friend was smiling.

"Okay: hoverboard." She sat up and glanced at the screen. Even without much work, Shay's face was already welcoming, vulnerable, healthy . . . pretty. "Don't you think you're beautiful?"

Shay didn't look, just shrugged. "That's not me. It's some committee's idea of me."

Tally smiled and hugged her.

"It will be you, though. *Really* you. Soon."

PRETTY BORING

"I think you're ready."

Tally cruised to a stop—right foot down, left foot up, bend the knees.

"Ready for what?"

Shay drifted slowly past, letting the breeze tug her along. They were as high up and far out as hoverboards would go, just above treetop level, at the edge of town. It was amazing how quickly Tally had gotten used to being up high, with nothing but a board and bracelets between her and a long fall.

The view from up here was fantastic. Behind them the spires of New Pretty Town rose from the center of town, and around them was the greenbelt, a swath of forest that separated the middle and the late pretties from the youngsters. Older generations of pretties lived out in the suburbs, hidden by the hills, in rows of big houses separated by strips of private garden for their littlies to play in.

Shay smiled. "Ready for a night ride."

"Oh. Look, I don't know if I want to cross the river again," Tally said, remembering her promise to Peris. She and Shay had shown each other a lot of tricks over the last three weeks, but they hadn't been back into New Pretty Town since the night they'd met. "Until we get turned, of course. After last time, the wardens are probably all—"

"I wasn't talking about New Pretty Town," Shay interrupted. "That place is boring, anyway. We'd have to sneak around all night."

"Okay. You mean just board around Uglyville."

Shay shook her head, still coasting gradually away on the breeze.

Tally shifted her weight on the board uncomfortably. "Where else is there?"

Shay put her hands in her pockets and spread her arms, turning her dorm's team jacket into a sail. The breeze pulled her farther away from Tally. By reflex, Tally tipped her toes forward so that her board would keep up.

"Well, there's out there." Shay nodded at the open land before them.

"The suburbs? That's dullsville."

"Not the burbs. Past them." Shay slid her feet in opposite directions, to the very edges of the board. Her skirt caught the cool evening wind, which tugged her away even faster. She was drifting toward the outer edge of the greenbelt. Off-limits.

Tally planted her feet and dipped the board, and pulled up next to her friend. "What do you mean? Outside the city completely?"

"Yeah."

"That's crazy. There's nothing out there."

"There's plenty out there. Real trees, hundreds of years old. Mountains. And the ruins. Ever been there?"

Tally blinked. "Of course."

"I don't mean on a school trip, Tally. You ever been there at night?"

Tally brought her board to a sharp halt. The Rusty Ruins were the remains of an old city, a hulking reminder of back when there'd been way too many people, and everyone was incredibly stupid. And ugly. "No way. Don't tell me you have."

Shay nodded.

Tally's mouth dropped open. "That's impossible."

"You think you're the only one who knows good tricks?"

"Well, maybe I believe you," Tally said. Shay had that look on her face, the one Tally had learned to watch out for. "But what if we get busted?"

Shay laughed. "Tally, there's nothing out there, like you just said. Nothing and no one to bust us."

"Do hoverboards even work out there? Does anything?"

"Special ones do, if you know how to trick them, and where to ride. And getting past the burbs is easy. You take the river the whole way. Farther upstream it's white water, too rough for skimmers."

Tally's mouth dropped open again. "You really have done this before."

A gust of wind billowed in Shay's jacket, and she slid farther away, still smiling. Tally had to lean her board into motion again to stay within earshot. A treetop brushed her ankles as the ground below them started to rise.

"It'll be really fun," Shay called.

"Sounds too risky."

"Come on. I've been wanting to show you this since we met. Since you told me you crashed a pretty party—and pulled a fire alarm!"

Tally swallowed, wishing she'd told the whole truth about that night—about how it had all just sort of *happened*. Shay seemed to think she was the world's biggest daredevil now. "Well, I mean, that alarm thing was partly an accident. Kind of."

"Yeah, sure."

"I mean, maybe we should wait. It's only a couple of months now."

"Oh, that's right," Shay said. "A couple of months and we'll be stuck inside the river. Pretty and boring."

Tally snorted. "I don't think it's exactly boring, Shay."

"Doing what you're supposed to do is *always* boring. I can't imagine anything worse than being required to have fun."

"I can," Tally said quietly. "Never having any."

"Listen, Tally, these two months are our last chance to do anything really cool. To be ourselves. Once we turn, it's new pretty, middle pretty, late pretty." Shay dropped her arms, and her board stopped drifting. "Then dead pretty."

"Better than dead ugly," Tally said.

Shay shrugged and opened her jacket into a sail again. They

weren't far from the edge of the greenbelt now. Soon Shay would get a warning. Then her board would tattle.

"Besides," Tally argued, "just because we get the operation doesn't mean we can't do stuff like this."

"But pretties never do, Tally. Never."

Tally sighed, tipping her feet again to follow. "Maybe that's because they have better stuff to do than kid tricks. Maybe partying in town is better than hanging out in a bunch of old ruins."

Shay's eyes flashed. "Or maybe when they do the operation—when they grind and stretch your bones to the right shape, peel off your face and rub all your skin away, and stick in plastic cheekbones so you look like everybody else—maybe after going through all that you just aren't very interesting anymore."

Tally flinched. She'd never heard the operation described that way. Even in bio class, where they went into the details, it didn't sound that bad. "Come on, we won't even know it's happening. You just have pretty dreams the whole time."

"Yeah, sure."

A voice came into Tally's head: *"Warning, restricted area."* The wind was turning cold as the sun dropped.

"Come on, Shay, let's go back down. It's almost dinner."

Shay smiled and shook her head, and pulled off her interface ring. Now she wouldn't hear the warnings. "Let's go tonight. You can ride almost as well as me now."

"Shay."

"Do this with me. I'll show you a roller coaster."

"What's a—"

"Second warning. Restricted area."

Tally stopped her board. "If you keep going, Shay, you'll get busted and we won't be doing anything tonight."

Shay shrugged as the wind tugged her farther away.

"I just want to show you something that's my idea of fun, Tally. Before we go all pretty and only get to have everybody else's idea of fun."

Tally shook her head, wanting to say that Shay had already taught her how to hoverboard, the coolest thing she'd ever learned. In less than a month she'd come to feel like they were best friends. Almost like when she'd met Peris as a littlie, and they'd known instantly they'd be together forever. "Shay . . ."

"Please?"

Tally sighed. "Okay."

Shay dropped her arms and dipped her toes to bring the board to a halt. "Really? Tonight?"

"Sure. Rusty Ruins it is."

Tally told herself to relax. It wasn't that big a deal, really. She broke rules all the time, and everyone went to the ruins once a year on school trips. It couldn't be dangerous or anything.

Shay zoomed back from the edge of the belt, swooping up beside Tally to put her arm around her. "Wait until you see the river."

"You said it's got white water?"

"Yeah."

"Which is what?"

Shay smiled. "It's water. But much, much better."

RAPIDS

"Good night."

"Sleep tight," replied the room.

Tally pulled on a jacket, clipped her sensor to her belly ring, and opened the window. The air was still, the river so flat that she could make out every detail of the city skyline mirrored in it. It looked like the pretties were having some sort of event. She could hear the roar of a huge crowd across the water, a thousand cheers rising and falling together. The party towers were dark under the almost full moon, and the fireworks all shimmering hues of blue, climbing so high that they exploded in silence.

The city had never looked so far away.

"I'll see you soon, Peris," she said quietly.

The roof tiles were slick with a late evening rain. Tally climbed carefully to the corner of the dorm where it was brushed by an old sycamore tree. The handholds in its branches felt solid and familiar, and she descended quickly into the darkness behind a recycler.

When she'd cleared the dormitory grounds, Tally looked back. The pattern of shadows that led away from the dorm seemed so convenient, almost intentional. As if uglies were supposed to sneak out every once in a while.

Tally shook her head. She was starting to think like Shay.

They met at the dam, where the river split in two to encircle New Pretty Town. Tonight, there weren't any river skimmers out to disturb the darkness, and Shay was practicing moves on her board when Tally walked up.

"Should you be doing that here in town?" Tally called over the roar of water rushing through the dam's gates.

Shay danced, shifting her weight back and forth on the floating board, dodging imaginary obstacles. "I was just making sure it worked. In case you were worried."

Tally looked at her own board. Shay had tricked the safety governor so it wouldn't tattle when they flew at night, or crossed the boundary out of town. Tally wasn't so much worried about it squealing on them as whether it would fly at all. Or let her fly into a tree. But Shay's board seemed to be hovering just fine.

"I boarded all the way here, and nobody's come to get me," Shay said.

Tally dropped her board to the ground. "Thanks for making sure. I didn't mean to be so wimpy about this."

"You weren't."

"Yeah, I was. I should tell you something. That night, when you met me, I kind of promised my friend Peris I wouldn't take any big risks. You know, in case I really got in trouble, and they got really mad."

"Who cares if they get mad? You're almost sixteen."

"But what if they get mad enough that they won't make me pretty?"

Shay stopped bouncing. "I've never heard of that happening."

"I guess I haven't either. But maybe they wouldn't tell us if it had. Anyway, Peris made me promise to take it easy."

"Tally, do you think maybe he just said that so you wouldn't come around again?"

"Huh?"

"Maybe he made you promise to take it easy so you wouldn't bother him anymore. To make you afraid to go to New Pretty Town again."

Tally tried to answer, but her throat was dry.

"Listen, if you don't want to come, that's fine," Shay said. "I mean it, Squint. But we're not going to get caught. And if we do, I'll take the blame." She laughed. "I'll tell them I kidnapped you."

Tally stepped onto her board and snapped her fingers. When she reached Shay's eye level she said, "I'm coming. I said I would."

Shay smiled and took Tally's hand for a second, squeezing.

"Great. It's going to be fun. Not new pretty fun—the real kind. Put these on."

"What are they? Night vision?"

"Nope. Goggles. You're going to love the white water."

They hit the rapids ten minutes later.

Tally had lived her whole life within sight of the river. Slow-moving and dignified, it defined the city, marking the boundary between worlds. But she'd never realized that a few kilometers upstream from the dam, the stately band of silver became a snarling monster.

The churning water really was white. It crashed over rocks and through narrow channels, catapulted up into moonlit sprays, split apart, rejoined, and dropped down into boiling cauldrons at the bottom of steep falls.

Shay was skimming just above the torrent, so low that she lifted a wake every time she banked. Tally followed at what she guessed was a safe distance, hoping her tricked-up board was still reluctant to crash into the darkness-cloaked rocks and tree branches. The forest to either side was a black void full of wild and ancient trees, nothing like the generic carbon-dioxide suckers that decorated the city. The moonlit clouds above glowed through their branches like a ceiling of pearl.

Every time Shay screamed, Tally knew she was about to follow her friend through a wall of spray leaping up from the maelstrom. Some shone like white lace curtains in the moonlight, but others struck unexpectedly from the darkness. Tally also found herself crashing through the arcs of cold water rising from Shay's board when it dipped or banked, but at least she knew when a turn was coming.

The first few minutes were sheer terror, her teeth clenched so hard that her jaw ached, her toes curled up inside her special new grippy shoes, her arms and even fingers spread wide for balance. But gradually Tally grew accustomed to the darkness, the roar of water below, the unexpected slap of cold spray against her face. It was wilder, and faster, and farther than she'd ever flown before. The river wound into the dark forest, cutting its serpentine route into the unknown.

Finally, Shay waved her hands and pulled up, the back of her board dipping low into the water. Tally climbed to avoid the wake, spinning her board in a tight circle to bring it to a smooth halt.

"Are we there?"

"Not quite. But look." Shay pointed back the way they'd come.

Tally gasped as she took in the view. The distant city was a bright coin nestled in darkness, the fireworks of New Pretty Town the barest cold-blue shimmer. They must have climbed a long way up; Tally could see patches of moonlight rolling slowly across the low hills around the city, pushed along by the light wind that barely tugged at the clouds.

She'd never been beyond the city limits at night, had never seen it lit up like this from afar.

Tally pulled off her spattered goggles and took a deep breath. The air was full of sharp smells, evergreen sap and wildflowers, the electric smell of churning water.

"Nice, huh?"

"Yeah," Tally panted. "Much better than sneaking around New Pretty Town."

Shay grinned happily. "I'm really glad you think so. I've been wanting to come out here so bad, but not alone. You know?"

Tally looked at the surrounding forest, trying to peer into the black spaces between the trees. This was really the wild, where anything could be hidden, not a place for human beings. She shivered at the thought of being there alone. "Where to now?"

"Now we walk."

"Walk?"

Shay eased her board to the shore and stepped off. "Yeah, there's a vein of iron about half a kilometer that way. But nothing between here and there."

"What are you talking about?"

"Tally, hoverboards work on magnetic levitation, right? So there's got to be some kind of metal around or they don't hover."

"I guess so. But in town—"

"In town, there's a steel grid built into the ground, no matter where you go. Out here, you have to be careful."

"What happens if your board can't hover anymore?"

"It falls down. And your crash bracelets don't work either."

"Oh." Tally stepped from her board and held it under one arm. All her muscles were sore from the wild ride here. It was good to be on solid ground. The rocks felt reassuringly the-opposite-of-hovery under her shakey legs.

After a few minutes' walking, though, the board started to

grow heavy. By the time the noise of the river had faded to a dull roar behind them, it felt like a plank of oak under her arm.

"I didn't know these things weighed so much."

"Yeah, this is what a board weighs when it's not hovering. Out here, you find out that the city fools you about how things really work."

The sky was getting cloudier, and in the darkness the cold seemed more intense. Tally hoisted the board up to get a better grip, wondering if it was going to rain. She was already wet enough from the rapids. "I kind of like being fooled about some things."

After a long scramble through the rocks, Shay broke the silence. "This way. There's a natural vein of iron underground. You can feel it in your crash bracelets."

Tally held out one hand and frowned, unconvinced. But after another minute she felt a faint tugging in her bracelet, like a ghost pulling her forward. Her board started to lighten, and soon she and Shay had hopped on again, coasting over a ridge and down into a dark valley.

Onboard, Tally found the breath to ask a question that had been bugging her. "So if hoverboards need metal, how do they work on the river?"

"Panning for gold."

"What?"

"Rivers come from springs, which come from inside mountains. The water brings up minerals from inside the earth. So there's always metals at the bottom of rivers."

"Right. Like when people used to pan for gold?"

"Yeah, exactly. But, actually, boards prefer iron. All that glitters is not hovery."

Tally frowned. Shay sometimes talked in a mysterious way, like she was quoting the lyrics of some band no one else listened to.

She almost asked, but Shay came to a sudden halt and pointed downward.

The clouds were breaking, and moonlight shot through them to fall across the floor of the valley. Hulking towers rose up, casting jagged shadows, their human-made shapes obvious against the plain of treetops rippling in the wind.

The Rusty Ruins.

THE RUSTY RUINS

A few blank windows stared down on them in silence from the husks of the giant buildings. Any glass had long since shattered, any wood had rotted, and nothing remained but metal frames, mortar, and stone crumbling in the grip of invading vegetation. Looking down at the black, empty doorways, Tally's skin crawled with the thought of descending to peer into one.

The two friends slid between the ruined buildings, riding high and silent as if not to disturb the ghosts of the dead city. Below them the streets were full of burned-out cars squeezed together between the looming walls. Whatever had destroyed this city, the people had tried to escape it. Tally remembered from her last school trip to the ruins that their cars couldn't hover. They just rolled along on rubber wheels. The Rusties had been stuck down in these streets like a horde of rats trapped in a burning maze.

"Uh, Shay, you're pretty sure our boards aren't suddenly going to conk out, right?" she called softly.

"Don't worry. Whoever built this city loved to waste metal. They aren't called the Rusty Ruins because some guy called Rusty discovered them."

Tally had to agree. Every building sported jagged spurs of metal sticking from its broken walls, like bones jutting from a long-dead animal. She remembered that the Rusties didn't use hoverstruts; every building was squat, crude, and massive, and needed a steel skeleton to keep it from falling down.

And some of them were so *huge.* The Rusties didn't put their factories underground, and they all worked together like bees in a hive instead of at home. The smallest ruin here was bigger than the biggest dorm in Uglyville, bigger even than Garbo Mansion.

Seeing them now, at night, the ruins felt much more real to Tally. On school trips, the teachers always made the Rusties out to be so stupid. You almost couldn't believe people lived like this, burning trees to clear land, burning oil for heat and power, setting the atmosphere on fire with their weapons. But in the moonlight she could imagine people scrambling over flaming cars to escape the crumbling city, panicking in their flight from this untenable pile of metal and stone.

Shay's voice pulled Tally from her reverie. "Come on, I want to show you something."

Shay cruised to the edge of the buildings, then out over the trees.

"Are you sure we can—"

"Look down."

Below, Tally saw metal glinting through the trees.

"The ruins are much bigger than they let on," Shay said. "They just keep that part of the city standing for school trips and museum stuff. But it goes on forever."

"With lots of metal?"

"Yeah. Tons. Don't worry, I've flown all over the place."

Tally swallowed, keeping an eye out for signs of ruin below, glad that Shay was moving at a nice, slow speed.

A shape emerged from the forest, a long spine that rose and fell like a frozen wave. It led away from them, off into the darkness.

"Here it is."

"Okay, but what is it?" Tally asked.

"It's called a roller coaster. Remember, I told you I'd show you one."

"It's pretty. But what's it for?"

"For having fun."

"No way."

"Yeah, way. Apparently, the Rusties did have some fun. It's like a track. They would stick ground cars to it and go as fast as they could. Up, down, around in circles. Like hoverboarding, without hovering. And they made it out of some really unrusty kind of steel—for safety, I guess."

Tally frowned. She'd only imagined the Rusties working in the giant stone hives and struggling to escape on that last, horrible day. Not having fun.

"Let's do it," Shay said. "Let's roller coaster."

"How?"

"On your board." Shay turned to Tally and said seriously, "But you've got to go fast. It's dangerous unless you're really moving."

"Why?"

"You'll see."

Shay turned away and sped down the roller coaster, flying just above the track. Tally sighed and leaned hard after her. At least the thing was metal.

It also turned out to be a great ride. It was like a hoverboard course made solid, complete with tight, banked turns, sharp climbs followed by long drops, even loops that took Tally upside down, her crash bracelets activating to keep her on board. It was amazing what good shape it was in. The Rusties must have built it out of something special, just as Shay had said.

The track went much higher than a hoverboard could go on its own. On the roller coaster, hoverboarding really was like being a bird.

It wound around in a wide, slow arc, circling back toward where they'd started. The final approach began with a huge climb.

"Take this part fast!" Shay shouted over her shoulder as she zoomed ahead.

Tally followed at top speed, rocketing up the spindly track. She could see the ruins in the distance: broken, black spires against the trees. And behind them, a moonlit glimmer that might have been the sea. This *was* really high!

She heard a scream of pleasure as she reached the top. Shay had disappeared. Tally leaned forward to speed up.

Suddenly, the board dropped out from under her. It simply fell away from her feet, leaving her flying through midair. The track below her had disappeared.

Tally clenched her fists, waiting for the crash bracelets to kick in and haul her up by her wrists. But they had become as useless as the board, just heavy strips of steel dragging her toward the ground. "Shay!" she screamed as she fell into blackness.

Then Tally saw the framework of the roller coaster ahead. Only a short segment was missing.

Suddenly, the crash bracelets pulled her upward, and she felt the solid surface of the hoverboard coming up from under her feet. Her momentum had carried her to the other side of the gap! The board must have sailed along with her, just below her feet for those terrifying seconds of free fall.

She found herself cruising down the track, to where Shay was waiting at the bottom. "You're insane!" she shouted.

"Pretty cool, huh?"

"No!" Tally yelled. "Why didn't you tell me it was *broken*?"

Shay shrugged. "More fun that way?"

"More *fun*?" Her heart was beating fast, her vision strangely clear. She was full of anger and relief and . . . joy. "Well, kind of. But you *suck*!"

Tally stepped from the board and walked across the grass on rubbery legs. She found a broken stone big enough to sit on, and lowered herself shakily onto it.

Shay jumped off her board. “Hey, sorry.”

“That was horrible, Shay. I was *falling*.”

“Not for long. Like, five seconds. I thought you said you’d bungee jumped off a building.”

Tally glared at Shay. “Yeah, I did, but I *knew* I wasn’t going to splat.”

“True. But, you see, the first time someone showed me the roller coaster, they didn’t tell me about the gap. And I thought it was pretty cool, finding out that way. Best time’s the first time. I wanted you to feel it too.”

“You thought falling was *cool*?”

“Well, maybe at first I was pretty angry. Yeah, I definitely was.” Shay smiled broadly. “But I got over it.”

“Give me a second on that one, Skinny.”

“Take your time.”

Tally’s breathing slowed, and her heart gradually stopped trying to beat its way out of her chest. But her brain stayed as clear as it had for those seconds of free fall, and she found herself wondering who had found the roller coaster first, and how many other uglies had come here since. “Shay, who showed you all this?”

“Friends, older than me. Uglies like us, who try to figure out how stuff works. And how to trick it.”

Tally looked up at the ancient, serpentine shape of the roller coaster, the vines crawling up its framework. “I wonder how long uglies have been coming here.”

“Probably a long time. You pass along stuff. You know, one person figures out how to trick their board, the next finds the rapids, the next makes it to the ruins.”

"Then somebody gets brave enough to jump the gap in the roller coaster." Tally swallowed. "Or jumps it accidentally."

Shay nodded. "But they all get turned pretty in the end."

"Happy ending," Tally said.

Shay shrugged.

"How do you know it's called a 'roller coaster,' anyway? Did you look it up somewhere?"

"No," Shay said. "Someone told me."

"But how'd they know?"

"This guy knows a lot of stuff. Tricks, stuff about the ruins. He's really cool."

Something about Shay's voice made Tally turn and take her hand. "But he's pretty now, I guess."

Shay pulled away and bit a fingernail. "No. He's not."

"But I thought all your friends—"

"Tally, will you make me a promise? A real promise."

"Sure, I guess. What kind of promise?"

"You can never tell anyone what I'm about to show you."

"It doesn't involve free fall, does it?"

"No."

"Okay. I swear." Tally held up her hand with the scar she and Peris had made. "I'll never tell anyone."

Shay looked into her eyes for a moment, searching hard, then nodded. "All right. There's someone I want you to meet. Tonight."

"Tonight? But we won't get back into town until—"

"He's not in town." Shay smiled. "He's out here."

WAITING FOR DAVID

"This is a joke, right?"

Shay didn't answer. They were back in the heart of the ruins, in the shadow of the tallest building around. She was staring up at it with a puzzled expression on her face. "I think I remember how to do this," she said.

"Do what?"

"Get up there. Yeah, here it is."

Shay eased her board forward, ducking to pass through a gap in the crumbling wall.

"Shay?"

"Don't worry. I've done this before."

"I think I already had my initiation for tonight, Shay." Tally wasn't in the mood for another one of Shay's jokes. She was tired, and it was a long way back to town. And she had cleanup duty tomorrow at her dorm. Just because it was summer didn't mean she could sleep all day.

But Tally followed Shay through the gap. Arguing would probably take longer.

They rose straight into the air, the boards using the metal skeleton of the building to climb. It was creepy being inside, looking out of the empty windows at the ragged shapes of other buildings. Like being a Rusty ghost watching as its city crumbled over the centuries.

The roof was missing, and they emerged to a spectacular view. The clouds had all disappeared, and moonlight brought the ruins into sharp relief, the buildings like rows of broken teeth. Tally saw that it really had been the ocean she'd glimpsed from the roller coaster. From up here, the water shone like a pale band of silver in the moonlight.

Shay pulled something from her shoulder pack and tore it in half.

The world burst into flame.

"Ow! Blind me, why don't you!" Tally cried, covering her eyes.

"Oh, yeah. Sorry." Shay held the safety sparkler at arm's length. It crackled to full strength in the silence of the ruins, casting flickering shadows through the interior of the ruin. Shay's face looked monstrous in the glare, and sparks floated downward to be lost in the depths of the wrecked building.

Finally, the sparkler ran out. Tally blinked, trying to clear the spots from before her eyes. Her night vision ruined, she could hardly see anything except the moon in the sky.

She swallowed, realizing that the sparkler would have been seen from anywhere in the valley. Maybe even out to sea. "Shay, was that a signal?"

"Yeah, it was."

Tally looked down. The dark buildings below were filled with phantom flickers of light, echoes of the sparkler burned into her eyes. Suddenly very aware of how blind she was, Tally felt a drop of cold sweat creep down her spine. "Who are we meeting, anyway?"

"His name's David."

"David? That's a weird name." It sounded made up, to Tally. She decided again that this was all a joke. "So he's just going to show up here? This guy doesn't really live in the ruins, does he?"

"No. He lives pretty far away. But he might be close by. He comes here sometimes."

"You mean, he's from another city?"

Shay looked at her, but Tally couldn't read her expression in the darkness. "Something like that."

Shay returned her gaze to the horizon, as if looking for a signal in answer to her own. Tally wrapped herself in her jacket. Standing still, she began to realize how cold it had become. She wondered how late it was. Without her interface ring, she couldn't just ask.

The almost full moon was descending in the sky, so it had to be past midnight, Tally remembered from astronomy. That was one thing about being outside the city: It made all that nature stuff they taught in school seem a lot more useful. She remembered now how rainwater fell on the mountains, and soaked into the ground before bubbling up full of minerals. Then it made its way back to the sea, cutting rivers and canyons into the earth over the centuries. If you lived out here, you could ride your hoverboard along the rivers, like in the really old days before the Rusties, when the not-as-crazy pre-Rusties traveled around in small boats made from trees.

Her night vision gradually returned, and she scanned the horizon. Would there really be another flare out there, answering Shay's? Tally hoped not. She'd never met anyone from another city. She knew from school that in some cities they spoke other languages, or didn't turn pretty until they were eighteen, and other weird stuff like that. "Shay, maybe we should head home."

"Let's wait a while longer."

Tally bit her lip. "Look, maybe this David isn't around tonight."

"Yeah, maybe. Probably. But I was hoping he'd be here." She turned to face Tally. "It would be really cool if you met him. He's . . . different."

"Sounds like it."

"I'm not making this up, you know."

"Hey, I believe you," Tally said, although with Shay, she was never totally sure.

Shay turned back to the horizon, chewing on a fingernail. "Okay, I guess he's not around. We can go, if you want."

"It's just that it's really late, and a long way back. And I've got cleanup tomorrow."

Shay nodded. "Me too."

"Thanks for showing me all this, Shay. It was all really incredible. But I think one more cool thing would kill me."

Shay laughed. "The roller coaster didn't kill you."

"Just about."

"Forgive me for that yet?"

"I'll let you know, Skinny."

Shay laughed. "Okay. But remember not to tell anyone about David."

"Hey, I promised. You can trust me, Shay. Really."

"All right. I do trust you, Tally." She bent her knees, and her board started to descend.

Tally took one last look around, taking in the ruins splayed out below them, the dark woods, the pearly strip of river stretching toward the glowing sea. She wondered if there was anyone out there, really, or if David was just some story that uglies made up to scare one another.

But Shay didn't seem scared. She seemed genuinely disappointed that no one had answered her signal, as if meeting David would have been even better than showing off the rapids, the ruins, and the roller coaster.

Whether he was real or not, Tally thought, David was very real to Shay.

They left through the gap in the wall and flew to the outskirts of the ruins, then followed the vein of iron up out of the valley. At the ridge, the boards started to stutter, and they stepped off. Tired as Tally was, carrying the board didn't seem so impossible this time. She had stopped thinking of it as a toy, like a littlie's balloon. The hoverboard had become something more solid, something that obeyed its own rules, and that could be dangerous, too.

Tally figured that Shay was right about one thing: Being in the city all the time made everything fake, in a way. Like the buildings and bridges held up by hoverstruts, or jumping off a rooftop with a bungee jacket on, nothing was quite real there. She was glad Shay had taken her out to the ruins. If nothing else, the mess left by the Rusties proved that things could go terribly wrong if you weren't careful.

Close to the river the boards lightened up, and the two of them jumped on gratefully.

Shay groaned as they got their footing. "I don't know about you, but I'm not taking another step tonight."

"That's for sure."

Shay leaned forward and eased her board out onto the river, wrapping her dorm jacket around her shoulders against the spray of the rapids. Tally turned to take one last look back. With the clouds gone, she could just see the ruins from here.

She blinked. There seemed to be the barest flicker coming from over where the roller coaster had been. Maybe it was just a trick of the light, a reflection of moonlight from some exposed piece of unrusted metal. "Shay?" she said softly.

"You coming or what?" Shay shouted over the roar of the river.

Tally blinked again, but couldn't make out the flicker anymore. In any case, they were too far away. Mentioning it to Shay would only make her anxious to go back. There was no way Tally was making the hike again.

And it probably was nothing.

Tally took a deep breath and shouted, "Come on, Skinny. Race you!" She urged her board onto the river, cutting into the cold spray and for a moment leaving a laughing Shay behind.

FIGHT

"Look at them all. What dorks."

"Did we ever look like that?"

"Probably. But just because we were dorks doesn't mean they're not."

Tally nodded, trying to remember what being twelve was like, what the dorm had looked like on her first day there. She remembered how intimidating the building had seemed. Much bigger than Sol and Ellie's house, of course, and bigger than the huts that littlies went to school in, one teacher and ten students to each one.

Now the dorm seemed so small and claustrophobic. Painfully childish, with its bright colors and padded stairs. So boring during the day and easy to escape at night.

The new uglies all stuck together in a tight group, afraid to stray too far from their guide. Their ugly little faces peered up at the dorm's four-story height, their eyes full of wonder and terror.

Shay pulled her head back in through the window. "This is going to be so fun."

"It'll be one orientation they won't forget."

Summer was over in two weeks. The population of Tally's dorm had been steadily dropping for the last year as seniors turned sixteen. It was almost time for a new batch to take their place. Tally watched the last few uglies make their way inside, gawky and nervous, unkempt and uncoordinated. Twelve was definitely the turning point, when you changed from a cute littlie into an oversize, undereducated ugly.

It was a stage of life she was glad to be leaving behind.

"You sure this thing is going to work?" Shay asked.

Tally smiled. It wasn't often that Shay was the cautious one. She pointed at the collar of the bungee jacket. "You see that little green light? That means it's working. It's for emergencies, so it's always ready to go."

Shay's hand slipped under the jacket to pull at her belly sensor, which meant she was nervous. "What if it knows there's no real emergency?"

"It's not that smart. You fall, it catches you. No tricks necessary."

Shay shrugged and put it on.

They'd borrowed the jacket from the art school, the tallest building in Uglyville. It was a spare from the basement, and they hadn't even had to trick the rack to get it free. Tally definitely didn't want to get caught messing around with fire alarms, in case the wardens connected her to a certain incident in New Pretty Town back at the beginning of summer.

Shay pulled an oversize basketball jersey over the bungee jacket. It was in her dorm's colors, and none of the teachers here knew her face very well. "How's that look?"

"Like you've gained weight. It suits you."

Shay scowled. She hated being called Stick Insect, or Pig-Eyes, or any of the other things uglies called one another. Shay sometimes claimed that she didn't care if she ever got the operation. It was crazy talk, of course. Shay wasn't exactly a *freak*, but she was hardly a natural-born pretty. There'd only been about ten of those in all of history, after all. "Do *you* want to do the jump, Squint?"

"I have both been there and done that, Shay, before I even met you. And you're the one who had this brilliant idea."

Shay's scowl faded into a smile. "It is brilliant, isn't it?"

"They'll never know what hit them."

They waited until the new uglies were in the library, scattered around the worktables to watch some orientation video. Shay and Tally lay on their stomachs on the top floor of the stacks, where the dusty old paper books were stored, peering through the guardrails down at the group. They waited for the tour leader to quiet the chattering uglies.

"This is almost too easy," Shay said, penciling a pair of fat, black eyebrows over her own.

"Easy for you. You'll be out the door before anyone knows what's happened. I've got to make it all the way down the stairs."

"So what, Tally? What are they going to do if we get caught?"

Tally shrugged. "True." But she pulled on her mousy brown wig anyway.

Over the summer, as the last few seniors turned sixteen and pretty, the tricks had grown worse and worse. But nobody ever seemed to get punished, and Tally's promise to Peris seemed ages ago. Once she was pretty, nothing she'd done in this last month would matter. She was anxious to leave it all behind, but not without a big finish.

Thinking of Peris, Tally stuck on a big plastic nose. They'd raided the drama room at Shay's dorm the night before and were loaded with disguises. "Ready?" she asked. Then she giggled at the nasal twang the fake nose gave her voice.

"Hang on." Shay grabbed a big, fat book from the shelf. "Okay, showtime."

They stood up.

"Give me that book!" Tally shouted at Shay. "It's mine!"

She heard the uglies below fall silent, and had to resist looking down to see their upturned faces.

"No way, Pignose! I checked it out first."

"Are you kidding, Fattie? You can't even read!"

"Oh, yeah? Well, read *this*!"

Shay swung the book at Tally, who ducked. She snatched it away and swung back, catching Shay solidly on her upraised forearms. Shay rolled back at the impact, spinning over the railing.

Tally leaned forward, watching wide-eyed as Shay tumbled down toward the library's main floor, three stories below. The new uglies screamed in unison, scattering away from the flailing body plummeting toward them.

A second later the bungee jacket activated, and Shay bobbed back up in midair, laughing maniacally at the top of her lungs. Tally waited another moment, watching the uglies' horror dissolve into confusion as Shay bounced again, then righted herself on one of the tables and headed for the door.

Tally dropped the book and dashed for the stairs, leaping a flight at a time until she reached the back exit of the dorm.

"Oh, that was perfect!"

"Did you see their faces?"

"Not actually," Shay said. "I was kind of busy watching the floor coming at me."

"Yeah, I remember that from jumping off the roof. It does catch your attention."

"Speaking of faces, love the nose."

Tally giggled, pulling it off. "Yeah, no point in being uglier than usual."

Shay's face clouded. She wiped off an eyebrow, then looked up sharply. "You're not ugly."

"Oh, come on, Shay."

"No, I mean it." She reached out and touched Tally's real nose. "Your profile is great."

"Don't be weird, Shay. I'm an ugly, you're an ugly. We will

be for two more weeks. It's no big deal or anything." She laughed. "You, for example, have one giant eyebrow and one tiny one."

Shay looked away, stripping off the rest of her disguise in silence.

They were hidden in the changing rooms beside the sandy beach, where they'd left their interface rings and a spare set of clothes. If anyone asked, they'd say they were swimming the whole time. Swimming was a great trick. It hid your body-heat signature, involved changing clothes, and was a perfect excuse for not wearing your interface ring. The river washed away all crimes.

A minute later they splashed out into the water, sinking the disguises. The bungee jacket would go back to the art school basement that night.

"I'm serious, Tally," Shay said once they were out in the water. "Your nose isn't ugly. I like your eyes, too."

"My eyes? Now you're totally crazy. They're way too close together."

"Who says?"

"Biology says."

Shay splashed a handful of water at her. "You don't believe all that crap, do you—that there's only one way to look, and everyone's programmed to agree on it?"

"It's not about believing, Shay. You just *know* it. You've seen pretties. They look . . . wonderful."

"They all look the same."

"I used to think that too. But when Peris and I would go into town, we'd see a lot of them, and we realized that pretties do look different. They look like themselves. It's just a lot more subtle, because they're not all freaks."

"We're not freaks, Tally. *We're* normal. We may not be gorgeous, but at least we're not hyped-up Barbie dolls."

"What kind of dolls?"

She looked away. "It's something David told me about."

"Oh, great. David again." Tally pushed away and floated on her back, looking up at the sky and wishing this conversation would end. They'd been out to the ruins a few more times, and Shay always insisted on setting off a sparkler, but David had never showed. The whole thing gave Tally the creeps, waiting around in the dead city for some guy who didn't seem to exist. It was great exploring out there, but Shay's obsession with David had started to sour it for Tally.

"He's real. I've met him more than once."

"Okay, Shay, David's real. But so is being ugly. You can't change it just by wishing, or by telling yourself that you're pretty. That's why they invented the operation."

"But it's a trick, Tally. You've only seen pretty faces your whole life. Your parents, your teachers, everyone over sixteen. But you weren't *born* expecting that kind of beauty in everyone, all the time. You just got programmed into thinking anything else is ugly."

"It's not programming, it's just a natural reaction. And more important than that, it's fair. In the old days it was all random—some people *kind* of pretty, most people ugly all their lives. Now everyone's ugly . . . until they're pretty. No losers."

Shay was silent for a while, then said, "There are losers, Tally."

Tally shivered. Everyone knew about uglies-for-life, the few people for whom the operation wouldn't work. You didn't see them around much. They were allowed in public, but most of them preferred to hide. Who wouldn't? Uglies might look goofy, but at least they were young. *Old* uglies were really unbelievable.

"Is that it? Are you worried about the operation not working? That's silly, Shay. You're no freak. In two weeks you'll be as pretty as anyone else."

"I don't want to be pretty."

Tally sighed. This again.

"I'm sick of this city," Shay continued. "I'm sick of the rules and boundaries. The last thing I want is to become some empty-headed new pretty, having one big party all day."

"Come on, Shay. They do all the same stuff we do: bungee jump, fly, play with fireworks. Only they don't have to sneak around."

"They don't have the imagination to sneak around."

"Look, Skinny, I'm with you," Tally said sharply. "Doing tricks is great! Okay? Breaking the rules is fun! But eventually you've got to do something besides being a clever little ugly."

"Like being a vapid, boring pretty?"

"No, like being an adult. Did you ever think that when you're pretty you might not *need* to play tricks and mess things up? Maybe just being ugly is why uglies always fight and pick on one another, because they aren't happy with who they are. Well, I want to be happy, and looking like a real person is the first step."

"I'm not afraid of looking the way I do, Tally."

"Maybe not, but you are afraid of growing up!"

Shay didn't say anything. Tally floated in silence, looking up at the sky, barely able to see the clouds through her anger. She wanted to be pretty, wanted to see Peris again. It seemed like forever since she'd talked to him, or to anyone else except Shay. She was sick of this whole ugly business, and just wanted it to end.

A minute later, she heard Shay swimming for shore.

LAST TRICK

It was strange, but Tally couldn't help feeling sad. She knew she'd miss the view from this window.

She'd spent the last four years looking out at New Pretty Town, wanting nothing more than to cross the river and not come back. That's probably what had tempted her through the window so many times, learning every trick she could to sneak closer to the new pretties, to spy on the life she would eventually have.

But now that the operation was only a week away, time seemed to be moving too fast. Sometimes, Tally wished that they could do the operation gradually. Get her squinty eyes fixed first, then her lips, and cross the river in stages. Just so she wouldn't have to look out the window one last time and know she'd never see this view again.

Without Shay around, things felt incomplete, and she'd spent even more time here, sitting on her bed and staring at New Pretty Town.

Of course, there wasn't much else to do these days. Everyone in the dorm was younger than Tally now, and she'd already taught all of her best tricks to the next class. She'd watched every movie her wallscreen knew about ten times, all the way back to some old black-and-white ones in an English she could barely understand. There was no one to go to concerts with, and dorm sports were boring to watch now that she didn't know anyone on the teams. All the other uglies looked at her enviously, but no one saw much point in making friends. Probably it was better to get the operation over with all at once. Half the time, she wished the doctors would just kidnap her in the middle of the night and do it. She could imagine a lot worse things than waking up pretty one morning. They said at school that they could make the operation work on fifteen-year-olds now. Waiting until sixteen was just a stupid old tradition.

But it was a tradition nobody questioned, except the occasional ugly. So Tally had a week to go, alone, waiting.

Shay hadn't talked to her since their big fight. Tally had tried to write a ping, but working it all out on-screen just made her angry again. And it didn't make much sense to sort it out now. Once they were both pretty, there wouldn't be anything to fight about anymore. And even if Shay still hated her, there was always Peris and all their old friends, waiting across the river for her with their big eyes and wonderful smiles.

Still, Tally spent a lot of time wondering what Shay was going to look like pretty, her skin-and-bones body all filled out, her already full lips perfected, and the ragged fingernails gone forever. They'd probably make her eyes a more intense shade of green. Or maybe one of the newer colors—violet, silver, or gold.

"Hey, Squint!"

Tally jumped at the whisper. She peered into the darkness and saw a form scuttling toward her across the roof tiles. A smile broke onto her face. "Shay!"

The silhouette paused for a moment.

Tally didn't even bother to whisper. "Don't just stand there. Come in, stupid!"

Shay crawled into the window, laughing, as Tally gathered her into a hug, warm and joyful and solid. They stepped back, still holding each other's hands. For a moment, Shay's ugly face looked perfect.

"It's so great to see you."

"You too, Tally."

"I missed you. I wanted to—I'm so sorry about—"

"No," Shay interrupted. "You were right. You made me think. I was going to write you, but it was all . . ." She sighed.

Tally nodded, squeezing Shay's hands. "Yeah. It sucked."

They stood in silence for a moment, and Tally glanced past her friend out the window. Suddenly, the view of New Pretty Town didn't seem so sad. It looked bright and tempting, as if all the hesitation had drained out of her. The open window was exciting again. "Shay?"

"Yeah?"

"Let's go somewhere tonight. Do some major trick."

Shay laughed. "I was kind of hoping you'd say that."

Tally noticed the way Shay was dressed. She was wearing serious trick-wear: all black clothes, hair tied back tight, a knapsack over one shoulder. She grinned. "Already got a plan, I see. Great."

"Yeah," Shay said softly. "I've got a plan."

She walked over to Tally's bed, unslinging the knapsack from her shoulder. Her footsteps squeaked, and Tally smiled when she saw that Shay was wearing grippy shoes. Tally hadn't been on a hoverboard in days. Flying alone was all the hard work and only half the fun.

Shay dumped the contents of the knapsack out onto the bed, and pointed. "Position-finder. Firestarter. Water purifier." She picked up two shiny wads the size of sandwiches. "These pull out into sleeping bags. And they're really warm inside."

"Sleeping bags? Water purifier?" Tally exclaimed. "This must be some kind of awesome multiday trick. Are we going all the way to the sea or something?"

Shay shook her head. "Farther."

"Uh, cool." Tally kept her smile on her face. "But we've only got six days till the operation."

"I know what day it is." Shay opened a waterproof bag and spilled its contents alongside the rest. "Food for two weeks—dehydrated. You just drop one of these into the purifier and add water. Any kind of water." She giggled. "The purifier works so well, you can even pee in it."

Tally sat down on the bed, reading the labels on the food packs. "Two weeks?"

"Two weeks for two people," Shay said carefully. "Four weeks for one."

Tally didn't say anything. Suddenly, she couldn't look at the stuff on the bed, or at Shay. She stared out the window, at New Pretty Town, where the fireworks were starting.

"But it won't take two weeks, Tally. It's much closer."

A plume of red soared up in the middle of town, tendrils of fireworks drifting down like the leaves of a giant willow tree. "What won't take two weeks?"

"Going to where David lives."

Tally nodded, and closed her eyes.

"It's not like here, Tally. They don't separate everyone, uglies from pretties, new and middle and late. And you can leave whenever you want, go anywhere you want."

"Like where?"

"Anywhere. Ruins, the forest, the sea. And . . . you never have to get the operation."

"You *what*?"

Shay sat next to her, touching Tally's cheek with one finger. Tally opened her eyes. "We don't have to look like everyone else, Tally, and act like everyone else. We've got a choice. We can grow up any way we want."

Tally swallowed. She felt like speech was impossible, but knew she had to say something. She forced words from her dry throat. "Not be pretty? That's crazy, Shay. All the times you talked that way, I thought you were just being stupid. Peris always said the same stuff."

"I *was* just being stupid. But when you said I was afraid of growing up, you really made me think."

"*I* made you think?"

"Made me realize how full of crap I was. Tally, I've got to tell you another secret."

Tally sighed. "Okay. I guess it can't get any worse."

"My older friends, the ones I used to hang out with before I met you? Not all of them wound up pretty."

"What do you mean?"

"Some of them ran away, like I am. Like I want us to."

Tally looked into Shay's eyes, searching for some sign that this was all a joke. But the intense look on her face held firm. She was dead serious.

"You know someone who actually ran away?"

Shay nodded. "I was supposed to go too. We had it all planned, about a week before the first of us turned sixteen. We'd already stolen survival gear, and told David that we were coming. It was all set up. That was four months ago."

"But you didn't . . ."

"Some of us did, but I chickened out." Shay looked out the window. "And I wasn't the only one. A couple of the others stayed and turned pretty instead. I probably would have too, except I met you."

"*Me?*"

"All of a sudden I wasn't alone anymore. I wasn't afraid to go back out to the ruins, to look for David again."

"But we never . . ." Tally blinked. "You finally found him, didn't you?"

"Not until two days ago. I've been out every night since we . . . since our fight. After you said I was afraid to grow up, I realized you were right. I'd chickened out once, but I didn't have to again."

Shay grasped Tally's hand, and waited until their eyes were locked. "I want you to come, Tally."

"No," Tally said without thinking. Then she shook her head. "Wait. How come you never *told* me any of this before?"

"I wanted to, except you would have thought I was crazy."

"You *are* crazy!"

"Maybe. But not that way. That's why I wanted you to meet David. So you'd know that it's all real."

"It doesn't seem real. I mean, what is this place you're talking about?"

"It's just called the Smoke. It's not a city, and nobody's in charge. And nobody's pretty."

"Sounds like a nightmare. And how do you get there, walk?"

Shay laughed. "Are you kidding? Hoverboards, like always. There are long-distance boards that recharge on solar, and the route's all worked out to follow rivers and stuff. David does it all the time, as far as the ruins. He'll take us to the Smoke."

"But how do people *live* out there, Shay? Like the Rusties? Burning trees for heat and burying their junk everywhere? It's wrong to live in nature, unless you want to live like an animal."

Shay shook her head and sighed. "That's just school-talk, Tally. They've still got technology. And they're not like the Rusties, burning trees and stuff. But they don't put a wall up between themselves and nature."

"And everyone's ugly."

"Which means no one's ugly."

Tally managed to laugh. "Which means no one's *pretty,* you mean."

They sat in silence. Tally watched the fireworks, feeling a thousand times worse than she had before Shay had appeared at the window.

Finally, Shay said the words Tally had been thinking. "I'm going to lose you, aren't I?"

"You're the one who's running away."

Shay brought her fists down onto her knees. "It's all my fault. I should've told you earlier. If you'd had more time to get used to the idea, maybe . . ."

"Shay, I never would have gotten used to the idea. I don't want to be ugly all my life. I want those perfect eyes and lips, and for everyone to look at me and gasp. And for everyone who sees me to think *Who's that?* and want to get to know me, and listen to what I say."

"I'd rather *have* something to say."

"Like what? 'I shot a wolf today and ate it'?"

Shay giggled. "People don't eat wolves, Tally. Rabbits, I think, and deer."

"Oh, gross. Thanks for the image, Shay."

"Yeah, I think I'll stick to vegetables and fish. But it's not about camping out, Tally. It's about becoming what I want to become. Not what some surgical committee thinks I should."

"You're still yourself on the inside, Shay. But when you're pretty, people pay more attention."

"Not everyone thinks that way."

"Are you sure about that? That you can beat evolution by being smart or interesting? Because if you're wrong . . . if you don't come back by the time you're twenty, the operation won't work as well. You'll look wrong, forever."

"I'm not coming back. Forever."

Tally's voice caught, but she forced herself to say it: "And I'm not going."

They said good-bye under the dam.

Shay's long-range hoverboard was thicker, and glimmered with the facets of solar cells. She'd also stashed a heated jacket and hat under the bridge. Tally guessed that winters at the Smoke were cold and miserable.

She couldn't believe her friend was really going.

"You can always come back. If it sucks."

Shay shrugged. "None of my friends has."

The words gave Tally a creepy feeling. She could think of a lot of horrible reasons to explain why no one had come back. "Be careful, Shay."

"You too. You're not going to tell anyone about this, right?"

"Never, Shay."

"You swear? No matter what?"

Tally raised her scarred palm. "I swear."

Shay smiled. "I know. I just had to ask again before I . . ." She pulled out a piece of paper and handed it to Tally.

"What's this?" Tally opened it up and saw a scrawl of letters. "When did you learn to write by hand?"

"We all learned while we were planning to leave. It's a good idea if you don't want minders sniffing your diary. Anyway, that's for you. I'm not supposed to leave any record of where I'm going, so it's in code, kind of."

Tally frowned, reading the first line of slanted words. "'Take the coaster straight past the gap'?"

"Yeah. Get it? Only you could figure it out, in case someone finds it. You know, if you ever want to follow me."

Tally started to say something, but couldn't. She managed to nod.

"Just in case," Shay said.

She jumped onto her board and snapped her fingers, securing her knapsack over both shoulders. "Good-bye, Tally."

"Bye, Shay. I wish . . ."

Shay waited, bobbing just a bit in the cool September wind. Tally tried to imagine her growing old, wrinkled, gradually ruined, all without ever having been truly beautiful. Never learning how to dress properly, or how to act at a formal dance. Never having anyone look into her eyes and be simply overwhelmed.

"I wish I could have seen what you would look like. Pretty, I mean."

"Guess you'll just have to live with remembering my face this way," Shay said.

Then she turned and her hoverboard climbed away toward the river, and Tally's next words were lost on the roar of the water.

OPERATION

When the day came, Tally waited for the car alone.

Tomorrow, when the operation was all over, her parents would be waiting outside the hospital, along with Peris and her other older friends. That was the tradition. But it seemed strange that there was no one to see her off on this end. No one said good-bye except a few uglies passing by. They looked so young to her now, especially the just-arrived new class, who gawked at her like she was an old pile of dinosaur bones.

She'd always loved being independent, but now Tally felt like the last littlie to be picked up from school, abandoned and alone. September was a crappy month to be born.

"You're Tally, right?"

She looked up. It was a new ugly, awkwardly exploding into unfamiliar height, tugging at his dorm uniform like it was already too tight.

"Yeah."

"Aren't you the one who's going to turn today?"

"That's me, Shorty."

"So how come you look so sad?"

Tally shrugged. What could this half-littlie, half-ugly understand, anyway? She thought about what Shay had said about the operation.

Yesterday they'd taken Tally's final measurements, rolling her all the way through an imaging tube. Should she tell this new ugly that sometime this afternoon, her body was going to be opened up, the bones ground down to the right shape, some of them stretched or padded, her nose cartilage and cheekbones stripped out and replaced with programmable plastic, skin sanded off and reseeded like a soccer field in spring? That her eyes would be laser-cut for a lifetime of perfect vision, reflective implants inserted under the iris to add sparkling gold flecks to their indifferent brown? Her muscles all trimmed up with a night of electrocize and all her baby fat sucked out for good? Teeth replaced with ceramics as strong as a suborbital aircraft wing, and as white as the dorm's good china?

They said it didn't hurt, except the new skin, which felt like a killer sunburn for a couple of weeks.

As the details of the operation buzzed around in her head, she could imagine why Shay had run away. It did seem like a lot to go through just to look a certain way. If only people were smarter, evolved enough to treat everyone the same even if they looked different. Looked ugly.

If only Tally had come up with the right argument to make her stay.

The imaginary conversations were back, but much worse than they had been after Peris had left. A thousand times she'd fought with Shay in her head—long, rambling discussions about beauty, biology, growing up. All those times out in the ruins, Shay had made her points about uglies and pretties, the city and the outside, what was fake and what was real. But Tally had never once realized her friend might actually run away, giving up a life of beauty, glamour, elegance. If only she'd said the right thing. *Any*thing.

Sitting here, she felt as if she'd hardly tried.

Tally looked the new ugly in the eye. "Because it all comes down to this: Two weeks of killer sunburn is worth a lifetime of being gorgeous."

The kid scratched his head. "Huh?"

"Something I should have said, and didn't. That's all."

The hospital hovercar finally came, settling onto the school grounds so lightly that it hardly disturbed the fresh-mown grass.

The driver was a middle pretty, radiating confidence and authority. He looked so much like Sol that Tally almost called her father's name.

"Tally Youngblood?" he said.

Tally had already seen the flash of light that had read her eyeprint, but she said, "Yes, that's me," anyway. Something about the middle pretty made it hard to be flippant. He was wisdom personified, his manner so serious and formal that Tally found herself wishing she had dressed up.

"Are you ready? Not taking much."

Her duffel bag was only half-full. Everyone knew that new pretties wound up recycling most of the stuff they brought over the river, anyway. She'd have all new clothes, of course, and all the new pretty toys she wanted. All she'd really kept was Shay's handwritten note, hidden among a bunch of random crap. "Got enough."

"Good for you, Tally. That's very mature."

"That's me, sir."

The door closed, and the car took off.

The big hospital was on the bottom end of New Pretty Town. It was where everyone went for serious operations: littlies, uglies, even late pretties from way out in Crumblyville coming in for life-extension treatments.

The river was sparkling under a cloudless sky, and Tally allowed herself to be swept away by the beauty of New Pretty Town. Even without the nighttime lights and fireworks, the city's surfaces shone with glass and metal, the unlikely spindles of party towers casting thin shadows across the island. It was so much more vibrant than the Rusty Ruins, Tally suddenly saw. Not as dark and mysterious, perhaps, but more alive.

It was time to stop sulking about Shay. Life was going to be one big party from now on, full of beautiful people. Like Tally Youngblood.

The hovercar descended onto one of the red *X*s on the hospital roof, and Tally's driver escorted her inside, taking her to a waiting room. An orderly looked up Tally's name, flashed her eye again, and told her to wait.

"You'll be okay?" the driver asked.

She looked up into his clear, soft eyes, wanting him to stay. But asking him to wait with her didn't seem very mature. "No, I'm fine. Thanks." He smiled and went away.

No one else was in the waiting room. Tally settled back and counted the tiles on the ceiling. As she waited, the conversations with Shay in her head came back again, but they weren't so troubling here. It was too late for second thoughts now.

Tally wished there was a window to look out onto New Pretty Town. She was so close now. She imagined tomorrow night, her first night pretty, dressed in new and wonderful clothes (her dorm uniforms all shoved down the recycler), looking out from the top of the highest party tower she could find. She would watch as lights-out fell across the river, bedtime for Uglyville, and know that she still had all night with Peris and her new friends, all the beautiful people she would meet.

She sighed.

Sixteen years. Finally.

Nothing happened for a long hour. Tally drummed her fingers, wondering if they always kept uglies waiting this long.

Then the man came.

He looked strange, unlike any pretty Tally had ever seen. He was definitely of middle age, but whoever had done his operation had botched it. He was beautiful, without a doubt, but it was a terrible beauty.

Instead of wise and confident, the man looked cold, commanding, intimidating, like some regal animal of prey. When he walked up, Tally started to ask what was going on, but a glance from him silenced her.

She had never met an adult who affected her this way. She always felt respect when face-to-face with a middle or late pretty. But in the presence of this cruelly beautiful man, respect was saturated with fear.

The man said, “There’s a problem with your operation. Come with me.”

She went.

SPECIAL CIRCUMSTANCES

This hovercar was larger, but not as comfortable.

The trip was much less pleasant than Tally's first ride that day. The strange-looking man flew with an aggressive impatience, dropping like a rock to cut between flight lanes, banking as steeply as a hoverboard with every turn. Tally had never been airsick before, but now she clutched the seat restraints, her knuckles white and eyes fixed on the solid ground below. She caught one last glimpse of New Pretty Town receding behind them.

They headed downriver, across Uglyville, over the greenbelt and farther out to the transport ring, where the factories stuck their heads aboveground. Beside a huge, misshapen hill, the car descended into a complex of rectangular buildings, as squat as ugly dorms and painted the color of dried grass.

They landed with a painful bump, and the man led her into one of the buildings, and down into a murk of yellow-brown hallways. Tally had never seen so much space painted in such putrid colors, as if the building were designed to make its occupants vaguely nauseated.

There were more people like the man.

They were all dressed in formals, raw silks in black and gray, and their faces had the same cold, hawkish look. Both the men and women were taller than pretty standard, and more powerfully built, their eyes as pale as an ugly's. There were a few normal people as well, but they faded into insignificance next to the predatory forms moving gracefully through the halls.

Tally wondered if this was someplace where people were taken when their operations went wrong, when beauty turned cruel. Then why was she here? She hadn't even had the operation yet. Tally swallowed. What if these terrible pretties had been made this way intentionally? When they had measured her yesterday, had they determined that she would never fit the vulnerable, doe-eyed pretty mold? Maybe she'd already been chosen to be remade for this strange, other world.

The man stopped outside a metal door, and Tally halted behind him. She felt like a littlie again, jerked along by a minder on an invisible string. All her ugly senior's confidence had evaporated the moment she'd seen him back at the hospital. Four years of tricks and independence gone.

The door flashed his eye and opened, and he pointed for her to go in. Tally realized he hadn't said a word since collecting her at the hospital. She took a deep breath, which made the paralyzed muscles in her chest flinch with pain, and managed to croak, "Say please."

"Inside," was his answer.

Tally smiled, silently declaring a small victory that she had made him speak again, but she did as she was told.

"I'm Dr. Cable."

"Tally Youngblood."

Dr. Cable smiled. "Oh, I know who you are."

The woman was a cruel pretty. Her nose was aquiline, her teeth sharp, her eyes a nonreflective gray. Her voice had the same slow, neutral cadence as a bedtime book. But it hardly made Tally sleepy. An edge was hidden in the voice, like a piece of metal slowly marking glass.

"You have a problem, Tally."

"I had kind of guessed that, uh . . ." It was strange, not knowing the woman's first name.

"Dr. Cable will do."

Tally blinked. She'd never called anyone by their last name in her life.

"Okay, Dr. Cable." She cleared her throat and managed to say more, in a dry voice. "My problem right now is that I don't know what's going on. So . . . why don't you tell me?"

"What do you think's going on, Tally?"

Tally closed her eyes, taking a rest from the sharp angles of the woman's face. "Well, that bungee jacket *was* a spare, you know, and we did put it back on the recharge pile."

"This isn't about some ugly-trick."

She sighed and opened her eyes. "No, I didn't think so."

"This is about a friend of yours. Someone missing."

Of course. Shay's disappearing trick had gone too far, leaving Tally to explain. "I don't know where she is."

Dr. Cable smiled. Only her top teeth showed when she did. "But you do know something."

"Who are you, anyway?" Tally blurted. "Where am I?"

"I'm Dr. Cable," the woman said. "And this is Special Circumstances."

First Dr. Cable asked her a lot of questions. "You didn't know Shay long, did you?"

"No. Just this summer. We were in different dorms."

"And you didn't know any of her friends?"

"No. They were all older than her. They'd already turned."

"Like your friend Peris?"

Tally swallowed. How much did this woman know about her? "Yeah. Like Peris and me."

"But Shay's friends didn't wind up pretty, did they?"

Tally took a slow breath, remembering her promise to Shay. She didn't want to lie, though. Dr. Cable would know if she did, Tally was sure. She was in enough trouble already. "Why wouldn't they?"

"Did she tell you about her friends?"

"We didn't talk about stuff like that. We just hung out. Because . . . it hurt being alone. We were just into playing tricks."

"Did you know she'd been in a gang?"

Tally looked up into Dr. Cable's eyes. They were almost as big as a normal pretty's, but they angled upward like a wolf's.

"A gang? How do you mean?"

"Tally, did you and Shay ever go to the Rusty Ruins?"

"Everyone does."

"But did you ever *sneak out* to the ruins?"

"Yeah. A lot of people do."

"Did you ever meet anyone there?"

Tally bit her lip. "What's Special Circumstances?"

"Tally." The edge in her voice was suddenly sharp as a razor blade.

"If you tell me what Special Circumstances is, I'll answer you."

Dr. Cable sat back. She folded her hands and nodded. "This city is a paradise, Tally. It feeds you, educates you, keeps you safe. It makes you pretty."

Tally couldn't help looking up hopefully at this.

"And our city can stand a great deal of freedom, Tally. It gives youngsters room to play tricks, to develop their creativity and independence. But occasionally bad things come from *outside* the city."

Dr. Cable narrowed her eyes, her face becoming even more like a predator's. "We exist in equilibrium with our environment, Tally, purifying the water that we put back in the river, recycling the biomass, and using only power drawn from our own solar footprint. But sometimes we can't purify what we take in from the outside. Sometimes there are threats from the environment that must be faced."

She smiled. "Sometimes there are Special Circumstances."

"So, you guys are like minders, but for the whole city."

Dr. Cable nodded. "Other cities sometimes pose a challenge. And sometimes those few people who live outside the cities can make trouble."

Tally's eyes widened. *Outside* the cities? Shay had been telling the truth—places like the Smoke really existed.

"It's your turn to answer my question, Tally. Did you ever meet anyone in the ruins? Someone not from this city? Not from any city?"

Tally grinned. "No. I never did."

Dr. Cable frowned, her eyes darting downward for a second, checking something. When they returned to Tally, they had grown even colder. Tally smiled again, certain now that Dr. Cable knew when she was telling the truth. The room must be reading her heartbeat, her sweat, her pupil dilation. But Tally couldn't tell what she didn't know.

The razor blade slid back into the woman's voice. "Don't play games with me, Tally. Your friend Shay will never thank you for it, because you'll never see her again."

The thrill of her small victory disappeared, and Tally felt her smile fade.

"Six of her friends disappeared, Tally, all at once. None of them has ever been found. Another two who were meant to join them chose not to throw their lives away, however, and we discovered a little about what had happened to the others. They didn't run away on their own. They were tempted by someone from outside, someone who wanted to steal our cleverest little uglies. We realized that this was a special circumstance."

One word sent ice down Tally's spine. Had Shay really been *stolen*? What did Shay or any ugly really know about the Smoke?

"We've been watching Shay since then, hoping she might lead us to her friends."

"So why didn't you . . . ," Tally blurted out. "You know, *stop* her!"

"Because of you, Tally."

"Me?"

Dr. Cable's voice softened. "We thought she had made a friend, a reason to stay here in the city. We thought she'd be okay."

Tally could only close her eyes and shake her head.

"But then Shay disappeared," Dr. Cable continued. "She turned out to be trickier than her friends. You taught her well."

"*I* did?" Tally cried. "I don't know any more tricks than most uglies."

"You underestimate yourself," Dr. Cable said.

Tally turned away from the vulpine eyes, shut out the razor-blade voice. This was *not* her fault. She had decided to stay here in the city, after all. She wanted to become pretty. She'd even tried to convince Shay.

But failed.

"It's not my fault."

"Help us, Tally."

"Help you what?"

"Find her. Find them all."

She took a deep breath. "What if they don't want to be found?"

"What if they do? What if they were lied to?"

Tally tried to remember Shay's face that last night, how hopeful she had been. She'd wanted to leave the city as much as Tally wanted to be pretty. However stupid the choice seemed, Shay had made it with her eyes open, and had respected Tally's choice to stay.

Tally looked up at Dr. Cable's cruel beauty, at the puke-yellow-brown of the walls. She remembered all the tricks Special Circumstances had played on her today—how they'd kept her waiting for an hour in the hospital, waiting and thinking she would soon be pretty, the brutal flight here, and all the cruel faces in the halls—and she decided. "I can't help you," Tally said. "I made a promise."

Dr. Cable bared her teeth. This time, it wasn't even a mockery of a smile. The woman became nothing but a monster, vengeful and inhuman. "Then I'll make you a promise too, Tally Youngblood. Until you do help us, to the very best of your ability, you will never be pretty."

Dr. Cable turned away.

"You can die ugly, for all I care."

The door opened. The scary man was outside, where he'd been waiting all along.

UGLY FOR LIFE

They must have forewarned the minders about her return. All the other uglies were gone, off on some unscheduled school trip. But they hadn't found out in time to save her stuff. When Tally reached her old room, she saw that everything had been recycled. Clothes, bedding, furniture, the pictures on the wallscreen—it had all reverted back to Generic Ugly. It even looked as if somebody else had been briefly moved in, then out again, leaving a strange drink can in the fridge.

Tally sat down on the bed, too stunned to cry. She knew she would start bawling soon, probably losing it at the worst possible time and place. Now that the encounter with Dr. Cable was over, her anger and defiance were fading, and there was nothing left to sustain her. Her stuff was gone, her future was gone, only the view out the window remained.

She sat and stared, having to remind herself every few minutes that it had all really happened: the cruel pretties, the strange buildings on the edge of town, the terrible ultimatum from Dr. Cable. Tally felt as if some wild trick had gone horribly wrong. A weird and horrible new reality had opened up, devouring the world she knew and understood.

All she had left was the small duffel bag she'd packed for the hospital. She couldn't even remember carrying it all the way back here. Tally pulled out the few clothes, which she'd shoved in at random, and found Shay's note.

She read it, looking for clues.

Take the coaster straight past the gap,
until you find one that's long and flat.
Cold is the sea and watch for breaks.
At the second make the worst mistake.
Four days later take the side you despise,
and look in the flowers for fire-bug eyes.
Once they're found, enjoy the flight.
Then wait on the bald head until it's light.

Hardly any of it made sense to her, only bits and pieces. Shay had obviously meant to hide the meaning from anyone else reading it, using references only the two of them would understand. Her paranoia made a lot more sense now. Having met Dr. Cable,

Tally could see why David wanted to keep his city—or camp, or whatever it was—a secret.

As Tally held the note, she realized that it was what Dr. Cable had wanted. The woman had been sitting across the room from the letter the whole time, but they'd never bothered to search her. That meant that Tally had kept Shay's secret, and that she still had something to bargain with.

It also meant that Special Circumstances could make mistakes.

Tally saw the other uglies come back in before lunchtime. As they filed off the school transport, all of them craned their necks to look up at her window. A few pointed before she ducked back into the shadows. Minutes later Tally could hear kids in the hall outside, growing silent as they passed her door. A few even giggled, as new uglies always did when tried to keep quiet.

Were they *laughing* at her?

Her rumbling stomach reminded Tally that she hadn't eaten breakfast, or dinner the night before. You weren't supposed to have food or water for sixteen hours before the operation. She was starving.

But she stayed in her room until lunch was over. She couldn't face a cafeteria full of uglies watching her every move, wondering what she had done to deserve her still-ugly face. When she couldn't stand her hunger anymore, Tally stole upstairs to the roof deck, where they put out leftovers for whoever wanted them.

A few uglies saw her in the hall. They clammed up and stood

aside as Tally passed, as if she were contagious. What had the minders told them? Tally wondered. That she'd pulled one too many tricks? That she was inoperable, an ugly-for-life? Or just that she was a Special Circumstance?

Everywhere she went, eyes looked away, but it was the most *visible* she'd ever felt.

A plate was set out for her on the roof deck, sealed in plastic wrap, her name stuck to it. Someone had noticed that she hadn't eaten. And, of course, everyone would realize that she was in hiding.

The sight of the plate of food, wilted and solitary, made the suppressed tears well up in her eyes. Tally's throat burned as if she'd swallowed something sharp, and it was all she could do to get back to her room before she burst into loud, jagged sobs.

When she got there, Tally found that she hadn't forgotten to bring the plate. She ate while she cried, tasting the salt of her tears in every bite.

Her parents came by about an hour later.

Ellie swept in first, gathering Tally into a hug that emptied her lungs and lifted her feet off the ground. "Tally, my poor baby!"

"Now don't injure the girl, Ellie. She's had a tough day."

Even without oxygen, it felt good inside the crushing embrace. Ellie always smelled just right, like a mom, and Tally always felt like a littlie in her arms. Released after what was probably a solid minute, but still too soon, Tally stepped back, hoping that she wouldn't cry again. She looked at her parents sheepishly, wondering what they must be thinking. She felt like a total failure. "I didn't know you guys were coming."

"Of course we came," Ellie said.

Sol shook his head. "I've never heard of anything like this happening. It's ridiculous. And we'll get to the bottom of it, don't you worry!"

Tally felt a weight lift from her shoulders. Finally there was someone else on her side. Her father's middle-pretty eyes twinkled with calm certainty. There was no question that he would sort everything out.

"What did they tell you?" Tally asked.

Sol gestured, and Tally sat down on the bed. Ellie settled beside her while he paced back and forth across the small room.

"Well, they told us about this Shay girl. Sounds like she's a lot of trouble."

"Sol!" Ellie interrupted. "The poor girl's missing."

"Sounds like she wants to be missing."

Her mother pursed her lips in silence.

"It's not her fault, Sol," Tally said. "She just didn't want to turn pretty."

"So, she's an independent thinker. Fine. But she should have had better sense than to drag someone else down with her."

"She didn't drag me anywhere. I'm right here." Tally looked out the window at the familiar view of New Pretty Town. "Where I'll be forever, apparently."

"Now, now," Ellie said. "They said that once you've helped them find this Shay girl, everything should go ahead as normal."

"It won't make any difference if the operation happens a few days late. It'll be a great story when you're old." Sol chuckled.

Tally bit her lip. "I don't think I can help them."

"Well, you just do your best," Ellie said.

"But I can't. I mean, I promised Shay that I wouldn't tell anyone her plans."

They were silent for a moment.

Sol sat down, taking one of her hands in his. They felt so warm and strong, almost as wrinkled as a crumbly's from days spent working in his wood shop. Tally realized that she hadn't visited her parents since the week of summer break, when she'd mostly been anxious to get back to hanging out with Shay full-time. But it was good to see them now.

"Tally, we all make promises when we're little. That's part of being an ugly—everything's exciting and intense and important, but you have to grow out of it. After all, you don't owe this girl anything. She's done nothing but cause you trouble."

Ellie took her other hand. "And you'll only be helping her, Tally. Who knows where she is now and what's happening to her? I'm surprised you let her run off like that. Don't you know how dangerous it is out there?"

Tally found herself nodding. Looking into Sol's and Ellie's faces, everything seemed so clear. Maybe cooperating with Dr. Cable would really be helping Shay, and would set things back on course for herself. But the thought of Dr. Cable made her wince. "You should have seen these people. The ones investigating Shay? They look like . . ."

Sol laughed. "I guess it would be a bit of a shock at your age, Tally. But of course we old folks know all about Special Circumstances. They may be tough, but they're just doing their jobs, you know. It's a tough world out there."

Tally sighed. Maybe her reluctance was just because the cruel pretties had scared her so much. "Have you ever met them? I couldn't believe the way they looked."

Ellie furrowed her brow. "Well, I can't say I've actually *met* one."

Sol frowned, then broke into a laugh. "Well, you wouldn't *want* to meet one, Ellie. And Tally, if you do the right thing now, you probably won't ever meet one again. That sort of business is something we can all do without."

Tally looked at her father, and for a moment she saw something other than wisdom and confidence in his expression. It was almost too easy the way Sol laughed off Special Circumstances, dismissing everything that went on outside the city. For the first time in her life, Tally found herself listening to a middle pretty without being completely reassured, a realization that made her dizzy. And she couldn't shake the thought that Sol knew nothing about the outside world Shay had fled to.

Maybe most people just didn't *want* to know. Tally had been taught all about the Rusties and early history, but at school they never said a single thing about people living outside the cities right now, people like David. Until she'd met Shay, Tally had never thought about it either.

But she couldn't dismiss the whole thing the way her father had.

And she had made Shay a solemn promise. Even if she was

just an ugly, a promise was a promise. "Guys, I'm going to have to think about this."

For a moment, an awkward silence filled the room. She'd said something they hadn't expected.

Then Ellie laughed and patted her hand. "Well, of course you do, Tally."

Sol nodded, back in command. "We know you'll do the right thing."

"Sure. But in the meantime," Tally said, "maybe I could come home with you?"

Her parents shared another look of surprise.

"I mean, it's really weird being here now. Everyone knows that I . . . I'm not scheduled for classes anymore, so it would just be like coming home for autumn break, but a little early."

Sol recovered first, and patted her shoulder. "Now, Tally, don't you think it would be even stranger for you out in Crumblyville? I mean, there's no other kids out there this time of year."

"You're much better off here with the other children, darling," Ellie added. "You're only a few months older than some of them. And goodness, we don't have your room ready at all!"

"I don't care. Nothing could be worse than this," Tally said.

"Oh, just order up some more clothes, and get that wallscreen back the way you want it," Sol said.

"I didn't mean the room—"

"In any case," Ellie interrupted, "why make a fuss? This'll all be over in no time. Just have a nice chat with Special Circumstances, tell them everything, and you'll be headed where you really want to be."

They all looked out the window at the towers of New Pretty Town.

"I guess so."

"Sweetheart," Ellie said, patting her leg, "what other choice do you have?"

PERIS

During the daytime, she hid in her room.

Going anywhere else was pure torture. The uglies in her own dorm treated her like a walking disease, and anyone else who recognized her sooner or later asked, "Why aren't you pretty yet?"

It was strange. She'd been an ugly for four years, but a few extra days had brought home to her exactly what the word really meant. Tally peered into her mirror all day, noting every flaw, every deformity. Her thin lips pursed with unhappiness. Her hair grew even frizzier because she kept running her hands through it in frustration. A trio of zits exploded across her forehead, as if marking the days since her sixteenth birthday. Her watery, too-small eyes glared back at her, full of anger.

Only at night could she escape from the tiny room, the nervous stares, her own ugly face.

She fooled the minders and climbed out as usual, but she didn't feel much like any real tricks. There was no one to visit, no one to play a prank on, and the idea of crossing the river was too painful to consider. She had gotten a new hoverboard, and tricked it up like Shay had taught her, so at least she could fly at night.

But flying didn't feel the same. She was alone, it was getting cold at night, and no matter how fast she flew, Tally was trapped, and she knew it.

The fourth night in ugly exile she took her board up into the greenbelt, staying at the edge of town. She whipped it back and forth past the dark columns of tree trunks, shooting through them at top speed, so fast that her hands and face collected dozens of scratches from the branches blurring by.

After a few hours' flying had worn away some of her anguish, Tally had a happy realization: This was the best she'd ever ridden; she was almost as good as Shay now. Never once did the board dump her for getting too close to a tree, and her shoes held on to its grippy surface like they were glued there. She worked up a sweat even in the autumn chill, riding until her legs were tired, her ankles aching, her arms sore from being spread out like wings guiding her through the dark forest. If she rode this hard all night, Tally thought, maybe tomorrow she could sleep the hideous daylight away.

She flew until exhaustion forced her home.

When she crawled back into her room at dawn, someone was waiting there.

• • •

"Peris!"

His features burst into a radiant smile, big eyes flashing beautifully in the early light. But when he looked closer, his expression changed. "What happened to your face, Squint?"

Tally blinked. "Haven't you heard? They didn't do the—"

"Not that." Peris reached up and touched her cheek, which smarted under his fingertips. "You look like you've been juggling cats all night."

"Oh, yeah." Tally ran her fingers through her hair, and rummaged through a drawer. She pulled a medspray out, closed her eyes, and squirted herself in the face.

"Ow!" she yelped in the few seconds before the anesthetic kicked in. She sprayed her scratched hands as well. "Just a little midnight hoverboarding."

"A little past midnight, don't you think?"

Out the window, the sun was just beginning to turn the towers of New Pretty Town pink. Cat-vomit pink. She looked at Peris, exhausted and confused. "How long have you been here?"

He shifted uncomfortably in her window chair. "Long enough."

"Sorry. I didn't know you were coming."

He raised his eyebrows in beautiful anguish. "Of course I came. The moment I figured out where you were, I came."

Tally turned away, unlacing her grippy shoes as she collected herself. She'd felt so abandoned since her birthday, it had never occurred to her that Peris would want to see her, especially not here in Uglyville. But here he was, worried, anxious, lovely.

"It's good to see you," she said, feeling tears come into her eyes. They were red and puffy most of the time these days.

He beamed up at her. "You too."

The thought of what she must look like was too much. Tally collapsed onto the bed, covering her face with her hands and sobbing. Peris sat next to her and held her for a while as she cried, then wiped her nose and sat her up. "Look at you, Tally Youngblood."

She shook her head. "Please don't."

"You're an absolute mess."

Peris found a brush and ran it through her hair. She couldn't meet his eyes, and stared at the floor.

"So, do you always go hoverboarding in a blender?"

She shook her head, lightly touching the scratches on her face. "Just tree branches. At high speed."

"Oh, so getting yourself killed is your next brilliant trick. I guess that would just about top your current one."

"My current what?"

Peris rolled his eyes. "This whole trick where you haven't turned pretty yet. Very mysterious."

"Yeah. Some trick."

"When did *you* get modest, Squint? All my friends are fascinated."

She turned her puffy eyes to her friend, trying to figure out if he was kidding.

"I mean, I already told everyone about you after that fire alarm thing, but they're *really* dying to meet you now," he continued.

"There's even a rumor that Special Circumstances is involved."

Tally blinked. Peris was serious.

"Well, that's true," she said. "They're the reason I'm still ugly."

Peris's big eyes widened even more. "Really? That is so bubbly!"

She sat up and frowned. "Did *everyone* know about them but me?"

"Well, I had no idea what anyone was talking about. Apparently, Specials are like gremlins; you blame them when anything weird happens. Some people think they're totally bogus, and no one I know has actually *seen* a Special."

Tally sighed. "Just my luck, I guess."

"So they're real?" Peris lowered his voice to a whisper. "Do they really look different? You know, *not* pretty."

"It's not that they're not pretty, Peris. But they're really . . ." Tally looked at him, gorgeous and hanging on every word. It felt so perfect to be sitting next to him, talking and touching, as if they'd never been apart. She smiled. "They're just not as pretty as you."

He laughed. "You'll have to tell me all about it. But don't you dare tell anyone else. Not yet. Everyone's going to be so intrigued. We can throw a big party when you get yourself prettied up."

She tried to smile. "Peris . . ."

"I know, you're probably not supposed to talk about it. But once you're across the river, just drop a few hints about Special-you-know-what and you'll get invited to all the parties! Just make sure you take me with you." He leaned closer. "There's even a rumor that all the bubbly jobs go to people who had tricky records as kids. But that's years from now. The main thing is to get you pretty already."

"But, Peris," she said, her stomach starting to hurt. "I don't think I'll . . ."

"You'll love it, Tally. Being pretty's the best thing ever. And I'll enjoy it about a million times more once you're there with me."

"I can't."

He frowned. "Can't what?"

Tally looked up at Peris, clutching his hand. "You see, they want me to tattle on a friend of mine. Someone I got to know really well. After you left."

"Tattle? Don't tell me this is all about some ugly-trick."

"Sort of."

"So, tattle away. How big a deal can it be?"

Tally turned away. "It's important, Peris. It's more than a trick. I made my friend a promise that I'd keep a secret for her."

His eyes narrowed, and for a moment he looked like the old Peris: serious, thoughtful, even a little bit unhappy. "Tally, you made me a promise too."

She swallowed and stared back at him. His eyes shone with tears.

"You promised you wouldn't do anything stupid, Tally. That you'd be with me soon. That we'd be pretty together."

She touched the scar on her palm, still there, even though Peris's had been rubbed away. He reached over and held her hand. "Best friends forever, Tally."

She knew that if she looked into his eyes again, it would be all over. One glance, and her resistance would evaporate. "Best friends forever?" she said.

"Forever."

She took a deep breath and let herself stare into his eyes. He looked so sad, so vulnerable and wounded. So perfect. Tally imagined herself by his side, just as beautiful, spending every day doing nothing but talking and laughing and having fun.

"You'll keep your promise, Tally?"

A shudder of exhaustion and relief went through her. She had it now, an excuse to break her vow. She'd made that promise to Peris, just as real, before she'd ever met Shay. She had known him for years, and Shay for only a few months.

And Peris was right here, not out in some strange wilderness, and was looking at her with those eyes . . .

"Of course."

"Really?" He smiled, and it was as bright as the daybreak outside.

"Yeah." The words came out so easily. "I'll be there as soon as I can. I promise."

He sighed and hugged her tight, rocking her softly. Tears rose up in her again.

Peris finally released her, and looked out at the sunny day.

"I should go." He waved at the door. "You know, before the . . . thingies . . . all wake up."

"Of course."

"It's almost past my bedtime, and you've got a big day ahead of you."

Tally nodded. She'd never felt so exhausted. Her muscles ached, and her face and hands had started stinging again. But she was overwhelmed with relief. This nightmare had begun three months ago, when Peris went across the river. And soon it would end.

"Okay, Peris. I'll see you soon. As soon as possible."

He hugged her again, kissed her salty, scratched cheeks, and whispered, "Maybe in just a couple of days. I'm so excited!"

He said good-bye and left, checking both ways down the corridor before departing. Tally looked out the window for another glance at Peris, and realized that a hovercar was waiting for him below. Pretties really did get whatever they wanted.

Tally wanted nothing more than to fall asleep, but acting on her decision couldn't wait. She knew that with Peris gone, the doubts would come back again and haunt her. She couldn't stand another day like this, not knowing if her ugly purgatory would ever end. And she'd promised Peris she'd be with him as soon as possible.

"I'm sorry, Shay," Tally said quietly.

Then she picked up her interface ring from where it had lain on the bedside table all night, and slipped it on. "Message to Dr. Cable, or whomever," she said to it. "I'll do what you want. Just let me sleep for a while. Message over."

Tally sighed, and let herself fall back onto the bed. She knew she should spray her scratches again before passing out, but the thought of moving made her whole body ache. A few dozen scratches wouldn't keep her from sleeping today. Nothing would.

Seconds later, the room spoke. "Reply from Dr. Cable: A car will be sent for you, arriving in twenty minutes."

"No," she mumbled, but realized that it would be useless to argue. Special Circumstances would come, they would wake her up, they would take her.

Tally decided to try for a few minutes of sleep. It would be better than nothing.

But for the next twenty minutes, she never once shut her eyes.

INFILTRATOR

The cruel pretties seemed even more unearthly to exhausted eyes. Tally felt like a mouse in a cage full of hawks, just waiting for one to swoop down and take her. The trip in the hovercar had been even more sickening this time.

She focused on the nausea eating away at her stomach, trying to forget why she was here. As Tally and her escort made their way down the hall, she tried to pull herself together, tucking in her shirt and tugging at her hair.

Dr. Cable certainly didn't look like she'd just gotten up. Tally tried without success to imagine what a tousled Dr. Cable would look like. Her darting, metal-gray eyes hardly seemed as if they would ever close long enough to sleep.

"So, Tally. You've reconsidered."

"Yes."

"And you'll answer all our questions now? Honestly and of your own free will?"

Tally snorted. "You're not giving me a choice."

Dr. Cable smiled. "We always have choices, Tally. You've made yours."

"Great. Thanks. Look, just ask your questions."

"Certainly. First of all, what on earth happened to your face?"

Tally sighed, one hand touching the scratches. "Trees."

"Trees?" Dr. Cable raised an eyebrow. "Very well. On a more important subject, what did you and Shay talk about the last time you saw her?"

Tally closed her eyes. This was it, the moment when she would break her vow to Shay. But a small voice in her exhausted brain reminded her that she was also keeping a promise. Now she could finally join Peris.

"She talked about going away. Running away with someone called David."

"Ah, yes, the mysterious David." Dr. Cable leaned back. "And did she say where she and David were going?"

"A place called the Smoke. Like a city, only smaller. And no one was in charge there, and no one was pretty."

"And did she say where it was?"

"No, she didn't, not really." Tally sighed and pulled Shay's crumpled note from her pocket. "But she left me these directions."

Dr. Cable didn't even look at the note. Instead, she pushed a piece of paper from her side of the desk over to Tally's. Through bleary eyes, Tally saw that it was a 3-D copy of the note, perfect down to the slight incisions of Shay's labored penmanship on the paper.

"We took the liberty of making a copy of that the first time you were here."

Tally glared at Dr. Cable, realizing she'd been duped. "Then why do you need me? I don't know anything more than what I just said. I didn't ask her to tell me any more. And I didn't go with her, because I just . . . wanted . . . to be *pretty*!" A lump rose in her throat, but Tally decided that under no circumstances—special or not—was she going to cry in front of Dr. Cable.

"I'm afraid that we find the instructions on the note rather cryptic, Tally."

"You and me both."

Dr. Cable's hawk-eyes narrowed. "They seem to be designed to be read by someone who knows Shay quite well. By you, perhaps."

"Yeah, well, I get some of it. But after the first couple of lines, I'm lost."

"I'm sure it's very difficult. Especially after a long night of . . . trees. I still think you can help us, however."

Dr. Cable opened a small briefcase on the desk between them. Tally's tired brain struggled to make sense of the objects in the case. A firestarter, a crumpled sleeping bag . . .

"Hey, that's like the survival stuff that Shay had."

"That's right, Tally. These ranger kits go missing every so often. Usually just about the same time that one of our uglies disappears."

"Well, mystery solved. Shay was all ready to travel to the Smoke with a bunch of that stuff."

"What else did she have?"

Tally shrugged. "A hoverboard. A special one, with solar."

"Of course a hoverboard. What is it about those things and miscreants? And what did Shay plan to eat, do you suppose?"

"She had food in packets. Dehydrated."

"Like this?" Dr. Cable produced a silvery food pack.

"Yeah. She had enough for four weeks." Tally took a deep breath. "Two weeks, if I'd gone along. More than enough, she said."

"Two weeks? Not so very far." Dr. Cable pulled a black knapsack from beside her desk and started to pack the various objects into it. "You might just make it."

"Make it? Make *what*?"

"The trip. To the Smoke."

"Me?"

"Tally, only you can understand these directions."

"I told you: I don't know what they mean!"

"But you will, once you're on the journey. And if you're . . . properly motivated."

"But I already told you everything you wanted to know. I gave you the note. You promised!"

Dr. Cable shook her head. "My promise, Tally, was that you wouldn't be pretty until you helped us to the very best of your ability. I have every confidence that this is within your ability."

"But why me?"

"Listen carefully, Tally. Do you really think that this is the first time we've been told about David? Or the Smoke? Or found some scrawled directions about how to get there?"

Tally flinched at the razor-blade voice, turning away from the anger on the woman's cruel face. "I don't know."

"We've seen all this before. But whenever we go ourselves, we find nothing. Smoke, indeed."

The lump had returned to Tally's throat. "So how am I supposed to find anything?"

Dr. Cable pulled the copy of Shay's note toward herself. "This last line, where it says to 'wait on the bald head,' clearly refers to a rendezvous point. You go there, you wait. Sooner or later, they'll pick you up. If I send a hovercar full of Specials, your friends will probably be a bit suspicious."

"You mean, you want me to go *alone*?"

Dr. Cable took a deep breath, a disgusted look on her face. "This isn't very complicated, Tally. You have had a change of heart. You have decided to run away, following your friend Shay. Just another ugly escaping the tyranny of beauty."

Tally looked up at the cruel face through a prism of gathering tears. "And then what?"

Dr. Cable pulled another object from the briefcase, a necklace with a little heart pendant. She pressed on its sides, and the heart clicked open. "Look inside."

Tally held the tiny heart up to her eye. "I can't see anything . . . ow!"

The pendant had flashed, blinding her for a moment. The heart made a little beep.

"The finder will only respond to your eye-print, Tally. Once it's activated, we'll be there within a few hours. We can travel very quickly." Cable dropped the necklace onto the desk. "But don't activate it until you're in the Smoke. This has taken us some time to set up. I want the real thing, Tally."

Tally blinked away the afterimage of the flash, trying to force her exhausted brain to think. She realized now that this had never been simply a matter of answering questions. They had always wanted her as a spy, an infiltrator. She wondered just how long this had been planned. How many times had Special Circumstances tried to get an ugly to work for them before? "I can't do this."

"You can, Tally. You must. Think of it as an adventure."

"Please. I've never even spent the whole night outside the city. Not alone."

Dr. Cable ignored the sob that had cut through Tally's words. "If you don't agree right now, I'll find someone else. And you'll be ugly forever."

Tally looked up, trying to see through the tears that were flowing freely now, to peer past Dr. Cable's cruel mask and find the truth. It was there in her dull, metal-gray eyes, a cold, terrible surety unlike anything a normal pretty could ever convey. Tally realized that the woman meant what she said.

Either Tally infiltrated the Smoke and betrayed Shay, or she'd be an ugly for life.

"I have to think."

"Your story will be that you ran away the night before your birthday," Dr. Cable said. "That means you've already got to make up for four lost days. Any more delays, and they won't believe you. They'll guess what happened. So decide now."

"I can't. I'm too tired."

Dr. Cable pointed at the wallscreen, and an image appeared. Like a mirror, but in close-up, it showed Tally as she looked right now: puffy-eyed and disheveled, exhaustion and red scratches marking her face, her hair sticking out in all directions, and her expression turning horrified as she beheld her own appearance.

"That's you, Tally. Forever."

"Turn it off . . ."

"Decide."

"Okay, I'll do it. Turn it off."

The wallscreen went dark.

Part II
THE SMOKE

There is no excellent beauty
that hath not some strangeness in the proportion.
—Francis Bacon, *Essays, Civil and Moral*, “Of Beauty”

LEAVING

Tally left at midnight.

Dr. Cable had demanded that no one be told about her mission, even the dorm minders. It was fine if Peris spread rumors—no one believed the gossip of new pretties, anyway. But not even her parents would be officially informed that Tally had been forced to run away. Except for her little heart pendant, she was on her own.

She slipped out the usual way, out the window and down behind the recycler. Her interface ring remained on the bedside table, and Tally carried nothing but the survival knapsack and Shay's note. She almost forgot her belly sensor, but clipped it on just before she left. The moon was about half-full and growing. At least she'd have some light as she traveled.

A special long-range hoverboard was waiting under the dam. It hardly moved when she stepped on. Most boards gave a little as they adjusted to a rider's weight, bouncing like a diving board, but this one was absolutely firm. She snapped her fingers, and it rose under her, steady as concrete under her feet.

"Not bad," she said, then bit her lip. Since Shay had run away ten days ago, she'd started talking to herself. That wasn't a good sign. She was going to be completely alone for at least a few days now, and the last thing she needed was more imaginary conversations.

The board eased forward smoothly, climbing the embankment to the top of the dam. Once on the river, Tally pushed it faster, leaning forward until the river was a shining blur beneath her feet. The board didn't seem to have a speed governor—no safety warning sounded. Perhaps its only limits were the open space in front of her, metal in the ground below, and Tally's feet staying on board.

Speed was everything if she was going to make up for the last four days in limbo. If Tally showed up too long after her birthday, Shay might realize that her operation had been delayed. From there, she might guess that Tally wasn't an ordinary runaway.

The river passed beneath her faster and faster, and she reached the rapids in record time. Drops of spray stung like hailstones when she hit the first falls, and Tally leaned back to slow herself a bit. Still, she was taking the rapids faster than she ever had before.

Tally realized that this hoverboard was no ugly toy. It was the real thing. On its front end a half circle of lights glowed, giving feedback from the board's metal detector, which constantly searched ahead to see if there was enough iron in the ground to stay aloft. The lights stayed on solidly as she climbed the rapids, and Tally hoped that Shay was right about metal deposits being found in every river. Otherwise, this could be a very long trip.

Of course, at this speed she wouldn't have time to stop if the lights suddenly went out. Which would make it a very short trip.

But the lights stayed on, and Tally's nerves were soothed by the roar of white water, the cold slap of spray in her face, the thrill of bending her body through curve after curve in the moon-speckled darkness. The board was smarter than her old one, learning her moves in a matter of minutes. It was like graduating from a tricycle to a motorbike: scary, but thrilling.

Tally wondered if the route to the Smoke had a lot of rapids to ride. Maybe this really would be an adventure. Of course, at the end of the journey there would only be betrayal. Or worse, she would discover that Shay's trust in David had been misplaced, which could mean . . . anything. Probably something horrible.

She shivered, deciding not to think about that possibility again.

When Tally reached the turnoff, she slowed and turned the board around, taking a last look at the city. It shone brilliantly in the dark valley, so distant that she could blot it out with one hand. In the clear night air, Tally could make out individual fireworks unfolding like bright flowers, everything in perfect miniature. The wild around her seemed so much larger, the churning river full of power, the forest huge with the secrets hidden in its black depths.

She allowed herself a long stare at the city lights before she stepped onto shore, wondering when she would see her home again.

On the trail, Tally wondered how often she'd have to walk. The trip up the rapids had been the fastest she had ever flown, even quicker than the Special Circumstances hovercar dodging through city traffic. After that rush of speed, carrying the knapsack and board felt like being turned into a slug.

But soon enough the Rusty Ruins appeared below, and the board's metal detector guided Tally to the natural vein of iron. She rode it down toward the crumbling towers, her nerves growing jumpy as the ruins rose up to blot out the half-moon. The broken buildings surrounded her, the scorched and silent cars passing below. Peering through the empty windows made her feel how alone she was, a solitary wanderer in an empty city.

"Take the coaster straight past the gap," she said aloud, an incantation to keep away any Rusty ghosts. At least that much of the note was crystal clear: The "coaster" had to be the roller coaster.

When the towering ruins gave way to flatter ground, Tally opened up the hoverboard. Reaching the roller coaster, she took the entire circuit at full speed. Maybe "straight past the gap" was the only important part of the clue, but Tally had decided to treat the note like a magic spell. Leaving out any part might make the whole thing meaningless.

And it felt good to ride fast and hard again, leaving the ghosts of the Rusty Ruins behind. As she whipped around tight turns and down steep descents, the world whirling around her, Tally felt like something caught in the wind, not knowing which direction the journey would ultimately take her.

A few seconds before she took the jump across the gap, the metal-detector lights winked out. The board dropped away, and her stomach seemed to go with it, leaving a hollow feeling inside. Her suspicion had proved right—at top speed, there hadn't been much warning.

Tally flew through the air in the silent darkness, the rush of her passage the only sound. She remembered her first time across the gap, how angry she'd been. A few days later it had turned into a joke between them, typical ugly stuff. But now Shay had done it again, disappearing like the track below, leaving Tally in free fall.

A count of five later, the lights flickered on, and the crash bracelets steadied her as the board reactivated, rising smoothly up under her feet with reassuring solidness. At the bottom of the hill the track turned, climbing into a steep corkscrew of turns. But Tally slowed and kept going ahead, murmuring, "straight past the gap."

The ruins continued under her feet. Out here they were almost completely submerged, only a few shapeless masses rising through the grasp of vegetation. But the Rusties had built solidly, in love with their wasteful skeletons of metal. The lights on the front of her board stayed bright.

"Until you find one that's long and flat," Tally said to herself. She had memorized the note backward and forward, but repeating the words hadn't made their meaning any clearer.

"One *what*?" was the question. A roller coaster? A gap? The first would be silly. Where would be the point of a long, flat roller coaster? A long, flat gap? Maybe that would describe a canyon, complete with a handy river at the bottom. But how could a canyon be flat?

Maybe "one" meant a one, like the number. Should she be looking for something that looked like a one? But a one was just a straight line, anyway, kind of long and flat already. So was *I,* the Roman numeral for one, except for the crossbars on top and bottom. Or the dot on the top if it was a small *i.*

"Thanks for the great clue, Shay," Tally said aloud. Talking to herself didn't seem like such a bad idea there in the outer ruins, where the relics of the Rusties struggled against the grip of creeping plants. Anything was better than ghostly silence. She passed concrete plains, vast expanses cracked by thrusting grasses. The windows of fallen walls stared up at her, sprouting weeds as if the earth had grown eyes.

She scanned the horizon, looking for clues. There was nothing long and flat that she could see. Peering down at the ground passing below, Tally could hardly make out anything in the weed-choked darkness. She might zoom right past whatever the clue referred to and not even know it, and have to retrace her path in daylight. But how would she know when she'd gone too far? "Thanks, Shay," she repeated.

Then she spotted something on the ground, and stopped.

Through the shroud of weeds and rubble, geometrical shapes had appeared—a series of rectangles in a line. She lowered the board and saw that below her was a track with metal rails and wooden crossbars—like the roller coaster, but much bigger. And it went in a straight line, as far as she could see.

"Take the coaster straight past the gap, until you find one that's long and flat."

This thing was a roller coaster, but long and flat.

"But what's it *for*?" she wondered aloud. What fun was a roller coaster without any turns or climbs?

She shrugged. However the Rusties got their kicks, this was perfect for a hoverboard. The track stretched off in two directions, but it was easy enough to tell which one to take. One led back the way she'd come, toward the center of the ruins. The other headed outward, northward and angling toward the sea.

"Cold is the sea," she quoted from the next line of Shay's note, and wondered how far north she was going.

Tally brought the hoverboard up to speed, pleased that she'd found the answer. If all of Shay's little riddles were this easy to solve, this whole trip was going to be a breeze.

SPAGBOL

She made good time that night.

The track zoomed along beneath her, tracing slow arcs around hills, crossing rivers on crumbling bridges, always headed toward the sea. Twice it took her through other Rusty ruins, smaller towns further along in their disintegration. Only a few twisted shapes of metal remained, rising above the trees like skeletal fingers grasping at the air. Burned-out groundcars were everywhere, choking the streets out of town, twisted together in the collisions of the Rusties' last panic.

Near the center of one ruined town, she discovered what the long, flat roller coaster was all about. In a nest of tracks tangled up like a huge circuit board, she found a few rotting roller-coaster cars, huge rolling containers full of Rusty stuff, unidentifiable piles of rust and plastic. Tally remembered now that Rusty cities weren't self-sufficient, and were always trading with one another, when they weren't fighting over who had more stuff. They must have used the flat roller coaster to move trade from town to town.

As the sky began to grow light, Tally heard the sound of the sea in the distance, a faint roar coming from across the horizon. She could smell salt in the air, which brought back memories of going to the ocean with Ellie and Sol as a littlie.

"Cold is the sea and watch for breaks," Shay's note read. Soon, Tally would be able to see the waves breaking on the shore. Maybe she was close to the next clue.

Tally wondered how much time she'd made up with her new hoverboard. She increased its speed, wrapping her dorm jacket around herself in the predawn chill. The track was slowly climbing now, cutting through formations of chalky rock. She remembered white cliffs towering over the ocean, swarming with seabirds nesting in high caves.

Those camping trips with Sol and Ellie felt as if they'd happened a hundred years ago. She wondered if there was some operation that could make her back into a littlie again, forever.

Suddenly, a gap opened up in front of Tally, spanned by a crumbling bridge. An instant later she saw that the bridge didn't make it all the way across, and there was no river full of metal deposits beneath it to catch her. Just a precipitous drop to the sea.

Tally spun her board sideways into a skid. Her knees bent under the force of braking, her grippy shoes squealing as they slipped across the riding surface, her body turning almost parallel to the ground.

But the ground was gone.

A deep chasm opened up under her, a fissure cut into the cliffs by the sea. Boiling waves crashed into the narrow channel, their whitecaps glowing in the darkness, their hungry roars reaching her ears. The board's metal-detector lights flickered out one by one as Tally left the splintered end of the iron bridge behind.

She felt the board lose purchase, slipping downward.

A thought flashed through her mind: If she jumped now, she could make a grab for the end of the broken bridge. But then the hoverboard would tumble into the chasm behind her, leaving her stranded.

The board finally halted in its slide out into midair, but Tally was still descending. The last fingers of the crumbling bridge were *above* her now, out of reach. The board inched downward, metal-detector lights flickering off one by one as the magnets lost their grip. She was too heavy. Tally slipped off the knapsack, ready to hurl it down. But how could she survive without it? Her only choice would be to return to the city for more supplies, which would lose two more days. A cold wind off the ocean blew up the chasm, goose-pimpling her arms like the chill of death.

But the breeze buoyed the hoverboard, and for a moment she neither rose nor fell. Then the board started to slip downward again. . . .

Tally thrust her hands into the pockets of her jacket and spread her arms, making a sail to catch the wind. A stronger gust struck, lifting her slightly, taking some weight off the board, and one of the metal-detector lights flickered stronger.

Like a bird with outstretched wings, she began to rise.

The lifters gradually regained purchase on the track, until the hoverboard had brought her level with the broken end of the bridge. She coaxed it carefully back over the cliff's edge, a huge shiver passing through her body as the board passed over solid ground. Tally stepped off, legs shaking.

"Cold is the sea and watch for *breaks,*" she said hoarsely. How could she have been so stupid, speeding up just when Shay's note said to be careful?

Tally collapsed onto the ground, suddenly dizzy and tired. Her mind replayed the chasm opening up, the waves below smashing indifferently against the jagged rocks. *She* could have been down there, battered again and again until there was nothing left.

This was the wild, she reminded herself. Mistakes had serious consequences.

Even before Tally's heart had stopped pounding, her stomach growled.

She reached into her knapsack for the water purifier, which she'd filled at the last river, and emptied the muck-trap. A spoonful of brown sludge that it had filtered from the water glopped out. "Eww," she said, opening the top to peer in. It looked clear, and smelled like water.

She took a much needed drink, but saved most to make dinner, or breakfast, whatever it was. Tally planned to do most of her traveling at night, letting the hoverboard recharge in sunlight, wasting no time.

Reaching into the waterproof bag, she pulled out a food packet at random. "'SpagBol,'" she read from the label, and shrugged. Unwrapped, it looked and felt like a finger-size knot of dried yarn. She dropped it into the purifier, which made burbling noises as it came to a boil.

When Tally glanced out at the glowing horizon, her eyes opened wide. She'd never seen dawn from outside the city before. Like most uglies, she was rarely up early enough, and in any case the horizon was always hidden behind the skyline of New Pretty Town. The sight of a real sunrise amazed her.

A band of orange and yellow ignited the sky, glorious and unexpected, as spectacular as fireworks, but changing at a stately, barely perceptible pace. That's how things were out here in the wild, she was learning. Dangerous or beautiful. Or both.

The purifier pinged. Tally opened the top and looked inside. It was noodles with a red sauce, with small kernels of soymeat, and it smelled delicious. She looked at the label again. "SpagBol . . . spaghetti Bolognese!"

She found a fork in the knapsack and ate hungrily. With the sunrise warming her and the crash of the sea rumbling below, it was the best meal she'd had for ages.

The hoverboard still had some charge left, so after breakfast she decided to keep moving. She reread the first few lines of Shay's note:

Take the coaster straight past the gap,
until you find one that's long and flat.
Cold is the sea and watch for breaks.
At the second make the worst mistake.

If "the second" meant a second broken bridge, Tally wanted to run into it in daylight. If she'd spotted the gap a split second later, she would have ended up so much SpagBol at the bottom of the cliffs.

But her first problem was getting across the chasm. It was much wider than the gap in the roller coaster, definitely too far to jump. Walking looked like the only way around. She hiked inland through the scrubby grass, her legs grateful for a stretch after the long night on board. Soon the chasm closed, and an hour later she had hiked back up the other side.

Tally flew much slower now, eyes fixed ahead, daring only an occasional glimpse at the view around her.

Mountains rose up on her right, tall enough that snow capped their tops even in the early autumn chill. Tally had always thought of the city as huge, a whole world in itself, but the scale of everything out here was so much grander. And so beautiful. She could see why people used to live out in nature, even if there weren't any party towers or mansions. Or even dorms.

The thought of home, however, reminded Tally how much her sore muscles would love a hot bath. She imagined a giant bathtub, like they had in New Pretty Town, with whirlpool jets and a big packet of massage bubbles dissolving in it. She wondered if the water purifier could boil enough water to fill a tub, in the unlikely event that she found one. How did they bathe in the Smoke? Tally wondered what she'd smell like when she arrived, after days without a bath. Was there soap in the survival kit? Shampoo? There certainly weren't any towels. Tally had never realized how much *stuff* she'd needed before.

The second break in the track came up after another hour: a crumbling bridge over a river that snaked down from the mountains.

Tally came to a controlled stop and peered over the edge. The drop wasn't as bad as the first chasm, but it was still deep enough to be deadly. Too wide to jump. Hiking around it would take forever. The river gorge stretched away, with no easy way down in sight.

"At the second make the worst mistake," she murmured.

Some clue. Anything she did right now would be a mistake. Her brain was too tired to handle this, and the board was short on power, anyway.

Midmorning, it was time to sleep.

But first she had to unfold the hoverboard. The Special who'd instructed her had explained that it needed as much surface area in the sun as possible while it recharged. She pulled the release tabs, and it came apart. It opened like a book in her hands, becoming two hoverboards, then each of those opened up, and then those, unfolding like a string of paper dolls. Finally, Tally had eight hoverboards connected side-to-side, twice as wide as she was tall, no thicker than a stiff sheet of paper. The whole thing fluttered in the stiff ocean breeze like a giant kite, though the board's magnets kept it from blowing away.

Tally laid it flat, stretched out in the sun, where its metallic surface turned jet black as it drank in solar energy. In a few hours it would be charged up and ready to ride again. She just hoped it would go back together as easily as it had pulled apart.

Tally pulled out her sleeping bag, yanked it out of its pack, and wriggled inside, still in her clothes. "Pajamas," she added to her list of things she missed about the city.

She made a pillow of her jacket, struggled out of her shirt, and covered her head with it. She could already feel a hint of burn on her nose, and realized she had forgotten to stick on a sunblock patch after daybreak. Perfect. A little red and flaking skin should go quite nicely with the scratches on her ugly face.

Sleep didn't come. The day was getting warm, and it felt weird lying there in the open. The cries of seabirds rang in her head. Tally sighed and sat up. Maybe if she had a little more to eat.

She pulled out food packets one by one. The labels read:

SpagBol
SpagBol
SpagBol
SpagBol
SpagBol . . .

Tally counted forty-one more packets, enough for three SpagBols a day for two weeks. She leaned back and closed her eyes, suddenly exhausted. "Thank you, Dr. Cable."

A few minutes later, Tally was asleep.

THE WORST MISTAKE

She was flying, skimming the ground with no track under her, not even a hoverboard, keeping herself aloft by sheer willpower and the wind in her outspread jacket. She skirted the edge of a massive cliff that overlooked a huge, black ocean. A flock of seabirds pursued her, their wild screams beating at her ears like Dr. Cable's razor-edged voice.

Suddenly, the stony cliffs beneath her cracked and fissured. A huge rift opened up, the ocean rushing in with a roar that drowned the seabirds' cries. She found herself tumbling through the air, falling down toward the black water.

The ocean swallowed her, filling her lungs, freezing her heart so that she couldn't cry out. . . .

"No!" Tally shouted, sitting bolt upright.

A cold wind off the sea struck her face, clearing her head. Tally looked around, realizing that she was up on the cliffs, tangled in her sleeping bag. Tired, hungry, and desperate to pee, but not falling into oblivion.

She took a deep breath. The seabirds still cried around her, but in the distance.

That last dream had been only one of many falling nightmares.

Night was coming, the sun setting over the ocean, turning the water bloodred. Tally pulled her shirt and jacket on before daring to emerge from the sleeping bag. The temperature seemed to be dropping by the minute, the light fading before her eyes. She hurried to get ready to go.

The hoverboard was the tricky part. Its unfolded surface had gotten wet, covered with a fine layer of ocean spray and dew. Tally tried to wipe it off with her jacket sleeve, but there was too much water and not enough jacket. The wet board folded up easily enough, but it felt too heavy when she was done, as if the water was still trapped between the layers. The board's operation light turned yellow, and Tally looked closely. The sides of the board were gradually oozing the water away. "Fine. Gives me time to eat."

Tally pulled out a packet of SpagBol, then realized that her purifier was empty. The only ready source of water was at the bottom of the cliff, and there was no way down. She wrung out her wet jacket, which produced a few good *squooshes,* then scraped off handfuls of the water oozing from the board until the purifier was half-full. The result was a dense, overspiced SpagBol that required lots of chewing.

By the time she was done with the unhappy meal, the board's light had turned green.

"Okay, ready to go," Tally said to herself. But where? She stood still, pondering, one foot on the board and one on the ground.

Shay's note read, "At the second make the worst mistake."

Making a mistake shouldn't be that hard. But what was the *worst* mistake? She'd almost killed herself once today already.

Tally remembered her dream. Falling into the gorge would count as a pretty bad mistake. She stepped onto the board and edged it to the crumbling end of the bridge, looking down to where the river met the sea far below.

If she climbed down, her only possible path would be to follow the river upstream. Maybe that's what the clue meant. But the steep cliff showed no obvious path, not even a handhold.

Of course, a vein of iron in the cliff might carry her down safely. Her eyes scanned the walls of the gorge, searching for the reddish color of iron. A few spots looked promising, but in the growing darkness, she couldn't be certain.

"Great." Tally realized that she'd slept too long. Waiting for dawn would be twelve hours lost, and she didn't have any more water.

The only other option was to hike upriver atop the cliff. But it might be days before she reached a place to climb down. And how would she see it at night?

She had to make up time, not blunder around in the dark.

Tally swallowed, coming to a decision. There had to be a way down on her board. Maybe she was making a mistake, but that's what the clue called for. She edged the board off the bridge until it began to lose purchase. It slipped down the cliffside, descending faster as it left the metal of the track behind.

Tally's eye searched desperately for any sign of iron in the cliff. She eased the board forward, bringing it closer to the wall of stone, but saw nothing. A few of the board's metal-detector lights flickered out. Any lower, and she was going to fall.

This wasn't going to work. Tally snapped her fingers. The board slowed for a second, trying to climb, but then shivered and continued to descend.

Too late.

Tally spread her jacket, but the air in the gorge was still. She spotted a rusty-looking streak in the wall of stone and coaxed the board closer, but it turned out to be just a slimy smear of lichen. The board slipped downward faster and faster, the metal-detector lights flickering out one by one.

Finally, the board went dead.

Tally realized that this mistake might be her last.

She fell like a rock, down toward the crashing waves. Just like in the dream, her voice felt choked by a freezing hand, as if her lungs were already filled with water. The board tumbled below her, spinning like a falling leaf.

Tally closed her eyes, waiting for the shattering impact of cold water.

Suddenly, something grabbed her by the wrists and yanked her up cruelly, spinning her in the air. Her shoulders screamed with pain, and she spun once all the way around like a gymnast on the rings.

Tally opened her eyes and blinked. She was being lowered onto the hoverboard, which waited rock-steady just above the water.

"What the . . . ?" she wondered aloud. Then, as her feet came to rest, Tally realized what had happened.

The river had caught her. It had been dumping metal deposits there for centuries, or however long rivers lasted, and the board's magnets had found purchase just in time.

"Saved, more or less," Tally muttered. She rubbed her shoulders, which ached from being caught by the crash bracelets, and wondered how far you had to fall before the bracelets would rip your arms out of their sockets.

But she'd made it down. The river stretched out in front of her, winding its way into the snowcapped mountains. Tally shivered in the ocean breeze and pulled her soggy jacket tighter around her.

"'Four days later take the side you despise,'" she quoted Shay's note. "Four days. Might as well get started."

After her first sunburn, Tally stuck a sunblock patch onto her skin every morning at dawn. But even with only a few hours in the sun each day, her already brown arms gradually deepened in color.

SpagBol never again tasted as good as it had that first time on the cliffs. Tally's meals ranged from decent to odious. The worst were SpagBol breakfasts, around sunset, when the mere thought of more noodles made her never want to eat again. She almost wished she would run out of the stuff and be forced to either catch a fish and cook it, or simply starve, losing her ugly-fat the hard way.

What Tally really dreaded was running out of toilet paper. Her only roll was already half-gone, and she rationed it strictly now, counting the sheets. And every day, she smelled a little worse.

On the third day up the river, she decided to take a bath.

Tally awoke, an hour before sunset as usual, feeling sticky inside the sleeping bag. She'd washed her clothes that morning and left them to dry on a rock. The thought of getting into clean clothes with dirty skin made her flesh crawl.

The water in the river was fast-moving, and left almost nothing in the muck-trap of the purifier, which meant it was clean. It was icy cold, though, probably fed by melting snow in the approaching mountains. Tally prayed it would be slightly less freezing late in the day, after the sun had had a chance to warm it up.

The survival kit did have soap, it turned out—a few disposable packets tucked into a corner of the knapsack. Tally clenched one in her hand as she stood at the edge of the river, wearing nothing but the sensor clipped to her belly ring, shivering in the cool breeze.

"Here we go," she said, trying to keep her teeth from chattering.

She put one foot in and jumped back from the icy streak of agony that shot into her leg. Apparently, there would be no easing slowly into the water. She had to take a running jump.

Tally walked along the riverbank, searching for a good place to leap in, slowly gathering her courage. She realized she'd never been naked outside before. In the city, everywhere outdoors was public, but she hadn't seen another human face for days. The world seemed to belong to her. Even in the cool air, the sun felt wonderful on her skin.

She clenched her teeth and faced the river. Standing here pondering the wild wasn't going to get her clean. Just a few steps and a leap, and gravity would do the rest.

She counted down from five, then counted down from ten, neither of which worked. Then she realized that she was getting cold just standing there.

Finally, Tally jumped.

The freezing water closed like a fist around her. It paralyzed every muscle, turning her hands into shivering claws. For a moment, Tally wondered how she would make it back to shore. Maybe she would just expire here, slipping under the icy water forever.

She took a deep, shuddering breath, reminding herself that the people before the Rusties must have taken baths in freezing streams all the time. Tally clenched her teeth to stop them chattering, and dipped her head under the water and out, whipping wet hair onto her back.

A few moments later an unlikely kernel of warmth ignited in her stomach, as if the icy water had activated some secret reserve of energy within her body. Her eyes opened wide, and she found herself whooping with excitement. The mountains, towering above her after three nights' travel inland, seemed suddenly crystal clear, their snowy peaks catching the last rays of the setting sun. Tally's heart pounded fiercely, her blood spreading unexpected warmth throughout her body.

But the burst of energy was burning quickly. She fumbled the soap packet open, squishing it between her fingers, across her skin, and into her hair. Another dunking and she was ready to get out.

Looking back at the shore, Tally realized that she'd been carried away from her camp by the river's current. She swam a few strokes upstream, then trudged toward the rocky shore.

Waist-high in the water, already shivering from the breeze on her wet body, Tally heard something that made her heart freeze.

Something was coming. Something big.

THE SIDE YOU DESPISE

Thunder came from the sky, like a giant drum beating fiercely and fast, forcing its way into her head and chest. It seemed to rattle the whole horizon, making the surface of the river shimmer with every thud.

Tally crouched low in the water, sinking to her neck just before the machine appeared.

It came from the direction of the mountains, flying low and kicking up dust in a dozen separate windstorms in its wake. It was much bigger than a hovercar, and a hundred times louder. Apparently without magnets, it beat the air into submission with a half-invisible disk shimmering in the sun.

When the machine reached the river, it banked into a turn.

Its passage churned the water, sending out circular waves as if some huge stone were skimming across the surface. Tally saw people inside, looking down at her camp. The unfolded hoverboard pitched in the windstorm, its magnets fighting to keep it on the ground. Her knapsack disappeared in the dust, and she saw clothing, the sleeping bag, and packets of SpagBol scattering in the machine's wake.

Tally sank lower into the frantic water, struck by the thought that she would be left here, naked and alone, with nothing. She was already half frozen.

But the machine dipped forward, just like a hoverboard, and moved on. It headed toward the sea, vanishing as quickly as it had appeared, leaving her ears pounding and the river's surface boiling.

Tally crept out shivering. Her body felt ice cold, her fingers barely able to clench into a fist. She made her way back to her camp, grasping clothes to her body, putting them on before the setting sun could dry her. She sat and wrapped her arms around herself until the shaking stopped, glancing fearfully at the red horizon every few seconds.

The damage was less than she'd feared. The hoverboard's operation light was green, and her knapsack, dusty but unharmed. After a search for SpagBol and a count of the remaining packets, Tally found that she had lost only two. But the sleeping bag was shredded. Something had chopped it to pieces.

Tally swallowed. There was nothing left of the bag bigger than a handkerchief. What if she had been in it when the machine had come?

She folded the hoverboard quickly and packed everything away. The board was ready to go almost instantly. At least the strange machine's windstorm had dried it off.

"Thanks a lot," Tally said as she stepped on, leaning forward as the sun began to set. She was anxious to leave the campsite behind her as quickly as possible, in case they came back.

But who were they? The flying machine had been just like what Tally imagined when her teachers had described Rusty contraptions: a portable tornado crashing along, destroying everything in its path. Tally had read about aircraft that shattered windows as they flew past, armored war vehicles that could drive straight through a house.

But the Rusties had been gone a long time. Who would be stupid enough to rebuild their insane machines?

Tally rode into the growing darkness, her eyes peeled for any signs of the next clue—"Four days later take the side you despise"—and for whatever other surprises the night would bring.

One thing was certain now: She wasn't alone out here.

Later that night, the river branched in two.

Tally cruised to a halt, surveying the junction. One of the branches was clearly larger, the other more like a broad stream. A "tributary," she remembered, was the name for a small river that fed into a larger one.

Probably she should just stay on the main river. But she'd been traveling for just three days, and her hoverboard was a lot faster than most. Maybe it was time for the next clue.

"Four days later take the side you despise," Tally muttered.

She peered at the two rivers in the light from the moon, which was almost full now. Which river did she despise? Or which one would Shay *think* she despised? They both looked pretty ordinary to her. She squinted into the distance. Maybe one led toward something despicable that would be visible in daylight.

But waiting would mean losing a night's travel, and sleeping in the cold and dark without a sleeping bag.

Tally reminded herself that the clue might not be about this junction. Maybe she should just stay on the big river until something more obvious came up. Why would Shay call the two rivers "sides," anyway? If she'd meant this junction, wouldn't it be "take the direction you despise"?

"The side you despise," Tally mumbled, remembering something.

Her fingers went to her face. When she had showed Shay her pretty morphos, Tally had mentioned how she always started by doubling her left side—that she had always hated the right side of her face. Which was exactly the sort of thing that Shay would remember.

Was this Shay's way of telling her to take a right?

Branching to the right was the smaller river, the tributary. The mountains were closer in that direction. Maybe she was drawing near the Smoke.

She stared at the two rivers in the darkness, one big and one small, and remembered Shay saying that pretty symmetry was silly, because she'd rather have a face with two different sides.

Tally hadn't realized it at the time, but that had been an important conversation for Shay, the first time she had talked about wanting to stay ugly. If only Tally had noticed at the time, maybe she could have talked Shay out of running away. And they'd both be in a party tower right now, together and pretty.

"Right it is." Tally sighed, and eased her board onto the smaller river.

By the time the sun rose, Tally knew she had made the right choice.

As the tributary climbed its way into the mountains, the fields around her filled with flowers. Soon the brilliant white bonnets were as thick as grass, driving every other color from the landscape. In the dawn light, it was as if the earth were glowing from within.

"'And look in the flowers for fire-bug eyes,'" Tally said to herself, wondering if she should get off the board. Maybe there was some kind of bug with fiery eyes she should be looking for.

She drifted to shore and stepped off.

The flowers came right up to the edge of the water. Tally knelt to inspect one closely. The five long white petals curved delicately up from the stem and around its mouth, which contained just a hint of yellow deep inside. One of the petals below the mouth was longer, arching down almost to the ground. Motion caught her eye, and she spotted a small bird hovering among the flowers, flitting from one to the next to alight on the longest petal, thrusting its beak into one after another.

"They're so beautiful," she said. And there were so many of them. She wanted to lie down in the flowers and sleep.

But she couldn't see anything that might be "fire-bug eyes." Tally stood, scanning the horizon. Nothing met her gaze but hills, blinding white with flowers, and the glimmering river climbing up into the mountains. It all looked so peaceful, a different world from the one that the flying machine had shattered last night.

She stepped back on the board and continued, slower now as she looked carefully for whatever might fit Shay's clue, remembering to stick on a sunblock patch as the sun rose higher.

The river climbed higher into the hills. From up there, Tally saw bare stretches among the flowers, expanses of dry, sandy earth. The patchy landscape was a strange sight, like a beautiful painting that someone had taken sandpaper to.

She got off her board several times to inspect the flowers, looking for insects or anything else that might match the words "fire-bug eyes." But as the day wore on, nothing made sense.

By the time noon approached the tributary was gradually growing smaller. Sooner or later, she would reach its source, a mountain spring or melting snowdrift, and then she'd have to walk. Tired after the long night, she decided to make camp.

Her eyes scanned the sky, wondering if any more of the Rusty flying machines were around. The idea of another one crashing into her in her sleep terrified her. Who knew what the people inside the thing wanted? If she hadn't been hidden in the water the night before, what would they have done with her?

One thing was certain: The shiny solar cells of the hoverboard would be obvious from the air. Tally checked the charge; more than half remained thanks to her slow speed and the bright sun now overhead. She unfolded the hoverboard, but only halfway, and hid it among the tallest flowers she could find. Then she hiked to the top of a nearby hill. From up there Tally could keep her eye on the hoverboard, and hear and see anything approaching from the air. She decided to repack her knapsack before she went to sleep, so she could bolt at a moment's notice.

It was the best she could do.

After a mildly revolting packet of SpagBol, Tally curled up in a spot where the white flowers were tall enough to hide her. The breeze stirred their long stalks, and shadows danced on her closed eyelids.

Tally felt strangely exposed without her sleeping bag, lying there in her clothes, but the warm sun and the long night's travel put her quickly to sleep.

When she awoke, the world was on fire.

FIRESTORM

At first there was a sound like a roaring wind in her dreams.

Then a tearing noise filled the air, the crackle of dry brush inflamed, and the smell of smoke swept over Tally, bringing her suddenly and completely awake.

Billowing clouds of smoke surrounded her, blotting out the sky. A ragged wall of flame moved through the flowers, giving off a wave of blistering heat. She grabbed her knapsack and stumbled down the hill away from the fire.

Tally had no idea in which direction the river lay. Nothing was visible through the dense clouds. Her lungs fought for air in the foul brown smoke.

Then she spotted a few rays from the setting sun breaching the billows, and she oriented herself. The river was back toward the flame, on the other side of the hill.

Tally retraced her path to the top of the hill and peered down through the smoke. The fire was growing stronger. Fingers of it shot up the hill, leaping from one beautiful flower to another, leaving them scorched and black. Tally caught the glimmer of the river through the smoke, but the heat pushed her back.

She stumbled down the other side again, coughing and spitting, one thought in her mind: Was her hoverboard already engulfed in flames?

Tally had to get to the river. The water was the only place safe from the rampaging fire. If she couldn't go over the hill, maybe she could go around.

She descended the slope at full tilt. There were a few spots burning on this side, but nothing like the galloping flame behind her. She reached level ground and made her way around the base of the hill, crouching low to the ground to duck under the smoke.

Halfway around, she reached a blackened patch where the fire had already passed. The brittle stems of flowers crunched under her shoes, and the heat coming off the scorched earth stung her eyes.

Her footsteps ignited with flame as she ran through the blackened flowers, like stabbing a poker into a slumbering fire. She felt her eyes drying, her face blistering.

Moments later, Tally spotted the river. The fire stretched in an unbroken wall across the opposite shore, a roaring wind pressing at its back and sending embers flying across to alight on the near side.

A rolling billow of smoke surged toward her, choking and blinding her until it passed.

When her eyes could open again, Tally spotted the shiny solar surface of her hoverboard. She ran toward it, ignoring the burning flowers in her path.

The board seemed untouched by the flame, protected by good luck and the layer of dew it collected every nightfall.

She quickly folded the board and stepped onto it, not waiting for the yellow light to turn green. The heat had mostly dried it already, and it rose into the air at her command. Tally took the board over the river, just above the water, and skimmed her way upstream, looking for a break in the wall of fire to her left.

Her grippy shoes were ruined, their soles cracked like sun-baked mud, so she flew slowly, scooping up handfuls of water to soothe her burning face and arms.

A noise thundered to life on Tally's left, unmistakable even above the roar of the fire. She and the board were caught in a sudden wind, shoved back toward the other shore. Tally leaned hard against it and stuck a foot into the water to slow the board. She clung tightly with both hands, desperately fighting being thrown into the river.

The smoke suddenly cleared, and a familiar shape loomed out of the darkness. It was the flying machine, its thundering beat now obvious above the raging fire. Sparks jumped across the river as the machine's windstorm stirred the fire to a new intensity.

What were they *doing*? she wondered. Didn't they realize they were spreading the fire?

Her question was answered a moment later when a gout of

flame shot from the machine, squirting across the river to ignite another patch of flowers.

They had set the fire, and were driving it on in every way they could.

The flying machine thundered closer, and she glimpsed an inhuman face staring at her from the pilot seat. She turned her board to fly away, but the machine lifted up into the air, passing right over her, and suddenly the wind was too great.

Tally pitched off and into the water. Her crash bracelets caught for a moment, holding her up above the waves, but then the wind caught the hoverboard, much lighter without her on it, and spun it away like a leaf.

She sank into the deep water in the middle of the river, knapsack and all.

It was cool and quiet under the waves.

For a few endless moments, Tally felt only relief to have escaped the searing wind, the thundering machine, the blistering heat of the firestorm. But the weight of the crash bracelets and knapsack pulled her down fast, and panic welled up in her pounding chest.

She thrashed in the water, climbing up toward the flickering lights of the surface. Her wet clothes and gear dragged at her, but just as her lungs were about to burst, she broke the surface into the maelstrom. Tally gulped a few breaths of smoky air, then was slapped in the face by a wave. She coughed and sputtered, struggling to stay afloat.

A shadow passed over her, blacking out the sky. Then her hand struck something—a familiar grippy surface. . . .

Her hoverboard had come back to her! Just the way it always did when she spilled. The crash bracelets lifted her up until she could grab on to it, her fingers clinging to its knobbly surface as she gasped for air.

A high-pitched whine came from the nearby shore. Tally blinked away water from her eyes and saw that the Rusty machine had landed. Figures were jumping from the machine, spraying white foam at the ground as they crashed through the burning flowers and into the river. They were headed for her.

She struggled to climb onto the board.

"Wait!" the nearest figured called.

Tally rose shakily to her feet, trying to keep steady on the wet surface of the board. Her hard-baked shoes were slippery, and her sodden knapsack seemed to weigh a ton. As she leaned forward, a gloved hand reached up to grab the front of the board. A face came up from the water, wearing some sort of mask. Huge eyes stared up at her.

She stomped at the hand, crunching the fingers. They slipped off, but her weight was thrown too far forward, and the board tipped its nose into the water.

Tally tumbled into the river again.

Hands grabbed at her, pulling her away from the hoverboard. She was hoisted out of the water and onto a broad shoulder. She caught glimpses of masked faces: huge, inhuman eyes staring at her unblinkingly.

Bug eyes.

BUG EYES

They pulled her to the shore and out of the water, hauling her to the flying machine.

Tally's lungs felt full of water and smoke. She could hardly take a breath without a wracking cough shaking her whole body.

"Put her down!"

"Where the hell did she come from?"

"Give her some oh-two."

They flopped Tally onto her back on the ground, which was thick with the white foam. The one who'd carried her pulled off his bug-eyed mask, and Tally blinked.

He was a pretty. A new pretty, every bit as beautiful as Peris.

The man plunged the mask over her face. Tally fought weakly

for a moment, but then cold, pure air surged into her lungs. Her head grew light as she gratefully sucked it down.

He pulled the mask off. "Not too much. You'll hyperventilate."

She tried to speak but could only cough.

"It's getting bad," another figure said. "Jenks wants to take her back up."

"Jenks can wait."

Tally cleared her throat. "My board."

The man smiled beautifully and glanced up. "It's headed over. Hey! Somebody stick that thing to the chopper! What's your name, kid?"

"Tally." Cough.

"Well, Tally, are you ready to move? The fire won't wait."

She cleared her throat and coughed again. "I guess so."

"Okay, come on." The man helped her up and pulled her toward the machine. She found herself pushed inside, where the noise was much less, crowded into the back with three others in bug-eyed masks. A door slammed shut.

The machine rumbled, and then Tally felt it lift from the ground. "My board!"

"Relax, kid. We got it." The woman pulled her mask off. She was another young pretty.

Tally wondered if these were the people in the clue. The "fire-bug eyes." Was she supposed to be looking for *them*?

"Is she going to make it?" a voice popped through the cabin.

"She'll live, Jenks. Make the usual detour, and work the fire a little on the way home."

Tally looked down as the machine climbed. Their flight followed the course of the river, and she saw the fires spreading across to the other shore, driven by the wind of its passage. Occasionally, the craft would shoot out a gout of flame.

She looked at the faces of the crew. For new pretties, they seemed so determined, so focused on their task. But their actions were madness. "What are you guys doing?" she said.

"A little burning."

"I can see that. But *why*?"

"To save the world, kid. But hey, we're real sorry about your getting in the way."

They called themselves rangers.

The one who'd pulled her from the river was called Tonk. They all spoke with an accent, and came from a city Tally had never heard of.

"It's not too far from here," Tonk said. "But we rangers spend most of our time out in the wild. The fire helicopters are based in the mountains."

"The fire *whats*?"

"Helicopters. That's what you're sitting in."

She looked around at the rattling machine, and shouted over the noise, "It's so Rusty!"

"Yeah. Vintage stuff, a few pieces of it are almost two hundred years old. We copy the parts as they wear out."

"But why?"

"You can fly it anywhere, with or without a magnetic grid. And it's the perfect thing for spreading fires. The Rusties sure knew how to make a mess."

Tally shook her head. "And you spread fires because . . ."

He smiled and lifted one of her shoes, pulling a crushed but unburned flower from the sole. "Because of *phragmipedium panthera,*" he said.

"Excuse me?"

"This flower used to be one of the rarest plants in the world. A white tiger orchid. In Rusty days, a single bulb was worth more than a house."

"A house? But there's zillions of them."

"You noticed?" He held up the flower, staring into its delicate mouth. "About three hundred years ago, some Rusty figured a way to engineer the species to adapt to wider conditions. She messed with the genes to make them propagate more easily."

"Why?"

"The usual. To trade them for lots of stuff. But she succeeded a little too well. Look down."

Tally peered out the window. The machine had gained altitude and left the firestorm behind. Below were endless fields of white, interrupted only by a few barren patches. "Looks like she did a good job. So what? They're nice."

"One of the most beautiful plants in the world. But too successful. They turned into the ultimate weed. What we call a monoculture. They crowd out every other species, choke trees and grass, and nothing eats them except one species of hummingbird, which feeds on their nectar. But the hummingbirds nest in trees."

"There aren't any trees down there," Tally said. "Just the orchids."

"Exactly. That's what monoculture means: Everything the same. After enough orchids build up in an area, there aren't enough hummingbirds to pollinate them. You know, to spread the seeds."

"Yeah," Tally said. "I know about the birds and the bees."

"Sure you do, kid. So the orchids eventually die out, victims of their own success, leaving a wasteland behind. Biological zero. We rangers try to keep them from spreading. We've tried poison, engineered diseases, predators to target the hummingbirds . . . but fire is the only thing that really works." He turned the orchid over in his hand and held up a firestarter, letting the flame lick into its mouth. "Have to be careful, you know?"

Tally noticed the other rangers were cleaning their boots and uniforms, searching for any trace of the flowers among the mud and foam. She looked down at the endless white. "And you've been doing this for . . ."

"Almost three hundred years. The Rusties started the job, after they figured out what they'd done. But we'll never win. All we can hope to do is contain the weed."

Tally sat back, shaking her head, coughing once more. The flowers were so beautiful, so delicate and unthreatening, but they choked everything around them.

The ranger leaned forward, handing her his canteen. She took it and drank gratefully.

"You're headed to the Smoke, aren't you?"

Tally swallowed some water the wrong way and sputtered. "Yeah. How'd you know?"

"Come on. An ugly waiting around in the flowers with a hoverboard and a survival kit?"

"Oh, yeah." Tally remembered the clue: "Look in the flowers for fire-bug eyes." They must have seen uglies before.

"We help the Smokies out, and they help us out," Tonk said. "They're crazy, if you ask me—living rough and staying ugly. But they know more about the wild than most city pretties. It's kind of admirable, really."

"Yeah," she said. "I guess so."

He frowned. "You guess so? But you're headed there. Aren't you sure?"

Tally realized that this was where the lies started. She could hardly tell the rangers the truth: that she was a spy, an infiltrator. "Of course I'm sure."

"Well, we'll be setting you down soon."

"In the Smoke?"

He frowned again. "Don't you know? The location's a big secret. Smokies don't trust pretties. Not even us rangers. We'll take you to the usual spot, and you know the rest, right?"

She nodded. "Sure. Just testing you."

The helicopter landed in a swirl of dust, the white flowers bending in a wide circle around the touchdown spot.

"Thanks for the ride," Tally said.

"Good luck," Tonk said. "Hope you like the Smoke."

"Me too."

"But if you change your mind, Tally, we're always looking for volunteers in the rangers."

Tally frowned. "What's a volunteer?"

The ranger smiled. "That's when you pick your own job."

"Oh, right." Tally had heard you could do that in some cities. "Maybe. In the meantime, keep up the good work. Speaking of which, you're not setting any fires around here, are you?"

The rangers laughed, and Tonk said, "We just work the edges of the infestation, to keep the flowers from spreading. This spot is right smack in the middle. No hope left."

Tally looked around. There wasn't a glimpse of any color but white as far as she could see. The sun had set an hour ago, but the orchids glowed like ghosts in the moonlight. Now that she knew what they were, the sight chilled Tally. What had he called it? Biological zero.

"Great."

She jumped out of the helicopter and yanked her hoverboard from the magnetic rack next to the door. She backed away, careful to crouch as the rangers had warned her to.

The machine whined back to life, and she peered upward into the shimmering disk. Tonk had explained that a pair of thin blades, spinning so quickly that you couldn't see them, carried the craft through the air. She wondered if he'd been kidding. It just looked like a typical force field to her.

The wind grew crazed again as the machine reared up, and she held on to her board tightly, waving until the aircraft disappeared into the dark sky. She sighed.

Alone again.

Looking around, she wondered how she could find the Smokies in this featureless desert of orchids.

"Then wait on the bald head until it's light," was the last line of Shay's note. Tally scanned the horizon, and a relieved smile broke onto her face.

A tall, round hill rose up not far away. It must have been one of the places where the engineered flowers had first taken root. The top half of the hill was dying, nothing left but bare soil, ruined by the orchids.

The cleared area looked just like a bald head.

She reached the bald hilltop in a few hours.

Her hoverboard was useless there, but the hiking was easy in the new shoes the rangers had given her, her own so burned that they had fallen apart in the helicopter. Tonk had also filled her purifier with water.

The ride in the helicopter had begun to dry out Tally's clothing, and the hike had done the rest. Her knapsack had survived the dunking, even the SpagBol remaining dry in its waterproof bag. The only thing lost to the river was Shay's note, reduced to a soggy wad of paper in her pocket.

But she had almost made it. As she looked out from the hilltop, Tally realized that, except for the burn blisters on her hands and feet, some bruises on her knees, and a few locks of hair that had gone up in smoke, she had pretty much survived. As long as the Smokies knew where to find her, and believed her story that she was an ugly coming to join them, and didn't figure out that she was actually a spy, then everything was just great.

She waited on the hill, exhausted but unable to sleep, wondering if she could really do what Dr. Cable wanted. The pendant around her neck had also survived the ordeal. Tally doubted a little water would have ruined the device, but she wouldn't know until she reached the Smoke and activated it.

She hoped for a moment that the pendant wouldn't work. Maybe one of the bumps along the way had broken its little eye-reader and it would never send its message back to Dr. Cable. But that was hardly worth hoping for. Without the pendant, Tally was stuck out here in the wild forever. Ugly for life.

Her only way home was to betray her friend.

LIES

A couple of hours after dawn, they came and got her.

Tally saw them hiking through the orchids, four figures carrying hoverboards and dressed all in white. Broad white hats in a dappled pattern hid their heads, and she realized that if they ducked down into the flowers, they would practically disappear.

These people went to a lot of trouble to stay hidden.

As the party drew close, she recognized Shay's pigtails bobbing under one of the hats and waved frantically. Tally had planned to take the note literally and wait on the hilltop, but at the sight of her friend, she grabbed her board and dashed down to meet them.

Infiltrator or not, Tally couldn't wait to see Shay.

The tall, lanky form broke from the others and ran toward her, and the two embraced, laughing.

"It *is* you! I knew it was!"

"Of course it is, Shay. I couldn't stand missing you." Which was pretty much true.

Shay couldn't stop smiling. "When we spotted the helicopter last night, most people said it had to be another group. They said you'd taken too long, and that I should give up."

Tally tried to smile back, wondering if she hadn't made up enough time. She could hardly admit starting four days *after* her sixteenth birthday.

"I kind of got turned around. Could your note have been any more obscure?"

"Oh." Shay's face fell. "I thought you'd understand it."

Unable to bear Shay blaming herself, Tally shook her head. "Actually, the note was okay. I'm just a moron. And the biggest problem was when I got to the flowers. The rangers didn't see me at first, and I almost got roasted."

Shay's eyes widened as she took in Tally's scratched and sun-burned face, the blisters on her hands, and her patchy, scorched hair. "Oh, Tally! You look like you went through a war zone."

"Just about."

The other three uglies walked up. They stood back a bit, one boy holding a device in the air. "She's carrying a bug," he said.

Tally's heart froze. "A what?"

Shay gently took Tally's board from her and handed it to the boy. He swept his device across it, nodded, and pulled one of the stabilizer fins off. "Here it is."

"They sometimes put trackers on the long-range boards," Shay said. "Trying to find the Smoke."

"Oh, I'm really . . . I didn't know. I swear!"

"Relax, Tally," the boy said. "It's not your fault. Shay's board had one too. That's why we meet you newbies down here." He held up the bug. "We'll take it away in some random direction and stick it on a migrating bird. See how the Specials like South America." The Smokies all laughed.

He stepped closer and swept the device up and down her body. Tally flinched when it passed close to the pendant. But he smiled. "It's okay. You're clean."

Tally sighed with relief. Of course, she hadn't activated the pendant yet, so his device couldn't detect it. The other bug was just Dr. Cable's way of misleading the Smokies, getting them to drop their guard. Tally herself was the real danger.

Shay stepped up next to the boy, taking his hand in hers. "Tally, this is David."

The boy smiled again. He was an ugly, but he had a nice smile. And his face held a kind of confidence that Tally had never seen in an ugly before. Maybe he was a few years older than she was. Tally had never watched anyone mature naturally past age sixteen. She wondered how much of being ugly was just an awkward age.

Of course, David was hardly a pretty. His smile was crooked, and his forehead too high. But, uglies or not, it was good to see

Shay, David—all of them. Except for a couple of stunned hours with the rangers, she hadn't seen human faces in what seemed like years.

"So, what've you got?"

"Huh?"

Croy was one of the other uglies who'd come to meet her. He also looked older than sixteen, but it didn't suit him like it did David. Some people needed the operation more than others. He reached out a hand for her knapsack.

"Oh, thanks." Her shoulders were sore from being strapped to the thing for the last week.

He pulled it open as they hiked, looking inside. "Purifier. Position-finder." Croy pulled out the waterproof bag and opened it. "SpagBol! Yum!"

Tally groaned. "You can have it."

His eyes widened. "I can?"

Shay pulled the knapsack away from him. "No, you can't."

"Listen, I've eaten that stuff three times a day for the past . . . what seems like forever," Tally said.

"Yeah, but dehydrated food's hard to get in the Smoke," Shay explained. "You should save it to trade."

"Trade?" Tally frowned. "What do you mean?" In the city, uglies might trade chores or stuff they'd stolen, but trade *food*?

Shay laughed. "You'll get used to the idea. In the Smoke, things don't just come out of the wall. You've got to hang on to the stuff you brought with you. Don't go giving it away to anyone who asks." Shay glared at Croy, who looked down sheepishly.

"I was going to give her something for it," he insisted.

"Sure you were," David said.

Tally noticed his hand on Shay's shoulder, touching her softly as they hiked. She remembered the way Shay had always talked about David, kind of dreamily. Maybe it wasn't just the promise of freedom that had brought her friend here.

They reached the edge of the flowers, a dense growth of trees and brush that started at the foot of a towering mountain.

"How do you keep the orchids from spreading?" Tally asked.

David's eyes lit up, as if this was his favorite subject. "This old-growth forest stops them. It's been around for centuries, probably even before the Rusties."

"It's got lots and lots of species," Shay said. "So it's strong enough to keep out the weed." She looked at David for approval.

"The rest of this land used to be farms or grazing pasture," he continued, gesturing back at the expanse of white behind them. "The Rusties had already broken its back before the weed arrived."

A few minutes into the forest, Tally realized why the orchids were no match for it. The tangled brush and thick trees were knotted together into an impassable wall on either side. Even on the narrow path, she was constantly shoving past branches and twigs, tripping over roots and rocks. She'd never seen any woodlands this raw and inhospitable. Vines dotted with cruel thorns ran through the semidarkness like barbed wire. "You guys *live* in here?"

Shay laughed. "Don't worry. We've got a ways to go. We're just making sure you weren't followed. The Smoke's much higher, where the trees aren't so intense. But the creek's coming up. We'll be on board soon."

"Good," Tally said. Her feet were already chafing in the new shoes. But they were warmer than her destroyed grippies, she realized, and were better for hiking. She wondered what would have happened if the rangers hadn't given them to her. How did you get new shoes in the Smoke? Trade someone all your food? Make them yourself? She looked down at the feet ahead of her, David's, and saw that his shoes did look handmade, like a couple of pieces of leather crudely sewn together. Strangely, though, he moved gracefully through the undergrowth, silent and sure while the rest of them crashed along like elephants.

The very idea of making a pair of shoes by hand boggled her mind.

It didn't matter, Tally reminded herself, taking a deep breath. Once in the Smoke, she could activate the pendant and be home within a day, maybe within hours. All the food and clothes she would ever need, hers for the asking. Her face pretty at long last, and Peris and all their old friends around her.

Finally, this nightmare would be over.

Soon, the sound of running water filled the forest, and they reached a small clearing. David pulled his device out again, pointing it back toward the path. "Still nothing." He grinned at Tally. "Congratulations, you're one of us now."

Shay giggled and hugged Tally again as the others readied their boards. "I still can't believe you came. I thought I'd messed everything up, waiting so long to tell you about running away. And I was so stupid, getting into a fight instead of just telling you what I was going to do."

Tally shook her head. "You'd said everything already, I just wasn't listening. Once I realized you were serious, I needed a chance to think about it. It just took me a while . . . every minute, until the last night before my birthday." She took a deep breath, wondering why she was saying all this, lying to Shay when she didn't really have to. She should just shut up, get to the Smoke, and get it over with. But Tally found herself continuing. "Then I realized I'd never see you again if I didn't come. And I'd always wonder."

That last part was true, at least.

As they boarded higher up into the mountain the creek widened, cutting an archway of trees into the dense forest. The gnarled, smaller trees became taller pines, the undergrowth thinning, the brook breaking into occasional rapids. Shay cried out as she rode through the spray of churning white water.

"I've been dying to show you this! And the *really* good rapids are on the other side."

Eventually, they left the creek, following a vein of iron over a ridge. From the top, they looked down into a small valley that was mostly clear of forest.

Shay held Tally's hand. "There it is. Home."

The Smoke lay below them.

THE MODEL

The Smoke really was smoky.

Open fires dotted the valley, surrounded by small groups of people. The scents of wood smoke and cooking drifted up to Tally, smells that made her think of camping and outdoor parties. In addition to the smoke there was a morning mist in the air, a white finger creeping down into the valley from a bank of clouds nestled against the mountain higher up. A few solar panels glimmered feebly, gathering what sun was reflected from the mist. Garden plots were planted in random spots between the buildings, twenty or so one-story structures made from long planks of wood. There was wood everywhere: in fences; as cooking spits; laid down in walkways over muddy patches; and in big stacks by the fires. Tally wondered where they had found so much wood.

Then she saw the stumps at the edges of the settlement, and gasped. "Trees . . . ," she whispered in horror. "You cut down trees."

Shay squeezed her hand. "Only in this valley. It seems weird at first, but it's the way the pre-Rusties lived too, you know? And we're planting more on the other side of the mountain, pushing into the orchids."

"Okay," Tally said doubtfully. She saw a team of uglies moving a felled tree, pushing it along on a pair of hoverboards. "There's a grid?"

Shay nodded happily. "Just in places. We pulled up a bunch of metal from a railroad, like the track you came up the coast on. We've laid out a few hoverpaths through the Smoke, and eventually we'll do the whole valley. I've been working on that project. We bury a piece of junk every few paces. Like everything here, it's tougher than you'd think. You wouldn't *believe* how much a knapsack full of steel weighs."

David and the others were already headed down, gliding single file between two rows of rocks painted a glowing orange. "That's the hoverpath?" Tally asked.

"Yeah. Come on, I'll take you down to the library. You've got to meet the Boss."

The Boss wasn't really in charge here, Shay explained. He just acted like it, especially to newbies. But he was in command of the library, the largest of the buildings in the settlement's central square.

The familiar smell of dusty books overwhelmed Tally at the library door, and as she looked around, she realized that books were pretty much all the library had. No big airscreen, not even private workscreens. Just mismatched desks and chairs and rows and rows of bookshelves.

Shay led her to the center of it all, where a round kiosk was inhabited by a small figure talking on an old-fashioned handphone. As they drew closer, Tally felt her heart starting to pound. She'd been dreading what she was about to see.

The Boss was an *old* ugly. Tally had spotted a few from a distance on the way in, but had managed to turn her eyes away. But here was the wrinkled, veined, discolored, shuffling, horrific truth, right before her eyes. His milky eyes glared at them as he berated whoever was on the phone, in a rattling voice and waving one claw at them to go away.

Shay giggled and pulled her toward the shelves. "He'll get to us eventually. There's something I want to show you first."

"That poor man . . ."

"The Boss? Pretty wild, huh? He's, like, *forty*! Wait until you talk to him."

Tally swallowed, trying to erase the image of his sagging features from her mind. These people were insane to tolerate that, to *want* it. "But his face . . . ," Tally said.

"That's nothing. Check these out." Shay sat her down at a table, turned to a shelf, and pulled out a handful of volumes in protective covers. She plonked them in front of Tally.

"Books on paper? What about them?"

"Not books. They're called 'magazines,'" Shay said. She opened one and pointed. Its strangely glossy pages were covered with pictures. Of people.

Uglies.

Tally's eyes widened as Shay turned the pages, pointing and giggling. She'd never seen so many wildly different faces before. Mouths and eyes and noses of every imaginable shape, all combined insanely on people of every age. And the *bodies.* Some were grotesquely fat, or weirdly overmuscled, or uncomfortably thin, and almost all of them had wrong, ugly proportions. But instead of being ashamed of their deformities, the people were laughing and kissing and posing, as if all the pictures had been taken at some huge party. "Who are these freaks?"

"They aren't freaks," Shay said. "The weird thing is, these are famous people."

"Famous for what? Being hideous?"

"No. They're sports stars, actors, artists. The men with stringy hair are musicians, I think. The really ugly ones are politicians, and someone told me the fatties are mostly comedians."

"That's funny, as in strange," Tally said. "So this is what people looked like before the first pretty? How could anyone stand to open their eyes?"

"Yeah. It's scary at first. But the weird thing is, if you keep looking at them, you kind of get used to it."

Shay turned to a full-page picture of a woman wearing only some kind of formfitting underwear, like a lacy swimsuit.

"What the . . . ," Tally said.

"Yeah."

The woman looked like she was starving, her ribs thrusting out from her sides, her legs so thin that Tally wondered how they didn't snap under her weight. Her elbows and pelvic bones looked sharp as needles. But there she was, smiling and proudly baring her body, as if she'd just had the operation and didn't realize they'd sucked out way too much fat. The funny thing was, her face was closer to being pretty than any of the rest. She had the big eyes, smooth skin, and small nose, but her cheekbones were too tight, the skull practically visible beneath her flesh. "What on earth is she?"

"A model."

"Which is what?"

"Kind of like a professional pretty. I guess when everyone else is ugly, being pretty is sort of, like, your job."

"And she's in her underwear because . . . ?" Tally began, and then a memory flashed into her mind. "She's got that disease! The one the teachers always told us about."

"Probably. I always thought they made that up to scare us."

Back in the days before the operation, Tally remembered, a lot of people, especially young girls, became so ashamed at being fat that they stopped eating. They'd lose weight too quickly, and some would get stuck and would keep losing weight until they wound up like this "model." Some even died, they said at school. That was one of the reasons they'd come up with the operation. No one got the disease anymore, since everyone knew at sixteen they'd turn beautiful. In fact, most people pigged out just before they turned, knowing it would all be sucked away.

Tally stared at the picture and shivered. Why go back to *this*?

"Spooky, huh?" Shay turned away. "I'll see if the Boss is ready yet."

Before she disappeared around a corner, Tally noticed how skinny Shay was. Not diseased skinny, just ugly skinny—she'd never eaten much. Tally wondered if, here in the Smoke, Shay's undereating would get worse and worse, until she wound up starving herself.

Tally fingered the pendant. This was her chance. Might as well get it over with now.

These people had forgotten what the old world was really like. Sure, they were having a great time camping out and playing hide-and-seek, and living out here was a great trick on the cities. But somehow they'd forgotten that the Rusties had been insane, almost destroying the world in a million different ways. This starving almost-pretty was only one of them. Why go back to that?

They were already cutting down *trees* here.

Tally popped open the heart pendant, looking down into the little glowing aperture where the laser waited to read her eye-print. She brought it closer, her hand shaking. It was foolish to wait. This would only get harder.

And what choice did she have?

"Tally? He's almost—"

Tally snapped closed the pendant and shoved it into her shirt.

Shay smiled slyly. "I noticed that before. What gives?"

"What do you mean?"

"Oh, come on. You never wore anything like that before. I leave you alone for two weeks and you get all romantic?"

Tally swallowed, looking down at the silver heart.

"I mean, it's a really nice necklace. Beautiful. But who gave it to you, Tally?"

Tally found she couldn't bring herself to lie. "Someone. Just someone."

Shay rolled her eyes. "Last-minute fling, huh? I always thought you were saving yourself for Peris."

"It's not like that. It's . . ."

Why not tell her? Tally asked herself. She'd figure it out when the Specials came roaring in, anyway. If she knew, Shay could at least prepare herself before this fantasy world came tumbling down. "I have to tell you something."

"Sure."

"My coming here is kind of . . . the thing is, when I went to get my—"

"What are you *doing*?"

Tally jumped at the craggy voice. It was like an old, broken version of Dr. Cable's, a rusty razor blade drawn across her nerves.

"Those magazines are over three centuries old, and you're not wearing gloves!" The Boss shuffled over to where Tally was sitting, producing white cotton gloves and pulling them on. He reached around her to close the one she was reading.

"Your fingers are covered with very nasty acids, young lady. You'll rot away these magazines if you're not careful. Before you go nosing around in the collection, you come to me!"

"Sorry, Boss," Shay said. "My fault."

"I don't doubt it," he snapped, reshelving the magazines with elegant, careful movements at odds with his harsh words. "Now, young lady, I suppose you're here for a work assignment."

"Work?" Tally said.

They both looked down at her puzzled expression, and Shay burst into laughter.

WORK

The Smokies all had lunch together, just like at an ugly dorm.

The long tables had clearly been cut from the hearts of trees. They showed knots and whorls, and wavy tracks of grain ran down their entire length. They were rough and beautiful, but Tally couldn't get over the thought that the trees had been taken alive.

She was glad when Shay and David took her outside to the cooking fire, where a group of younger uglies hung out. It was a relief to get away from the felled trees, and from the disturbing older uglies. Out here, at least, any of the Smokies could pass as a senior. Tally didn't have much experience in judging an ugly's age, but she turned out to be more or less right. Two had just arrived from another city, and weren't even sixteen yet. The other three—Croy, Ryde, and Astrix—were friends of Shay's, from the group that had run away together back before Tally and Shay had first met.

Here in the Smoke only five months, Shay's friends already had a hint of David's self-assurance. Somehow, they carried the authority of middle pretties without the firm jaw, the subtly lined eyes, or the elegant clothing. They spent lunch talking about projects they were up to. A canal to bring a branch of the creek closer to the Smoke; new patterns for the sheep wool their sweaters were made from; a new latrine. (Tally wondered what a "latrine" was.) They seemed so serious, as if their lives were a really complicated trick that had to be planned and replanned every day.

The food was serious too, and was piled on their plates in serious quantities. It was heavier than Tally was used to, the tastes too rich, like whenever her food history class tried to cook their own meals. But the strawberries were sweet without sugar, and although it seemed weird to eat it plain, the Smokies' bread had its own flavor without anything added. Of course, Tally would have happily devoured anything that wasn't SpagBol.

She didn't ask what was in the stew, though. The thought of dead trees was enough to deal with in one day.

As they emptied their plates, Shay's friends started pumping Tally for news from the city. Dorm sports results, soap opera story lines, city politics. Had she heard of anyone else running away? Tally answered their questions as best she could. No one tried to hide their homesickness. Their faces looked years younger as they remembered old friends and old tricks.

Then Astrix asked about her journey here to the Smoke.

"It was pretty easy, really. Once I got the hang of Shay's directions."

"Not that easy. Took you what, ten days?" David asked.

"You left the night before our birthday, right?" Shay said.

"Stroke of midnight," Tally said. "Nine days . . . and a half."

Croy frowned. "It took a while for the rangers to find you, didn't it?"

"I guess so. And they almost roasted me when they did. They were doing a huge burn that got out of control."

"Really? Whoa." Shay's friends looked impressed.

"My board almost burned. I had to save it and jump in the river."

"Is that what happened to your face?" Ryde asked.

Tally touched the peeling skin on her nose. "Well, that's kind of . . ." *Sunburn,* she almost said. But the others' faces were rapt. She'd been alone so long, Tally found herself enjoying being the center of attention.

"The flames were all around me," she said. "My shoes melted crossing this big patch of burning flowers."

Shay whistled. "Incredible."

"That's weird. The rangers usually keep an eye out for us," David said.

"Well, I guess they missed me." Tally decided not to go into the fact that she'd intentionally hidden her hoverboard. "Anyway, I was in the river, and I'd never even seen a helicopter—except for the day before—and this thing came thundering out of the smoke, driving the fire toward me. And of course I had no idea the rangers were the good guys. I thought they were Rusty pyromaniacs risen from the grave!"

Everyone laughed, and Tally felt herself enjoying the warmth of the group's attention. It was like telling everyone at dorm about a really successful trick, but much better, because she really had survived a life-or-death situation. David and Shay were hanging on to every word. Tally was glad she hadn't activated the pendant yet. She could hardly sit here enjoying the Smokies' admiration if she'd just betrayed them all. She decided to wait until tonight, when she was alone, to do what she had to.

"That must have been creepy," David said, his voice pulling her away from uncomfortable thoughts, "being alone in the orchids for all those days, just waiting."

She shrugged. "I thought they were kind of pretty. I didn't know about the whole superweed thing."

David frowned at Shay. "Didn't you tell her *anything* in your note?"

Shay flushed. "You told me not to write anything that would give the Smoke away, so I put it in code, sort of."

"It sounds like your code almost got her killed," David said, and Shay's face fell. He turned to Tally. "Hardly anyone ever makes the trip alone. Not their first time out of the city."

"I'd been out of the city before." Tally put her arm around Shay's shoulder comfortingly. "I was fine. It was just a bunch of pretty flowers to me, and I started with two weeks of food."

"Why did you steal all SpagBol?" Croy asked. "You must love the stuff." The others joined in his laughter.

Tally tried to smile. "I didn't even notice when I pinched it. Three SpagBols a day for nine days. I could hardly stomach the stuff after day two, but you get so hungry."

They nodded. They all knew about hard traveling, and hard work, too, apparently. Tally had already noticed how much everyone had consumed for lunch. Maybe Shay wasn't so likely to get the not-eating disease. She had cleaned her heaping plate.

"Well, I'm glad you made it," David said. He reached across and touched the scratches on Tally's face softly. "Looks like you had more adventures than you're telling us."

Tally swallowed and shrugged, hoping she looked modest.

Shay smiled and hugged David. "I knew you'd think Tally was awesome."

A bell rang across the grounds, and they hurried to finish their food.

"What's that?" she asked.

David grinned. "That's back to work."

"You're coming with us," Shay said. "Don't worry, it won't kill you."

On the way to work, Shay explained more about the long, flat roller coasters called railroads. Some stretched across the entire continent, one small part of the Rusty legacy still scarring the land. But unlike most ruins, the railroads were actually useful, and not just for hoverboarding. They were the main source of metal for the Smokies.

David had discovered a new railroad track a year or so earlier.

It didn't run anywhere useful, so he had drawn up a plan to plunder it for metal and build more hoverpaths in and around the valley. Shay had been working on the project since she'd come to the Smoke ten days before.

Six of them took their boards up and out the other side of the valley, down a stream churning with white water, and along a razor-sharp ridge filled with iron ore. From there, Tally finally understood how far up the mountain she'd come since leaving the coast. The whole continent seemed to be spread out before them. A thin bank of clouds below the ridge mirrored the heavier layer overhead, but forests, grasslands, and the shimmering arcs of rivers were visible through the misty veil. The sea of white orchids could still be glimpsed from this side of the mountain, glowing like an encroaching desert in the sun.

"Everything's so big," Tally murmured.

"That's what you can never tell from inside," Shay said. "How small the city is. How small they have to make everyone to keep them trapped there."

Tally nodded, but she imagined all those people let loose in the countryside below, cutting down trees and killing things for food, crashing across the landscape like some risen Rusty machine.

Still, she wouldn't have traded anything for this moment, standing there and looking down at the plains spread out below. Tally had spent the last four years staring at the skyline of New Pretty Town, thinking it was the most beautiful sight in the world, but she didn't think so anymore.

• • •

Lower down and halfway around the mountain, another river crossed David's railroad track. The route there from the Smoke twisted in all directions, taking advantage of veins of iron, rivers, and dry creek beds, but they'd never had to leave their boards. Walking wouldn't be an option, Shay explained, when they came back loaded with heavy metal.

The track was overgrown with vines and stunted trees, every wooden cross-tie in the grip of a dozen tentacles of vegetation. The forest had been hacked away in patches surrounding a few missing segments of rail, but it held the rest firmly in its grasp.

"How are we going to get any of this out?" Tally asked. She kicked at a gnarled root, feeling puny against the strength of the wild.

"Watch this," Shay said. She pulled a tool from her backpack, an arm-length pole that telescoped out almost to Tally's height. Shay twisted one end, and four short struts unfolded from the other like the ribs of an umbrella. "It's called a powerjack, and it can move just about anything."

Shay twisted the handle again, and the ribs retracted. Then she thrust one end of the jack under a cross-tie. With another twist of her wrist, the pole began to shudder, and a groaning sound came from the wood. Shay's feet slipped backward, but she leaned her weight into the pole, keeping it wedged under the cross-tie. Slowly, the ancient wood began to rise, tearing free from plants and earth, bending the rail that lay across it. Tally saw the struts of the power-jack unfolding underneath the tie, gradually forcing it up, the rail above beginning to pull free of its moorings.

Shay grinned up at her. "I told you."

"Let me try," Tally said, holding out her hand, eyes wide.

Shay laughed and pulled another powerjack from her backpack. "Take that tie there, while I keep this one up."

The powerjack was heavier than it looked, but its controls were simple. Tally pulled it open and jammed it under the tie that Shay had indicated. She turned the handle slowly, until the jack started to shudder in her hands.

The wood began to shift, the stresses of metal and earth twisting in her hands. Vines tore from the ground, and Tally could feel their complaints through the soles of her shoes, like a distant earthquake rumbling. A metal shriek filled the air as the rail began to bend, pulling free of vegetation and the rusty spikes that had held it down for centuries. Finally, the jack had opened to its full extent, the rail still only half-free from its ancient bonds. She and Shay struggled to pull their jacks out.

"Having fun?" Shay asked, wiping sweat from her brow.

Tally nodded, grinning. "Don't just stand there, let's finish the job."

DAVID

A few hours later, a pile of scrap metal stood in one corner of the clearing. Each segment of rail took an hour to get free, and required all six of them to carry. The railroad ties sat in another pile; at least all the Smokies' wood didn't come from live trees. Tally couldn't believe how much they had salvaged, literally tearing the track from the forest's grasp.

She also couldn't believe her hands. They were red and raw, screaming with pain and covered with blisters.

"Looks pretty bad," David said, glancing over Tally's shoulder as she stared at them in amazement.

"*Feels* pretty bad," she said. "But I didn't notice until just now."

David laughed. "Hard work's a good distraction. But maybe

you should take a break. I was just about to scout up the line for another spot to salvage. Want to come?"

"Sure," she said gratefully. The thought of picking up the powerjack again made her hands throb.

Leaving the others at the clearing, they hoverboarded up and over the gnarled trees, following the barely visible track below into dense forest. David rode low in the canopy, gracefully avoiding branches and vines as if this were a familiar slalom course. Tally noticed that, like his shoes, his clothes were *all* handmade. City clothing only used seams and stitching for decoration, but David's jacket seemed to be cut together from a dozen patches of leather, all different shades and shapes. Its patchwork appearance reminded her of Frankenstein's monster, which led to a terrible thought.

What if it were made of *real* leather, like in the olden days? Skins.

She shuddered. He couldn't be wearing a bunch of dead animals. They weren't savages here. And she had to admit that the coat fit him well, the leather following the line of his shoulders like an old friend. And it fended off the whips of branches better than her microfiber dorm jacket.

David slowed as they came into a clearing, and Tally saw that they had reached a wall of solid rock. "That's weird," she said. The railroad track seemed to plunge straight into the mountain, disappearing into a pile of boulders.

"The Rusties were serious about straight lines," David said. "When they built rails, they didn't like to go around stuff."

"So they just went *through*?"

David nodded. "Yeah. This used to be a tunnel, cut right into the mountain. It must have collapsed sometime after the Rusty panic."

"Do you think there was anyone . . . inside? When it happened, I mean."

"Probably not. But you never know. There could be a whole trainload of Rusty skeletons in there."

Tally swallowed, trying to imagine whatever was in there, flattened and buried for centuries in the dark.

"The forest's a lot clearer around here," David said. "Easier to work through. I'm just worried about these boulders collapsing if we start prying rails up."

"They look pretty solid."

"Oh, yeah? Check this out," David said. He stepped off his board onto a boulder, and deftly climbed to a spot that lay shadowed in the setting sun.

Tally angled her board closer and jumped onto a large rock next to David. When her eyes adjusted to the darkness, she saw that a long space extended back between the boulders. David crawled inside, his feet disappearing into the darkness.

"Come on," his voice called.

"Um, there isn't really a trainload of dead Rusties in there, right?"

"Not that I've found. But today might be our lucky day."

Tally rolled her eyes and lowered herself onto her belly. She crawled inside, the cool weight of the rocks settling over her.

A light flicked on ahead. She could see David sitting up in a small space, a flashlight glowing in his hand. She pulled herself in and took a seat next to him on a flat bit of rock. Giant shapes were stacked above them. "So the tunnel didn't collapse completely."

"Not at all. The rock cracked into pieces, some big and some small." David pointed the flashlight down through a chink between where they sat. Tally squinted into the darkness and saw a much bigger open space below. A glint of metal revealed a segment of track.

"Just think. If we could get down there," David said, "we wouldn't have to pull up all those vines. All that track just waiting for us."

"Just a hundred tons of rock in the way, is all."

He nodded. "Yeah, but it would be worth it." He pointed the flashlight upward at his face, making himself hideous. "No one's been down there for hundreds of years."

"Great." Tally's skin tingled, her eyes picking out the dark fissures all around them. Maybe no human beings had been there for a long time, but lots of things liked to live in cool, dark caves.

"I keep thinking," David said, "the whole thing might tumble open if we could just move the exact right boulder. . . ."

"And not the exact wrong one, the one that makes the whole thing crush us?"

David laughed and pointed the flashlight so that it lit her face rather than his. "I thought you might say that."

Tally peered through the darkness, trying to make out his expression. "What do you mean?"

"I can see that you're struggling with this."

"Struggling? With what?"

"Being here in the Smoke. You're not sure about it all."

Tally's skin tingled again, but not from the thought of snakes or bats or long-dead Rusties. She wondered if David had somehow already figured out she was a spy. "No, I guess I'm not sure," she said evenly.

She caught a glimmer of reflected light from David's eyes as he nodded. "That's good. You take this seriously. A lot of kids come out here and think it's all fun and games."

"I don't think that for a minute," she said softly.

"I can tell. It's not just a trick to you, like it is to most runaways. Even Shay, who really believes the operation is wrong, doesn't get how deadly serious the Smoke is."

Tally didn't say anything.

After a long moment of silence in the dark, David continued. "It's dangerous out here. The cities are like these boulders. They may seem solid, but if you start messing with them, the whole pile could crumble."

"I think I know what you mean," Tally said. Since the day she'd gone to get her operation, she'd felt the massive weight of the city looming over her, and had learned firsthand how much places like the Smoke threatened people like Dr. Cable. "But I don't really understand why they care so much about you guys."

"It's a long story. But part of it is . . ."

She waited for a moment before saying, "Is what?"

"Well, this is a secret. I don't usually tell people until they've been here for a while. Years. But you seem . . . serious enough to handle it."

"You can trust me," Tally said, then immediately wondered why. She was a spy, an infiltrator. She was the last person David should trust.

"I hope I can, Tally," he said, reaching out to her. "Feel the palm of my hand."

She took it, running her fingers over the flesh. It was as rough as the wood grain of the table in the dining hall, the skin along his thumb as hard and dry as leather cracking with age. No wonder he could work all day and not complain. "Wow. How long does it take to get calluses like that?"

"About eighteen years."

"About . . . ?" She stopped in disbelief, then compared the horn of his palm with her own tender, blistered flesh. Tally could feel it there, the grueling afternoon of real work she'd put in today, but stretched across a lifetime. "But how?"

"I'm not a runaway, Tally."

"I don't understand."

"My parents were runaways, not me."

"Oh." She felt stupid now, but it had never once occurred to her. If you could live in the Smoke, you could raise children here too. But she hadn't seen any littlies. And the whole place seemed so tenuous, so temporary. It would be like having a child on a camping trip. "How did they manage? Without any doctors, I mean."

"They are doctors."

"Huh. But . . . hang on. Doctors? How old were they when they ran away?"

"Old enough. They weren't uglies anymore. I think it's called being a middle pretty?"

"Yeah, at least." New pretties worked or studied, if they wanted to, but few people got serious about a profession until their middle years. "Wait. What do you mean they *weren't* uglies?"

"They weren't. But they are now."

Tally tried to get her mind to process his words. "You mean, they never did the third operation? They still look middle, even though they're crumblies?"

"No, Tally. I told you: They're doctors."

A shock ran through her. This was more stunning than the felled trees or the cruel pretties; as overwhelming as anything she'd felt since Peris had gone away. *"They reversed the operation?"*

"Yes."

"They cut each other? Out here in the wild? To make themselves . . ." Her throat closed on the word, as if she was going to gag.

"No. They didn't use surgery."

Suddenly the dark cave seemed to be crushing her, squeezing the air from her chest. Tally forced herself to breathe.

David pulled his hand away, and with a corner of her panicked mind Tally realized she'd held on to it all that time.

"I shouldn't have told you all this."

"No, David, I'm sorry. I didn't mean to get all hyperventilated."

"It's my fault. You just got here, and I dumped all this on you."

"But I do want you to . . ."—she fought saying it, but lost—"to trust me. To tell me this stuff. I do take it seriously." That much was true.

"Sure, Tally. But maybe that's enough for now. We should get back." He turned and crawled toward the sunlight.

As she followed, Tally thought of what David had said about the boulders. However massive, they were ready to topple if you pushed them the wrong way. Ready to crush you.

She felt the pendant swinging from her neck, a tiny but insistent pull. Dr. Cable would be impatient by now, waiting for the signal. But David's revelation had suddenly made everything much more complicated. The Smoke wasn't just a hideout for assorted runaways, she realized now. It was a real town, a city in its own right. If Tally activated the tracker, it wouldn't just mean the end of Shay's big adventure. It would be David's home taken from him, his whole *life* stripped away.

Tally felt the weight of the mountain pressing down upon her, and found that she was still struggling to breathe as she pulled herself out into the sunlight.

HEARTTHROB

Around the fire at dinner that night, Tally told the story of how she'd hidden in the river when the rangers' helicopter first appeared. She had everyone wide-eyed again. Apparently, she'd had one of the more exciting journeys to the Smoke.

"Can you imagine? I'm naked and crouching down in the water, and this Rusty machine is destroying my camp!"

"Why didn't they land?" Astrix asked. "Didn't they see your stuff?"

"I thought they did."

"The rangers only pick up uglies in the white flowers," David explained. "That's the rendezvous spot we tell runaways to use. They can't just pick up anyone, or they might accidentally bring a spy here."

"I guess you wouldn't want that," Tally said softly.

"Still, they should be more careful with those helicopters," Shay said. "Someone's going to get chopped to pieces one day."

"Tell me about it. The wind almost took my hoverboard away," Tally said. "It lifted my sleeping bag right off the ground and up into the blades. It was totally shredded." She was pleased by the amazement on the faces of her audience.

"So where'd you sleep?" Croy asked.

"It wasn't that bad. It was only for—" Tally stopped herself just in time. She'd spent one night without the sleeping bag, but in her cover story she'd spent four days in the orchids. "It was warm enough."

"You'd better get a new one before bedtime," David said. "It's a lot colder up here than down in the weeds."

"I'll take her over to the trading post," Shay said. "It's like a requisition center, Tally. Only when you get something, you have to leave something else behind as payment."

Tally shifted uncomfortably in her seat. She still hadn't gotten used to the idea that you had to *pay* for things here. "All I've got is SpagBol."

Shay smiled. "That's perfect to trade with. We can't make dehydrated food here, except fruit, and traveling with regular food is a total pain. SpagBol's good as gold."

After dinner, Shay took her to a large hut near the center of town. The shelves were full of things made in the Smoke, along with a few objects that had come from the cities. The city-made stuff was mostly shabby and worn, repaired again and again, but the handmade things fascinated Tally. She ran her still-raw fingers across the clay pots and wooden tools, amazed at how each had its own texture and weight. Everything seemed so heavy and . . . serious.

An older ugly was running the place, but he wasn't as scary as the Boss. He brought out woolen gear and a few silvery sleeping bags. The blankets, scarves, and gloves were beautiful, in subdued colors and simple patterns, but Shay insisted that Tally get a city-made sleeping bag. "Much lighter, and it squishes up small. Much better for when we go exploring."

"Of course," Tally said, trying to smile. "That'll be great."

She wound up trading twelve packets of SpagBol for another sleeping bag, and six for a handmade sweater, which left her with eight. She couldn't believe that the sweater, brown with bands of pale red and green highlights, cost half as much as the sleeping bag, which was threadbare and patched.

"You're just lucky you didn't lose your water purifier," Shay said as they walked home. "Those things are impossible to trade for."

Tally's eyes widened. "What happens if they break?"

"Well, they say you can drink water from the streams without purifying it."

"You're kidding."

"Nope. A lot of the older Smokies do," Shay said. "Even if they've got a purifier, they don't bother."

"Yuck."

Shay giggled. "Yeah, no kidding. But hey, you can always use mine."

Tally put a hand on Shay's shoulder. "Same goes for mine."

Shay's pace slowed. "Tally?"

"Yeah?"

"You were going to say something to me, back in the library, before the Boss started yelling at you."

Tally's stomach sank. She pulled away, her fingers automatically going to the pendant at her neck.

"Yeah," Shay said. "About that necklace."

Tally nodded, but didn't know how to start. She still hadn't activated the pendant, and since her conversation with David, she wasn't sure she could. Maybe if she returned to the city in a month, starving and empty-handed, Dr. Cable would take mercy on her.

But what if the woman kept her promise, and Tally never got the operation? In twenty-something years, she would be lined and wrinkled, as ugly as the Boss, an outcast. And if she stayed here in the Smoke, she'd be sleeping in an old sleeping bag and dreading the day her water purifier broke down.

She was so tired of lying to everyone. "I haven't told you everything," she started.

"I know. But I think I've got it figured out."

Tally looked at her friend, afraid to speak.

"I mean, it's pretty obvious, right? You're all upset because you broke your promise to me. You didn't keep the Smoke a secret."

Tally's mouth fell open.

Shay smiled, taking her hand. "As you got closer to your birthday, you decided you wanted to run away. But in the meantime, you met someone. Someone important. The same someone who gave you that heart necklace. So you broke your promise to me. You told that someone where you were going."

"Um, kind of," Tally managed.

Shay giggled. "I *knew* it. That's why you've been all nervous. You want to be here, but you also wish you were somewhere else. With someone else. And before you ran away, you left directions, a copy of my note, in case your new heartthrob wants to join us. Am I right or am I right?"

Tally bit her lip. Shay's face glowed in the moonlight, obviously thrilled with herself for figuring out Tally's big secret. "Uh, you're partly right."

"Oh, Tally." Shay grabbed both her shoulders. "Don't you see that it's okay? I mean, I did the same thing."

Tally frowned. "What do you mean?"

"I wasn't supposed to tell anyone I was coming here. David made me promise I wouldn't even tell you."

"Why?"

Shay nodded. "He hadn't met you, and wasn't sure if he could trust you. Normally, runaways only recruit old friends, people they've tricked with for years. But I'd only known you since the beginning of summer. And I never once mentioned the Smoke to you until the day before I left. I was never brave enough, in case you said no."

"So you weren't supposed to tell me?"

"No way. So when you actually showed up, it made everyone nervous. They don't know whether they can trust you. Even David's been acting weird around me."

"Shay, I'm so sorry."

"It's not your fault!" Shay shook her head vigorously. "It's mine. I screwed everything up. But so what? Once they get to know you, they'll think you're really cool."

"Yeah," Tally said softly. "Everyone's been really nice." She wished she had activated the pendant the moment she'd gotten there. In only one day she'd begun to realize that it wasn't just Shay's dream she'd be betraying. Hundreds of people had made a life in the Smoke.

"And I'm sure your someone will be cool too," Shay said. "I can't wait till we're all together."

"I don't know if . . . that's going to happen." There had to be some other way out of this situation. Maybe if she went to another city . . . or found the rangers again and told them that she wanted to volunteer, they'd make her pretty. But she hardly knew anything about their city, except that she didn't know anyone there. . . .

Shay shrugged. "Maybe not. But I wasn't sure you'd come either." She squeezed Tally's hand. "I'm really glad you did, though."

Tally tried to smile. "Even though I got you into trouble?"

"It's not such a big deal. I think everyone's way too paranoid around here. They spend all this time disguising the place so satellites can't see it, and they mask the handphone transmissions so they won't be intercepted. And all the secrecy about runaways is way overdone. And dangerous. Just think—if you hadn't been smart enough to figure out my directions, you could be halfway to Alaska by now!"

"I don't know, Shay. Maybe they know what they're doing. The city authorities can be pretty tough."

Shay laughed. "Don't tell me you believe in Special Circumstances."

"I . . ." Tally closed her eyes. "I just think that the Smokies have to be careful."

"Okay, sure. I'm not saying we should advertise. But if people like you and me want to come out here and live differently, why shouldn't we? I mean, no one has the right to tell us we have to be pretty, right?"

"Maybe they're just worried because we're kids. You know?"

"That's the problem with the cities, Tally. Everyone's a kid, pampered and dependent and pretty. Just like they say in school: Big-eyed means vulnerable. Well, like you once told me, you have to grow up sometime."

Tally nodded. "I know what you mean, how the uglies here are more grown up. You can see it in their faces."

Shay pulled Tally to a stop and looked at her closely for a second. "You feel guilty, don't you?"

Tally looked back into Shay's eyes, speechless for a moment. She suddenly felt naked in the cold night air, as if Shay could see straight through her lies.

"What?" she managed.

"Guilty. Not just that you told your someone about the Smoke, but that they might actually come. Now that you've seen the Smoke, you're not sure if that was such a good idea." Shay sighed. "I know it seems weird at first, and it's a lot of hard work. But I think you'll eventually like it."

Tally looked down, feeling tears welling into her eyes. "It's not that. Well, maybe it is. I just don't know if I can . . ." Her throat felt too full to speak. If she said another word, she'd have to tell Shay the truth: that she was a spy, a traitor sent there to destroy everything around them.

And that Shay was the fool who had led her there.

"Hey, it's okay." Shay gathered Tally in her arms, rocking her gently as Tally began to cry. "I'm sorry. I didn't mean to unload everything on you at once. But I've felt kind of distant from you since you got here. It feels like you're not sure you want to look at me."

"I should tell you everything."

"Shhh." Tally felt Shay's fingers stroking her hair. "I'm just glad you're here."

Tally let herself cry, burying her face in the scratchy wool sleeve of her new sweater, feeling Shay's warmth against her, and feeling awful about every gesture of kindness from her friend.

With half her mind, Tally was actually glad she'd come and seen all this. She could have lived her whole life in the city and never seen this much of the world. With the other half, Tally still wished she had activated the pendant the moment she'd arrived in the Smoke. It would have been so much easier that way.

But there was no way back in time now. She had to decide whether to betray the Smoke or not, completely understanding what it would do to Shay, to David, to everyone here.

"It's okay, Tally," Shay murmured. "You'll be okay."

SUSPICION

As the days passed, Tally fell into the routines of the Smoke.

There was something comforting about the exhaustion of hard work. All her life, Tally had been troubled by insomnia, lying awake most nights thinking about arguments she'd had, or wanted to have, or things she should have done differently. But here in the Smoke her mind shut off the moment her head hit the pillow, which wasn't even a pillow, just her new sweater stuffed into a cotton bag.

Tally still didn't know how long she was going to stay there. She hadn't come to a decision about whether to activate the pendant, but she knew that thinking about it all the time would drive her crazy. So she decided to put it out of her mind. One day she might wake up and realize that she couldn't stand to live her entire life as an ugly, no matter who it hurt or what it cost . . . but for the moment, Dr. Cable could wait.

Forgetting her troubles was easy in the Smoke. Life was much more intense than in the city. She bathed in a river so cold that she had to jump in screaming, and she ate food pulled from the fire hot enough to burn her tongue, which city food never did. Of course, she missed shampoo that didn't sting her eyes, and flush toilets (she'd learned to her horror what "latrines" were), and mostly medspray. But however blistered her hands became, Tally felt stronger than ever before. She could work all day at the railroad site, then race David and Shay home on hoverboards, her backpack full of more scrap metal than she could have lifted a month before. She learned from David how to repair her clothes with a needle and thread, how to tell raptors from their prey, and even how to clean fish, which turned out to be not nearly as bad as cutting them up in bio class.

The physical beauty of the Smoke also cleared her mind of worries. Every day seemed to change the mountain, the sky, and the surrounding valleys, making them spectacular in a completely new way. Nature, at least, didn't need an operation to be beautiful. It just was.

One morning on the way to the railroad track, David pulled his board up alongside Tally's. He rode silently for a while, taking the familiar turns with his usual grace. Over the last two weeks, she'd learned that his jacket was actually made of leather, real dead animals, but she'd gradually gotten used to the idea. The Smokies hunted, but they were like the rangers, killing only species that didn't belong in this part of the world or that had gotten out of control thanks to the Rusties' meddling. With its random patches, the jacket would probably look silly on anyone else. But it suited David, somehow, as if growing up here in the wild allowed him to fuse with the animals that had donated their skins to his clothes. And it probably didn't hurt that he had actually made the jacket himself.

He spoke up suddenly. "I've got a present for you."

"A present? Really?"

By now, Tally understood that nothing in the Smoke ever lost its value. Nothing was discarded or given away just because it was old or broken. Everything was repaired, refitted, and recycled, and if one Smokey couldn't put it to use, it was traded to another. Few things were given away lightly.

"Yeah, really." David angled closer and handed her a small bundle.

She unwrapped it, following the familiar route down the stream almost without looking. It was a pair of gloves, handmade in light brown leather.

She shoved the bright, city-made wrapping paper into her pocket, then pulled the gloves onto her blistered hands. "Thanks! They fit perfectly."

He nodded. "I made them when I was about your age. They're a little small for me these days."

Tally smiled, wishing she could hug him. When they spread their arms to take a hard turn, she held his hand for a second.

Flexing her fingers, Tally found that the gloves were soft and pliant, the palms worn pale from years of use. White lines across the finger joints revealed how they had fitted David's hands. "They're wonderful."

"Come on," David said. "It's not like they're magic or anything."

"No, but they've got . . . something." History, Tally realized. In the city, she'd owned lots of things—practically anything she wanted came out of the wall. But city things were disposable and replaceable, as interchangeable as the T-shirt, jacket, and skirt combinations of dorm uniforms. Here, in the Smoke, objects grew old, carrying their histories with them in dings and scratches and tatters.

David chuckled at her and sped up, joining Shay at the front of the pack.

When they got to the railroad site, David announced that they had to clear more track, using vibrasaws to cut through the vegetation that had grown up around the metal rails.

"What about the trees?" Croy asked.

"What about them?"

"Do we have to chop them down?" Tally asked.

David shrugged. "Scrub trees like this aren't good for much. But we won't waste them. We'll take them back to the Smoke for burning."

"Burning?" Tally said. The Smokies usually only cut down trees from the valley, not the rest of the mountain. These trees had been growing there for decades, and David wanted to use them just to cook a meal? She looked at Shay for support, but her friend's expression was carefully neutral. She probably agreed, but didn't want to argue with David in front of everyone about how to run his project.

"Yes, burning," he said. "And after we've salvaged the track, we'll replant. Put a row of useful trees where the railroad used to be."

The five others looked at him silently. He spun a saw in his hand, anxious to get started, but aware he didn't have their full support yet.

"You know, David," Croy said. "These trees aren't useless. They protect the underbrush from sunlight, which keeps the soil from eroding."

"Okay, you win. Instead of planting some other kind of tree, we'll let the forest take back the land. All the crappy scrub and underbrush you want."

"But do we have to clear-cut them?" Astrix asked.

David took a slow breath. "Clear-cutting" was the word for what the Rusties had done to the old forests: felling every tree, killing every living thing, turning entire countries into grazing land. Whole rain forests had been consumed, reduced from millions of interlocking species to a bunch of cows eating grass, a vast web of life traded for cheap hamburgers.

"Look, we're not clear-cutting. All we're doing is pulling out the garbage that the Rusties left behind," David said. "It just takes a little surgery to do it."

"We could chop around the trees," Tally said. "Only cut into them where we need to. Like you said: surgery."

"Okay, fine." He chuckled. "Let's see what you think of these trees after you've had to hack a few out of the ground."

He was right.

The vibrasaw purred through heavy vines, parted tangled underbrush like a comb through wet hair, and sliced cleanly through metal when the odd misstroke brought the cutting edge down onto the track. But when its teeth met the gnarled roots and twisted branches of the scrub trees, it was a different story.

Tally grimaced as her saw bounced across the hard wood again, spitting bits of bark at her face, its low hum transformed into a protesting howl. She struggled to force the edge down into the tough old branch. One more cut and this section of track would be clear.

"Going good. You almost got it, Tally."

She noticed that Croy stood well back, poised to jump if the saw somehow slipped from her hands. She could see now why David had wanted to chop the scrub trees into pieces. It would have been a lot easier than reaching through the tangle of roots and branches, trying to bring the vibrasaw to bear against a precise spot.

"Stupid trees," Tally muttered, gritting her teeth as she plunged the blade down again.

Finally, the saw found purchase in the wood, letting out a high-pitched scream as it bit into the branch. Then it slipped through, free for a second before it thrust, spitting and screeching, into the dirt below.

"Yeah!" Tally stepped back, lifting her goggles, the saw powering down in her hands.

Croy stepped forward and kicked the section of branch away from the track. "Perfect surgical slice, Doctor," he said.

"I think I'm getting the hang of this," Tally said, wiping her brow.

It was almost noon, and the sun was beating down into the clearing mercilessly. She pulled off her sweater, realizing that the morning chill was long gone. "You were right about the trees giving shade."

"You said it," Croy said. "Nice sweater, by the way."

She smiled. Along with her new gloves, it was her prized possession. "Thanks."

"What did it cost you?"

"Six SpagBols."

"A little pricey. Pretty, though." Croy caught her eye. "Tally, remember that first day you got here? When I kind of grabbed your knapsack? I really wouldn't have taken your stuff. Not without giving you something for it. You just surprised me when you said I could have everything."

"Sure, no problem," she said. Now that she'd worked with Croy, he seemed like a nice enough guy. She'd rather have been teamed up with David or Shay, but those two were cutting together today. And it was probably time she got to know some of the other Smokies better.

"And you got a new sleeping bag, too, I hope."

"Yeah. Twelve SpagBols."

"Must be almost out of trade."

She nodded. "Only eight left."

"Not bad. Still, I bet you didn't realize on your way here that you were eating your future wealth."

Tally laughed. They crouched under the partly cut tree, pulling handfuls of cut vines from around the track.

"If I'd known how valuable food packets were, I probably wouldn't have eaten so many, starving or not. I don't even like it anymore. The worst was SpagBol for breakfast."

"Sounds good to me." Croy chuckled. "This section look clear to you?"

"Sure. Let's start on the next one." She handed him the saw.

Croy did the easy part first, attacking the underbrush with the humming saw. "So, Tally, there's one thing that's kind of confusing."

"What's that?"

The saw glanced off metal, sending up a smattering of sparks.

"The first day you were here, you said you left the city with two weeks of food."

"Yeah."

"If it took you nine days to get here, you should only have had five days of food left. Maybe fifteen packets altogether. But I remember on that first day, when I looked into your bag, I was, like, 'She's got tons!'"

Tally swallowed, trying not to show any expression.

"And it turns out I was right. Twelve plus six plus eight is . . . twenty-six?"

"Yeah, I guess."

He nodded, working the saw carefully beneath a low branch. "I thought so. But you left the city *before* your birthday, right?"

Tally thought fast. "Sure. But I guess I didn't really eat three meals every day, Croy. Like I said, I was pretty sick of SpagBol after a while."

"Seems like you didn't eat much at all, for such a long trip."

Tally struggled to do the math in her head, to figure out what sort of numbers would add up. She remembered what Shay had said that first night: Some Smokies were suspicious of her, worried that she might be a spy. Tally had thought they all accepted her by now. Apparently not.

She took a deep breath, trying to keep the fear out of her voice. "Look, Croy, let me tell you something. A secret."

"What's that?"

"I probably left the city with more than just two weeks' worth of food. I never really counted."

"But you kept saying—"

"Yeah, I might have exaggerated a little, just to make the trip sound more interesting, you know? Like I could have run out of food when the rangers didn't turn up. But you're right, I always had plenty."

"Sure." He looked up at her, smiling gently. "I thought maybe so. Your trip did sound a little bit too . . . interesting to be true."

"But most of what I said was—"

"Of course." The saw whined to a stop in his hand. "I'm sure most of it was. Question is, how much?"

Tally met his piercing eyes, struggling to think of what to say.

It was nothing but a few extra food packets, hardly proof that she was a spy. She should just laugh it off. But the fact that he was dead right silenced her.

"You want the saw for a while?" he said mildly. "Clearing this up is hard work."

Since they were clearing brush, there was no load of metal to take back at midday, so the railroad crew had brought their lunch out with them: potato soup, and bread with salty olives dotted through it. Tally was glad when Shay took her lunch away from the rest of the group, to the edge of the dense forest. She followed, settling next to her friend in the dappled light. "I need to talk to you, Shay."

Shay, not looking at her, sighed softly as she tore her bread into pieces. "Yeah, I guess you do."

"Oh. Did he talk to you, too?"

Shay shook her head. "He didn't have to say anything."

Tally frowned. "What do you mean?"

"I mean it's obvious. Ever since you got here. I should have seen it right away."

"I never—" Tally started, but her voice betrayed her. "What are you saying? You think Croy's right?"

Shay sighed. "I'm just saying that—" She stopped and turned to face Tally. "Croy? What about Croy?"

"He was talking to me before lunch, and he noticed my sweater and asked if I got a sleeping bag. And he figured that after nine days getting here I had too much SpagBol left."

"You had too much *what*?" Shay's expression was one of total confusion. "What on earth are you talking about?"

"Remember when I got here? I told everyone that . . ." Tally trailed off, for the first time noticing Shay's eyes. They were lined with red, as if she hadn't slept. "Wait a second, what did you think I was talking about?"

Shay held out a hand, fingers splayed. "This."

"What?"

"Hold out yours."

Tally opened one hand, making a mirror image of Shay's.

"Same size," Shay said. She turned both her palms up. "Same blisters, too."

Tally looked down and blinked. If anything, Shay's hands were in worse shape, red and dry and cracked with the ragged edges of burst blisters. Shay always worked so hard, diving in first, always taking the hardest jobs.

Tally's fingers went to the gloves tucked into her belt. "Shay, I'm sure David didn't mean to—"

"I'm sure he did. People always think long and hard about gifts in the Smoke."

Tally bit her lip. It was true. She pulled the gloves from her belt. "You should take them."

"I. Don't. Want. Them."

Tally sat back, stunned. First Croy, now this.

"No, I guess you don't." She dropped the gloves. "But Shay, shouldn't you talk to David before you go nuts about this?"

Shay chewed at a fingernail, shaking her head. "He doesn't talk to me that much anymore. Not since you showed up. Not about anything important. He's got stuff on his mind, he says."

"Oh." Tally gritted her teeth. "I never . . . I mean, I like David, but . . ."

"It's not your fault, okay? I know that." Shay reached out and gave Tally's heart-shaped pendant a little flick. "And besides, maybe your mysterious someone will show up, and it won't matter anyway."

Tally nodded. True enough, once the Specials got here, Shay's romantic life would be the least of anyone's worries.

"Have you even mentioned that to David? It seems like it might be an issue."

"No. I haven't."

"Why not?"

"It just never came up."

Shay's mouth tightened. "That's convenient."

Tally let out a groan. "But Shay, you said it yourself: I wasn't supposed to be giving out directions to the Smoke. I feel really bad about the whole thing. I'm not going to go advertising it."

"Except by wearing that thing around your neck. Which didn't do much good, though, since apparently David didn't notice it."

Tally sighed. "Or maybe he doesn't care, because this is all just in your . . ." She couldn't finish. It wasn't just in Shay's head; she could see it now, and feel it too. When David showed her the railway cave, and told her his secret about his parents, he had trusted her, even when he shouldn't have. And now this present. Could it really be just Shay overreacting?

In a quiet part of her mind, Tally realized that she hoped it wasn't.

She took a deep breath, expelling the thought. "Shay, what do you want me to do?"

"Just tell him."

"Tell him what?"

"About why you wear that heart. About your mysterious someone."

Too late, Tally felt the expression on her face.

Shay nodded. "You don't want to, do you? That's pretty clear."

"No, I will. Really."

"Sure you will." Shay turned away, pulling a hunk of bread from her soup and taking a vicious bite.

"I *will.*" Tally touched her friend's shoulder, and instead of pulling away, Shay turned back to her, her expression almost hopeful.

Tally swallowed. "I'll tell him everything, I promise."

BRAVERY

That night at dinner, she ate alone.

Now that she'd spent a day cutting trees herself, the wooden table in the dining hall no longer horrified her. The grain of the wood felt reassuringly solid, and tracing its whorls with her eyes was easier than thinking.

For the first time, Tally noticed the sameness of the food. Bread again, stew again. A couple of days ago, Shay had explained that the plump meat in the stew was rabbit. Not soy-based, like the dehydrated meat in her SpagBol, but real animals from the overcrowded pen on the edge of the Smoke. The thought of rabbits being killed, skinned, and cooked suited her mood. Like the rest of her day, this meal tasted brutal and serious.

Shay hadn't talked to her after lunch, and Tally had no idea what to say to Croy, so she'd worked the rest of the day in silence. Dr. Cable's pendant seemed to grow heavier and heavier, wound around her neck as tightly as the vines, brush, and roots grasping the railroad tracks. It felt as if everyone in the Smoke could see what the necklace really was: a symbol of her treachery.

Tally wondered if she could ever stay there now. Croy suspected what she was, and it seemed like it would be only a matter of time before everyone else knew. All day long a terrible thought had kept crossing her mind: Maybe the Smoke was where she really belonged, but she'd lost her chance by going there as a spy.

And now Tally had come between David and Shay. Without even trying, she'd shafted her best friend. Like walking poison, she killed everything.

She thought of the orchids spreading across the plains below, choking the life out of other plants, out of the soil itself, selfish and unstoppable. Tally Youngblood was a weed. And, unlike the orchids, she wasn't even a pretty one.

Just as she finished eating, David sat down across from her. "Hey."

"Hi." She managed to smile. Despite everything, it was a relief to see him. Eating alone had reminded her of the days after her birthday, trapped as an ugly when everyone knew she should be pretty. Today was the first time she'd felt like an ugly since coming to the Smoke.

David reached across and took her hand. "Tally, I'm sorry."

"You're sorry?"

He turned her palm up to reveal her freshly blistered fingers.

"I noticed you didn't wear the gloves. Not after you had lunch with Shay. It wasn't hard to guess why."

"Oh, yeah. It's not that I didn't like them. I just couldn't."

"Sure, I know. This is all my fault." He looked around the crowded hall. "Can we get out of here? I've got something to tell you."

Tally nodded, feeling the cold pendant against her neck and remembering her promise to Shay. "Yeah. I've got something to tell you, too."

They walked through the Smoke, past cook fires being extinguished with shovelfuls of dirt; windows coming alight with candles and electric bulbs; and a handful of young uglies pursuing an escaped chicken. They climbed the ridge from which Tally had first looked down on the settlement, and David led her along it to a cool, flat outcrop of stone where a view opened up between the trees. As always, Tally noticed how graceful David was, how he seemed to know every step of the path intimately. Not even pretties, whose bodies were perfectly balanced, designed for elegance in every kind of clothing, moved with such effortless control.

Tally deliberately turned her eyes away from him. In the valley below, the orchids glowed with pale malevolence in the moonlight, a frozen sea against the dark shore of the forest.

David started talking first. "Did you know you're the first runaway to come here all alone?"

"Really?"

He nodded, still staring down at the white expanse of flowers. "Most of the time, I bring them in."

Tally remembered Shay, the last night they'd seen each other in the city, saying that the mysterious David would take her to the Smoke. Back then Tally had hardly believed there was such a person. Now, sitting next to her, David seemed very real. He took the world more seriously than any other ugly she'd ever met—more seriously, in fact, than middle pretties like her parents. In a funny way, his eyes held the same intensity that the cruel pretties' had, though without their coldness.

"My mother used to in the old days," he said. "But now she's too old."

Tally swallowed. They always explained in school about how uglies who didn't have the operations eventually became infirm. "Oh, I'm so sorry. How old is she, anyway?"

He laughed. "She's plenty fit, but uglies have an easier time trusting someone like me, someone their own age."

"Oh, of course." Tally remembered her reaction to the Boss that first day. Only a couple of weeks later she was much more used to all the different kinds of faces that age created.

"Sometimes, a few uglies will make it on their own, following coded directions like you did. But it's always been three or four in a group. No one's ever come all alone."

"You must think I'm an idiot."

"Not at all." He took her hand. "I think it was really brave."

She shrugged. "It wasn't that bad a trip, really."

"It's not the traveling that takes courage, Tally. I've done much longer trips on my own. It's leaving home." He traced a line on her sore hand with a finger. "I can't imagine having to walk away from the Smoke, away from everything I've ever known, realizing I'd probably never come back."

Tally swallowed. It hadn't been easy. Of course, she hadn't really had a choice.

"But you left your city, the only place you'd ever lived, all alone," David continued. "You hadn't even met a Smokey, someone to convince you firsthand that it was a real place. You did it all on trust, because your friend asked you. I guess that's why I feel I can trust you."

Tally looked out at the weeds, feeling worse with every word David said. If he only knew the real reason she was there.

"When Shay first told me you were coming, I was really angry at her."

"Because I might have given the Smoke away?"

"Partly. And partly because it's really dangerous for a city-bred sixteen-year-old to cross hundreds of miles alone. But mostly I thought it was a wasted risk, because you probably wouldn't even make it out of your dorm window."

He looked up at her, squeezing her hand softly. "I was amazed when I saw you running down that hill."

Tally smiled. "I was a pretty sorry sight that day."

"You were so scratched up, your hair and clothes all singed from that fire, but you had the biggest smile on your face." David's face seemed to glow in the soft moonlight.

Tally closed her eyes and shook her head. Great. She was going to get an award for bravery when she should really be kicked out of the Smoke for treachery.

"You don't look quite so happy now, though," he said softly.

"Not everyone thinks it's great that I came here."

He laughed. "Yeah, Croy told me about his big revelation."

"He did?" She opened her eyes.

"Don't listen to him. From the moment you got here, he was suspicious about your coming alone. He thought you must have had help along the way. City help. But I told him he was crazy."

"Thanks."

He shrugged. "When you and Shay saw each other, you were so happy. I could tell that you'd really missed her."

"Yeah. I was worried about her."

"Of course you were. And you were brave enough to come looking yourself, even if it meant walking away from everything you'd ever known, alone. You didn't really come because you wanted to live in the Smoke, did you?"

"Um . . . what do you mean?"

"You came to see if Shay was all right."

Tally looked into David's eyes. Even if he was completely wrong about her, it felt good to bask in his words. Up until now, the whole day had been tainted by suspicion and doubt, but David's face shone with admiration for what she had done. A feeling spread through her, a warmth that pushed away the cold wind cutting across the ridge.

Then Tally trembled inside, realizing what the feeling was. It was that same warmth she'd felt talking to Peris after his operation, or when teachers looked at her with approval. It was not a feeling she'd ever gotten from an ugly before. Without large, perfectly shaped eyes, their faces couldn't make you feel that way. But the moonlight and the setting, or maybe just the words he was saying, had somehow turned David into a pretty. Just for a moment.

But the magic was all based on lies. She didn't deserve the look in David's eyes.

She turned to face the ocean of weeds again. "I bet Shay wishes she'd never told me about the Smoke."

"Maybe right now. Maybe for a while," David said. "But not forever."

"But you and she . . ."

"She and I." He sighed. "Shay changes her mind pretty quickly, you know."

"What do you mean?"

"The first time she wanted to come to the Smoke was back in spring. When Croy and the others came."

"She told me. She chickened out, right?"

David nodded. "I always figured she would. She just wanted to run away because her friends were. If she stayed in the city, she'd be left all alone."

Tally thought of her friendless days after Peris's operation. "Yeah. I know that feeling."

"But she never showed up that night. Which happens. I was really surprised to see her in the ruins a few weeks ago, suddenly convinced she wanted to leave the city forever. And she was already talking about bringing a friend, even though she hadn't said a word to you yet." He shook his head. "I almost told her to just forget about it, to stay in the city and become pretty."

She took a deep breath. Everything would have been so much easier if David had done exactly that. Tally would be pretty right now, high up in a party tower with Peris and Shay and a bunch of new friends at this very moment. But the image in her mind didn't give Tally the thrill it usually did; it just fell flat, like a song she'd heard too many times.

David squeezed her hand. "I'm glad I didn't."

Something made Tally say, "Me too." The words amazed her, because somehow they felt true. She looked at David closely, and the feeling was still there. She could see that his forehead was too high, that a small scar cut a white stroke through his eyebrow. And his smile was pretty crooked, really. But it was as if something had changed inside Tally's head, something that had turned his face pretty to her. The warmth of his body cut the autumn chill, and she moved closer.

"Shay's tried hard to make up for chickening out that first time, and for giving you directions when she promised me she wouldn't," he said. "Now she's decided the Smoke is the greatest place in the world. And that I'm the best person in the world for bringing her here."

"She really likes you, David."

"And I really like her. But she's just not . . ."

"Not what?"

"Not serious. Not you."

Tally turned away, her head swimming. She knew she had to keep her promise now, or she never would. Her fingers went to the pendant. "David . . ."

“Yeah, I noticed that necklace. After your smile, it was the second thing I noticed about you.”

“You know someone gave it to me.”

“That’s what I figured.”

“And I . . . I told them about the Smoke.”

He nodded. “I figured that, too.”

“You’re not mad at me?”

He shrugged. “You never promised me anything. I hadn’t even met you.”

“But you still . . .” David was gazing into her eyes, his face glowing again. Tally looked away, trying to drown her uncanny pretty feelings in the sea of white weeds.

David sighed softly. “You left a lot of things behind when you came here—your parents, your city, your whole life. And you are starting to like the Smoke, I can tell. You get what we’re doing here in a way that most runaways don’t.”

“I like the way it feels here. But I might not . . . stay.”

He smiled. “I know. Listen, I’m not rushing you. Maybe whoever gave you that heart is coming, maybe not. Maybe you’ll go back to them. But in the meantime, could you do something for me?”

“Sure. I mean, what?”

He stood, offering her his hand. “I’d like you to meet my parents.”

THE SECRET

They descended the ridge on the far side, down a steep, narrow path. David led her quickly in the darkness, finding footing on the almost invisible trail without hesitation. It was all Tally could do to keep up.

The whole day had been one shock after another, and now to top it all off she was going to meet David's parents. That was the last thing she'd expected after showing him her pendant and telling him she hadn't kept the Smoke a secret. His reactions were different from those of anyone she'd ever met before. Maybe it was because he'd grown up out here, away from the customs of the city. Or maybe he was just . . . different.

They left the familiar ridge line far behind, and the mountain rose steeply to one side.

"Your parents don't live in the Smoke?"

"No. It's too dangerous."

"Dangerous how?"

"It's part of what I was telling you your first day here, in the railroad cave."

"About your secret? How you were raised in the wild?"

David stopped for a moment, turning back to face her in the darkness. "There's more to it than that."

"What?"

"I'll let them tell you. Come on."

A few minutes later, a small square filled with faint light appeared, hovering in the darkness of the mountainside. Tally saw that it was a window, a light inside glowing deep red through a closed curtain. The house seemed half buried, as if it had been wedged into the mountain.

When they were still a stone's throw away, David stopped. "Don't want to surprise them. They can be jumpy," he said, then shouted, "Hello!"

A moment later a doorway opened, letting out a shaft of light.

"David?" a woman's voice called. The door opened wider until the light spilled across them. "Az, it's David."

As they drew closer, Tally saw that she was an old ugly. Tally couldn't tell if she was younger or older than the Boss, but she certainly wasn't as terrifying to look at. Her eyes flashed liked a pretty's, and the lines of her face disappeared into a welcoming smile as she gathered her son into a hug.

"Hi, Mom."

"And you must be Tally."

"Nice to meet you." She wondered if she should shake hands or something. In the city, you never spent much time with other uglies' parents, except when you hung out at friends' houses during school breaks.

The house was much warmer than the bunkhouse, and the timber floors weren't nearly as rough, as if David's parents had lived there so long, their feet had worn them smooth. The house somehow felt more solid than any building in the Smoke. It was really cut into the mountain, she saw now. One of the walls was exposed stone, glistening with some kind of transparent sealant.

"Nice to meet you, too, Tally," David's mother said. Tally wondered what her name was. David always referred to them as "Mom" and "Dad," words Tally hadn't used for Sol and Ellie since she was a littlie.

A man appeared, shaking David's hand before turning to her. "Good to meet you, Tally."

She blinked, her breath catching, for a moment unable to speak. David and his father somehow looked . . . alike.

It didn't make any sense. There had to be more than thirty years between them, if his father really had been a doctor when David was born. But their jaws, foreheads, even their slightly lop-sided smiles were all so similar.

"Tally?" David said.

"Sorry. You just . . . you look the same!"

David's parents burst into laughter, and Tally felt her face turning red.

“We get that a lot,” his father said. “You city kids always find it a shock. But you know about genetics, don’t you?”

“Sure. I know all about genes. I knew two sisters, uglies, who looked almost the same. But parents and children? That’s just weird.”

David’s mother forced a serious expression onto her face, but the smile stayed in her eyes. “The features that we take from our parents are the things that make us different. A big nose, thin lips, high forehead—all the things that the operation takes away.”

“The preference toward the mean,” his dad said.

Tally nodded, remembering school lessons. The overall average of human facial characteristics was the primary template for the operation. “Sure. Average-looking features are one of the things people look for in a face.”

“But families pass on nonaverage looks. Like our big noses.” The man tweaked his son’s nose, and David rolled his eyes. Tally realized that David’s nose was much bigger than any pretty’s. Why hadn’t she noticed that before now?

“That’s one of the things you give up, when you become pretty. The family nose,” his mother said. “Az? Why don’t you turn up the heat.”

Tally realized that she was still shivering, but not from the cold outside. This was all so weird. She couldn’t get over the similarity between David and his father. “That’s okay. It’s lovely in here, uh . . .”

“Maddy,” the woman said. “Shall we all sit down?”

• • •

Az and Maddy apparently had been expecting them. In the front room of the house, four antique cups were set out on little saucers. Soon a kettle began to whistle softly on an electric heater, and Az poured the boiling water into an antique pot, releasing a floral scent into the room.

Tally looked around her. The house was unlike any other in the Smoke. It was like a standard crumbly home, filled with impractical objects. A marble statuette stood in one corner, and rich rugs had been hung on the walls, lending their colors to the light in the room, softening the edges of everything. Maddy and Az must have brought a lot of things from the city when they ran away. And, unlike uglies, who had only their dorm uniforms and other disposable possessions, the two had actually spent half a lifetime collecting things before escaping the city.

Tally remembered growing up surrounded by Sol's woodwork, abstract shapes fashioned from fallen branches she would collect from parks as a littlie. Maybe David's childhood hadn't been completely different from her own. "This all looks so familiar," she said.

"David hasn't told you?" Maddy said. "Az and I come from the same city as you. If we'd stayed, we might have been the ones to turn you pretty."

"Oh, I guess so," Tally murmured. If they'd stayed in the city, there would have been no Smoke, and Shay never would have run away.

"David says that you made it all the way here on your own," Maddy said.

She nodded. "I was following a friend of mine. She left me directions."

"And you decided to come alone? Couldn't you wait for David to come around again?"

"There wasn't time to wait," David explained. "She left the night before her sixteenth birthday."

"That's leaving things until the last minute," Az said.

"But very dramatic," Maddy said approvingly.

"Actually, I didn't have much choice. I hadn't even heard of the Smoke until Shay, my friend, told me she was leaving. That was about a week before my birthday."

"Shay? I don't believe we've met her," Az said.

Tally looked at David, who shrugged. He had never brought Shay here? She wondered for a moment what had really gone on between David and Shay.

"You certainly made up your mind quickly, then," Maddy said.

Tally brought her mind back to the present. "I had to. I only had one chance."

"Spoken like a true Smokey," Az said, pouring a dark liquid from the kettle into the cups. "Tea?"

"Uh, please." Tally accepted a saucer and felt the scalding heat through the thin, white material of the cup. Realizing that this was one of those Smokey concoctions that burned your tongue, she sipped carefully. Her face twisted at the bitter taste. "Ah. I mean . . . sorry. I've never had tea before, actually."

Az's eyes widened. "Really? But it was very popular back when we lived there."

"I've heard of it. But it's more of a crumbly drink. Um, I mean, mostly only late pretties drink it." Tally willed herself not to blush.

Maddy laughed. "Well, we're pretty crumbly, so I guess it's okay for us."

"Speak for yourself, my dear."

"Try this," David said. He dropped a white cube into Tally's tea. The next time she drank, a sweetness had spread through it, cutting the bitterness. It was possible to sip the stuff now without grimacing.

"David's told you a little about us, I suppose," Maddy said.

"Well, he said you ran away a long time ago. Before he was born."

"Oh, did he?" Az said. The expression on his face was exactly like David's when a member of the railroad crew did something thoughtless and dangerous with a vibrasaw.

"I didn't tell her everything, Dad," David said. "Just that I grew up in the wild."

"You left the rest to us?" Az said a bit stiffly. "Very good of you."

David held his father's gaze. "Tally came here to make sure her friend was okay. All the way here alone. But she might not want to stay."

"We don't force anyone to live here," Maddy said.

"That's not what I mean," David said. "I think she should know, before she decides about going back to the city."

Tally looked from David to his parents, quietly amazed. The way they communicated was so strange, not like uglies and crumblies at all. It was more like uglies arguing. Like equals.

"I should know what?" she asked softly.

They all looked at her, Maddy and Az measuring her with their eyes.

"The big secret," Az said, "the one that made us run away almost twenty years ago."

"One we usually keep to ourselves," Maddy said evenly, her eyes on David.

"Tally deserves to know," David said, his eyes locked with his mother's. "She'll understand how important it is."

"She's a kid. A city kid."

"She made it here alone, with only a bunch of gibberish directions to guide her."

Maddy scowled. "You've never even been to a city, David. You have no idea how coddled they are. They spend their whole lives in a bubble."

"She survived alone for nine days, Mom. Made it through a brush fire."

"Please, you two," Az interjected. "*She* is sitting right here. Aren't you, Tally?"

"Yeah, I am," Tally said quietly. "And I wish you'd tell me what you're talking about."

"I'm sorry, Tally," Maddy said. "But this secret is very important. And very dangerous."

Tally nodded her head, looking down at the floor. "Everything out here is dangerous."

They were all silent for a moment. All Tally heard was the tinkle of Az stirring his tea.

"See?" David said finally. "She understands. You can trust her. She deserves to know the truth."

"Everyone does," Maddy said quietly. "Eventually."

"Well," Az said, then paused to sip his tea. "I suppose we'll have to tell you, Tally."

"Tell me *what*?"

David took a deep breath. "The truth about being pretty."

PRETTY MINDS

"We were doctors," Az began.

"Cosmetic surgeons, to be precise," Maddy said. "We've both performed the operation hundreds of times. And when we met, I had just been named to the Committee for Morphological Standards."

Tally's eyes widened. "The Pretty Committee?"

Maddy smiled at the nickname. "We were preparing for a Morphological Congress. That's when all the cities share data on the operation."

Tally nodded. Cities worked very hard to stay independent of one another, but the Pretty Committee was a global institution that made sure pretties were all more or less the same. It would ruin the whole point of the operation if the people from one city wound up prettier than everyone else.

Like most uglies, Tally had often indulged the fantasy that one day she might be on the Committee, and help decide what the next generation would look like. In school, of course, they always managed to make it sound really boring, all graphs and averages and measuring people's pupils when they looked at different faces.

"At the same time, I was doing some independent research on anesthesia," Az said. "Trying to make the operation safer."

"Safer?" Tally asked.

"A few people still die each year, as with any surgery," he said. "From being unconscious so long, more than anything else."

Tally bit her lip. She'd never heard that. "Oh."

"I found that there were complications from the anesthetic used in the operation. Tiny lesions in the brain. Barely visible, even with the best machines."

Tally decided to risk sounding stupid. "What's a lesion?"

"Basically it's a bunch of cells that don't look right," Az said. "Like a wound, or a cancer, or just something that doesn't belong there."

"But you couldn't just *say* that," David said. He rolled his eyes toward Tally. "Doctors."

Maddy ignored her son. "When Az showed me his results, I started investigating. The local committee had millions of scans in its database. Not the stuff they put in medical textbooks, but raw data from pretties all over the world. The lesions turned up everywhere."

Tally frowned. "You mean, people were sick?"

"They didn't seem to be. And the lesions weren't cancerous, because they didn't spread. Almost everyone had them, and they were always in exactly the same place." She pointed to a spot on the top of her head.

"A bit to the left, dear," Az said, dropping a white cube into his tea.

Maddy obliged him, then continued. "Most importantly, almost everyone all over the world had these lesions. If they were a health hazard, ninety-nine percent of the population would show some kind of symptoms."

"But they weren't natural?" Tally asked.

"No. Only post-ops—pretties, I mean—had them," Az said. "No uglies did. They were definitely a result of the operation."

Tally shifted in her chair. The thought of a weird little mystery in everyone's brain made her queasy. "Did you find out what caused them?"

Maddy sighed. "In one sense, we did. Az and I looked very closely at all the negatives—that is, the few pretties who didn't have the lesions—and tried to figure out why they were different. What made them immune to the lesions? We ruled out blood type, gender, physical size, intelligence factors, genetic markers—nothing seemed to account for the negatives. They weren't any different from everyone else."

"Until we discovered an odd coincidence," Az said.

"Their jobs," Maddy said.

"Jobs?"

"Every negative worked in the same sort of profession," Az said. "Firefighters, wardens, doctors, politicians, and anyone who worked for Special Circumstances. Everyone with those jobs didn't have the lesions; all the other pretties did."

"So you guys were okay?"

Az nodded. "We tested ourselves, and we were negative."

"Otherwise, we wouldn't be sitting here," Maddy said quietly.

"What do you mean?"

David spoke up. "The lesions aren't an accident, Tally. They're part of the operation, just like all the bone sculpting and skin scraping. It's part of the way being pretty changes you."

"But you said not everyone has them."

Maddy nodded. "In some pretties, they disappear, or are intentionally cured—in those whose professions require them to react quickly, like working in an emergency room, or putting out a fire. Those who deal with conflict and danger."

"People who face challenges," David said.

Tally let out a slow breath, remembering her trip to the Smoke. "What about rangers?"

Az nodded. "I believe I had a few rangers in my database. All negatives."

Tally remembered the look on the faces of the rangers who had saved her. They had an unfamiliar confidence and surety, like David's, completely different from the new pretties she and Peris had always made fun of.

Peris . . .

Tally swallowed, tasting something more bitter than tea in

the back of her throat. She tried to remember how Peris had acted when she'd crashed the Garbo Mansion party. She'd been so ashamed of her own face, it was hard to remember anything specific about Peris. He'd looked so different and, if anything, he seemed older, more mature.

But in some way, they hadn't connected . . . it was as if he'd become a different person. Was it only because since his operation they had lived in different worlds? Or had it been something more? She tried to imagine Peris coping out here in the Smoke, working with his hands and making his own clothes. The old, ugly Peris would have enjoyed the challenge. But what about pretty Peris?

Her head felt light, as if the house were in an elevator heading swiftly downward.

"What do the lesions do?" she asked.

"We don't know exactly," Az said.

"But we've got some pretty good ideas," David said.

"Just suspicions," Maddy said. Az looked uncomfortably down into his tea.

"You were suspicious enough to run away," Tally said.

"We had no choice," Maddy said. "Not long after our discovery, Special Circumstances paid a visit. They took our data and told us not to look any further or we'd lose our licenses. It was either run away, or forget everything we'd found."

"And it wasn't something we could forget," Az said.

Tally turned to David. He sat beside his mother, grim-faced, his cup of tea untouched before him. His parents were still reluctant to say everything they suspected. But she could tell that David saw no need for caution. "What do you think?" she asked him.

"Well, you know all about how the Rusties lived, right?" he said. "War and crime and all that?"

"Of course. They were crazy. They almost destroyed the world."

"And that convinced people to pull the cities back from the wild, to leave nature alone," David recited. "And now everybody is happy, because everyone looks the same: They're all pretty. No more Rusties, no more war. Right?"

"Yeah. In school, they say it's all really complicated, but that's basically the story."

He smiled grimly. "Maybe it's not so complicated. Maybe the reason war and all that other stuff went away is that there are no more controversies, no disagreements, no people demanding change. Just masses of smiling pretties, and a few people left to run things."

Tally remembered crossing the river to New Pretty Town, watching them have their endless fun. She and Peris used to boast they'd never wind up so idiotic, so shallow. But when she'd seen him . . . "Becoming pretty doesn't just change the way you look," she said.

"No," David said. "It changes the way you think."

BURNING BRIDGES

They stayed up late into the night, talking with Az and Maddy about their discoveries, their escape into the wild, and the founding of the Smoke. Finally, Tally had to ask the question that had been on her mind since she'd first seen them.

"So how did you two change yourselves back? I mean, you were pretty, and now you're . . ."

"Ugly?" Az smiled. "That part was simple. We're experts in the physical part of the operation. When surgeons sculpt a pretty face, we use a special kind of smart plastic to shape the bones. When we change new pretties to middle or late, we add a trigger chemical to that plastic, and it becomes softer, like clay."

"Eww," Tally said, imagining her face suddenly softening so she could squish it around to a different shape.

"With daily doses of this trigger chemical, the plastic will gradually melt away and be absorbed into the body. Your face goes back to where it started. More or less."

Tally's eyebrows rose. "More or less?"

"We can only approximate the places where bone was shaved away. And we can't make big changes, like someone's height, without surgery. Maddy and I have all the noncosmetic benefits of the operation: impervious teeth, perfect vision, disease resistance. But we look pretty close to the way we would have without the operation. As far as the fat that was sucked out"—he patted his stomach—"that proves very easy to replace."

"But *why*? Why would you want to be ugly? You were doctors, so there was nothing wrong with your brains, right?"

"Our minds are fine," Maddy answered. "But we wanted to start a community of people who didn't have the lesions, people who were free of pretty thinking. It was the only way to see what difference the lesions really made. That meant we had to gather a group of uglies. Young people, recruited from the cities."

Tally nodded. "So you had to become ugly too. Otherwise, who'd trust you?"

"We refined the trigger chemical, created a once-a-day pill. Over a few months, our old faces came back." Maddy looked at her husband with a twinkle in her eye. "It was a fascinating process, actually."

"It must have been," Tally said. "What about the lesions? Can you create a pill that cures them?"

They were both silent for a moment, then Maddy shook her head. "We didn't find any answers before Special Circumstances showed up. Az and I are not brain specialists. We've worked on the question for twenty years without success. But here in the Smoke we've *seen* the difference that staying ugly makes."

"I've seen that myself," Tally said, thinking of the differences between Peris and David.

Az raised an eyebrow. "You catch on pretty fast, then."

"But we know there's a cure," David said.

"How?"

"There has to be," Maddy said. "Our data showed that everyone has the lesions after their first operation. So when someone winds up in a challenging line of work, the authorities somehow cure them. The lesions are removed secretly, maybe even fixed with a pill like the bone plastic, and the brain returns to normal. There must be a simple cure."

"You'll find it one day," David said quietly.

"We don't have the right equipment," Maddy said, sighing. "We don't even have a pretty human subject to study."

"But hang on," Tally said. "You used to live in a city full of pretties. When you became doctors, your lesions went away. Didn't you notice that you were changing?"

Maddy shrugged. "Of course we did. We were learning how the human body worked, and how to face the huge responsibility of saving lives. But it didn't feel as if our brains were changing. It felt like growing up."

"Oh. But when you looked around at everyone else, how

come you didn't notice they were . . . brain damaged?"

Az smiled. "We didn't have much to compare our fellow citizens with, only a few colleagues who seemed different from most people. More engaged. But that was hardly a surprise. History would indicate that the majority of people have always been sheep. Before the operation, there were wars and mass hatred and clear-cutting. Whatever these lesions make us, it isn't a far cry from the way humanity was in the Rusty era. These days we're just a bit . . . easier to manage."

"Having the lesions is normal now," Maddy said. "We're all used to the effects."

Tally took a deep breath, remembering Sol and Ellie's visit. Her parents had been so sure of themselves, and yet in a way so clueless. But they'd *always* seemed that way: wise and confident, and at the same time disconnected from whatever ugly, real-life problems Tally was having. Was that pretty brain damage? Tally had always thought that was just how parents were *supposed* to be.

For that matter, shallow and self-centered was how brand-new pretties were supposed to be. As an ugly, Peris had made fun of them—but he hadn't waited a moment to join in the fun. No one ever did. So how could you tell how much was the operation and how much was just people going along with the way things had always been?

Only by making a whole new world, which is just what Maddy and Az had begun to do.

Tally wondered which had come first: the operation or the lesions? Was becoming pretty just the bait to get everyone under the knife? Or were the lesions merely a finishing touch on being pretty? Perhaps the logical conclusion of everyone looking the same was everyone thinking the same.

She leaned back in her chair. Her eyes were blurry, and her stomach clenched whenever she thought about Peris, her parents, and every other pretty she'd ever met. How different were they? she wondered. How did it feel to be pretty? What was it really like behind those big eyes and exquisite features?

"You look tired," David said.

She laughed softly. It seemed like weeks since she and David had arrived there. A few hours of conversation had changed her world. "Maybe a little."

"I guess we'd better go, Mom."

"Of course, David. It's late, and Tally has a lot to digest."

Maddy and Az stood, and David helped Tally up from the chair. She said good-bye to them in a daze, flinching inside when she recognized the expression in their old and ugly faces: They felt *sorry* for her. Sad that she'd had to learn the truth, sad that they'd been the ones to tell her. After twenty years, maybe they'd gotten used to the idea, but they still understood that it was a horrible fact to learn.

Ninety-nine percent of humanity had had something done to their brains, and only a few people in the world knew exactly what.

"You see why I wanted you to meet my parents?"

"Yeah, I guess I do."

Tally and David were in the darkness, climbing the ridge back toward the Smoke, the sky full of stars now that the moon had set.

"You might have gone back to the city not knowing."

Tally shivered, realizing how close she had come so many times. In the library, she'd actually opened the pendant, almost holding it to her eye. And if she had, the Specials would have arrived within hours.

"I couldn't stand that," David said.

"But some uglies must go back, right?"

"Sure. They get bored with camping out, and we can't make them stay."

"You let them go? When they don't even know what the operation really means?"

David stopped and took hold of Tally's shoulder, anguish on his face. "Neither do we. And what if we told everyone what we suspect? Most of them wouldn't believe us, but others would go charging back to the city to rescue their friends. And eventually, the cities would find out what we were saying, and would do everything in their power to hunt us down."

They already are, Tally said to herself. She wondered how many other spies the Specials had blackmailed into looking for the Smoke, how many times they'd come close to finding it. She wanted to tell David what they were up to, but how? She couldn't explain that she had come here as a spy, or David would never trust her again.

She sighed. That would be the perfect way to stop herself from coming between him and Shay.

"You don't look very happy."

Tally tried to smile. David had shared his biggest secret with her; she should tell him hers. But she wasn't brave enough to say the words. "It's been a long night. That's all."

He smiled back. "Don't worry, it won't last forever."

Tally wondered how long it was until dawn. In a few hours she'd be eating breakfast alongside Shay and Croy, and everyone else she had almost betrayed, almost condemned to the operation. She flinched at the thought.

"Hey," David said, lifting her chin with his palm. "You did great tonight. I think my parents were impressed."

"Huh? With me?"

"Of course, Tally. You understood immediately what this all means. Most people can't believe it at first. They say the authorities would never be so cruel."

She smiled grimly. "Don't worry, I believe it."

"Exactly. I've seen a lot of city kids come through here. You're different from the rest of them. You can see the world clearly, even if you did grow up spoiled. That's why I had to tell you. That's why . . ."

Tally looked into his eyes and saw that his face was glowing again—touching her in that pretty way she'd felt before.

"That's why you're beautiful, Tally."

The words made her dizzy for a moment, like the falling feeling of looking into a new pretty's eyes. "Me?"

"Yes."

She laughed, shaking her head clear. "What, with my thin lips and my eyes too close together?"

"Tally . . ."

"And my frizzy hair and squashed-down nose?"

"Don't say that." His fingers brushed her cheeks where the scratches were almost healed, and ran fleetingly across her lips. She knew how callused his fingertips were, as hard and rough as wood. But somehow their caress felt soft and tentative.

"That's the worst thing they do to you, to any of you. Whatever those brain lesions are all about, the worst damage is done before they even pick up the knife: You're all brainwashed into believing you're ugly."

"We are. Everyone is."

"So you think I'm ugly?"

She looked away. "It's a pointless question. It's not about individuals."

"Yes it is, Tally. Absolutely."

"I mean, no one can really be . . . you see, biologically, there're certain things we all—" The words choked off. "You really think I'm beautiful?"

"Yes."

"More beautiful than Shay?"

They both stood silent, their mouths gaping. The question had popped out of Tally before she could think. How had she uttered something so horrible?

"I'm sorry."

David shrugged, turned away. "It's a fair question. Yes, I do."

"Do what?"

"I think you're more beautiful than Shay." He said it so matter-of-factly, as if talking about the weather.

Tally's eyes closed, every bit of exhaustion from the long day crashing into her at once. She saw Shay's face—too thin, eyes too far apart—and an awful feeling welled up inside her. The warmth she'd felt from David was crushed by it.

Every day of her life she'd insulted other uglies and had been insulted in return. Fattie, Pig-Eyes, Boney, Zits, Freak—all the names uglies called one another, eagerly and without reserve. But equally, without exception, so that no one felt shut out by some irrelevant mischance of birth. And no one was considered to be even remotely beautiful, privileged because of a random twist in their genes. That was why they'd made everyone pretty in the first place.

This was not fair.

"Don't say that. Please."

"You asked me."

She opened her eyes. "But it's horrible! It's wrong."

"Listen, Tally. That's not what's important to me. What's inside you matters a lot more."

"But *first* you see my face. You react to symmetry, skin tone, the shape of my eyes. And you decide what's inside me, based on all your reactions. You're programmed to!"

"*I'm* not programmed. I didn't grow up in a city."

"It's not just culture, it's evolution!"

He shrugged in defeat, the anger draining from his voice. "Maybe some of it is." He chuckled tiredly. "But you know what first got me interested in you?"

Tally took a deep breath, trying to calm herself. "What?"

"The scratches on your face."

She blinked. "The *what*?"

"These scratches." He softly touched her cheek again.

She shook away the electric feeling his fingers left behind. "That's nuts. Imperfect skin is a sign of a poor immune system."

David laughed. "It was a sign that you'd been in an adventure, Tally, that you'd bashed your way across the wild to get here. To me, it was a sign that you had a good story to tell."

Her outrage faded. "A good story?" Tally shook her head, a laugh building inside her. "Actually, my face got scratched up back in the city, hoverboarding through some trees. At high speed. Some adventure, huh?"

"It does tell a story, though. As I thought the first time I saw you—you take risks." His fingers wound into a lock of her singed hair. "You're still taking risks."

"I guess so." Standing here in the darkness with David felt like a risk, like everything was about to change again. He still had the look in his eye, the pretty look.

Maybe he really could see past her ugly face. Maybe what was inside her did matter to him more than anything else.

Tally stepped onto a fist-size stone on the path and found an uneasy balance on it. They were eye to eye now.

She swallowed. "You really think I'm beautiful."

"Yes. What you do, the way you think, makes you beautiful."

A strange thought crossed her mind, and Tally said, "I'd hate it if you got the operation." She couldn't believe she was saying it. "Even if they didn't do your brain, I mean."

"Gee, thanks." His smile shone in the darkness.

"I don't want you to look like everyone else."

"I thought that was the point of being pretty."

"I did too." She touched his eyebrow where the line of white cut through it. "So how'd you get that scar?"

"An adventure. A good story. I'll tell you sometime."

"You promise?"

"I promise."

"Good." She leaned forward, her weight pressing into him, and as her feet gradually slipped down the stone, their lips met. His arms wrapped around her and pulled her closer. His body was warm in the predawn cold, and formed something solid and certain in Tally's shaken reality. She held on tightly, amazed at how intense the kiss became.

A moment later, she pulled away to take a breath, thinking for just a second how odd this was. Uglies did kiss each other, and a lot more, but it always felt as if nothing counted until you were a pretty.

But this counted.

She pulled David toward her again, her fingers digging into the leather of his jacket. The cold, her aching muscles, the awful thing she had just learned, all of it just made this feeling stronger.

Then one of his hands touched the back of her neck, traced the slender chain there, down to the cold, hard metal of the pendant.

She stiffened, and their lips parted.

"What about this?" he said.

She enclosed the metal heart in her fist, her other arm still wrapped around him. There was no way she could tell David about Dr. Cable now. He would pull away, maybe forever. The pendant was still between them.

Suddenly, Tally knew what to do. It was perfect. "Come with me."

"Where?"

"To the Smoke. I have to show you something."

She pulled him up the slope, scrambling until they reached the top of the ridge.

"Are you okay?" he asked, panting. "I didn't mean to—"

"I'm great." She smiled broadly at him, then peered down on the Smoke. A single campfire burned near the center of town, where the night-watch gathered to warm up every hour or so. "Come on."

Suddenly, it seemed important to get there fast, before her certainty faded, before the warm feeling inside her could give way to doubt. She scrambled down between the painted stones of the hoverboard path, David struggling to keep up. When her feet reached level ground, she ran, heedless of the dark and silent huts on either side, seeing only the firelight ahead. Her speed was effortless, like hoverboarding on an open straightaway.

Tally ran until she reached the fire, skidding to a halt against its cushion of heat and smoke. She reached up to unclasp the pendant's chain.

"Tally?" David ran up panting, confusion on his face. He tried breathlessly to say more.

"No," she said. "Just watch."

The pendant swung by its chain in her fist, sparkling red in the firelight. Tally focused all her doubts on it, all her fear of discovery, her terror at Dr. Cable's threats. She clutched the pendant, squeezing the unyielding metal until her muscles ached, as if forcing into her own mind the almost unthinkable fact that she might really remain an ugly for life. But somehow not ugly at all.

She opened her hand and threw the necklace into the center of the fire.

It landed on a crackling log, the metal heart burning black for a moment, then gradually turning yellow and white in the heat. Finally, a small *pop* came from it, as if something trapped inside had exploded, and it slid from the log and disappeared among the flames.

She turned to David, her vision spotted with sinuous shapes from staring into the fire. He coughed at the smoke. "Wow. That was dramatic."

Tally suddenly felt foolish. "Yeah, I guess so."

He moved closer. "You really meant that. Whoever gave it to you—"

"Doesn't matter anymore."

"What if they come?"

"No one's coming. I'm sure of it."

David smiled and gathered Tally into a hug, pulling her away from the edge of the fire. "Well, Tally Youngblood, you certainly know how to make a point. You know, I would have believed you if you just told me—"

"No, I had to do it like this. I had to burn it. To know for sure."

He kissed her forehead and laughed. "You're beautiful."

"When you say that, I almost . . . ," she whispered.

Suddenly, a wave of exhaustion struck Tally, as if her last bit of energy had gone into the fire with the pendant. She was tired from the wild run here, from the long night with Maddy and Az, from a hard day's work. And tomorrow she would have to face Shay again, and explain what had happened between her and David. Of course, the moment Shay saw that the pendant was gone from around Tally's neck, she would know.

But at least she'd never know the real truth. The pendant was charred beyond recognition, its true purpose hidden forever. Tally slumped into David's arms, closing her eyes. The image of the glowing heart was burned into her vision.

She was free. Dr. Cable would never come here now, and no one could ever take her away from David or the Smoke, or do to Tally's brain whatever the operation did to pretties'. She was no longer an infiltrator. She finally belonged here.

Tally found herself crying.

David silently walked her to the bunkhouse. At the door, he leaned forward to kiss her, but she pulled away and shook her head. Shay was just inside. Tally would have to talk to her tomorrow. It wouldn't be easy, but Tally knew she could face anything now.

David nodded, kissed his finger, and traced one of the remaining scratches on her cheek. "See you tomorrow," he whispered.

"Where are you going?"

"For a walk. I need to think."

"Don't you ever sleep?"

"Not tonight." He smiled.

Tally kissed his hand and slipped inside, where she kicked off her shoes and crawled into bed with her clothes on, falling asleep in seconds, as if the weight of the world had lifted from her shoulders.

The next morning she awoke to chaos, the sounds of running, shouting, and the scream of machines invading her dreams. Out the bunkhouse window, the sky was full of hovercars.

Special Circumstances had arrived.

Part III

INTO THE FIRE

Beauty is that Medusa's head
Which men go armed to seek and sever.
It is most deadly when most dead.
And dead will stare and sting forever.
—Archibald MacLeish, "Beauty"

INVASION

Tally turned from the window and saw nothing but empty beds. She was alone in the bunkhouse.

She shook her head, foggy from sleep and disbelief. The ground rumbled beneath her bare feet, and the bunkhouse shuddered around her. Suddenly, the plastic in one of the windows shattered, and the muffled cacophony from outside rushed in to batter her ears. The entire building shook as if it would collapse.

Where was everyone? Had they already fled the Smoke, leaving her there to face this invasion alone?

Tally ran for the door and threw it open. Before her, a hovercar was landing, blinding her for a moment with a face full of dust. She recognized the machine's cruel lines from the Special

Circumstances car that had first taken her to see Dr. Cable. But this one was equipped with four shimmering blades—one each where the wheels of a groundcar would be—a cross between a normal hovercar and the rangers' helicopter.

It could travel anywhere, Tally realized, inside a city or out in the wild. She remembered Dr. Cable's words: *We'll be there in a few hours.* Tally forced the thought from her head. This attack couldn't have anything to do with her.

The hovercar struck the dusty ground with a thud. This was no time to stand there wondering. She turned and ran.

The camp was a chaos of smoke and running figures. Cooking fires had been blown from their pits, and scattered embers burned everywhere. Two of the encampment's big buildings were ablaze. Chickens and rabbits scampered underfoot, dust and ashes coiled in rampant whirlwinds. Dozens of Smokies ran about, some trying to put out the fires, some trying to escape, some simply panicking.

Through everything else, the forms of cruel pretties moved. Their gray uniforms passed like fleeting shadows through the confusion. Graceful and unhurried, as if unaware of the chaos around them, they set about subduing the panicking Smokies. They moved in a blur, without any weapons that Tally could see, leaving everyone in their wake lying on the ground, bound and dazed.

They were superhumanly fast and strong. The Special operation had given them more than just terrible faces.

Near the mess hall, about two dozen Smokies were making a stand, holding off a handful of Specials with axes and makeshift clubs. Tally made her way toward the fight, and the incongruous smells of breakfast reached her through the choking haze of smoke. Her stomach growled.

Tally realized that she had slept through the breakfast call, too exhausted to wake up with everyone else. The Specials must have waited until most of the Smokies were gathered in the mess hall before launching their invasion.

Of course. They wanted to capture as many Smokies as possible in a single stroke.

The Specials weren't attacking the large group at the mess hall. They waited patiently in a ring around the building while their numbers increased, more hovercars landing every minute. If anyone tried to get past the cordon, they reacted swiftly, disarming and incapacitating whoever dared to run. But most of the Smokies were too shocked to resist, paralyzed by the terrible faces of their opponents. Even here, most people had never seen a cruel pretty.

Tally pinned herself against a building, trying to disappear next to a stack of firewood. She shielded her eyes from the dust storm, searching for an escape route. There was no way to get into the center of the Smoke, where her hoverboard lay on the broad roof of the trading post, charging in the sun. The forest was the only way out.

A stretch of uncleared trees lay at the closest edge of town, only a twenty-second dash away. But a Special stood between her and the border of dense trees and brush, waiting to intercept any stray Smokies. The woman's eyes scanned the approach to the forest, her head moving from side to side in a weirdly regular motion, like someone watching a slow-motion tennis match without much interest.

Tally crept closer, staying pressed against the building. A hovercar passed overhead, blowing a maelstrom of dust and loose wood chips into her eyes.

When she could see again, Tally found an aging ugly crouching next to her, against the wall.

"Hey!" he hissed.

She recognized the sagging features, the bitter expression.

It was the Boss.

"Young lady, we have a problem." His harsh voice cut through the cacophony of the attack.

She glanced in the direction of the waiting Special. "Yeah, I know."

Another hovercar roared over them, and he pulled her around the corner of the building and down behind a drum that collected rainwater from the gutters.

"You noticed her too?" He grinned, showing a missing tooth. "Maybe if we both run at once, one of us might make it. If the other puts up a fight."

Tally swallowed. "I guess." She peered out at the Special, who stood as calmly as a crumbly waiting for a pleasure ferry. "But they're pretty fast."

"That depends." He dropped the duffel bag from his shoulder. "There're two things I keep ready for emergencies."

The Boss unzipped the bag and pulled out a plastic container big enough for a sandwich. "This is one." He popped open one corner of the top, and a puff of dust rose up. A second later, a wave of fire rushed into Tally's head. She covered her face, eyes watering, and tried to cough up the finger of flame that had crawled down her throat.

"Not bad, eh?" the Boss chuckled. "That's pure habanero pepper, dried and ground down to dust. Not too bad in beans, but hell in your eyes."

Tally blinked away her tears and managed to speak. "Are you nuts?"

"The other thing is this bag, which contains a representative sample of two hundred years of Rusty-era visual culture. Priceless and irreplaceable artifacts. So which do you want?"

"Huh?"

"Do you want the habanero pepper or the bag of magazines? Do you want to get caught while taking out our Special friend? Or save a precious piece of human heritage from these barbarians?"

Tally coughed once more. "I guess . . . I want to escape."

The Boss smiled. "Good. I'm sick of running. Sick of losing my hair too, and being short-sighted. I've done my bit, and you look pretty fast."

He handed her the duffel bag. It was heavy, but Tally had grown stronger since she'd come to the Smoke. Magazines were nothing compared with scrap metal.

She thought of the first day she had arrived there, seeing a magazine for the first time in the library, realizing with horror what humanity had once looked like. The pictures had made her sick that first day, and now here she was ready to save them.

"Here's the plan," the Boss said. "I'll go first, and when that Special grabs me, I'll give her a face full of pepper. You run straight and fast and don't look back. Got that?"

"Yeah."

"With any luck, we both might make it. Though I wouldn't mind a face-lift. Ready?"

Tally pulled the bag farther up on her shoulder. "Let's go."

"One . . . two . . ." The Boss paused. "Oh, dear. There's a problem, young lady."

"What?"

"You haven't got any shoes."

Tally looked down. In her confusion, she had stumbled barefoot out of the bunkhouse. The packed dirt of the Smoke compound was easy enough to walk on, but in the forest . . .

"You won't make it ten meters, kid."

The Boss pulled the duffel bag away from her and handed her the plastic container. "Now get going."

"But I . . . ," Tally said. "I don't want to go back to the city."

"Yes, young lady, and I wouldn't mind getting some decent dental work. But we all have to make sacrifices. Starting *now*!" On the last word, he shoved her out from behind the drum.

Tally stumbled forward, utterly exposed in the middle of the street. The roar of a hovercar seemed to pass right over her head, and she instinctively ducked, dashing toward the cover of the forest.

The Special cocked her head toward Tally, calmly folded her arms, and frowned like a teacher spotting littlies playing where they shouldn't.

Tally wondered if the pepper would do anything to the woman. If it affected the Special like it had Tally, she might still make it into the forest. Even if she was supposed to be the bait. Even if she had no shoes.

Even if it turned out David had already been caught and she'd never see him again . . .

The thought unleashed a sudden torrent of anger inside her, and she ran straight at the woman, the container clenched in both hands.

A smile broke out on the Special's cruel features.

A split second before they collided, the Special seemed to disappear, slipping out of sight like a coin in a magician's hand. In her next stride Tally felt something hard connect with her shin, and pain shot up her leg. Her body tumbled forward, hands reaching out to break her fall, the container slipping from her grasp.

She hit the ground hard, skidding on her palms. As she rolled through the dirt, Tally glimpsed the Special crouching behind her. The woman had simply ducked, invisibly fast, and Tally had tripped over her like some awkward littlie in a brawl.

Shaking her head and spitting the dirt out of her mouth, Tally spotted the container just out of reach. She scrambled toward it, but a staggering weight crashed down on her, driving her face-first into the ground. She felt her wrists pulled back and bound, hard plastic cuffs cutting into her flesh.

She struggled, but couldn't move.

Then the awful weight lifted, and a nudge from a boot flipped her over effortlessly. The Special stood over her, smiling coldly, holding the container. "Now, now, ugly," the cruel pretty said. "You just calm down. We don't want to hurt you. But we will if we have to."

Tally started to speak, but her jaw clenched with pain. It had plowed into the ground when she'd fallen.

"What's so important about this?" the Special asked, shaking the container and trying to peer through its translucent plastic.

Out of the corner of her eye, Tally saw the Boss making his way toward the forest. His run was slow and tortured, the duffel bag too heavy for him.

"Open it and see," Tally spat painfully.

"I will," she said, still smiling. "But first things first." She turned her attention toward the Boss, and her posture suddenly transformed into something animal, crouched and coiled like a cat ready to spring.

Tally rolled back onto her shoulders, thrashing out wildly with both feet. Her kick connected with the container, and it popped open, a puff of brownish-green dust spraying out over the Special.

For a second, a disbelieving expression spread over the woman's face. She made a gagging noise, her whole body shuddering. Then her eyes and fists clamped shut, and she screamed.

The sound wasn't human. It cut into Tally's ears like a vibrasaw striking metal, and every muscle in her body fought to get free of the handcuffs, her instincts demanding that she cover her ears. With another wild kick, she rolled herself over and stumbled to her feet, staggering in the direction of the forest.

A tickle grew in Tally's throat as the pepper dust dispersed on the wind. She coughed as she ran, eyes watering and stinging until she was half-blind. With her hands tied behind her, Tally lurched into the brush off-balance, tumbling to the ground as her bare feet caught on something in the dense vegetation.

She struggled forward, trying to drag herself out of sight.

Blinking away tears, she saw that the Special's inhuman scream had been some kind of alarm. Three more of the cruel pretties had responded. One led the pepper-covered Special away at arm's length, and the others approached the forest.

Tally froze, the brush barely concealing her.

Then she felt a tickle in her throat, a slowly growing irritation. Tally held her breath, closing her eyes. But her chest began to shudder, her body twitching, demanding to expel traces of the pepper from her lungs.

She *had* to cough.

Tally swallowed again and again, hoping spit could put out the fire in her throat. Her lungs demanded oxygen, but she didn't dare breathe. One of the Specials was only a stone's throw away, scanning the forest with slow back-and-forth sweeps of his head, his eyes searching the dense trees relentlessly.

Gradually, painfully, the flames seemed to expire in Tally's chest, the cough dying a quiet death inside her. She relaxed, finally letting out her breath.

Over the thunder of hovercars and crackle of burning buildings and sounds of battle, the Special somehow heard her soft exhalation. His head turned swiftly, eyes narrowing, and in what seemed like a single motion he was by her side, a hand on the back of her neck. “You’re a tricky one,” he said.

She tried to answer, but wound up coughing savagely instead, and he forced her face down in the dirt before she could manage another breath.

THE RABBIT PEN

They marched her to the rabbit pen, where about forty handcuffed Smokies sat inside the wire fence. A dozen or so Specials stood in a cordon around them, watching their captives with empty expressions. By the entrance to the compound a few rabbits hopped aimlessly, too addled by their sudden freedom to make a break for it.

The Special who had captured Tally took her to the end farthest from the gate, where a handful of Smokies with bloody noses and black eyes were clustered.

"Armed resistor," he said to the two cruel pretties who guarded this end of the pen, and shoved her down to the ground among the others.

She stumbled and fell onto her back, where her weight stretched the cuffs painfully across her wrists. When she struggled to turn over, a foot planted itself into her back and pushed her up. For a moment, she thought the shoe belonged to a Special, but it was one of the other Smokies, helping her up the only way he could. She managed to sit up cross-legged.

The wounded Smokies around her smiled grimly, nodding encouragement.

"Tally," someone hissed.

She struggled to turn toward the voice. It was Croy, a cut over his eye bleeding down onto his cheek, one side of his face covered with dirt. He scooted himself a bit closer. "You resisted?" he said. "Huh. Guess I was wrong about you."

Tally could only cough. Traces of the burning pepper seemed stuck in her lungs, like the embers of a fire that wouldn't go out. Tears still streamed from her eyes.

"I noticed you slept through breakfast call this morning," he said. "Then when the Specials came, I figured you'd picked an awfully convenient time to disappear."

She shook her head, forced words through the cinders in her throat. "I was out late with David. That's all." Speaking made her sore jaw ache.

Croy frowned. "I haven't seen him all morning."

"Really?" She blinked away tears. "Maybe he got away."

"I doubt anyone did." Croy jutted his chin toward the gate of the pen. A large group of Smokies was on its way, guarded by a squad of Specials. Among them, Tally recognized faces from those who'd made a stand at the mess hall.

"They're just mopping up now," he said.

"Have you seen Shay?"

Croy shrugged. "She was at breakfast when they attacked, but I lost track of her."

"What about the Boss?"

Croy looked around. "No."

"I think he got away. He and I made a run together."

A dark smile crossed Croy's face. "That's funny. He always said he wouldn't mind getting captured. Something about a face-lift."

Tally managed to smile. But then she thought about the brain lesions that went along with becoming pretty, and a shiver passed through her body. She wondered how many of these captives knew what was really going to happen to them.

"Yeah, the Boss was going to give himself up, to help me get away, but I couldn't have made it through the forest."

"Why not?"

She wriggled her toes. "No shoes."

Croy raised an eyebrow. "You picked the wrong day to sleep late."

"I guess so."

Outside the overcrowded rabbit pen, the new arrivals were being organized into groups. A pair of Specials moved through the pen, flashing a reader into the bound Smokies' eyes, taking them outside one by one.

"They must be separating everyone by city," Croy said.

"Why?"

"To take us home," he said coldly.

"Home," she repeated. Just last night, that word had changed its meaning in her mind. And now *home* was destroyed. It lay around her in ruins, burning and captured.

She scanned the captives, looking for Shay and David. The familiar faces in the crowd were haggard, dirty, crumpled by shock and defeat, but Tally realized that she no longer thought of them as ugly. It was the cold expressions of the Specials, beautiful though they were, that seemed horrific to her now.

A disturbance caught her eye. Three of the invaders were carrying a struggling figure, bound hand and foot, through the pen. They marched straight to the resistors' corner and dumped her onto the ground.

It was Shay.

"Watch this one."

The two Specials guarding them glanced at the still writhing figure. "Armed resistor?" one asked.

There was a pause. Tally saw that one of the Specials had a bruise marring his pretty face.

"Unarmed. But dangerous."

The three left their captive behind, their cruel grace marked with a touch of hurry.

"Shay!" Croy hissed.

Shay rolled herself over. Her face was red, her lips puffy and bleeding. She spat, saliva trailing from her mouth to a bloodred glob on the dusty ground.

"Croy," she managed with a thick tongue.

Then her eyes fell on Tally.

"*You!*"

"Uh, Shay . . . ," Croy began.

"You did this!" Her whole body writhed like a snake in its death throes. "Stealing my boyfriend wasn't enough? You had to betray the whole Smoke!"

Tally closed her eyes and shook her head. It couldn't be true. She had destroyed the pendant. The fire had consumed it.

"Shay!" Croy said. "Calm down. Look at her. She fought them."

"Are you blind, Croy? Look around you! *She* did this!"

Tally took a deep breath and forced herself to look at Shay. Her friend's eyes burned with hatred.

"Shay, I swear to you, I didn't. I never . . ." Her voice faltered.

"Who else could have led them here?"

"I don't know."

"We can't blame each other, Shay," Croy said. "It could've been anything. A satellite image. A scouting mission."

"A spy."

"Will you *look at her,* Shay?" Croy cried. "She's tied up, like us. She resisted!"

Shay slammed her eyes shut and shook her head.

The two Specials with the eye-reader had reached the resistors' corner of the pen. One stood back while the other stepped forward warily. "We don't want to hurt you," she announced. "But we will if we have to."

The cruel pretty grabbed Croy's chin and flashed the reader in his eye. She looked at its readout.

"Another one of ours," she said.

The other Special raised an eyebrow. "Didn't know we had so many runaways."

The two hauled Croy to his feet and marched him toward the largest group of Smokies outside. Tally bit her lip. Croy was one of Shay's old friends, so these two Specials were from her own city. Maybe all the invaders were.

It had to be a coincidence. This couldn't be her fault. She'd seen the pendant burn!

"So you've got Croy on your side too now, I see," Shay hissed.

Tears began to fill Tally's eyes, but not from the pepper this time. "Look at me, Shay!"

"He suspected you from the beginning. But I told him every time, 'No, Tally's my friend. She'd never do anything to hurt me.'"

"Shay, I'm not lying."

"How did you change Croy's mind, Tally? The same way you changed David's?"

"Shay, I never meant for that to happen."

"So where were you two last night?"

Tally swallowed, trying to hold her voice steady. "Just talking. I told him about my necklace."

"That took all night? Or did you just decide to make your move before the Specials came? One last game with him. With me."

Tally lowered her head. "Shay . . ."

A hand grabbed her chin and forced it up. She blinked, and a dazzling red light flashed.

The Special looked at the device closely. "Hey, it's her."

Tally shook her head. "No."

The other Special looked at the readout, nodding confirmation. "Tally Youngblood?"

She didn't answer. They lifted her to her feet and dusted her off.

"Come with us. Dr. Cable wants to see you immediately."

"I knew it," Shay hissed.

"No!"

They pulled Tally toward the gate of the pen. She twisted her head around to look back, trying to think of words that would explain.

Shay glared up at her from the ground, bloody teeth gritted, her eyes falling to Tally's bound wrists. A second later, Tally felt the pressure release, and her hands popped apart. The Specials had cut her handcuffs.

"No," she said softly.

One of the Specials squeezed her shoulder. "Don't worry, Tally, we'll have you home in no time."

The other chimed in. "We've been looking for this bunch for years."

"Yeah, good work."

IN CASE OF DAMAGE

They took her to the library. It had been transformed into a headquarters for the invasion, the long tables filled with portable workscreens manned by Specials, its usual quiet replaced by a buzz of clipped exchanges and commands. The razor voices of the cruel pretties set Tally's teeth on edge.

Dr. Cable waited at one of the long tables. Reading an old magazine, she seemed almost relaxed, at a remove from the activity around her.

"Ah, Tally." She bared her teeth in an attempt at a smile. "Nice to see you. Sit down."

Tally wondered what was behind the doctor's greeting. The

Specials had treated Tally like an accomplice. Had some signal from the pendant reached them before she had destroyed it?

In any case, her only chance of escape was to play along. She pulled out a chair and sat down.

"Goodness. Look at you," Dr. Cable said. "For someone who wants to be a pretty, you're always such a sight."

"I've had a rough morning."

"You seem to have been in a scrape."

Tally shrugged. "I was just trying to get out of the way."

"Indeed." Dr. Cable placed the magazine facedown on the table. "That's something you don't seem to be very good at."

Tally coughed twice, the last bit of pepper leaving her lungs. "I guess not."

Dr. Cable glanced at her workscreen. "I see we had you among the resistors?"

"Some of the Smokies already suspected me. So when I heard you guys coming, I tried to get out of town. I didn't want to be around when everyone realized what was happening. In case they got mad at me."

"Self-preservation. Well, at least you're good at something."

"I didn't ask to come here."

"No, and you took your time, too." Dr. Cable leaned back, making a steeple of her long, thin fingers. "How long have you been here exactly?"

Tally forced herself to cough again, wondering if she dared lie. Her voice, still harsh and uneven from inhaling the pepper, wasn't likely to give her away. And although Dr. Cable's office back in the city might be one big lie detector, this table and chair were solid wood, without any tricks inside.

But Tally hedged. "Not that long."

"You didn't get here as quickly as I'd hoped."

"I almost didn't make it at all. And when I did, it was ages after my birthday. That's why they suspected me."

Dr. Cable shook her head. "I suppose I should have been worried about you, out in the wild all alone. Poor Tally."

"Thanks for your concern."

"I'm sure you would have used the pendant if you'd gotten into any real trouble. Self-preservation being your one skill."

Tally sneered. "Unless I'd fallen off a cliff. Which almost happened."

"We still would have come for you. If the pendant had been damaged, it would have sent a signal automatically."

The words sunk in slowly: *If the pendant had been damaged . . .* Tally gripped the edge of the table, trying not to show any emotion.

Dr. Cable narrowed her eyes. She might not have machines to read Tally's voice and heartbeat and sweat, but her own perceptions were alert. She'd chosen those words to provoke a reaction. "Speaking of which, where is it?"

Tally's fingers went to her neck. Of course, Dr. Cable had noticed the pendant's absence immediately. Her questions had been leading to this moment. Tally's brain raced for an answer. The handcuffs were off. She had to get out of there, to the trading post. Hopefully, her hoverboard still lay on the roof, unfolded and charging in the morning sun. "I hid it," she said. "I was scared."

"Scared of what?"

"Last night, after I was sure this really was the Smoke, I activated the pendant. But they have this thing that detects bugs. They found the one on my board—the one you put there without telling me."

Dr. Cable smiled, spreading her hands helplessly.

"That almost blew the whole thing," Tally continued. "So after I activated the pendant, I got scared they'd know a transmission had been sent. I hid it, in case they came looking."

"I see. A certain amount of intelligence sometimes accompanies a strong sense of self-preservation. I'm glad you decided to help us."

"Like I had a choice?"

"You always had a choice, Tally. But you made the right choice. You decided to come here and find your friend, to save her from a life of being ugly. You should be happy about that."

"I'm thrilled."

"So pugnacious, you uglies. Well, you'll be growing up soon."

A chill went down Tally's spine at the words. To Dr. Cable, "growing up" meant having your brain changed.

"There's just one more thing you have to do for me, Tally. Do you mind getting the pendant from where you've hidden it? I don't like to leave loose ends lying around."

Tally smiled. "I'd be happy to."

"This officer will accompany you." Dr. Cable lifted a finger, and a Special appeared at her side. "And just to keep you safe from your Smokey friends, we'll make it look like you've been a brave resistor."

The Special pulled Tally's hands together behind her back, and she felt plastic bite into her wrists again.

She took a breath, her pulse pounding in her head, then forced herself to say, "Whatever."

"This way."

Tally led the Special toward the trading post, taking in the situation. The Smoke had been beaten into silence. Fires were left to burn freely. Some were already exhausted, clouds of smoke still rising from the blackened wood and swirling through the camp.

A few faces turned to look up with suspicion at Tally. She was the only Smokey still walking around. Everyone else was on the ground, handcuffed and under guard, most of them gathered near the rabbit pen.

She tried to give those who saw her a grim smile, hoping they noticed that she was handcuffed just like they were.

When they reached the trading post, Tally looked up. "I hid it on the roof."

The Special eyed the building suspiciously. "All right, then," he said. "You wait here. Sit down and don't stand up."

She shrugged, kneeling carefully.

The Special swung himself onto the roof with an ease that made Tally shiver. How was she going to overcome this cruel pretty? Even if her hands weren't tied, he was bigger, stronger, faster.

A moment later, his head stuck out over the edge. "Where is it?"

"Under the rapchuck."

"The what?"

"The *rapchuck*. You know, the old-fashioned thingie where the roofline connects with the abbersnatch."

"What the hell are you talking about?"

"It's Smokey slang, I guess. Let me show you."

A fleeting expression crossed the Special's impassive face—annoyance mixed with suspicion. But he leaped down again and stacked a couple of crates. He jumped onto them and pulled Tally up, sitting her on the edge of the roof as if she weighed nothing. "You touch one of those hoverboards, I'll put you on your face," he threatened casually.

"There're hoverboards up here?"

He leaped past her and hauled her onto the roof. "Find it."

"No problem." She walked gingerly up the slanted roof, exaggerating the difficulty of balancing without her hands. The solar cells of the recharging hoverboards were blindingly bright in the sun. Tally's board lay too far away, on the other side of the roof, and it was unfolded into eight sections. Folding it back up would take a solid minute. But Tally saw one nearby, Croy's maybe, that had only been unfolded once. Its light was green. One kick to close it and the board would be ready to fly.

But Tally couldn't fly with her hands bound. She'd fall off on the first turn.

She took a deep breath, ignoring the part of her brain that saw only the distance to the ground. As long as the Special was as fast and strong as he seemed . . .

"I'm wearing a bungee jacket," she lied to herself. "Nothing can possibly happen."

Tally let her bare feet trip, and tumbled down the slope.

The rough shingles battered Tally's knees and elbows as she rolled, letting out a cry of pain. She fought to stay on the roof, her feet scrambling against the wood to slow herself down.

Just as she reached the edge, an iron grip fastened onto her shoulder. She rolled off into space, the ground looming below. But Tally jerked to a halt, her arm wrenching in its socket, and she heard the Special's razor voice curse.

She swung for a moment, her fall arrested, then they both started to slip.

She could hear the Special's fingers and feet scrabbling for purchase. However strong he might be, there was nothing for him to hold on to. Tally was going to fall.

But at least she was going to take him with her.

Then a grunt came from the Special, and Tally felt herself being pulled up in a mighty heave. She was thrown back onto the roof, and a shadow passed over her. Something hit the ground below. The Special had thrown himself off the roof to save her!

She rolled up into a crouch, stood, and lifted half of Croy's hoverboard with one foot, flipping it closed. A noise came from the edge of the roof, and Tally stepped away from Croy's board.

The Special's fingers appeared, then his body swung into view. He was completely unhurt.

"Are you okay?" she asked. "Wow. You guys are strong. Thanks for saving me."

He looked at her coolly. "Just get what we came for. And try not to kill yourself."

"Okay." Tally turned, managed to get a foot tangled on a shingle, and teetered again. The Special had her in his arms in a second. Finally, she heard real anger in his voice. "You uglies are so . . . incompetent!"

"Well, maybe if you could—"

Even before it was out of her mouth, she felt the pressure on her wrists disappear. She brought her hands around in front, rubbing her shoulders. "Ow. Thanks."

"Listen," he said, the razors in his cruel voice sharper than ever, "I don't want to hurt you, but—"

"You will if you have to." Tally smiled. He was standing in exactly the right place.

"Just get whatever Dr. Cable wants. And don't you dare touch one of those hoverboards."

"Don't worry, I don't have to," she said, and snapped the fingers of both hands as loudly as she could.

Croy's hoverboard jumped into the air, knocking the Special's feet out from under him. The man rolled off the roof again, and Tally leaped onto the board.

RUN

Tally had never ridden a hoverboard barefoot before. Young Smokies had all kinds of competitions, carrying weights or riding double, but no one was ever *that* stupid.

She almost fell off on the first turn, zooming down a new path they'd spiked with scrap metal only a few days before. The moment the board banked, her dirty feet skidded across the surface, spinning her halfway around. Her arms flailed wildly, but somehow Tally kept her footing, shooting across the compound and over the rabbit pen.

A ragged cheer rose up below as the captives below saw her fly past and realized that someone was making an escape. Tally was too busy staying on board to glance down.

Regaining her balance, Tally realized she wasn't wearing crash bracelets. Any fall would be for real. Her toes gripped the board, and she vowed to take the next turn more slowly. If the sky had been cloudy this morning, the sun wouldn't have burned the dew off Croy's board yet. She'd be lying in a crumpled heap in the pen, probably with a broken neck. It was lucky she, like most young Smokies, slept with her belly sensor on.

Already, the whine of hovercars taking off came from behind.

Tally knew only two ways out of the Smoke by hoverboard. Instinctively, she headed for the railroad tracks where she worked every day. The valley dropped behind her, and she managed to make the tight turn onto the white-water stream without falling off. With no knapsack and her heavy crash bracelets missing, Tally felt practically naked.

Croy's board wasn't as fast as hers, and it didn't know her style. Riding it was like breaking in new shoes—while running for your life.

Over the water, spray struck her face, hands, and feet. Tally knelt, grasping the edge of the board with wet hands, flying as low as she dared. Down here, the spray might make it even harder to ride, but the barrier of the trees kept her invisible. She dared a glance backward. No hovercars had appeared yet.

As she shot down the winding stream, swerving through the familiar hard turns, Tally thought of all the times she and David and Shay had raced each other to the work site. She wondered where David was. Back in camp, bound and ready to be taken to a city he'd never seen before? Would he have his face filed down and replaced by a pretty mask, his brain turned into whatever mush the authorities decided would be acceptable for a former renegade raised in the wild?

She shook her head, forcing the image from her mind. David hadn't been among the captured resistors. If he'd been caught, he definitely would have put up a fight. He must have escaped.

The roar of a hovercar passed overhead, the shock wave of its passage almost throwing Tally from the board. A few seconds later, she knew it had spotted her, its screaming turn echoing through the forest as it cut back to the river.

Shadows passed over Tally, and she glanced up to see two hovercars following her, their blades shimmering as bright as knives in the midmorning sun. The hovercars could go anywhere, but Tally was limited by her magnetic lifters. She was trapped on the route to the railroad.

Tally remembered her first ride out to Dr. Cable's office, the violent agility of the hovercar with its cruel pretty driver. In a straight line, they were much faster than any board. Her only advantage was that she knew this path backward and forward.

Fortunately, it was hardly a straight line.

Tally gripped the board with both hands and jumped from the river to the ridge line. The cars disappeared into the distance, overshooting as she skimmed the iron vein. But Tally was out in the open now, the plains spreading out below her as huge as ever.

She noticed fleetingly that it was a perfect day, not a cloud in the sky.

Tally lay almost flat to cut down wind resistance, coaxing every ounce of speed from Croy's board. It didn't look like she'd make it to the next cover before the two cars had swung around.

She wondered how they planned to capture her. Use a stunner? Throw a net? Simply bowl her over with their shock waves? At this speed and without crash bracelets, anything that knocked Tally off the board would kill her.

Maybe that was just fine with them.

The scream of their blades came from her right, louder and louder.

Just before the sound reached her, Tally dragged herself into a full hoverskid, her momentum crushing her down into the board. The two hovercars shot past ahead, missing by a mile, but the wind of their passage spun her around in circles. The board flipped over and then back upright, Tally hanging on with both arms as the world spun wildly around her.

She regained control and urged it forward again, bringing it back to full speed before the hovercars could turn back around. The Specials might be faster, but her hoverboard was more maneuverable.

As the next turn drew near, the hovercars were headed straight for her, moving slower now, their pilots realizing that at top speed they would overshoot her every time.

Let them try to fly below tree level, though.

Now riding on her knees, gripping the board with both hands, Tally twisted into the next turn, dropping to skim just above the cracked dirt of the dry creek bed. She heard the whine of the hovercars steadily build.

They were tracking her too easily, probably using her body heat to pick her out among the trees, like the minders back home. Tally remembered the little portable heater she'd used to sneak out of the dorm so many times. If only she had it now.

Then Tally remembered the caves that David had shown her on her first day in the Smoke. Under the cold stones of the mountain, her body heat would disappear.

She ignored the sound of her pursuers, shooting down the creek bed and across a spur of ore, then onto the river that led to the railroad. She careened along above the water, and the hovercars stayed above tree height, patiently waiting for her to run out of cover.

As the turnoff to the railroad approached, Tally increased her speed, skimming the water as fast as she dared. She took the turn at full skid and hurtled down the track.

The cars swept away down the river. The Specials might have expected her to turn off on another river, but the sudden appearance of an old railroad track had surprised them. If she could make it to the mountain before the hovercars completed their slow turns, she would be safe.

Just in time, Tally remembered the spot where they had pulled up the track for scrap metal, and angled her board for a stomach-wrenching moment of freefall, soaring over the gap in a high arc. The lifters found metal again, and thirty seconds later she came to a skidding halt at the end of the line.

Tally jumped from the hoverboard, turned it around, and gave it a shove back toward the river. Without her crash bracelets to pull it back, the board would drift along the straight line of the railroad until it reached the break, where it would drop to the ground.

Hopefully, the Specials would think she'd fallen off, and start their search back there.

Tally crawled up the boulders and into the cave, scrambling back into the darkness. She pulled herself as far as she could go, hoping that the tons of stone overhead would be enough to hide her from the Specials. When the tiny aperture of light at the mouth of the cave had shrunk to the size of an eye, Tally dropped to the stone, panting, her hands still shaking from the flight, telling herself again and again that she'd made it.

But what had she made it to? She had no shoes, no hoverboard, no friends, not even a water purifier or a packet of SpagBol. No home to go back to.

Tally was completely alone. "I'm so dead," she said aloud.

A voice came out of the dark.

"Tally? Is that *you*?"

AMAZING

Hands grasped Tally's shoulders in the darkness.

"You made it!" It was David's voice.

In her surprise, Tally couldn't speak, but pulled him close, burying her face in his chest.

"Who else is with you?"

She shook her head.

"Oh," David whispered. Then his grip tightened as the cave shuddered around them. The roar of a hovercar passed slowly overhead, and Tally imagined the Specials' machines searching every crevice in the rock for signs of their prey.

Had she led them to David? That would be perfect, her final betrayal.

The low rumble of pursuit passed over them again, and David pulled her deeper into the blackness, down a long, twisting path that grew colder and darker. A stillness settled around her, damp and chill, and Tally imagined again the trainload of dead Rusties buried among the stones.

They waited in silence for what seemed like hours, holding each other, not daring to speak until long after the sounds of the cars had faded.

Finally David whispered, "What's happening back at the Smoke?

"The Specials came this morning."

"I know. I saw." He held her tighter. "I couldn't sleep, so I took my board up the mountain to watch the sunrise. They went right over me, twenty hovercars at once coming across the ridge. But what's happening now?"

"They put everyone in the rabbit pen, separating us into groups. Croy said they're going to take us all back to our cities."

"Croy? Who else did you see?"

"Shay, a couple of her friends. The Boss might have made it out. He and I made a break together."

"What about my parents?"

"I don't know." She was glad for the darkness. The fear in David's voice was painful enough. His parents had founded the Smoke, and they knew the secret of the operation. Whatever punishment awaited the other Smokies, it would be a hundred times worse for them.

"I can't believe it finally happened," he said softly.

Tally tried to think of something comforting to say. All she could see in the darkness was Dr. Cable's mocking smile.

"How did you get away?" he asked.

She pulled his hands to feel her wrists, where the plastic bracelets of the handcuffs remained. "I cut through these, got up onto the roof of the trading post, and stole Croy's hoverboard."

"With Specials guarding you?"

She bit her lip, saying nothing.

"That's amazing. My mother says they're superhuman. Their second operation augments all their muscles and rewires their nervous system. And they're so scary-looking, a lot of people just panic the first time they see one." He held her tighter. "But I should have known you would escape."

Tally closed her eyes, which made no difference in the utter darkness. She wished they could stay in there forever, never having to face what was outside. "It was just good luck."

Tally was amazed that she was lying again, already. If she had only told the truth about herself in the first place, the Smokies would have known what to do with the pendant. They could have attached it to some migratory bird, and Dr. Cable would be on her way to South America instead of in the library overseeing the destruction of the Smoke.

But Tally knew she couldn't tell the truth, not now. David would never trust her again, not after she'd destroyed his home, his family. She'd already lost Peris, Shay, and her new home. She couldn't bear to lose David as well.

And what good would a confession do now? David would be

left alone, and so would she, when they most needed each other.

His hands ran across her face. "You still amaze me, Tally."

She felt herself shudder, the words twisting in her like a knife.

In that moment, Tally made a deal with herself. Eventually she would have to tell David what she had unwittingly done. Not now, but someday. When she'd made things better, fixed part of what she had destroyed, maybe then he would understand. "We'll go after them," she said. "Rescue them."

"Who? My parents?"

"They came from my city, right? So that's where they'll take them. And Shay and Croy, too. We'll rescue them all."

David laughed bitterly. "Us two? Against a bunch of Specials?"

"They won't expect us."

"But how will we find them? I've never been inside a city, but I hear they're pretty big. More than a million people."

Tally took a slow breath, once again remembering her first trip out to Dr. Cable's office. The low, dirt-colored buildings at the edge of the city, past the greenbelt and among the factories. The huge, misshapen hill nearby. "I know where they'll be."

"You what?" David pulled away from their embrace.

"I've been there. Special Circumstances headquarters."

There was a moment of silence. "I thought they were secret. Most of the kids who come out here don't even believe in them."

She went on, quietly horrified that another lie was coming into her head with such ease. "A while ago I pulled a really bad trick, the kind that gets you special attention." She rested her head against David again, glad that she couldn't see his trusting expression. "I snuck into New Pretty Town. That's where you live right after the operation, having fun all the time."

"I've heard of it. And uglies aren't allowed in, right?"

"Yeah. It's a pretty serious trick. Anyway, I wore this mask and crashed a party. They almost caught me, so I grabbed a bungee jacket."

"Which is?"

"Like a hoverboard, but you wear it. It was invented for escaping tall buildings in a fire, but new pretties use it mostly for goofing around. So I grabbed one, pulled a fire alarm, and jumped off the roof. It freaked a lot of people out."

"Right. Shay told me the whole story on our way to the Smoke, saying you were the coolest ugly in the world," he said. "But all I was thinking was that things must be *really* boring in the city."

"Yeah, I guess so."

"But you got caught? Shay didn't mention that."

The lie took form as she spoke, pulling on as many strands of truth as it could reach. "Yeah, I thought I'd gotten away, but they found my DNA or something. A few days later they took me to Special Circumstances, introduced me to this scary woman. I think she was in charge there. It was the first time I'd ever seen Specials."

"Are they really that bad up close?"

She nodded in the dark. "They're beautiful, absolutely. But in a cruel, horrible way. The first time's the worst. They only wanted to scare me, though. They warned me I'd be in big trouble if I ever got caught again. Or if I ever told anyone. That's why I never mentioned it to Shay."

"That explains a lot."

"About what?"

"About you. You always seemed to know how dangerous it was here in the Smoke. Somehow, you understood what the cities were really like, even before my parents told you the truth about the operation. You were the only runaway I ever met who really got it."

Tally nodded. That much was true. "I get it."

"And you still want to go back there for my parents and Shay? To risk getting caught? To risk your mind?"

A sob broke in her voice. "I have to." *To make it up to you.*

David held her tighter, tried to kiss her. She had to turn her face away, tears finally coming.

"Tally, you are amazing."

RUIN

They didn't leave the cave until the next morning.

Tally squinted in the dawn light, eyes scanning the sky for a fleet of hovercars suddenly rising above the trees. But they hadn't heard any sound of a search all night. Maybe now that the Smoke was destroyed, catching the last few runaways wasn't worth the trouble.

David's hoverboard had spent the night hidden in the cave, and hadn't had any sunlight for a whole day now, but it had just enough charge to get them back up the mountain. They rode to the river. Tally's stomach rumbled after a whole day without food, but the first thing she needed was water. Her mouth was so dry, she could hardly talk.

David knelt at the bank and dipped his head under the icy

water. Tally shivered at the sight. Without a blanket or shoes, she'd frozen in the cave all night long, even huddled in David's arms. She needed warm food in her before she could face anything colder than the morning breeze.

"What if the Smoke's still occupied?" she asked. "Where will we get food?"

"You said they put prisoners in the rabbit pen? Where'd the rabbits go?"

"All over."

"Exactly. They should be everywhere by now. And they aren't hard to catch."

She grimaced. "Well, okay. As long as we cook them."

David laughed. "Of course."

"I've never actually started a fire," she admitted.

"Don't worry. You're a natural." He stepped onto his board and held out his hand.

Riding double was something Tally had never done before, and she found herself glad she was with David and not just anyone. She stood in front of him, bodies touching, her arms out, his hands around her waist. They negotiated the turns without words, Tally shifting her weight gradually, waiting for David to follow her lead. As they slowly got the hang of it, their bodies began to move together, threading the board down the familiar path as one.

It worked, as long as they went slowly, but Tally kept her ears open for sounds of pursuit. If a hovercar appeared, a full-speed escape was going to be tricky.

They smelled the Smoke long before they saw it.

• • •

From high up the mountain, the buildings had the look of a burned-out campfire, smoking, crumbling, blackened through and through. Nothing moved in the compound, except a few pieces of paper stirred by the wind.

"Looks like it burned all night," Tally said.

David nodded, speechless. Tally grasped his hand, wondering what it was like to see your childhood home reduced to a smoking ruin.

"I'm so sorry, David," she said.

"We have to go down. I need to see if my parents . . ." He swallowed the words.

Tally searched for signs of anyone remaining in the Smoke. It seemed entirely deserted, but there might be a few Specials in hiding, waiting for stragglers to reappear. "We should wait."

"I can't. My parents' house is on the other side of the ridge. Maybe the Specials didn't see it."

"If they missed it, Maddy and Az will still be there."

"But what if they ran?"

"Then we'll find them. In the meantime, let's not get caught ourselves."

David sighed. "All right."

Tally held his hand tight. They unfolded the hoverboard and waited as the sun climbed, watching for any sign of a human being below. Occasionally, the embers of the fires flared to life in the breeze, the last standing columns of wood collapsing one by one, crumbling into ash.

A few animals rummaged for food, and Tally watched in silent horror as a stray rabbit was taken by a wolf, the short struggle leaving only a patch of blood and fur. This was what was left of nature, raw and wild, only hours after the Smoke had fallen.

"Ready to go down?" David asked after an hour.

"No," Tally said. "But I never will be."

They approached slowly, ready to turn and fly if any Specials appeared. But when they reached the edge of town, Tally felt her anxiety turn to something worse: a horrible certainty that no one remained there.

Her home was gone, replaced by nothing but charred wreckage.

At the rabbit pen, footprints showed where groups of Smokies had been moved in and out through the gates, a whole community turned into cattle. A few rabbits still hopped around on the dirt.

"Well, at least we won't starve," David said.

"I guess not," Tally said, although the sight of the Smoke had stilled her hunger. She wondered how David always managed to think practical thoughts, no matter what horrors were in front of him. "Hey, what's that?"

At one corner of the pen, just outside the fence, clusters of little shapes lay on the ground.

They edged the board closer, David squinting through a drifting wall of smoke. "It looks like . . . shoes."

Tally blinked. He was right. She lowered the board and jumped off, running to the spot.

Tally looked around in amazement. Around her were scattered

twenty or so pairs of shoes, in all sizes. She fell to her knees to look closer. The laces were still tied, as if the shoes had been kicked off by people whose hands were bound behind them. . . .

"Croy recognized me," she murmured.

"What?"

Tally turned to David. "When I escaped, I flew right over the pen. Croy must have seen it was me. He knew I didn't have shoes. We joked about it."

She imagined the Smokies, helplessly awaiting their fate, making one last gesture of defiance. Croy would have kicked his own shoes off, then whispered to whomever he could: "Tally's free, and barefoot." They'd left her with a score of pairs to pick from, the only way they could help the one Smokey they'd seen escape.

"They knew I'd come back here." Her voice faltered. What they didn't know was who had betrayed them.

She picked a pair that looked about the right size, with grippy soles for hoverboarding, and pulled them on. They fit, even better than the ones the rangers had given her.

Jumping back on the board, Tally had to hide the pained expression on her face. This is what it would be like from now on. Every gesture of kindness from her victims would only make her feel worse. "Okay, let's go."

The hoverpath wound through the smoking camp, over what streets remained between the charred ruins. Beside a long building, now little more than a ridge of blackened rubble, David pulled the board to a halt.

"I was afraid of this."

Tally tried to picture what had stood there. Her knowledge of the Smoke had evaporated, the familiar streets reduced to an unrecognizable sprawl of ash and embers.

Then she saw a few blackened pages fluttering in the wind. The library.

"They didn't take the books out before they . . . ," she cried. "But why?"

"They don't want people to know what it was like before the operation. They want to keep you hating yourselves. Otherwise, it's too easy to get used to ugly faces, *normal* faces."

Tally turned around to look into David's eyes. "Some of them, anyway."

He smiled sadly.

Then a thought crossed her mind. "The Boss was running away with some old magazines. Maybe he escaped."

"On foot?" David sounded dubious.

"I hope so." She leaned, and the board slid toward the edge of town.

A blotch of pepper still marked the ground where she had fought the Special. Tally jumped off, trying to remember exactly where the Boss had escaped into the forest.

"If he got away, he must be long gone," David said.

Tally pushed her way into the brush, looking for signs of a struggle. The morning sun was streaming through the leaves, and a trail of broken bushes cut into the forest. The Boss had been none too graceful, leaving a path like a charging elephant.

She found the duffel bag half-hidden, shoved under a moss-covered fallen tree. Zipping it open, Tally saw that the magazines were still there, each one lovingly wrapped in its own plastic cover. She slung the bag over her shoulder, glad to have salvaged something from the library, a small victory over Dr. Cable.

A moment later, she found the Boss.

He lay on his back, his head turned at an angle that Tally instantly knew was utterly wrong. His fingers were clenched, the nails bloody from clawing at someone. He must have fought to distract them, maybe to keep them from finding the duffel bag. Or maybe for Tally's sake, having seen that she'd reached the forest too.

She remembered what the Specials had said to her more than once: *We don't want to hurt you, but we will if we have to.*

They'd been serious. They always were.

She stumbled back out of the forest, stunned, the bag still hanging from her shoulder.

"You found something?" David asked.

She didn't answer.

He saw the expression on her face and jumped down from the board. "What happened?"

"They caught him. They killed him."

David looked at her, his mouth open. He took a slow breath. "Come on, Tally. We have to go."

She blinked. The sunlight seemed wrong, twisted out of shape, like the Boss's neck. As if the world had become horribly distorted while she was among the trees. "Where?" she murmured.

"We have to go to my parents' house."

MADDY AND AZ

David took the board over the ridge so fast that Tally thought she would tumble off. She sank her fingertips into David's jacket to steady herself, thankful for the new shoes' grippy soles. "Listen, David. The Boss fought them, that's why they killed him."

"My parents would fight too."

She bit her lip and focused her whole mind on staying on board. When they reached the closest approach of the hoverpath to his parents' house, David jumped off and dashed down the slope.

Tally realized that the board still wasn't fully charged, and took a moment to unfold it before following, in no hurry to discover what the Specials had done to Maddy and Az. But when she thought of David finding his parents on his own, Tally ran after him.

It took her long minutes to find the path in the dense brush. Two nights ago they had come in the dark, and from a different direction. She listened for David, but couldn't hear anything. But then the wind shifted, and the smell of smoke came through the trees.

Burning the house hadn't been easy.

Set into the mountain, the stone walls and roof had provided no fuel for the fire. But the attackers had evidently thrown something inside that had contained its own fuel. The windows were blown outward, glass littering the grass in front of the house, nothing left of the door but a few charred scraps swinging on their hinges in the breeze.

David stood in front, unable to cross the threshold.

"Stay here," Tally said.

She stepped through the doorway, but the air overpowered her for the first moments. Morning light slanted in, picking out floating particles of ash. They swirled around Tally, little spiral galaxies set in motion by her passage.

The blackened floorboards crumbled under her feet, burned away to bare stone in some places. But some things had survived the fire. She remembered the marble statuette from her visit, and one of the rugs hanging on the wall remained mysteriously untouched. In the parlor, a few teacups stood out white against the charred furniture. Tally picked one up, realizing that if these cups had survived, a human body would leave more than traces.

She swallowed. If David's parents had been here, whatever was left of them would be easy to find.

Deeper into the house, in a small kitchen, city-made pots and pans hung from the ceiling, their warped, blackened metal still shining through in a few spots. Tally noted a bag of flour, and a few pieces of dried fruit somehow made her empty stomach growl.

The bedroom was last.

The stone ceiling was low and angled, the paint cracked and blackened from the heat of a raging fire. Tally felt the heat still rising from the bed, the straw mattress and thick quilts fuel for the conflagration.

But Az and Maddy had not been there. There was nothing in the room that could have been human remains. Tally sighed with relief and made her way back outside, rechecking every room.

She shook her head as she stepped through the door. "Either the Specials took them, or they got away."

David nodded and pushed past her. Tally collapsed on the ground and coughed, her lungs finally protesting against the smoke and dust particles she had inhaled. Her hands and arms were black with soot, she realized.

When David came out, he held a long knife. "Hold out your hands."

"What?"

"The handcuffs. I can't stand them."

She nodded and held out her hands. He carefully threaded the blade between flesh and plastic, working it back and forth to saw the cuffs.

A solid minute later, he pulled the knife away in frustration. "It's not working."

Tally looked closer. The plastic had hardly been marked. She hadn't seen how the Special had snipped her handcuffs in two behind her, but it had only taken a moment. Perhaps they'd used a chemical trigger.

"Maybe it's some kind of aircraft plastic," she said. "Some of that stuff is stronger than steel."

David frowned. "So how did you get them apart?"

Tally opened her mouth, but nothing came out. She could hardly tell him that the Specials had released her themselves.

"And why do you have two cuffs on each wrist, anyway?"

She looked down dumbly, remembering that they'd handcuffed her first when she was captured, then again in front of Dr. Cable, before taking her to look for the pendant.

"I don't know," Tally managed. "I guess they double-cuffed us. But breaking out was easy. I cut them on a sharp rock."

"That doesn't make sense." David looked at the knife. "Dad always said this was the most useful thing he'd ever brought from the city. It's all high-tech alloys and monofilaments."

She shrugged. "Maybe the part that joined the cuffs was made out of different stuff."

He shook his head, not quite accepting her story. Finally, he shrugged. "Oh well, we'll just have to live with them. But one thing's for sure: My parents didn't get away."

"How do you know?"

He held up the knife. "If he'd had any warning, my dad never would have left without this. The Specials must have surprised them completely."

"Oh. I'm sorry, David."

"At least they're alive."

He looked into her eyes, and Tally saw that his panic had faded. "So, Tally, do you still want to go after them?"

"Yes, of course."

David smiled. "Good." He sat next to her, looking back at the house and shaking his head. "It's funny, Mom always warned me that this would happen. They tried to prepare me the whole time I was growing up. And for a long while I believed them. But after all those years, I started to wonder. Maybe my parents were just being paranoid. Maybe, like runaways always said, Special Circumstances wasn't real."

Tally nodded silently, not trusting herself to speak.

"And now that it's happened, it seems even less real."

"I'm sorry, David." But he could never know how sorry. Not until she'd helped save his parents, at least. "Don't worry, we'll find them."

"One stop to make first."

"Where?"

"As I said, my parents were ready for this, ever since they founded the Smoke. They made preparations."

"Like making sure you could take care of yourself," she said, touching the soft leather of his handmade jacket.

He smiled at her, rubbing soot from her cheek with one finger. "They did a lot more than that. Come with me."

• • •

In a cave near the house, the opening so small that Tally had to crawl inside on her belly, David showed her the cache of gear his parents had tended for twenty years.

There were water purifiers, direction finders, lightweight clothes, and sleeping bags—by Smokey standards, an absolute fortune in survival equipment. The four hoverboards had old-fashioned styling, but they were fitted with the same features as the one Dr. Cable had supplied Tally with for the trip to the Smoke, and there was a package of spare belly sensors, sealed against moisture. Everything was of the highest quality.

"Wow, they did plan ahead."

"Always," he said. He picked up a flashlight and tested its beam against the stone. "Every time I came here to check on all this stuff, I would imagine this moment. A million times I planned exactly what I would need. It's almost like I imagined it so much that it *had* to happen."

"It's not your fault, David."

"If I'd been here—"

"You'd be in a Special Circumstances hovercar right now, handcuffed, not likely to rescue anyone."

"Yeah, and instead, I'm here." He looked at her. "But at least you are too. You're the one thing I never imagined, all those times. An unexpected ally."

She managed to smile.

He pulled out a big waterproof bag. "I'm starving."

Tally nodded, and her head swam for a moment. She hadn't eaten since dinner two nights before.

David rummaged through the bag. "Plenty of instant food. Let's see: VegiRice, CurryNoods, SwedeBalls, Pad-Thai . . . any favorites?"

Tally took a deep breath. Back to the wild.

"Anything but SpagBol."

THE OIL PLAGUE

Tally and David left at sunset.

Each of them rode two hoverboards. Pressed together like a sandwich, the paired boards could carry twice as much weight, most of it in saddlebags slung on the underside. They packed everything useful they could find, along with the magazines the Boss had saved. Whatever happened, there would be no point in returning to the Smoke.

Tally took the river down the mountain carefully, the extra weight swaying below her like a ball and chain around both ankles. At least she was wearing crash bracelets again.

Their journey would follow a path very different from the one Tally had taken there. That route had been designed to be easy to follow, and had included a helicopter ride with the rangers. This one wouldn't be as direct. Overloaded as they were, Tally and David couldn't manage even short distances on foot. Every inch of the journey had to be over hoverable land and water, no matter how far it took them out of their way. And after the invasion, they would be giving any cities a wide berth.

Fortunately, David had made the journey to and from Tally's city dozens of times, alone and with inexperienced uglies in tow. He knew the rivers and rails, the ruins and natural veins of ore, and dozens of escape routes he'd devised in case he was ever pursued by city authorities.

"Ten days," he announced when they started. "If we ride all night and stay low during the day."

"Sounds good," Tally said, but she wondered if that would be soon enough to save anyone from the operation.

Around midnight the first night of travel, they left the brook that led down to the bald-headed hill, and followed a dry creek bed through the white flowers. It took them to the edge of a vast desert.

"How do we get through that?"

David pointed at dark shapes rising up from the sand, a row of them receding into the distance. "Those used to be towers, connected by steel cables."

"What for?"

"They carried electricity from a wind farm to one of the old cities."

Tally frowned. "I didn't know the Rusties used wind power."

"They weren't all crazy. Just most of them." He shrugged. "You've got to remember, we're mostly descended from Rusties, and we're still using their basic technology. *Some* of them must have had the right idea."

The cables still lay buried in the desert, protected by the shifting sands and a near-total absence of rainfall. In spots, they had broken or rusted through, so Tally and David had to ride carefully, eyes glued to the boards' metal detectors. When they reached a gap they couldn't jump, they would unroll a long piece of cable David carried, then walk the boards along it, guiding them like reluctant donkeys across some narrow footbridge before rolling it up again.

Tally had never seen a real desert before. She'd been taught in school that they were full of life, but this one was like the deserts she'd imagined as a littlie—featureless humps stretching into the distance, one after another. Nothing moved but slow snakes of sand borne by the wind.

She only knew the name of one big desert on the continent. "Is this the Mojave?"

David shook his head. "This isn't nearly that big, and it isn't natural. We're standing where the white weed started."

Tally whistled. The sand seemed to go forever. "What a disaster."

"Once the undergrowth was gone, replaced by the orchids, there was nothing to hold the good soil down. It blew away, and all that's left is sand."

"Will it ever be anything but desert?"

"Sure, in a thousand years or so. Maybe by then someone will have found a way to stop the weed from coming back. If we haven't, the process will just start all over again."

They reached a Rusty city around daybreak, a cluster of unremarkable buildings stranded on the sea of sand.

The desert had invaded over the centuries, dunes flowing through the streets like water, but the buildings were in better shape than other ruins Tally had seen. Sand wore away the edges of things, but it didn't tear them down as hungrily as rain and vegetation.

Neither of them was tired yet, but they couldn't travel during the day; the desert offered no protection from the sun, nor any concealment from the air. They camped in the second floor of a low factory building that still had most of its roof. Ancient machines, each as big as a hovercar, stood silent around them.

"What was this place?" Tally asked.

"I think they made newspapers here," David said. "Like books, but you threw them away and got a new one every day."

"You're kidding."

"Not at all. And you thought we wasted trees in the Smoke!"

Tally found a patch of sun shining through where the roof had collapsed, and unfolded the hoverboards to recharge. David pulled out two packets of EggSal.

"Will we make it out of the desert tonight?" she asked, watching David coax their last few drops of bottled water into the purifiers.

"No problem. We'll hit the next river before midnight."

She remembered something that Shay had said a long time ago, the first time she'd shown Tally her survival gear. "Can you really pee in a purifier? And then drink it, I mean?"

"Yeah. I've done it."

Tally grimaced and looked out the window. "Okay, I shouldn't have asked."

He came up behind her, laughing softly, placing his hands on her shoulders. "It's amazing what people will do to survive," he said.

She sighed. "I know."

The window overlooked a side street, partly protected from the encroaching desert. A few burned-out groundcars stood half-buried, their blackened frames stark against the white sand.

She rubbed the handcuff bracelets still encircling her wrists. "The Rusties sure wanted to survive. Every ruin I've seen, those cars are always all over, trying to get out. But they never seem to make it."

"A few of them did. But not in cars."

Tally leaned back into his reassuring warmth. The morning sun was hours away from burning off the chill of the desert.

"It's funny. At school, they never talk much about how it happened—the last panic, when the Rusty world fell apart. They shrug and say that all their mistakes just kept adding up, until it all collapsed like a house of cards."

"That's only partly true. The Boss had some old books about it."

"What did they say?"

"Well, the Rusties did live in a house of cards, but someone gave it a pretty big shove. No one ever found out who. Maybe it was a Rusty weapon that got out of control. Maybe it was people in some poor country who didn't like the way the Rusties ran things. Maybe it was just an accident, like the flowers, or some lone scientist who wanted to mess things up."

"But what happened?"

"A bug got loose, but it didn't infect people. It infected petroleum."

"Oil got infected?"

He nodded. "Oil is organic, made from old plants and dinosaurs and stuff. Somebody made a bacterium that ate it. The spores spread through the air, and when they landed in petroleum, processed or crude, they sprouted. Like a mold or something. It changed the chemical composition of the oil. Have you ever seen phosphorus?"

"It's an element, right?"

"Yeah. And it catches fire on contact with air."

Tally nodded. She remembered playing with the stuff in chem class, wearing goggles and talking about all the tricks you could do with it. But no one ever thought of a trick that wouldn't kill someone.

"Oil infected by this bacterium was just as unstable as phosphorus. It exploded on contact with oxygen. And as it burned, the spores were released in the smoke, and spread on the wind. Until the spores got to the next car, or airplane, or oil well, and started growing again."

"Wow. And they used oil for everything, right?"

David nodded. "Like those cars down there. They must have been infected as they tried to get out of town."

"Why didn't they just *walk*?"

"Stupid, I guess."

Tally shivered again, but not from the cold. It was hard to think of the Rusties as actual people, rather than as just an idiotic, dangerous, and sometimes comic force of history. But there were human beings down there, whatever was left of them after a couple of hundred years, still sitting in their blackened cars, as if still trying to escape their fate.

"I wonder why they don't tell us that in history class. They usually love any story that makes the Rusties sound pathetic."

David lowered his voice. "Maybe they didn't want you to realize that every civilization has its weakness. There's always one thing we depend on. And if someone takes it away, all that's left is some story in a history class."

"Not us," she said. "Renewable energy, sustainable resources, a fixed population."

The two purifiers pinged, and David left her to get them. "It doesn't have to be about economics," he said, bringing the food over. "The weakness could be an idea."

She turned to take her EggSal, cupping its warmth in her hands, and saw how serious he looked. "So, David, is that one of the things you thought about all those years, when you imagined the Smoke being invaded? Did you ever wonder what would turn the cities into history?"

He smiled and took a big bite.

"It gets clearer every day."

FAMILIAR SIGHTS

They reached the edge of the desert the next night, on schedule, then followed a river for three days, all the way to the sea. It took them still farther north, and the October chill turned as cold as any winter Tally had ever felt. David unpacked city-made arctic gear of shiny silver Mylar, which Tally wore over her handmade sweater, her only possession left from the Smoke. She was glad she'd dropped off to sleep in it the night before the Specials had invaded, so it hadn't been lost that day like everything else.

The nights spent on board seemed to pass quickly. On this journey, there were none of Shay's cryptic clues to puzzle through, no brush fires to escape, and no antique Rusty machines descending to scare her to death. The world seemed to be empty except for the occasional ruins, as if Tally and David were the last people alive.

They augmented their diet with fish caught from the river, and Tally roasted a rabbit on a fire she'd built herself. She watched David repair his leather clothes and decided she would never be able to manage a needle and thread well. He taught her how to tell time and direction from the stars, and she showed him how to open the expert software in the boards to optimize them for night travel.

At the sea they turned south, heading down the northern reaches of the same coastal railway that Tally had followed on her way to the Smoke. David said it had once stretched unbroken all the way back to Tally's home city and beyond. But now there were large gaps in the track, and new cities built on the sea, so they had to travel inland more than once. But David knew the rivers, the spurs of the railroad, and the other metal paths the Rusties had left behind, so they made good time toward their goal.

Only the weather stopped them. After a few days' travel down the coast, a dark and threatening mountain of clouds appeared over the ocean. At first, the storm seemed reluctant to come ashore, building up its nerve over a slow twenty-four hours, the air pressure changing in a way that made the hoverboards jittery to ride. The storm gave plenty of warning, but when it finally arrived, it was much worse than Tally had imagined weather could be.

She'd never faced the full force of a hurricane, except from within the solid structures of her inland city. It was another lesson in nature's savage power.

For three days Tally and David huddled in a plastic tent in the shelter of a rock outcrop, burning chemical glowsticks for heat and light, hoping the magnets in the hoverboards wouldn't bring down a lightning strike. For the first hours, the drama of the storm kept them fascinated, amazed at its power, wondering when the next peal of thunder would shake the cliffs. Then the driving rain became simply monotonous, and they spent a whole day talking to each other about anything and everything, but especially their childhoods, until Tally was sure that she understood David better than anyone she'd ever known. On their third day trapped in the tent they had a terrible fight—Tally could never remember about what—that ended when David stormed out and stood alone in the icy wind for a solid hour. When he finally returned, it took him hours to stop shivering, even wrapped in her arms. "We're taking too long," he finally said.

Tally squeezed tighter. It took time to prepare subjects for the operation, especially if they were older than sixteen. But Dr. Cable wouldn't wait forever to turn David's parents. Every day the storm delayed them, there was a greater chance that Maddy and Az had already gone under the knife. For Shay, the perfect age for turning, the odds were even worse.

"We'll get there, don't worry. They measured me every week for a year before I was supposed to turn. It takes time to do it right."

A shudder passed through his body.

"Tally, what if they don't bother to do it right?"

The storm ended the next morning, and they emerged to find that the world's colors had been transformed. The clouds were bright pink, the grass an unearthly green, and the ocean darker than Tally had ever seen it, marked only by the foam crests of waves and a peppering of driftwood driven into the sea by the wind. They rode all day to make up for lost time, in a state of shock, amazed that the world could still exist after the storm.

Then the railway turned inland, and a few nights later they reached the Rusty Ruins.

The ruins looked smaller, as if the spires had shrunk since Tally had left them behind more than a month before, headed to the Smoke with nothing but Shay's note and a knapsack full of SpagBol. As she and David passed through the dark streets, the ghosts of the Rusties no longer seemed to threaten from the windows.

"The first time I came here at night, this place really scared me," she said.

David nodded. "It's kind of creepy how well preserved it is. Of all the ruins I've seen, it looks the most recent."

"They sprayed it with something to keep it up for school trips." And that was her city in a nutshell, Tally realized. Nothing left to itself. Everything turned into a bribe, a warning, or a lesson.

They stowed most of their gear in a collapsed building far from the center, a crumbling place that even truant uglies would probably avoid, packing only water purifiers, a flashlight, and a few food packets. David had never been any closer to the city than the ruins, so Tally took the lead for once, following the vein of iron that Shay had shown her months before.

"Do you think we'll ever be friends again?" she asked as they hiked toward the river, lugging their boards for the first time the entire trip.

"You and Shay? Of course."

"Even after . . . you and me?"

"Once we've rescued her from the Specials, I figure she'll forgive you for just about anything."

Tally was silent. Shay had already guessed that Tally had betrayed the Smoke. She doubted anything would ever make up for that.

Once they reached the river, they shot down the white water at top speed, glad to be finally free of the heavy saddlebags. With the spray hitting her face, the roar of water all around her, Tally could almost imagine this was one of her expeditions, back when she was a carefree city kid and not a . . .

What was she now? No longer a spy, and she couldn't call herself a Smokey anymore. Hardly a pretty, but she didn't feel like an ugly, either. She was nothing in particular. But at least she had a purpose.

The city came into view.

"There it is," she called to David over the churning water. "But you've seen cities before, right?"

"I've been this close to a few. But not much closer."

Tally gazed down at the familiar skyline, the slender trails of fireworks silhouetting the party towers and mansions. She felt a pang of something like homesickness, but much worse. The sight of New Pretty Town had once filled her with longing. Now the skyline was like a vacant shell, all its promises gone. Like David, she had lost her home. But unlike the Smoke, her city still existed, right in front of her eyes—but emptied of everything it had once meant.

"We've got a few hours before sunrise," she said. "Want to take a look at Special Circumstances?"

"The sooner the better," David said.

Tally nodded, her eyes tracing the familiar patterns of light and darkness surrounding the city. There was time to make it there and back before daybreak.

"Let's go."

They followed the river as far as the ring of trees and brush that separated Uglyville from the suburbs. The greenbelt was the best place to travel without being seen, and a good ride as well.

"Don't go so fast!" David hissed from behind as she whipped through the trees.

She slowed down. "You don't have to whisper. No one comes here at night. It's ugly territory, and they're all in bed, unless they're tricking."

"Okay," he said. "But shouldn't we be more careful about hoverpaths?"

"Hoverpaths? David, hoverboards work *everywhere* in the city. There's a metal grid under the whole thing."

"Oh, right."

Tally smiled. She had been so used to living in David's world, it was good to be explaining things to him for once. "What's the matter," she taunted, "can't keep up?"

David grinned. "Try me."

Tally turned and shot ahead, cutting a zigzag path between the tall poplars, letting her reflexes guide her.

She remembered her two hovercar rides to Special Circumstances. They'd flown across the greenbelt on the far side of town, then out to the transport ring, the industrial zone between the middle-pretty suburbs and outer Crumblyville. The hard part would be getting across the burbs, a risky place to have an ugly face. Luckily, middle pretties went to bed early. Most of them, anyway.

She raced David halfway around the greenbelt, until the lights of the big hospital sat directly across the river from them. Tally remembered that first terrible morning, yanked away from the promised operation, flown out to be interrogated, her future pulled out from under her. She made a grim face, realizing that this time she was actually going out *looking* for Special Circumstances.

A tingle passed through her as they left the greenbelt. A minuscule part of Tally still expected her interface ring to warn her that she was leaving Uglyville. How had she worn that stupid thing for sixteen years? It had seemed such a part of her back then, but now the idea of being tracked and monitored and advised every minute of the day repelled Tally.

"Stick close," she said to David. "This is the part where you should whisper."

As a littlie, Tally had lived in the middle-pretty burbs with Sol and Ellie. But back then her world had been pathetically tiny: a few parks, the path to littlie school, one corner of the greenbelt where she would sneak in to spy on uglies. Like the Rusty Ruins, the neat row houses and gardens seemed much smaller to her now, an endless village of dollhouses.

They skimmed the rooftops, crouching low. If anybody was awake, going for a late-night run or walking a dog, they wouldn't be looking up, hopefully. Their boards barely a hand's breadth above the housetops, the patterns of shingles passed underneath hypnotically. All they encountered were nesting birds and a few cats, who flew or scrambled out of their way in surprise.

The burbs ended suddenly, a last band of parks fading into the transport ring, where underground factories stuck their heads aboveground and cargo trucks drove concrete roads all day and night. Tally lofted her board and gained speed.

"Tally!" David hissed. "They'll see us!"

"Relax. Those trucks are automatic. Nobody comes out here, especially at night."

He stared down at the lumbering vehicles nervously.

"Look, they don't even have headlights." She pointed down at a giant road-train passing below, the only light coming from it a dim red flicker from underneath, the navigation laser reading the bar codes painted onto the road.

They rode on, David still anxious at the sight of moving vehicles below.

Soon, a familiar landmark rose above the industrial wasteland.

"See that hill? Special Circumstances is just below it. We'll climb up top and take a look."

The hill was too steep to put a factory on, and apparently too big and solid to flatten with explosives and bulldozers, so it stood out on the flat plain like a lopsided pyramid, steep on one side and sloping on the other, covered with scrub and brown grass. They skimmed up the sloping side, dodging a few boulders and hard-scrabble trees, until they reached the top.

From this height, Tally could see all the way back to New Pretty Town, the glowing disk of the island about as big as a dinner plate. The outer city was in darkness, and below her, the low, brown buildings of Special Circumstances were lit only with the harsh glare of security lights. "Down there," she said, her voice falling to a whisper.

"Doesn't look like much."

"Most of it's underground. I don't know how far down it goes."

They stared at the cluster of buildings in silence. From up here, Tally could see the perimeter wire clearly, stretching around the buildings in an almost perfect square. That meant serious security. There weren't many barriers in the city—not that you could see, anyway. If you weren't supposed to be someplace, your interface ring just politely warned you to move along.

"That fence looks low enough to fly over."

Tally shook her head. "It's not a fence, it's a sensor wire. You get within twenty meters of it and the Specials will know you're there. Same goes if you touch the ground inside it."

"Twenty meters? Too high to clear on boards. So what do we do, knock on the gate?"

"There's no gate that I can see. I went in and out by hovercar."

David drummed his fingers on his board. "What about stealing one?"

"A hovercar?" Tally whistled. "That'd be a pretty good trick. I knew uglies who used to go joyriding, but not in Special Circumstances hovercars."

"It's too bad we can't just jump down."

Tally narrowed her eyes. "Jump?"

"From here. Get on our hoverboards back at the bottom of the hill, zoom up at maximum speed, then jump off from about this spot. We'd probably hit that big building dead center."

"Dead is right. We'd splat."

"Yeah, I guess. Even with crash bracelets, our arms would probably yank out of their sockets after a fall like that. We'd need parachutes."

Tally looked down, plotting trajectories from the hilltop, shushing David when he started to speak again, the wheels of her brain spinning. She remembered the party at Garbo Mansion, which seemed like years ago.

Finally, she allowed herself to smile.

"Not parachutes, David. Bungee jackets."

ACCOMPLICES

"There's enough time, if we hurry."

"Enough time to what?"

"To drop by the Uglyville art school. They have bungee jackets in the basement. A whole rack of spares."

David took a deep breath. "Okay."

"You're not scared, are you?"

"I'm not . . ." He grimaced. "It's just that I've never seen this many people before."

"People? We haven't seen anyone."

"Yeah, but all those houses on the way here. I keep thinking of people living in every single one, all crowded together like that."

Tally laughed. "You think the burbs are crowded? Wait until we get to Uglyville."

They headed back, taking the rooftops at top speed. The sky was pitch-black, but by now Tally could read the stars well enough to know that the first notes of dawn were only a couple of hours away.

Reaching the greenbelt, they turned back the way they'd come, neither of them speaking, concentrating instead on navigating through the trees. This arc of the belt brought them through Cleopatra Park, where Tally threaded the slalom poles for old times' sake. Her instincts twitched as they passed the path down to her old dorm. For a split second, it felt as if she could make the turnoff, climb in through her window, and go to bed.

Soon, the jumbled spires of the Uglyville art school rose up, and Tally brought the two of them to a halt.

This part was easy. It seemed like a million years ago that Tally and Shay had borrowed one of the school's bungee jackets for their final trick, Shay's leap onto the new uglies in the dorm library. Tally retraced her steps to the exact window they'd jimmied, a dirty, forgotten pane of glass concealed behind decorative bushes, and found that it was still unlocked.

Tally shook her head. This sort of burglary had seemed so daring two months before. Back then, the library stunt was the wildest prank she and Shay could dream up. Now she saw tricks for what they were: a way for uglies to blow off steam until they reached sixteen, nothing but a meaningless distraction until their mutinous natures were erased by adulthood, and the operation.

"Give me the flashlight. And wait here."

She slipped in, found the rack of spares, grabbed two bungee jackets, and was out in less than a minute. When she pulled herself out of the window, she found David staring at her with wide eyes. "What?" she asked.

"You're just so . . . good at all this. So confident. It makes me nervous just being inside city limits."

She grinned. "This is no big deal. Everyone does it."

Still, Tally was happy to impress David with her burglary skills. In the last few weeks he'd taught her how to build a fire, scale a fish, pitch a tent, and read a contour map. It was nice to be the competent one for a change.

They crept back to the greenbelt and reached the river before the sky had even shown a sliver of pink. Zooming past the white water and onto the vein of ore, they sighted the ruins just as the sky was beginning to change.

On the hike down, Tally asked, "Tomorrow night, then?"

"No point in waiting."

"No." And there was every reason to attempt the rescue soon. It had been more than two weeks since the invasion of the Smoke.

David cleared his throat. "So, how many Specials do you think will be in there?"

"When I was there, a lot. But that was during the day. I assume they have to sleep sometime."

"So it'll be empty at night."

"I doubt that. But maybe just a few guards." She didn't say more. Even one Special would be more than a match for a pair of uglies. No amount of surprise would make up for the cruel pretties' superior strength and reflexes. "We'll just have to make sure they don't see us."

"Sure. Or hope they've got something else to do that night."

Tally trudged ahead, exhaustion taking over now that they were safely out of the city, her confidence ebbing with every step. They'd traveled all this way without thinking very hard about the task ahead of them. Rescuing people from Special Circumstances wasn't just another ugly-trick, like stealing a bungee jacket or sneaking up the river. It was serious business.

And although Croy, Shay, Maddy, and Az were probably all prisoners in those horrible underground buildings, there was always the possibility that the Smokies had been taken somewhere else. And even if they hadn't, Tally had no idea exactly where they'd be inside the warren of puke-brown hallways.

"I just wish we had some help," she said softly.

David's hand settled on her shoulder, bringing her to a halt. "Maybe we do."

She looked at him questioningly, then followed his gaze down toward the ruins. At the top of the highest spire, the last few flickers of a safety sparkler were sputtering out.

There were uglies down there.

"They're looking for me," he said.

"So what do we do?"

"Is there any other way back to the city?" David asked.

"No. They'll come hiking right up this path."

"Then we wait."

Tally squinted, peering at the ruins. The sparkler had faded, and nothing was visible in the dawn light just starting to spill across the sky. Whoever was down there had waited until the last possible minute to head for home.

Of course, if they were looking for David, these uglies were potential runaways. Rebellious seniors, not that worried about missing breakfast.

She turned to David. "So, I guess uglies are still looking for you. And not just here."

"Of course," he said. "The rumors will go on for generations, in cities all over, whether I'm around or not. Lighting a sparkler doesn't usually get an answer, so it'll be a long time before even the uglies I've met figure out I'm not showing up. And most of them already don't even think the Smoke—"

His voice caught, and Tally took his hand. For a moment he'd forgotten that the Smoke didn't, in fact, exist anymore.

They waited in silence, until the sound of scrambling feet came across the rocks. It sounded like three or so uglies, talking in low tones as if still wary of the ghosts of the Rusty ruins.

"Watch this," David whispered, pulling a flashlight from his pocket. He stood and pointed the light up at his own face, switching it on.

"Looking for me?" he said in a loud, commanding voice.

The three uglies froze, wide-eyed and open-mouthed. Then the boy dropped his board, and it crashed onto the stones beside him, breaking their paralysis.

"Who are you?" one of the girls managed.

"I'm David."

"Oh. You mean you're . . ."

"Real?" He switched off the light and grinned. "Yeah, I get that question a lot."

Their names were Sussy, An, and Dex, and they had been coming to the ruins for a month now. They'd heard rumors about the Smoke for years, since an ugly in their dorm had run away.

"I'd just moved to Uglyville," Sussy said, "and Ho was a senior. When he disappeared, everyone had these crazy theories about where he'd gone."

"Ho?" David nodded. "I remember him. He stayed for a few months, then changed his mind and came back. By now, he's a pretty."

"But he really made it? To the Smoke?" An asked.

"Yeah. I took him there."

"Wow. So it's real." An shared an excited look with her two friends. "We want to see it too."

David opened his mouth, then closed it. His eyes drifted away to one side.

"You can't," Tally spoke up. "Not right now."

"Why not?" Dex asked.

Tally paused. The truth, that the Smoke had been destroyed by an armed invasion, seemed too far-fetched. A few months ago, she wouldn't have believed what her own city was capable of. And if she admitted that the Smoke was gone, the rumor would make its way down through generations of uglies. Dr. Cable's work would be complete, even if a few rescued Smokies somehow managed to create another community in the wild. "Well," she started, "every so often the Smoke has to move, to stay secret. Right now, it doesn't really exist. Everyone's scattered, so we're not recruiting."

"The whole place moves?" Dex said. "Whoa."

An frowned. "Hang on. If you're not recruiting, then why are you here?"

"To do a trick," Tally said. "A really big one. Maybe you could help us. And then when the Smoke is back on its feet, you'll be the first to know."

"You want us to help? Like an initiation?" Dex asked.

"No," David said firmly. "We don't make anyone do anything to get into the Smoke. But if you do want to help, Tally and I would appreciate it."

"We just need a diversion," Tally said.

"Sounds like fun," An said. She looked at the others, and they waggled their heads.

Up for anything, Tally thought, just like she used to be herself. They were definitely seniors, less than a year behind her, but she was amazed at how young they seemed.

David stared at Tally along with the others, waiting for the rest of her idea. She had to come up with a diversion right away. A good one. Something that would intrigue the Specials enough to investigate.

Something that would make Dr. Cable herself take notice.

"Well, you'll need a lot of sparklers."

"No problem."

"And you know how to get into New Pretty Town, right?"

"New Pretty Town?" An looked at her friends. "But don't the bridges report everyone who crosses the river?"

Tally smiled, always happy to teach someone a new trick.

OVER THE EDGE

The two waited all day in the Rusty Ruins, patches of sunlight crawling across the floor through the crumbling roof, like slow searchlights marking the hours. It took Tally ages to get to sleep, imagining the leap from the hilltop down into uncertainty. Finally she passed out, too tired to dream.

Awakening at dusk, she found that David had already packed two knapsacks with everything they might need during the rescue. They hoverboarded to the edge of the ruins, riding two sand-wiched hoverboards each. Hopefully, they would need the extra boards when they emerged from Special Circumstances, escapees in tow.

Eating breakfast by the river, Tally took time to appreciate her SwedeBalls. If they got caught tonight, at least she would never have dehydrated food again. Sometimes Tally felt she could almost accept brain damage if it meant a life without reconstituted noodles.

As darkness fell, Tally and David reached the white water, and they passed through the greenbelt at the very moment the lights winked off in Uglyville. By midnight, they were atop the hill overlooking Special Circumstances.

Tally pulled out her binoculars and trained them inward, toward New Pretty Town, where the party towers were just coming alight.

David blew into his hands, his breath visible in the October chill. "You really think they'll do it?"

"Why not?" she said, watching the dark spaces of the city's largest pleasure garden. "They seemed into it."

"Yeah, but aren't they taking a big risk? I mean, they just met us."

She shrugged. "An ugly lives for tricks. Haven't you ever done something just because a mysterious stranger intrigued you?"

"I gave my gloves to one once. But it got me into all kinds of trouble."

She lowered the binoculars and saw that David was smiling. "You don't look as nervous tonight," she said.

"I'm glad we're finally here, finally ready to *do* something. And after those three kids agreed to help us, I feel like . . ."

"Like this might actually work?"

"No, something better." He looked down at the Special

Circumstances compound. "They were so ready to help, just to make trouble, just to play a trick. At first, it killed me to hear you act like the Smoke still existed. But if there are enough uglies like them, maybe it will again."

"Of course it will," she said softly.

David shrugged. "Maybe, maybe not. But even if we blow it tonight, and both wind up under the knife, at least someone will still keep fighting. Making trouble, you know?"

"I hope it's us, making trouble," Tally said.

"Me too." He drew Tally closer, and kissed her. When he released her, Tally took a deep breath and closed her eyes. It felt better to kiss him, more real, now that she was about to begin undoing the damage she had done.

"Look," David said.

In the dark spaces of New Pretty Town, something was happening.

She raised her binoculars.

A shimmering line cut its way across the black expanse of the pleasure garden, like a bright fissure opening in the earth. Then more lines appeared, one by one, tremulous arcs and circles sweeping through the darkness. The various segments seemed to sparkle into existence in random order, but they eventually formed letters, and words.

Finally, the whole glittering thing was finished, some parts of it newly sprung to life, the first few lines already starting to fade as the sparklers exhausted themselves. But for a few moments, Tally could read the whole thing, even without her binoculars. From

Uglyville, it must have been huge, visible to anyone staring longingly out their window. It said: THE SMOKE LIVES.

As Tally watched it fade, breaking down into random lines and arcs again as the sparklers extinguished, she wondered if the words were really true.

"There they go," David said.

Below them, a large circular opening had appeared in the largest building's roof, and three hovercars rose up through the gap in quick succession, screaming toward the city. Tally hoped that An, Dex, and Sussy had followed her advice and were long gone from New Pretty Town. "Ready?" she said.

In answer, David tightened the straps of his bungee jacket and jumped onto his boards.

They rode down the hill, turned around, and started back up.

For the tenth time, Tally checked the light on the collar of her jacket. It was still green, and she could see David's light bobbing along beside her. No excuses now.

They gained speed as they climbed toward the dark sky, the entire hill like a giant ramp before them. The wind pushed Tally's hair back, and she blinked as bugs pinged against her face. She slid carefully toward the front of the paired boards, the toes of one grippy shoe sticking out past the riding surface.

Then the horizon seemed to slip away in front of her, and Tally crouched, ready to jump.

The ground disappeared.

Tally pushed off with all her strength, forcing her hoverboards down the steep side of the hill, where they would bring themselves to a halt. She and David had switched off their crash bracelets—they didn't want the boards following them over the wire. Not yet.

Tally soared into midair, still climbing for a few more seconds. The outer city lay below her, a vast patchwork of light and dark. She spread her arms and legs.

At the peak of her arc, the silence seemed to overwhelm everything—her stomach-churning weightlessness, the mix of excitement and fear rushing through her, the wind against her face. Tally tore her eyes from the silently waiting earth and dared a glance at David. Hardly an arm's length away, he was looking back at her, his face alight.

She grinned at him and turned back to see that the ground was approaching now, the speed of her fall building slowly. As she'd calculated, they were coming down right in the middle of the wire. Tally began to anticipate the sickening jolt of her bungee jacket pulling her up.

For long moments nothing happened, except the ground getting closer, and Tally wondered again if bungee jackets could handle a fall from this distance. A hundred versions of what a hard landing would feel like managed to squeeze into her head. Of course, it probably wouldn't feel like anything.

Ever again.

The ground grew closer and closer, until Tally was certain something had gone wrong. Then, with sudden violence, the straps of the jacket came alive, cutting cruelly into her thighs and shoulders, crushing the air from her lungs, the pressure building as if a huge rubber band were wrapped around her, trying to bring her to a halt. The bare dirt of the compound rushed up toward her, looking flat and packed and *hard,* the jacket fighting her momentum desperately now, crushing her like a fist in its grasp.

Finally, the invisible rubber band stretching toward its breaking point, she slowed to a shuddering halt within reach of the ground, pulling her hands back to keep from touching it, her eyeballs straining forward as if they wanted to pop out of her skull.

Then her fall reversed, and she pulled back upward, hover-bouncing head over heels, sky and horizon spinning around her like a playground ride. Tally had no idea where David was—or where up and down were, for that matter. This jump was ten times her plunge off Garbo Mansion. How many bounces would it take to come to a stop?

Now she was falling again, the dirt of the compound replaced by a building below her. One foot almost touched down onto the roof, but Tally was pulled up again, still barreling forward with the momentum of her leap off the hill.

She managed to orient herself, sorting out up and down just in time to see the edge of the roof coming toward her. She was overshooting the building. . . .

Flailing in the grasp of the jacket, flying helplessly upward and then down again, she passed the roof's edge. But her outstretched hand caught a rain gutter, bringing Tally to a sudden halt. "Phew," she said, looking down.

The building wasn't very tall, and Tally would bounce in her jacket if she fell, but the moment her feet touched the ground, the wire would sound an alarm. She gripped the rain gutter with both hands.

But the bungee jacket, satisfied that her fall had stopped, was shutting itself down, gradually returning her to normal weight. She struggled to pull herself up onto the roof, but the heavy knapsack full of rescue equipment dragged her downward. It was like trying to do a pull-up wearing lead shoes.

She hung there, out of ideas, waiting to fall.

Footsteps came toward her along the roof, and a face appeared. David.

"Having trouble?"

She grunted an answer, and he reached over, grabbing a strap of the knapsack. The weight mercifully lifted from her shoulders, and Tally pulled herself over the edge.

David sat back onto the roof, shaking his head. "So, Tally, you used to do that for *fun*?"

"Not every day."

"Didn't think so. Can we rest for a minute?"

She scanned the rooftop. No one coming, no alarms ringing. Apparently, the wire wasn't built to sense them up there. Tally smiled.

"Sure. Take two minutes, if you want. It looks like the Specials weren't expecting anyone to jump out of the sky."

INSIDE

The roof of Special Circumstances had looked flat and featureless from way up on top of the hill. But standing on it, Tally could see air vents, antennae, maintenance hatchways, and of course the big circular door that the hovercars had come through, now closed. It was a wonder neither she nor David had cracked their heads hover-bouncing across it.

"So how do we get in?" David asked.

"We should start with this." She pointed toward the hovercar door.

"Don't you think they'll notice if we come through there and we're not a hovercar?"

"Agreed. But what if we jam the door? If any more Specials show up, we don't want to make it easy for them to come in after us."

"Good idea." David searched through his knapsack, bringing out what looked like a tube of hair gel. He squeezed out white goo along the edges of the door, careful not to let any touch his fingers.

"What's that?"

"Glue. The nano kind. You can stick your shoes to the ceiling with this stuff and hang upside down."

Tally's eyes widened. She'd heard rumors of tricks you could play with nanotech glue, but uglies weren't allowed to requisition it. "Tell me you haven't done that."

He smiled. "I had to leave them up there. Waste of good shoes. So how do we get down?"

Tally pulled a powerjack from her pack and pointed. "We take the elevator."

The big metal box sticking up from the roof looked like a storage shed, but the double doors and eye-reader gave it away. Tally squinted, making sure the reader didn't flash her, and worked her powerjack between the doors. They crumpled like foil.

Through the doors, a dark shaft dropped away to nothingness. Tally clicked her tongue, and the echoes indicated that it was a long way down. She glanced at her collar light. Still green.

Tally turned to David. "Wait for me to whistle."

She stepped off into thin air.

Falling down the shaft was much scarier than leaping off Garbo Mansion, or even flying into space from the hilltop. The darkness offered no clue how deep the shaft was, and it felt to Tally as if she might fall forever.

She sensed the walls rushing past, and wondered if she was drifting toward one side as she fell, about to crash against it. She imagined herself bouncing from one wall to another all the way down, coming to a soft landing already broken and bleeding.

Tally kept her arms close to her sides.

At least she was sure the jacket would work in here. Elevators used the same magnetic lifters as any other hovercraft, so there was always a solid metal plate at the bottom.

After a long count of five, the jacket gripped Tally. She bounced twice, straight up and down, then settled onto a hard surface and found herself in silence and absolute blackness. Stretching out her hands, she felt the four walls around her. Nothing suggested the inside of closed doors. Her fingers came away greasy.

Tally peered upward. A tiny shaft of light shone above, and she could just make out David's face peering down. She pursed her lips to whistle, but stopped.

A muffled sound came from below her feet. Someone talking.

She crouched, trying to grasp the words. But all Tally could hear was the razor sound of a cruel pretty's voice. The mocking tone reminded her of Dr. Cable.

Without warning, the floor dropped out from under her. Tally struggled to keep her footing. When the elevator stopped again, one of her ankles twisted painfully under her weight, but she managed not to fall.

The sound below her faded. One thing was certain now: The complex wasn't empty.

Tally lifted her head and whistled, then huddled in one corner of the shaft, hands covering her head, counting.

Five seconds later, a pair of feet dangled next to her, then jerked back up, the beam of David's flashlight swinging around drunkenly. Gradually, he settled beside her. "Wow. It's dark down here."

"Shhh," she hissed.

He nodded, sweeping the flashlight around the shaft. Just above them, it fell on the inside of closed doors. Of course. Standing on the elevator's roof, they were midway between floors.

Tally interlaced her fingers, locking her hands together to give David a boost up to where he could wedge the powerjack between the doors. They crumpled open with a metal screech that set her hair on end. He pulled himself through, then extended his hand back down to her. Tally grabbed it and pulled, her grippy shoes squeaking on the walls of the elevator shaft like a herd of panicked mice.

Everything was making too much noise.

The hallway was dark. Tally tried to convince herself that no one had heard them yet. Maybe this whole floor was empty at night.

She pulled out her own flashlight, pointing it at the doors as they walked down the hall. Small brown labels marked each of them.

"Radiology. Neurology. Magnetic Imaging," she read softly. "Operating Theater Two."

She looked at David. He shrugged and gave the door a push. It opened.

"I guess when you're in an underground bunker, there's no point in locking up," he said softly. "After you."

Tally crept inside. The room was big, the walls lined with dark and silent machines. An operating tank stood in the middle, the liquid drained out of it, tubes and electrodes hanging loosely in a puddle at the bottom. A metal table glistened with the cruel shapes of knives and vibrasaws.

"This looks like photos Mom showed me," David said. "They do the operation here."

Tally nodded. Doctors only put you in a tank if they were doing major surgery.

"Maybe this is where they make Specials special," she said. The thought didn't cheer her up.

They returned to the hall. A few doors later, they found a room labeled MORGUE.

"Do you . . . ," she started to ask.

David shook his head. "No."

They searched the rest of the floor. Basically, it was a small, well-equipped hospital. There were no torture chambers or prison cells. And no Smokies.

"Where to now?"

"Well," Tally said. "If you were the evil Dr. Cable, where would you put your prisoners."

"The evil who?"

"Oh. That's her name, the woman who runs this place. I remember from when I got busted."

David frowned, and Tally wondered if she'd said too much.

Then he shrugged. "I guess I'd put them in the dungeon."

"Okay. Down, then."

They found a set of fire stairs that led down, but they ended after only one flight. Apparently, they had reached the bottom floor of Special Circumstances.

"Careful," Tally whispered. "Before, I heard people getting out of the elevator below me. They must be somewhere down here."

This floor was lit by a soft glowstrip running down the middle of the hallway. A cold finger crept down Tally's spine as she read the labels on the doors.

"Interrogation Room One. Interrogation Room Two. Isolation Room One," she whispered, her flashlight flickering across the words like an anxious firefly. "Disorientation Room One. Oh, David, they must be down here somewhere."

He nodded, and pushed one of the doors softly, but it didn't budge. He ran his fingers around the edge, searching for a place where the powerjack could get purchase.

"Don't let the eye-reader flash you," Tally warned softly. She pointed at the little camera by the door. "If it thinks it sees an eye, it'll read your iris and check with the big computer."

"It won't have any record of me."

"And that will freak it out totally. Just don't get too close. It's automatic."

"Okay," David said, nodding. "These doors are too smooth, anyway. No place to fit a jack in. Let's keep looking."

Farther down the hall, a label caught Tally's eye. "Long-Term Detention," she whispered. The door had a long expanse of blank wall on either side, as if the room behind it was bigger than the others. She put her ear to it, listening for any hint of sound.

She heard a familiar voice. It was coming closer. "David!" she hissed, pulling away from the door and throwing herself against the wall. David looked around frantically for a place to hide. Both of them were in plain view.

The door slid open, and Dr. Cable's malevolent voice poured out.

"You're simply not trying hard enough. You just have to convince her that—"

"Dr. Cable," Tally said.

The woman spun to face Tally, her hawklike features twisted in surprise.

"I'd like to give myself up."

"Tally Youngblood? How—"

From behind, David's powerjack thudded against the side of Dr. Cable's head, and she slumped to the floor.

"Is she . . . ," David stammered. His face was white.

Tally knelt and turned Dr. Cable's head to inspect the wound. No blood, but she was out cold. No matter how formidable cruel pretties were, surprise still had its advantages. "She'll be okay."

"Dr. Cable? What's going—"

Tally turned toward the voice, her eyes taking in the young woman before her.

She was tall and elegant, every feature perfection. Her eyes—deep and soulful, flecked with copper and gold—widened with a troubled look. Her generous lips parted wordlessly, and she raised one graceful hand. Tally's heart almost stopped at the beauty of her confusion.

Then recognition filled the woman's face, her broad smile illuminating the darkness, and Tally felt herself smiling in return. It felt good to make this woman happy.

"Tally! It *is* you."

It was Shay. She was pretty.

RESCUE

"Shay . . ."

"You made it!" Shay's stunning smile faded as she looked down at the crumpled form of Dr. Cable. "What's with her?"

Tally blinked, awed by the transformation of her friend. Shay's beauty seemed to snuff out everything inside Tally; her fear, surprise, and excitement fled, leaving nothing but amazement. "You . . . turned."

"Duh," she said. "David! You're both okay!"

"Uh, hi." His voice was dry, his hands shaking as they gripped the powerjack. "We need your help, Shay."

"Yeah, I guess you do." She looked down at Dr. Cable again and sighed. "You guys still know how to make trouble, I see."

Tally averted her eyes from Shay's beauty, trying to focus her thoughts. "Where's everyone else? David's parents? Croy?"

"Right in here." Shay gestured over one shoulder. "All locked up. Dr. C has been totally bogus to us."

"Keep her here," David said. He pushed past Shay and through the door. Tally saw a row of small doors inside the long room, each with a tiny window set in it.

Shay beamed at her. "I'm so glad you're all right, Tally. The thought of you all alone in the wild . . . of course, you weren't alone, were you?"

Meeting Shay's eyes, Tally was overwhelmed all over again. "What did they do to you?"

Shay smiled. "Besides the obvious?"

"Yeah. I mean, no." Tally shook her head, not knowing how to ask Shay if she was brain damaged. "Are any of the rest of them . . ."

"Pretty? No. I got to be first, because I made the most trouble. You should have seen me kicking and biting." Shay chuckled.

"They forced you."

"Yeah, Dr. C can be a major pain. It's kind of a relief, though."

Tally swallowed. "A relief . . ."

"Yeah, I hated this place. The only reason I'm here is that Dr. C wanted me to come by and talk to the Smokies."

"You live in New Pretty Town," Tally said softly. She tried to see past the beauty, to find whatever was behind Shay's wide, perfect eyes.

"Yeah. I just came from the *best* party."

Tally finally heard how slurred Shay's words were. She was

drunk. Maybe that was why she was acting so strangely. But she had called the others "the Smokies." She wasn't one of them anymore.

"You go to parties, Shay? While everyone here is locked up?"

"Well, I guess so," Shay said defensively. "I mean, they'll all get out once they turn. Once Cable gets over her stupid power trip." She looked at the unconscious form on the floor and shook her head. "She's going to be in a bad mood tomorrow, though. Thanks to you two."

The sound of complaining metal came from the detention room. Tally heard more voices.

"Of course, sounds like no one'll be around to see it," Shay said. "So how are you two doing, anyway?"

Tally opened her mouth, closed it, then managed to answer. "We're . . . good."

"That's great. Listen, sorry I was such a pain about all that. You know what uglies are like." Shay laughed. "Well, of course you do!"

"So you don't hate me?"

"Don't be silly, Tally!"

"I'm glad to hear that." Of course, Shay's blessing was meaningless. It wasn't forgiveness, just brain damage.

"You did me a big favor, getting me out of that Smoke place."

"You can't really believe that, Shay."

"What do you mean?"

"How could you change your mind so quickly?"

Shay laughed. "It took exactly one hot shower to change my mind." She reached out and touched Tally's hair, tangled and knotted from two weeks of camping out and riding all day. "Speaking of showers, *you* are a total mess."

Tally blinked. Hot tears were forcing themselves into her eyes. Shay had wanted so much to keep her own face, to live on her own terms outside the city. But that desire had been extinguished.

"I didn't mean to . . . betray you," she said softly.

Shay glanced over her shoulder, then turned back and smiled. "He doesn't know that you were working for Dr. C, does he? Don't worry, Tally," she whispered, putting one elegant finger to her lips. "Your ugly little secret is safe with me."

Tally swallowed, wondering if Shay had found out the whole story. Maybe Dr. Cable had told them all what she'd done.

A buzzing sound came from beside Dr. Cable. On the work tablet she had been carrying, a request light blinked with an incoming call.

Tally picked up the tablet and handed it to Shay. "Talk to them!"

Shay winked, pushed a button, and said, "Hey, it's me, Shay. No, I'm sorry, Dr. Cable's busy. Doing what? Well, it's complicated . . ." She muted the device. "Shouldn't you be rescuing people or something, Tally? That is the point of this little trick, right?"

"You'll stay here?"

"Duh. This looks bubbly. Just because I'm pretty doesn't mean I'm *totally* boring."

Tally brushed past her and into the room. Two doors had been ripped open, David's mother and another Smokey freed. The two were dressed in orange jumpsuits, with stunned and sleepy looks on their faces. David was working another door, his powerjack thrust into a small slot at floor level.

Tally saw Croy's face peering wide-eyed through one of the tiny windows, and planted her powerjack under his door. It whined to life, and the thick metal screeched as it bent upward. "David, they know something's up!" she called.

"Okay. We're almost done here."

Her jack had wrenched a small gap in the metal, not big enough. Tally reset the tool, and the metal groaned again. Her days of pulling up railroad ties soon paid off, the jack tearing a hole the size of a doggy door.

Croy's arms appeared, then his head, his jumpsuit ripping on jagged spurs of metal as he wriggled. Maddy grabbed his hands and pulled him through. "That's everyone who's left," she said. "Let's go."

"What about Dad!" David cried.

"We can't help him." Maddy ran into the hall.

Tally and David shared an anxious look, and followed.

Maddy was dashing down the hall toward the elevator, dragging Shay by the wrist behind her. Shay stabbed the tablet's talk button and said, "Wait a second, I think she's just coming back now. Hold please." She giggled and muted the device again.

"Bring Cable!" Maddy called. "We need her!"

"Mom!" David ran after her.

Tally looked at Croy, then down at Dr. Cable's crumpled form.

Croy nodded, and they each took a wrist, dragging the woman along the slick floor at a trot, Tally's grippy shoes squealing.

When the party reached the elevator, Maddy grabbed Dr. Cable by the collar and pulled her up to the eye-reader. The woman groaned once, softly. Maddy carefully pried open one of her eyes, and the elevator pinged, its doors sliding open.

Maddy tugged off the doctor's interface ring and dropped her to the floor, then pulled Shay inside. Tally and the other Smokies followed, but David stood his ground. "Mom, where's Dad?"

"We can't help him." Maddy yanked the tablet away from Shay and cracked it against the wall, then pulled David in against his protests. The doors closed, and the elevator asked, "Which floor?"

"Roof," Maddy said, the interface ring still in her hand. The elevator began to move, Tally's ears complaining at the swift ascent.

"What's our escape plan?" Maddy snapped. The glazed look was completely gone from her eyes, as if she'd gone to sleep last night expecting to be rescued this morning.

"Uh, hoverboards," Tally managed to answer. "Four of them." Realizing that she hadn't done so yet, Tally adjusted her crash bracelets to call them in.

"Oh, cool!" Shay said. "You know, I haven't been boarding since I left the Smoke?"

"There's seven of us," Maddy said. "Tally, you take Shay. Astrix and Ryde, double up. Croy, you go alone and throw them off the track. David, I'll ride with you."

"Mom . . . ," David pleaded, "if he's pretty, can't you cure him? Or at least try?"

"Your father's not pretty, David," she answered softly. "He's dead."

GETAWAY

"Give me a knife." Maddy held out her hand, ignoring the shocked look on her son's face.

Tally scrambled through her knapsack. She passed her multi-knife to Maddy, who pulled out a short blade and cut a piece from the arm of her jumpsuit. When the elevator reached roof level, its doors slid halfway open and groaned to a halt, revealing the uneven hole Tally had torn to gain entry. They slipped through one by one and ran for the edge of the roof.

A hundred meters away, Tally saw the hoverboards cruising across the compound, called by her crash bracelets. Alarms were ringing all around them now. If by some magic the Specials hadn't noticed the escape so far, the riderless boards had tripped the wire.

Tally spun around, looking for David. He was stumbling along at the back of the group, half in a daze. She caught him by his shoulders. "I'm so sorry."

He shook his head. Not at her, not at anything in particular.

"I don't know what to do, Tally."

She took his hand. "We have to run. That's all we can do right now. Follow your mother."

He looked into her eyes, his face wild. "Okay." He started to say more, but the words were drowned out by a noise like huge fingernails scraping metal. The hovercar door was fighting against the nanotech glue, setting the whole roof shuddering.

Maddy, last out of the elevator, had jimmied its door open with a powerjack. Its voice kept repeating, "Elevator requested."

But there were other ways onto the roof. Maddy turned to David. "Glue down those hatches so they can't get out."

His gaze cleared for a moment, and he nodded.

"I'll get the boards," Tally said, turning to dash for the edge of the roof. When she reached it, she jumped into space, hoping her bungee jacket still had some charge.

After one bounce, Tally was on the ground running. The boards sensed her crash bracelets and sped toward her.

"Tally! Look out!"

She looked over her shoulder at Croy's shout. A squad of Specials was headed toward her across the compound, an open door behind them at ground level. They ran inhumanly fast, covering the ground with long, loping strides.

The boards nudged her calves from behind, like dogs ready

to play. Tally leaped up, teetering for a moment with one foot on each pair of sandwiched boards. She'd never heard of anyone riding four boards at once. But the closest cruel pretty was only a few strides away.

Tally snapped her fingers and rose swiftly into the air.

The Special jumped, amazingly high, the fingers of one outstretched hand just brushing the front edge of the boards. The contact set them wobbling beneath Tally. It was like standing on a trampoline while someone else jumped on it. The other Specials watched from the ground below, waiting for her to fall.

But Tally regained her balance and leaned forward, heading back toward the building. The boards picked up speed, and seconds later Tally leaped off onto the roof, kicking one pair of hoverboards to Croy. He pulled them apart while she separated the other two.

"Go now," Maddy said. "Take this."

She handed Tally a swatch of orange fabric, a small bit of circuitry visible on one side. Tally noticed that Maddy had cut pieces from the forearms of all the jumpsuits.

"There's a tracker in that cloth," Maddy said. "Drop it somewhere to throw them off."

Tally nodded, looking around for David. He was running toward them, his face set into a grim mask, the tube of glue crushed and empty in his hand. "David—," she started.

"Go!" Maddy shouted, pushing Shay onto the board behind Tally.

"Um, no crash bracelets?" Shay said, her feet unsteady. "This is not my first party tonight, you know."

"I know. Hold on," Tally said, and shot away from the roof.

The two of them teetered for a moment, almost losing their balance. But Tally steadied herself, feeling Shay's arms wrap tightly around her waist.

"Whoa, Tally! Slow down!"

"Just hang on."

Tally leaned into a turn, sickened by the sluggishness of the board. Not only was it carrying two, but Shay's wobbly moves were freaking it out.

"Don't you remember how to ride?"

"Sure!" Shay said. "Just a little rusty, Squint. Plus a little too much to drink tonight."

"Just don't fall off. It'll hurt."

"Hey! I didn't ask to be rescued!"

"No, I guess you didn't." Tally looked down as they soared over Crumblyville, skipping the greenbelt to head straight back toward the river. If Shay hit the ground at this speed, she'd be worse than hurt. She'd be dead.

Like David's father. Tally wondered how he'd died. Had he tried to escape the Specials, like the Boss? Or had Dr. Cable done something to him? One thought stuck in her mind: However it had happened, it was her fault.

"Shay, if you fall off, take me with you."

"What?"

"Just hold on to me and don't let go, no matter what. I'm wearing a bungee jacket and bracelets. We should bounce." Probably. Unless the jacket pulled her one way and the bracelets the other.

Or Tally's and Shay's combined weight was too much for the lifters.

"So give me the bracelets, silly."

Tally shook her head. "No time to stop."

"Guess not. Our Special friends are going to be royally pissed." Shay clung tighter.

They were almost at the river, with no sign of pursuit behind them. The nanotech glue must have been putting up quite a fight. But Special Circumstances had other hovercars—the three they'd seen leave earlier, at least—and regular wardens had them too.

Tally wondered if Special Circumstances would call for help from the wardens, or whether they'd keep the whole situation a secret. What would the wardens think of the underground prison? Did the regular city government know what the Specials had done to the Smoke, or to Az?

Water flashed below her, and Tally dropped the swatch of orange cloth as they turned. It fluttered away, down toward the river. The current would take it back toward the city, in the opposite direction of their escape route.

Tally and David had agreed to rendezvous upriver, a long way past the ruins, where he had found a cave years before. Because its entrance was covered by a waterfall, it would shelter them from heat sensors. From there, they could hike back to the ruins to retrieve the rest of their equipment, and then . . .

Rebuild the Smoke? Seven of them? With Shay as their honorary pretty? Tally realized that they hadn't made plans beyond tonight. The future hadn't seemed real until now.

Of course, they still might all be caught.

"You think it's true?" Shay shouted. "What Maddy said?"

Tally dared a glance back at Shay. Her pretty face looked worried.

"I mean, Az was fine when I visited a few days ago," Shay said. "I thought they were going to make him pretty. Not *kill* him."

"I don't know." It was hardly something Maddy would lie about. But maybe she was mistaken.

Tally leaned forward, skimming the river low and fast, trying to leave the cold feeling in her stomach behind. Spray struck their faces as they hit the white water. Shay had started to ride properly, leaning with the slow arcs of the river's bends. "Hey, I remember this!" she shouted.

"Do you remember anything else from before your operation?" Tally yelled over the roar of water.

Shay ducked behind Tally as they struck a wall of spray. "Of course, silly."

"You hated me. Because I stole David from you. Because I betrayed the Smoke. Remember?"

Shay was silent for a moment, only the roar of white water and the rushing wind around them. Finally, she leaned closer, her voice thoughtful in Tally's ear. "Yeah, I know what you mean. But that was all ugly stuff. Crazy love and jealousy and needing to rebel against the city. Every kid's like that. But you grow up, you know?"

"You grew up because of an operation? Doesn't that strike you as weird?"

"It wasn't because of the operation."

"Then why?"

"It was just good to come home, Tally. It made me realize how crazy the whole Smoke thing was."

"What happened to biting and kicking?"

"Well, it took a few days to sink in, you know."

"Before or after you became pretty?"

Shay went silent again. Tally wondered if you could talk somebody out of their brain damage.

She pulled a position-finder from her pocket. The coordinates for the cave were still half an hour away. A glance over her shoulder didn't reveal any hovercars, not yet. If all four boards took different routes to the river, and all of them dropped their trackers in different places, the Specials were going to have a confusing night.

There were also Dex, Sussy, and An, who'd promised to tell every tricky ugly they knew to go for a ride tonight. The greenbelt would be crowded.

Tally wondered how many uglies had seen the burning letters in New Pretty Town, how many of them knew what the Smoke was, or were coming up with their own stories to explain the mysterious message. What new legends had she and David created with their little diversion?

When they reached a calmer part of the river, Shay spoke up again. "So, Tally?"

"Yeah?"

"Why do you want me to hate you?"

"I don't want you to hate me, Shay." Tally sighed. "Or maybe I do. I betrayed you, and I feel horrible about it."

"The Smoke wasn't going to last forever, Tally. Whether you turned us in or not."

"I didn't turn you in!" Tally cried. "Not on purpose, anyway. And the whole thing with David was just an accident. I didn't mean to hurt you."

"Of course not. You're just confused."

"*I'm* confused?" Tally groaned. "You're the one who . . ." She trailed off. How could Shay not understand that she'd been changed by the operation? Not just been given a pretty face, but also a . . . pretty mind. Nothing else could explain how quickly she'd changed, abandoning the rest of them for parties and hot showers, leaving her friends behind, just as Peris had so many months ago.

"Do you love him?" Shay asked.

"David? I, uh . . . maybe."

"That's sweet."

"It's not *sweet*. It's real!"

"Then why are you ashamed of it?"

"I'm not . . . ," Tally sputtered. She lost concentration for a moment, and the back of the board dipped low, sending a sheet of water up behind them. Shay whooped and held tighter. Tally gritted her teeth and took them a bit higher.

When Shay had stopped laughing, she said, "And you think *I'm* confused?"

"Listen, Shay, there's one thing I'm not confused about. I didn't want to betray the Smoke. I was blackmailed into going there as a spy, and when I sent for the Specials, it was an accident, really. But I'm sorry, Shay. I'm sorry I ruined your dream." Tally felt herself crying, the tears driven backward by the wind. The trees rushed past in the darkness for a while.

"I'm just glad you two made it back to civilization," Shay said softly, holding on tight. "And I'm not sorry about what happened. If that makes you feel any better."

Tally thought of the lesions on Shay's brain, the tiny cancers or wounds or whatever they were, that she didn't even know she had. They were in there somewhere, changing her friend's thoughts, warping her feelings, gnawing at the roots of who she was. Making her forgive Tally.

"Thanks, Shay. But no, it doesn't."

NIGHT ALONE

Tally and Shay made it to the cave first.

Croy arrived a few minutes later, without warning, he and his board hurtling through the waterfall in a sudden explosion of splashing and cursing. He tumbled into the darkness, his body rolling across the stone floor with a series of sickening thuds.

Tally scrambled from the back of the cave, a flashlight in one hand.

Croy shook his head and groaned. "I lost them."

Tally looked at the entrance of the cave, the sheet of water a solid curtain against the night. "I hope so. Where's everybody else?"

"Don't know. Maddy told us all to go different ways. Since I was flying solo, I went all the way around the greenbelt first to get them off track." He laid his head back, still panting. A position-finder fell from one of his hands.

"Wow. You went fast."

"You're telling me. No crash bracelets."

"Been there. At least you had shoes on," Tally said. "Did any-one chase you?"

He nodded. "I held on to my tracker as long as I could. Got most of the Specials to follow me. But there were a whole bunch of hoverboard riders in the belt. You know, city kids. The Specials kept getting us confused."

Tally smiled. Dex, An, and Sussy had done their work well.

"Are David and Maddy okay?"

"I wouldn't know about okay," he said softly. "But they got off right after you, and it didn't look like anyone was following them. Maddy said they were heading straight for the ruins. We're sup-posed to meet them there tomorrow night."

"Tomorrow?" Tally said.

"Maddy wanted to be alone with David for a while, you know?"

Tally nodded, but her heart wrenched inside her. David needed her. At least, she hoped he did. The thought of him dealing with Az's death without her made the icy feeling in her stomach drop a few more degrees.

Of course, Maddy was there. Az had been her husband, after all, and Tally had only met the man once. But still.

She sighed. Tally tried to remember the last words she'd said to David, and wished they'd been more comforting. There hadn't even been time to hold him. Since the invasion of the Smoke, Tally hadn't been separated from David for longer than that hour in the storm, and now she wouldn't see him for a whole day.

"Maybe I should go to the ruins. I could hike out there tonight."

"Don't be crazy," Croy said. "The Specials are still out looking."

"But just in case they need anything . . ."

"Maddy said to tell you no."

Astrix and Ryde showed up a half hour later, coming into the cave more gracefully than Croy, but with their own stories of running from hovercars. The pursuit had been confused, the Specials overwhelmed by everything that had happened that night.

"They never even got close," Astrix said.

Ryde shook his head. "They were all over the place."

"It's like we won a battle, you know?" Croy said. "We beat them in their own city. Made them look like fools."

"Maybe we don't have to hide in the wild anymore," Ryde said. "It could be like when we were uglies, playing tricks. But telling the whole city the truth."

"And if we get caught, Tally can come and rescue us!" Croy shouted.

Tally tried to smile at their cheers, but knew she wouldn't feel good about anything until she saw David again. Not until tomorrow night. She felt exiled, shut out from the one thing that really mattered.

Shay had fallen asleep in a small crevice after complaining about the dampness and her hair, asking when they were going to take her home. Tally crawled back to where her friend lay and snuggled up next to her, trying to forget the damage that had been done to Shay's mind. At least Shay's new body wasn't as painfully skinny; she felt soft and warm in the damp cold of the cave. Cradled against her, Tally managed to stop shivering.

But it was a long time before she fell asleep.

She woke up to the smell of PadThai.

Croy had found the food packets and purifier in her knapsack and was making food with water from the fall, apparently trying to placate Shay.

"A little escape was one thing, but I didn't know you guys were going to drag me all the way out here. I'm through with this whole rebellion thing, I've got a wicked hangover, and I really need to wash my hair."

"There's a waterfall right there," Croy said.

"But it's cold! I'm so *over* this camping-out bogusness."

Tally crawled out into the big part of the cave, every muscle stiff, every rock she'd slept on imprinted on her. Through the curtain of the waterfall, dusk was falling. She wondered if she'd ever be able to sleep at night again.

Shay was squatting on a rock, digging into the PadThai, complaining that it wasn't spicy enough. Bedraggled, in dirty party clothes, her hair stuck to her face, she was still stunning. Ryde and Astrix watched her silently, a bit awestruck by her looks. They were two of Shay's old friends who'd run away to the Smoke the time she'd chickened out, so it must have been months since they'd seen a pretty face. Everyone seemed willing to let her go on complaining.

One thing about being pretty, people put up with your annoying habits.

"Morning," said Croy. "SwedeBalls or VegiRice?"

"Whatever's faster." Tally stretched her muscles. She wanted to get to the ruins as soon as possible.

When darkness fell, Tally and Croy crept out from behind the waterfall. There was no sign of Specials in the sky. She doubted anyone was searching this far out. Forty minutes from the city on a fast board was a long way.

They gave the all-clear, and everyone rode farther upriver, to a place where the river's course twisted closer to the ruins. A long hike followed, the four uglies sharing the load of boards and supplies. Shay had stopped complaining, settling into a pouty, hungover silence. The walk seemed easy for her. Her wiry fitness from hard work at the Smoke hadn't faded in two weeks, and the operation actually firmed up a new pretty's muscles, at least for a while. Although Shay announced once that she wanted to go home, heading back on her own didn't seem to have entered her mind.

Tally wondered what they were going to do with her. She knew there was no simple fix. Maddy and Az had worked for twenty years to no avail. But they couldn't leave Shay like this.

Of course, the moment she was cured, her hatred for Tally would return.

Which was worse: a friend with brain damage, or one who despised you?

• • •

They reached the edge of the ruins after midnight, and boarded down to the abandoned building where Tally and David had camped.

David was waiting outside.

He looked exhausted, the dark lines under his eyes visible even in starlight. But he embraced Tally the moment she stepped from the board, his arms tight around her, and she hugged him back hard. "Are you okay?" she whispered, then felt idiotic. What was he supposed to say to that? "Oh, David, of course you're not. I'm sorry, I—"

"Shhh. I know." He pulled away and smiled.

Relief flowed through Tally, and she squeezed David's hands, confirming the realness of him. "I missed you," she said.

"Me too." He kissed her.

"You two are just so cute," Shay said, combing her hair with her fingers after the windy ride.

"Hi, Shay." David gave her a tired smile. "You guys look hungry."

"Only if you have any non-bogus food," Shay said.

"Afraid not. Three kinds of reconstituted curry."

Shay groaned and pushed past him into the crumbling building. His eyes followed her, but without any of the awe still in Ryde's and Astrix's faces. It was as if David didn't see her beauty.

He turned back. "We finally got some luck."

Tally looked into his lined, fatigued face. "Really?"

"We got that tablet working, the one Dr. Cable was carrying.

Mom was yanking the phone part out so they couldn't track us through it, and she got it to display Cable's work data."

"About what?"

"All her notes on making pretties into Specials. Not just the physical part"—he pulled her closer—"but also how the brain lesions work. It's everything my parents weren't told when they were doctors!"

Tally swallowed. "Shay . . ."

He nodded. "Mom thinks she can find a cure."

HIPPOCRATIC OATH

They stayed at the edge of the Rusty Ruins.

Occasionally, hovercars would pass over the crumbling city, threading a slow search pattern across the sky. But the Smokies were old hands at hiding from satellites and aircraft. They placed red herrings across the ruins—chemical glowsticks that gave off human-size pockets of heat—and covered the windows of their building with sheets of black Mylar. And of course the ruins were very large; finding seven people in what had once been a city of millions was no simple matter.

Every night, Tally watched the influence of the "New Smoke" grow. A lot of uglies had seen the burning message on the night of the escape, or had heard about it, and the nightly pilgrimages out to the ruins slowly increased, until sparklers wavered atop high buildings from midnight until dawn. Tally, Ryde, Croy, and Astrix made contact with the city uglies, starting new rumors, teaching new tricks, and offering glimpses of the ancient magazines the Boss had salvaged from the Smoke. If they doubted the existence of Special Circumstances, Tally showed them the plastic handcuff bracelets still encircling her wrists, and invited them to try to cut the cuffs off.

One new legend towered above all the rest. Maddy had decided that the brain lesions couldn't be kept a secret anymore; every ugly had the right to know what the operation really entailed. Tally and the others spread the rumor among their city friends: Not just your face was changed by the knife. Your personality—the real you inside—was the price of beauty.

Of course, not every ugly believed such an outrageous tale, but a few did. And some sneaked across to New Pretty Town in the dead of night to talk to their older friends face-to-face, and decided for themselves.

The Specials sometimes tried to crash the party, setting traps for the New Smokies, but someone always gave a warning, and no hovercar could ever catch a board among winding streets and rubble. The New Smokies learned the nooks and crannies of the ruins as if they'd been born there, until they could disappear in a heartbeat.

Maddy worked on the brain cure, using materials salvaged from the ruins or brought by city uglies willing to borrow from hospitals and chem classes. She withdrew from the rest of them, except for David. She seemed particularly cool to Tally, who felt guilty for every moment she spent with David, now that his mother was alone. None of them ever talked about Az's death.

Shay stayed with them, complaining about the food, the ruins, her hair and clothes, and having to look at all the ugly faces around her. But she never seemed bitter, only perpetually annoyed. After the first few days she didn't even talk about leaving. Perhaps the brain damage made her pliant, or the fact that she hadn't lived in New Pretty Town for long. She still remembered them all as friends. Tally sometimes wondered if Shay secretly enjoyed having the only pretty face in their little rebellion. Certainly, she didn't do any more work than she would have in the city; Ryde and Astrix obeyed her every command.

David helped his mother, searching the ruins for salvage, and taught wilderness survival tricks to any ugly who wanted to learn. But in the two weeks after his father's death, Tally found herself missing the days when it had been just the two of them.

Twenty days after the rescue, Maddy announced that she had found a cure.

"Shay, I want to explain this to you carefully."

"Sure, Maddy."

"When you had the operation, they did something to your brain."

Shay smiled. "Yeah, right." She looked across at Tally, wearing a familiar expression. "That's what Tally keeps telling me. But you guys don't understand."

Maddy folded her hands. "What do you mean?"

"I *like* the way I look," Shay insisted. "I'm happier in this body. You want to talk about brain damage? Look at you all, running around these ruins playing commando. You're all full of schemes and rebellions, crazy with fear and paranoia, even jealousy." Her eyes skipped back and forth between Tally and Maddy. "That's what being ugly does."

"And how do you feel, Shay?" Maddy asked calmly.

"I feel bubbly. It's nice not being all raging with hormones. Of course, it kind of sucks being out here instead of in the city."

"No one's keeping you here, Shay. Why haven't you left?"

Shay shrugged. "I don't know. . . . I'm worried about you guys, I guess. It's dangerous out here, and messing with Specials isn't a good idea. You should know that by now, Maddy."

Tally took a sharp breath, but Maddy's expression didn't change. "And you're going to protect us from them?" she asked calmly.

Shay shrugged. "I just feel bad about Tally. If I hadn't told her about the Smoke, she'd be pretty right now instead of living in this dump. And I figure eventually she'll decide to grow up. We'll go back together."

"You don't seem to want to decide for yourself."

"Decide what?" Shay rolled her eyes, looking at Tally to confirm what a bore this was. The two of them had plowed through this conversation a dozen times before, until Tally had realized there was no convincing Shay that her personality had changed. To Shay, her new attitude was simply the result of growing up, moving on, leaving all the overheated emotions of ugliness behind.

"You weren't always this way, Shay," David said.

"No, I used to be ugly."

Maddy smiled gently. "These pills won't change the way you look. They'll only affect your brain, undoing what Dr. Cable did to the way your mind works. Then you can decide for yourself how you want to look."

"Decide? After you've messed with my brain?"

"Shay!" Tally said, forgetting her promise to remain silent. "We're not the ones messing with your brain!"

"Tally," David said softly.

"That's right, *I'm* the one who's crazy." Shay's voice took on the tone of her daily round of complaining. "Not you guys, who live in a broken-down building on the edge of a dead city, slowly turning into freaks when you could be beautiful. Yeah, I'm crazy all right . . . for trying to help you!"

Tally sat back and crossed her arms, silenced by Shay's words. Whenever they had this conversation, reality became a little unhinged, as if she and the other New Smokies might really be the insane ones. It felt like Tally's horrible first days in the Smoke, when she hadn't known whose side she was on.

"How are you helping us, Shay?" Maddy asked calmly.

"I'm trying to get you to understand."

"Just like you did when Dr. Cable used to bring you by my cell?"

Shay's eyes narrowed, confusion clouding her face, as if her memories of the underground prison didn't fit in with the rest of her pretty worldview.

"I know Dr. C was horrible to you," she said. "The Specials are psychos—just look at them. But that doesn't mean you have to spend your whole lives running away. That's what I'm saying. Once you turn, Specials won't mess with you."

"Why not?"

"Because you won't make trouble anymore."

"Why not?"

"Because you'll be *happy*!" Shay took a couple of deep breaths, and her usual calm returned. She smiled, beautiful again. "Like me."

Maddy picked up the pills on the table in front of her. "You won't take these willingly?"

"No way. You said they're not even safe."

"I said there was a small chance something could go wrong."

Shay laughed. "You *must* think I'm nuts. And even if those pills work, look what they're supposed to do. From what I can tell, 'cured' means being a jealous, self-important, whiny little ugly-brain. It means thinking you've got all the answers." She crossed her arms. "In a lot of ways, you and Dr. Cable are alike. You're both convinced you've personally got to change the world. Well, I don't need that. And I don't need those."

"Okay, then." Maddy picked up the pills and put them in her pocket. "That's all I have to say."

"What do you mean?" Tally asked.

David squeezed her hand. "That's all we can do, Tally."

"What? You said we could cure her."

Maddy shook her head. "Only if she wants to be cured. These

are experimental, Tally. We can't give them to someone against her will. Not when we don't know if they'll work."

"But her mind . . . she's got the lesions!"

"Hello," Shay called. "*She* is sitting right here."

"Sorry, Shay," Maddy said mildly. "Tally?"

Maddy pulled aside the Mylar barrier, stepping out onto what the New Smokies called the balcony. It was really just part of the top floor of the building, where the roof had entirely collapsed, leaving sweeping views of the ruins.

Tally followed. Behind her, Shay was already talking about what was for dinner. David came out a moment later.

"So, we give her the pills secretly, right?" Tally whispered.

"No," Maddy said firmly. "We can't. I'm not going to do medical experiments on unwilling subjects."

"Medical experiments?" Tally swallowed.

David took her hand. "You can't know for sure how something like this will work. It's only a one-percent chance, but it could screw up her brain forever."

"It's already screwed up."

"But she's happy, Tally." David shook his head. "And she can make decisions for herself."

Tally pulled her hand away, staring out over the city. A sparkler was already showing on the tall spire, uglies come to gossip and trade. "Why did we even have to ask? *They* didn't get her permission when they did this to her!"

"That's the difference between us and them," Maddy said. "After Az and I found out what the operation really meant, we realized we'd been party to something horrible. People had had their minds changed without their knowledge. As doctors, we took an ancient oath never to do anything like that."

Tally looked into Maddy's face. "But if you weren't going to help Shay, why did you bother finding a cure?"

"If we knew the treatment would work safely, then we could give it to Shay and see how she felt about it later. But to test it, we need a willing subject."

"Where are we ever going to find one? Anyone who's pretty is going to say no."

"Maybe for right now, Tally. But if we keep making inroads into the city, we might find a pretty who wants out."

"But we *know* Shay's crazy."

"She's not crazy," Maddy said. "Her arguments make sense, in fact. She's happy as she is, and doesn't want to take a deadly risk."

"But she's not really herself. We *have* to change her back."

"Az died because someone thought like that," Maddy said grimly.

"What?"

David put his arm around her. "My father . . ." He cleared his throat, and Tally waited in silence. Finally he would tell her how Az had died.

He took a slow breath before continuing. "Dr. Cable wanted to turn them all, but she was worried that Mom and Dad might talk about the brain lesions, even after the operation, because they'd been focused on them for so long." David's voice trembled, but it was soft and careful, as if he didn't dare put any emotion into the words. "Dr. Cable was already working on ways to change memories, a way of erasing the Smoke forever from people's minds. When they took my father for the operation, he never came back."

"That's awful," Tally whispered. She gathered him into a hug.

"Az was the victim of a medical experiment, Tally," Maddy said. "I can't do the same thing to Shay. Otherwise, she'd be right about me and Dr. Cable."

"But Shay ran away. She didn't want to become pretty."

"She doesn't want to be experimented on, either."

Tally closed her eyes. Through the Mylar shade, she could hear Shay telling Ryde about the hairbrush she'd made. For days she'd proudly shown the little brush, made of splinters of wood shoved into a lump of clay, to anyone who would listen. As if it were the most important thing she'd ever done.

They had risked everything to rescue her. But they had nothing to show for it. Shay would never be the same.

And it was all Tally's fault. She'd come to the Smoke, and had brought the Specials, leaving Shay an empty-headed pretty, and Az dead.

She took a deep breath. "Okay, you've got a willing subject."

"What do you mean, Tally?"

"Me."

CONFESSIONS

"What?" David said.

"Your taking the pills won't prove anything, Tally," Maddy said. "You don't have the lesions."

"But I will have them. I'll go back to the city and get caught, and Dr. Cable will give me the operation. In a few weeks, you come and get me. Give me the cure. You've got your subject."

The three of them stood there in silence. The words had poured out of Tally of their own accord. She could hardly believe she'd uttered them.

"Tally . . ." David shook his head. "That's crazy."

"It's not crazy. You need a willing subject. Someone who agrees *before* they become pretty that they want to be cured, experimental or not. It's the only way."

"You can't give yourself up!" David cried.

Tally turned toward Maddy. "You said you're ninety-nine percent sure these pills will work, right?"

"Yes. But the one percent could leave you a vegetable, Tally."

"One percent? Compared to breaking into Special Circumstances, that's a breeze."

"Tally, stop it." David took her shoulders. "It's too dangerous."

"Dangerous? David, you can get across into New Pretty Town no problem. City uglies do it all the time. Just grab me out of my mansion and stick me on a board. I'll come with you, just like Shay did. Then you cure me."

"What if the Specials decide to change your memory? Like they did my father's?"

"They won't," Maddy said.

David stared at his mother in surprise.

"They didn't bother with Shay. She remembers the Smoke just fine. Az and I were the only ones they were worried about. Because we'd been focused on the brain lesions for half our lives, they figured we'd never shut up about them, even as pretties."

"Mom!" David cried. "Tally's not going anywhere."

"And besides," Maddy continued, "Dr. Cable wouldn't do anything to hurt Tally."

"Stop talking like this is going to happen!"

Tally looked into Maddy's eyes. The woman nodded. She knew.

"David," Tally said. "I have to do this."

"Why?"

"Because of Shay. It's the only way that Maddy will cure her. Right?"

Maddy nodded.

"You don't have to save Shay," David said slowly and evenly. "You've done enough for her. You followed her to the Smoke, rescued her from Special Circumstances!"

"Yeah, I've done a lot for her." Tally took a breath. "I'm the reason she's like this, pretty and brainless."

David shook his head. "What are you talking about?"

She turned to him, taking his hand. "David, I didn't come to the Smoke just to make sure Shay was okay. I came to bring her back to the city." She sighed. "I came to betray her."

Tally had imagined telling her secret to David so many times, rehearsing this speech to herself almost every night, that she could hardly believe this wasn't just another nightmare in which the truth was forced from her. But as the reality of the moment sank in, she found the words spilling out in a torrent.

"I was a spy for Dr. Cable. That's how I knew where Special Circumstances was. That's why the Specials came to the Smoke. I brought a tracker with me."

"You're not making any sense," David said. "You fought when they came. You escaped. You helped rescue my mother . . ."

"I'd changed my mind. And I never meant to activate the tracker, honestly. I wanted to live in the Smoke. But the night before the invasion, after I found out about the lesions . . ."

She closed her eyes. "After we kissed, I accidentally set it off."

"What?"

"My locket. I didn't mean to. I wanted to destroy it. But I'm the one who brought the Specials to the Smoke, David. I'm the reason why Shay is pretty. It's my fault your father's dead."

"You're making this up! I'm not going to let you—"

"David," Maddy said sharply, silencing her son, "she's not lying."

Tally opened her eyes. Maddy was looking at her sadly.

"Dr. Cable told me everything about how she manipulated you, Tally. I didn't believe her at first, but the night you rescued us, she'd just brought Shay down to confirm it."

Tally nodded. "Shay knew I was a traitor, at the end."

"She still knows," Maddy said. "But it doesn't matter to her anymore. That's why Tally has to do this."

"You're both crazy!" David shouted. "Look, Mom, just get off your high horse and give Shay the pills." He reached out his hand. "I'll do it for you."

"David, I won't let you turn yourself into a monster. And Tally's made her choice."

David looked at them both, unable to believe any of it. Finally, he found words. "You were a spy?"

"Yes. At first."

He shook his head.

"Son." Maddy stepped forward, trying to hold him.

"No!" He turned and ran, tearing the Mylar shade down and leaving the others inside speechless; even Shay was shocked into silence.

Before Tally could follow, Maddy took her arm in a firm grip. "You should go to the city now."

"Tonight? But—"

"Otherwise, you'll talk yourself out of it. Or David will."

Tally pulled away. "I have to say good-bye to him."

"You have to go."

Tally stared at Maddy and slowly realized the truth. Although the woman's gaze held more sadness than anger, there was something cold in her eyes. David might not blame her for Az's death, but Maddy did.

"Thank you," Tally said softly, forcing herself to hold Maddy's gaze.

"For what?"

"For not telling him. For letting me do it myself."

Maddy shook her head, managing a smile. "David needed you these last two weeks."

Tally swallowed and stepped away, looking at the city. "He still needs me."

"Tally—"

"I'll go tonight, all right? But I know that David will be the one who brings me back."

DOWN THE RIVER

Before leaving, Tally wrote a letter to herself.

It was Maddy's idea, to put her consent in writing. That way, even as a pretty, unable to comprehend why she would ever want her brain fixed, Tally could at least read her own words and know what was about to happen.

"Whatever makes you feel better," Tally said. "As long as you cure me, no matter what I say. Don't leave me like Shay."

"I'll cure you, Tally. I promise. I just need written consent." Maddy handed her a pen and a small, precious piece of paper.

"I never learned penmanship," Tally said. "They don't require it anymore."

Maddy shook her head sadly and said, "Okay. You dictate, and I'll write it."

"Not you. Shay can write it for me. She took a class, back when she was trying to get to the Smoke." Tally remembered the scrawl of Shay's directions to the Smoke, clumsy but readable.

The letter didn't take long. Shay giggled at Tally's heartfelt words, but she wrote them down as directed. There was something earnest in the way she put stylus to paper, like a littlie learning how to read.

When they were finished, David still hadn't come back. He'd taken one of the hoverboards in the direction of the ruins. As she put away her things, Tally kept glancing at the window, hoping he would return.

But Maddy was probably right. If Tally saw him again, she would just talk herself out of this. Or maybe David would stop her.

Or worse, maybe he wouldn't.

But no matter what David said now, he would always remember what she had done, the lives she had cost with her secrets. This was the only way Tally could be certain that he had forgiven her. If he came to rescue her, she would know.

"So, let's get moving," Shay said when they were done.

"Shay, I'm not going to be gone forever. I'd rather you . . ."

"Come on. I'm sick of this place."

Tally bit her lip. What was the point of giving herself up if Shay was coming too? Of course, they could always snatch her away again as well. Once the cure was proven to work, they could give it to anyone. Or everyone.

"The only reason I've been hanging around this dump is to try to get you to come back," Shay said, then lowered her voice. "You know, it's my fault you're not already pretty. I messed up everything by running away. I owe you."

"Oh, Shay." Tally's head began to spin. She closed her eyes.

"Maddy always says I can go anytime. You don't want me to go back all alone, do you?"

Tally tried to imagine Shay hiking to the river alone. "No, I guess not." She looked at her friend's face and saw a spark in her eyes, something real ignited by the idea of going on a trip with Tally.

"Please! We'll have a blast in New Pretty Town."

Tally spread her hands. "Okay. I guess I can't stop you."

They rode together on one hoverboard. Croy came along on another, to take the boards back when they reached the city's edge.

He didn't talk the whole way down. The other New Smokies had all heard the fight outside, and finally knew what Tally had done. It must have been worse for Croy. He had suspected, and she'd lied to him face-to-face. He was probably wishing he'd stopped Tally himself before she'd had a chance to betray them all.

When they reached the greenbelt, though, he forced himself to look at her. "What did they do to you, anyway? To make you do something like that?"

"They said I couldn't turn, until I'd found Shay."

He looked away, staring at the lights of New Pretty Town,

bright in the clear cold of a November night. "So you're finally getting your wish."

"Yeah. I guess."

"Tally's going to be pretty!" Shay said.

Croy ignored her and looked at Tally again. "Thanks for rescuing me, though. That was some trick you guys pulled off. I hope that . . ." He shrugged, and shook his head. "See you later."

"I hope so."

Croy stuck the boards together and headed back up the river.

"This is going to be the best!" Shay said. "I can't wait for you to meet all my new friends. And you can finally introduce me to Peris."

"Sure."

They walked down toward Uglyville until they found themselves in Cleopatra Park. The earth was hard underneath their feet in the late autumn chill, and they huddled close against the cold. Tally wore her Smoke-made sweater. She'd wanted Maddy to keep it for her, but she'd left her microfiber jacket behind instead. City-made clothes were too valuable to waste on someone going back to civilization.

"You see, I was already getting popular," Shay was saying. "Having a criminal past is the only way into the really good parties. I mean, no one wants to hear about what classes you took in ugly school." She giggled.

"We should be a hit, then."

"Duh. When we tell everyone about your kidnapping me right out of Special Circumstances headquarters? And how I talked you into escaping from that band of freaks? But we're going to have to tone it down, Squint. No one's ever going to believe the truth!"

"No, you're right about that."

Tally thought of the letter she'd left with Maddy. Would *she* even believe the truth in a few weeks' time? How would the words of a fugitive, desperate, tragic ugly look through pretty eyes?

For that matter, what was David going to look like after she'd been surrounded by new pretty faces twenty-four hours a day? Would she really believe all that stuff about ugliness again, or would she remember how someone could be beautiful even without surgery? Tally tried to picture David's face, but it hurt to think of how long it would be before she saw him again.

She wondered how long it would take after the operation, before she would stop missing David. It might be a few days before the lesions completely took hold of her, Maddy had warned. But that didn't mean it was her own mind, changing itself.

Maybe if she decided to go on missing him, no matter what, Tally could keep her mind from changing. Unlike most people, she *knew* about the lesions. Maybe she could beat them.

A dark shape passed overhead, a warden's hovercar, and Tally instinctively froze. The city uglies had said there were more patrols out these days. The regular authorities had finally noticed that things were changing.

The hovercar halted, then settled softly onto the earth next to them. A door slid open, and a blinding light popped on. "All right, you kids . . . oh, sorry, miss."

The light was on Shay's face. Then it flicked across to Tally.

"What are you two . . . ?" The warden's voice stumbled. Didn't this beat everything? A pretty and an ugly taking a stroll together. The warden came closer, confusion all over his middle-pretty face.

Tally smiled. At least she was causing trouble to the end.

"I'm Tally Youngblood," she said. "Make me pretty."

PRETTIES

To the Australian SF community for all your acceptance and support

Part I

SLEEPING BEAUTY

Remember that the most beautiful
things in the world are the most useless.
—John Ruskin, *The Stones of Venice, I*

CRIMINAL

Getting dressed was always the hardest part of the afternoon.

The invitation to Valentino Mansion said semiformal, but it was the *semi* part that was tricky. Like a night without a party, "semi" opened up too many possibilities. Bad enough for boys, for whom it could mean jacket and tie (skipping the tie with certain kinds of collars), or all white and shirtsleeves (but only on summer afternoons), or any number of longcoats, waistcoats, tailcoats, kilts, or really nice sweaters. For girls, though, the definition simply exploded, as definitions usually did here in New Pretty Town.

Tally almost preferred formal white-tie or black-tie parties. The clothes were less comfortable and the parties no fun until everyone got drunk, but at least you didn't have to think so hard about getting dressed.

"Semiformal, *semi*formal," she said, her eyes drifting over the expanse of her open closet, the carousel stuttering back and forth as it tried to keep up with Tally's random eyemouse clicks, setting clothes swaying on their hangers. Yes, "semi" was definitely a bogus word.

"Is it even a word?" Tally asked aloud. "'Semi'?" It felt strange in her mouth, which was dry as cotton because of last night.

"Only half of one," the room said, probably thinking it was clever.

"Figures," Tally muttered.

She collapsed back onto her bed and stared up at the ceiling, feeling the room threaten to spin a little. It didn't seem fair, having to get worked up over half a word. "Make it go away," she said.

The room misunderstood, and slid shut the wall over her closet. Tally didn't have the strength to explain that she'd really meant her hangover, which was sprawled in her head like an overweight cat, sullen and squishy and disinclined to budge.

Last night, she and Peris had gone skating with a bunch of other Crims, trying out the new rink hovering over Nefertiti Stadium. The sheet of ice, held aloft by a grid of lifters, was thin enough to see through, and was kept transparent by a horde of little Zambonies darting among the skaters like nervous water bugs. The fireworks exploding in the stadium below made it glow like some kind of schizoid stained glass that changed colors every few seconds.

They all had to wear bungee jackets in case anyone broke through. No one ever did, of course, but the thought that at any moment the world could fall away with a sudden *crack* kept Tally drinking plenty of champagne.

Zane, who was pretty much the leader of the Crims, got bored and tipped a whole bottle onto the ice. He said that alcohol had a lower freezing point than water, so it might send someone tumbling down into the fireworks. But he hadn't poured out enough to save Tally's head this morning.

The room made the special sound that meant another Crim was calling.

"Hey."

"Hey, Tally."

"Shay-la!" Tally struggled up onto one elbow. "I need help!"

"The party? I know."

"What's the deal with *semi*formal, anyway?"

Shay laughed. "Tally-wa, you are so missing. Didn't you get the ping?"

"What ping?"

"It went out *hours* ago."

Tally glanced at her interface ring, still on her bedside table. She never wore it at night, an old habit from when she'd been an ugly, sneaking out all the time. It sat there softly pulsing, still muted for sleeptime. "Oh. Just woke up."

"Well forget semi anything. They changed the bash to fancy dress. We have to come up with *costumes*!"

Tally checked the time: just before five in the afternoon. "What, in three hours?"

"Yeah, I know. I'm all over the place with mine. It's so shaming. Can I come down?"

"Please."

"In five?"

"Sure. Bring breakfast. Bye."

Tally let her head fall back onto the pillow. The bed was spinning like a hoverboard now, the day just starting and already wiping out.

She slipped on her interface ring and listened angrily as the ping played, saying that no one would be admitted tonight without a really bubbly costume. Three hours to come up with something decent, and everyone else had a huge head start.

Sometimes, it felt like being a *real* criminal had been much, much simpler.

Shay had breakfast in tow: lobster omelettes, toast, hash browns, corn fritters, grapes, chocolate muffins, and Bloodies—more food than a whole packet of calorie purgers could erase. The overburdened tray shivered in the air, its lifters trembling like a littlie arriving at school, first day ever.

"Um, Shay? Are we going as blimps or something?"

Shay giggled. "No, but you sounded bad. And you have to be bubbly tonight. All the Crims are coming to vote you in."

"Great, bubbly." Tally sighed, relieving the tray of a Bloody Mary. She frowned at the first sip. "Not salty enough."

"No problem," Shay said, scraping off the caviar decorating an omelette and stirring it in.

"Ew, fishy!"

"Caviar is good with anything." Shay took another spoonful and put it straight into her mouth, closing her eyes to chew the little fish eggs. She twisted her ring to start some music.

Tally swallowed and drank more Bloody, which at least stopped the room from spinning. The chocolate muffins were starting to smell good. Then she'd move on to the hash browns. Then the omelette; she might even try the caviar. Breakfast was the meal when Tally most felt like she had to make up for the time she'd lost out in the wild. A good breakfast binge made her feel in control, as if a storm of city-made tastes could erase the months of stews and SpagBol.

The music was new and made her heart beat faster. "Thanks, Shay-la. You are totally life-saving."

"No problem, Tally-wa."

"So where were you last night, anyway?"

Shay just smiled, like she'd done something bad.

"What? New boy?"

Shay shook her head. Batted her eyes.

"You didn't surge again, did you?" Tally asked, and Shay giggled. "You *did.* You're not supposed to more than once a week. Could you be any more missing?"

"It's okay, Tally-wa. Just local."

"Where?" Shay's face didn't look any different. Was the surgery hidden under her pajamas?

"Look closer." Shay's long lashes fluttered again.

Tally leaned forward, staring into the perfect copper eyes, wide and speckled with jewel dust, and her heart beat still faster. A month after coming to New Pretty Town, Tally was still awestruck by other pretties' eyes. They were so huge and welcoming, bright with interest. Shay's lush pupils seemed to murmur, *I'm listening to you. You fascinate me.* They narrowed down the world to only Tally, all alone in the radiance of Shay's attention.

It was even weirder with Shay, because Tally had known her back in ugly days, before the operation had made her this way.

"Closer."

Tally took a steadying breath, the room spinning again, but in a good way. She gestured for the windows to transpare a little more, and in the sunlight she saw the new additions. "Ooh, pretty-making."

Bolder than all the other implanted glitter, twelve tiny rubies ringed each of Shay's pupils, glowing softly red against emerald irises.

"Bubbly, huh?"

"Yeah. But hang on . . . are the bottom-left ones different?" Tally squinted harder. One jewel in each eye seemed to be flickering, a tiny white candle in the coppery depths.

"It's five o'clock!" Shay said. "Get it?"

It took Tally a second to remember how to read the big clock tower in the center of town. "Um, but that's seven. Wouldn't bottom-*right* be five o'clock?"

Shay snorted. "They run counterclockwise, silly. I mean, so boring otherwise."

A laugh bubbled up in Tally. "So wait. You have jewels in your eyes? And they tell time? And they go *backward*? Isn't that maybe *one* thing too many, Shay?"

Tally immediately regretted what she'd said. The expression that clouded Shay's face was tragic, sucking away the radiance of a moment before. She looked about to cry, except without puffy eyes or a red nose. New surge was always a delicate topic, like a new hairstyle, almost.

"You hate them," Shay softly accused.

"Of course I don't. Like I said: *totally* pretty-making."

"Really?"

"Very. And it's *good* they go backward."

Shay's smile returned, and Tally breathed a sigh of relief, still not believing herself. It was the kind of mistake only brand-new pretties made, and she'd had the operation over a month ago. Why was she still saying bogus things? If she made a comment like that tonight, one of the Crims might vote against her. It only took one veto to shut you out.

And then she'd be alone, almost like running away again.

Shay said, "Maybe we should go as clock towers tonight, in honor of my new eyeballs."

Tally laughed, knowing the lame joke meant she was forgiven. She and Shay had been through a lot together, after all. "Have you talked to Peris and Fausto?"

Shay nodded. "They said we're all supposed to dress criminal. They've got an idea already, but it's secret."

"That's so bogus. Like *they* were such bad boys. All they ever did in the ugly days was sneak out and maybe cross the river a few times. They never even made it to the Smoke."

The song ended just then, and Tally's last word fell into sudden silence. She tried to think of what to say, but the conversation just faded out, like fireworks in a dark sky. The next song seemed to take a long time to start.

When it did, she was relieved and said, "Crim costumes should be easy, Shay-la. We're the two biggest criminals in town."

Shay and Tally tried for two hours, making the hole in the wall spit out costumes and trying them on. They thought of bandits, but didn't really know what one looked like—in all the old bandit movies in the wallscreen, the bad guys didn't look Crim, just retarded. Pirates were much better dressing, but Shay didn't want to wear a patch over one of her new eyeballs. Going as hunters was another idea, but the hole in the wall had this thing about guns, even fake ones. Tally thought of famous dictators from history, but most of them turned out to be men and fashion-missing.

"Maybe we should be Rusties!" Shay said. "In school, they were always the bad guys."

"But they mostly looked like us, I thought. Except ugly."

"I don't know, we could cut down trees or burn oil or something."

Tally laughed. "This is a costume, Shay-la, not a lifestyle."

Shay spread her arms and said more things, trying to be bubbly. "We could smoke tobacco? Or drive cars?"

But the hole in the wall wouldn't give them cigarettes or cars.

It was fun, though, hanging out with Shay and trying things on, then snorting and giggling and tossing the costumes back into the recycler. Tally loved seeing how she looked in new clothes, even silly ones. Part of her could still remember back before, when looking in the mirror had been painful, her eyes too close together and nose too small, hair frizzy all the time. Now it was like someone gorgeous stood across from Tally, following her every move—someone whose face was in perfect balance, whose skin glowed even with a total hangover, whose body was beautifully proportioned and muscled. Someone whose silvery eyes matched anything she wore.

But someone with bogus taste in costumes.

After two hours they were lying on the bed, which was spinning again.

"Everything sucks, Shay-la. Why does everything suck? They'll never vote me in if I can't even come up with a non-bogus costume."

Shay took her hand. "Don't worry, Tally-wa. You're already famous. There's no reason to be nervous."

"That's easy for you to say." Even though they'd been born on the same day, Shay had become pretty weeks and weeks before Tally. She'd been a full-fledged Crim for almost a month now.

"It's not going to be a problem," Shay said. "Anyone who used to hang out with Special Circumstances is a natural Crim."

A feeling went through Tally when Shay said that, like a ping, but hurting. "Still. I hate not being bubbly."

"It's Peris's and Fausto's fault for not telling us what they're wearing."

"Let's just wait till they get here. And copy them."

"They deserve it," Shay agreed. "Want a drink?"

"I think so."

Tally was too spinning to go anywhere, so Shay told the breakfast tray to go and get some champagne.

• • •

When Peris and Fausto came in, they were on fire.

It was really just sparklers wound into their hair and stuck onto their clothes, making safety flames flicker all over them. Fausto kept laughing because it tickled. They were both wearing bungee jackets—their costume was that they'd just jumped from the roof of a burning building.

"Fantastic!" Shay said.

"Hysterical," Tally agreed, but then asked, "but how is that Crim?"

"Don't you remember?" Peris said. "When you crashed a party last summer, and got away by stealing a bungee jacket and jumping off the roof? Best ugly trick in history!"

"Sure . . . but why are you on fire?" Tally asked. "I mean, it's not Crim if the building's really on fire."

Shay was giving Tally a look like she was saying something bogus again.

"We couldn't just wear bungee jackets," Fausto said. "Being on fire is much bubblier."

"Yeah," Peris said, but Tally could tell he saw what she meant, and was sad now. She wished she hadn't mentioned it. Stupid Tally. The costumes really were bubbly.

They put the sparklers out to save them for the party, and Shay told the hole in the wall to make two more jackets.

"Hey, that's copying!" Fausto complained, but it turned out not to matter. The hole wouldn't do costume bungee jackets, in case someone forgot and jumped off something and splatted. It couldn't make a real jacket; you had to ask Requisition for anything complicated or permanent. And Requisition wouldn't send any up because there wasn't a fire.

Shay snorted. "The mansion is being totally bogus today."

"So where'd you get those?" Tally asked.

"They're real." Peris smiled, fingering his jacket. "We stole them from the roof."

"So they *are* Crim," Tally said, and jumped off the bed to hug him.

With Peris in her arms, it didn't feel like the party was going to suck, or that anyone was going to vote against her. His big brown eyes beamed down into hers, and he lifted her up and squeezed her hard. She'd always felt this close to Peris back in ugly days, playing tricks and growing up together. It was bubbly to feel this way right now.

All those weeks that Tally had been lost in the wild, all she'd ever wanted was to be back here with Peris, pretty in New Pretty Town. It was totally stupid being unhappy today, or any day. Probably just too much champagne. "Best friends forever," she whispered to him, as he set her down.

"Hey, what's this thing?" Shay said. She was deep in Tally's closet, poking around for ideas. She held up a shapeless mass of wool.

"Oh, that." Tally let her arms fall from around Peris. "That's my sweater from the Smoke, remember?" The sweater looked strange, not like she remembered. It was messy, and you could see where human hands had knitted the different pieces together. People in the Smoke didn't have holes in the wall—they had to make their own things, and people, it turned out, weren't very good at making things.

"You didn't recycle it?"

"No. I think it's made of weird stuff. Like, the hole can't use it."

Shay held the sweater to her nose and inhaled. "Wow. It still smells like the Smoke. Campfires and that stew we always ate. Remember?"

Peris and Fausto went over to smell it. They'd never been out of the city, except for school trips to the Rusty Ruins. They certainly hadn't gotten as far as the Smoke, where everyone had to work all day making stuff, and growing (or even killing) their own food, and everyone stayed ugly after their sixteenth birthday. Ugly until they died, even.

Of course, the Smoke didn't exist anymore, thanks to Tally and Special Circumstances.

"Hey, I know, Tally!" Shay said. "Let's go as Smokies tonight!"

"That would be totally criminal!" Fausto said, his eyes full of admiration.

The three looked at Tally, all of them thrilled with the idea, and even though another nasty ping went through her, she knew it would be bogus not to agree. And that with a totally bubbly costume like a real-life Smokey sweater to wear, there was no way anyone would vote against her, because Tally Youngblood was a natural Crim.

BASH

The bash was in Valentino Mansion, the oldest building in New Pretty Town. It sprawled along the river only a few stories high, but was topped by a transmission tower visible halfway across the island. Inside, the walls were made of real stone, so the rooms couldn't talk, but the mansion had a long history of giant and fabulous bashes. The wait to become a Valentino resident was at least forever.

Peris, Fausto, Shay, and Tally walked down through the pleasure gardens, which were already bubbling with people headed to the bash. Tally saw an angel with beautiful feathered wings that must have been requisitioned *months* ago, which was so cheating, and a bunch of new pretties wearing fat-suits and masks that gave them triple chins. A mostly naked clique of Bashers were pretending to be pre-Rusties, building bonfires and drumming, establishing their own little satellite party, which was what Bashers always did.

Peris and Fausto kept arguing about exactly when to light themselves on fire again. They wanted to make an entrance but also save their sparklers for the other Crims. As they got closer to the mansion's noise and glimmer, Tally's nerves started to jump. The Smokey costumes didn't look like much. Tally wore her old sweater and Shay a copy, along with rough pants, knapsacks, and handmade-looking shoes that Tally had described to the hole in the wall, remembering someone wearing them in the Smoke. For unbathed authenticity they had rubbed dirt into their clothes and faces, which had seemed bubbly during the walk down, but now just felt dirty.

At the door were two Valentinos dressed up as wardens, making sure no one got inside without a costume. They stopped Fausto and Peris at first, but laughed when the two set themselves on fire, waving them through. They just shrugged at Shay and Tally, but let them in.

"Wait till the other Crims see us," Shay said. "They'll get it."

The four pushed through the crowds and into a total confusion of costumes. Tally saw snowmen, soldiers, thumbgame characters, and a whole Pretty Committee of scientists carrying facegraphs. Historical figures were everywhere in crazy clothes from all over the world, which reminded Tally how different from one another everyone used to look back when there were way too many people. A lot of the older new pretties were dressed in modern costumes: doctors, wardens, builders, or politicians—whatever they hoped to become after having the middle-pretty operation. A bunch of firefighters laughingly tried to extinguish Peris's and Fausto's flames, but only succeeded in annoying them.

"Where are they?" Shay kept asking, but the stone walls didn't answer. "This is so missing. How do people live here?"

"I think they carry handphones all the time," Fausto said. "We should have requed one."

The problem was that in Valentino Mansion you couldn't just call people by asking—the rooms were old and dumb, so it was like being outside. Tally placed one palm against the wall as they walked, liking how cool the ancient stones felt. For a moment, they reminded her of things out in the wild, rough and silent and unchanging. She wasn't really dying to find the other Crims; they'd all be looking at her and wondering how to vote.

They wandered the crowded hallways, peeking into rooms full of old-timey astronauts and explorers. Tally counted five Cleopatras and two Lillian Russells. There were even a few Rudolph Valentinos; it turned out the mansion was named after a natural pretty from back in the Rusty days.

Other cliques had organized theme costumes—teams of Jocks carrying hockey sticks and wobbly on hoverskates, Twisters as sick puppies wearing big cone-shaped plastic collars. And of course the Swarm was everywhere, all jabbering to one another on their interface rings. Swarmers had skintennas surged into them so they could call one another from anywhere, even inside Valentino Mansion's dumb walls. The other cliques always made fun of the

Swarm, who were afraid to go anywhere except in giant groups. They were all dressed as houseflies with big bug eyes, which at least was sense-making.

No other Crims appeared among the tumult of costumes, and Tally began to wonder if they'd all ditched the party rather than vote for her. Paranoid thoughts began to plague her, and she kept catching glimpses of someone lurking in the shadows, half-hidden by the crowds, but always there. Every time she turned around, though, the gray silk costume slipped out of sight.

Tally couldn't tell whether it was a boy or a girl. The figure wore a mask, scary but also beautiful, its cruel wolf eyes glinting in the low, flickering party lights. The plastic face jarred something in Tally, a painful memory that took a moment to gel.

Then she realized what the costume was supposed to be: an agent of Special Circumstances.

Tally leaned back against one of the cool stone walls, remembering the gray silk coveralls that Specials wore and the cruel pretty faces they were given. The sight made her head spin, which was the way Tally always felt when she thought back to her days in the wild.

Seeing the costume here in New Pretty Town didn't make any sense. Besides herself and Shay, hardly anyone had ever seen a Special. To most people they were just rumors and urban legends, blamed whenever anything weird happened. Specials kept themselves well hidden. Their job was to protect the city from outside threats, like soldiers and spies back in the days of the Rusties, but only total criminals like Tally Youngblood ever met them in person.

Still, someone had done a pretty good job on the costume. He or she must have seen a real Special at some point. But why was the figure *following her*? Every time Tally turned, it was there, moving with the terrible and predatory grace she remembered from being hunted through the ruins of the Smoke on that awful day when they had come to take her back to the city.

She shook her head. Thinking of those days always brought up bogus memories that didn't fit together. The Specials hadn't hunted Tally, of course. Why would they? They'd *rescued* her, bringing her home after she'd left the city to track down Shay. The thought of Specials always left her spinning, but that was just because their cruel faces were designed to freak you out, the same way that looking at regular pretties made you feel good.

Maybe the figure wasn't following her at all; maybe it was more than one person, some clique all dressed the same and spread out across the party, which made it feel like one of them was lurking her. That idea was a lot less crazy-making.

She caught up with the others, and joked with them as they searched for the rest of the Crims. But as Tally kept one eye out for figures in the shadows, she slowly became sure that it wasn't a clique. There was always exactly one, not talking to anybody, totally lurking. And the way the figure moved, so gracefully . . .

Tally told herself to calm down. Special Circumstances had no reason to follow her. And it made no sense for a Special to come to a costume party dressed as *a Special.*

She forced a laugh from herself. It was probably one of the other Crims playing a joke on her, one who'd heard Shay's and Tally's stories a hundred times and knew all about Special Circumstances.

If so, it would be totally bogus to go all brain-missing in front of everyone. Better to ignore the fake Special altogether.

Tally looked down at her own costume, and wondered if the Smokey clothes were helping to freak her out. Shay had been right: The smell of the old, handmade sweater brought back their time outside the city, days of backbreaking work and nights staying warm by the campfire, mingled with memories of the aging ugly faces that still brought her awake screaming sometimes.

Living in the Smoke had totally done a job on Tally's head.

No one else mentioned the figure. Were they all in on the joke? Fausto kept worrying that his sparklers were going to run out before any of the other Crims saw them. "Let's see if they're in one of the spires," he said.

"At least we can call them from a real building," Peris agreed.

Shay snorted and headed toward the nearest door. "Anything to get out of this bogus pile of rocks."

The party was spilling outside, anyway, expanding beyond the ancient stone walls. Shay led them toward a party spire at random, through a cluster of Hairdos with beehive wigs, each with its own swarm of bumblebees, which were really micro-lifters painted yellow and black in holding patterns around their heads.

"They didn't get the buzzing sound right," Fausto said, but Tally could tell he was impressed by the costumes. The sparklers in his hair were sputtering out, and people were looking at him like, *huh?*

From inside the party tower, Peris called Zane, who said the Crims were all right upstairs. "Good guess, Shay."

The four of them crammed into the elevator with a surgeon, a trilobite, and two drunken hockey players struggling to stay upright on hoverskates.

"Get that nervous look off your face, Tally-wa," said Shay, squeezing her shoulder. "You'll be in, no problem. Zane likes you."

Tally managed a smile, wondering if that was really true. Zane was always asking her about ugly days, but he did that with everyone, sucking up the Crims' stories with his gold-flecked eyes. Did he really think that Tally Youngblood was anything special?

It was clear that someone did—as the elevator doors closed, Tally glimpsed gray silk slipping gracefully through the crowd.

LURKER

Most of the other Crims had come as lumberjacks, dressed in plaid and grotesquely muscle-padded, holding big fake chainsaws and glasses of champagne. There were also butchers, a few smokers who'd made their own fake cigarettes, and a hangman with a long noose draped over her shoulder. Zane, who knew a lot about history, had come as some dictator's assistant who wasn't totally fashion-missing, all in tight black with a bubbly red armband. He'd done costume surge to make his lips thin and cheeks sunken, which made him look kind of like a Special.

They all laughed at Peris's costume, and tried to relight Fausto, but only managed to burn a few wisps of his hair, which was totally bogus-smelling. It took an anxious moment for them to figure out

Tally's and Shay's costumes, but soon the other Crims were crowding in to touch the rough fibers of the handmade sweater and asking if it was itchy. (It was, but Tally shook her head.)

Shay stood close to Zane and got him to notice her new eye surge.

"Think they're pretty-making?" she asked.

"I give them fifty milli-Helens," he said.

This went totally missing on everyone.

"A milli-Helen is enough beauty to launch exactly one ship," Zane explained, and the older Crims all laughed. "Fifty's pretty good."

Shay smiled, Zane's praise lighting her face up like champagne.

Tally tried to be bubbly, but the thought of the costumed Special lurking her was too dizzy-making. After a few minutes, she escaped onto the party spire's balcony to fill her lungs with cold, fresh air.

A few hot-air balloons were tethered to the spire, hovering like huge black moons in the sky. The Hot-airs riding in one gondola were shooting roman candles at the others, laughing as the safety flames roared across the darkness. Then one of the balloons began to rise, the roar of its burner audible above the party noise, its tether dropping to slap against the spire. It lifted on a tiny finger of flame, finally disappearing into the distance. If Shay hadn't introduced her to the Crims, Tally figured she would have been a Hot-air. They were always drifting off into the night and landing at random places, calling a hovercar to pick them up from some distant suburb or even past the city limits.

Staring out over the river toward the darkness of Uglyville made Tally's brain much less spinning. It was strange. Her time in the wild was so fuzzy, but Tally could perfectly remember being a young ugly, watching the lights of New Pretty Town from her dorm window and dying to turn sixteen. She had always imagined herself here on this side, in some high tower, with fireworks going off around her, surrounded by pretties and pretty herself.

Of course, the Tally of those fantasies had usually been wearing a ball gown—not a woolen sweater and work pants, her face smeared with dirt. She fingered a thread working its way free of the weave, wishing that Shay hadn't found the sweater tonight. Tally wanted to leave the Smoke behind, to escape all the tangled memories of running and hiding and feeling like a betrayer. She hated glancing every minute at the elevator door, wondering if the costumed Special had followed her up here. She wanted to feel totally belonging somewhere, not waiting for the next disaster to strike.

Maybe what Shay kept saying was right, and tonight's vote would fix all that. The Crims were one of the tightest cliques in New Pretty Town. You had to be voted in, and once you were a Crim, you could always depend on friends and parties and bubbly conversation. No more running for Tally.

The only catch was, no one could join who hadn't been totally tricky in their ugly days, with good stories to tell about sneaking out and hoverboarding all night and running away. Crims were pretties who hadn't forgotten being uglies, who still enjoyed the practical jokes and criminal tricks that made Uglyville, in its own way, bubbly.

"What would you give the view?" It was Zane, suddenly next to her, looking all of his two-meter maximum pretty height in the ancient black uniform.

"Give it?"

"A hundred milli-Helens? Five hundred? Maybe a whole Helen?"

Tally took a steadying breath, looking down at the dark river. "I'd give it none. It's Uglyville, after all."

Zane chuckled. "Now, Tally-wa, there's no reason to be nasty about our ugly little brothers and sisters. It's not their fault they aren't as pretty as you." He pushed a stray lock of Tally's hair back around her ear.

"Not them, the place. Uglyville is a prison." The words felt wrong in her mouth, too serious for a bash.

But Zane didn't seem to mind. "You escaped, didn't you?" He stroked the sweater's strange fibers, like the rest of them kept doing. "Was the Smoke any better?"

Tally wondered if he wanted a real answer. She was nervous about saying something bogus. If Zane thought Tally was missing, vetoes would rain down no matter what Shay and Peris had promised.

She looked up into his eyes. They were a shimmering metallic gold, reflecting the fireworks like tiny mirrors, and something behind them seemed to pull at Tally. Not just the usual pretty magic, but something that felt serious, as if the bash around them had disappeared. Zane always listened raptly to her Smoke stories. He'd heard them all by now, but maybe there was something more he wanted to know.

"I left the night before my sixteenth birthday," she said. "So I wasn't exactly escaping Uglyville."

"That's right." Zane released her from his gaze and looked out across the river. "You were running from the operation."

"I was following Shay. I had to stay ugly to find her."

"To rescue her," he said, then trained his golden eyes on her again. "Was that really it?"

Tally nodded carefully, last night's champagne spinning her head. Or maybe tonight's. She looked at the empty glass in her hand and wondered how many she'd had.

"It was just a thing I had to do." As she said the words, Tally knew that they sounded bogus.

"A special circumstance?" Zane asked, his smile wry.

Tally's eyebrows lifted. She wondered what tricks Zane had pulled back when he was an ugly. He didn't tell that many stories himself. Though he wasn't that much older than her, Zane never seemed to have to prove that he was a real Crim, he just was.

Even with his lips thinned by costume surge, he was beautiful. His face had been sculpted into more extreme shapes than most, as if the doctors had wanted to push the Pretty Committee's specs to the limit. His cheekbones were as sharp as arrowheads underneath his flesh, and his eyebrows arched absurdly high when he was amused. Tally saw with sudden clarity that if any of his features were shifted a few millimeters he would look terrible, and yet at the same time it was impossible to imagine that he had ever been an ugly.

"Did you ever go to the Rusty Ruins?" she asked. "Back when you were . . . young?"

"Almost every night, last winter."

"In *winter*?"

"I love the ruins covered with snow," he said. "It makes the edges softer, adding mega-Helens to the view."

"Oh." Tally remembered traveling across the wild in early autumn, how cold it had been. "Sounds totally . . . freezing."

"I could never get anyone else to come with me." His eyes narrowed. "When you talk about the ruins, you never mention meeting anyone there."

"Meeting someone?" Tally closed her eyes, finding herself suddenly balance-missing. She leaned against the balcony rail and took a deep breath.

"Yeah," he said. "Did you ever?"

The empty champagne glass slipped from her hand and tumbled into the blackness.

"Look out below," Zane murmured, a smile on his lips.

A tinkling crash rose up from the darkness, surprised laughter spreading from it like ripples from a stone in water. It sounded a thousand kilometers away.

Tally took in more breaths of the cold night air, trying to regain her composure. Her stomach was doing flip-flops. It was so shaming to be like this, about to throw breakfast after a few lousy glasses of champagne.

"It's okay, Tally," Zane whispered. "Just let yourself be bubbly."

Tally realized how bogus that was, having to be *told* to stay bubbly. But even through his costume surge, Zane's gaze had softened, as if he really did want her to relax.

She turned away from the drop into emptiness, gripping the guardrail with both hands behind her. Shay and Peris were also out on the balcony now; she was surrounded by all her new Crim friends, protected and part of the group. But they were watching her carefully too. Maybe everyone was expecting something special from her tonight.

"I never saw anyone out there," Tally said. "Someone was supposed to come, but never did."

She didn't hear Zane's response.

The lurker had appeared again—across the crowded spire, standing still and staring straight at her. The mask's flashing eyes seemed to acknowledge her gaze for a moment, then the figure turned and slipped among the white coats of the costumed Pretty Committee, disappearing behind their giant facegraphs of every major pretty type. And even though Tally realized it was a bogus thing to do, she pushed away from Zane and through the crowd, because there was no way she could pull herself together tonight until she found out who this person was, Crim or Special or random new pretty. She had to know why someone was throwing Special Circumstances in her face.

Tally dodged between white coats and bounced like a pinball through a clique all dressed in fat-suits, their softly padded bellies spinning her in circles. She bowled over most of a hockey team, who wobbled on their slippy hoverskates like littlies. Glimpses of gray silk teased Tally from just ahead as she ran, but the crowd was thick and in frantic motion, and by the time she reached the central column of the spire, the figure had disappeared.

Glancing at the lights above the elevator door, she saw that it was on its way up, not down. The fake Special was still around, somewhere in the spire.

Then Tally noticed the door to the emergency stairs, bright red and plastered with warnings that an alarm would sound if you opened it. She looked around again—still no gray figure. Whoever it was *had* to have escaped down the stairs. Alarms could be switched off; she'd pulled that trick herself a million times as an ugly.

Tally reached out toward the door, her hand shaking. If a siren started blaring, everyone would be staring at her and whispering as the wardens arrived and evacuated the tower. It would be a really bubbly end to her career as a Crim.

Some Crim, she thought. She'd be a pretty bogus criminal if she couldn't set off an alarm every once in a while.

She pushed the door open. It didn't make a sound.

Tally stepped into the stairwell. The door closed behind her, muffling the tumult of the party. In the sudden quiet, she could feel her heart pounding in her chest and hear her own breath, still ragged from the chase. The beat of the music seemed to leak under the door, making the concrete floor shudder.

The figure sat on the stairs, a few steps up. "You made it." It was a boy's voice, indistinct behind the mask.

"Made it where? This party?"

"No, Tally. Through the door."

"It wasn't exactly locked." She tried to stare her way through the jeweled eyes of the mask. "Who are you?"

"You don't recognize me?" He sounded genuinely puzzled, as if he were an old friend, someone who wore a mask all the time. "What do I look like?"

Tally swallowed and said softly, "Special Circumstances."

"Good. You remember." Tally could hear the smile in his voice. He was talking slowly and carefully, as if she were some kind of idiot.

"Of course I remember. Are you one of them? Do I know you?" Tally couldn't recall any individual Specials; in her memory, their faces all ran together into one cruel and pretty blur.

"Why don't you take a look?" The figure didn't move to take off his mask. "Go ahead, Tally."

Suddenly, she realized what was going on here. Recognizing what the costume meant, chasing him across the party, braving the alarmed door—all of it had been a test. Some kind of recruitment. He was sitting there wondering if she would dare pull off his mask.

Tally was sick of tests. "Just stay away from me," she said.

"Tally—"

"I don't want to work for Special Circumstances. I just want to live here in New Pretty Town."

"I'm not—"

"Leave me alone!" she shouted, clenching her fists. The cry echoed off the concrete walls, leaving a moment of silence, as if it had surprised them both. The music from the party drifted through the stairwell, muffled and timid.

Finally, a sigh came through the mask, and he held up a crude leather pouch. "I have something for you. If you're ready for it. Do you want it, Tally?"

"I don't want anything from . . ." Tally's voice trailed off. Soft shuffling sounds came from below them. Not the party. Someone was coming up the stairs.

The two of them moved at the same time, peering over the handrail down the narrow stairwell shaft. A long way down, Tally saw flashes of gray silk and hands grasping the rails, half a dozen people climbing the stairs incredibly fast, their footsteps barely audible over the muffled music.

"See you later," the figure said, standing.

Tally blinked. He pushed her aside, spooked by the sight of real Specials. So who was he? Before his fingers reached the doorknob, Tally snatched the mask from his face.

He was an ugly. A *real* ugly.

His face was nothing like the costumed fatties done up for the bash, with their big noses or squinty eyes. It wasn't just exaggerated features that made him different; it was everything, as if he were made of some utterly different substance. In those seconds, Tally's pretty-perfect eyesight caught every gaping pore, the random tangles in his hair, the crude imbalance of his disjointed face. Her skin crawled at his imperfections, the tufts of teenage beard, his unsurged teeth, the eruptions on his forehead screaming out disease. She wanted to pull away, to put distance between herself and his unlucky, unclean, unhealthy *ugliness.*

But somehow she knew his name. . . .

"Croy?" she said.

FALL

"Later, Tally," Croy said, snatching back his mask. He yanked open the door, and the noise of the party rushed into the stairwell as he darted through, the gray silk of his costume disappearing into the crowd.

Tally just stood there as the door swung closed again, too stunned to move. Like her old sweater, she'd remembered ugliness all wrong: Croy's face was much worse than her mental image of the Smokies. His crooked smile, his dull eyes, the way his sweating skin carried angry red marks where the mask had pressed against it . . .

But then the door slammed itself shut, and among the echoes Tally heard the footsteps still climbing toward her, real Specials on their way up, and for the first time all day, a clear thought went through her head.

Run.

She pulled open the door and plunged into the crowd.

The elevator was just spilling open, and Tally stumbled into a clique of Naturals plastered with brittle leaves, walking last days of autumn who shed yellows and reds as she shoved through them. She managed to keep her footing—the floor was sticky with spilled champagne—and caught another glimpse of the gray silk.

Croy was headed toward the balcony and the Crims.

She tore after him. Tally didn't want anyone lurking her, panicking her at parties, tangling her memories when she needed to be bubbly. She had to catch Croy and tell him never to follow her again.

This wasn't Uglyville or the Smoke—he had no right to be here. He had no business stepping out of her ugly past.

And there was another reason she was running: the Specials. It had only taken a glimpse of them to put every cell in her body on high alert. Their inhuman speed repelled her, like watching a cockroach skitter across a plate. Croy's movements might have seemed unusual, his Smokey confidence standing out in a party full of new pretties, but the Specials were another species altogether.

Tally burst out onto the balcony just in time to see Croy leap up onto the rail, waving his arms for a precarious moment. Then he got his balance, bent his knees, and pushed off into the night.

She ran to the spot and leaned over. Croy was tumbling downward out of sight, his form swallowed by the darkness below.

After a sickening moment he reappeared, head over heels, gray silk catching the light of fireworks as he hoverbounced toward the river.

Zane stood beside her, looking down. "Hmm, the invitation didn't say 'bungee jackets required,'" he murmured. "Who was that, Tally?"

She opened her mouth, but an alarm began to howl.

Tally spun around and saw the crowd parting. The group of Specials were pouring through the stairwell door, slicing their way through confused new pretties. Their cruel faces weren't costumes any more than Croy's ugliness had been, and they were just as shocking to look at. The wolflike eyes sent a chill through Tally, and their advance, as purposeful and dangerous as a hunting cat's, made her body scream to keep running.

At the other end of the balcony she saw Peris, standing frozen next to the rail, awestruck by the spectacle. His safety sparklers were sputtering out at last, but the light on his bungee jacket collar glowed bright green.

Tally pushed toward him through the other Crims, judging the angles, knowing exactly when to jump. For a moment, the world became strangely clear, as if the sight of Croy's ugliness and the cruel-pretty Specials had removed some barrier between her and the world. Everything was bright and harsh, the details so sharp that Tally squinted as if dashing into a freezing wind.

She hit Peris just right, her arms wrapping around his shoulders, her momentum lifting both of them up and over the balcony railing. They tumbled out of the light and into blackness, Peris's costume flaring up one last time in the wind of their descent, the safety sparks bouncing from her face as cool as snowflakes.

He was half-screaming and half-laughing, as if enduring an annoying but invigorating practical joke—cold water over the head.

Halfway down it occurred to Tally that the bungee jacket might not catch them both.

She squeezed harder, and heard Peris grunt as the lifters kicked in. The jacket pulled him upright, almost wrenching Tally's shoulders from their sockets. Her muscles were still powerful from their weeks of manual labor in the Smoke—if anything, the operation had tuned them up—but she barely kept her grip as the jacket absorbed the velocity of their fall. Her arms slipped farther down until they were wrapped around Peris's waist, her fingers painfully entangled in the jacket's straps.

As they came to a shuddering halt, Tally's feet brushed the grass, and she let go.

Peris shot back up into the air, his knee catching Tally's brow and sending her staggering back into the darkness. She lost her footing, landing on a drift of fallen leaves that crunched beneath her.

For a moment Tally lay still. The pile of leaves smelled softly of earth and rot, like something old and tired. She blinked as something trickled into one eye. Maybe it was raining.

She looked up at the party tower and the distant hot-air balloons, blinking and catching her breath. She could make out a few figures peering down from the bright balcony ten stories above. Tally wondered if any of them were Specials.

Peris was nowhere to be seen. She remembered bungee jumping as an ugly, how a jacket would carry you down a slope. He must have bounced down toward the river after Croy.

Croy. She wanted to say something to him. . . .

Tally struggled to her feet and faced the river. Her head throbbed, but the clarity that had come over her as she'd thrown herself off the balcony hadn't faded. Her heart pounded as a burst of fireworks lit the sky, casting pink light and sudden shadows through the trees, every blade of grass in sharp relief.

Everything felt very real: her intense revulsion at Croy's ugly face, her fear of the Specials, the shapes and smells around her. It felt as if a thin plastic film had been peeled from her eyes, leaving the world with razored edges.

She ran downhill, toward the mirrored band of the river and the darkness of Uglyville. "Croy!" she cried.

The pink flower in the sky faded, and Tally tripped over the winding roots of an old tree. She stumbled to a halt.

Something was gliding up out of the darkness.

"Croy?" The fireworks had left green spots scattered across her vision.

"You don't give up, do you?"

He was on a hoverboard a meter off the ground, feet spread for balance, looking comfortable. His gray silks had been replaced with pitch-black, his cruel pretty mask discarded. Behind him, two other black-clad figures rode, younger uglies wearing dorm uniforms and nervous looks.

"I wanted . . ." Her voice trailed off. She'd followed him

to say, *Go away, leave me alone, never come back.* To scream it at him. But everything had become so clear and intense . . . what she wanted now was to hold on to this bright focus. Croy's invasion of her world was a part of that, she somehow knew.

"Croy, they're coming," one of the younger uglies said.

"What did you want, Tally?" he asked calmly.

She blinked, uncertain, worried that if she said the wrong thing, the clarity might go away—the barrier would close again.

She remembered what he'd offered in the stairwell. "You had something to give me?"

He smiled, and pulled the old leather pouch from his belt. "This? Yeah, I think you're ready for it. Only one problem: You'd better not take it from me right now. Wardens are coming. Maybe Specials."

"Yeah, in about ten seconds," the nervous ugly complained.

Croy ignored him. "But we'll leave it for you at Valentino 317. Can you remember that? Valentino 317."

She nodded, then blinked again. Her head felt light.

Croy frowned. "I hope so." He spun his board around in one graceful movement, and the other two uglies followed suit. "Later. And sorry about your eye."

They darted away toward the river, veering off in three different directions as they disappeared into the darkness.

"Sorry about my what?" she asked softly.

Then Tally found herself blinking again, her vision blurring. She reached up to touch her forehead. Her fingers came away sticky, and more dark blotches dripped into her palm as she stared at it dumbfounded.

She finally felt the pain, her head throbbing in time with her heartbeat. The collision with Peris's knee must have opened up her forehead. Her fingers traced a line of blood that dripped around her brow and down one cheek, as hot as tears.

Tally sat down on the grass, suddenly shaking all over.

Fireworks lit the sky again, turning the blood on her hand bright red, each drop a little mirror reflecting the explosion overhead. There were hovercars in the sky now, lots of them.

Tally felt something slipping away as she bled, something she'd wanted to keep hold of . . .

"Tally!"

Looking up, she saw Peris, chuckling as he climbed the hill.

"Now that was *not* a bubbly move, Tally-wa. I almost wound up in the river!" He mimed drowning, grasping at water and slipping under.

She found herself giggling at his performance, her weird shakiness turning bubbly now that Peris was here. "What's the matter? Can't you swim?"

He laughed and sank to the grass beside her, fighting with the straps of the bungee jacket. "I'm not dressed for it." He rubbed one shoulder. "Also . . . *ow* on the clinginess."

Tally tried to remember why jumping off the tower had seemed like such a good idea, but the sight of her own blood had left her brain-missing, and she just wanted to sleep. Everything was harsh and shiny. "Sorry."

"Just warn me next time." Fireworks exploded overhead, and Peris squinted at her, his face beautifully puzzled. "What's with the blood?"

"Oh, yeah. Your knee whacked into me when you bounced. Isn't it bogus?"

"Not very pretty-making." He reached out and squeezed her arm softly. "Don't worry, Tally. I'll ping a warden car. There's tons out tonight."

But one was already coming. It passed silently overhead, running lights casting a red tinge on the grass around them. A spotlight picked them out. Tally sighed, letting the uncomfortable shininess of everything slip away. She realized now why it had been such a bogus day. She'd been trying way too hard, worrying about how the Crims would vote and what to wear, more serious than bubbly. No wonder the party-crashers had driven her over the edge.

She giggled. Literally over the edge.

But everything was okay now. With the uglies and cruel pretties gone and Peris here to take care of her, a restful feeling settled over Tally. Funny how that kick to the head had left her brain-missing for a moment, actually talking to those uglies like they mattered.

The hovercar landed nearby, and two wardens jumped out and headed over, one with a first-aid kit in hand. Maybe while they were fixing her head, Tally thought, she could get some eye surge like Shay's. Not exactly the same, which would be bogus, but sort of matching.

She looked up into the wardens' middle-pretty faces, calm and wise and knowing what to do. The look of concern on their faces made the blood all over her face feel less shaming.

They gently led her to the car and sprayed new skin onto the wound, giving her a pill to stop the swelling. When she asked about bruises, they laughed and said the operation took care of that. No more bruises ever.

Because it was a head wound, they gave Tally a neural exam, waving a glowing red pointer back and forth while they tracked her eyemouse. The test seemed pretty retarded, but the wardens said it proved she didn't have a concussion or brain damage. Peris told a story about when he'd walked into a glass door at Lillian Russell Mansion and had to stay awake or die, and they all laughed.

Then the wardens asked a few questions about the tricking uglies who'd come across the river that night and caused all the trouble. "Did you know any of them?"

Tally sighed, not really wanting to get into it. It was totally shaming to be the cause of the uglies' party-crashing. But it was middle pretties asking, and you couldn't blow them off. They always knew what they were doing, and it would be bogus to tell a lie straight to their calm, authoritative faces.

"Yeah. I kind of remembered one of them. Croy."

"He was from the Smoke, wasn't he, Tally?"

She nodded, feeling stupid wearing the Smokey sweater with dirt and blood all over it. It was all Valentino Mansion's fault for switching the dress code: There was nothing more bogus than still being in a costume after you'd left a party.

"Do you know what he wanted, Tally? Why he was here?"

She looked at Peris for help. He was hanging on every word, his luminous eyes bugging wide. It made her feel important.

She shrugged. "Just ugly tricks, that's all. Showing off in front of his friends, probably." Which sounded bogus. Croy didn't live in Uglyville, after all. He was a Smokey, from out in the wild between cities. The two with him might have been city kids just tricking, but Croy had definitely had a plan.

But the wardens only smiled and nodded, believing her. "Don't worry, it won't happen again. We'll be keeping an eye on you to make sure it doesn't."

She smiled back at them, and they took her home.

When Tally made it to her room, there was a ping from Peris, who'd gone back to the party.

"Guess what?" he yelled. Crowd sounds and music bled in around the words, making Tally wish she'd gone back to the bash, even with sprayed-on skin all over her forehead.

She frowned and flopped onto her bed as the message continued: "When I got back, the Crims had already voted! They thought it was totally bubbly that real-life Specials were at the party, and our dive off the tower got *six hundred* milli-Helens from Zane! You are so Crim! See you tomorrow. Oh yeah, and don't get that scar erased until everyone's seen it. Best friends forever!"

As the message ended, Tally felt the bed spin a little. She closed her eyes and let out a long, slow sigh of relief. Finally, she was a full-fledged Crim. Everything she'd ever wanted had come to her at last. She was beautiful, and she lived in New Pretty Town with Peris and Shay and tons of new friends. All the disasters and terrors of the last year—running away to the Smoke, living there in pre-Rusty squalor, traveling back to the city through the wilds—somehow all of it had worked out.

It was so wonderful, and Tally was so exhausted, that belief took a while to settle over her. She replayed Peris's message a few times, then pulled off the smelly Smokey sweater with shaking hands and threw it into the corner. Tomorrow, she would *make* the hole in the wall recycle it.

Tally lay back and stared at the ceiling for a while. A ping from Shay came, but she ignored it, setting her interface ring to sleep-time. With everything so perfect, reality seemed somehow fragile, as if the slightest interruption could imperil her pretty future. The bed beneath her, Komachi Mansion, and even the city around her—all of it felt as tenuous as a soap bubble, shivering and empty.

It was probably just the knock to her head causing the weird missingness that underlay her joy. She only needed a good night's sleep—and hopefully no hangover tomorrow—and everything would feel solid again, as perfect as it really was.

Tally fell asleep a few minutes later, happy to be a Crim at last.

But her dreams were totally bogus.

ZANE

So, there was this beautiful princess.

She was locked in a high tower, one with stone walls and cold, empty rooms that couldn't talk. There was no elevator or even fire stairs, so Tally wondered how the princess had gotten up there.

But there she was, at the top. No bungee jacket and fast asleep.

The tower was guarded by a dragon. It had jeweled eyes and hungry, cruel features, and moved with a brutal suddenness that made Tally's stomach churn. Even dreaming, she recognized exactly what the dragon was. It was a cruel pretty, an agent of Special Circumstances, or maybe a bunch of them all rolled up into one gray and silk-scaled serpent.

And you couldn't have this dream without a prince.

He made it past the dragon, not so much slaying as creeping, finding chinks in the ancient stone wall to slip his fingers into, because it was old and crumbling. He climbed the tower's daunting height easily, sparing only an amused look down at the dragon, which had been distracted by a host of playful rats scurrying through its claws.

The prince made it in through the high stone window and swept the princess into a kiss, which woke her up, and that was the whole story. Getting back down and past the dragon didn't turn out to be an issue, because this was a dream and not a movie or even a fairy tale, and it was all over with one big kiss, a classic happy ending.

Except for one thing.

The prince was totally ugly.

Tally woke up with a throbbing head.

Catching her reflection in the mirror wall, she remembered that the headache wasn't just a hangover. And discovered that getting kicked in the head was not pretty-making. As the wardens last night had warned might happen, the sprayed-on skin above her eye had turned an angry red. She'd have to go to a surge office to get the scar completely erased.

But Tally decided not to fix it yet. Like Peris had said, it did look really criminal. She smiled, remembering her new status. The scar was perfect.

There was a mountain of pings from other Crims, drunken congratulations and reports of more wild behavior as the party had gone on (though nothing as bubbly as her dive off the tower with Peris). Tally listened to the messages with eyes closed, sinking into the crowd noises in the background, loving how connected she was to the others even though she'd come home early. That's what being voted into a clique meant: knowing you had friends whatever you did.

Zane had left three messages in all, the last one asking if Tally wanted to have breakfast this morning. He didn't sound as drunk as the rest of them, so maybe he was already awake.

When she pinged him, he answered. "How are you?"

"Face-missing," she said. "Did Peris tell you how my head got bonked?"

"Yeah. You were actually bleeding?"

"Very."

"Whoa." Zane's voice was breathy in her ear, his usual cool overwhelmed. "Nice dive, though. Glad you didn't . . . you know, die."

Tally smiled. "Thanks."

"So, did you read the weirdness about the party?"

There'd been a news-ping among Tally's messages, but she hadn't felt up to reading. "What weirdness?"

"Someone hacked the mail yesterday and sent out that new invitation, the one that changed the dress code to costumes. Everyone on the Valentino Bash Committee thought it was someone else who'd done it, so they all just went along. But nobody knows who actually wrote it. Dizzying, huh?"

Tally blinked, the room suddenly out of focus. Dizzying was right. The world seemed to turn around her, as if she were inside the stomach of something big and out of control. Only uglies did stuff like hack mail. And she could only think of one person who would want the Valentino party turned into a costume bash: Croy with his cruel-pretty mask and weird offers.

Which meant it all had to do with Tally Youngblood.

"That is deeply bogus, Zane."

"Totally. You hungry?"

She nodded, feeling her head begin to throb again. Out the window, the Garbo Mansion party towers rose up, tall and spindly. Tally stared at them, as if fixing her gaze could make the world less spinning. She had to be overreacting; everything wasn't about her, after all. It could have just been pointlessly tricking uglies, or someone on the Valentino Bash Committee going brain-missing.

But even if it had been simply a mistake, Croy had to have been ready with that costume. In the Rusty Ruins and wilderness where Smokies hid, there weren't any holes in the wall; you had to make your own things, which took time and effort. And Croy hadn't chosen just any costume. . . . Tally remembered the cold, jeweled eyes and felt faint.

Maybe food would fix her.

"Yeah, deeply hungry. Let's have breakfast."

They met in Denzel Park, a pleasure garden that snaked from the center of New Pretty Town down to Valentino Mansion. The mansion itself was hidden by trees, but the transmission tower on top was visible, the old-fashioned Valentino flag whipping in the cold wind. In the garden, the damage from the night before was mostly cleared up, except for a few blackened patches left by the Bashers' bonfires. A maintenance robot hovered above one circle of ashes, turning the soil over with careful movements of its claws, spraying seeds into the scorched earth.

Zane's suggestion of a picnic had raised Tally's eyebrows (a motion that was totally *ouch*), but walking down in the fresh air did help clear her head. The pills the wardens had given her muted the pain of her wound, but had no effect on her general fuzziness. The rumor in New Pretty Town was that doctors knew how to fix hangovers, but kept the cure a secret on principle.

Zane arrived on time, breakfast bobbing softly behind him in the cool breeze. As he grew near, his eyes widened at the scar on her forehead. One of his hands reached out, almost as if he wanted to touch it.

"Pretty bogus, huh?" she said.

"Totally criminal-looking," he said, still wide-eyed.

"Not so many milli-Helens, though, is it?"

He looked thoughtful for a moment. "I wouldn't measure it in Helens. I'm not quite sure what I'd use instead, though. Something bubblier."

Tally smiled: Peris had been right about not fixing her face right away. In his fascination with the scar, Zane was extra beautiful, and his expression gave her a tingly feeling—like being at the center of everything, but without the spinning.

Zane's costume surge had worn off; his lips returned to normal pretty fullness. Still, he always looked extreme in daylight. His face was all contrasts, his chin and cheekbones sharp, his forehead high.

His skin was the same olive as everyone's, but in the sun, against his dark hair, it somehow looked pale. The operation guidelines wouldn't let you have jet-black hair, which the Committee thought was too extreme, but Zane dyed his with calligraphy ink. On top of that, he didn't eat much, keeping his face gaunt, his stare intense. Of all the pretties Tally had met since her operation, he was the only one whose looks really stood out.

Maybe that was why he was the head Crim—you had to be different from everyone else to really be a criminal. His gold eyes flickered as they searched for a spot, coming to rest in the dappled shadow of a broad oak tree.

They sat down on the grass and leaves, and Tally breathed in the scent of dew and earth. Breakfast settled between them, giving off warmth from the glowing elements that kept the scrambled eggs and hash browns from going cold and slimy.

Tally piled up a heated plate with eggs and cheese and slices of avocado, and shoved half a muffin into her mouth. Looking up at Zane, she saw that he held nothing but a cup of coffee, and she wondered if eating like a greedy pig was a bogus move.

But what did it matter? She was a Crim now, she reminded herself, all voted on and full-fledged. And Zane had asked her here, after all, wanting to hang out. It was time to stop worrying about being accepted and start enjoying herself. There were worse things than sitting in a perfect park, being closely watched by a beautiful boy.

Tally consumed the rest of the muffin, which was totally steaming inside and marbled with half-melted chocolate, and picked up her fork to attack the eggs. She hoped that the breakfast had some calorie-purgers packed with it. They worked better if you took them right after eating, and she was going to eat a lot. Maybe losing blood made you starving.

"So last night, who was that guy?" Zane asked.

Still chewing, Tally only shrugged, but he waited patiently for her to swallow.

"Just some crashing ugly," she finally said.

"Figured that. Who else would Specials be chasing? I mean, was he someone you knew?"

Tally looked away. It was embarrassing to have your ugly life follow you across the river, at least in person. But Peris had heard her telling the wardens about it last night, so lying to Zane would be bogus. "Yeah, I guess I knew him. From the Smoke. This guy called Croy."

An odd look passed over Zane's face. His gold eyes stared into the distance, searching for something. A moment later, he nodded. "I knew him too."

Tally froze, her fork halfway to her mouth. "You're kidding."

Zane shook his head.

"But I thought you never ran away," Tally said.

"No, I didn't." He pulled up his legs and hugged his knees with one long arm, taking a sip of coffee. "Not any farther than the Rusty Ruins, anyway. But Croy and I were friends back when we were littlies, and we lived in the same ugly dorm."

"That's . . . funny." Tally finally took the bite of eggs, chewing them slowly. The city had a million people in it, and Zane had known Croy. "What are the odds of that?" she said softly.

Zane shook his head again. "Not a coincidence, Tally-wa."

Tally stopped chewing, the eggs tasting funny in her mouth, like everything was going to get all spinning again. The world had gone totally missing on coincidences lately.

"How do you mean?"

Zane leaned forward. "Tally, you know that Shay lived in my dorm, right? Back when we were uglies?"

"Sure," she said. "That's how she hooked up with you guys after coming here." Tally paused a moment, then felt a realization starting to fall slowly into place. Memories from the Smoke always came back at a brain-missing pace, like bubbles rising up through some thick, viscous liquid.

"Out in the Smoke," she said carefully, "Shay introduced me to Croy. They were old friends. So you three all knew one another?"

"Yeah, we did." Zane grimaced, as if something rotten had crawled into his coffee.

Tally looked down at her food unhappily. As Zane continued, it was just like the night before, the whole bogus story of the past summer pushing uncomfortably back into her head.

"There were six of us in my dorm," he said. "We called ourselves Crims back then, too. We did all the usual ugly tricks: sneaking out at night, hacking the dorm minders, coming across the river to spy on new pretties."

Tally nodded, remembering Shay's stories about before the two of them had met. "And going out to the Rusty Ruins?"

"Yeah, after some older uglies showed us how." He looked up the hill at the towering center of New Pretty Town. "Being out there makes you realize how big the world is. I mean, twenty million people used to live in that old Rusty city. Compared with that, this place is tiny."

Tally closed her eyes and put her fork onto her plate, her appetite fading. After everything that had happened last night, maybe breakfast with Zane hadn't been such a good idea. Sometimes he seemed to think he was still an ugly, trying to stay bubbly, pushing back against the easy fun of being pretty. That was why he was great at leading the Crims, of course. But one-on-one, he could be dizzy-making.

"Yeah, but the Rusties all died," she said quietly. "There were too many of them, and they were totally stupid."

"I know, I know. They almost destroyed the world," he recited, then sighed. "But sneaking out to the ruins was the most exciting thing I'd ever done."

Zane's eyes flashed as he said this, and Tally remembered her own trips to the ruins, how the empty majesty of the ghost-city had kept every nerve in her body on high alert. The feeling that real danger might be lurking out there, unlike the harmless thrill of a hot-air ascent or a bungee jump.

She shivered, recalling some of that old excitement as she met Zane's stare. "I know what you mean."

"And I knew I'd never go there again after the operation. New pretties don't do anything that tricky. So when I got close to turning sixteen, I started thinking about leaving the city, going into the wilderness. At least for a while."

Tally nodded slowly. She remembered Shay saying the same

things back when they'd met, the words that had started her down the path to the Smoke. "And you talked Shay and Croy and the rest of them into coming along?"

"I tried." He laughed. "At first they thought I was crazy, because you can't live in the wild. But then we met this guy out there who—"

"Stop," Tally said. Suddenly her heart was beating fast, like when you took a purger and your metabolism kicked up to burn the calories. She felt a dampness on her face, the breeze suddenly cold. She felt moisture on her cheeks, but pretty faces didn't sweat. . . .

Tally blinked, her fists clenching until fingernails drove into her palms. The world had changed somehow. Pinpoints of sunlight cut harshly through the leaves overhead as she tried to take deep, slow breaths. She remembered now that the same thing had happened last night, when she'd seen Croy.

"Tally?" Zane said.

She shook her head, not wanting him to say anything. Not about meeting someone in the Rusty Ruins. She found herself speaking quickly to keep him quiet, repeating what Shay had told her. "You heard about the Smoke, right? Where people lived like pre-Rusties and were ugly for life. So you all decided to go there. But when the time came to run, most of you chickened out. Shay told me about that night: She was all packed and everything, but in the end she got too scared to go."

Zane nodded, looking down into his coffee.

"So you bailed too, didn't you?" Tally said. "You were supposed to run away that time?"

"Yeah," he said flatly. "I didn't go, even though the whole thing was my idea. And I became pretty, right on schedule."

Tally looked away, unable to keep herself from remembering that summer. Shay's friends had all run off to the Smoke or turned pretty, leaving her alone in Uglyville. That's when she and Tally had met, becoming best friends. And when Shay's second attempt at running away had succeeded, Tally had been sucked into the whole mess.

She let out a slow breath, telling herself to calm down. Last summer might have been a nightmare, but it was also why she was a Crim now, and not just some boring brand-new pretty trying to get into a lame non-bubbly clique. Maybe it had been worth it all to wind up here, pretty and popular.

She looked at Zane, his beautiful eyes still staring into the dregs of his coffee, and felt herself relax. She smiled. He looked so tragic sitting there, dark eyebrows arched in despair, still regretting that he'd bailed on running away to the Smoke. She reached out to take his hand.

"Hey, it's no big deal. It wasn't that great out there. Mostly it was getting sunburned and bitten by bugs."

His eyes rose to meet hers. "At least you took the chance, Tally. You were brave enough to find out for yourself."

"I didn't have a choice, really. I had to go find Shay." She shivered, pulling her hand away. "I'm just lucky I made it back."

Zane moved closer and reached out, his delicate fingers tracing the sprayed-on skin over her scar, his golden eyes wide. "I'm glad you did."

She smiled, touching the back of his hand. "Me too."

Zane's fingers slid into her hair, and he gently pulled her closer. She closed her eyes, letting his lips press against hers, reaching up to feel the smooth, flawless skin of his cheek.

Tally's heart was beating hard again, her mind racing even as her lips parted. Reality was shifting around her once more, but this time she liked the feeling.

When she'd arrived in New Pretty Town, Peris had warned Tally about sex. Getting too close to other pretties could be overwhelming when you were brand-new. It took time to get used to all the gorgeous faces, the perfect bodies, the luminous eyes. When everyone was beautiful, you could wind up falling in love with the first pretty you kissed.

But maybe it was time. She had been here a month, and Zane was special. Not just because he led the Crims and looked different from everyone else, but the way he tried to stay bubbly, to bend the rules. It made him even prettier than the others, somehow.

And of all the unexpected turns in the last twenty-four hours, this was the nicest. Kissing Zane was dizzy-making, but not like she was falling into darkness. His lips were warm and soft and perfect, and she felt safe.

After a long moment, the two pulled a little apart, Tally's eyes still closed. She felt his breath against her, his hand warm and soft on the back of her neck. "David," she whispered.

BUBBLY-MAKING

Zane pulled back, his eyes narrowing.

"Oh, I'm sorry," Tally sputtered. "I don't know what . . ."

As she trailed off, Zane nodded slowly. "No, that's okay."

"I didn't mean to . . . ," Tally started again, but Zane waved her silent, a thoughtful look spreading across his beautiful features. He stared at the ground, pulling up blades of grass between two fingers.

"I remember now," he said.

"Remember what?"

"That was his name."

"Whose name?"

Zane spoke in quiet, even tones, as if trying not to wake someone sleeping nearby. "He was the one who was supposed to take us to the Smoke. David."

Tally heard herself gasp softly. Her eyes were squinting, as if the sun had been turned up a notch. She could still feel the ghost of Zane's lips on hers, the warmth where his hands had touched her, but suddenly she was shivering.

She took Zane's hand. "I didn't mean to say that."

"I know. But things come back sometimes." He looked up from the grass, his golden eyes flashing. "Tell me about David."

Tally swallowed and turned away.

David. She could see him now, his funny big nose and high forehead. The handmade shoes he wore, and a jacket made out of dead animal skins sewn together. David had grown up out in the Smoke, had never set foot in a city his whole life. His face was ugly from top to bottom, tanned imperfectly by the sun, with a scar that went through his eyebrow . . . but remembering him sparked something inside Tally.

She shook her head, amazed. Somehow, she'd forgotten David.

"You met him in the Rusty Ruins, right?" Zane pressed her.

"No," she said. "I'd heard about him from Shay, and she tried to signal him once. But he never showed up. He was the one who took Shay to the Smoke, though."

"He was supposed to take me, too." Zane sighed. "But you went to the Smoke on your own, didn't you?"

"Yeah. But when I got there, he and I . . ." Tally remembered now. It all seemed a million years ago, but she could see herself—

her ugly self—kissing David, traveling with him across the wilderness for weeks alone. A weird ping of memory moved through her, how strong and never-ending being with him had felt back then.

And then, somehow, he'd disappeared.

"Where is he now?" Zane asked. "Did the Specials catch him when they took down the Smoke?"

She shook her head. Her other memories of David were tricky and faded, but the moment when they had parted was simply . . . gone. "I don't know."

Tally felt faint, the world growing unsteady for the hundredth time that day. She reached out toward the breakfast tray, but Zane took her hand. "No, don't eat."

"What?"

"Don't eat anything else, Tally. In fact, take a couple of these." He pulled a packet of calorie-purgers from his pocket—four had already been punched out.

"It helps if your heart's beating faster." He punched out two more, and bolted them down with a drink of coffee.

"Helps *what*?" she asked.

Zane pointed at his head. "Thinking. Hunger focuses your mind. Any kind of excitement works, actually." He grinned, and pressed the packet into her hand. "Like kissing someone new. That works really well."

Tally gazed down at the calorie-purgers, uncomprehending. The shiny foil glimmered painfully in the sun, and the packet's edges felt sharp as razors.

"But I've eaten hardly anything. Not enough to gain weight."

"It's not about losing weight. I need to talk to you, Tally. I need you with me for another minute. I've been waiting for someone like you for a long time. I need you . . . bubbly."

"Purgers are supposed to make me bubbly?"

"They help. I'll explain later. Just trust me, Tally-wa." His gaze remained on her, almost crazily intense, like when he explained some new trick idea to the Crims. It could be hard to resist Zane when he was like this, even if he wasn't making any sense.

"Okay, I guess." With clumsy fingers, she punched out two purgers and brought them to her mouth, but hesitated. You weren't supposed to take them if you hadn't eaten. It was dangerous. Back in the Rusty days—before the operation, when everyone had been ugly—there had been a disease where people deliberately didn't eat. They were so afraid of getting fat that they got way too skinny, sometimes even starving themselves to death in a world full of food. It was one of the scary things the operation had gotten rid of.

But a couple of purgers wouldn't kill her. When Zane handed Tally his coffee, she washed them down, then grimaced at the acid taste.

"Strong coffee, huh?" he said, grinning.

After a moment, her heart started beating fast, her metabolism kicking up. Her vision stayed sharp. Like the night before, she felt as if a thin film of plastic between her and the rest of the world were being peeled away. She squinted harder in the bright sunlight.

"Okay," Zane said. "What's the last thing you remember about David?"

Tally tried to steady her shaking hands, ransacking her brain to fight through the fog around her ugly memories. "We were all out in the ruins," she said. "You remember Shay's story about how we kidnapped her?"

Zane nodded, though Shay had more than one way of telling that story. In some versions, Shay had been kidnapped by Tally and the Smokies right from Special Circumstances headquarters. In other versions, she left the city to rescue Tally from the Smokies, and the two of them escaped back to the city together. Of course, Shay's weren't the only stories that changed sometimes. Crims always exaggerated stuff about the old days, because making it bubbly was the point. But Tally had a feeling that Zane wanted the truth.

"The Specials had destroyed the Smoke," she continued. "But there were a few of us still hiding out in the ruins."

"The New Smoke. That's what the uglies were calling you."

"That's right. But how did you know about that? Weren't you pretty by then?"

Zane grinned. "You think you're the only brand-new pretty I ever got to tell me stories, Tally-wa?"

"Oh." Remembering the kiss of a moment before, Tally wondered exactly how Zane had gotten the others to remember their ugly days.

"But why did you come back to the city?" he asked. "Don't tell me Shay actually rescued you."

Tally shook her head. "I don't think so."

"Did the Specials catch you? Did they get David, too?"

"No." The word reached her lips without hesitation. However fuzzy her memories were, David was still out there somewhere, she knew. In her mind she could see him clearly now, hiding in the ruins.

"Tell me, Tally, why did you come back here and give yourself up?"

Zane still held her hand, was squeezing it hard as he waited for an answer. His face was close again, gold eyes luminous in the dappled shade, drinking in everything she said. But somehow, the memories wouldn't come. Thinking about those times was like banging her head against a wall.

She chewed her lip. "How come I can't remember? What's wrong with me, Zane?"

"That's a good question. But whatever it is, it's wrong with all of us."

"Who? The Crims?"

He shook his head, glancing up at the party spires that loomed over them. "Not just us. Everyone. At least, everyone here in New Pretty Town. Most people won't even talk about when they were uglies. They say they don't want to discuss boring kid stuff."

Tally nodded. She had figured that out pretty quickly about New Pretty Town—outside the Crims, talking about ugly days was totally fashion-missing.

"But when you push them," Zane continued, "it turns out most of them *can't* remember."

Tally frowned. "But us Crims always talk about the old days."

"We were all troublemakers," Zane said. "So we have exciting stuff stored in our heads. But you have to keep telling those stories, listening to one another, and breaking the rules. You have to stay bubbly, or you'll gradually forget everything from back then. Permanently."

Returning his powerful gaze, she suddenly realized something. "That's what the Crims are for, isn't it?"

He nodded. "That's right, Tally—to keep from forgetting, and to help me figure out what's wrong with us."

"How did you . . . what makes you so different?"

"Another good question. Maybe I was just born this way, or maybe it's because I made myself a promise after I chickened out that night last spring: One day I'm going to leave the city, pretty or not." Zane's voice faded on the last words, and he breathed out through his teeth. "It just turned out to be a lot harder than I thought. Things were getting seriously boring there for a while, and I was starting to forget." He brightened. "But then you showed up, with your screwy stories that don't make sense. Things are definitely bubbly now."

"I guess they are." Tally looked down at her hand in his. "One more question, Zane-la?"

"Sure." He smiled. "I like your questions."

Tally looked away, a little embarrassed. "When you kissed me just then, was that to help you stay bubbly and to make me remember better? Or was it . . ." She trailed off, looking nervously into his eyes.

Zane grinned. "What do you think?" But he didn't give her a chance to answer. He took her shoulders and pulled her close again, and kissed her deeper this time, the warmth of his lips mixing with the strength of his hands on her, the taste of coffee and the smell of his hair.

When it was done, Tally leaned back, breathing hard because the kiss had been totally oxygen-missing. But it had made her bubbly, more than the calorie-purging pills or even jumping off the party spire the night before. And she remembered another thing that should have been totally obvious to mention before now, but somehow hadn't been.

And it was going to make Zane totally happy.

"Last night," Tally said, "Croy told me they had something for me, but he didn't say what. He was going to leave it here in New Pretty Town, hidden so the wardens wouldn't find it."

"Something from the New Smoke?" His eyes grew wide. "Where?"

"Valentino 317."

VALENTINO 317

"Wait a second," Zane said. He pulled off her interface ring and then his own, and led her deeper into the pleasure garden. "Better lose these," he said. "Don't want them following."

"Oh, right." Tally remembered ugly days, how easy it was to trick the dorm minders. "The wardens last night—they said they were going to keep an eye on me."

Zane chuckled. "They're *always* keeping an eye on me."

He threaded the rings onto two tall reeds, which bowed under the weight of the metal bands. "The wind will move them every now and then," he explained. "That way, it won't look like we took them off."

"But won't it look weird? Us staying in one place for so long?"

"It *is* a pleasure garden." Zane laughed. "I've spent my share of time in here."

A nasty ping went through Tally, but she didn't let it show. "What about finding them again?"

"I know this place. Quit worrying."

"Oh. Sorry."

He turned to her and laughed. "Nothing to be sorry for. This is the best breakfast I've had in ages."

They left the rings and headed down toward the river and Valentino Mansion, Tally wondering what they would discover in Room 317. In most mansions, each room had its own name—Tally's room in Komachi was called Etcetera; Shay's was Bluesky—but Valentino was so old that the rooms had numbers. Valentinos always made a big deal out of stuff like that, sticking to the ancient traditions of their crumbling home.

"Tricky place to hide it," Zane said as they approached the sprawling mansion. "Easier to keep secrets where the walls don't talk."

"That's probably why they hacked a Valentino bash and not one in some other mansion," Tally said.

"Except I had to go and screw everything up," Zane said.

Tally looked at him. "You?"

"We started off down in the stone mansion, but when we couldn't find you guys anywhere, I said we should go up into the new party spire so the smart walls would find you."

"We had the same idea," Tally said.

Zane shook his head. "Yeah, well, if we'd all stayed down in Valentino, the Specials wouldn't have spotted Croy so fast. He would have had time to talk to you."

"So they can listen through the walls?"

"Yeah." Zane grinned. "Why do you think I suggested a picnic on this bogusly cold day."

Tally nodded, thinking it through. The city interface brought you pings, answered your questions, reminded you of appointments, even turned the lights on and off in your room. If Special Circumstances wanted to watch you, they'd know everything you did and half of what you were thinking. She remembered talking to Croy up in the spire, her interface ring on her finger, the walls catching every word. . . . "Do they watch *everybody*?"

"No, they couldn't, and most people aren't worth watching. But some of us get special treatment. As in Special Circumstances."

Tally swore. The Specials had shown up so quickly last night. She'd only had a few minutes with Croy, as if they'd been waiting close by. Maybe they'd already spotted that the party had been hacked. Or maybe they were never very far away from Tally Youngblood. . . .

She looked into the trees. Shadows shifted in the wind, and she imagined gray shapes flitting among them. "I don't think last night was because of you, Zane. It was my fault."

"How do you mean?"

"It's always my fault."

"That's bogus, Tally," Zane said softly. "There's nothing wrong with being special."

His voice trailed off as they passed through the main arch of Valentino Mansion. Within the cool stone walls, it was as silent as a tomb.

"The party was still going when we left," Zane whispered. "They probably all just went to bed."

Tally nodded. There weren't even any maintenance robots at work yet. Bits of torn costumes littered the hallways. Spilled drinks filled the air with a sickly sweet perfume, and the floor was sticky underfoot. The glamour of the party had been stripped away, like bubbliness turned into a hangover.

Her finger felt naked without an interface ring, bringing back memories of sneaking across the river as an ugly, the terror of being caught. But fear kept her bubbly, her senses sharp enough to hear stray party rubbish shifting in the drafty corridors, to separate the raisiny scent of spilled champagne from the stale funk of beer. Besides their own footsteps, the mansion was silent.

"Whoever lives in 317 is going to be asleep," Tally whispered.

"Then we'll wake them up," Zane said softly, eyes flashing in the semidarkness.

The ground-floor rooms were all numbered in the one hundreds, so they looked for a way up. New elevators had been added to the mansion at some point, but without interface rings, the doors wouldn't open for them. A set of stone stairs brought Tally and Zane to the third floor, across from 301. The numbers counted up as they walked down the hall, odds on one side and evens on the other. Zane squeezed her hand when they reached 315.

But the next room was numbered 319.

They retraced their steps, checking the other side of the hall, but found only doors numbered 316, 318, and 320. Searching the rest of the floor, they found more 320s and the 330s, odd and even, but no Valentino 317.

"This is a bubbly puzzle," Zane said, chuckling to himself.

Tally sighed. "Maybe it was all a joke."

"You think the New Smokies would hack a citywide invitation, sneak across the river, and crash a party just to waste our time?"

"Probably not," Tally admitted, but she felt something in her starting to fade. She found herself wondering if this whole expedition was kind of lame, looking for some big secret that *uglies* had left behind. Sneaking around in someone else's mansion was pretty bogus, after all. "You think breakfast is still warm?" she asked.

"Tally . . ." Zane turned his intense gaze on her. With trembling hands, he pushed her hair behind her ears. "Stay with me."

"I'm right here," she said.

He drew closer, until his lips almost brushed hers. "I mean, stay bubbly."

Tally kissed him, and with the pressure of his lips the world sharpened again. She pushed the hunger out of her mind and said, "Okay. What about the elevator?"

"Which one?"

She led him back to the space between Valentino 315 and 319. The long expanse of stone wall was interrupted by an elevator door.

"There used to be a room here," she said.

"But they got rid of it when they put in the elevator." Zane laughed. "Lazy pretties. Can't climb two flights of stairs."

"So maybe 317 is the elevator now."

"Well, that's bogus," Zane said. "We can't make it come without our rings."

"We could wait around until someone else calls the elevator, and slip in."

Zane looked up and down the empty hallway, piled with plastic cups and torn paper decorations. "Hours from now," he said, sighing. "When we won't be bubbly anymore."

"Yeah. Not bubbly." A layer of fuzziness was starting to sink across Tally's vision again, and her stomach growled in a food-missing way, which called up the mental image of a warm chocolate muffin. She shook her head to clear it, visualizing a Special Circumstances uniform instead. Last night the sight of gray silk had focused her mind, had propelled her after Croy and into the fire stairwell. The whole thing had been a test to see how well her brain was working. Maybe this was another test. A bubbly puzzle, as Zane had said.

She stared at the elevator door. There had to be a way inside.

Slowly, a memory came to her. It was from back in the ugly days, but not so long ago. Tally remembered falling down a lightless shaft. It was one of the stories that Shay always liked to hear her tell, about how Tally and David had snuck into Special Circumstances headquarters. . . . "The roof," Tally said.

"What?"

"You can climb down into an elevator shaft from the roof. I've done it."

"Really?"

Instead of answering, Tally kissed him again. She couldn't remember exactly how, but knew that if she just stayed bubbly, it would come back to her. "Follow me."

Getting up to the roof wasn't as simple as she'd expected—the stairs they had taken up stopped at the third floor. Tally frowned, frustration deadening everything again. In Komachi Mansion, getting up to the roof was easy. "This is bogus. What do they do if there's a fire?"

"Stone doesn't burn," Zane said. He pointed at a small window at the end of the hall, sunlight streaming in through its stained-glass panels. "That's the way out." He strode toward it.

"What? Climb up the outside wall?"

Zane stuck his head out and looked down, letting out a long whistle. "Nothing like heights to keep you bubbly."

Tally frowned, unsure whether or not she wanted to be *that* bubbly.

Zane pulled himself up onto the sill and leaned out, grasping the top of the window. He stood carefully, slowly rising until Tally could see only his boots standing on the stone ledge outside. Her heart began to race again, until she could feel it beating in her fingertips. The world became as sharp as icicles.

For a long time his feet were motionless, then they shuffled closer to the edge, until only Zane's toes rested on the stone, precariously balanced.

"What are you doing up there?"

In answer, his boots lifted slowly into the air. Then Tally heard the muffled sound of soles scrabbling on stone. She stuck her head through and peered up.

Above her, Zane dangled from the edge of the roof, his feet swinging and scraping. Then one of his boots found purchase in a crack between the stones, and he hauled himself over and out of sight.

A moment later, his face appeared, grinning from ear to ear. "Come on up!"

Tally pulled her head in and took a deep breath, placing her hands on the ledge. The stone was rough and cold. The wind whistling through the window made the tiny hairs on her arms stand up.

"Stay bubbly," Tally said softly. She pulled herself up to sit in the window, the stone cold against her thighs, and took a quick glance at the ground. It was a long way down to the scattered leaves and tree roots that would break her fall. The wind picked up, making nearby branches wave, and Tally could see every twig. The smell of pine tree sharpened in her nostrils. Bubbly was not going to be a problem.

She slid one foot out onto the ledge, then the other.

Standing up was the scariest part. Tally clutched the window frame with one hand as she rose, the other feeling for a handhold on the outside wall. She didn't dare let herself look down again. The cool stone was pocked with holes and cracks, but none seemed large enough for more than fingertips.

When her legs had straightened all the way, Tally found herself paralyzed for a moment. She swayed slightly in the breeze, like an unsupported tower built too tall.

"Pretty bubbly-making, huh?" Zane's voice came from above. "Just grab the ledge."

She tore her gaze from the wall in front of her and looked up. The edge of the roof was just out of reach. "Hey, this isn't fair. You're taller than me."

"No problem." He lowered one hand.

"Are you sure you can hold me?"

"Come on, Tally-wa. What's the point of having all those new pretty muscles if you don't use them for anything."

"Like getting killed?" she said under her breath, but reached up to take his hand.

Her new muscles were stronger than she'd thought, though. With her fingers locked around Zane's wrist, Tally pulled herself easily up from the window ledge. Her free hand grasped the roof's edge, and one toe managed to get purchase in a crack in the mansion wall. With a grunt, Tally was up, rolling over the ledge and onto the roof. She sprawled on the reassuringly solid stone, giggling with the rush of relief that swept through her.

Zane grinned. "It's true, what I said before."

She looked up at him questioningly.

"I've been waiting for someone like you."

Pretties didn't blush—not in an ugly-making way, at least—but Tally rolled to her feet to hide her reaction. The bubbliness of their death-defying climb had made Zane's gaze too intense. She stood to take in the view.

From the roof, Tally could see the spires of New Pretty Town still towering over them, the green trails of pleasure gardens snaking up the central hill. Across the river, Uglyville was already awake. A soccer field full of just-turned-uglies swarmed around a black-and-white ball, and the wind carried to her ears the sound of a whistle being furiously blown. The view seemed terribly close and in focus, her nervous system still ringing, echoing from the moments she'd swung from Zane's hand.

The stone roof was flat, marked only by the spinning heads of three air vents, the towering transmission mast, and a metal shack no bigger than an ugly's closet. Tally pointed at the latter. "That's right above the elevator."

They crossed the roof. In the shack's ancient door, a rust-covered sheet of metal like those that littered the ruins, letters had been painstakingly scratched: VALENTINO 317.

"Very non-bogus, Tally," Zane said, grinning. He yanked at the door, but a shiny chain snapped taut with a screeched complaint. "Hmm."

Tally looked at the device that kept the chain from slipping, wracking her still-spinning brain. "That's called a . . . padlock, I think." She felt the smooth steel object between her fingers, trying to remember how they worked. "They had them in the Smoke, to secure stuff that people might steal."

"Great. All this and we still need our rings."

Tally shook her head. "Smokies don't use interface rings, Zane. To open a padlock, you need a . . ." She searched her memory for another old word, then found it. "There must be a key somewhere."

"A key? Like a password?"

"No. This kind of key is a little metal thing. You stick it in and turn, which makes the lock pop open."

"What does it look like?"

"A flat piece of steel, about as long as your thumb, with teeth."

Zane giggled at this image, but started looking around.

Tally stared at the door. The shack was obviously much older than the chain that held it shut. She wondered what it had been used for. Leaning close to the narrow gap Zane had opened, Tally sheltered her gaze with both hands and peered into the blackness. Her eyes adjusted slowly, until she could make out dark shapes within.

There seemed to be a huge pulley and a crude mechanical engine, like the kind they used out in the Smoke. The elevator had once moved up and down on a chain. This shack was old; it must have been abandoned after lifters had been invented, which was ages ago. Modern elevators ran on the same principle as hoverboards and bungee jackets. (Which was a *lot* safer than dangling from a chain. . . . Tally shivered at the thought.) When lifters had been added, the old mechanism must have been left up here on the roof to rust.

She yanked at the padlock again, but it held firm. Heavy and crude, the lock looked out of place here in the city. When wardens wanted to secure something, they stuck up a sensor that would tell you to keep out. Only New Smokies would have used a padlock made of metal.

Croy had told her to come here, so there had to be a key around somewhere.

"Another stupid test," she muttered.

"A what?" Zane asked. Looking for the key, he had climbed on top of the shack.

"Like Croy dressing up as a Special," she explained. "And making us find Valentino 317. The key has to be tricky to get hold of, because it's all a test. Their point is to make it *hard* to find this thing that Croy left for me. They don't want us to find it unless we're bubbly."

"Or maybe," Zane said, perching on one edge of the shack, "they want the search to *make* us bubbly, so we're thinking clearly when we find it."

"Whatever it is," Tally said, and sighed. She felt annoyance rising in her, along with the feeling that this test would never end, that every solution would just lead to another level of problems, like some stupid thumbgame. Maybe the smartest move would be to blow it all off and just have breakfast. Why was she trying to prove herself to the New Smokies, anyway? They didn't matter. She was beautiful and they were ugly.

But Zane's brain was still spinning. "So they'd hide the key somewhere that would be extra tricky to get to. But what would be trickier than climbing up here?"

Tally's eyes swept the roof, until they found the spindly transmission tower. At its top, twenty stories above them, the Valentino flag whipped in the wind. At the sight of it, the world grew crisp again, and she smiled.

"Climbing up there."

THE HIGH TOWER

The transmission tower was the newest piece of Valentino Mansion, made of steel painted over with white polymers to keep rust at bay. It was part of the system that tracked people's interface rings, supposedly to help find anyone who got lost or injured outside a smart building.

White struts loomed over Tally and Zane, crisscrossing like a cat's cradle, shining in the sun like porcelain. The tower didn't look hard to climb, except for the fact that it was five times as tall as Valentino Mansion, even taller than a party spire. As she stared up into its heights, a low rumble sounded in Tally's stomach. She was pretty sure it wasn't hunger. "At least there's no dragon guarding it," she said.

Zane lowered his anxious gaze from the tower. "Huh?"

Tally shook her head. "Just something from a dream I had."

"You really think the key's up there?"

"I'm afraid so."

"The New Smokies climbed all that way?"

Old memories came back. "No. They could've hoverboarded up the side. Boards can go that high if they stay close enough to a big piece of metal."

"You know, we could requisition a hoverboard . . . ," Zane said quietly.

She looked at him with surprise.

He muttered, "Of course, that wouldn't be very bubbly, would it?"

"It wouldn't. And anything that flies has a minder. Do you know how to trick a hoverboard's safety governor?"

"Used to, but I can't remember."

"Me either. Okay, then. We climb."

"Okay," he said. "But first . . ." He reached for Tally's hand, drew her to him, and they kissed again.

She blinked once, then felt a grin spreading on her face. "Just to keep us bubbly."

The first half was easy.

Tally and Zane stayed together, climbing opposite sides of the tower, finding ready handholds in the weave of struts and cables. The wind kicked up now and then, playfully tugging at Tally in a way that was nervous-making, but all it took was a quick glance downward to focus her mind.

Halfway up, she could already see the whole of Valentino Mansion, the pleasure gardens spread out in every direction, even the hovercar pads atop the central hospital where they did the operation. The river glittered as the sun climbed toward noon, and across the water, in Uglyville, Tally saw her old dorm hulking among the trees. On the soccer field, a few uglies were watching them and pointing, probably wondering who was climbing the tower.

Tally wondered how long it would be before someone on this side of the river noticed their ascent and pinged the wardens.

With her new muscles, the climb wasn't physically demanding. But as the two of them neared the top, the tower grew narrower, the handholds less sure. The polymer coating was slick, still wet in a few corners where the morning sun hadn't yet dried the dew. Microwave dishes and thick skeins of braided cables crowded the struts, and doubts began to creep through Tally's mind. Was the key really up here? Why would the New Smokies make her risk her life just to pass a test? As the climb grew trickier and the drop more panic-making, Tally found herself wondering how she'd wound up here on this tall and windy spike.

The night before, her only goal had been to become a Crim, pretty and popular, surrounded by a clique of new friends. And she'd managed to get everything she'd wanted—on top of which, Zane had kissed her, a bubbly development she hadn't even imagined before this morning.

Of course, getting what you wanted never turned out the way you'd thought it would. Being a Crim wasn't about being satisfied, and hanging out with Zane apparently involved risking your life and not eating breakfast. Tally had only been voted in last night, and here she was having to prove herself again.

And for what? Did she really want to unlock the rusty shack below? Whatever was in there could only make her head more spinning, and was certain to remind her of David and the Smoke and everything she'd left behind. It felt as if every time she took a step forward into her new life, something sucked her back toward ugly days.

With her mind tangled by these questions, Tally put her foot wrong.

The sole of one shoe slipped from a thick cable coated in slick plastic, sending her flailing legs away from the tower, yanking her hands from their grip on a strut that was still wet with dew. Tally tumbled downward, the feeling of free fall surging through her body, familiar from all the times she had wiped out on a hoverboard or thrown herself from the top of a building.

Her instincts told her to relax, until she realized the big difference between this fall and all those others: Tally wasn't wearing crash bracelets or a bungee jacket. This time she was *really* falling; nothing was going to catch her.

Her brand-new pretty reflexes kicked into gear, and her hands flew out to grab a passing braid of cable. Tally's palms slid down the plastic insulation, the friction burning her skin as if the cable had burst into flame. Her legs swung in toward the tower—knees bent, body turning—and Tally absorbed the impact against the metal with her hip, a blow that shook her whole frame but didn't loosen the grip of her burning fingers.

Tally's feet scrabbled to gain purchase, their soles finding a wide strut and mercifully taking most of the weight from her hands. She wrapped her arms around the cable, every muscle tense, barely hearing Zane's shouts above her, and gazed out over the river, amazed at her own vision.

Everything shone, as if diamonds had been scattered across Uglyville. Her mind felt clean, like the air after a morning rain, and Tally understood at last why she had climbed up here. Not to impress Zane or the Smokies, or to pass any test, but because some part of her had wanted this moment, this clarity she hadn't felt since the operation. This was way beyond bubbly.

"Are you okay?" came a distant cry.

She looked back up at Zane. Seeing how far she'd fallen, Tally swallowed, but still managed a smile. "I'm bubbly. Totally. Wait up."

She climbed fast now, ignoring her bruised hip. Her scorched palms complained every time they closed around a handhold, but within a minute she was alongside Zane again. His golden eyes were wider than ever, as if her fall had scared him worse than it had Tally.

She smiled again, realizing that it probably had. "Come on." She left him behind, pulling herself up the last few meters.

Reaching the top, Tally found a black magnet stuck to the bottom of the flagpole, a shiny new key clinging to it. She carefully pulled the key off and slipped it into her pocket while the Valentino flag snapped overhead, the sound as crisp as clothes fresh out of the wall.

"Got it!" she yelled, and started down, passing Zane before he'd even moved, the shocked expression still frozen on his face.

• • •

It wasn't until she stood on the roof again that Tally realized how sore her muscles were. Her heart was still pounding, and the world remained crystalline. She pulled the key from her pocket, tracing its teeth with one trembling fingertip, her senses registering every detail of the metal's jagged edge.

"Hurry up!" she cried to Zane, who was still only halfway down. He started to climb faster, but Tally snorted and spun on one heel, striding toward the shack.

The padlock popped open when she turned the key, the rusty door groaning with age as its bottom edge skidded across the stone. Tally stepped inside, blind for a moment in the darkness, seeing red traces that pulsed with her heartbeat, full of excitement. If the Smokies had arranged all this to make her bubbly, they'd gotten what they wanted.

The little room smelled very old, the air inside warm and still. As Tally's eyes adjusted, she could see the flaking graffiti that filled every centimeter of wall space, layer upon layer of slogans, scrawled tags, and the names of couples proclaiming their love. Some of the dates included years that made no sense, until Tally realized that they were written in Rusty style, counting all the old centuries before the collapse. The crumbling elevator machinery was decorated with still more graffiti, and the floor littered with ancient contraband: old cans of spray-paint, crushed and empty tubes of notoriously sticky nano-glue, burned-out fireworks smelling like old campfires. Tally saw a yellowed rectangle of paper, squashed and blackened at one end, like a picture of a cigarette from a Rusty history book. She picked it up and sniffed, dropping it when her stomach heaved at the stench.

A cigarette? This place was older than lifters, she reminded herself, maybe even older than the city itself, a strange, forgotten piece of history. She wondered how many generations of uglies and tricky new pretties like the Crims had made it theirs.

The pouch Croy had shown her rested on one of the old rusted gears of the elevator mechanism, waiting.

Tally picked it up. The old leather felt strange in her hands, sending her mind back to the worn textures of the Smoke. She opened it and pulled out a sheet of paper. A small, skittering sound came from the stone floor, and she realized something tiny had fallen from the pouch—two things, in fact. Tally knelt down and squinted, feeling the cool stone with her still burning palms until she found two little white pills.

She stared at them, feeling a memory at the edge of her awareness.

The room darkened, and she looked up. Zane was in the doorway, panting, his eyes flashing in the gloom. "Gee. Thanks for waiting, Tally."

She didn't say anything. He took a step in and knelt beside her.

"You okay?" His hand came to rest on her shoulder. "Didn't hit your head in that fall, did you?"

"No. Just cleared it up. I found this." She handed the sheet of paper to Zane, who smoothed it out and held it up to the light streaming through the door. It was covered with an almost unreadable scrawl.

Tally looked down again at the pills in her hand. Tiny and white, they looked like a pair of purgers. But Tally was pretty sure they would do more than burn calories. She remembered something. . . .

Zane slowly lowered the sheet of paper, his eyes wide. "It's a letter, and it's addressed to you."

"A letter? Who from?"

"You, Tally." His voice echoed softly from the metal walls of the shack. "It's from you."

NOTE TO SELF

Dear Tally,

You're me.

Or I guess another way to say it is, I'm you—Tally Youngblood. Same person. But if you're reading this letter, then we're also two different people. At least, that's what us New Smokies are guessing has happened by now. You've been changed. That's why I'm writing to you.

I wonder if you remember writing these words. (Actually, I'm telling Shay to write them. She did handwriting in school.) Do they seem like a diary entry from back when you were a littlie, or like someone else's diary altogether?

If you can't remember writing this letter *at all,* then we're both in big trouble. Especially me. Because not being remembered by myself would mean that the me who wrote this letter has been erased somehow. Ouch. And maybe that means I'm dead, sort of. So please *try* to remember, at least.

Tally paused and traced the scrawled words with one finger, trying to remember dictating them. Shay liked to demonstrate how they could make letters with a stylus, one of the tricks she'd learned in preparation for their trip to the Smoke. She had left a note for Tally telling how to follow her there. But was this really Shay's handwriting?

More important, were the words true? Tally really couldn't remember. She took a breath and kept on reading. . . .

But, anyway, here's what I'm trying to tell you: They did something to your brain—*our* brain—and that's why this letter may seem kind of weird to you.

We (that's "we" as in us out in the New Smoke, not "we" as in you and me) don't know exactly how it works, but we're pretty sure that *something* happens to everyone who has the operation. When they make you pretty, they also add these lesions (tiny scars, sort of) to your brain. It makes you different, and not in a good way. Look in the mirror, Tally. If you're pretty, you've got them.

Tally heard a sharp intake of breath next to her ear. She turned to find Zane reading over her shoulder. "Looks like you may be right about us pretties," she said.

He nodded slowly. "Yeah. Great." He pointed at the next paragraph. "But how about that?"

She dropped her eyes to the page again.

> The good news is, there's a cure. That's why David came and got you, to give you the pills that will fix your brain. (I really hope you remember David.) He's a good guy, even if he had to kidnap you to get you here. Trust him. It might be scary to be out here, away from the city, wherever the New Smokies are hiding you, but the people who gave you the lesions will be looking, and you have to be kept safe until you're cured.

Tally stopped reading. "Kidnapped me?"

"Looks like there's been a change of plan since you wrote this," Zane said.

Tally felt funny for a moment, the image of David now stronger in her head. "*If* I wrote this. And *if* it's true. Anyway, Croy came to see me, not . . . David." As she said his name, memories surged through Tally: David's hands roughened from years of work, his jacket made from sewn-together skins, the white scar that went through his eyebrow. A feeling like panic began to well up in her. "What happened to David, Zane? Why didn't he come?"

He shook his head. "I don't know. Were you and he . . . ?"

Tally looked down at the letter again. It blurred before her, and a single teardrop fell onto the paper. Ink bled into the spattered mark, turning the tear black. "I'm pretty sure we were." Her voice was rough, memories tangled inside her. "But something happened."

"Oh?"

"I don't know what." Tally wondered why she couldn't remember. Was it really because of *lesions*—the scars on her brain that the note had warned about? Or did she simply not want to?

"What's that in your hand, Tally?" Zane asked.

She opened her reddened palm to reveal the tiny white pills resting there. "The cure. Let me finish this." She took a steadying breath.

> One more thing—Maddy (David's mom, who came up with the cure) says I have to add this, something about "informed consent":
>
> I, Tally Youngblood, hereby give my permission for Maddy and David to give me the pills that cure being pretty-minded. I realize this is a test on an unproven drug, and it all might go horribly wrong. Brain-dead wrong.
>
> Um, sorry about that last part. That's the risk we have to take. That's why I gave myself up to become pretty, so we could test the pills and save Shay and Peris, and everyone else in the world who's had their brain messed with.
>
> So you have to take them. For me. Sorry in advance

if you don't want to, and David and Maddy force you to.

You'll be better off, I promise.

Good luck.

Love,

Tally

Tally let the paper fall onto her lap. Somehow, the scrawled words had sucked the clarity out of the world, making her head-spinning and fuzzy again. Her heart was still pounding, but not in that beautiful way it had when she'd caught herself falling from the tower. It felt more like panic, as if she were locked inside the little metal shack.

Zane let out a low whistle. "So that's why you came back."

"You believe this, don't you?"

His eyes flashed gold in the darkness. "Of course. It all makes sense now. Why you can't remember David or coming back to the city. Why Shay has so many mixed-up stories about those days. Why the New Smokies are so interested in you."

"Because I'm brain damaged?"

Zane shook his head. "We're *all* brain damaged, Tally. Just like I thought. But you gave yourself up on purpose, knowing there's a cure." He pointed at the pills in her hand. "*Those* are the reason why you're here."

She stared down at the pills, which looked small and insignificant in the gloom of the shack. "But the letter said they might not even work. I might wind up brain-dead. . . ."

He took her wrist lightly. "If you don't want to take them, Tally, I will."

She closed her hand. "I can't let you do that."

"But this is what I've been waiting for. A way to escape prettiness, to be bubbly all the time!"

"*I* wasn't waiting for this," Tally cried. "I didn't want anything but to be a Crim!"

He pointed at the letter. "Yes, you did."

"That wasn't me. She says so herself."

"But you—"

"Maybe I changed my mind!"

"*You* didn't change your mind. The operation did."

She opened her mouth, but nothing came out.

"Tally, you gave yourself up, knowing you'd have to risk the cure. That's amazingly brave." Zane reached out and touched her face, his eyes shining in the shaft of sunlight that streamed across him. "But if you don't want to, let me take the risk for you."

Tally shook her head, wondering what she was more afraid of: the pills going wrong on her, or watching Zane turn into a vegetable in her place. Or maybe what she really feared was finding out what had happened to David. If only Croy had left her alone, or if she'd never found Valentino 317. If she could just forget the pills and stay dumb and pretty, none of this would ever worry her again. "I just want to forget David."

"Why?" Zane leaned closer. "What did he do to you?"

"Nothing. He didn't do anything. But why did Croy leave these pills for me instead of him coming and taking me away? What if he's—"

The shack shuddered for a moment, silencing her. They both looked up; something big had passed overhead.

"A hovercar . . . ," Tally whispered.

"Probably just flying over. As far as they know, we're in the pleasure garden."

"Unless someone saw us up on the . . ." She fell silent as a cloud of dust stirred in through the half-opened door, glowing in the shaft of sunlight. "It's landing."

"They know we're here," Zane said, and started tearing up the letter.

"What are you *doing*?"

"We can't let them find this," he said. "They can't know there's a cure." He stuffed a piece of the letter into his mouth, grimacing at the taste.

She looked at the pills in her hand. "What about these?"

He swallowed the paper with a tortured expression. "I have to take them, *now*." He bit off another piece of the letter and started chewing.

"They're so small," she said. "We could hide them."

He shook his head, swallowing again. "Getting caught without rings is pretty obvious, Tally. They'll want to know what we were up to. When you get some food in you, you won't be as bubbly—you might chicken out and hand over the pills."

The sound of footsteps approached across the roof outside.

Zane yanked the door almost shut, pulling the ends of the chain through to the inside and snapping the padlock closed, plunging them into darkness. "That won't stop them for long. Give me the pills. If they work, I promise I'll make sure you—"

A voice called from outside, and something cold crawled down Tally's spine. The voice had an edge, like razors in her ears. They weren't wardens outside. This was a Special Circumstance.

In the gloom of the shack, the pills stared up at her like two soulless white eyes. Tally was somehow certain that the words in the letter were her own, begging her to take them. Maybe when she did, everything would be clear and bubbly all the time, like Zane said.

Or maybe they wouldn't work, and would leave her a hollow, brain-dead shell.

Or maybe it was David who was dead. Tally wondered if after today part of her would always remember his face, no matter what she did. And unless she took the pills, she would never know the truth.

Tally started to bring them to her mouth, but found she couldn't. She imagined her brain unraveling. Being erased, like that other Tally who had written the letter. She looked into Zane's pleading, beautiful eyes. He had no doubts, at least.

Maybe she didn't have to do this alone. . . .

The door made a sharp screech as someone tried to pull it open, snapping the chain taut. A blow landed on the door, the sound booming like fireworks in the little metal shack. Specials were strong, but could they beat down a metal door?

"*Now,* Tally," Zane whispered.

"I can't."

"Then give them to me."

She shook her head and leaned closer, whispering to stay unheard under the thundering blows against the door. "I can't do that to you, Zane, and I can't do this alone. Maybe if we each took one . . ."

"What? That's crazy. We don't know how that will—"

"We don't know *anything,* Zane."

The pounding stopped, and Tally shushed his reply. Specials weren't just strong and fast, they had the sharp hearing of predators.

Suddenly, a bright light sparked through the gap in the door, throwing wildly jittering shadows into the shack, leaving tracers on Tally's vision. The cutting tool hissed as it burned into the chain, and the smell of molten metal reached her nostrils. The Specials would be inside in seconds.

"Together," she whispered, handing one of the pills to Zane. With a deep breath she placed the other on her tongue. Bitterness exploded through her mouth, like biting into a seed inside a grape. She swallowed the pill, which trailed an acid taste down her throat.

"Please," she pleaded softly. "Do this with me."

He sighed and took the pill, grimacing at the taste. He stared at her, shaking his head. "That may have been very stupid, Tally."

She tried to smile. "At least we were stupid together." Leaning forward, she grasped the back of his neck and kissed him. David hadn't come to rescue her. He was either dead or he must not care what happened to her. He was ugly, and Zane was beautiful, and bubbly, and he was here. "We need each other now," she said.

They were still kissing when the Specials burst in.

Part II

THE CURE

and kisses are a better fate
than wisdom
—e. e. cummings, "since feeling is first"

BREAKTHROUGH

Overnight, the first freeze of winter had come. The trees shone like glass, bare branches alight with icicles. Glittering black fingers stretched across the window, cutting the sky into sharp little pieces.

Tally pressed one hand against the pane, letting the chill leak through the glass and into her palm. The bracing cold made the afternoon light sharper, as brittle as she imagined the icicles outside to be. It focused the part of her mind that still wanted to sink back into pretty dreams.

When she finally pulled her hand away from the window, a fuzzy outline showed its imprint on the glass, then slowly faded.

"Blurry Tally is no more," she said, then grinned, placing her icy palm against Zane's cheek.

"What the . . . ," he muttered, stirring just enough to nudge her hand away.

"Wake up, pretty-head."

His eyes opened a slit. "Make it dark," he told his interface cuff.

The room obeyed, opaquing the window.

Tally frowned. "Another headache?" Zane still sometimes got crippling migraines that could put him out for hours, but they weren't as bad as the first weeks after he'd taken the pill.

"No," he murmured. "Sleepy."

She reached for the manual controls, setting the window back to transparent. "Then it's time to get up. We'll be late for ice skating."

He squinted at her through one eye. "Ice skating is bogus."

"Sleeping's bogus. Get up and be bubbly."

"Bubbly is bogus."

Tally raised one eyebrow, which didn't hurt anymore. She'd been a good pretty and had her forehead all fixed, though she'd memorialized the scar with a flash tattoo: black Celtic swirls just above her eye that spun in time with her heartbeat. For good measure, she'd gotten eye surge exactly like Shay's, backward-running clocks and everything.

"Bubbly is *not* bogus, lazy-face." Tally placed her hand against the window again to recharge its iciness. Her interface cuff sparkled in the sun like the frozen trees below, and for the millionth time she searched for any seam in its metal surface. But the cuff seemed to have been forged from one piece of steel, perfectly fitted to the oval of her wrist. She pulled at it softly, feeling the slightest give; she was growing skinnier every day. "Coffee, please," she said sweetly to the cuff.

Brewing smells began to percolate into the room, and Zane stirred again. When her hand had grown sufficiently cold, Tally placed it on his bare chest. He flinched but didn't fight back, just squeezed two fistfuls of sheet and took a shuddering breath. His eyes opened, their gold irises shining like the cold winter sun. "Now *that* was bubbly."

"I thought bubbly was bogus."

He smiled and shrugged drowsily.

Tally smiled back. Zane was extra beautiful when he first woke up. The edges of sleep softened his intense stare, leaving his severe features almost vulnerable-looking, like a lost and hungry boy. Tally never mentioned this fact, of course, or Zane would probably have gotten surge to fix it.

She made her way to the coffeemaker, stepping over the piles of unrecycled clothes and dirty dishes that occupied every square centimeter of floor. As always, Zane's room was a wreck. His closet lay half-open, too overflowing to shut properly. It was an easy room to hide things in.

Sipping her coffee, Tally told the hole in the wall to make their usual skating ensembles: heavy plastic jackets lined with fake rabbit fur; knee-padded pants for bad falls; black scarves; and, most important, thick gloves that reached halfway to their elbows. While the hole was spitting out clothes, she took Zane his coffee, which finally dragged him to consciousness.

Zane and Tally skipped breakfast—a meal they hadn't eaten for the last month—and layered up in the elevator down to the front door of Pulcher Mansion, speaking fluent pretty along the way.

"Did you see the frost, Zane-la? So icy-making."

"Winter is totally bubbly."

"Totally. Summer is just too . . . I don't know. *Warming* or something."

"Utterly."

They smiled pleasantly at the door minder and went out into the cold, pausing for a moment on the mansion's front steps. Tally handed Zane her coffee mug and pulled her gloves up inside her sleeves, covering the interface cuff on her left arm with two layers. Then she wrapped that arm with the black scarf to seal the cuff tightly. She took both coffees from Zane, watching steam curl up from the trembling black pools while he did the same with his own gloves.

When he was done, Tally spoke, not too loudly. "I thought we were supposed to act normal today."

"I am acting normal."

"Come on. 'Bubbly is bogus'?"

"What? Too much?"

She shook her head, giggled, and pulled him toward the floating rink.

It had been one month since they'd taken the pills, and Tally and Zane weren't brain-dead yet. The first few hours, though, had been totally bogus. The Specials had searched them and Valentino 317 madly, putting everything they found in little plastic bags. They'd barked a million questions in their grating Special voices, trying to find out why a pair of new pretties would climb the transmission tower. Tally tried to tell them they'd just wanted privacy, but no explanation satisfied the Specials.

Finally, some wardens showed up with the abandoned interface rings, medspray for Tally's palms, and muffins. Tally ate her long-delayed breakfast like a hungry dog until all her bubbliness went away, then smiled prettily and asked to be taken to surge for the previous night's scar. After another really boring hour or so, the Specials let the wardens take her to the hospital with Zane in tow.

That was mostly it, except for the interface cuffs. The doctors slipped Tally's on during her eyebrow surge, and Zane awoke the next morning to find himself wearing one. They worked just like interface rings, except they could send voice-pings from anywhere, like a handphone. That meant the cuffs heard you talking even when you went outside and, unlike rings, they didn't come off. They were manacles with an invisible chain, and no tool Tally and Zane had yet tried could cut them open.

Unexpectedly, the cuffs also became the fashion item of the season. Once the other Crims saw them, it was all Zane could do to keep everyone from requisitioning their own. He got the hole in the wall to make a bunch of nonworking copies and passed them out. Over the next few weeks, word spread that the cuffs were some new marker of criminality, signifying that you had scaled the transmission tower on top of Valentino Mansion; it turned out that hundreds of new pretties had witnessed Tally's and Zane's climb, pinging one another to run to windows and check out the show. Within a few weeks, only the most fashion-missing went around without some kind of metal cuff locked onto their wrists, and minders had to be installed to keep new pretties off the tower.

People were starting to point out Tally and Zane when they were in public, and there were more Crim wannabees every day. It was like everybody wanted to be bubbly.

Tally was nervous about the breakthrough, but she and Zane didn't say much on the way to the skating rink. Although their cuffs couldn't hear anything while wrapped up in the heavy winter gear, silence was a habit that had begun to follow them everywhere. Tally had grown used to communicating in other ways: winks and rolled eyes and silently mouthed words. Living in an unspoken conspiracy filled every gesture with significance, charged every shared touch with unspoken meaning.

Inside the glass elevator that carried them up to the floating sheet of ice, looking down on the great bowl of Nefertiti Stadium, Zane took Tally's hand. His eyes flashed, as they did before a sudden, unexpected trick, like a snowball ambush from the roof of Pulcher Mansion. His playful glance was perfectly timed to settle Tally's nerves a little. It wouldn't do for the other Crims to see her anxious, after all.

Most of them were already there, trading in boots for ice skates, finding bungee jackets in the right size. A few newly voted-in Crims were warming up, looking wobbly ankled on the floating ice, the sound of their skates like a library minder telling you to shush.

Shay glided over to gather Tally in a hug, coming to a halt mostly by bumping into her. "Hey, Skinny-wa."

"Hey, Squint-la," Tally retorted, giggling. Ugly nicknames were back in fashion, but Shay and Tally had switched their old names now that Tally was losing weight. Going food-missing sucked, but sooner or later she hoped to be thin enough to slip the cuff from her wrist.

She saw that Shay had wrapped a black scarf around her forearm in solidarity. Shay also sported a version of Tally's flash tattoo, a nest of snakes coiling around one brow and down her cheek. A lot of the Crims had new facial tattoos with heart-rate triggers—you could see at a glance how bubbly they were. Self-heated coffee mugs sent clouds of steam into the air above the pack of Crims, and everyone's tattoos were spinning.

A chorus of hellos rose up as Tally and Zane were spotted, excitement rising in the pack. Peris glided over with a bungee jacket and Tally's usual skates in hand.

"Thanks, Nose," Tally said, kicking her boots off and sitting down on the ice. Here at the rink, hoverskates weren't allowed; real metal blades glittered in the wintry light like daggers. Tally drew her laces up tight. "Got your flask?" she asked Peris.

He pulled it out. "Double vodka."

"Very thawing." Tally and Zane had stopped drinking alcohol, which turned out to make you more pretty-minded than bubbly, but strong spirits had other uses here on the ice.

She held out her gloved hands, and Peris pulled her up, her momentum sending the two of them into a slippery little waltz.

Giggling, they steadied themselves against each other.

"Don't forget your jacket, Skinny," he said.

She took it from him and tied the straps. "That would be bogus, wouldn't it?"

Peris nodded nervously.

"Any word from our friends across the river?" she asked, her voice dropping to just above a whisper.

"Not a ping. They're still totally missing."

Tally frowned. Croy's visit was a month ago now, and the New Smokies hadn't shown themselves since. The silence was ominous, unless this was another of their annoying tests. Either way, she was itching to go looking, once she got this stupid cuff off. "How's Fausto going on tricking that hoverboard?"

Peris only shrugged, looking distractedly at the other Crims, who were invading the rink, laughing and screaming, slashing through the little Zambonies that skittered about polishing the ice.

Tally checked the flash tattoo on Peris's forehead—a third eye that blinked with his heartbeat—and looked into his gorgeous eyes, brown and soft and depthless. Peris seemed bubblier than he had a month ago—all the Crims did—but Tally no longer saw improvement in him from day to day. It was so much harder for the rest of them who hadn't had the pills, who weren't half-cured like Tally and Zane. They could get excited in the short term, but it was hard to keep them focused.

Well, the breakthrough would give them a jolt.

"It's okay, Nose. Let's skate." Tally pushed off against the flat of one blade, building up speed as she swept around the rink's outer edge. She looked down through the mottled window of ice underfoot. The hoverlifters that held the floating rink up in the air were easy to see, spaced in a grid a few meters apart and sending out a sunburst of refrigeration tendrils. Much farther below, the broad oval of the sports stadium was visible, softly out of focus like the world through a pretty-minded haze. The stadium lights were coming on, warming up for the soccer game scheduled in forty-five minutes. As always, there would be fireworks before it started, once the crowd was in their seats. Very pretty-making.

The sky above was an uninterrupted expanse of blue, except for a few hot-air balloons tethered to the tallest party spires. When it was airborne, the skating rink was the highest thing in New Pretty Town. Tally could glimpse the entire city spread out below.

She skated after Zane, catching him as he rounded a turn. "Everybody seem bubbly to you?"

"Mostly nervous." He gracefully reversed, skating backward as easily as breathing. His operation-augmented muscles had been freed from pretty timidity and sloth. He could hold a handstand without trembling, climb up to his window in Pulcher Mansion in seconds, and outrun the monorail that brought crumblies from the burbs into the central hospital. He never broke a sweat and could hold his breath for two solid minutes.

Watching him perform these feats, Tally remembered the Rangers who'd rescued her from a brushfire on her journey to the Smoke. Zane was as physically confident as they had been—fast and strong, but without the twitching inhumanity of Special Circumstances agents. Tally was no slouch herself, but somehow the cure had taken Zane's strength and coordination to a new level. She loved gliding across the ice with him, skating circles around the others, being the graceful center of the Crims' motley vortex of flashing blades.

"Anything from the New Smoke?" he asked, barely audible over the swoosh of skates.

"Peris says nothing."

Zane swore and took a tight turn, spraying ice on a non-Crim struggling slowly along the side of the rink.

Tally caught up to him. "We have to be patient, Zane. We'll get these things off."

"I'm tired of being patient, Tally." He looked down through the ice. The stadium below was teeming, the growing audience awaiting the first game of the intercity play- offs. "How long?"

"Any minute now," she said.

As the words left her mouth the first fireworks exploded below, instantly transforming the rink into a mottled palette of reds and blues. A second later, a tardy boom shuddered up through the ice, followed by a long *ahhh* of appreciation from the crowd.

"Here we go," Zane said with a grin, his irritation erased.

Tally squeezed his hand and then let him skate away, gliding to a halt in the center of the rink, the farthest point from the supporting hoverstructure around the ice. She raised one hand and waited as the other Crims gathered in a tight pack around her.

"Flasks," she said softly, and heard the whisper spread through the pack.

Flashes of metal caught the sun, and Tally heard the rasp of tops being unscrewed. Her heart was beating fast, her senses sharpened by anticipation. Everyone's tattoos were totally spinning. She saw Zane gathering speed along the outside of the rink.

"Pour," she said softly.

A liquid sound spread through the pack of Crims, double vodka and straight ethyl alcohol gurgling out. Tally thought she heard a creak, the slightest of complaints from the ice as its freezing point was lowered by the spirits.

Even in the old days, Zane had always dreamed of pulling something like this, sometimes pouring champagne on the ice while the Crims skated. But the cure had made him serious; he'd even run a test in the small fridge in his room. He'd filled a tray of ice cubes, each one with a slightly different mix of vodka and water, and stuck it in the freezer. The all-water cube had frozen normally, but those with more alcohol in them got slushier and slushier, leaving the final all-vodka cube completely liquid.

Tally looked down at the layer of spirits slowly spreading across the ice through their skates, melting away the marks of blades and falls. The stadium came into heart-pounding focus, until Tally could see every detail of a rising plume of green and yellow fireworks. When the thunderous boom reached her ears, another ominous creak sounded. The fireworks display was building in intensity, ramping up for the finale.

Tally raised her hand for Zane.

He rounded the next turn, then headed toward them, skating hard. She felt a shimmer of panic in the pack around her, like a herd of gazelles spotting some big cat in the distance. A few Crims took last slugs from their flasks, then squirted boxes of orange juice into them to erase the evidence of what they'd done.

Tally grinned, imagining the pretty befuddlement she would put on for the wardens: *We were all just standing there talking and minding our own business, not even skating, and suddenly . . .*

"Watch out!" Zane cried, and the pack split in half, opening to create a path for him.

He skated into its center and jumped into the air inhumanly high, eyes and blades flashing, then brought his skates down hard onto the ice, all his weight behind them.

Zane instantly disappeared from view with a noise like breaking glass, and Tally heard the crack spreading with a sound that built like the shriek of a falling tree out in the Smoke. For a strange split second she was pushed up into the air as a large plate of ice teeter-tottered on the fulcrum of a lifter, but then it snapped in half and Tally was falling, her stomach lurching up into her throat. Gloved hands grabbed her coat from every direction in a moment of group panic, then a whoop rose up as the middle of the rink gave way altogether, icy shards and Crims and Zambonies all tumbling down toward the green grass of the soccer field, ten thousand faces staring up at them in shock.

Now *this* was bubbly.

BOUNCE

For a moment it was quiet.

All around her, shattered ice fell without a sound, catching the stadium lights as it spun. Wind tore the war cries from the Crims' mouths. The crowd below looked up in stunned silence. Tally spread her arms to slow her fall, clutching the precious seconds with cupped fingers. This part of a bungee jump was always like flying.

Then a burst of light and sound sent Tally spinning, ears pummeled and eyes forced shut by blinding streaks of brilliance. After a few stunned seconds, she shook her head and opened her eyes: Rainbow shards of fire traveled away in every direction, as if Tally were at the center of an exploding galaxy. More booms thundered above her, unleashing a steady rain of incandescence. She realized what had happened. . . .

The grand finale of the fireworks show had detonated just as the pack of falling Crims had broken through the ice. The timing of the breakthrough had been a little too perfect.

One sizzling flare clung to her bungee jacket, burning with the cool insistence of safety fireworks, tickling her face with cast-off sparks. Tally flailed her arms to right herself, but the ground was already rushing up, only seconds away. She was still out of control when the straps of the bungee jacket bit into her, bringing her headfirst plummet to a halt a few meters from the ground.

As the jacket yanked Tally upright and back into the air, she rolled into a ball in case anything big was still falling. The possibility of one of them catching a chunk of ice or a tumbling Zamboni had always been the nervous-making part of this plan. But Tally made the bounce unscathed, and as she reached its apex she heard the *ahhh* of the crowd's vast confusion. They knew something had gone wrong.

She and Zane had thought about hacking the scoreboard to show a message at this moment, to penetrate the crowd's pretty haze while their heads were spinning. But then the wardens would know the breakthrough had been planned, which would lead to all sorts of bogus complications.

The New Smokies would hear about this trick one way or another, and they, at least, would know what it meant. . . .

The cure had worked. The New Smoke had allies inside the city. The sky was falling.

• • •

Tally's hoverbouncing came to a stop about midfield, on grass littered with broken ice, shuddering Zambonies, giggling Crims, and the few innocent skaters who'd fallen through, no doubt suddenly glad that bungee jackets were required in the rink. She looked around for Zane, and saw that his momentum had carried him down the field and into one of the goals. She ran toward that end, checking on Crims along the way. Everyone's tattoos were pulsing madly, spinning with the anti-pretty magic of the breakthrough. But nobody was hurt beyond a few bruises or a little singed hair.

"It worked, Tally!" Fausto said softly as she passed, staring with amazement at a chunk of ice in his hand. She kept running.

Zane was laughing hysterically, tangled up in the net. When he saw Tally, he cried out a long, "Go-o-o-o-al!"

She thudded to a halt, relieved, and let herself enjoy the bubbliness of everything, the world transformed around her. It was as if she could take in the whole audience at a glance, every expression crystal clear in the unreal sharpness of the stadium lights. Ten thousand faces stared back at her, awestruck and amazed.

Tally imagined herself making a speech right now, telling them all about the operation, the lesions, the terrible price of being pretty—that lovely meant brainless, and that their easy lives were empty. The bedazzled crowd looked as if they would listen.

She and Zane had wanted to signal the New Smokies, but that hadn't been the only goal of the breakthrough. A trick on this scale would jazz up the Crims for a few days, they knew, but would a truly bubbly experience permanently change pretties who hadn't taken the pills? From the look in Fausto's eyes, Tally thought it might. And now, seeing the faces of the crowd—new and middle pretties and even crumblies all head-spinning together—she wondered if the falling sky had awakened something larger.

The city had definitely noticed. Wardens were streaming onto the field, first-aid kits in hand. Tally had never seen such panicked expressions on middle pretties. Like the crowd, they all looked stunned that anything could have gone so totally wrong here in the city. The hovercameras that had been ready to record the play-off game were panning across the field, taking in the wreckage. By the end of the day, Tally realized, this trick would be broadcast in every city on the globe.

She took a deep breath. It felt like setting off her first firework as a littlie, amazed that one little press of a button could make so much noise, wondering if she was going to get in trouble. As her euphoria wore off, Tally couldn't shake the feeling that, no matter how carefully they had covered up the trick, someone was going to know the breakthrough had been planned.

Suddenly, Tally needed Zane's touch, his silent reassurance, and she ran the rest of the distance to the goal. He was being untangled from the torn net, a pair of wardens treating his face with medspray. Tally pushed them aside and took Zane into her arms.

There were wardens everywhere, so she spoke in pretty. "Bubbly-making, huh!"

"Utterly," he said. Zane didn't have any flash tattoos, but Tally could feel his heart pounding through the heavy winter coat.

"Are you broken anywhere?"

"No. Just ouching." He touched one side of his face gingerly; it bore red lines in the pattern of the net. "Looks like we scored."

She giggled and kissed his wounded cheek as softly as she could, then brought her lips to his ear. "It worked. It really worked. It's like we can do anything."

"We can."

"After this, the New Smokies *have* to know the cure works. They'll send us more pills, and we can change everything."

He pulled away and nodded, then leaned closer to kiss her ear softly and murmur, "And if they don't notice this, we'll just have to go out looking for them."

PARTY CRASH

That night was all about champagne. Although they'd sworn off drinking, Tally and Zane felt as if they had to toast the Crims' survival of the Great Collapse of Nefertiti Stadium.

They had all practiced for tonight, every reaction rehearsed, so there was no mention of spirits poured onto the ice, no gloating about a plan that had worked perfectly—just the excited chatter of new pretties recovering from a bubbly and unexpected departure from the norm.

Everyone told and retold the story of their own fall—the shudder of cracking ice, the dazzling interior of the fireworks display, the yank of bungee jackets, and, after it was all over, alarmed calls from crumbly parents who had seen the whole thing replayed again and again on every channel. Most of the Crims had been interviewed for the feeds, telling their stories with expressions of innocent surprise. The newsfeed story was spreading and mutating: calls for resignations from the city architecture board, a total rescheduling of the soccer play-offs, and the closure of the floating rink forever (a bogus side effect that Tally hadn't anticipated).

But it didn't take long for the feeds to get repetitious—even your own face on a wallscreen was boring after you'd seen it fifty times—so Zane led them outside to build a bonfire in Denzel Park.

The Crims stayed bubbly, their flash tattoos spinning in the firelight as they retold their stories. They all were speaking fluent pretty in case anyone was listening, but Tally heard more than vapid nonsense in their words. It was like the way she and Zane spoke to each other, always aware of the cuffs but loading their pretty-talk with meaning. The silent conspiracy that they had shared was growing beyond the two of them. As Tally stared into the flames, listening to the Crims around her, she began to believe that the bubbly-making excitement of the breakthrough really would stick. Maybe people could *think* their way out of being pretty-minded, no pills required.

"Better drink that champagne, Skinny," Zane said, his fingers drifting along the back of her neck to interrupt her thoughts. "I hear that alcohol evaporates totally quickly."

"Evaporates? That's terrible." Tally made a serious face, and held her champagne up to the firelight. The news was giving hourly updates on the breakthrough investigation. A bunch of engineers were trying to figure out how twenty centimeters of lifter-supported ice could have buckled under the weight of a few dozen people. Blame had been assigned to shock waves from the fireworks show, heat from the stadium lights, even sympathetic vibrations from skaters moving in tandem like marching soldiers. But none of the experts had guessed that the real reason for the breakthrough had evaporated into thin air.

She raised her glass, clinking it against Zane's. He drained his glass, then took hers, splashing some champagne into his. "Thanks, Skinny," he said.

"For what?"

"For sharing."

She gave him a pretty smile. He meant the pills they'd split, of course, not the champagne. "Anytime. I'm glad there was enough for two."

"Bubbly luck how it worked out."

She nodded. The cure hadn't been perfect, but considering they'd each only had half a dose, the test had been a success. The cure had affected Zane almost instantly, shattering his pretty-mindedness in a few days. Tally's pill had worked more slowly, and she still woke up fuzzy most mornings, needing Zane to remind her to think bubbly thoughts. The good part was, she never got Zane's awful headaches.

"It's better shared, I think," Tally said, clinking his glass again. She remembered the warning in the letter from herself, and shivered despite the fire. Maybe two pills was actually too much, and if Tally had taken both she would have been brain-dead by now.

Zane pulled her closer. "Like I said . . . thanks." He kissed her, his lips warm in the cold night air, eyes flickering with bonfire reflections, and held his mouth to hers for a long time. Between the oxygen-missing kiss and the champagne, Tally felt herself getting pretty-minded, the edges of the firelit party turning fuzzy. Which maybe wasn't always a bad thing. . . .

Zane finally let her go and turned toward the bonfire, nuzzling her ear to whisper, "We have to get these things off."

"Shhh." Even with winter coats and gloves covering their cuffs, Tally felt a little too famous at the moment to make plans out loud. The Crims had already thrown rocks to drive away one hover-camera covering the party for some follow-up story on the rink collapse.

"It's driving me crazy, Tally."

"Don't worry. We'll figure it out." *Just stop talking,* she pleaded silently.

Zane kicked a fallen branch into the bonfire. As it burst into flame, he let out a pained sound.

"Zane?"

He shook his head, fingers at his temples. Tally swallowed. Another headache. Sometimes they ended after a few seconds, sometimes they lasted for hours.

"No. I'm okay." He sucked in a deep breath.

"You know, you could go to a doctor," she whispered.

"Forget that! They'll know I'm cured."

She pulled him closer to the crackle of the fire and pressed her lips to his ear. "I told you about Maddy and Az, David's parents? They were doctors—surgeons—and for a long time even they didn't know about the brain lesions. They just thought most people were stupid. A regular doctor won't think there's anything wrong with fixing you."

Zane shook his head furiously and turned to whisper in her ear. "It won't stop with a regular doctor, Tally. New pretties don't get sick."

She looked around the fire at the glowing faces. The Crims wound up at the hospital often enough, but only for injuries, not illness. The operation boosted your immune system, strengthened your organs, fixed your teeth forever. An unhealthy new pretty was such a rarity, there would probably be a ton of tests. And if Zane's headaches persisted, the test results would be passed on to experts.

"They're keeping an eye on us already," he whispered. "We can't afford anyone poking around inside my head." He flinched again, pain contorting his features.

"We should go home," she said softly.

"You stay. I can make it to Pulcher okay."

She groaned and pulled him away from the fire. "Come on."

He let her lead him into the darkness, circling around the other Crims. Shay called out to them, but Tally waved her away, saying, "Too much champagne." Shay smiled sympathetically and turned back to the fire.

They trudged home, the bare ground glistening with frost in the moonlight, the cold wind sharp after the lulling heat of the fire. The night was beautiful, but Tally could only wonder about what was happening inside Zane's head. Was it just a minor side effect of the cure? Or a sign of something gone terribly wrong?

"Don't worry, Zane," she said, just above a whisper. "We'll figure this out. Or we'll get out of here and get help from the Smokies. This is Maddy's cure—she'll know what's going on."

He didn't answer, just stumbled up the hill beside her.

When Pulcher Mansion came into view, Zane pulled her to a halt. "Go back to the party. I can make it home okay from here." His voice was too loud.

She looked around, but they were alone—no pretties or hovercams in sight. "I'm worried about you," she whispered.

He lowered his voice. "It's silly to worry, Skinny. It's just a headache. Same thing as always. Probably because I was pretty longer than you." He forced a smile. "It's just taking me longer to get used to having a brain again."

"Come on. Let's get you in bed."

"No, you go back. I don't want them to know about . . . this."

"I won't say anything," Tally whispered. They had told no one about the cure, not until they absolutely trusted that the other Crims were bubbly enough to keep their mouths shut. "I'll just say you drank too much."

"Fine, but go back to the party," he said firmly. "You have to keep them bubbly. Make sure they don't get drunk and start saying stupid things."

Tally looked back at the fire, just visible through the trees below. With enough champagne, someone might start bragging. She looked back at Zane. "You'll be okay?"

He nodded. "Better already."

She took a breath of the cold air. He didn't look any better. "Zane . . ."

"Listen, I'll be fine. And no matter what happens, I'm glad we took the pills."

Tally took a deep breath to steady herself. "What do you mean, 'no matter what happens'?"

"I don't mean tonight. Just whenever. You know."

Tally looked into his gold-flecked eyes, and saw in them the pain he was silently carrying. Whatever was happening to Zane, staying bubbly wasn't worth losing him. She shook her head. "No, I don't know."

He sighed. "I guess that was a stupid way to put it. I'm fine."

"I'm worried about you."

"Just go back to the party."

Tally sighed softly. There was no point in arguing. She held up one arm, indicating the scarf wrapped around her wrist. "Okay. But if you feel worse, ping me."

He smiled bitterly. "At least those things are good for something."

She kissed him softly, then watched him trudge up to the door of the mansion and inside.

On the lonely trip back down to the party, the air seemed to grow colder. Tally almost wished she could be pretty-minded again, just for one night, instead of having to keep watch on the Crims. From the very first kiss, being with Zane had made things complicated.

She sighed. Maybe that was the way it always worked.

Zane would never go to a doctor, Tally knew. If his headaches turned into something worse, could she *make* him go? Of course, Zane was right: Any doctor who could fix his problem could probably figure out what had caused it, and that was someone who could make Zane pretty-minded again.

If only Croy hadn't disappeared. Tally wondered how long it would take for the New Smokies to get in touch with them now. After the breakthrough, they had to realize the cure had worked. Even if wherever they were hiding didn't have newsfeeds, every ugly in the world would be chattering about the rink collapse, talking about Tally Youngblood looking innocent on their wallscreens.

Of course, she and Zane still had to escape the city. Tally had no idea how to get the cuffs off. As they grew thinner, it *seemed* like the rings of steel were closer to coming off, but how long was it going to take? Tally didn't much like being in a race between her own starvation and Zane's brain melting.

And when they escaped, she didn't want to go without the other Crims. Peris and Shay, at least. The Crims were so bubbly tonight, they'd probably all jump on hoverboards and head out if she said the word. But how bubbly would they be tomorrow?

Suddenly, Tally felt exhausted. There were too many things to juggle. Too many worries all falling on her alone. All she'd wanted was to become a Crim, to feel safe inside a clique of friends, and now she'd found herself in charge of a rebellion.

"Your friend have too much champagne?"

Tally froze. The words had come out of the darkness, cutting her ears like fingernails scraping metal.

"Hello?"

A figure emerged from the shadows in a hooded winter coat, moving with total silence through the fallen leaves. The woman stood in a shaft of moonlight, ten centimeters taller than Tally, taller even than Zane. She had to be a Special.

Tally forced herself to relax, trying to conquer her nerves and make her face melt into the soft expression of a brand-new pretty. "Shay? Is that you being all scary-making?" she said angrily.

The figure took another step forward into the light of a walkway torch. "No, Tally. It's me." The woman pulled off her hood.

It was Dr. Cable.

THE DRAGON

"Do I know you?"

Dr. Cable smiled coldly. "I'm sure you remember me, Tally."

Tally took a step back, letting some of her fear show; even the most innocent new pretty would be frightened by the sight of Dr. Cable. Her cruel features, exaggerated by the moonlight, made her look like a beautiful woman half transformed into a werewolf.

Memories flooded into Tally's mind. Being trapped in Dr. Cable's office that awful first time they'd met, learning of the existence of Special Circumstances, and then again when she had agreed to find and betray Shay, the price for becoming pretty. Then, in the Smoke, after Cable had followed Tally with an army of Specials to burn her new home to the ground.

"Yeah," Tally said. "I think I remember. I used to know you, right?"

"Indeed, you did." Cable's sharp teeth glowed in the moonlight. "But what's more important, Tally, is that I know you."

Tally managed a vacant smile. Dr. Cable no doubt remembered their last meeting—Tally and David's rescue of the Smokies—when it had been necessary to crack her on the head.

Dr. Cable gestured at the black scarf that bound Tally's cuff tightly under her glove and winter coat. "Interesting way to wear a scarf."

"What, are you fashion-missing? Everybody does this."

"But I imagine you started the trend. You always were tricky."

Tally beamed prettily. "I guess. I used to play all kinds of tricks back when I was ugly."

"Nothing like today, though."

"Oh, you saw the feeds? Wasn't that totally *bogus*? The ice just falling out from under us like that!"

"Yes . . . just like that." Dr. Cable's eyes narrowed. "I must admit, at first you had me fooled. That floating rink was a typical architectural folly designed to amuse new pretties. An accident waiting to happen. But then I thought about the timing—the stadium full, a hundred cameras ready."

Tally blinked, shrugged. "I bet it was those fireworks. You could feel them right through the ice. Who's missing idea was that?"

Dr. Cable nodded slowly. "An almost believable accident.

And then I saw your face on the newsfeeds, Tally. All wide-eyed and innocent and telling your *bubbly* little tale." Cable's upper lip curled into something that was not a smile. "And I realized that you were still playing tricks."

Tally felt something punch into her stomach, something from ugly days: the old feeling of being caught. She tried to turn her fear into a look of surprise. "Me?"

"That's right, Tally: you. Somehow."

Under Dr. Cable's gaze, Tally imagined herself being hauled into the depths of Special Circumstances, the cure reversed, her memories erased again. Or maybe this time they wouldn't bother returning her to New Pretty Town at all. She tried to swallow, but her mouth felt full of cotton. "Yeah, right. Like everything's *my* fault," she managed.

Dr. Cable stepped closer, and Tally fought to hold her ground, though her whole body screamed *run.* The woman gazed at her coldly, as if peering at a specimen cut open on a table. "I certainly hope that it was your fault."

Tally frowned. "You hope what?"

"Let's speak frankly, Tally Youngblood. I've had enough of your pretty act. I'm not here to take you away to my dungeon."

"You're not?"

"Do you really think I care if you break things in New Pretty Town?"

"Um . . . kind of?"

Dr. Cable snorted. "Maintenance is not my department. Special

Circumstances is only interested in outside threats. The city can take care of itself, Tally. There are so many safety backups, it's hardly worth worrying about. Why do you think skaters on that rink had to wear bungee jackets?"

Tally blinked. It hadn't crossed her mind to wonder about the jackets; everything was always ultra-safe in New Pretty Town, otherwise new pretties would kill themselves left and right. She shrugged. "In case the lifters failed? Like in a power blackout?"

Cable let out a razor-sharp laugh that lasted less than a second. "There hasn't been a blackout in a hundred and fifty years." She shook her head at the thought and continued. "Knock down anything you want, Tally. I don't care about your little tricks . . . except for what they reveal about you."

The woman's gaze focused on her once more, and Tally again had to fight the urge to run. She wondered if this was simply a way to get her to admit what the Crims had done. Probably she'd said too much already. But something about Dr. Cable's cold stare—her razor voice, her predatory movements, her very existence in the world—made it impossible for Tally to act pretty-minded. By now, any real new pretty would have fled screaming or dissolved into a puddle on the spot.

Besides, if Special Circumstances really wanted Tally to confess her tricks, they wouldn't have bothered with a conversation.

"So why are you here?" Tally said in her normal voice, trying hard to keep it steady.

"I've always admired your survival instinct, Tally. You were a good little traitor when you had to be."

"Uh, thanks . . . I guess."

Cable nodded. "And now it turns out you have more of a brain than I gave you credit for. You resist conditioning very well."

"*Conditioning.* That's what you call it?" Tally swore. "Like it's a hair treatment or something?"

"Amazing." Dr. Cable leaned close again, her eyes focusing on Tally's as if trying to bore through to her brain. "Somewhere in there, you're still a tricky little ugly, aren't you? Most impressive. I could use you, I think."

Tally felt a flush of anger, a fire inside her head. "Um, like, didn't you *already* use me?"

"So, you do remember. Superb." The woman's cruel-pretty eyes, flat and lusterless and cold, somehow showed pleasure. "I know that was an unpleasant experience, Tally. But it was necessary. We needed to take our children back from the Smoke, and only you could help us. But I do apologize."

"Apologize?" Tally said. "For blackmailing me into betraying my friends, for destroying the Smoke, for killing David's father?" She felt an expression of disgust on her face. "I don't think you'll be using me, Dr. Cable. I've already done you enough favors."

The woman only smiled again. "I agree. So it's time I did you a favor. What I am offering is something quite . . . bubbly."

The word on Cable's thin, cruel lips made Tally laugh dryly. "What would you know about being bubbly?"

"You'd be surprised. We at Special Circumstances know all about sensations, especially the ones you and your so-called Crims are always searching for. I can give it to you, Tally. All day, every day, bubblier than you can imagine. The real thing. Not just an escape from the haze of being pretty—something better."

"What are you talking about?"

"Remember flying on a hoverboard, Tally?" Cable said, her dull eyes igniting with cold fire. "That feeling of being alive? Yes, we can make people pretty inside—empty and lazy and vapid—but we can also make them *bubbly,* as you call it. More intense than you ever felt as an ugly, more alive than a wolf taking its prey, even bubblier than ancient Rusty soldiers killing one another over some plot of oil-rich desert. Your senses sharper, your body faster than any athlete's in history, your muscles as strong as any human's in the world."

The woman's razor voice fell silent, and Tally could suddenly hear the night around them perfectly—icicles dripping against hard ground, trees creaking in the wind, the bonfire below spitting out random showers of sparks. She could hear the party perfectly: Crims shouting about the exploits of the day, arguing about who had bounced highest or landed hardest. Cable's words had left the world as sharp as broken crystal.

"You should see the world as I see it, Tally."

"You're offering me a . . . job? As a Special?"

"Not a job. A whole new being." Dr. Cable said each word with deliberate care. "You can be one of us."

Tally was breathing hard, her pulse pounding through her entire body, as if the very idea was already changing her. She bared her teeth at Dr. Cable. "You think I'd work for you?"

"Consider your other choice, Tally. Spending your life looking for cheap thrills, managing a few moments at a time truly awake. Never clearing your head completely. But you'd make a fine Special. Traveling to the Smoke on your own was impressive; I always had hopes for you. But now that I see you're still tricky even after the operation"—Dr. Cable shook her head—"I realize that you're a natural. Join us."

A ping went through Tally as she understood something at last. "Tell me something. What were you like as an ugly?"

"Outstanding, Tally." The woman barked her one-second laugh. "You already know the answer, don't you?"

"You were tricky."

Cable nodded. "I was just like you. All of us were. We went to the ruins, tried to run farther, had to be brought back. That's why we let uglies play their little tricks—to see who's cleverest. To see which of you fights your way out of the cage. That's what your rebellion is all about, Tally—graduating to Special Circumstances."

Tally closed her eyes, and knew the woman was telling the truth. She remembered being an ugly, how easy it had always been to fool the dorm minders, how everyone always found ways around the rules. She took a deep breath. "But why?"

"Because someone has to keep things under control, Tally."

"That's not what I meant. What I want to know is, why do you do it to pretties? Why change their brains?"

"Goodness, Tally, isn't that obvious?" Dr. Cable shook her head in disappointment. "What do they teach in school these days?"

"That the Rusties almost destroyed the world," Tally recited.

"There's your answer."

"But we're better than them, we leave the wild alone, we don't strip-mine or burn oil. We don't have wars. . . ." Tally's voice sputtered out as she began to see.

Dr. Cable nodded. "*We* are under control, Tally, because of the operation. Left alone, human beings are a plague. They multiply relentlessly, consuming every resource, destroying everything they touch. Without the operation, human beings always become Rusties."

"Not in the Smoke."

"Think back, Tally. The Smokies clear-cut the land, they killed animals for food. When we landed, they were *burning trees.*"

"Not that many." Tally heard her voice break.

"What if there had been millions of Smokies? *Billions* of them, soon enough? Outside of our self-contained cities, humanity is a disease, a cancer on the body of the world. But we . . ." She reached out and stroked Tally's cheek, her fingers strangely hot in the winter air. "Special Circumstances . . . *we* are the cure."

Tally shook her head, stumbling back from Dr. Cable. "Forget it."

"This is what you've always wanted."

"You're wrong!" Tally shouted. "All I ever wanted was to be pretty. You're the one who keeps *getting in my way*!"

Her cry left them both in surprised silence, the last words echoing through the park. A hush settled over the party below, everyone probably wondering who was screaming her head off up in the trees.

Dr. Cable recovered first, sighing softly. "Goodness, Tally.

Relax. There's no need to shout. If you don't want what I'm offering, I'll leave you to your party. Feel free to age into a smug middle pretty. Soon enough, being bubbly won't matter so much; you'll forget this little conversation."

Tally held the doctor's cruel-pretty stare, almost wanting to tell her about the cure, to spit it back in her face. Tally's mind wasn't going to fade away, not tomorrow, not in fifty years; she wasn't going to forget who she was. And she didn't need Special Circumstances to feel alive.

Her throat still stung from yelling, but Tally said hoarsely, "Never."

"All I ask is that you think about it. Take your time deciding—it's all the same to me. Just remember the way it felt falling through that ice. You can have that feeling every second." Dr. Cable waved a hand casually. "And if it makes a difference, I may even find space for your friend Zane. I've had my eye on him for some time. He was once of help to me."

A chill went through Tally, and she shook her head. "No."

Dr. Cable nodded. "Yes. Zane was very forthcoming about David and the Smoke, that time he didn't run away."

She turned and disappeared into the trees.

BREAKUP

Tally stumbled back to the party.

The bonfire had grown bigger, its heat pushing back the revelers into a wide circle. Someone had requisitioned industrial-size logs of peat, big enough to burn through the Crims' collective carbon allowance for a month. The fire was topped off with fallen branches gathered from the park, and the hiss of still-green wood reminded Tally of cook-fires in the Smoke, when the water inside fresh-cut trees would boil, steam spitting out as if giving voice to the angry spirits of the forest.

She looked up at the column of smoke rising, ominously dark against the sky. That's how the Smoke had gotten its name. As Dr. Cable had said, the Smokies burned trees ripped alive from the ground. Human beings had been pulling that particular trick for thousands of years; a few centuries before, they'd almost put enough carbon in the air to screw up the climate for good. Only when someone had released an oil-transforming bacteria into the air had Rusty civilization been brought to a halt, and the planet saved.

And now, at their bubbliest, the Crims were instinctively headed in the same direction. Suddenly, the warm, cheery fire just made Tally feel worse.

She listened to the voices around her—bragging about how far they'd hoverbounced on the soccer field, debating who'd done the best interview for the feeds. Her unhappy conversation with Dr. Cable had left Tally's senses sharpened; she could separate every sound, tease apart every strand of conversation. Suddenly the Crims all sounded foolish, repeating the stories of their petty victories to one another again and again. Just like pretties.

"Skinny?"

She turned from the fire to find Shay next to her.

"Is Zane okay?" Shay peered closer, and her eyes widened. "Tally-wa, you look . . ."

Tally didn't need her to finish, she could see it in Shay's eyes: She looked terrible. Tally smiled tiredly at this news. That was part of the cure, of course. She might still be gorgeous—her bone structure perfect, her skin flawless—but Tally's face revealed the turmoil inside. Now that she could think unpretty thoughts, she would no longer be beautiful every minute of the day. Anger, fear, and anxiety were not pretty-making.

"Zane's all right. It's just me."

Shay leaned her weight against Tally, putting an arm around her. "Why so sad, Skinny? Tell me."

"It's just"—she glanced around at the boasting Crims—"it's everything, kind of."

Shay lowered her voice. "I thought today went perfectly."

"Sure. Perfect."

"Until Zane went and drank too much, of course. That's all it was, right?"

Tally made a noncommittal sound. She didn't want to lie to Shay. Eventually, she would tell her all about the cure, which would mean explaining Zane's headaches.

Shay sighed, squeezing Tally harder. There was a moment of silence, and then she asked, "Skinny, what happened to you guys up there?"

"Up where?"

"You know—when you climbed the transmission tower. It changed you, somehow."

Tally played with the scarf around her wrist, wishing she could tell her friend everything. But it was too risky to share news of the cure until they were safely outside the city. "I don't know what to say, Squint. It was really bubbly-making up there. You can see the whole island, and you can fall at any moment. Die, even. That makes a difference."

"I know," Shay whispered.

"You know what?"

"How it feels. I climbed the tower. Fausto and I figured out how to hack the minders, and last night I decided to go for it. To make myself bubbly for the breakthrough."

"Really?" Tally stared at her. Shay's face glowed with pride in the firelight, her implanted eye-jewels glittering. All the Crims were changing, but if Shay was hacking minders and scaling the Valentino tower, she was way ahead of the rest of them. "That's great. And you climbed up *at night*?"

"Only way to get away with it, since you and Zane got so totally busted. Fausto said I should wear a bungee jacket, but I wanted to do it like you did. I could have fallen—died, like you said. I even cut myself on a cable." With a smile, she showed a red mark that stretched across her palm, but then paused a moment, unpretty lines appearing on her forehead. "But it was kind of disappointing."

"How?"

"It didn't change me as much as I thought it would."

Tally shrugged. "Well, everyone's different. . . ."

"I suppose so," Shay said softly. "But it made me wonder . . . It wasn't just you guys climbing the tower, was it? There was something else that happened that day, Skinny. You'd never even hung out alone with Zane before, but since then you two have your own secret club, smiling at your own jokes and whispering all the time. You never go anywhere without each other."

"Squint . . . ," Tally said, and sighed. "Sorry if we've been all coupley. But, you know, it's my first crush as a pretty."

Shay stared at the fire. "That's what I thought, at first. But it's gone way past that, Tally. You're so different from the rest of us—both of you." Her voice rose above a whisper. "Zane gets those weird headaches that he tries to hide, and that was you screaming a minute ago, wasn't it?"

Tally swallowed.

"What changed you guys that day?"

Tally pointed at her wrist. "Shhh."

"Don't shush me! *Tell* me."

Tally looked around them nervously. The fire consumed more fallen branches, hissing loudly, and most of the Crims were singing drinking songs. No one had heard Shay's outburst, but Tally could feel the hard metal of the cuff around her wrist, always listening. "I can't tell you, Squint."

"Yes, you can." Shay's face seemed to change in the firelight, the pretty softness burning away as her anger grew. "You see, Tally, I remembered some things when I was up in that tower, staring down at the ground and wondering if I was going to die. And then I remembered a few more while I was falling through the ice and bouncing on the soccer field. A lot of things came back from ugly days. Isn't that great?"

Tally turned away from the harsh expression on Shay's face. "Yeah, sure it is."

"Glad you agree. So here's what I remembered: It's because of you that I'm here in the city, Tally. All those stories I used to tell? They were bogus. What really happened is that you followed me out to the Smoke to betray me, right?"

Tally felt it again, the same gut-punch as when she'd seen Dr. Cable in the trees: caught. From the moment she'd felt the pills working on her, Tally had known somewhere inside her that this moment would come, that Shay would eventually remember what had really happened back when they were uglies. But Tally hadn't expected it so soon. "Yeah, I followed you to bring you back here. It's my fault, what happened to the Smoke. The Specials tracked me there."

"Right, you betrayed us. *After* you stole David from me, of course." Shay laughed bitterly. "I hate to bring the whole David thing up, but who knows if I'll remember it tomorrow, you know? So I thought I'd mention it while I'm bubbly."

Tally turned to her. "You'll remember it."

Shay only shrugged. "Maybe. But tricks like today's don't come around that often. So you might be off the hook again by tomorrow."

Tally took a deep breath, inhaling the smell of wood smoke, burning peat, pine needles, and spilled champagne. The firelight revealed everything as bright as day, even the whorls of her fingerprints. She didn't know what to say.

"Look at me," Shay said. Her flash tattoo was spinning hard, its halo of snakes blurring together like the spokes of a bicycle wheel. "Tell me what happened to you that day. Keep me bubbly. You owe me."

Tally swallowed. She and Zane had promised each other not to tell anyone—not yet. But neither of them had realized how far Shay had come—bubbly enough to climb the tower on her own, to finally remember what had really happened back in ugly days. Probably she could keep a secret, and telling her about the cure would give her hope, at least. It was the only way Tally could begin to make up for what she'd done.

And Shay was right: Tally owed her.

"Okay. Something else happened that day."

Shay nodded slowly. "I thought so. What was it?"

Tally pointed at Shay's scarf, and together they pulled it off and wrapped it tightly around Tally's wrist, another layer over the cuff. After another breath, she said in the softest whisper she could manage, "We found a cure."

Shay's eyes narrowed. "It's about starving yourself, isn't it?"

"No. Well, that helps. Hunger, coffee, playing tricks—all that stuff Zane's been doing for months. But the real cure is . . . simpler than that."

"What is it? I'll do it."

"You can't."

"The *hell* with you, Tally!" Shay's eyes flashed. "If you can do it, I can!"

Tally shook her head. "It's a pill."

"A pill? Like vitamins?"

"No, a special pill. Croy brought it to me, the night of the Valentino bash. Try to remember, Shay. Before you and I came back to the city, Maddy had figured out how to reverse the operation. You helped me write a letter, remember?"

Shay's face went blank for a moment, then she frowned. "That's when I was pretty."

"Right. After we rescued you, when we were hiding out in the ruins."

"Funny, those days are harder to remember than back when I was ugly." Shay shook her head.

"Well, Maddy figured out a cure. But it was untested, dangerous. She wouldn't give it to you because you refused. You wanted to stay pretty. So I had to give myself up to test it. That's why I'm here."

"And Croy brought it to you *a month* ago?"

Tally nodded, taking Shay's hand. "And it works. You've seen how it changed me and Zane. It makes us bubbly all the time. So once we get out of here, you can—" Shay's expression brought Tally to a halt. "What's the matter?"

"You and Zane both took some?"

"Yeah," Tally said. "There were two pills, and we split them. I was afraid to do it on my own."

Shay turned to the fire, pulling her hand away. "I can't believe you, Tally."

"What?"

Shay whirled to face her. "Why him? Why didn't you ask *me*?"

"But I—"

"You're supposed to be my friend, Tally. I've done everything for you. I was the one who first told you about the Smoke. I was the one who introduced you to David. And when you came to New Pretty Town, I helped you become one of the Crims. Did it even *occur* to you to share the cure with me? It's your fault I'm like this, after all!"

Tally shook her head. "There wasn't time . . . I didn't even—"

"No, of course you didn't," Shay spat. "You barely even knew Zane, but he was the leader of the Crims, so hooking up with him was the next trick on your list. Just like David out in the Smoke. That's why you split the cure with him."

"It wasn't like that!" Tally cried.

"*You* are like that, Tally. You have *always* been like that! No cure is going to make you any different—you were busy betraying people a long time ago. You didn't need any operation to make you selfish and shallow and full of yourself. *You already were.*"

Tally tried to answer, but something horrible rose up in her throat, choking off her words. Then she noticed the quiet around them, and realized that Shay had been yelling. The other Crims looked on in puzzlement, only the hiss of the fire filling the silence. Pretties didn't fight. They hardly ever argued, and they certainly never shouted at one another in the middle of a party. That sort of obnoxious behavior was strictly for uglies.

She looked down at her wrist, wondering if Shay's raised voice had gotten through the layers of cloth and plastic. If so, it would all end tonight.

Shay pulled away and whispered fiercely, "I may be my pretty self again tomorrow, Tally. But I'll remember this, I swear. No matter what sweet things I say to you, trust me, I am *not* your friend." She turned and walked into the trees, thrashing through frozen branches.

Tally looked around at the other Crims, the champagne glasses in their hands glittering sharply in the moonlight, reflecting the wasteful fire. She felt alone and exposed with all of them staring at her. But after a few more horrible moments of silence, they turned away and started telling breakthrough stories again.

Tally's head spun. The change in Shay had been so shocking, so complete, and she hadn't even taken a pill. A few minutes of real anger had transformed her from a placid pretty to a wild beast. . . . It didn't make sense.

Suddenly, Tally remembered Dr. Cable's last words, about Zane helping Special Circumstances. After his friends had run away, he must have been taken to see her, confessing everything he knew about the Smoke and the mysterious David who took uglies there. Maybe that was what had kept him bubbly all these months—his shame about not running away, his guilt over having betrayed his friends to Dr. Cable.

Of course, Tally had her own guilty secrets. So she'd stayed bubbly too, never quite fitting in, never quite sure of what she wanted, no matter how much champagne she drank. Old and ugly emotions were always waiting, hidden inside, ready to change her.

And Shay had been transformed as well—not by guilt, but by buried anger. Concealed behind her pretty smiles were suppressed memories of the betrayals that had cost her David, the Smoke, and finally her freedom. All it had taken was climbing up the tower and falling through the ice—enough stimulation to break the logjam in her memories—to bring that anger to the surface. And now she hated Tally.

Maybe Shay wouldn't need the pills at all—maybe old memories from ugly days were enough. Perhaps, thanks to every terrible thing that Tally Youngblood had ever done to her, Shay would find her own way to a cure.

RAIN

Tally woke up with an ugly mind.

It was what she used to call bubbly—the gray morning light somehow bright and glittery, sharp enough to cut flesh. The rain beat against Zane's window in malicious, half-frozen drops, tapping like impatient fingernails.

But Tally didn't mind the rain. It blurred the city's spires and gardens, reducing the view to gray and green blotches, the lights of other mansions casting halos on the wet glass.

The downpour had started late the night of the party, finally extinguishing the Crims' bonfire, as if Dr. Cable had called the heavens down to drown their celebration. For the two days since, Tally and Zane had been trapped inside, unable to speak freely within the smart walls of Pulcher Mansion. She hadn't even had a chance to tell him about Shay's outburst of old memories, or about meeting Dr. Cable in the woods. Not that she was looking forward to revealing what she'd confessed to Shay, or bringing up what Cable had told her about Zane's past.

This morning had brought another mountain of pings, but Tally couldn't face any more requests to join the Crims. The stadium collapse and the last two days of feed coverage had made them the hottest clique in New Pretty Town, but a bunch of new members was exactly what the Crims didn't need. What they needed was to stay bubbly. Tally worried, though, that a third day stuck inside by the rain would bore everyone back into being pretty-heads.

Zane was already awake, sipping coffee and staring out the window, absently spinning his cuff with one finger. He glanced at her as she stirred, but didn't make a sound. The silence between them since they'd been cuffed had felt conspiratorial, their secret whispers intimate, but Tally wondered if talking so little was gradually shutting them off from each other. Shay had been right about one thing: Tally had hardly known Zane before that day they'd climbed the tower. What Dr. Cable had told her made Tally realize that she still didn't know him very well.

But once the cuffs were off and they were outside the city, their memories freed from the blur of pretty-headedness, there would be nothing to stop them from telling each other everything.

"Bogus weather, huh?" she said.

"Just a few degrees colder and it'd be snowing."

Tally brightened. "Yeah, snow would be totally pretty-making."

She fished a dirty T-shirt from the floor, wadded it up, and threw it at his head. "Snowball fight!"

He let it bounce off him, smiling softly. Zane's headache from the night of the party had passed, but it had left him in a serious mood. Without having said a word, they both knew they would have to escape the city soon.

It all came down to the cuffs.

Tally gave hers an experimental pull. It slipped from her wrist onto her hand, catching only centimeters from coming off. She'd hardly eaten anything the day before, determined to fade away to nothing if that's what it took to get the thing off, but Tally wondered if she would ever be skinny enough. The cuff's circumference looked just smaller than the width of the bones in her hand, a measurement that no amount of starvation was going to alter.

She stared at the red marks left by the metal. The big bone that was the joint of her left thumb was most of the problem. Tally envisioned pulling the thumb back hard enough to snap the bone, leaving room for the cuff to slip off, and couldn't imagine anything more painful.

A ping came from the door, and Tally sighed. Someone had gotten sick of being ignored and had come around in person.

"We're not here, are we?" Zane said.

Tally shrugged. Not if it was Shay outside, or some wannabe trying to get into the Crims. Come to think of it, there was no one she was in the mood to see.

The ping came again.

"Who is it, anyway?" Tally asked the room, but the room didn't know. Which meant whoever it was wasn't wearing their interface ring.

"That's . . . interesting," Zane said. They looked at each other for a moment, and Tally felt the moment when curiosity got the better of them.

"Okay, open up," she told the room.

The door slid away to reveal Fausto, looking like a kitten pulled out of a river. His hair was plastered to his head, his clothing soaked, but his eyes were bright. Under his arms he carried two hoverboards, their knobbly surfaces dripping water on the floor.

He walked into the room without a word and dropped the boards. They came to a hovery stop at knee height, while Fausto unloaded four crash bracelets and two belly sensors from his pockets. He took one of the boards and turned it over, gesturing at the access panel on its bottom. Tally rolled out of bed to take a closer look. The nuts securing the panel were stripped, and two red wires snaked out, their ends twisted together and sealed with black tape.

Fausto mimed pulling the wires apart, then opened his hands in a gesture that meant, *Where is it?* He grinned.

Tally nodded slowly. Fausto was still bubbly from the breakthrough, his flash tattoo spinning. He, at least, hadn't wasted the last rainy days and nights. These boards were tricked up, ugly-style. When the wires were disconnected, their governors and trackers would crash, freeing the boards from the city interface.

Once they'd gotten rid of the cuffs, Zane and Tally could fly anywhere they wanted.

"Awesome," she said aloud, not caring if the walls heard it.

• • •

They didn't wait for sunshine.

Flying through the rain was like standing under a freezing shower. The hole in the wall had coughed up goggles and grippy shoes, so it was possible to stay on board, but just barely. The high winds plastered Tally's soaking winter coat against her skin, pulling her hood back from her head and threatening to spill her on every turn.

Her reflexes from ugly days hadn't disappeared, though. If anything, the operation had improved her balance, and the almost freezing rain kept Tally from slipping into a pretty haze, even with her coat's heating turned to maximum. With a pounding heart and chattering teeth, her mind stayed crystal clear.

She and Zane shot down to the river at treetop level, following the winding path of Denzel Park. The branches danced in the wind under them, like flailing hands trying to reach up and drag them down. As Tally leaned into turns, cutting the wind with her hands, the last traces of her morning pretty-mindedness disappeared. The weight of the sensor clipped to her belly ring—which told the board where her center of gravity was—brought back memories of expeditions to the Rusty Ruins with Shay, reminding her how easy it had been to sneak out of the city back in ugly days.

Only the inescapable presence of the interface cuff spoiled her mood. The crash bracelets were big enough to fit over the metal ring, their soft, smart plastics conforming to its shape. Still, Tally imagined the manacle cutting into her flesh.

They reached the river and turned onto it, skimming under bridges, her board slapping the churning whitecaps stirred up by the wind. Laughing maniacally, Zane pulled in front of Tally and dipped his board's tail into the water, sending up a wall of spray.

She crouched low on the board, ducking the worst of the water, and tipped it forward to shoot into the lead. Banking across Zane's path, she slapped the river with her board, raising up a wall of water in front of him. She heard him whoop as he zoomed straight through it.

Soaking and panting hard, Tally wondered if this is what it would be like to be a Special—her senses sharp, every moment intense, her body a perfectly tuned machine. She remembered Maddy and Az saying that Specials didn't have the lesions—they were cured.

Of course, there was a price for being Special—the small matter of a new face: wolflike teeth and cold, dull eyes that terrified everyone you met. And the horror-movie look was nothing compared with having to work for Special Circumstances—tracking down runaway uglies and crushing anyone the city felt threatened by.

And what if the Special operation changed your mind in some other way: making you obedient instead of empty-headed? With all that speed and strength, running away from the city would be easy, but what if the Special operation put something like the cuff *inside* you, something that would always tell them where you were?

A faceful of water reminded Tally to keep her mind on the

game, and she shot high into the air, soaring over a footbridge. Below, Zane was looking back uncertainly, trying to figure out where she'd disappeared to.

Tally dropped down just ahead of him, hitting the river with a sound like a face being slapped, throwing up an explosion of water. But she knew instantly she'd hit too fast. At this speed, the water was as hard as concrete, and her feet slipped at the impact—Tally felt herself sliding off. . . .

She was falling for a moment, then the crash bracelets kicked in, gripping her wrists cruelly and spinning her to a safe halt.

She wound up waist-deep in the freezing water, hanging from the bracelets, crying out as she discovered a whole new level of being soaked. She was glad to see that her attack had also dumped Zane.

"*Really* bubbly move, Skinny!" he shouted, pulling himself back onto his hoverboard. Too out of breath to answer, she crawled onto hers and lay on her stomach, laughing. The two of them wordlessly coasted over to the ground to recover their breath.

On the muddy riverbank, they huddled close for warmth. Her heart still pounded, the expanse of rain-struck water stretched before them like a field of glittering flowers.

"So beautiful," Tally said, trying to imagine what it would be like in the wild with Zane, feeling this way every day, free from the mind-numbing restrictions of the city.

Her wrist was throbbing, and she pulled her crash bracelet off to take a look. In the wipeout, the metal cuff underneath had cut into her skin. Tally gave it a tug, but even with her soaking skin, it stopped at its usual spot.

"Still stuck," she said.

Zane took her hand and said softly, "Don't push it, Tally." He covered the cuff with her coat and whispered, "You'll only make your wrist swell up."

She swore, pulling on her hood. The rain beat on the plastic, impatient fingers drumming on her head. "I thought maybe with the water . . ."

"Nah. Cold makes metal contract, so they're probably tighter out here."

Tally looked at Zane, raising an eyebrow. "So," she whispered, "do they get bigger when they get hot?"

He was silent for a moment. Then, so softly that she could barely hear him above the rain, he whispered, "If they got *really* hot? I guess they'd get a little bigger."

"How much?"

He shrugged, the gesture almost invisible under his winter coat, but he was interested now. "How much heat can you stand?"

"You're not talking about a candle, are you?"

Zane shook his head. "Something much hotter than that. Something we could control, so it wouldn't roast our hands off. We'd still get burned, though."

She looked at the bulge in her sleeve and sighed. "Beats breaking your own thumb, I guess."

"Doing what?"

"Just something I was . . ." Her voice trailed off.

Zane's gaze followed hers across the river. On the opposite bank, two figures on hoverboards stood watching them, faceless in their hooded raincoats.

Tally fought to keep her voice down. "Smokies?"

Zane shook his head. "Those are dorm jackets."

"What would city uglies be doing out in this rain?"

He stood up. "Maybe we should ask."

CUTTERS

On the Uglyville side of the river, the four of them sheltered together under a tarp covering a paper recycler, hidden from view and out of the rain. The two uglies weren't wearing rings, Tally was glad to see; the four of them wouldn't be recorded by the city interface as having hung out together.

"Is that really you, Tally?" the girl whispered.

"Uh, yeah. Recognize me from the feeds?"

"No! It's me, Sussy. And this is Dex," she said. "Don't you remember us?"

"Remind me."

The girl just stared. She was wearing a crude leather strap around her neck, which looked like the sort of thing a Smokey might own—handmade and discolored by age. Where had she gotten it?

"We helped you with that 'New Smoke Lives' thing, remember?" the boy offered. "Back when you were . . . ugly."

An image came slowly into Tally's mind: huge burning letters lit as a diversion while she and David had broken into Special Circumstances. These were two of the uglies who had organized that trick, and then helped them hide out in the Rusty Ruins, bringing news and supplies from the city, playing more tricks to keep the wardens and Specials busy.

"You really forgot us," Dex said. "So it's true. They do something to your brains."

"Yeah, it's true," Zane said. "But a little softer, please." The rain was as loud as a jet engine on the plastic tarp, making it hard to hear. The two uglies needed reminding to keep their voices down.

Dex's stare dropped to Tally's wrist, covered by a crash bracelet and bound in a scarf, as if he didn't believe the cuff was really under there, listening. "Sorry."

When his eyes crept back up to stare at her face, Dex couldn't hide his amazement at her transformation. Sussy was silent—awestruck and hanging on every word. Under their gaze, Tally felt self-conscious and weirdly powerful. It was obvious the two would do anything she or Zane asked. Back when her brain had been prettified, she'd felt entitled to this sort of awe. But now, with her head clear, it was kind of embarrassing.

But talking to the two uglies was less awkward than it might have been. Tally's unpretty thoughts over the last month had made it easier to look at their imperfect faces. They didn't horrify her as much as her first glance at Croy had. The tiny gap between Sussy's two front teeth seemed more charming than revolting, and even Dex's zits didn't make her skin crawl.

"But the damage wasn't permanent," Zane was saying. "We're starting to get smarter. Which, by the way, is not something you can spread around to everyone, okay?"

The two nodded dumbly, and Tally wondered if hinting about the cure to random uglies was worth the risk. Of course, enlisting Sussy and Dex might be the quickest way to get a message to the New Smoke.

"What's the news from the ruins?" she asked.

Sussy leaned closer, remembering to whisper. "That's why we came down here. As far as we could tell, the New Smokies had all disappeared. Until last night."

"What happened last night?" Tally asked.

"Well, since they went missing, we've been going to the ruins every few nights," Dex said. "To check out the old spots, light sparklers. But we haven't seen anything all month."

Tally and Zane shared a glance. A month ago was about the same time Croy had left the pills for Tally to find. The timing probably wasn't a coincidence.

"But last night we found some stuff in an old hideout," Sussy said. "Burned-out lightsticks and some old magazines."

"Old magazines?" Tally asked.

"Yeah," Sussy said. "From the Rusty era. Those ones that showed how ugly everyone used to be."

"I don't think the New Smokies would have left those lying around," Tally said. "Those are precious. I knew someone who died to save them. So they must be back."

"But they're lying low," Dex said. "Playing it safe."

"Why?" Zane said softly. "And for how long?"

"How would we know?" Dex said. "That's why we came down here today. We were going to sneak over in the rain and find you, Tally. We thought you guys might have a clue."

"After you were all over the news the other day, we figured something was up," Sussy added. "Like, that stadium thing was a trick, right?"

"Glad you noticed," Tally said. "The New Smokies were supposed to notice too. Apparently, they did."

"We figured you knew something about it," Sussy said. "Especially after we spotted some of your pretty friends out here in Uglyville."

Tally frowned. "Pretties? Out here?"

"Yeah, in Cleopatra Park. I recognized a couple of them from the feeds. I think they were Crims. That's your clique, right?"

"Yeah, but . . ."

Sussy frowned. "You didn't know?"

Tally shook her head. After the last couple of days, she had gotten a few pings from other Crims—mostly complaints about the rain. But no one had said anything about going to Uglyville.

"What were they up to?" Zane asked.

Dex and Sussy looked at each other, unhappy expressions on their faces.

"Um, we're not sure," Sussy said. "They wouldn't talk to us, just chased us off."

Tally let out a slow breath through her teeth. Pretties were allowed on this side of the river—they could go anywhere they wanted in the city—but they never came to Uglyville. Which meant that Cleopatra Park would be a great place for a pretty to find some privacy, especially in the driving rain. But privacy for what?

"Didn't you tell everyone to lie low for a while?" Zane asked her.

"Yeah, I did." Tally wondered which of the Crims was behind this. And what "this" was.

"Take us there," she said.

Sussy and Dex led them up toward the park, flying slowly in the steady rain. Figuring that someone was monitoring the cuffs' positions, Tally had asked them to take an indirect route. The journey wound through half-familiar sights of her childhood: ugly dorms and schools, sodden parks, and empty soccer fields.

Despite the downpour, there were a few uglies out. One bunch was taking turns skidding down a hill, screaming as they ran to throw themselves onto a mudslide. A few played tag in a dorm courtyard, slipping and falling and winding up just as muddy as the first group. They were all having too much fun to notice the four hoverboarders gliding silently past.

Tally wondered if she'd had that much fun as an ugly. All she could recall from those days was dying to turn pretty, to get across the river and leave all this behind. Floating above the earth, her perfect face hidden by a hood, she felt like some risen spirit, enviously watching the living and trying to remember what it was like to be one of them.

Cleopatra Park, high in the greenbelt on the outer edge of Uglyville, was empty. The walking paths had been transformed into small creeks carrying the rain down toward the swollen river. The wildlife seemed to be in hiding except for a few miserable-looking birds that clung to the branches of the great pines that drooped low under their loads of water.

Sussy and Dex brought them to a clearing marked with slalom flags, and Tally felt a flush of recognition. "This is one of Shay's favorite spots. She taught me to hoverboard here."

"Shay?" Zane said. "But she'd tell us if she was up to some kind of trick, wouldn't she?"

"Um, maybe not," Tally said softly. No pings had come from Shay since the fight. "I've been meaning to tell you, Zane: She's kind of pissed off at me right now."

"Wow," Sussy said. "I thought pretties all liked each other."

"Usually, they do." Tally sighed. "Welcome to the new world."

Zane narrowed his eyes. "I think Tally and I need to talk." He glanced at the two uglies.

It took them a moment to realize what he meant, but then Sussy said, "Oh, sure. We'll be going. But what if . . . ?"

"If the New Smokies show up again, send me a ping," Tally said.

"Doesn't the city read your mail?"

"Probably. Don't say anything except that you saw us on the feeds and you want to join the Crims when you turn sixteen. Leave the real message hidden under that recycler, and I'll send someone to pick it up. Got that?"

"Got it," Sussy said with a gap-toothed smile. Tally figured the two would be headed out to the ruins every night now, rain or not, looking for the New Smokies, happy to have a mission.

She gave them a pretty smile. "Thanks for everything."

Tally and Zane sat in silence for a minute after the uglies had left, watching the clearing from a thick stand of trees. The plastic slalom flags drooped miserably in the rain, the wind barely lifting them. Rainwater gathered in spots, the shallow pools reflecting the gray sky like rippling mirrors. Tally remembered flying between the flags on her hoverboard in ugly days, learning to bank and turn. Back when she and Shay were really friends . . .

It was impossible to guess why Shay would be visiting this spot. Maybe it was nothing but a few Crims practicing their hoverboarding, figuring it was a great way to stay bubbly. No big deal.

As they sat, Tally realized she was out of excuses for not telling Zane everything. It was time to admit what she'd done to the Smoke and how she'd told Shay about the cure, and past time to bring up what Dr. Cable had revealed about Zane. But Tally wasn't looking forward to the conversation, and being soaking wet and cold wasn't helping. Her coat's heating was already turned up to maximum. The bubbliness from hoverboarding had worn off, replaced by Tally's anger at herself for having waited this long. The always-listening cuffs made it too easy to avoid mentioning uncomfortable subjects.

"So what happened between you and Shay?" Zane said. His voice stayed soft, but carried an edge of frustration.

"Her memories are starting to come back." Tally stared into a mud puddle before her, watching drops that had made their way down through the soaked pine trees distort its surface. "On the night of the breakthrough, she got really mad at me. She blames me for the Specials finding the Smoke. Which, I guess, is pretty much what happened. I betrayed them."

He nodded. "I figured that. All the stories you two told—back before the cure—they had you rescuing her from the Smoke. That sounds like pretty-talk for betrayal."

Tally looked up at him. "So you knew?"

"That you'd gone undercover for Special Circumstances? I'd guessed it."

"Oh." Tally didn't know whether to feel relieved or ashamed. Of course, Zane had cooperated with Dr. Cable himself, so maybe he understood. "I didn't want to do it, Zane. I mean, at first I went out there to bring Shay back, so they'd make me pretty, but then I changed my mind. I wanted to stay in the Smoke. I tried to destroy the tracker they'd given me, but I wound up setting it off. Even when I tried to do the right thing, I betrayed everyone."

Zane faced her, his eyes intense under his hood. "Tally, we're all manipulated by the people who run this city. Shay should know that."

"I wish that was all," Tally said. "I also stole David from her. Back when we were in the Smoke."

"Oh, him again." Zane shook his head. "Well, I guess she's

pretty pissed off at you right now. At least that'll keep her bubbly."

"Yeah, really bubbly." Tally swallowed. "And there's one more thing that's got her mad."

He waited silently, rain dripping from his hood.

"I told her about the cure."

"*You what?*" Zane's whisper cut through the rain like a hiss of steam.

"I had to." Tally spread her hands imploringly. "She had it halfway figured out already, Zane, and was thinking she could cure herself. She climbed the Valentino tower like we did, thinking that was what had changed us. But of course it didn't work, not like the pills. She kept asking me what happened to us. She said I owed her, after everything I did to her back in ugly days."

Zane swore under his breath. "So you told her about the pills? Great. That's one more thing that can go wrong."

"But she's totally bubbly, Zane. I don't think she'll give us away," Tally said, then shrugged. "If anything, finding out about the pills made her furious enough to stay bubbly for life."

"Furious? Because you're cured and she's not?"

"No." Tally sighed. "Because *you* are."

"What?"

"I owed *her*, and *you* got the other pill."

"But there wasn't time to—"

"I know that, Zane. But she doesn't. To her, it looks like . . ." She shook her head, feeling hot tears in her eyes. The rest of her was so cold, her fingers were slowly going numb. She began to tremble.

"It's okay, Tally." Zane reached out and took her hand, squeezing hard through the thick glove.

"You should have heard her, Zane. She really hates me."

"Listen, I'm sorry about that. But I'm glad it was me."

She looked up, her vision blurring with tears. "Yeah. Thanks for all the headaches, you mean."

"Better than staying a pretty-brain," he said. "But that's not what I meant. That day was about more than just finding those pills. I'm glad about . . . you and me."

She looked up and found him smiling. His fingers, still interlaced with hers, also trembled in the cold. Tally managed to smile back. "Me too."

"Don't let Shay make you feel bad about us, Tally."

"Of course not." She shook her head, realizing how much she meant it. Whatever Shay thought, Zane had been the right person to share the cure with. He had kept her bubbly, pushing her to pass the Smokies' tests, pressing her to dare the unproven pills. Tally had found more than a cure for pretty-headedness that day—she'd found someone to move forward with, past everything that had gone wrong last summer.

It had been littlie days when Peris had promised to stay her best friend forever—but the day he'd turned sixteen, Peris had left her behind in Uglyville. Then Tally had lost Shay's friendship, betraying her to Special Circumstances and stealing David from her. Now even David was gone, missing somewhere in the wild and half-erased from her memories. He hadn't even bothered to bring her the pills—he'd left that job to Croy. Tally could guess what that meant.

But Zane . . .

Tally stared into his golden, perfect eyes. He was here with her right now, in the flesh, and she'd been stupid to let what was between them get tangled up in her messy past. "I should have told you about Shay earlier. But the smart walls . . ."

"It's okay. But you can trust me. Always."

She pressed his hand in both of hers. "I know."

He reached up to touch her face. "We didn't really know each other very well that day, did we?"

"We took a chance, I guess. Weird how that happened."

He laughed. "I think that's the way it always happens. Usually without mysterious pills or Special Circumstances pounding on the door. But it's always taking a risk, when you . . . kiss someone new."

Tally nodded, and leaned forward. Their lips met, the kiss slow and intense in the chill of the rain. She could feel him trembling, and the muddy ground beneath them was cold, but their two hoods joined to block out the world, making a space that became warm from their mingling breath.

Tally whispered, "I'm so glad it was you with me that day."

"Me too."

"I—Ah!" She pulled away, wiping at her face. A trickle of water had crawled inside Tally's hood and was running down her cheek like a cold, malevolent tear.

He laughed and stood up, pulling her to her feet. "Come on, we can't stay here forever. Let's go back to Pulcher and get breakfast, and some dry clothes."

"I wasn't uncomfortable."

He smiled, but indicated his wrist and lowered his voice. "If we sit in one place too long, someone might get curious about what the big deal is out here in Uglyville."

"Whatever it is," she whispered.

But Zane was right. They should go home. They hadn't eaten anything all day except for a few calorie-purgers and some coffee. Their winter coats were heated, but between the physical effort of hoverboarding and the shock of getting dumped into the freezing river, Tally was starting to feel exhaustion and cold down in her bones. Hunger, the cold, and the kiss were all dizzy-making.

Zane snapped his fingers, and his board rose into the air.

"Wait a second," she said softly. "There's one more thing I should tell you about the night of the breakthrough."

"Okay."

"After I took you home . . ." The thought of Dr. Cable's feral face made her shiver, but Tally took a calming breath. She'd been stupid not to drag Zane outside sooner, getting him away from Pulcher Mansion's smart walls to tell him about her encounter with the doctor. She didn't want any secrets between them.

"What's wrong, Tally?"

"She was waiting for me . . . ," she said. "Dr. Cable."

The name made Zane's face go blank for a moment, then he nodded. "I remember her."

"You do?"

"She's kind of hard to forget," Zane said. He paused, staring out into the clearing. Tally wondered if he was going to say more.

Finally, she said, "She made me a weird sort of offer. She wanted to know if I—"

"Shhh!" he hissed.

"What—," she began, but Zane silenced her with a gloved hand. He turned and crouched in the mud, pulling her down beside him. Through the trees, a group of figures were marching into the clearing. They moved slowly, huddled in almost identical winter gear, their left wrists wrapped in black scarves. But Tally recognized one of them instantly, copper eyes bright and flash tattoo spinning in the cold.

It was Shay.

RITUAL

Tally counted ten of them, slogging with quiet determination across the muddy ground. They reached the middle of the clearing and arranged themselves in a wide circle around one of the slalom flags. Shay moved to stand in the center, turning slowly, peering at the others from under her hood. The others settled into place about an arm's length apart, facing Shay and waiting silently.

After a long moment motionless, she dropped her winter coat to the ground, pulling off her gloves and spreading her arms. She wore only trousers, a sleeveless white T-shirt, and the fake metal cuff on her left wrist. Tipping her head back, she let the rain pound against her face.

Tally shivered and gathered her own coat tighter around her. Was Shay trying to freeze herself to death?

The other figures did nothing for a moment. Then, slowly and with awkward glances at one another, they followed her example, pulling off coats and gloves and sweaters. As their hoods came down, Tally recognized two more Crims. Ho was there—one of Shay's old friends who had run away to the Smoke only to come back on his own. Tally also recognized Tachs, who'd joined the clique a few weeks before she had.

But the other seven pretties weren't Crims at all. They placed their coats on the ground gingerly, hugging themselves against the bitter cold. When Ho and Tachs spread their arms, the others followed reluctantly. Rain ran down their faces and plastered the white shirts to their skin.

"What are they doing?" Zane whispered.

Tally only shook her head. She noticed that Shay had gotten new surge, some sort of raised tattoo hash marks on her arms. They extended from elbow to wrist, and Ho and Tachs seemed to have copied the design.

Shay began to speak, facing upward, addressing the flag overhead like a crazy person talking to nobody in particular. Her voice didn't carry across the clearing except for a word here and there. Tally couldn't make sense of it—the cadence sounded like a chant, almost like the prayers that Rusties and pre-Rusties had once offered up to their invisible superheroes in the sky.

After a few minutes, Shay fell silent, and again the group stood without saying a word, all shivering in the cold except the apparently insane Shay. Tally realized that the non-Crims all had flash tattoos on their faces, fresh-looking surge that glistened in the rain. She guessed that since the stadium disaster, swirly face tattoos must be the rage, but it was an awfully big coincidence that all seven of the unknown pretties had them.

"Those pings from wannabees," she whispered. "Shay's been recruiting."

"But why?" Zane hissed. "We all agreed that newbies were the last thing we need right now."

"Maybe she needs them."

"For what?"

A shiver went through Tally. "For this."

Zane swore. "We'll just veto them."

Tally shook her head. "I don't think she cares about vetoes. I'm not sure if she's still a—"

Shay's voice cut through the rain again. She reached into her back pocket and produced an object that glittered coldly in the gray light. It unfolded into a long knife.

Tally's eyes widened, but none of the pretties in the circle looked surprised; their expressions revealed a mix of queasy fear and excitement.

Holding the knife aloft, Shay spoke more words in the same slow, deliberate cadence, and Tally heard one repeated enough to make it out.

It sounded like "Cutters."

"Let's get out of here," she said so softly that Zane must not have heard. She wanted to climb on her hoverboard and flee, but Tally found she couldn't move, or look away, or close her eyes.

Shay took the knife with her left hand and placed its edge against her right forearm, the wet metal gleaming. She raised both arms, turning slowly, fixing each of the others with her burning gaze. Then she looked up into the rain.

The movement was so slight that Tally hardly saw it from their hiding place, but she knew what had happened from the reactions of the others. Their bodies shuddered, eyes widening with horrified fascination—like Tally, they couldn't look away.

Then she saw the blood begin to trickle from the wound. It ran thinly in the rain, spreading down Shay's upraised arm and onto her shoulder, reaching her shirt, spreading a color that was more pink than red.

She turned around once to give them all a good look, her slow, deliberate movements as disturbing as the blood running down her arm. The others were shivering visibly now, shooting furtive glances at one another.

Shay finally lowered her arm, swaying a little on her feet, and held out the knife. Ho stepped forward to take it from her, and she took his place in the circle.

"What is this?" Zane whispered.

Tally shook her head and closed her eyes. The rain became suddenly deafening around her, but she heard her own words through the torrent. "This is Shay's new cure."

• • •

The others followed one by one.

Tally kept on expecting them to run, thinking that if only one of them would make a break for it, the rest would scatter into the forest like scared rabbits. But something—the bleak setting, the spirit-sapping rain, or maybe the crazed expression on Shay's face—bound them to their spots. They all watched, and then, one by one, they cut themselves. And as each did so, their faces transformed to become more like Shay's: ecstatic and insane.

With every cut, Tally felt something hollowing out inside her. She couldn't forget that there was more to this ritual than madness. She remembered the night of the costume party. Her fear and panic had made her bubbly enough to pursue Croy, but had left her still pretty-minded. It wasn't until after Peris's knee had struck her as he hoverbounced—opening up her eyebrow—that Tally's head had really become clear.

Shay had admired that scar; she'd been the one to suggest getting a tattoo to commemorate it. Apparently she'd also understood how that injury had changed Tally, leading her to Zane, to the top of the transmission tower, and finally to the cure.

And now Shay was sharing her knowledge.

"This is our fault," Tally whispered.

"What?"

Tally opened her gloved hands toward the tableaux before them. She and Zane had given Shay what she needed to spread this cure: citywide fame, hundreds of pretties all dying to become Crims—bleeding to become Crims.

Or whatever they were becoming. "Cutters," Shay had said.

"She's not one of us anymore."

"Why are we just sitting here?" Zane hissed. His fists were clenched, his face reddening in the shadow of his hood.

"Zane, calm down." Tally took his hand.

"We should make her . . ." His voice trailed off with a choked-sounding cough, his eyes wide.

"Zane?" she whispered.

He was struggling for breath, hands clutching at empty air.

"Zane!" Tally cried aloud. She grabbed his other hand, staring into his bulging eyes. He wasn't breathing.

Tally glanced into the clearing, desperate for help from someone, anyone—even the Cutters. A few of the distant figures had heard her cry, but they only stared wide-eyed at her, blood flowing and flash tattoos spinning, too zoned out to be of any help.

She reached for her cuff, tearing off the black scarf to send a distress ping. But Zane's hand reached out to grab her. He shook his head painfully. "No."

"Zane, you need help!"

"I'm okay. . . ." The words tore from his throat.

She paused a moment, imagining him dying here in her arms. But if she called the wardens, they might both wind up under the surgeon's knife, pretty-minded for good—leaving Shay's cure as the only one in town. "All right," she said. "But I'm taking you to the hospital."

"No!"

"Not inside. Just as close as we can get. We'll wait there and see what happens."

Tally rolled Zane onto her hoverboard and snapped her fingers, watching as it rose into the air. She lay on top of him, feeling the board settle uneasily under their combined weight. The lifters held, and she pushed forward carefully.

As the board began to move, she glanced back at the clearing. All ten of them were staring at Tally and Zane now. Shay was walking toward them, her glare as cold as the rain.

Suddenly, Tally was overwhelmed with fear, the same terror she felt at the sight of Specials. She pushed off hard with her feet, leaning forward and climbing into the trees, leaving the place behind.

The ride down to the river was terrifying. Zane's limbs sprawled out in all directions, his shifting weight threatening to tip the board over with every turn. Tally wrapped her arms around him, fingernails scraping across the board's knobbly underside. She steered with her flailing legs, her turns as wide as a stumbling drunk's. The cold rain spat into her face, and Tally remembered the goggles in her coat pocket, but there was no way of getting at them without stopping.

And there wasn't time to stop.

They hurtled among the trees, the board picking up speed as they descended toward the river. Pine branches, heavy and glistening with captured raindrops, reared up out of the rain to slash her face. When they finally burst out of Cleopatra Park, Tally cut across a belt of muddy sports fields at top speed, angling toward the far end of the central island.

At this distance, the hospital was invisible in the driving rain, but Tally spotted the running lights of a hovercar headed in that direction. It was moving fast and high, probably an ambulance taking someone in. Squinting against the barrage of freezing rain, she managed to keep her eyes on it, following its course. As the hovercar pulled out of sight, they reached the river, and the overweighted board began to lose lift over the open water.

Tally realized too late what was happening: The buried metal grid that magnetic lifters used to push against was lower here—in the ground under ten meters of water. As they neared the middle of the river, the board descended closer and closer to the cold and choppy surface.

Halfway across, the board struck water with a slap, Zane's hands bouncing off the river as if it was solid. But the hoverboard rebounded into the air, and as the far shore grew closer, the lifters gained purchase and carried them higher.

"Tally . . . ," a croaking voice came from beneath her.

"It'll be okay, Zane. I've got you."

"Yeah. Feels very under control."

Tally dared a glance down at him. His eyes were open, his face no longer red. She realized that his chest rose and fell beneath her, his breathing normal. "Just relax, Zane. I'll stop when we're close to the hospital."

"Don't take me there."

"I'm just taking you closer. In case."

"In case what?" he said raggedly.

"In case you stop breathing again! Now *shut up*!"

He fell obediently silent, his eyes closing.

As the river's rain-spattered surface shot by underneath them, the lights of the hospital rose up, its dark bulk reassuringly close. Tally spotted the flashing yellow lights of the emergency bay, but pulled off the river before they reached it, climbing the bank slowly. She brought the board to rest in the shelter of a rack of empty ambulances, the hovercars stacked three high in their giant metal frame, apparently awaiting some major disaster.

When the board settled, Zane rolled off onto the wet ground with a groan.

She kneeled next to him. "Talk to me."

"I'm fine," he said. "Except my back."

"Your back? What . . ."

"I think it has to do with riding a hoverboard on it." He snorted. "And under you."

She took his face in her hands, staring into his pupils. He looked exhausted and bedraggled, but he smiled and winked at her tiredly.

"Zane . . ." She felt herself starting to cry again, tears running hot among the cold raindrops. "What's happening to you?"

"Like I said: I think we need some breakfast."

Sobs wracked her body. "But . . ."

"I know." He put his hands on her shoulders. "We have to get out of here."

"But what about the New Smo—"

His hand shot up to cover her mouth, muffling her next words. She pulled away in surprise. Zane pushed himself up on one elbow, staring at her cuff, which was uncovered in the rain. She'd taken her glove off to make a call when his attack had started.

"Oh . . . I'm sorry."

He shook his head, pulling her closer and whispering, "It's okay."

Tally closed her eyes, trying to remember what they had said on the mad trip here. "We argued about taking you to the hospital," she whispered.

He nodded and stood shakily, saying aloud, "Well, since we're here." He turned and punched his fist against the metal of the ambulance rack. It rebounded with a dull ring.

"Zane!"

He doubled over with pain, then shook his head, waving his wounded hand in the air for a moment. He regarded the blood on the knuckles. "As I said, since we came all this way, I might as well get this looked at. But next time *ask me,* okay?"

She stared at him, finally understanding. For a moment, she'd thought Shay's insanity was contagious. But a wounded hand was a plausible reason for their wild ride here, and would square with most of what the cuff had heard. Tally could also tell the wardens that they hadn't eaten in a couple of days. Maybe a vitamin- and blood-sugar drip in Zane's arm would help his headache.

He still looked like crap, muddy and soaking wet, but he walked without any stagger. In fact, Zane seemed pretty bubbly after cracking his hand. Maybe Shay wasn't as insane as she looked—at least she knew what worked.

"Come on," he said.

"Want a ride?" Tally asked, pointing. The second hoverboard was coasting toward them across the grass, having followed the signal in Zane's crash bracelets.

"I think I'll walk," he said, trudging toward the flashing lights of the emergency bay. Tally saw then that his hands shook, and how pale he was. And she resolved that the next time he had an attack, she was calling the wardens.

Even the cure wasn't worth dying for.

HOSPITAL

It turned out that Zane's punch had broken three bones in his hand, which were going to take half an hour to fix.

Tally shared the waiting room with two brand-new pretties waiting for a friend with a broken leg—something about running down wet stairs outside Lillian Russell Mansion. She ignored the details of the story, scarfing down cookies and coffee with lots of milk and sugar, luxuriating in the hospital's warmth and total absence of pounding rain. The rare sensation of calories entering her body softened the world a little, but Tally was glad for a few moments of pretty haze. Her memories of what Shay and company were up to in Cleopatra Park were all too clear.

"So what happened to *you*?" one of the pretties finally asked, the emphasis on the last word indicating her soaked and muddy clothes, exhausted expression, and generally shaming appearance.

Tally shoved a chocolate-chip cookie into her mouth and shrugged. "Hoverboarding."

The other pretty elbowed her friend, widening her eyes and angling one nervous thumb at Tally.

"What?" he said.

"Shhh!"

"*What?*"

The second pretty sighed. "Sorry," she said to Tally. "My friend is brand-new. And totally *brain-missing.*" She explained to him in a whisper, *"That's Tally Youngblood."*

The first one opened his mouth wide, then shut it.

Tally just smiled and stuffed another cookie into her face. *Of course* you'd run into Tally Youngblood in the emergency bay, they were thinking. Where else? They were probably wondering what piece of major architecture had crumbled under her this time.

Though her celebrity kept the two mercifully quiet, their furtive glances were unsettling. These two pretties weren't the type to become Cutters, Tally was fairly certain. But she couldn't escape the realization that her criminal notoriety was feeding Shay's little project, creating pretties hungry to explore a certain kind of bubbliness. Even full of coffee, milk, and cookies, Tally's stomach began to feel sour as she wondered if trips to the emergency bay were going to be the rage this winter.

"Tally?" An orderly stood by the waiting room door, beckoning her in. Finally. Tally was ready to get out of this place.

"Take care, kids," she said to the pretties, and followed the orderly down the hall.

When the door closed behind her, Tally realized that she hadn't been taken to the outpatient center. The orderly had brought her to a small room dominated by a huge, cluttered desk. A wallscreen showed a grassy field on a sunny day—the sort of visuals they showed in littlie school right before nap time.

"Been out in the rain?" the orderly said brightly, pulling off his powder blue paper robe. He was wearing a suit underneath—*semi*formal, her brain informed her—and Tally realized that he wasn't an orderly at all. He had the beaming smile favored by politicians, nursery teachers, and headshrinks.

She sat in the chair across from him, her damp clothes squelching. "You totally guessed it."

He smiled. "Well, accidents happen. You were wise to bring your friend in. And lucky me, being here when you did. The thing is, I've been trying to get in touch with you, Tally."

"You have?"

"Indeed." He smiled again. There was a species of middle pretty who smiled at everything: happy smile, disappointed smile, you're-in-trouble smile. His was welcoming and enthusiastic, trustworthy and calm, and it set Tally's teeth on edge. He was the sort of middle pretty Dr. Cable had promised Tally she would become: smug and self-assured, his handsome face marked with just the right lines of laughter, age, and wisdom.

"You haven't been opening your mail the last couple of days, have you?" he said.

She shook her head. "Too many bogus pings. From being on the feeds, you know? Totally famous-making."

The words earned Tally a proud smile. "I suppose it's all been very exciting for you and your friends."

She shrugged, going for false modesty. "It was bubbly at first, but now it's getting bogus. So, who are you again?"

"Dr. Remmy Anders. I'm a trauma counselor here on the hospital staff."

"Trauma? Is this about the stadium thing? Because I'm totally—"

"I'm sure you're fine, Tally. It's a friend of yours I've been wanting to ask you about. Frankly, we're a little worried."

"About who?"

"Shay."

Behind her pretty expression, a serious ping went through Tally. She tried to keep her voice steady. "Why Shay?"

Slowly, as if controlled by a remote, Dr. Anders's concerned smile bent into a frown. "There was a disturbance the other night at your little bonfire party. An argument between you and Shay. Quite troubling."

Tally blinked, stalling as she recalled Shay screaming at her by the fire. Even under all those layers, the cuff must have heard how upset Shay had been—way beyond the usual soft-spoken tiff between new pretties. Tally tried to recall exactly what Shay had shouted, but the combination of champagne and horrible guilt wasn't very memory-improving. She shrugged. "Yeah. She was pretty drunk. Me too."

"It didn't sound very happy-making."

"Dr. Remmy, are you, like, spying on us? That's bogus."

The counselor shook his head and went back to the concerned smile. "We have had a particular interest in all of you who suffered that unfortunate accident. It can sometimes be difficult to recover from frightening and unexpected events. That's why I've been assigned as your post-stress counselor."

Tally pretended not to notice that he'd totally dodged the spying question—she already knew the answer, anyway. Special Circumstances might not care if the Crims knocked down New Pretty Town, but the wardens were always on the job. Given that the city was designed to keep people pretty-minded, it made sense that they would assign a counselor to anyone who'd had any serious bubbly-making experience. Dr. Anders was here to make sure that the breakthrough hadn't given the Crims any new and exciting ideas.

She summoned up a pretty smile. "In case we go crazy?"

Dr. Anders laughed. "Oh, we don't think you'll go crazy. I'm just here to make sure there aren't any long-term effects. Friendships can be negatively impacted by stress, you know."

She decided to throw Remmy a bone, and let her eyes widen. "So *that's* why she was being such a pain that night?"

He brightened. "Yes, it's all about stress, Tally. But remember, she probably didn't mean it."

"Well, I didn't go all crazy on *her.*"

Reassuring smile. "Everyone reacts differently to trauma, Tally. Not everyone's as tough as you. Instead of getting angry, why don't we think of this as an opportunity to show Shay your support. You're old friends, aren't you?"

"Yeah. Since we were uglies. Same birthday."

"That's wonderful. Old friends are best at times like these. What was the fight about?"

Tally shrugged. "I don't know. Nothing, really."

"Can you remember at all?"

Tally wondered if this room was rigged to polygraph her, and if so, how big a lie she could get away with. She closed her eyes, concentrating on the calories moving through her half-starved body, letting a pretty haze settle over herself.

"Tally?" he prompted.

She decided to give Dr. Anders a little bit of the truth. "It was just . . . old stuff."

He nodded, folding his hands in satisfaction. Tally wondered if she'd said too much. "From ugly days?" he asked.

She shook her head, not trusting her voice.

"How have you and Shay been getting along since that night?"

"Just fine."

He smiled happily, but Tally caught him glancing away into the middle distance—probably at an eyescreen that was invisible to her. Was he checking the city interface? It would know that she and Shay hadn't pinged each other since the party, and three whole days without any mail between them was pretty unusual. Or was Dr. Anders looking to see if her voice was wavering?

He gave his invisible data, or whatever it was, a small nod. "Has she seemed in better spirits to you since then?"

"She's okay, I guess." Just a little self-mutilation, crazy chanting, and maybe wanting to start her own very disturbing clique. "I haven't seen her since this bogus rain started coming down, actually. But me and her are best friends forever."

The last words came out wrong, Tally's voice sounding rough. She coughed a little, which was marked by a deepening of Dr. Anders's concerned smile. "I'm glad to hear that, Tally. And you're feeling all right as well, aren't you?"

"Bubbly," she said. "A little hungry, though."

"Yes, yes. You and Zane really must eat more. You're looking a bit thin, and I'm told his blood sugar was terribly low when he came in."

"I'll make sure he has some of those chocolate-chip cookies in the waiting room. They're awesome."

"A wonderful idea. You're a good friend, Tally." He stood, offering his hand. "Well, I see that Zane's all patched up, so I won't keep you. Thanks for your time, and make sure you let me know if you or any of your friends ever need to talk."

"Oh, I will," she said, giving the doctor her prettiest smile. "This has really been great."

Outside, the cold rain embraced Tally like an old and unavoidable friend, the discomfort almost a relief after Dr. Anders's radiant smiles. She told Zane about him on the way home. Although her cuff was bound up again, she spoke softly enough for the wind to tear her words away as they climbed into the gray sky.

He sighed when she was done. "Sounds like they're as worried about her as we are."

"Yeah. They must have heard our fight the other night. She was screaming at me in a very unpretty way."

"Perfect." His teeth were bared against the cold. It didn't look like the painkillers they'd given him for his hand were helping Zane's headache much. His feet shuffled on the board, finding their balance clumsily.

"I didn't say anything much. Just that she was drunk and acting up." Tally allowed herself a thin smile of self-congratulation. This one time, at least, she hadn't betrayed Shay. She hoped.

"Of course you didn't, Tally. Shay might need help, but not from some middle-pretty headshrink. What we have to do is get her out into the wild and give her the real cure. As soon as possible."

"Yeah. The pills are a lot better than cutting yourself." *If they don't wind up giving you brain damage,* she didn't add. Tally had decided not to tell Zane about her resolve to take him to the hospital the next time he had an attack; hopefully it wouldn't come to that. "So how were your doctors?"

"The usual. They spent the first hour lecturing me about eating more. When they finally got around to knitting my bones up, I was only unconscious about ten minutes. But other than being skinny, they didn't seem to notice anything weird about me."

"Good."

"Of course, that doesn't mean I'm fine. They didn't look at my head, after all, just my hand."

Tally took a deep breath. "Your headaches are getting worse, aren't they?"

"I think it was more hunger and cold than anything else."

She shook her head. "I haven't eaten anything today either, Zane, and you didn't see me—"

"Forget about my head, Tally! I'm not any worse or any better. It's Shay's arms I'm worried about." He angled his board closer and lowered his voice. "They're going to be keeping an eye on her, too, now. If your Dr. Remmy gets a good look at what she's been doing to herself, all hell will break loose."

"Yeah. I can't argue with that." Tally visualized the row of scars along Shay's arms. From a distance, she'd thought they were tattoos, but from close up, anyone would know what they were. If Dr. Anders saw them, Tally doubted very much that he would have a smile appropriate to the occasion. Alarms would go off all over the city, and the wardens' interest in everyone who'd been involved in the stadium disaster would go way off the scale.

Tally reached out and brought them to a stop, lowering her voice to just above a whisper. "We don't have much time, then. He could decide to talk to Shay any day now."

Zane took a deep breath. "You'll have to talk to Shay first. Tell her to lay off the cutting."

"Oh. Fun. What if she doesn't want to?"

"Tell her we're about to leave. Tell her we'll get her the real cure."

"Leave? How?"

"We just go—tonight, if we can. I'll pack up everything we need, you get the other Crims ready."

"What about these?" She was too exhausted to raise her swaddled wrist, but he took her meaning.

"We'll get them off. Tonight. There's a trick I've been saving."

"What trick, Zane?"

"I can't tell you yet. It'll work, though—it's just a little risky."

Tally frowned. She and Zane had tried every tool they could think of, and nothing had so much as scratched the cuffs. "What is it?"

"I'll show you tonight," he said, his jaw tight.

Tally swallowed. "Must be more than a little risky."

Zane stared at her, his face pale and half-starved, his eyes dull through the goggles. "Give the girl a hand." He chuckled. "Might need one."

Tally had to turn her eyes away from his smile.

CRUSHER

The shop shed wasn't far from the hospital, on the downstream end of New Pretty Town where the two arms of the river rejoined each other. This late at night, the lathes, imaging tables, and injection molds sat unused, the place almost empty. The only light came from the other end of the shed, where a middle pretty was blowing molten glass into shape.

"It's freezing in here," Tally said. She could see the words coiling from her mouth in the soft red glow of work lights. The rain had finally stopped while they were getting the Crims ready to run, but the air was still damp and chill. Even inside the shed, Tally, Fausto, and Zane were huddled in their winter coats.

"They've usually got smelting furnaces going," Zane said. "And some of these machines put out a ton of heat." He pointed at the two sides of the shed that were open to the night. "But the ventilation means no smart walls, see?"

"I see." Tally pulled her coat tighter around her, reaching into one pocket to turn up its heater.

Fausto pointed out a machine that looked like a huge press. "Hey, I remember playing with one of those back in ugly school, for industrial design class," Fausto said. "We made these lunch trays with runners on the bottom, for sliding on the snow."

"That's why I brought you along," Zane said, leading Tally and Fausto across the concrete floor.

The bottom part of the machine was a metal table, which seemed to be etched with a million tiny dots. Parallel with the table was suspended an identical expanse of metal.

"What? You want to use a crusher?" Fausto raised his eyebrows. Zane still hadn't told them what he was up to, but Tally didn't like the look of the massive machine.

Or its name, for that matter.

Zane put down the champagne bucket he'd brought, sloshing ice water onto the floor. He pulled a memory card from one pocket and shoved it into the crusher's reader slot. The machine booted up, lights winking around the edge and the floor rumbling powerfully under Tally's feet.

A ripple seemed to pass through the table, a wave traveling across the surface as if the metal had suddenly become liquid and alive.

When the movement subsided, Tally took a closer look at the

crusher's surface. The tiny etched-looking dots were in fact the tips of thin rods, which could be raised up and down to make shapes. She ran her fingers across the table, but the rods were so thin and perfectly aligned, it felt like smooth metal. "What's it for?"

"Stamping out stuff," Zane said. He pushed a button, and the table sprang to life again, a tiny, symmetrical collection of mountains rising up in its center. Tally noticed that identically shaped cavities had appeared in the upper surface of the crusher.

"Hey, that's my lunch tray," Fausto said.

"Of course. You thought I forgot? Those things were awesome for sledding," Zane said happily. He pulled a sheet of metal from under the machine and carefully aligned its edges to the table's.

"Yeah. I always wondered why they never mass-produced them," Fausto said.

"Too bubbly-making," Zane said. "But I bet some ugly reinvents them every few years. Heads up. I'm going to shoot it."

The other two each took a healthy step back.

Zane grasped two handles at the edge of the table, squeezing both at the same moment. The machine made a rumbling noise for a fraction of a second, then leaped suddenly into motion, the top half slamming down onto the lower with an earsplitting *clang*. The sound echoed through the shed, and Tally's ears were still ringing as the crusher's jaws slowly parted to reveal the sheet of metal.

"Sweet, isn't it?" Zane said. He picked up the sheet, whose contours had been reshaped by the impact. It looked like a lunch tray now, with little sections to divide a meal into salad, main, and dessert. Turning it over in his hands, Zane ran a finger down the grooves that marked the back side of the tray. "On good, powdery snow you could go a thousand klicks an hour on these babies."

Fausto's face had turned pale. "It won't work, Zane."

"Why not?"

"Too many safeties. Even if you could get one of us to—"

"Are you kidding, Zane?" Tally cried. "You are not sticking your hand in there. That thing'll take it off!"

Zane just smiled. "No, it won't. Like Fausto said: too many safeties." He pulled the memory card out of the crusher's reader slot and stuck another in. The table rippled again, leaving a set of sharp ridges at its edge, like a row of teeth. He placed his left wrist alongside the metal jaws. "It's hard to tell with the glove on, but see where it'll snip the cuff?"

"But what if it misses, Zane?" Tally said. She had to fight to keep her voice down. Their cuffs were bound as usual, but she didn't want the middle pretty at the other end of the shed to hear them.

"It doesn't miss. You can stamp out parts for a stopwatch with these things."

"It won't work at all," Fausto proclaimed. He stuck his own hand under the crusher. "Shoot it."

"I know, I know," Zane said, grasping the handles and squeezing.

"What?" Tally cried in horror, but the machine didn't move. A row of yellow lights flashed around its edge, and a tinny industrial voice said, "Clear, please."

"It detects humans," Fausto said. "Body heat."

Tally swallowed, her heart pounding in her chest as Fausto took his hand out from under the crusher. "Don't *do* that!"

"And even if you trick it, what's the point?" Fausto continued. "It'll only crush the cuff, which will squish your hand."

"Not at fifty meters per second. Look here." Zane leaned over the table, running one finger along the formation of teeth he had programmed. "That edge will cut it, or at least smack it hard enough to kill whatever's inside. Our cuffs will just be hunks of dead metal after this thing hits them."

Fausto leaned in to look closer, and Tally turned away from the sight of them with their heads between the metal jaws. *Dead metal.* She stared at the glassblower at the other end of the shed. Unaware of their insane conversation, the woman was calmly holding a chunk of glass inside a small, radiant furnace, turning it slowly over the flame.

Tally walked toward the woman until she was out of earshot of Zane and Fausto, then unwrapped her cuff. "Ping Shay."

"Not available. Message?"

Tally scowled, but said, "Yes. Listen, Shay, I know this is my eighteenth message today, but you've got to answer. I'm sorry we were spying on you, but . . ." Tally didn't know what to add, assuming that the wardens—maybe even Specials—might be listening. She could hardly explain that they were escaping tonight. "But we're worried about you. Get back to me as soon as you can. We need to talk . . . face-to-face."

Tally signed off and rewrapped the scarf around her wrist. Shay, Ho, and Tachs—the Cutters—had pulled a big disappearing act, refusing to answer any pings. Probably Shay was sulking about having her secret ceremony spied on. But hopefully one of the Crims would find them and tell them about tonight's escape.

Tally and Zane had spent the afternoon getting everyone ready. The Crims were packed up and positioned around the island, ready to start moving once the signal came from the shop shed that Tally and Zane were free.

The woman blowing glass had finished heating it up. She pulled the glowing mass from the furnace and began to blow into it through a long tube, making the molten material bubble up into sinuous shapes. Tally reluctantly turned away from the sight and returned to the crusher.

"But what about the safeties?" Fausto was arguing.

"I can get rid of my body heat."

"How?"

Zane kicked the champagne bucket. "Thirty seconds in ice water and my hand will be as cold as a chunk of metal."

"Yeah, but your hand is *not* a chunk of metal," Tally cried. "And neither is mine. That's the problem."

"Look, Tally, I'm not asking you to go first."

She shook her head. "I'm not going *at all,* Zane. Neither are you."

"She's right." Fausto was staring at the metal teeth rising up from the table, comparing them with their twins jutting down from the top half. "High marks for good design, but sticking your hand in there is crazy. If you've miscalculated by one centimeter, the crusher will hit bone. They told us about that in shop class. The shock wave will travel all the way up your arm, shattering everything along the way."

"Hey, if it misses, they'll put me back together. And it won't miss. I even made a different cast for your hand, Tally," Zane said, waving another memory card. "Since your cuff's smaller."

"If this goes wrong, they'll never fix you," she said quietly. "Not even the city hospital can rebuild a flattened hand."

"Not flattened," Fausto said. "Your bones will be *liquifacted,* Zane. That means the shock will *melt* them."

"Listen, Tally," Zane said, reaching down to fish the bottle out of the champagne bucket. "I didn't want to do this either. But I had an attack this morning, remember?" He popped the cork.

"You had a *what*?" Fausto said.

Tally shook her head. "We have to find some other way."

"There's no time," Zane said, taking a swig from the bottle. "So, Fausto, will you help?"

"Help?" Tally asked.

Fausto nodded slowly. "It takes two hands to shoot the crusher—another safety feature, so you can't leave one in there by accident. He needs one of us to pull the triggers." Fausto crossed his arms. "Forget it."

"And I'm not helping you either!" Tally said.

"Tally." Zane sighed. "If we don't leave the city tonight, I might as well stick my head in there. These headaches have been coming every three days or so, and now they're getting worse. We have to leave."

Fausto frowned. "What are you talking about?"

Zane turned to him. "Something's wrong with me, Fausto. That's why we have to go tonight. We think the New Smokies can help me."

"Why would you need them? What's wrong with you?"

"What's wrong with me is, I'm cured."

"Come again?"

Zane took a deep breath. "You see, we took these pills. . . ."

Tally groaned and turned away, realizing that another line was being crossed. First Shay, and now Fausto. Tally wondered how long it would be before all the Crims knew about the cure. Which would only make it more urgent for her and Zane to escape the city, no matter what they had to risk.

Tally watched the glassblower with growing unhappiness. She could sense Fausto's disbelief fading as Zane explained what had happened to the two of them over the last month: the pills, the growing bubbliness of the cure, and Zane's crippling headaches.

"So Shay was right about you guys!" he said. "That's why you're so different now. . . ."

Shay had been the only one to call Tally on it, but all the Crims must have seen the changes and wondered what had happened. They all wanted the strange new bubbliness that Tally and Zane had. Now that Fausto knew the cure existed, that it was as simple as swallowing a pill, maybe risking a couple of hands in the crusher wouldn't seem so crazy to him.

Tally sighed. Maybe it wasn't crazy. That very morning she had delayed taking Zane to the hospital, waiting outside in the rain for what might have been precious minutes—risking his life, not just a hand.

She swallowed. What was the word Fausto had used? *Liquifacted?*

The glass object was growing in the woman's grasp, bubbling into overlapping spheres that looked supremely delicate, impossible to repair if shattered. The woman held the glowing shape carefully; some things couldn't be put back together if you broke them.

Tally thought about David's father, Az. When Dr. Cable had tried to erase Az's memories, the process had killed him. The mind was even more fragile than the human hand—and none of them had a clue what was going on inside Zane's head.

She looked down at her own left glove, flexing the fingers slowly. Was she brave enough to put it in the crusher's metal jaws? Maybe.

"Are you sure we can find the New Smokies out there?" Fausto was saying to Zane. "I thought no one had seen them for a while."

"The uglies we met this morning said there were signs they'd come back."

"And they can cure you?"

Tally heard it then in Fausto's voice—he was justifying it to himself aloud, slowly but surely, and would eventually agree to shoot the crusher. It even made perfect sense, in a horrible way. There was a cure for Zane's condition somewhere out in the wild, and if they didn't get him to it, he was as good as dead, anyway.

What was risking a hand?

Tally turned and said, "I'll do it. I'll pull the triggers."

They looked at her in shocked silence for a moment, then Zane smiled. "Good. I'd rather it was you."

She swallowed. "Why?"

"Because I trust you. Don't want to be shaking."

Tally took a deep breath, fighting to keep tears from her eyes. "Thanks, I guess."

There was a moment of uncomfortable silence.

"Are you sure, Tally?" Fausto finally said. "I could do it."

"No. It should be me."

"Well, no sense waiting around." Zane dropped his winter coat to the floor. He unwrapped his scarf from his wrist and pulled off the glove that had covered his cuff. His bare left hand looked small and fragile next to the crusher's dark mass. Zane made a fist and thrust it into the ice bucket, wincing as the freezing water began to leach his body heat away. "Get ready, Tally."

She glanced at their backpacks on the floor, felt to make sure she was wearing her belly sensor, checked the hoverboards at the edge of the shed one more time; the wires under the boards were yanked apart, disconnected from the city grid. They were ready to go.

Tally looked at her cuff. Once Zane's was shattered, the tracking signal would be interrupted. They'd have to do hers right away and get moving. They would have a long run just to reach the edge of the city.

Two dozen Crims waited all over the island, ready to scatter into the wild and draw pursuit in every direction. Each carried a Roman candle with a special mix of colors—purple and green—to spread the signal once Zane and Tally were free.

Free.

Tally looked down at the crusher's controls and swallowed.

The two handles were cast in cheery bright yellow plastic and shaped like thumbgame joysticks, each with a fat trigger. When she took hold of them, the power of the idling machine shuddered in her hands, like the rumble of a suborbital plane passing overhead.

She tried to imagine herself pulling the triggers, and couldn't. Tally was out of arguments, though, and the time for discussion was past.

After thirty long seconds in the ice water, Zane pulled his hand out.

"Close your eyes in case the metal shatters. The cold will make it brittle," Zane said in a normal voice. It didn't matter what the cuff heard now, Tally realized. By the time anyone figured out what they were talking about, they'd be flying at top speed toward the Rusty Ruins.

Zane placed his wrist on the edge of the table, closing his eyes tightly. "Okay. Do it."

Tally took a deep breath, her hands trembling on the controls. She closed her eyes and thought, *Okay, do it now. . . .*

But her fingers didn't obey.

Her mind started to spin, thinking of everything that could go wrong. She imagined flying Zane to the hospital again, his left arm a mass of jelly. She imagined Specials bursting in at that moment and stopping them, having figured out what they were up to. She wondered if Zane had made all the right measurements, and if he'd remembered that the cuff would have shrunk a bit from the ice water.

Tally paused at that thought, thinking maybe she should ask

him. She opened her eyes. The wet cuff glimmered like a piece of gold in the crusher's yellow work lights.

"Tally . . . do it!"

Cold would make the metal contract, but heat . . . Tally glanced at the glassblower on the other side of the shed, blissfully unaware of the violent, horrible thing that was about to happen.

"Tally!" Fausto said softly.

Heat would make the cuff expand. . . .

The woman held the red-hot glass in her hands, turning it over to inspect it from every side. *How was she holding molten glass?*

"Tally," Fausto said. "If you want, I'll do—"

"Hang on," she said, taking her hands from the crusher's controls.

"What?" Zane cried.

"Stay here." She pulled the memory card from the crusher's slot, ignoring the sounds of protest behind her, and ran past hulking lathes and furnaces to the other side of the shed. At her approach, the woman looked up placidly, smiling with middle-pretty calm.

"Hello, dear."

"Hi. That's beautiful," Tally said.

The pleasant smile grew warmer. "Thank you."

Tally could see the woman's hands now, how they shimmered silver in the glowing red light. "You're wearing gloves, aren't you."

The woman laughed. "Of course! It's rather hot in that furnace, you know."

"But you can't feel it?"

"Not through these gloves. I think the material was invented for shuttles coming back through the atmosphere. It can reflect a couple of thousand degrees."

Tally nodded. "And they're really thin, aren't they? From across the room, I couldn't even tell you had them on."

"That's right." The woman nodded happily. "You can feel the texture of the glass right through them."

"Wow." Tally smiled prettily. The gloves would fit on *under* the cuffs, she could see now. "Where can I get a pair?"

The woman nodded at a cupboard. Tally opened it and found dozens of gloves crammed inside, their reflective material glittering like fresh snow. She pulled two out. "They're all the same size?"

"Yeah. They stretch to fit, all the way up past the elbows," the woman said. "Just make sure you throw them away after one use. They don't work very well the second time."

"No problem." Tally turned away with the gloves in a tight grip, relief flooding through her as she realized she wouldn't have to pull the triggers, wouldn't have to watch the crusher snap down on Zane's hand. A new and better plan unfolded in her mind like clockwork—she knew exactly where to find a powerful furnace, one they could take right to the edge of the city.

"Wait a second, Tally," the woman said, a troubled note entering her voice.

Tally froze, realizing that the woman had recognized her. Of course, everyone who watched the feeds knew Tally Youngblood's face now. She wracked her brain for an innocent reason for needing the gloves, but everything she thought of sounded totally bogus. "Um, yeah?"

"You've got two left gloves there." The woman laughed. "Not very useful, whatever trick you're planning."

Tally smiled, letting a slow chuckle escape her lips. *That's what* you *think.* But she turned back to the cupboard and fished out two right gloves. It wouldn't hurt to protect both hands. "Thanks for all your help," she said.

"No problem." The woman smiled beautifully, turning away, staring again into the curves of her piece of glass. "Just be careful."

"Don't worry," Tally said. "I always am."

HIJACKING

"Are you kidding? How do we requisition one in the middle of the night?" Fausto asked.

"We can't. We'll have to hijack it." Tally put a backpack over her shoulder, and snapped for her board to follow. "In fact, we should get a few. The more of us who go out that way, the better."

"Hijack?" Zane said, checking the rewrapped scarf around his forearm. "You mean steal them?"

"No, we'll ask nicely." She grinned. "Don't forget, Zane, we're the Crims. We're famous. Follow me."

Outside the shop shed, she jumped on board and headed up toward the center of the island, where the tops of the party spires were always surrounded by parasails, hot-air balloons, and fireworks. The other two scrambled to follow. "You pass the word to the rest of the Crims," she shouted to Fausto. "Tell them about the change in plans."

He glanced at Zane for approval, then nodded, relieved that the crusher concept had been replaced by something less violent. "How many of us do you want to go up with?"

"Nine or ten," she said. "Anyone who's not afraid of heights—the rest can go by hoverboard, as planned. We'll be ready in twenty minutes. Meet us in the center of town."

"I'll be there," Fausto said, and angled away into the night sky.

Tally turned to Zane. "You okay?"

He nodded, slowly flexing the fingers of his gloved hand. "I'll be fine. It's just taking me a second to switch gears."

She brought her board closer to Zane's, taking his bare hand. "It was brave, what you wanted to do."

He shook his head. "I guess it was stupid."

"Yeah, maybe. But if we hadn't gone to the shop, I wouldn't have thought of this."

He smiled. "I'm pretty glad you did, to tell you the truth." His hand flexed nervously again. Then he pointed ahead of them. "There's a couple."

She followed his gaze to the center of the island, where a pair of hot-air balloons floated like big bald heads above a party spire, the tethers that kept them in place catching the trembling light of safety fireworks.

"Perfect," she said.

"One problem," Zane said. "How do we get that high on hover-boards?"

She thought for a moment. "Very carefully."

They climbed higher than she ever had, rising slowly alongside the party spire, close enough to reach out and touch its concrete wall. The metal inside the building provided barely enough push for the boards' lifters, and Tally felt a nervous-making tremble under her feet, like standing at the end of the highest diving board as a littlie. After a slow minute, they reached the spot where one of the balloons was tethered to the tower. Tally touched the tether with her bare hand, feeling its rain-slick links. "No problem. It's metal."

"Yeah, but is it *enough* metal?" Zane asked.

Tally shrugged.

He rolled his eyes. "And you thought *my* plan was risky. Okay, I'll take the stupid-looking one." He slid around the tower's girth to where the other balloon bobbed in the breeze. Tally grinned, seeing that it was shaped like a giant pig's head, with protruding ears and two big eyes painted on the pink nylon of its envelope.

At least her own balloon was a normal color: silvery and reflective, with a blue stripe around its equator. From up in the gondola she heard the unmistakable sound of a champagne cork popping, then laughter. It wasn't far away, but getting up was going to be tricky.

Her eyes followed the length of the tether, which drooped down before curving up to where it was attached to the gondola's bottom. The sinuous line reminded her of the roller coaster out in the Rusty Ruins. Of course, the roller coaster had a lot more metal in it, almost as if it had been designed for hoverboarding. This slender length of chain would provide slim pickings for her board's magnetic lifters.

And, unlike the roller coaster, the tether was in constant motion; the balloon was drifting slowly downward as the air in its envelope cooled, but Tally knew it would suddenly jump up and pull the tether taut if the burner was ignited. Worse, the Hot-airs might get bored of hovering around and decide to go for a night ride, releasing the tether and leaving nothing between Tally and the ground.

Zane was right: This wasn't the easiest way to get hold of a balloon, but there was no time to requisition one properly, or wait for the Hot-airs in the gondola to get bored and decide to land. If they were going to make it to the Rusty Ruins before dawn, the escape had to start soon. Maybe someone would find Shay while this new plan was unfolding.

Tally crept farther up the spire wall, rising until the tether ring was just under the center of her board. She nudged herself away from the party spire, drifting out over open space, balancing her hoverboard across the tether like a tightrope walker on a plank of wood.

She moved slowly forward, the lifters straining and trembling, their invisible magnetic fingers pushing down the chain. Once or twice, the board actually scraped the links, sending a shudder through Tally. She saw the balloon dip a little as her weight disrupted the delicate balance between hot air and gravity.

Tally descended until she reached the halfway point, then began to climb toward the balloon. Her board trembled harder as it left the party spire behind, until she was certain the lifters were about to fail, dumping her into a fifty-meter fall. From this height, crash bracelets were much worse than a bungee jacket—being jerked to a halt by her wrists would probably dislocate a shoulder.

Of course, that was nothing compared to what the crusher might have done.

But the lifters didn't fail; the board continued to rise, climbing up toward the gondola of the balloon. She heard a few shouts from the party spire's balcony behind her, and knew she and Zane had been spotted. What sort of bubbly new game was this?

A face appeared over the edge of the gondola, looking down with a surprised expression.

"Hey, look! Someone's coming!"

"What? How?"

The other three pretties in the balloon crowded onto the near side to peer down at her, their shifting weight making the tether wobble. Tally swore as her board swayed perilously under her feet.

"Stay still up there!" she shouted. "And don't pull the burn chain!" Her barked commands were met by surprised silence, but at least they stopped moving around.

A minute later, Tally's shuddering board had pulled almost to within reach of the gondola. She bent her knees and jumped, in free fall for a sickening moment before her hands grasped the wicker rail. Hands reached down to help pull her up, and soon Tally was inside, facing four wide-eyed Hot-airs. Relieved of her weight, her board followed her up, and she pulled it in.

"Whoa! How'd you do that?"

"I didn't know hoverboards could come this high!"

"Hey, you're Tally Youngblood!"

"Who else?" She grinned and leaned over the side. The ground was coming closer, her weight and the board's tugging the balloon earthward. "Now, I hope you don't mind landing this thing. Me and my friends need to go for a little ride."

By the time the balloon was settling on the lawn in front of Garbo Mansion, a pack of Crims on hoverboards had arrived, Fausto at their head. Tally saw the pink-eared shape of Zane's balloon coming to rest nearby, bouncing slowly to a halt.

"Don't get out yet!" she told the hijacked Hot-airs. "We don't want this thing to shoot up into the air empty." They waited while Peris and Fausto cruised over and climbed into the gondola.

"How many will it hold, Tally?" Fausto said.

The gondola was made of wicker. She ran her hand across the woven cane, which was still the perfect substance if you wanted something strong, light, and flexible. "Let's take four in each."

"So what are you guys doing?" one of the Hot-airs got up enough nerve to ask.

"Wait and see," Tally said. "And when they interview you for the feeds, feel free to tell them all about it."

The four of them stared at her with widened eyes, realizing that they were going to be famous.

"But keep quiet for the next hour or so. Otherwise, our little trick won't work, and it won't be as bubbly a story."

They nodded obediently.

"How do you release the tether?" Tally asked, realizing that for all her plans to do so, she'd never been up in a balloon.

"Pull this cord to cut loose," one of the Hot-airs answered. "And push this button when you want a hovercar to come get you."

Tally smiled. That was one feature they wouldn't be needing.

Seeing her expression, one of the Hot-airs said, "Hey, you guys are going somewhere really far, aren't you?"

Tally paused for a moment, knowing that what she said would wind up on the feeds, and then be repeated down through generations of uglies and new pretties. It was worth the risk to tell the truth, she decided. These four wouldn't want to short-circuit their brush with criminal fame, so they wouldn't be talking to the authorities until it was way too late.

"We're going to the New Smoke," she said in a slow, clear voice. They stared at her with disbelief.

Chew on that, Dr. Cable! she thought happily.

The gondola shook, and Tally turned to find that Zane had jumped in. "Mind if I join you? There's four in my balloon," he said. "And we've got another bunch taking over one more."

"The rest are set to go out on our signal," Fausto said.

Tally nodded. As long as she and Zane escaped by balloon, it didn't matter how the others went. She looked up at the burner hanging over their heads, purring like an idling jet engine, waiting to heat the air in the envelope again. Tally just hoped it was powerful enough to expand the cuffs wider than their wrists, or at least destroy the transmitters in them.

She pulled the fire-resistant gloves from her pocket and handed a pair to Zane.

"Much better plan, Tally," he said, looking at the idling burner. "A furnace that can fly. We'll be at the edge of the city by the time we're free."

She smiled at him, then said to the Hot-airs, "Okay, guys. You can get out now. Thanks for all your help, and remember not to mention this to anyone for at least an hour."

They nodded and jumped out of the gondola one by one, retreating a few meters to give it room as it gained buoyancy, bobbing impatiently in the breeze.

"Ready?" she called to the pig-faced balloon. The Crims inside gave the thumbs-up. A third balloon was coming down not far away; they would be headed up soon. The more rogue balloons, the better. If they all left their interface rings in the gondolas when they jumped, the wardens would have a busy night.

"We're all set," Zane said softly. "Let's go."

Tally's eyes swept the horizon—taking in Garbo Mansion, the party spires, the lights of New Pretty Town—the world she had looked forward to her whole ugly life. She wondered if she would ever see the city again.

Of course, Tally had to return, if Shay still hadn't gotten the word. Her cutting was really just a struggle to be cured. There was no way Tally could leave her behind for good, whether Shay hated her or not.

"Okay, let's go," she said, then whispered, "Sorry, Shay. I'll come back for you."

She reached up and pulled the ascent chain. The burner burst into a full-throated roar, blistering heat washing over them, the envelope beginning to swell overhead. The balloon began to rise.

"Whoa!" Peris cried. "We are out of here!"

Fausto let out a whoop and pulled the release cord, the gondola bucking as the tether's weight fell away.

Tally locked eyes with Zane. They were rising fast now, passing the top of the party spire, a dozen pretties on its balcony drunkenly hailing them.

"I'm really leaving," Zane said softly. "Finally."

She grinned. There would be no backing out for Zane this time. She wouldn't let him.

The balloon quickly left the party spire below, rising higher than any building in New Pretty Town. Tally could see the silver band of river all around them, the darkness of Uglyville, and the dull lights of the burbs in every direction. Soon they would be high enough to glimpse the sea.

She released the ascent chain, silencing the burner. They didn't want to get too high. The balloons weren't fast enough to escape the wardens' hovercars; they would need their boards for that. Soon, they would have to jump, free-falling until their hoverboards could pick up the city's magnetic grid and catch them.

Not as simple as falling with a bungee jacket, but not too dangerous, she hoped. Looking down, Tally shook her head and sighed. Sometimes it felt like her life was a series of falls from ever-greater heights.

Tally could see that the wind was carrying them quickly now, pushing the balloon away from the sea, though, strangely, the air felt motionless around them. Of course, Tally realized, the balloon was moving along with the air currents, as if she were perfectly still, and the world sliding along beneath her.

The Rusty Ruins were slipping away behind them, but there were lots of rivers around the city, their beds filled with mineral deposits that could support a hoverboard. The Crims had planned on heading out in lots of directions—everyone knew how to get back to the ruins no matter where the wind took them.

Tally dropped her winter coat, crash bracelets, and gloves to the gondola's floor. Warmth still radiated from the glowing burner, so she didn't feel too cold. She pulled on her heat-resistant gloves, sliding the left one underneath the interface cuff, pulling it up past her elbow and almost to her armpit. Across from her, Zane was also getting ready.

Now to bring their cuffs within reach of the flame.

She looked up. The burner was held to the gondola by a frame with eight arms, stretching over them like a giant metal spider. She put one foot on the railing and held tightly to the burner frame, pulling herself up. From this precarious perch, Tally glanced down at the city passing below, hoping the balloon wasn't going to start rocking in some sudden wind.

She took a deep breath. "Fausto, the signal."

He nodded and lit his Roman candle, which began to hiss and to spit out green and purple flares. Tally watched the signal repeated by nearby Crims, and then spread across the island in a series of colored plumes. They were committed now.

"Okay, Zane," she said. "Let's get these things off."

BURNER

The four nozzles of the burner were barely a meter from her face, still glowing, radiating heat into the cold night air. Tally reached out and tapped one gingerly. The woman in the shop had been telling the truth. Tally could feel the burner's ridges through the heat-resistant fabric, her fingertips sensing a few stray bumps where it had been welded together. But she had no sense of temperature at all; the burner wasn't hot, or cold . . . nothing. The feeling was uncanny, as if her hand were immersed in body-temperature water.

She looked across at Zane, who had pulled himself up on the other side of the burner. "These things really work, Zane. I can't feel a thing."

He looked at his own gloved left hand, unconvinced. "Two thousand degrees, you said?"

"That's right." As long as you believed every statistic tossed off by a middle-pretty artist blowing glass in the middle of the night. "I'll go first," she offered.

"No way. We'll do it together."

"Don't be dramatic." Tally looked down at Fausto, whose face was as pale as when Zane's hand had been in the crusher. "Give the burner cord a little tug, as short as you can, on my signal."

"Hang on!" Peris said. "What are you guys doing?"

Tally realized that no one had brought Peris up to speed on the plan. He stared at her with a look of total confusion. Well, there wasn't time for explanations now. "Don't worry, we have gloves on," she said, and placed her left hand on the burner.

"Gloves?" Peris said.

"Yeah . . . special gloves. Hit it, Fausto!" Tally cried.

A wave of heat struck, the pure blue flame of the burner blindingly bright. Tally slammed her eyes shut, the inferno like a desert wind on the skin of her face. She ducked her head below the burner frame, and heard the cry of horrified surprise that escaped from Peris's lips.

A half-second later, the burner stopped.

Tally opened her eyes, yellow afterimages of the flame crowding her vision. But she saw her fingers flexing in front of her, still whole.

"My hand didn't feel a thing!" she shouted. She blinked away the dancing yellow spots, and saw that the metal of her cuff was glowing a bit. It didn't look any bigger, though.

"What are you *doing*?" Peris shouted. Fausto shushed him.

"All right," Zane said, thrusting his hand out over the burner. "Let's do it fast. They must know we're up to something by now."

Tally nodded—the cuff had to have felt the scorching burst of flame. Like the locket Dr. Cable had given Tally before her trip to the Smoke, it probably was designed to send some kind of signal if damaged. She took a deep breath of the cold night air, placing her hand over the burner again and ducking her head. "Okay, Fausto. Burn it until I say stop!"

Another wash of blistering heat poured over Tally. Peris stared up at her, his terrified expression turned demonic by the intense fire, and she had to look away from him. Above them, the envelope began to swell, and the balloon was tugged upward by its load of superheated air. The gondola swayed, testing Tally's grip on the burner frame.

Her left shoulder, covered only by her T-shirt, was taking the worst of the inferno. Past the glove's protection, her skin itched like a bad sunburn. Sweat trickled down her back in the relentless heat.

Weirdly, the parts of Tally that felt the furnace the least were her gloved hands, even her left, sitting in the inferno's very center. She imagined the cuff hidden within that blaze, turning red, then white . . . gradually expanding.

After what seemed like a solid minute, she yelled, "Okay, hold it!"

The burner stopped, and the air was instantly cool around her, the night suddenly black. Tally stood up from her crouch, feet still on the gondola's railing, and blinked, amazed at how still and silent it was with the raging flame extinguished.

She pulled her hand from the burner, expecting it to be a blackened stump, no matter what her nerve endings told her. But all five fingers wiggled in front of her. The cuff glowed blazing white, mesmerizing blue flickers traveling around its edge. The smell of molten metal struck her nose.

"Quick, Tally!" Zane yelled, jumping down into the gondola. He started tugging at his cuff. "Before they cool off."

She leaped down from the rail and started pulling—glad that she had brought two gloves for each of them. The cuff slid down her arm, but came to a halt as it always did, catching at the usual spot. She squinted at the glowing band, trying to see if it had grown. It seemed bigger, but maybe the heat-resistant glove was thicker than she'd thought, making up the difference.

Tally squeezed the fingers of her left hand together and tugged again; the cuff crept another centimeter along. Heat still radiated from the ring of metal, but it was gradually turning a dull red, its light fading. . . . As it cooled, would it shrink around her hand now, crushing her wrist?

She gritted her teeth and pulled once more, as hard as she could . . . and the cuff slipped off, dropping onto the floor of the gondola like a glowing coal.

"*Yes!*" Finally, she was free.

Tally looked up at the others. Zane was still struggling; Fausto and Peris were scrambling to avoid her glowing cuff as it rolled, steaming and hissing, across the gondola floor. "I did it," she said softly. "It's off."

"Well, mine's not," Zane grunted. His cuff was wedged around the thick of his wrist, its glow faded to a dull red. He swore and stepped back up onto the gondola's railing. "Hit it again."

Fausto nodded, and gave another long blast on the burner.

Tally turned away from the heat, looking down at the city, trying to clear the spots from her eyes. They were past the greenbelt now, over the burbs. She could see the factory belt coming up, dotted with industrial orange work lights, and past that the absolute blackness that marked the edge of the city.

They had to jump soon. In a few more minutes they would pass beyond the metal grid that underlay the city. Without the grid, their hoverboards wouldn't fly or even stop a fall, and they'd be forced to crash-land the balloon instead of bailing out.

She looked up at the swollen envelope, wondering how long it would take the still rising balloon to settle back to earth. Maybe if they could rip the envelope open somehow to get themselves down faster . . . but how hard would a torn balloon crash-land? And without working hoverboards, the four of them would have to hike until they reached a river, giving the wardens plenty of time to find the crumpled balloon and track them down.

"Come on, Zane!" Tally said. "We've got to hurry!"

"I'm hurrying! Okay?"

"What's that smell?" Fausto said.

"What?" Tally pulled back into the gondola, sniffing at the still, hot air.

Something was burning.

THE CITY'S EDGE

"It's us!" Fausto shouted. He jumped back, releasing the burner chain, staring down at the gondola floor.

Tally smelled it then: burning cane, like the smell of brush thrown onto a campfire. Somewhere under their feet, her red-hot cuff had ignited the wicker gondola.

She glanced up at Zane still perched on the railing—he ignored the others' panicked cries, tugging fiercely at his glowing cuff. Peris and Fausto were hopping around, trying to find the source of the smell.

"Relax!" she said. "We can always jump!"

"I can't! Not yet," Zane shouted, still struggling with the cuff. Peris looked as if he was about to leap out of the balloon without bothering to take his hoverboard.

Her vision was finally clearing from burner's glare, and Tally looked down at her feet. A bottle lay there, left behind by the Hot-airs. She reached for it with her gloved hands; it was full.

"Hold on, you guys," she said, and with a practiced motion twisted off the foil and placed both thumbs beneath the cork. She popped it, watching the cork soar into the dark void. "Everything's under control."

Froth bubbled out, and Tally put one thumb over the bottle's mouth. Shaking the bottle, she sprayed champagne across the floor of the gondola. An angry sizzle came from the smoldering flames.

"Got it!" Zane cried at that moment. His cuff fell off and rolled under her feet, and Tally calmly emptied the rest of the bottle onto it. The smell of molten metal rose up around her, tinged with an oddly sweet smell: boiled champagne.

Zane was staring with amazement at his freed left hand. He pulled off the heat-resistant gloves and tossed them overboard. "It worked!" he said, and swept Tally into a hug.

She laughed, letting the bottle drop to the floor and pulling off her own gloves. "Time for that later. Let's get out of here."

"Okay." He balanced his board on the gondola's railing, looking down. "Damn, that's a long fall."

Fausto tugged at a dangling cord. "I'll vent some hot air—maybe we can get a little lower."

"No time," Tally cried. "We're almost at the end of town. If we get separated, meet at the tallest building in the ruins. And remember: Don't let go of your board on the way down!"

They all scrambled to put on their backpacks, bumping into

one another in the small space, Zane and Tally struggling back into their winter coats and crash bracelets. Fausto pulled off his interface ring and threw it to the gondola floor, grabbed his board, and jumped out with a whoop. The balloon pitched upward as his weight left it behind.

When Zane was ready, he turned and kissed her. "We did it, Tally. We're free!"

She looked into his eyes, dizzy with the thought that they were finally here, at the edge of the city, at the beginning of freedom. "Yeah. We made it."

"See you down there." He looked over his shoulder at the distant earth, then turned back to her. "I love you."

"I'll see you down . . . ," she began, but the words sputtered out. It took a moment to replay in her mind what Zane had said. Finally she managed, "Oh. Me too."

He laughed, then let out a wordless cry as he tumbled over the rail, the gondola bucking again under its two remaining passengers.

Tally blinked, dazzled for a moment by Zane's unexpected words. But she shook her head to clear it. This was no time to get pretty-headed; she had to jump now.

She pulled the straps of her backpack tight, wrestling her hoverboard up onto the rail. "Hurry up!" she shouted at Peris.

He was just standing there, staring over the side.

"What are you waiting for?" she cried.

He shook his head. "I can't."

"You can do it. Your board will stop your fall—all you have to do is hang on!" she shouted. "Just jump! Gravity does the rest!"

"It's not the fall, Tally," Peris said. He turned to face her. "I don't want to leave."

"What?"

"I don't want to leave the city."

"But this is what we've been waiting for!"

"Not me." He shrugged. "I liked being a Crim, and being bubbly. But I never thought we'd get this far. I mean, like, leaving home forever?"

"Peris . . ."

"I know you've been out there before, you and Shay. And Zane and Fausto always talked about escaping. But I'm not like you guys."

"But you and me, we're . . ." Tally's voice caught. She was about to say "best friends forever," but the old words wouldn't come anymore. Peris had never been to the Smoke, had never tangled with Special Circumstances, had never even been in trouble. Everything had always gone smoothly for him. Their lives had been so different for so long.

"You're sure you want to stay?"

He nodded slowly. "I'm sure. But I can still help. I'll keep them busy for you. I'll stay airborne as long as I can, then push the pickup button. They'll have to come out and get me."

Tally started to argue, but she couldn't help remembering sneaking across the river right after Peris's operation, visiting him in Garbo Mansion. He had adjusted so quickly, loving New Pretty Town right from the beginning. Maybe the whole Crim thing had just been a joke to him. . . .

But she couldn't leave him here in the city alone. "Peris, think.

Without us around, you won't be bubbly anymore. You'll go back to being a pretty-head."

He smiled sadly. "I don't mind, Tally. I don't need to be bubbly."

"You don't? But don't you feel how much . . . *better* it is?"

He shrugged. "It's exciting. But you can't keep fighting the way things are forever. At some point, you have to . . ."

"Give up?"

Peris nodded, the smile still on his face, as if giving up wasn't really that bad, as if fighting was only worthwhile as long as it was amusing.

"Okay. Stay, then." She turned away, not trusting herself to say anything more. But when Tally looked down, all she saw was darkness. "Oh, crap," she said softly.

The city had run out. It was too late to jump.

Side by side, they stared into the darkness, the wind carrying them farther and farther away.

Peris finally broke the silence. "We'll come down eventually, right?"

"Not soon enough." She sighed. "The wardens probably already know that our cuffs are fried. They'll come looking for us soon. We're sitting ducks up here."

"Oh. I really didn't mean to screw things up for you."

"It's not your fault. I waited too long." Tally swallowed, wondering if Zane would ever find out what happened. Would he think she'd fallen to her death? Or would he guess that she'd chickened out, like Peris?

Whatever he thought, Tally saw their future fading out, disappearing like the distant lights of the city behind them. Who knew what Special Circumstances would do to her brain when they caught her again?

She looked at Peris. "I really thought you wanted to come."

"Listen, Tally. I just got caught up in everything. Being a Crim was exciting and you were my friends, my clique. What was I supposed to do? *Argue* against running away? Arguing's bogus."

She shook her head. "I thought you were bubbly, Peris."

"I am, Tally. But tonight is about as bubbly as I want to get. I like breaking the rules, but living out *there*?" He waved his hand at the wild below them, a cold, unfriendly sea of darkness.

"Why didn't you tell me before now?"

"I don't know. I guess it wasn't until we got up here that I realized you guys were so serious about . . . never coming back."

Tally closed her eyes, remembering what having a pretty mind was like—everything vague and fuzzy, the world nothing but a source of entertainment, the future nothing but a blur. A few tricks weren't enough to make everyone bubbly, she supposed; you had to *want* your mind to change. Maybe some people had always been pretty-heads, even back before the operation had been invented.

Maybe some people were happier being that way.

"But now you can stay with me," he said, putting his arm around her. "It'll be like it was supposed to be. You and me pretty—best friends forever."

Tally shook her head, a sickening feeling sweeping over her. "I am *not* staying, Peris. Even if they take me back tonight, I'll find a way to escape."

"Why are you so unhappy there?"

She sighed, looking out over the darkness. Zane and Fausto would already be headed toward the ruins, thinking she wasn't far behind. How had she let this opportunity slip away? The city always seemed to claim her in the end. Was she really like Peris, somewhere deep inside?

"Why am I unhappy?" Tally repeated softly. "Because the city makes you the way *they* want you to be, Peris. And I want to be myself. That's why."

He squeezed her shoulder and gave her a sad look. "But people are better now than they used to be. Maybe they have good reasons for changing us, Tally."

"Their reasons don't mean anything unless I have a choice, Peris. And they don't give anyone a choice." Tally shook his hand from her shoulder, staring back at the distant city. A set of winking lights was rising into the air, a fleet of hovercars gathering. She remembered that the Specials' cars were held aloft by spinning blades, like the Rusties' ancient helicopters, so they could fly beyond the grid. They must be headed this way, pursuing the final signals of the cuffs.

She had to get out of this balloon *now*.

Before he'd jumped, Fausto had tied off the descent cord, and hot air was spilling from the envelope every moment. But the balloon, superheated as they'd burned off the cuffs, was losing altitude so slowly . . . the ground hardly looked any closer.

Then Tally saw the river.

It stretched out below them, catching moonlight like a silver snake, winding out of the ore-rich mountains to make its way toward the sea. On its bed would be centuries' worth of metal deposits, enough to make her hoverboard fly. Maybe enough to catch her fall.

Maybe she could get her future back.

She pulled her board back up onto the rail. "I'm going."

"But, Tally. You can't—"

"The river."

Peris looked down, his eyes wide. "It looks so small. What if you miss?"

"I won't." She gritted her teeth. "You've seen those formation bungee jumpers, haven't you? They've only got their arms and legs to guide themselves down. I've got a whole hoverboard. It'll be like having wings!"

"You're crazy!"

"I'm leaving." She kissed Peris quickly, then threw one leg over the rail.

"Tally!" He grabbed her hand. "You could die! I don't want to lose you. . . ."

She shook him off violently, and Peris took a fearful step back. Pretties didn't like conflict. Pretties didn't take risks. Pretties didn't say no.

Tally was no longer pretty. "You already have," she said.

And, clutching her hoverboard, she threw herself into the void.

Part III
OUTSIDE

The beauty of the world . . . has two edges, one of laughter, one of anguish, cutting the heart asunder.
—Virginia Woolf, *A Room of One's Own*

DESCENT

Tally dropped into silence, spinning out of control.

After the stillness in the balloon, the rush of passing air built around her with unexpected strength, almost tearing the hoverboard from Tally's hands. She held it tightly to her chest, but the wind's fingers continued to search for purchase, hungry to pry away her only hope of survival. She clasped her hands around the board's underbelly, kicking her legs, trying to control the spinning. Gradually, the dark horizon steadied.

But Tally was upside down, looking up at the stars and hanging from the board. She could see the dark orb of the balloon above. Then its flame ignited, giving the envelope a silvery glow against the darkness, like a huge, dull moon in the sky. She guessed that Peris was headed upward to throw off the pursuit. At least he was trying to help.

His change of heart stung her, but she didn't have time to worry about it, not while plummeting toward the earth.

Tally struggled to turn herself over, but the hoverboard was wider than she was—it caught the air like a sail, threatening to pull itself from her grasp. It was like trying to carry a large kite in a strong wind, except that if she lost control of this particular kite, she'd be splattered all over the ground in about sixty seconds.

Tally tried to relax, letting herself hang there. Something was tugging at her wrist, she realized. Up here in the void, the board's lifters might be useless for flying, but they would still interact with the metal in her crash bracelets.

She adjusted her left bracelet to maximize the connection. Her grip on the board made surer, she straightened out her right arm into the rushing air. It was like riding in her parents' groundcar as a littlie, her hand stuck out a window. Flattening her palm increased the resistance, and Tally found herself slowly beginning to turn over.

A few seconds later, the hoverboard was beneath her.

Tally swallowed at the sight of the earth spread out below, vast and dark and hungry. The rushing cold seemed to cut straight through her coat.

She'd been falling for what felt like forever, but the ground didn't *look* any closer. There was nothing to give it scale except the winding river, still no bigger than a piece of ribbon. Tally angled her outstretched palm experimentally, and watched the curve of moonlit water turn clockwise beneath her. She pulled her arm in, and the river steadied.

Tally grinned. At least she had *some* control over her wild descent.

As she fell, the silvery band of river grew in size, first slowly, then faster, the dark horizon of earth expanding like some huge predator advancing toward her, blotting out the starlit sky. Clinging to the hoverboard with both hands, Tally discovered that her outstretched legs could guide her descent, keeping the river directly below her.

And then in the last ten seconds, she began to realize how large the river was, its surface wide and troubled. She saw things moving in it.

It grew, faster and faster. . . .

When the board's lifters kicked in, it was like a door slamming in her face, flattening her nose and breaking open her lower lip, the taste of blood instantly in her mouth. Her wrists were twisted cruelly by the crash bracelets, and her momentum squashed her against the braking hoverboard, forcing the breath from her lungs like a giant vice. She struggled to pull in a breath.

The hoverboard was slowing rapidly, but the river's surface still grew, stretching farther in all directions like a huge mirror full of starlight, until . . .

Slap!

The board struck the water like the flat of a giant hand, catching Tally's body with another battering jolt, an explosion of light and sound filling her head. And then she was underwater, ears filled with a dull roar. She let go of the board and clawed for the surface, her lungs emptied by the impact. Forcing her eyes open, Tally saw only the faintest glimmer of light filtering down through the murky river. Her arms struggled weakly, and the light grew slowly closer. Finally, she broke into the air, gasping and coughing.

The river raged around her, the swift current kicking up whitecaps in every direction. She dog-paddled hard, the weight of her pack trying to pull her back under. Her lungs sucked in air, and she coughed violently, tasting blood in her mouth.

Turning from side to side, Tally realized that she hit her mark too well—she was in the dead center of the river, fifty meters from either shore. She swore and kept paddling, waiting for a tug on her crash bracelets.

Where was her hoverboard? It should have found her by now.

It had taken so long for the lifters to kick in—Tally had expected to pull up in midair, not hit the river at speed. But after a few moments' thought, she realized what had happened. The river was deeper than she'd anticipated; the minerals on its floor were a long way below her kicking feet. She remembered how hoverboards sometimes got wobbly over the middle of the city river—too far from the mineral deposits for the lifters to work at full strength.

It was lucky the board had slowed her fall at all.

Tally looked around. Too dense to float, the hoverboard had probably sunk to the bottom, the raging current carrying her away from it. She turned up her crash bracelets' calling range to a whole kilometer, and waited for the board's nose to push itself above the surface.

Shapes bobbed along in the water all around her, knobby and irregular, like a flotilla of alligators in the fast-moving current. What were they?

Something nudged her. . . .

She spun around, but it was just an old tree trunk—not an alligator, and *not* her hoverboard. Tally grabbed on to it gratefully, though, already exhausted from paddling. In every direction were more trees, as well as branches, clots of reeds, masses of rotting leaves. The river was carrying all sorts of cargo on its surface.

The rain, Tally thought. Three days of downpour must have flooded the hills, washing all manner of stray matter down into the river, swelling its size and accelerating its current. The trunk she clung to was old and rotted black, but a few strands of green wood showed from a break. Had the flooding ripped it from the ground alive?

Tally's fingers traced where the tree had broken, and she saw that something unnaturally straight had struck it.

Like the edge of a hoverboard.

A few meters away, another log floated, cut with the same sharp edge. Tally's crash-landing had snapped the old, rotten tree in half. Her face was bleeding from the impact; she could still taste blood. So what damage had been done to the hoverboard?

Tally twisted the call controls of her crash bracelets higher, setting them to burn their batteries down. Every second, the current was carrying her farther from where she'd landed.

No hoverboard rose up above the surface, no tugging came at her wrists. As the minutes passed, Tally began to admit to herself that the board was dead, a piece of junk at the bottom of the river.

She switched her bracelets off and, still clinging to the log, began to kick her way toward shore.

The riverbank was slippery with mud, the ground saturated by the rains and the swollen river. Tally waded to shore in a small inlet, struggling through branches and reeds in the hip-deep water. It seemed the flood had collected everything that floated and dumped it in this one spot.

Including Tally Youngblood.

She stumbled up the bank, desperate to reach dry ground, every instinct impelling her to keep moving away from the rushing water. Her exhausted body felt full of lead, and Tally slid back down the slope, becoming covered with mud. Finally, she gave up and huddled on the muddy ground, shaking in the freezing cold. Tally couldn't remember feeling so tired since becoming a new pretty, as if the river had sucked away her body's vitality.

She took the firestarter from her backpack and, with trembling fingers, gathered a pile of washed-up twigs. But the wood was so wet from three days of rain that the firestarter's tiny flame only made the twigs hiss dully.

At least her coat was still working. She turned its heater up to full, not worrying about the batteries, and gathered herself into a ball.

Tally waited for sleep to come, but her body wouldn't stop trembling, like a fever coming on back in ugly days. But new pretties almost never got sick, unless she'd run herself too far down this last month—eating almost nothing, staying out in the cold, running on adrenaline and coffee, with hardly an hour in the last twenty-four when she hadn't been soaking wet.

Or was she finally getting the same reaction from the cure as Zane? Was the pill beginning to damage her brain, now that she was beyond any hope of medical care?

Tally's head pounded, fevered thoughts swirling through her. She had no hoverboard, no way of getting to the Rusty Ruins except on foot. No one knew where she was. The world had been emptied of everything but the wild, the freezing cold, and Tally Youngblood. Even the absence of the cuff on her wrist felt strange, like the gap left behind by a missing tooth.

Worst was the absence of Zane's body next to her. She'd stayed with him every night for the last month, and they'd spent most of every day together. Even in their enforced silence, she had grown used to his constant presence, his familiar touch, their wordless conversations. Suddenly he was gone, and Tally felt as if she'd lost some part of herself in the fall.

She had imagined this moment a thousand times, finally reaching the wild, free from the city at last. But never once had she imagined being here without Zane.

And yet here she was, utterly alone.

Tally lay awake a long time, replaying in her mind those last frantic minutes in the balloon. If she'd only jumped sooner, or had thought to look down before the city grid ran out. After what Zane had said, she shouldn't have hesitated, knowing that this escape was their only chance for freedom together.

Once again, things were screwed up, and it was all her fault.

Finally Tally's exhaustion overpowered her worries, and she drifted into troubled sleep.

ALONE

So, there was this beautiful princess.

She was locked in a high tower, one whose smart walls had clever holes in them that could give her anything: food, a clique of fantastic friends, wonderful clothes. And, best of all, there was this mirror on the wall, so that the princess could look at her beautiful self all day long.

The only problem with the tower was that there was no way out. The builders had forgotten to put in an elevator, or even a set of stairs. She was stuck up there.

One day, the princess realized that she was bored. The view from the tower—gentle hills, fields of white flowers, and a deep, dark forest—fascinated her. She started spending more time looking out the window than at her own reflection, as is often the case with troublesome girls.

And it was pretty clear that no prince was showing up, or at least that he was really late.

So the only thing was to jump.

The hole in the wall gave her a lovely parasol to catch her when she fell, and a wonderful new dress to wear in the fields and forest, and a brass key to make sure she could get back into the tower if she needed to. But the princess, laughing pridefully, tossed the key into the fireplace, convinced she would never need to return to the tower. Without another glance in the mirror, she strolled out onto the balcony and stepped off into midair.

The thing was, it was a long way down, a lot farther than the princess had expected, and the parasol turned out to be total crap. As she fell, the princess realized she should have asked for a bungee jacket or a parachute or *something* better than a parasol, you know?

She struck the ground hard, and lay there in a crumpled heap, smarting and confused, wondering how things had worked out this way. There was no prince around to pick her up, her new dress was ruined, and thanks to her pride, she had no way back into the tower.

And the worst thing was, there were no mirrors out there in the wild, so the princess was left wondering whether she in fact was still beautiful . . . or if the fall had changed the story completely.

When Tally awoke from this bogus dream, the sun was halfway across the sky.

She struggled to her feet, having to pry herself from the sucking embrace of the mud. At some point during the night, her winter coat had run out of charge. Without batteries, it was a cold thing clinging to her skin, still damp from her soaking in the river, and it smelled funny. Tally unstuck the coat from herself and laid it across the broad surface of a rock, hoping that the sun would dry it out.

For the first time in days the sky was cloudless. But in clearing, the air had turned crisp and cold—the warmer weather that had arrived with the rain had departed with it as well. The trees glittered with frost, and the mud under her feet sparkled, its thin layer of rime crackling underfoot.

Her fever had passed, but Tally felt dizzy standing, so she knelt beside her backpack to look through its contents—the sum of everything she possessed. Fausto had managed to gather up some of the usual Smokey survival gear: a knife, water filter, position-finder, firestarter, and some safety sparklers, along with a few dozen packets of soap. Remembering how valuable dehydrated food had been in the Smoke, Tally had packed three months' worth, which was all wrapped up in waterproof plastic, fortunately. When Tally saw the two rolls of toilet paper she'd brought, however, she let out a groan. They were soaked through, reduced to bloated, squishy blobs of white. She placed them on the rocks next to her jacket, but doubted that it was even worth drying them out.

She sighed. Even back in her Smokey days, she'd never gotten used to the leaf thing.

Tally found her pitiful pile of twigs, and remembered trying to light a fire the night before, too delirious to realize how stupid *that* would have been. The Special Circumstances hovercars that had come after the balloon would have easily spotted a fire in the darkness.

There was no evidence of pursuit in the sky this morning, but Tally decided to put some distance between herself and the river. Without a working heater in her jacket, she would need to build a fire that night.

But first things first, which meant food.

She trudged down to the river to fill the purifier, dried mud crumbling from her skin and clothing with every step. Tally had never been so dirty in her life, but she wasn't up to bathing in the freezing water, not without a fire to warm her up afterward. Last night's fever might have passed, thanks to her new-pretty immune system kicking in, but she didn't want to take any risks with her health out here.

Of course, Tally realized, it wasn't her own health she should be worrying about. Zane was somewhere out here too, maybe just as alone as she was. He and Fausto had jumped almost at the same moment, but they might have landed kilometers apart. If Zane had one of his attacks on the way to the ruins, with no one to help him . . .

Tally shook the thought from her head. All she could do right now for Zane or anyone else was get to the ruins herself. And that meant making food, not worrying about things she couldn't control.

The purifier took two fillings before it had strained enough pure water from the silty inlet to make a meal. She chose a packet of PadThai and set the purifier to boil; the smell of reconstituting noodles and spices soon rose from the gurgling water.

By the time the meal pinged that it was ready, Tally was ravenous. As she reached the end of the PadThai, she realized there was no longer any point in going hungry, and immediately boiled up a packet of CurryNoods. Starvation might have been useful for getting off the cuffs and staying bubbly, but her cuff was gone, and Tally now had the whole of the wild, dangerous and cold, to keep her bubbly. Not much chance of sinking into a pretty haze out here.

After breakfast, the position-finder offered up its bad news. Tally had to check her calculations twice before she believed the distance she'd traveled the night before. The winds from off the ocean had pushed the balloon a long way east, in the opposite direction from the Rusty Ruins, and then the river's current had carried her another long distance southward. She was more than a week's journey by foot to the ruins, if she went in a straight line. And straight lines wouldn't come into it: She had to go the long way around the city, staying in the forest to hide herself from searchers in the air.

Tally wondered how long the Specials would bother to keep looking for her. Luckily, they didn't know that her hoverboard had disappeared into the river, so they would assume she was flying, not trudging along on foot. As far as they knew, Tally would have to stay near the river or some other natural vein of mineral deposits.

The sooner she got away from the riverbank, the better.

Tally packed up her pitiful camp unhappily. Her backpack held more than enough food for the journey, and the hills would be full of ready water after the long rains, but she felt defeated already. From what Sussy and Dex had said, the New Smokies hadn't set up a permanent camp in the ruins. They might leave any day now, and she was a week away.

Her only hope was that Zane and Fausto would stay behind, waiting for her to show up. Unless they thought that she had been captured, or killed by the fall, or had simply chickened out.

No, she told herself, Zane wouldn't think that last one of her. He might be worried, but Tally knew that he would wait for her, however long it took.

She sighed as she tied the still-damp coat around her waist and hoisted her backpack onto her shoulders. There was no point wondering about where the others were; her only choice was to hike toward the ruins and trust that someone would be waiting when she arrived.

Tally had nowhere else to go.

The way through the forest was rugged, every step a battle. Back in the Smoke, Tally had mostly traveled by hoverboard. When she had been forced to hike cross-country, it had been on paths hacked through the trees. But this was nature in the raw, hostile and unrelenting. The dense undergrowth tugged at her feet, trying to trip her, throwing up thick bushes and ankle-twisting roots and impenetrable walls of thorn.

Among the trees, the downpour still echoed. Pine needles sparkled with frost, which the day's heat was slowly changing to water, generating a constant rain of chill, sparkling mist. It was like a magnificent ice palace, with spears of sunlight shooting between the trees, visible in the mist like lasers through smoke. But every time Tally dared disturb a branch, it unloaded its freight of freezing water onto her head.

She remembered traveling to the Smoke through the ancient forest that had been devastated by the Rusties' biologically engineered weeds. At least walking through that flattened landscape had been easier than this dense growth. Sometimes, you could almost see why the Rusties had tried so hard to destroy nature.

Nature could be a pain.

As she walked, the struggle between the forest and Tally began to feel more and more personal. The grasping brambles seemed almost conscious of her, corralling Tally the way they wanted her to go, no matter what her direction-finder said. The dense undergrowth would split open welcomingly, offering easy paths that wound pointlessly off her course. Hiking in a straight line was impossible. This was nature, not some Rusty superhighway cutting through mountains and across deserts without any regard for the terrain.

But as the afternoon progressed, Tally slowly became convinced that she was following an actual path, like the nature trails that the pre-Rusties had used a millennium before.

She remembered what David had told her out in the Smoke, that most of the pre-Rusty trails had originally been made by animals. Even deer, wolves, and wild dogs didn't want to fight their way through virgin growth. Just like people, animals stuck to the same paths for generation after generation, forging tracks through the forest.

Of course, Tally had always imagined that animal trails were something that only David could see. Having grown up in the wild, he was practically a pre-Rusty himself. But as the shadows lengthened around her, Tally found her path becoming easier and straighter, as if she had stumbled onto some uncanny fissure in the wild.

A gnawing feeling started in her stomach. The random sounds of dripping trees began to play with her mind, and Tally's nerves began to twitch, as if she was being watched.

It was probably just her perfect new-pretty eyesight helping her spot the subtle marks of animal passage. She must have picked up more skills than she knew out in the Smoke. This was an animal path. Certainly, no *people* could live out here. Not this close to the city, where they would have been detected by the Specials decades ago. Even out in the Smoke, no one knew of any other communities living outside the cities. Humanity had decided two centuries ago to leave nature alone.

Alone, Tally kept reminding herself. No one else was out here. Though, oddly, she couldn't decide whether being the only person in the forest made it feel less creepy, or more.

Finally, as the sky was fading to pink, Tally decided to come to a halt. She found an open clearing where the sun had beaten down all day, maybe drying out enough wood for a fire. The brutal hike had raised a sweat—Tally's shirt clung to her, and she'd never once worn her coat—but once the sun set, she knew the air would turn freezing cold again.

Finding dry twigs was easy, and Tally weighed a few small logs in her hand to find the lightest, which would contain the least water. All her Smokey knowledge seemed to have come back, with no scraps of pretty-mindedness remaining after the escape. Now that she was out of the city, the cure had settled over Tally's mind for good.

But she hesitated before putting the firestarter to the pile, paranoia staying her hand. The forest still made its sounds—dripping water, bird cries, the skitterings of small animals among the wet leaves—and it was easy to imagine something watching her from the darkened spaces between the trees.

Tally sighed. Maybe she still was a pretty-head, making up irrational stories about the empty forest. The longer she stayed alone out here, the more Tally understood why the Rusties and their predecessors had believed in invisible beings, praying to placate spirits as they trashed the natural world around them.

Well, Tally didn't believe in spirits. The only things she had to worry about were Specials, and they would be looking along the river, kilometers behind her. Darkness had fallen as she built the fire, and it was already halfway to freezing. She couldn't risk another fever out here in the wild, alone.

The firestarter flicked to life in her hand, and Tally held it to the twigs until a blaze erupted. She nursed the fire along with larger and larger branches until it was strong enough to ignite the lightest of her logs, then banked it with the others to dry them out.

Soon, the blaze was hot enough to push her back on her heels, and Tally felt warmth stealing into her bones for what seemed like the first time in days.

She smiled as she stared into the flames. Nature was tough, it could be dangerous, but unlike Dr. Cable or Shay or Peris—unlike people in general—it made sense. The problems it threw at you could be solved rationally. Get cold, build a fire. Need to get somewhere, walk there. Tally knew she could make it to the ruins, with or without a hoverboard under her. And from there she would eventually find Zane and the New Smoke, and everything would be all right.

Tonight, Tally realized happily, she was going to sleep well. Even without Zane beside her, she had made it through her first day of freedom in the wild, still bubbly and still in one piece.

She lay down, watching the fire's embers pulsing beside her, warm as old friends. After a while, her eyelids began to flicker, then to fall.

Tally was deep in pleasant dreams when the shrieking woke her.

HUNT

At first, she thought the forest was on fire.

There were flames moving through the trees, casting jittering shadows across the clearing, darting through the air like wild, burning insects. Shrieks rose up from every side, inhuman calls strung with meaningless words.

Tally staggered to her feet and stumbled straight into the remains of her fire. Kicked embers flared to life in all directions. She felt hot needles through the soles of her boots, and almost fell to her hands and knees among the glowing coals. Another shriek came from close by—a high-pitched cry of anger. A human form ran toward her, a torch raised in one hand. The torch hissed and sparked with every step, as if the flame were a living thing impelling its carrier onward.

The figure was swinging something across its path—a long, polished stick, gleaming in the firelight. Tally leaped back just in time, and the weapon whistled through empty air. She rolled backward on the ground, feeling the sting of the scattered embers in the middle of her back. Jumping to her feet, she spun away, dashing toward the trees. Another figure blocked her path, also brandishing a club.

His face was obscured by a beard, but even in the jittering torchlight Tally could see that he was an ugly—fat and with a bloated nose, the pale skin of his forehead pocked with disease. He had ugly reflexes, too: The swing of the club was slow and predictable. Tally rolled under the flailing weapon, lashing out with her feet to take his knees out from under him.

By the time she heard the thump of his body hitting the earth, Tally was up and running again, slashing through branches, angling toward the darkest part of the forest.

Another chorus of shrieks rose up behind her, the pursuers' torches casting flickering shadows onto the trees ahead. Tally crashed through the undergrowth almost blind, half-falling as she ran, wet branches whipping her face. A vine grasped her ankle, jerking Tally off-balance and throwing her to the ground. She stretched out both hands to catch herself, and felt one wrist bend too far backward with a wrenching burst of pain.

She cradled the injured hand for a moment, glancing back at the ugly hunters. They weren't as fast as Tally, but they ducked and weaved through the forest skillfully, knowing the way through the trees even in darkness. The hovering lights of their torches flowed into place around where Tally lay, the racket from their reedy cries surrounding her once more.

But what *were* they? They looked small in stature, and they yelled back and forth in some language she didn't recognize. Like pre-Rusty ghosts risen from the grave . . .

Whatever they were, there wasn't time to ponder the question. Tally rose to her feet and made another dash for the darkness, aiming for the gap between two torches.

The two hunters closed on her as she approached: bearded men, their ugly faces marked with scars and sores. Tally crashed between them, close enough to feel the heat of the torches. A wildly swung club caught her shoulder with a glancing blow, but Tally managed to keep her feet, and found herself stumbling down a hill into blackness.

The two cried out as they followed her, and more shrieks came from up ahead. How many of them were there? They seemed to be rising up from the ground itself.

Suddenly, her feet splashed into cold water, and Tally found herself slipping, falling into a shallow creek. Behind, her two closest pursuers tumbled down the slope, their torches spitting out sparks as they bumped trees and branches. It was a wonder the whole forest wasn't aflame.

Tally got to her feet and dashed down the streambed, thankful for the route it cut through the undergrowth. She stumbled on the slick, rocky bottom, but found herself outpacing the burning eyes that darted along either bank. If she could only reach some sort of open ground, Tally knew that she could outrun the smaller, slower uglies.

The sound of splashing feet came from behind her, and then a grunt and a stream of curses in their unknown tongue. One of them had fallen. Maybe she was going to make it.

Of course, her food and water purifier were in her backpack in the clearing, back among the shrieking, club-wielding uglies. Lost.

She forced the thought from her mind and kept running. Her wrist still throbbed from the fall, and she wondered if it was broken.

A loud roar rose up before Tally, the stream boiling around her ankles, the ground rumbling. Then suddenly the earth seemed to disappear from under her feet as she ran. . . .

Flailing through the air, Tally realized too late that the roar was behind her now—she'd run straight off the top of a waterfall. Her flight through emptiness lasted only a moment, then she hit water, a deep, churning pool that wrapped its chill around her, sound suddenly reduced to a low rumble in her ears. She felt herself hurtling downward into darkness and silence, slowly turning head over heels.

One shoulder brushed the bottom, and Tally pushed herself upward. She came up gasping, clawing at the water until her fingers found a rocky edge. Clinging to it, she pulled herself up into the shallows, on hands and knees, coughing and trembling.

Caught.

Torches hovered all around her, reflected in the churning water like swarms of fireflies. Tally raised her eyes and found at least a dozen pursuers glowering down from the stream's steep banks, their pale and ugly faces made even more hideous by the torchlight.

A man was standing in the stream in front of her—his fat belly and big nose marking him as the hunter she'd knocked over at the clearing. His bare knee was bleeding where she'd kicked it. He bellowed a wordless cry, raising his crude club high into the air.

Tally stared up at him in disbelief. Was he really going to hit her? Did these people murder total strangers for no reason at all?

But no blow came. As he stared down at her, fear gradually filled the man's expression. He thrust his torch toward her, and Tally shrank back, covering her face. The man sank to one knee before her, taking a closer look. She dropped her hands.

His milky eyes squinted in the torchlight, staring in confusion.

Did he *recognize* her?

Warily, Tally watched the thoughts racing across his exaggerated features: growing fear and doubt, and then a sudden realization that something terrible had happened . . .

The torch fell from his hand and into the stream, where it was extinguished with a strangled hiss and a puff of foul smoke. The man bellowed once more, this time as if in pain, the same word repeated again and again. He pitched forward, lowering his face almost into the water.

The others followed, dropping to their hands and knees, their torches falling to sputter against the ground. They all set up the same wailing cry, almost drowning out the roar of the waterfall.

Tally rose to her knees, coughing a little and wondering what the hell was going on.

Looking around, she noticed for the first time that all the hunters were men. Their clothes were irregular, far cruder than the Smokies' handmade clothing. They all had unhealthy marks on their faces and arms, and long beards that were matted and tangled. Their hair looked as if they'd never combed it in their lives. They were paler than pretty average, with the sort of freckly, pinkish skin of those occasional littlies born extra sensitive to the sun.

None of them stared back at her. Their faces were buried in their hands or pressed to the ground.

Finally, one of them crawled forward. He was thin and horribly wrinkled, his hair and beard white, and Tally remembered from her time in the Smoke that this was what *old* uglies looked like. Without the operation, their bodies grew decrepit, like ancient ruins abandoned by their builders. He trembled as he moved, either from fear or ill health, and stared closely at her for what seemed an endless time.

At last he spoke, his wavering voice barely audible above the waterfall. "I know little the gods' tongue."

Tally blinked. "You what?"

"We saw fire and thought outsider. Not a god."

All the others had gone silent, waiting fearfully, ignoring their torches guttering on the ground. Tally saw a bush crackle to life, but the man crouching next to it seemed too paralyzed by fear to move.

So she terrified them all of a sudden? Were these people crazy?

"Never gods use fire before. Please understand." His eyes begged her for forgiveness.

She stood unsteadily. "Um, that's okay. No problem."

The old ugly rose from his crouch so suddenly that Tally stepped backward, almost toppling back into the churning pool. He yelled a single word, and the hunters repeated it. The cry seemed to release them from their spell; they stood up, stamping out the small fires that had sprung up around their dropped torches.

Suddenly, Tally felt outnumbered again. "But, hey," she added, "just no more with the . . . clubs, okay?"

The old man listened, bowed, and yelled out more words in the unknown language. The hunters sprang into action: Some propped their clubs against trees and split them with a kick; others pounded them against the ground until they shattered, or threw the weapons off into the darkness.

The old man turned back to Tally, his hands spread open, clearly waiting for approval. His club lay split in two at her feet. The others raised their free hands, empty and open.

"Yeah," she said. "Much better."

The old man smiled.

And then she saw it, the familiar glimmer in his ancient, milky eyes. The same look Sussy and Dex had given her when they'd first seen her pretty face. The same awe and eagerness to please, the same instinctive fascination—the sure result of a century of cosmetic engineering and a million years of evolution.

Tally looked around at the others, and found all of them shrinking from her gaze. They could barely meet her huge, copper-flecked eyes, almost couldn't stand to face her beauty.

God, he'd said. The old Rusty word for their invisible superheroes in the sky.

This was their world out here—this raw, cruel wilderness with its disease and violence and animal struggle for survival. Like these people, this world was ugly. To be pretty was to be from somewhere beyond.

Out here, Tally was a god.

YOUNG BLOOD

The hunters' camp took about an hour to reach. With torches extinguished, the party followed pitch-black trails and waded down freezing streams, never uttering a word.

Tally's guides displayed a strange combination of crudity and skill. They were small and slow, a few even disfigured, shuffling along carrying all their weight on one leg. They smelled as if they never bathed, and wore shoes so poor, their feet were scarred. But they knew the forest, moving gracefully through the tangled undergrowth, guiding Tally unerringly through the darkness. The hunters didn't use direction-finders, or even pause to check the stars.

The suspicions that Tally had nursed the day before were proven right. These hills were laced with human-made paths. The trails she'd only half-glimpsed in daylight now seemed to open up magically in the darkness, the old man who led her taking turns and switchbacks without hesitation. The group moved in a single line, making no more noise than a snake among leaves.

The hunters had enemies, it seemed. After their cacophonous attack on Tally, she wouldn't have imagined them capable of stealth or cunning. But now they sent signals up and down the line with clicking sounds and birdlike chirps instead of words. They seemed perplexed whenever Tally tripped over an invisible root or vine, and nervous when she let out a string of curses as a result. They didn't like being unarmed, she realized. Perhaps they regretted breaking their weapons at the first sign of her displeasure.

Tough luck, Tally thought. No matter how friendly the hunters had become, she was glad they'd discarded the clubs, just in case they changed their minds. After all, if she hadn't fallen into the water, washing the day's mud and muck from her pretty face, Tally doubted she would be alive now.

Whoever the hunters' enemies were, the grudge was serious.

Tally smelled the village before they reached it. It made her nose wrinkle unhappily.

It wasn't just the scent of wood smoke, or the less welcome tang of animal slaughter, which she knew from watching rabbits and chickens killed for food back in the Smoke. The smell at the outskirts of the hunters' camp was much worse, reminding Tally of the outdoor latrines the Smokies had used. That was one aspect of camping she'd never quite gotten used to. Mercifully, the smell faded as the village came into sight.

The camp wasn't big—a dozen huts made of mud and reeds, a few sleeping goats tied to each, the furrows of vegetable plots casting ruffled shadows in the starlight. One big storehouse sat in the middle of everything, but there were no other large buildings that Tally could see.

The village's borders were marked by watch fires and armed guards. Having reached home, the hunters felt safe enough to raise their voices again, shouting the news that they'd brought back a . . . visitor.

People began to flow out of the huts, the hubbub growing as the village gradually awoke. Tally found herself at the center of a gathering crowd of curious faces. A circle formed around her, but the adult villagers never pressed too close, as if held back by the force field of her beauty. They kept their eyes averted.

The littlies, on the other hand, showed more courage. Some actually dared to touch her, darting out to lay a hand on her silvery jacket before retreating back into the crowd. It was strange seeing kids out here in the wild. Unlike their elders, the littlies looked almost normal to Tally. They were too young for their skin to show the ravages of bad nutrition and disease, and, of course, even in the city no one got the operation until they were sixteen. She was used to seeing asymmetrical faces and squinty eyes on littlies, and they were cute, anyway.

Tally knelt and reached out a hand, letting the bravest of them nervously stroke her palm.

She also saw women for the first time. Given that almost every man wore a beard, it was easy to tell the sexes apart. The women hung back in the crowd, tending to the smallest littlies and hardly daring a glance at Tally. A few were building a fire on a blackened pit in the middle of town. No men bothered to help them, she noticed.

Tally dimly remembered learning in school about the pre-Rusty custom of assigning different tasks to men and women. And it was usually women who got the crappy jobs, she recalled. Even some Rusties had doggedly clung to that little trick. The thought gave Tally a queasy feeling in her stomach, and she hoped similar rules didn't apply to gods.

She wondered exactly where the god idea had come from. Tally had her firestarter and other equipment in her backpack, recovered before she and the hunters had started on their way here. But none of them had seen those miracles yet. All it had taken was one glance. From what she knew of mythology, being divine meant more than having a pretty face.

Of course, she wasn't the first pretty they'd seen. At least some of them knew Tally's language. They might know something about high technology as well.

Someone shouted from the outskirts of the throng, and the crowd parted before her, growing silent. A man came into the circle, oddly shirtless in the cold. He walked with an air of unmistakable authority, striding right through Tally's divine force field and to within arm's length. He was almost her height, a giant among these people. He looked strong as well, wiry and hard, though Tally guessed that his reflexes were no match for hers. In the firelight, his eyes sparkled with curiosity rather than fear.

She had no idea what his age might be. His face had some of the lines of a middle pretty, but his skin looked better than most of the others'. Was he younger than most of them? Or simply healthier?

Tally also noticed that he wore a knife, the first metal tool she'd seen. Its handle shone with the matte black of plastic. She raised an eyebrow: The knife had to be city-made.

"Welcome," he said.

So he also spoke the gods' tongue. "Thanks. Um, I mean . . . thank you."

"We did not know you were coming. Not for many days."

Did gods usually call ahead before visiting? "Oh, sorry," she mumbled, but her response only seemed to confuse him. Maybe gods weren't supposed to apologize.

"We were confused," he said. "We saw your fire, and thought you were an outsider."

"Yeah, I got that. No harm done."

He tried to smile, but then frowned and shook his head. "We still do not understand."

You and me both.

The man's accent sounded slightly unusual, like someone from another city on the continent, but not from another civilization altogether. On the other hand, he seemed to lack words for the questions he wanted to ask, as if he wasn't accustomed to making small talk with gods. Possibly he was searching for: *What the hell are you doing here?*

Whatever concept of the divine these people had, Tally evidently wasn't fitting into it very well. And she had a feeling that if they decided she wasn't really a god, that would only leave one other category: outsider.

And outsiders got their heads caved in.

"Forgive us," he said. "We don't know your name. I am Andrew Simpson Smith."

A strange name for a strange situation, she thought. "I'm Tally Youngblood."

"Young Blood," he said, beginning to look a little happier. "So, you are a *young* god?"

"Uh, yeah, I guess. I'm only sixteen."

Andrew Simpson Smith closed his eyes, evidently relieved. Tally wondered if he wasn't very old himself. His earlier swagger seemed to abandon him during his moments of confusion, and he hardly had any beard yet. If you didn't notice the lines and a few pockmarks, his face could almost be an ugly of about David's age, maybe eighteen or so.

"Are you the . . . leader here?" she asked.

"No. He is headman." He pointed at the fat hunter with the bloated nose and bleeding knee, the one Tally had knocked down during the chase. The one who'd been totally about to cave her head in with his club. Great.

"I am the holy man," Andrew continued. "I learned the gods' tongue from my father."

"You speak it really well."

His face broke into a crooked-toothed smile. "I . . . thank you."

He laughed, then a look that was almost sly crossed his face. "You fell, didn't you?"

Tally held her injured wrist. "Yeah, during the chase."

"From the sky!" He looked around with a stagey bafflement, spreading his empty hands. "You have no hovercar. So you must have fallen!"

Hovercar? That was interesting. Tally shrugged. "Actually, I guess you've got me there. I did fall from the sky."

"Ahh!" He sighed with relief, as if the world was beginning to make sense again. He called out a few words to the crowd, who murmured sounds of understanding.

Tally found herself beginning to relax. They all seemed much happier now that her presence on earth had a perfectly rational explanation. Falling from the sky, they could deal with. And hopefully young gods were held to different standards of conduct.

Behind Andrew Simpson Smith, the fire exploded to life with a crackle. Tally smelled food, and heard the unmistakable squawk of a chicken being captured for slaughter. Apparently, divine visitation was a good enough excuse for a midnight feast.

The holy man spread one arm toward the fire, and the crowd parted again to open a path toward it. "Will you tell the story of falling? I will change your words to ours."

Tally sighed. She was exhausted, bewildered, and injured—her wrist still throbbed. She wanted nothing more than to curl up and sleep. But the fire looked warm and cheery after her soaking under the waterfall, and Andrew's expression was hard to resist.

She couldn't disappoint the whole village. There were no

wallscreens here, no newsfeeds or satellite bands, and touring soccer teams were no doubt few and far between. Just like back at the Smoke, that made stories a valuable commodity, and it probably wasn't very often that a stranger dropped in from the sky.

"Okay," she said. "One story, but then I'm passing out."

The whole village gathered around the fire.

The smells of roasting chicken came from long spits held over the flames, and earthen pots were shoved in among the coals, something white and yeasty-smelling gently rising in them. The men sat in the front row, eating noisily, wiping their greasy hands on their beards until they glowed in the firelight. Women tended to the food while littlies ran amok underfoot, the older ones feeding the fire with branches scavenged from the darkness. But when the signal went up that Tally was going to speak, everyone settled down.

Perhaps it was sharing a meal with her, or possibly young gods weren't so intimidating, but many of the villagers now dared to catch her eye, some even gazing unapologetically at her pretty face as they waited for the story.

Andrew Simpson Smith sat beside her, proudly ready to translate.

Tally cleared her throat, wondering how to explain her journey here in a way that would make sense to these people. They knew about hovercars and pretties, apparently. But did they know about Specials? What about the operation? The Crims? The Smoke?

The difference between bubbly and bogus?

Tally doubted her story would make any sense to them at all.

She cleared her throat again, looking down at the ground to escape their expectant gazes. She felt tired, almost pretty-headed from the night's interrupted sleep. The whole trip from the city to this fireside seemed almost like a dream.

A dream. She smiled at that thought, and gradually the words for her story began to find their way to her lips.

"Once upon a time, there was a beautiful young goddess," Tally said, then waited as her words were translated into the tongue of the villagers. The strange syllables that came from Andrew's mouth made this firelit setting even more dreamlike, until the story was flowing from her without effort.

"She lived in a high tower in the sky. It was a very comfortable tower, but there was no way down and out into the world. And one day the young goddess decided that she had better things to do than look at herself in the mirror. . . ."

REVENGE

Tally awoke to unfamiliar smells and sounds: sweat and morning breath, a soft chorus of snores and snuffling, the heavy, humid warmth of a small and crowded space.

She stirred in the darkness, and a ripple of movements spread out from her, intertwined bodies shifting to accommodate one another. Beneath the fur blankets, soft, comforting warmth suffused her senses. It felt almost like a pretty dream, except for the overwhelming smell of unwashed humans and the fact that Tally really had to pee.

She opened her eyes. Light filtered through the chimney, which was just a hole in the roof that let smoke out. Judging by the angle of the sun, it was midmorning; everyone was sleeping late. That was no surprise—the feast had lasted until dawn. Everyone told more stories after Tally's was over, competing to see whose tale could keep the sleepy god awake, with Andrew Simpson Smith tirelessly translating the whole time.

When at last they'd let her go to bed, Tally discovered that "bed" was in fact a foreign concept here. She had wound up sharing this hut with twenty other people. Apparently, in this village, staying warm on winter nights meant sleeping in piles, fur blankets strewn across everyone. It had been weird, but not weird enough to keep Tally awake another minute.

This morning, unconscious bodies lay all around her, more or less clothed, tangled up with one another and with the animal skins. But the casual contact hardly seemed sexual. It was just a way of keeping warm, like kittens in a pile.

Tally tried to sit up, and found an arm wrapped around her. It was Andrew Simpson Smith, snoring softly with his mouth half-open. She pushed his weight away from her, and he turned over without waking, draping his arm over the old man asleep on the other side of him.

As she moved through the semidarkness, Tally began to find the crowded hut dizzying. She had known that these people hadn't invented hoverboards or wallscreens or flush toilets, probably not even metal tools, but it had never occurred to Tally that there was ever anyone anywhere who hadn't invented *privacy.*

She made her way across the unconscious forms, stumbling over arms and legs and who-knew-what-else to reach the door. Stooping, she gratefully crawled out into the bright sun and fresh air.

The freezing cold goose-pimpled her bare arms and face, every breath carrying ice into her lungs. Tally realized that her coat was back in the hut, but she only wrapped her arms around herself, deciding she would rather shiver than run the gauntlet of all those sleeping bodies again. Out here in the cold, she felt her wrist throbbing from the fall the night before, and the sore muscles from the long day's hike. Maybe the human warmth of the hut hadn't been so bad, but first things first.

To find the latrine, Tally only had to follow her nose. It was nothing but a ditch, and the overwhelming smell made her glad for the first time that she had run away in winter. How did people live here in summer?

Tally had faced outdoor toilets before, of course. But the Smokies treated their waste, using a few simple, self-propagating nanos borrowed from city recycling plants. The nanos broke down sewage and routed it straight back into the soil, which helped produce the best tomatoes Tally had ever eaten. More important, they kept the latrines from raising a stink. The Smokies had almost all been born in cities, however much they loved nature. They were products of a technological civilization, and didn't like bad smells.

This village was another matter altogether, almost like the mythical pre-Rusties who had existed before high technology. What sort of culture had these people descended from? In school, they taught that the Rusties had incorporated everyone into their economic framework, destroying every other way of life—and although it was never mentioned, Tally knew that the Specials did pretty much the same thing. So where had these people come from? Had they returned to this way of life after the Rusty civilization crashed? Or had they lived out in the wild even before then? And why had the Specials left them alone?

Whatever the answers to these questions, Tally realized that she couldn't face the latrine ditch—she was too much of a city girl for that. She wandered farther back into the forest. Although she knew this had been frowned on in the Smoke, she hoped young gods got special dispensations here.

When Tally waved to a pair of watchmen on duty at the edge of town, they nodded back a bit nervously, averting their eyes and clumsily hiding their clubs behind them. The hunters were still wary of her, as if wondering why they hadn't gotten in trouble yet for trying to cave her head in.

Only a few meters into the trees, the village disappeared from view, but Tally wasn't worried about getting lost. Gusts of wind still brought smells of staggering intensity from the latrine trench, and she was still close enough to yell to the watchmen if she wound up hopelessly turned around.

In the bright sun, the night frost was melting, falling in a steady mist. The forest made soft shifting sounds, like her parents' old house when no one else was home. The shadows of leaves broke the outlines of the trees, making every shape indistinct, creating movement in the corner of her eye with every gust of wind. The feeling of being watched that she'd experienced the day before returned, and she found a spot and peed quickly.

But she didn't head straight back. It was pointless to let her imagination run away with her. A few moments of privacy were a luxury here. She wondered what lovers did when they wanted to be alone, and if anyone kept secrets for long in the village.

Over the last month, she'd gotten used to spending almost every minute with Zane. She could feel his absence right now; her body missed having his warmth next to her. But sharing sleeping quarters with a couple of dozen strangers was a strange and unexpected substitute.

Suddenly, Tally felt her nerves twitch, and she froze. Somewhere in her peripheral vision, something had shifted, not part of the natural play of sunlight and leaves and wind. Her eyes scanned the trees.

A laugh rolled from the forest.

It was Andrew Simpson Smith, crunching through the undergrowth with a big smile on his face.

"Were you spying on me?" she asked.

"Spying?" He said it as if he'd never heard the word, and Tally wondered if, with so little privacy, anyone here had even invented the concept of spying. "I woke when you left us, Young Blood. I thought maybe I would get to see you . . ."

She raised an eyebrow. "See me what?"

"Fly," he said sheepishly.

Tally had to laugh. The night before, no matter how she'd tried to explain it, Andrew Simpson Smith had never quite grasped the concept of hoverboarding. She had explained that younger gods didn't use hovercars very much, but the idea that there were different kinds of flying vehicles seemed to befuddle him.

He looked hurt by her amusement. Perhaps he thought Tally was hiding her special powers just to vex him.

"Sorry, Andrew. But like I kept saying last night, I can't fly."

"But in your story, you said you were going to join your friends."

"Yeah. But like I told you, my board's busted. And underwater. I'm afraid I'm stuck walking."

He seemed confused for a moment, perhaps amazed that divine contraptions could get broken. Then suddenly he beamed, revealing a missing tooth that made him look like a littlie. "Then I'll help you. We will walk there together."

"Uh, really?"

He nodded. "The Smiths are holy men. I am a servant of the gods, like my father was."

His voice fell flat on the last few words. Tally was amazed again at how easy it was to read Andrew's face. All the villagers' emotions seemed to live right on the surface, as if they had no more invented privacy in their thoughts than they had in their sleeping arrangements. She wondered if they ever lied to one another.

Of course, some pretties had lied to them at some point. Gods, indeed.

"When did your father die, Andrew? Not long ago, right?"

He looked up at her in wonder, as if she'd magically read his thoughts. "It was only a month ago, just before the longest night."

Tally wondered what the longest night was, but didn't interrupt.

"He and I were searching for ruins. The elder gods like us to find old and Rusty places for them, for study. We came upon outsiders."

"Outsiders? Like you mistook me for?"

"Yes. But this was no young god we found. It was a raiding party looking for a kill. We spotted them first, but their dogs had our scent.

And my father was old. Forty years, he had lived," he said proudly.

Tally let out a slow breath. All eight of her great-crumblies were still alive, and all in their hundred-teens.

"His bones had grown weak." Andrew's voice fell almost to a whisper. "Running in a stream, he turned his ankle. I had to leave him behind."

Tally swallowed, dizzy at the thought of someone dying from a sprained ankle. "Oh. I'm sorry."

"He gave me his knife before I left him." Andrew pulled it from his belt, and Tally got a closer look than the night before. It was a disposable kitchen knife with a notched, ragged blade. "Now I am the holy man."

She nodded slowly. The sight of the cheap knife in his hand reminded Tally of how her first encounter with these people had almost ended. She had almost met the same fate as Andrew's father. "But why?"

"Why, Young Blood? Because I was his son."

"No, not that," she said. "Why would the outsiders want to kill your father? Or anyone?"

Andrew frowned, as if this was an odd question. "It was their turn."

"Their *what*?"

He shrugged. "We had killed in the summer. The revenge was on them."

"You had killed . . . one of them?"

"Our revenge, for a killing in the early spring." He smiled coldly. "I was in that raiding party."

"So this is like payback? But when did the whole thing start?"

"Start?" He stared into the flat of the knife's blade, as if trying to read something in the mirror of its dull metal. "It has always been. They are outsiders." He smiled. "I was glad to see that it was you they brought home, and not a kill. So that it is still our turn, and I may still be there for my father's revenge."

Tally found herself speechless. In seconds, Andrew Simpson Smith had changed from a grieving son into some kind of . . . *savage.* His fingers had turned even paler, wrapped around the knife so tightly that the blood was forced from them.

She took her eyes from the weapon and shook her head. It wasn't fair to think of him as uncivilized. What Andrew was describing was as old as civilization itself. In school, they'd talked about this sort of blood feud. And the Rusties had only been worse, inventing mass warfare, creating more and more deadly technologies until they'd almost destroyed the world.

Still, Tally couldn't afford to forget how different these people were from anyone she'd ever known. She forced herself to stare at Andrew's grim expression, his weird delight in the heft of the knife in his hand.

Then she remembered Dr. Cable's words. *Humanity is a cancer, and we are the cure.* Violence was what the cities had been built to end, and part of what the operation switched off in pretties' brains. The whole world that Tally had grown up in was a firebreak against this awful cycle. But here was the natural state of the species, right in front of her. In running from the city, perhaps *this* was what Tally was running toward.

Unless Dr. Cable was wrong, and there was another way.

Andrew looked up from his knife and sheathed it, spreading his empty hands. "But not today. Today I will help you find your friends." He laughed, suddenly beaming again.

Tally breathed out slowly, for a moment wanting to reject his help. But she had no one else to turn to, and the forests between her and the Rusty Ruins were filled with hidden paths and natural dangers, and probably more than a few people who might think of her as an "outsider." Even if she wasn't being chased by a bloodthirsty raiding party, a sprained ankle alone in the freezing wilderness could prove fatal.

She needed Andrew Simpson Smith, it was that simple. And he had spent his life training to help people like her. Gods.

"Okay, Andrew. But let's leave today. I'm in a hurry."

"Of course. Today." He stroked the place where his slight beard was beginning to grow. "These ruins where your friends are waiting? Where are they?"

Tally glanced up at the sun, still low enough to indicate the eastern horizon. After a moment's calculation, she pointed off to the northwest, back toward the city and, beyond that, the Rusty Ruins. "About a week's walk that way."

"A week?"

"That means seven days."

"Yes, I know the gods' calendar," he said huffily. "But a whole *week*?"

"Yeah. That's not so far, is it?" The hunters had been tireless on their march the night before.

He shook his head, an awed expression on his face. "But that is beyond the edge of the world."

FOOD OF THE GODS

They left at noon.

The whole village turned out to see them off, bringing offerings for the trip. Most of the gifts were too heavy to carry, and Tally and Andrew politely turned them down. He did fill his pack, however, with the scary-looking strips of dried meat that were offered them. When Tally realized that the grisly stuff was meant to be eaten, she tried to hide her horror, but didn't do a very good job. The only gift she accepted was a wooden and leather slingshot offered by one of the older members of her littlie fan club. Tally remembered being pretty handy with slingshots back in her own littlie days.

The headman publicly bestowed his blessing on the journey, adding one last apology—translated by Andrew—for almost cracking open the head of such a young and pretty god. Tally assured him that her elders would never be told about the misunderstanding, and the headman seemed guardedly relieved. He then presented Andrew with a beaten copper bracelet, a mark of gratitude to the young holy man for helping to make up for the hunters' error.

Andrew flushed with pride at the gift, and the crowd cheered as he held it aloft. Tally realized that she had caused trouble here. Like wearing semiformal dress to a costume bash, her unexpected visit had thrown things out of whack, but Andrew's helping her was making everyone relax a little. Apparently, placating the gods was a holy man's most important job, which made Tally wonder how much city pretties interfered with the villagers.

Once she and Andrew were past the town limits, and their entourage of littlies had been called back home by anxious mothers, she decided to ask some serious questions. "So, Andrew, how many gods do you know . . . uh, personally?"

He stroked his non-beard, looking thoughtful. "Since my father's death no gods have come but you. None knows me as holy man."

Tally nodded. As she'd guessed, he was still trying to fill his father's shoes. "Right. But your accent's so good. You didn't learn to speak my language only from your father, did you?"

His crooked grin was sly. "I was never supposed to speak to the gods, only listen as my father attended them. But sometimes when guiding a god to a ruin or the nest of some strange new bird, I would speak."

"Good for you. So . . . what did you guys talk about?"

He was quiet for a moment, as if choosing his words carefully. "We talked about animals. When they mate and what they eat."

"That makes sense." Any city zoologist would love a private army of pre-Rusties to help them with fieldwork. "Anything else?"

"Some gods wanted to know about ruins, as I told you. I would take them there."

Ditto for archeologists. "Sure."

"And there is the Doctor."

"Who? The *Doctor*?" Tally froze in her tracks. "Tell me, Andrew, is this Doctor really . . . scary-looking?"

Andrew frowned, then laughed. "Scary? No. Like you, he's beautiful, almost hard to look upon."

She shuddered with relief, then smiled and raised an eyebrow. "You don't seem to find it too hard to look upon me."

His eyes fell to the ground. "I am sorry, Young Blood."

"Come on, Andrew, I didn't mean it." She took his shoulder lightly. "I was only kidding. Look upon me all you . . . um, whatever. And call me Tally, okay?"

"Tally," he said, trying out the name in his mouth. She dropped her hand from his shoulder, and Andrew looked at the place where she had touched him. "You are different from the other gods."

"I certainly hope so," she said. "So this Doctor guy looks normal? Or pretty, I mean? Or, anyway . . . godlike?"

"Yes. He is here more often than the others. But he does not care for animals or ruins. He asks only about the ways of the village. Who is courting, who is heavy with child. Which hunter might challenge the headman to a duel."

"Right." Tally tried to remember the word. "An anthro—"

"Anthropologist, they call him," Andrew said.

Tally raised an eyebrow.

He grinned. "I have good ears, my father always said. The other gods sometimes mock the Doctor."

"Huh." The villagers knew more about their divine visitors than the gods realized, it seemed. "So you've never met any gods who were really . . . scary-looking, have you?"

Andrew's eyes narrowed, and he started hiking again. Sometimes he took a long time to answer questions, as if being in a hurry was another thing the villagers hadn't bothered to invent. "No, I haven't. But my father's grandfather told stories about creatures with strange weapons and faces like hawks, who did the will of the gods. They took human form, but moved strangely."

"Kind of like insects? Fast and jerky?"

Andrew's eyes widened. "They are real, then? The Sayshal?"

"Sayshal? Oh. We call them Specials."

"They destroy any who challenge the gods."

She nodded. "That's them, all right."

"And when people disappear, they sometimes say it was the Sayshal who have taken them."

"Taken them?" *Where?* Tally wondered.

She fell silent, staring down at the forest path in front of her. If Andrew's great-grandfather had run into Special Circumstances, then the city had known about the village for decades, probably longer. The scientists who exploited these people had been doing so for a long time, and weren't above bringing in Specials to shore up their authority.

It seemed that challenging the gods was a risky business.

They hiked for a day, making good time across the hills. Tally was beginning to spot the trails of the villagers without Andrew's help, as if her eyes were learning how to see the forest better.

As night fell, they found a cave to make camp in. Tally started to collect firewood, but stopped when she noticed Andrew watching her with a mystified expression. "What's up?"

"A fire? Outsiders will see!"

"Oh, right. Sorry." She sighed, rubbing her hands together to drive the chill from her fingers. "So this revenge thing makes for some cold nights on the trail, doesn't it?"

"Being cold is better than being dead, Tally," he said, then shrugged. "And perhaps our journey will not last so long. We will reach the edge of the world tomorrow."

"Right, sure." During the day's hike, Andrew hadn't been convinced by Tally's description of the world: a planet 40,000 kilometers around, hanging in an airless void, with gravity making everyone stick to it. Of course, from his perspective it probably did sound pretty nutty. People used to get arrested for believing in a round world, they said in school—and it had usually been holy men doing the arresting.

Tally picked out two packages of SwedeBalls. "At least we don't have to build a fire to have hot food."

Andrew drew closer, watching her fill the purifier. He'd been chewing on dried meat all day, and was pretty excited about trying some "food of the gods." When the purifier pinged and Tally lifted the cover, his jaw dropped at the sight of steam rising from the reconstituted SwedeBalls. She handed it to him. "Go ahead. You first."

She didn't have to insist. Back in the village the men always ate first, and the women and littlies got leftovers. Tally was a god, of course, and in some ways they had treated her as an honorary man, but some habits died hard. Andrew took the purifier from her and stuck his hand in to grab a meatball. He yanked it out with a yelp.

"Hey, don't burn yourself," she said.

"But where is the fire?" he asked softly, sucking on his fingers as he held up the purifier to look for a flame underneath.

"It's electronic . . . a very small fire. Are you sure you don't want to try chopsticks?"

He experimented with the sticks hopelessly for a while, which allowed the SwedeBalls to cool, then finally dug in with his hands. A slightly disappointed expression crossed his face as he chewed. "Hmm."

"What's wrong?"

"I thought that food of the gods would be . . . better, somehow."

"Hey, this is *dehydrated* food of the gods, okay?"

Tally ate after he was done, but her CurryNoods were underwhelming after the feast of the night before. She remembered from her days in the Smoke how much better food could taste in the wild. Even fresh produce was never spectacular when it had been harvested from hydroponic tanks. And she had to agree with Andrew—dehydrated food was resolutely not divine.

The young holy man was surprised when Tally didn't want to sleep curled up with him—it was winter, after all. She explained that privacy was a god thing—he wouldn't understand—but he still moped at her as she chewed her toothpaste pill and found her own corner of the cave to sleep in.

It was the middle of the night when Tally awoke half-frozen, regretting her rudeness. After a long, silent session of self-recrimination, she sighed and crawled over to nestle against Andrew's back. He wasn't Zane, but the warmth of another person was better than lying on the stone floor shivering, miserable and alone.

When she awoke again at dawn, the smell of smoke filled the cave.

THE EDGE OF THE WORLD

Tally tried to cry out, but a hand was planted firmly over her mouth.

She was about to thrash out with her fists in the semidarkness, but some instinct told her not to—it was Andrew holding her. She could *smell* him, Tally realized. After two nights of sleeping next to each other, the back of her brain recognized his scent.

She relaxed, and he let go.

"What is it?" she whispered.

"Outsiders. Enough of them to build a fire."

She puzzled over this for a moment, then nodded: Because of the blood feud, only a large party of armed men would dare build a fire outside the safety of their village.

Tally sniffed the smoky air, detecting the smell of searing meat. The sounds of raucous conversation reached her ears. They must have camped close by after Tally and Andrew had gone to sleep, and now they were cooking breakfast.

"What do we do?"

"You stay here. I will see if I can find one alone."

"You're doing *what*?" she hissed.

He drew his father's knife. "This is my chance to settle the score."

"*Score?* What is this, a soccer game?" Tally whispered. "You'll get killed! Like you said, there must be lots of them."

He scowled. "I will only take one who is alone. I'm not a fool."

"Forget it!" She took hold of Andrew, locking her fingers around his wrist. He tried to pull away, but his wiry strength was no match for her postoperation muscles.

He glared at her, then spoke in a loud voice. "If we fight, they'll hear us."

"No kidding. *Shhh!*"

"Let me go!" His voice raised in volume again, and Tally realized that he would gladly shout if he had to. Honor compelled him to hunt the enemy, even if it jeopardized both their lives. Of course, the outsiders probably wouldn't hurt Tally once they saw her pretty face, but Andrew would be killed if they were caught, which was going to happen if he didn't shut up. She had no choice but to release his wrist.

Andrew turned away without another word and crawled from the cave, knife in hand.

Tally sat in the darkness, stunned, replaying their fight in her mind. What could she have said to him? What whispered arguments could overcome decades of blood feud? It was hopeless.

Maybe it went deeper than that. Tally remembered again her conversation with Dr. Cable, who had claimed that human beings always rediscovered war, always became Rusties in the end—the species was a planetary plague, whether they knew what a planet was or not. So what was the cure for *that,* except the operation?

Maybe the Specials had the right idea.

Tally crouched in the cave, miserable, hungry, and thirsty. Andrew's waterskin was empty, and there was nothing to do except wait for him to come back. Unless he wasn't coming back.

How could he just *leave* her here?

Of course, he'd had to leave his own father lying in a cold stream, injured and certain to be killed. Maybe anybody would want revenge after going through a thing like that. But Andrew wasn't looking for the men who'd killed his father, he was just out to murder a random stranger—anyone would do. It didn't make any sense.

The smells of cooking eventually faded. Creeping up to the mouth of the cave, Tally no longer heard any sounds from the outsider camp, only wind in the leaves.

Then she saw someone coming through the trees. . . .

It was Andrew. He was covered in mud, as if he'd been crawling around on his belly, but the knife clutched in his hand looked clean. Tally didn't see any blood on his hands. As he grew closer, she saw with relief that he wore an expression of disappointment.

"So, no luck?" she said.

He shook his head. "My father is not yet avenged."

"Tough. Let's get going."

He frowned. "No breakfast?"

Tally scowled. A moment ago he'd wanted nothing more than to ambush and murder some random stranger, and now his face looked like a littlie's whose promised ice cream had been snatched away.

"Too late for breakfast," she said, and pulled her backpack up onto her shoulder. "Which way to the edge of the world?"

They walked in silence until well past noon, when Tally's grumbling stomach finally forced a stop. She prepared VegiRice for them both, not in the mood for the taste of pseudomeat.

Andrew was like an anxious-to-please puppy, gamely trying to use chopsticks and making jokes about his clumsiness. But Tally couldn't bring herself to smile. The chill that had seeped into her bones while he was out looking for revenge hadn't gone away.

Of course, it wasn't completely fair being upset with Andrew. Probably he couldn't understand Tally's aversion to casual murder. He'd grown up with the cycle of revenge. It was just a part of his pre-Rusty life, like sleeping in piles or cutting down trees. He didn't see it as wrong any more than he could understand how utterly the latrine ditch revolted her.

Tally was different from the villagers—at least that much had changed in the course of human history. Maybe there was hope after all.

But she didn't feel much like talking it over with Andrew, or even giving him a smile.

"So what's beyond the edge of the world?" she finally said.

He shrugged. "Nothing."

"There must be *something.*"

"The world just ends."

"Have you been there?"

"Of course. Every boy goes, one year before you become a man."

Tally scowled—another boys-only club. "So what does it look like? A wide river? Some kind of cliff?"

Andrew shook his head. "No. It looks like the forest, like any other place. But it is the end. There are little men there, who make sure you go no farther."

"Little men, huh?" Tally remembered an old map on the library wall at her ugly school, the words "Here Be Dragons" written in flowery letters in all the blank spots. Maybe this world's edge was nothing more than the borderline of the villager's mental map of the world—like their need for revenge, they simply couldn't see beyond it. "Well, it won't be the end for me."

He shrugged again. "You are a god."

"Yeah, that's me. How far are we now?"

He glanced up at the sun. "We'll be there before nightfall."

"Good." Tally didn't want to spend another cold night huddled with Andrew Simpson Smith if she could help it.

They saw no more signs of outsiders over the next few hours, but the habit of silence had settled onto the journey. Even after Tally had decided she was no longer angry at Andrew, she found herself covering the kilometers without uttering a word. He looked dejected by her silent treatment, or maybe he was still moping about not getting his kill that morning.

A bad day all around.

Late afternoon shadows had begun to stretch behind them when he said, "We are close now."

Tally came to a halt for a drink of water, scanning the horizon. It looked like every other bit of forest she'd seen since falling from the sky. Perhaps the trees were thinning a little here, the clearings growing larger and almost bare of grass in the growing cold of winter. But it hardly looked like someone's idea of the end of the world.

Andrew walked more slowly as they continued, as if looking for signs among the trees. He sometimes glanced at the faraway hills to point out landmarks. Finally, he halted, staring with wide eyes into the forest.

Tally took a moment to focus, then saw something hanging from a tree. It looked like a doll, a human-shaped bundle of twigs and dried flowers, no bigger than a fist. It swayed in the breeze, like a little person dancing. She could see more of them stretching into the distance.

Tally had to smile. "So those are the little men?"

"Yes."

"And this is your edge of the world?" It looked like more of the same to her: dense undergrowth and trees filled with squawking birds.

"*The* edge, not mine. No one has ever passed beyond it."

"Yeah, right." Tally shook her head. The dolls probably just marked the territory of the next tribe over. She noticed a bird perched close to one, regarding the doll curiously, possibly wondering if it was edible.

She sighed and adjusted her backpack on her shoulder, striding toward the nearest doll. Andrew didn't follow, but he would catch up with her once his superstitions were disproved. Centuries before, Tally remembered, sailors had been afraid to sail into the deep ocean, thinking that sooner or later they would fall off the edge. Until someone tried it, and it turned out there were more continents out there.

On the other hand, maybe it would be better if Andrew didn't follow her. The last thing she needed was a traveling companion who was bent on revenge at any cost. The people beyond of the edge of world certainly hadn't had anything to do with the death of his father, but one outsider would be as good as another to Andrew.

As she grew nearer, Tally saw more of the dolls. They hung every few meters, marking some kind of border, like misshapen ornaments for an outdoor party. Their heads were at funny angles, she saw—the dolls all hung from their necks, nooses of rough twine around every one. She could understand how the villagers might find the little men creepy, and a slow chill ran down her spine. . . .

Then the tingling sensation moved to her fingers.

At first, Tally thought her arm had fallen asleep, pins and needles spreading from her shoulders down. She adjusted the backpack, trying to restore her circulation, but the tingling continued.

A few steps later, Tally heard the sound. A rumble seemed to come up from the earth itself, a note so low that she could feel it in her bones. It played across her skin, the world trembling around her. Tally's vision blurred, as if her eyes were vibrating in sympathy with the sound. She took another step forward, and it grew louder, now like a swarm of insects inside her head.

Something was very wrong here.

Tally tried to turn around, but found that her muscles had melted into water. Her backpack felt suddenly filled with stone, and the ground had become mush under her feet. She managed a staggering step backward, the sound fading a little as she moved away.

Holding up a hand in front of her face, she saw it trembling; maybe her fever had returned.

Or was it this place?

Tally stretched her arm out farther, and the vibrations in her fingertips increased, itching like an untended sunburn. The air itself was buzzing, growing worse with every centimeter her hand moved toward the dolls. It felt as if her flesh itself were repelled by them.

She gritted her teeth and took a defiant step forward, but the buzzing swarmed into her head, blurring her vision again. Her throat gagged on her next breath, as if the air were too electrified to breathe.

Tally staggered back from the dolls, sinking to her knees once the sound had faded. Tingles still ran across her skin, like a horde of ants swarming under her clothes. She tried to move farther, but her body refused.

Then she smelled Andrew again. His strong hands lifted her from the ground, and as he half-carried and half-dragged her away from the line of dolls, the riot of sensations slowly faded.

Tally shook her head, trying to clear the vibrating echoes. Her whole body was quivering inside. "That buzzing, Andrew . . . I feel like I swallowed a beehive."

"Yes. Buzzing, like bees." Andrew nodded, staring at his own hands.

"Why didn't you *tell* me?" she cried.

"But I did. I told you of the little men. I said you could not pass."

Tally scowled. "You could have been more specific."

He frowned, then shrugged. "It's the edge of the world. It has always been this way. How could you not know?"

She groaned in frustration, then sighed. Looking up at the closest doll, Tally finally noticed what she'd missed before. It seemed to be made of twigs and dried flowers—natural materials—but it showed no signs of weathering. All of the dolls Tally could see looked brand-new, not like handmade things that had hung for days in a torrential downpour. Unless someone had replaced every single one of them since the rains, the dolls were made of something hardier than twigs.

Something like plastic, maybe.

And inside them was something far more sophisticated, a security system powerful enough to cripple human beings, but clever enough not to harm the trees or the birds. Something that attacked the human nervous system, drawing an impassable border around the villagers' world.

Tally saw it then, why the Specials could allow the village to exist. This wasn't just a few stray people living in the wilderness; it was someone's pet anthropology project, a preserve of some kind. Or . . . what had the Rusties called them?

This was a reservation.

And Tally was trapped inside.

HOLY DAY

"You don't have a way across?" Andrew finally asked.

Tally sighed, shaking her head. Her outstretched fingers felt the tingling here, as they had every other spot she'd tried over the last hour. The line of dolls stretched unbroken as far as she could see, and all of them seemed to be in perfect working order.

She stepped back from the edge of the world, and the prickling in her hands subsided. After her first experience, Tally hadn't tested the barrier further than the tingling stage—once was enough for that—but she was fairly certain that all the other dolls had just as much punch as the one that had brought her to her knees. City machines could last a long time, and there was plenty of solar power up there in the trees.

"No. There's no way."

"I did not think so," Andrew said.

"You sound disappointed."

"I'd hoped you might show me . . . what is beyond."

She frowned. "I thought you didn't believe me, about there being more."

Andrew shook his head vigorously. "I believe you, Tally. Well, not about the airless void and *gravity,* but there must be something beyond. The city where you live must be real."

"Lived," she corrected him, sticking her fingers out again. The tingling traveled through them, feeling uncannily as if she'd sat on her hand for an hour or so. Tally stepped back and rubbed her arm. She had no idea what sort of technology the barrier was using, but it might not be very healthy to keep testing it. No point in risking permanent nerve damage.

The little dolls hung there, mocking her as they danced in the breeze. She was stuck here, inside Andrew's world.

Tally remembered all the tricks she'd pulled back in ugly days, sneaking out of dorms to cross the river at night, even crashing a party in Peris's mansion after he'd turned pretty. But her ugly skills didn't necessarily apply out here. As she'd learned in her conversation with Dr. Cable, the city was an easy place to trick. Security there was designed to stimulate uglies' creativity, not to fry anyone's nervous system.

But this barrier had been created to keep dangerous pre-Rusty villagers away from the city, to protect campers and hikers and anyone else who might have wandered out into nature. These dolls weren't likely to succumb to Tally's tinkering with the point of her knife.

The thought of ugly tricks sent Tally's hand to the slingshot in her back pocket. It seemed like an unlikely way to trick the edge of the world, but maybe the direct approach was worth a try.

She found a smooth, flat stone and loaded it up, the leather creaking as she drew it back. Tally let fly, but missed the nearest doll by a meter or so. "Guess I'm a little out of practice."

"Young Blood!" Andrew said. "Is that wise?"

She smiled. "Afraid I'll break the world?"

"The stories say that the gods put these here, to mark the edge of oblivion."

"Yeah, well. They're more like 'Keep Out' signs, or 'Keep In,' I guess—as in keeping you guys in your place. The world goes on for a whole lot farther, trust me. This is just a trick to keep you from knowing it."

Andrew looked away, and Tally thought he was going to argue some more, but instead he knelt and lifted a rock the size of his fist. He pulled back his arm, took aim, and hurled it. Tally saw from the moment it left his hand that the stone was dead on-target. It struck the nearest doll and sent it spinning, the noose tightening around its neck, then the doll spun the other way, unwinding like a top.

"That was brave of you," she remarked.

He shrugged. "As I said, Young Blood, I believe what you say. Maybe this isn't really the edge of the world. If that is true, I want to see beyond."

"Good for you." Tally stepped forward and thrust out a hand.

No change: Her fingertips buzzed with the latent energy in the air, the ants crawling up her arm until she pulled away. Of course. Any system designed to last for decades in the wild—surviving hail-storms, hungry animals, and lightning strikes—was probably more than a match for a few rocks.

"The little men are still doing their thing." She rubbed life back into her fingers. "I don't know how to get past this place, Andrew. But nice try."

He was staring down at his empty hand, as if a little surprised at himself for challenging the gods' work. "It is a strange thing to want to go past the edge of the world. Isn't it?"

She laughed. "Welcome to my life. But I'm sorry to bring you all this way for nothing."

"No, Tally. It was good to see."

She tried to read his expression, a mix of puzzlement and intensity. "To see what? Me getting serious nerve damage?"

He shook his head. "No. Your slingshot."

"Excuse me?"

"When I came here as a boy, I felt the little men crawling inside me and wanted to run back home." He looked at her, still puzzled. "But you wanted to sling a rock at them. You don't know some things that every child knows, but you are so certain about the shape of this . . . *planet.* You act as if . . ." He trailed off, his knowledge of the city language failing him.

"As if I see the world differently?"

"Yes," he said softly, his intense expression deepening. Most likely, Tally thought, it had never occurred to him before now that people could see reality in completely different ways. Between surviving outsider attacks and getting enough food to live, villagers probably didn't have a lot of time for philosophical disagreements.

"That's the way it feels," she said, "once you get off the reservation, I mean, once you go beyond the edge of the world. Speaking of which, do you know for sure that no matter what direction we walk in, we'll run into these little guys?"

Andrew nodded. "My father taught that the world is a circle, seven days' walk across. This is the nearest edge to our village. But my father once walked around the entire compass of the world."

"Interesting. You think he was looking for a way out?"

Andrew frowned. "He never said."

"Well, I guess he didn't find one. So how am I going to escape this world of yours and get to the Rusty Ruins?"

Andrew was silent for a while, but Tally could tell he was thinking, taking one of his interminable delays to ponder her question. Finally, he said, "You must wait for the next holy day."

"The next what?"

"The holy days mark when the gods visit. And they will come in hovercars."

"Oh, yeah?" Tally sighed. "I don't know if you've figured this out yet, Andrew, but I'm not supposed to be here. If any elder gods see me, I'm busted."

He laughed. "Do you think I'm a fool, Tally Young Blood? I listened to your story about the tower. I understand that you have been cast out."

"Cast out?"

"Yes, Young Blood. You bear this mark." His fingers brushed her left brow.

"Mark? Oh, right . . ." For the first time since meeting the villagers, Tally remembered her flash tattoo. "So you think this means something?"

Andrew bit his lip, dropping his eyes from her brow. "I am not sure, of course. My father never taught me of such things. But in my village, we only mark those who have stolen."

"Yeah, sure. But you thought I was . . . *marked* somehow?" He looked up sheepishly, and Tally rolled her eyes. No wonder the villagers had been so confused by her; they'd thought the flash tattoo was some kind of badge of shame. "Listen, it's just a fashion statement. Or, um, let me put that another way. It's just something me and my friends did to amuse ourselves. You notice how it moves sometimes?"

"Yes. When you are angry, or smiling, or thinking hard."

"Right. Well, that's called being 'bubbly.' Anyway, I *ran* away. I didn't get cast out."

"And they'll want to take you home, I understand. You see, when the gods come, they leave their hovercars behind when they walk in the forest. . . ."

Tally blinked, and then a smile spread across her face. "And you'd help me steal from the elder gods?"

He only shrugged.

"Won't they get cranky with you?"

Andrew sighed, stroking his non-beard as he considered this. "We must be careful. But I have noticed that the gods are not . . . perfect. You escaped their tower, after all."

"Well, well, imperfect gods." Tally allowed herself a chuckle. "What would your father say, Andrew?"

He shook his head. "I am not sure. But he isn't here. I am the holy man now."

That night, they camped near the barrier. Andrew said that no one—outsiders or otherwise—would be likely to venture this close to the dolls at night. It was a place of superstitious dread, on top of which, no one wanted to get their brains fried when they woke up and stumbled off into the darkness to pee.

The next morning they began a roundabout journey back to Andrew's village, taking their time, avoiding the outsiders' hunting grounds. It took three days, during which Andrew displayed his knowledge of the forest, mixing villager lore with scientific knowledge he'd picked up from the gods. He understood the water cycle, and a little about the food chain, but after a day of arguing about gravity, Tally gave up.

When they neared the village, it was still almost a week before the next holy day. Tally told Andrew to find her a cave to hide in, one near the clearing where the gods parked their hovercars. She had decided to stay out of sight. If none of the villagers knew she had returned, they couldn't give Tally away to the elder gods. And she didn't want anyone getting blamed for harboring a runaway.

Andrew headed back home, where he planned to tell how the Young Blood had passed through the edge of the world and to the beyond. Apparently, the villagers knew how to lie after all—at least the holy men did.

And his story would be true, once Tally got her hands on a hovercar. She was no expert at driving, but she'd taken the same safety course that every ugly took at fifteen: learning how to fly straight and level and how to land in an emergency. She knew that some uglies went trick-riding all the time, and said it was easy. Of course, they'd only stolen idiotproof cars that flew on the city grid.

Still, how much harder could it be than hoverboarding?

As Tally waited out the days in the cave, she couldn't stop wondering how the other Crims were. While her own survival had been an issue, it had been easy to forget them. But now that she had nothing to do all day but sit and watch the sky, Tally found herself slowly going crazy from worry. Had the Crims escaped the Specials' pursuit? Had they found the New Smokies yet? And, most important, how was Zane? She could only hope that Maddy had been able to fix whatever was wrong with him.

She remembered their last minutes before he'd jumped from the balloon—the last words he'd said. In all of Tally's tattered memories, she'd never experienced anything like that moment. It had felt beyond bubbly, beyond any trick, like the world would change forever.

And now she didn't even know whether he was still alive.

It didn't help Tally's state of mind that Zane and the other Crims had to be just as worried about her, wondering if she'd been recaptured or had fallen to her death. They would have expected to see her at the Rusty Ruins at least a week ago, and had to be thinking the worst by now.

How long would it be before even Zane gave up, deciding she

was dead? What if she never made it out of the reservation? No one's faith could last forever.

When she wasn't driving herself crazy, Tally also spent the time wondering about Andrew's confined world. How had it come to exist? Why were the villagers allowed to live out here, when the Smoke had been ruthlessly destroyed? Maybe it was the fact that the villagers were trapped, believing old legends and stuck in ancient blood feuds, while the Smokies had known the truth about the cities and the operation. But why keep a brutal culture alive, when the whole point of civilization was to curb the violent, destructive tendencies of human beings?

Andrew visited her every day, bringing her nuts and a few root vegetables to go with her dehydrated god-food. He wouldn't give up on bringing strips of dried meat until she tried it. It tasted like it looked—as salty as seaweed and harder than an old shoe—but she gratefully accepted his other offerings.

In return, Tally told him stories about home, especially those that showed how the city of the gods wasn't all divine perfection. She explained about uglies and the operation, how the beauty of gods was just a technological trick. The difference between magic and technology was lost on Andrew, but he listened intently. He'd inherited a healthy skepticism from his father, whose experiences with the gods, it turned out, hadn't always left the old holy man full of respect.

Andrew could be frustrating company, though. He made some brilliant leaps of insight, but other times he was just as thick as could be expected from someone who thought the world was flat—

especially when it came to the boys-in-charge thing, which she found particularly annoying. Tally knew she should be more understanding, but was only willing to cut Andrew so much slack; being born into a culture that assumed women were servants didn't make it okay to go along with the plan. After all, Tally had turned her back on everything she'd been raised to expect: an effortless life, perfect beauty, pretty-mindedness. It seemed like Andrew could learn to cook his own chickens.

Maybe the barriers around Tally's pretty world weren't as obvious as the little men hanging in the trees, but they were just as hard to escape. She remembered how Peris had chickened out as he'd looked down on the wild from the balloon, suddenly unwilling to jump and leave behind everything he'd known. Everyone in the world was programmed by the place they were born, hemmed in by their beliefs, but you had to at least *try* to grow your own brain. Otherwise, you might as well be living on a reservation, worshipping a bunch of bogus gods.

They arrived at dawn, right on schedule.

From overhead came the roar of two cars—the kind that Specials used, each with four lifting fans to carry it through the air. It was a noisy way to travel, the wind roiling the trees like a storm. From the mouth of her cave, Tally saw a huge cloud of dust rising up from the landing area, and then the whine of their rotors cycled down into a riot of frightened birdcalls. After almost two weeks of natural sounds, the powerful machines sounded strange to Tally's ears, like engines from another world.

She crept toward the clearing in the dawn light, moving in total silence. Rehearsing her approach every morning, Tally had become familiar with every tree along the way. For once, the elder gods were going to face someone who knew all their tricks, and a few of her own.

She watched from under cover at the clearing's edge. Four middle pretties were unpacking the cars' cargo holds, pulling out digging tools, hovercameras, and specimen cages, loading everything onto carts. The scientists looked like campers dressed in bulky winter gear, field glasses hanging around their necks, water bottles dangling from their belts. Andrew said they never stayed more than a day, but they looked ready for weeks in the wild. Tally wondered which one was the Doctor.

Andrew worked among the four pretties, lending a hand as they arranged their equipment, being a helpful holy man. When the carts were all packed with gear, he and the scientists pushed them into the forest, leaving Tally alone with the hovercars.

She hoisted her backpack and approached the clearing warily.

This was the trickiest part of the plan. Tally could only guess what sort of security the hovercars had on board. Hopefully the scientists hadn't thought to use more than childproof minders, the simple codes that kept littlies from flying off with a car. Surely the scientists wouldn't suspect the villagers of knowing the same tricks as a city kid like Tally.

Unless they'd been warned that there were runaways in the area . . .

That was nonsense, of course. No one knew Tally was stranded out here without a board, and she hadn't seen a hovercar since the night she'd left the city. If the Specials were looking for her, they weren't looking around here.

She reached one of the cars and peeked into its open cargo door, finding nothing but pieces of packing foam shifting in the soft breeze. A few more steps brought her to the window of the passenger cabin, also empty. She reached for the door handle.

A man's voice called from behind her.

Tally froze. After two weeks of sleeping rough, her clothes torn and dirty, she might pass for a villager from a distance. But once she turned around, her pretty face would give her away.

The voice called out again in the villagers' language, but it was inflected with a late pretty's gravelly air of authority. Footsteps were coming closer. Should she dive into the hovercar and try to make it away?

The words faded as the man grew closer. He had noticed her city clothes under all the dirt.

Tally turned around.

He was equipped like the others, with field glasses and a water bottle, his crumbly face a picture of surprise. He must have been sitting inside the other hovercar, moving a little slower than the rest of them—that's why he'd caught her.

"Good heavens!" he exclaimed, switching languages. "What are you doing out here?"

She blinked, pausing for a moment, a vacant look on her pretty face. "We were in a balloon."

"A balloon?"

"There was some kind of accident. But I don't remember exactly. . . ."

He took a step forward, then his nose wrinkled. Tally might look like a pretty, but she smelled like a savage. "I think I saw something on the feeds about balloons going wrong, but that was a couple of weeks ago! You couldn't have been here that . . ." He looked at her torn clothes, his nose wrinkling again. "But I suppose you have."

Tally shook her head. "I don't know how long it's been."

"You poor dear." Recovering from his surprise, he was now all late-pretty concern. "You're okay now. I'm Dr. Valen."

She smiled like a good pretty, realizing that this must be the Doctor. A bird-watcher probably wouldn't know the villagers' language, after all. This was the man in charge.

"It feels like I've been hiding out *forever,*" she said. "There are all these crazy people out here."

"Yes, they can be quite dangerous." He shook his head, as if still not believing that a young city pretty had survived out here for so long. "You're lucky to have stayed clear of them."

"Who are they?"

"They're . . . part of a very important study."

"A study? Of *what*?"

He chuckled. "Now, that's all very complicated. Perhaps I should tell someone we've found you. I'm sure everyone's very anxious to know if you're okay. What's your name?"

"What are you studying out here?"

He blinked, perplexed that a new pretty was asking questions instead of whining about getting home. "Well, we're looking at certain fundamentals of . . . human nature."

"Of course. Like violence? Revenge."

He frowned. "Yes, in a manner of speaking. But how . . . ?"

"I thought so." All at once, it was becoming clear. "You're studying violence, so you'd need a violent, brutal group of people, wouldn't you? You're an anthropologist?"

Confusion still played across his face. "Yes, but I'm also a doctor. A medical doctor. Are you sure you're all right?"

A realization hit Tally. "You're a brain doctor."

"We're called neurologists, actually." Dr. Valen warily turned to reach for the hovercar door. "But perhaps I should make that call. I didn't get your name."

"I didn't give it."

Her tone stopped him cold.

"Don't touch that door," she said.

He turned to face her again, his late-pretty composure crumbling. "But you're . . ."

"Pretty? Think again." She smiled. "I'm Tally Youngblood. My mind is very ugly. And I'm taking your car."

The Doctor was quite afraid of savages, it seemed—even beautiful ones.

He meekly allowed himself be locked into the cargo container of one of the hovercars, and handed over the take-off codes to the other. The security was nothing Tally couldn't have tricked herself, but it saved time. And the expression on Dr. Valen's face as he gave her the codes was pretty indeed. He was used to dealing with villagers in awe of his godhood. But one look at Tally's knife and he'd realized who was giving the orders.

The man answered a few more of Tally's questions, until no doubt remained in her mind what this reservation was all about. This had been the place where the operation had been developed, from which the first test subjects had been drawn. The purpose of the brain lesions was to deter violence and conflict, so who better to experiment on than people caught up in an endless blood feud? Like rabid enemies in a locked room, the tribes trapped within the ring of little men would reveal anything you wanted to know about the very human origins of bloodshed.

She shook her head. Poor Andrew. His whole world was an experiment, and his father had died in a conflict that meant precisely nothing.

Tally paused a moment in the hovercar before taking off, familiarizing herself with the controls. They seemed about the same as a city car, but she had to remember that this one wasn't idiotproof—it would fly into a mountain if you told it to. She would have to be careful in the high spires of the ruins.

The first thing she did was put her boot through the communication system; she didn't want the car telling the city authorities where it was.

"Tally!"

She started at the shout, peering out through the front windows. But it was only Andrew, and he was alone. She slid out of the driver's door, waving for him to be silent and pointing at the other car. "I've got the Doctor locked up," she hissed. "Don't let him hear your voice. What are you doing back here?"

He looked at the other hovercar, eyes widening at the thought of a god imprisoned within, and whispered, "I was sent back to see where he was. He said he would be just behind us."

"Well, he's not coming. And I'm about to leave."

He nodded. "Of course. Good-bye, Young Blood."

"Good-bye." She smiled. "I won't forget all your help."

Andrew was staring into her eyes, the familiar pretty-awed expression coming over his face. "I'll not forget you, either."

"Don't look at me that way."

"What way, Tally?"

"Like a . . . god. We're just humans, Andrew."

He looked at the ground, nodding slowly. "I know."

"Not very perfect humans, some of us worse than you could imagine. We've done awful things to your people for a long time now. We've used you."

He shrugged. "What can we do? You are so powerful."

"Yeah, we are." She took his hand. "But keep trying to get past the little men. The real world is huge. Maybe you can get far enough away that the Specials will stop looking for you. And I'll try to . . ." She didn't finish the promise. Try to do what?

A smile broke across Andrew's face, and he reached out to touch her flash tattoo. "You are bubbly now."

She nodded, swallowing.

"We will wait for you, Young Blood."

Tally blinked, then hugged him wordlessly. She slid back into the hovercar and started the rotors. As the whine of its engines built, she watched the birds scatter from the clearing, terrified by the roar of the gods' machine. Andrew backed away.

The car rose at her first touch on the controls, its power shuddering through her bones. The rotors whipped the treetops around her into a frenzy, but the car rose steadily, under control.

Tally looked down as the car cleared the trees, and saw Andrew waving up at her, his crooked, gap-toothed smile still hopeful. Tally knew that she would have to return, just like he'd said; she no longer had a choice. Someone had to help the people here escape the reservation, and they had no one else but Tally.

She sighed. At least one thing was consistent about her life: It just kept on getting more complicated.

THE RUINS

Tally reached the sea while the sun was still rising, painting the water pink through the low clouds out on the horizon.

She angled the machine northward in a slow, even turn. As she'd expected, this out-of-city car had a scary tendency to do whatever Tally asked of it. Her first turn had been sharp enough to bang her head against the driver's side window. This time, she was taking it easy.

As the car gradually climbed, she soon spotted the outskirts of the Rusty Ruins. A distance that would have taken a week on foot had shot by in a blur below Tally in less than an hour. When the sinuous shape of the ancient roller coaster came into view, she began to bank the craft inland.

Landing was the easy part. Tally pulled the emergency bar, the one they taught littlies to use if their driver had a heart attack or passed out. The car brought itself to a halt and began to descend. Tally had picked a flat spot, one of the many giant concrete fields that the Rusties built to park their groundcars in.

The vehicle settled onto the weed-choked ground, and Tally opened her door the moment the car bumped to a stop. If the other scientists had found the Doctor and made some sort of emergency call, the Specials would already be looking for her. The more distance she put between herself and the stolen hovercar, the better.

The spires of the ruins rose up before Tally, the tallest about an hour away on foot. She was, of course, arriving almost two weeks after the others. But hopefully they hadn't given up on her, or maybe they'd left a message of some kind.

Surely Zane would have stayed, waiting in the tallest building, unwilling to leave while there was still a chance she would show up.

Unless, of course, their escape had come too late for him.

Tally shouldered her backpack and started to walk.

The ruined streets were full of ghosts.

Tally had hardly ever walked in the city before. She had always cruised around on a hoverboard—ten meters up, at least—avoiding the burned-out cars down at ground level. In the last days of Rusty civilization, an artificial plague had spread across the world. It didn't infect human beings or animals, just petroleum, reproducing itself in the gas tanks of groundcars and jet aircraft, slowly making the infected oil unstable. Plague-transformed petroleum burst into flame when it came into contact with oxygen, and the oily smoke from the sudden fires spread the bacterial spores on the wind, into more gas tanks, more oil fields, until it had reached every Rusty machine across the globe.

The Rusties really hadn't liked walking, it turned out. Even after they'd figured out what the plague was doing, panicked citizens still jumped into their funny, rubber-wheeled groundcars, thinking to escape into the wild. If Tally looked hard enough, she could see crumbling skeletons through the smeared windows of the cars jammed onto the ruins' streets. Only a few of the people back then had been smart enough to *walk* out, and strong enough to survive the death of their world. Whoever had engineered the plague had definitely understood the Rusties' weakness.

"Boy, you guys were stupid," Tally muttered at the car windows, but calling them names didn't make the dead Rusties any less ominous. The few intact skulls just stared back at her with empty expressions.

Farther into the dead city, the buildings grew taller and taller, their steel frameworks rising up like the skeletons of giant and extinct creatures. Tally took a winding path through the narrow streets, looking for the tallest building in the ruins. The huge spire was easy to spot from a hoverboard, but from the ground the city was a tangled maze.

Then she turned a corner and saw it, chunks of old concrete clinging to the towering matrix of steel beams, the empty windows gazing down at her, jagged shapes of bright sky showing through. This was definitely the place—Tally remembered when Shay had taken her up to its top the first time she'd come out to the Rusty Ruins. There was only one problem.

How was she going to get up?

The innards of the building had long since rotted away. There were no stairs, and hardly any floors to speak of. The steel frame made it perfect for a hoverboard's magnetic lifters, but there was no way for a person to climb it without serious mountaineering gear. If Zane or the New Smokies had left a message for Tally, it would be up there, but she had no way of reaching it.

Tally sat down, suddenly exhausted. It was like the tower in her dream, without stairs or elevator, and she'd lost the key, which in this case was her hoverboard. All she could think of was to hike back to the stolen car and fly it up there. Maybe she could bring it close enough beside the building . . . but who would hold it in a steady hover while she climbed out onto the ancient steel frame?

For the thousandth time, Tally wished that her board hadn't been wrecked.

She stared up at the tower. What if no one was up there? What if, after traveling all this way, Tally Youngblood was still alone?

She got to her feet and yelled as loud as she could, "Heeeey!"

The sound echoed through the ruins, sending a flock of birds into flight from a distant rooftop.

"Hey! It's me!"

Once the echoes faded, there was no sound in answer. Tally's throat felt sore from yelling. She knelt to dig a safety flare out of her backpack. A fire would be pretty obvious down here in the shadows of the cavernous buildings.

She cracked the flare open, holding its hissing flame away from her face, then cried out again. "It's meeeee . . . Tally Youngblood!"

Something shifted in the sky above.

Tally blinked away the spots that the flare had left in her eyes and stared into the bright blue sky. A shape drifted away from the towering building, a tiny oval that began to grow slowly. . . .

The underside of a hoverboard. Someone was coming down!

Tally tossed the flare onto a pile of rocks, her heart pounding, suddenly realizing she had no idea who was descending to meet her. How had she been so dimwitted? It could be anyone up there on the board. If the Specials had caught the other Crims and made them talk, they would know this was the planned meeting place, and Tally's latest escape was about to come to a sudden end.

She told herself to calm down. It *was* a hoverboard, after all, and only one. Surely if Specials had been lying in wait, they would have rushed out from every direction in a bunch of hovercars.

In any case, there was no point in panicking. She wasn't likely to escape on foot now. The only thing to do was wait. The safety flare sizzled out to a sputtering death while the hoverboard descended slowly, hugging the metal frame of the building. Once or twice, Tally thought she saw a face peering over the edge, but against the bright sky it could have been anyone.

When it was only ten meters overhead, Tally found the nerve to cry out again. "Hello?" Her voice sounded shaky in her ears.

"Tally . . . ," someone called back, the voice familiar.

The hoverboard settled beside her, and Tally found herself staring into a thoroughly ugly face: the forehead too high, the smile crooked, a small scar cutting a white line through one eyebrow. She stared at him, blinking in the gloom of the broken city.

"David?" she said softly.

FACES

He stared at her, of course.

Even if she hadn't shouted out her name, David knew her voice. And he had been waiting for Tally, after all, so he must have known from the first cry who was down here. But the way he stared at her, it was as if he were seeing someone else.

"David," she said again. "It's me."

He nodded, still speechless. But it wasn't pretty-awe that had caught his tongue—that much Tally realized. His gaze seemed to be searching for something, trying to recognize what the operation had left of her old face, but his expression remained unsure . . . and a bit sad.

David was uglier than she remembered. In Tally's ugly-prince dreams, his imbalanced features had never been so disjointed, his unsurged teeth never so crooked or discolored. His blemishes weren't as bad as Andrew's, of course. He looked no worse than Sussy or Dex, city kids who'd grown up with toothpaste pills and sunblock patches.

But this was *David*, after all.

Even after her time with the villagers, many of them toothless and scarred, his face sent a shock through her. Not because he was hideous—he wasn't—but because he was simply . . . unimpressive.

Not an ugly prince. Just ugly.

And the weird thing was, even as she had these thoughts, her long-suppressed memories were finally flooding back. This was *David,* who had taught her how to make a fire, how to clean and cook fish, how to navigate by the stars. They had worked side by side, traveled together for weeks on end, and Tally had given up her city life to stay with him in the Smoke—she'd wanted to live with him forever.

All those memories had survived the operation, hidden somewhere inside her brain. But her life among the pretties must have changed something even more profound: the way she saw him, as if this wasn't the same David in front of her anymore.

Neither of them said anything for a while.

Finally, he cleared his throat. "We should probably get moving. They sometimes send patrols out around this time of day."

She looked at the ground. "Okay."

"I've got to do this first." He pulled a wandlike device from one pocket and swept it over her. It stayed silent.

"No bugs on me?" she said.

He shrugged. "Can't be too careful. You don't have a board?"

Tally shook her head. "It got damaged in the escape."

"Wow. Takes a lot to break a hoverboard."

"It was a long fall."

He smiled. "Same old Tally. I knew you'd show up, though. Mom said you'd probably . . ." He didn't finish.

"I'm fine." She looked up at him, unsure of how much to say. "Thanks for waiting."

They rode his board. Tally was taller than David now, so she stood behind him, hands around his waist. She'd abandoned her heavy crash bracelets before her long trek with Andrew Simpson Smith, but her sensor was still clipped to her belly ring, so the board could feel her center of gravity and compensate for the extra weight. Still, they went slowly at first.

The feel of David's body, the way he leaned into the turns, was so familiar—even the smell of him set her memories spinning. (Tally didn't want to think about how *she* smelled, but he didn't seem to have noticed.) She was amazed at how much was coming back; her memories of him seemed to have been ready and waiting, and were all flooding in now that he stood next to her. Here on the board, with David turned away from her, Tally's body cried out to hold him tight. She wanted to take back all the stupid, pretty-minded thoughts she'd had at her first glimpse of his face.

But was it just that he was ugly? Everything else had changed as well.

Tally knew she should be asking about the others, especially Zane. But she couldn't bring the name to her lips, couldn't speak at all. Just standing on the board with David was almost too much.

She kept wondering why it had been Croy who'd brought her the cure. In Tally's letter to herself, she had been so certain that David would be the one to rescue her. *He* was the prince of her dreams, after all.

Was he still angry that she had betrayed the Smoke? Did he blame her for his father's death? The same night she'd confessed everything to David, Tally had gone back to the city to give herself up, to become pretty so she could test the cure. She'd never had a chance to explain how sorry she was. They hadn't even said good-bye to each other.

But if David hated her, why had *he* been the one waiting in the ruins? Not Croy, not Zane—David. Her head was spinning, almost like being pretty-minded again, but without the happy part.

"It's not far," David said. "Maybe three hours, traveling tandem like this."

She didn't answer.

"I didn't think to bring another board. Should have known you wouldn't have one, since it took you so long to get here."

"I'm sorry."

"No big deal. We just have to fly a little slower."

"No. I'm sorry. For what I did." She fell silent. The words had exhausted her.

He let the board coast to a stop between two towering husks of metal and concrete, and they stood there for a long moment,

David still facing away. She rested one cheek on his shoulder, her eyes beginning to burn.

Finally, he said, "I thought I would know what to say. Once I saw you."

"Forgot about the new face, didn't you?"

"I didn't forget, exactly. But I didn't think it would be so . . . not you."

"Me either," Tally said, then realized her words wouldn't make sense to him. David's face hadn't changed, after all.

He turned around carefully on the board and touched her brow. Tally tried to look at him, but couldn't. She felt her flash tattoo pulsing under his fingers.

Tally smiled. "Oh, is that freaking you out? It's just a Crim thing, to see who's bubbly."

"Yeah, a tattoo keyed to your heartbeat. They told me. But I hadn't imagined one on you. It's so . . . weird."

"It's still me inside, though."

"It feels that way, flying together." He turned away, tilting the hoverboard forward and into motion.

Tally held him tighter now, not wanting him to turn around again. This was hard enough without the confused feelings that rose up every time she looked at him. He probably didn't want to look at her city-made face either, with its huge eyes and animated tattoo. One thing at a time. "Just tell me, David, why did Croy bring me the cure instead of you?"

"Things got messed up. I was going to come for you when I got back."

"Got back? From where?"

"I was away scouting another city, looking for more uglies to join us, when the Specials came in force. They started to make huge sweeps of the ruins, looking for us." He took her hand and pressed it to his chest. "My mom decided to get out of town for a while. We've been holed up in the wild."

"Leaving me stuck in the city," she said, and sighed. "Maddy wouldn't have much problem with that, I guess." Tally had little doubt that David's mother still blamed her for everything—the end of the Smoke, Az's death.

"She didn't have a choice," David protested. "There's never been so many Specials before. It was too dangerous to stay here."

Tally took a deep breath, remembering her little chat with Dr. Cable. "I guess Special Circumstances has been recruiting lately."

"But I hadn't forgotten about you, Tally. I'd made Croy promise to bring you the pills and your letter if anything happened to me, just to make sure you had a chance of escaping. When they started to pack up the New Smoke, he figured we might not be back for a while, so he snuck into the city."

"You told him to come?"

"Of course. He was my backup. I never would have left you alone in there, Tally."

"Oh." Dizziness swept over her again, as if the board were a feather spinning toward the ground. She closed her eyes and held David tighter, finally grasping the solidness and reality of him, more powerful than any memory. Tally felt something inside herself depart, a disquiet that she'd hardly known was there. The torment in her dreams, the worry that David had forsaken her, had all been over a mix-up, just plans that had gone wrong, like in old stories when a letter arrived too late or was sent to the wrong person, and the trick was not killing yourself over it.

David had wanted to come for her himself, it turned out.

"Of course, you weren't alone," he said softly.

Tally's body stiffened. By now he knew about Zane, of course. How was she supposed to explain that she'd simply *forgotten* David? It wouldn't sound like much of an excuse to most people, but he knew all about the lesions—his parents had raised him knowing what being pretty-minded meant. He had to understand.

Of course, in reality it wasn't as simple as that. Tally *hadn't* forgotten Zane, after all. She could see his beautiful face right now, gaunt and vulnerable, the way his golden eyes had flashed just before he jumped from the balloon. His kiss had given her the strength to find the pills; he had shared the cure with her. So what was she supposed to say?

The easiest thing was, "How is he?"

David shrugged. "Not great. But not too bad, considering. You're lucky it wasn't you, Tally."

"The cure is dangerous, isn't it? It doesn't work for some people."

"It works perfectly. Your pals have already all had it, and they're fine."

"But Zane's headaches . . ."

"More than just headaches." He sighed. "I'll let my mother explain it to you."

"But what . . ." Tally let her question fade into silence. She couldn't blame David for not wanting to talk about Zane. At least her unasked questions had all been answered. The other Crims had made it here and had hooked up with the Smokies; Maddy had been able to help Zane; the escape had worked perfectly. And now that Tally had made it to the ruins herself, everything was just fine and dandy. "Thank you for waiting for me," she said again, softly.

He didn't answer, and they flew the rest of the way without looking at each other once.

DAMAGE CONTROL

The path to the New Smokies' hiding place wound along streams and ancient railway beds, wherever there was enough metal to keep the hoverboard aloft. Finally, they climbed a small mountain far outside the Rusty Ruins, the board's lifters clinging to the fallen remains of an old cable car track, up to where a huge concrete dome, cracked open by the centuries, stood against the sky.

"What was this place?" Tally asked, her voice dry after three hours in silence.

"An observatory. There used to be a big telescope in that dome. But the Rusties took it out once the pollution from the city got too bad."

Tally had seen pictures of the sky filled with dirt and smoke—

they showed those a lot in school—but it was hard to imagine that the Rusties had really managed to change the color of the air itself. She shook her head. Everything that she thought her teachers had exaggerated about the Rusties always turned out to be true. The temperature had dropped steadily as they'd climbed the mountain, and the afternoon sky looked crystal clear to her.

"After the scientists couldn't see the stars anymore, the dome was just for tourists," David said. "That's what all these cable cars were for. Lots of ways down by hoverboard, if we ever need to get out of here fast, and we can see for miles in every direction."

"Fort Smokey, huh?"

"I guess. If the Specials ever find us, at least we've got a chance."

A lookout had evidently spotted them on the way up—people were spilling from the broken observatory as the hoverboard settled to the earth. Tally spotted the New Smokies—Croy, Ryde, and Maddy, along with a few uglies she didn't recognize—and the two dozen or so Crims who'd come along on the escape.

Tally searched for Zane's face among the crowd, but he wasn't there.

She jumped from the board, running to hug Fausto. He grinned at her, and she could see from his sharpened expression that he'd taken the pills. He wasn't just bubbly anymore; he was cured.

"Tally, you smell," he said, still grinning.

"Oh, yeah. Long trip. Long story."

"I knew you'd make it. But where's Peris?"

She took a deep breath of the cold mountain air.

"Chickened out, huh?" Fausto said before she could answer.

When she nodded, he added, "Always thought he would."

"Take me to Zane."

Fausto turned, gesturing toward the observatory. The others were hovering close, but looked a little put off by her bedraggled appearance and ripe smell. The Crims called out hellos, and she could see the uglies reacting to a new pretty face, their eyes widening even though she was a mess. Worked every time, even when they didn't think you were a god.

Tally paused to nod at Croy. "I haven't had a chance to thank you yet."

He raised an eyebrow. "Don't thank me. You did it yourself."

She frowned, noticing that Maddy was staring strangely at her. Tally ignored the look, not interested in what David's mother thought, and followed Fausto into the broken dome.

It was dark inside—a few lanterns were strung up around the edge of the huge, open hemisphere, and a narrow shaft of blinding sunlight streamed through the dome's great fissure. An open fire cast jittering shadows through the space, its smoke climbing lazily up through the crack overhead.

Zane lay on a pile of blankets by the fire, his eyes closed. He looked even thinner than when they'd been trying to starve the cuffs off, his eyes sunken into his head. The covers rose and fell softly with his breathing.

Tally swallowed. "But David said he was okay. . . ."

"He's stable," Fausto said, "which is good, considering."

"Considering *what*?"

Fausto spread his hands helplessly. "His brain."

A chill moved through Tally, the shadows in the corners of her eyes rippling for a moment. "What about it?" she said softly.

"You had to experiment, didn't you, Tally?" came a voice from the darkness. Maddy stepped into the light, David at her side.

Tally held her steely glare. "What are you talking about?"

"The pills I gave you were meant to be taken together."

"I know. But there were two of us . . ." Tally trailed off at David's expression. *And I was too scared to do it alone,* she added to herself, remembering the panic of those moments in Valentino 317.

"I suppose I should have known," Maddy said, shaking her head. "This was always a risk, letting a pretty-head treat herself."

"What was?"

"I never explained how the cure worked, did I?" Maddy said. "How the nanos remove the lesions from your brain? They break them down, like the pills that cure cancer."

"So what went wrong?"

"The nanos didn't stop. They went on reproducing, breaking down Zane's brain."

Tally turned to look at the form on the bed. His breathing seemed so shallow, the movement of his chest at the edge of perception.

She faced David. "But you said the cure worked perfectly."

He nodded. "It does. Your other friends are fine. But the two pills were *different.* The second pill, the one you took, is the cure for the cure. It makes the nanos self-destruct after they finish with the lesions. Without it, Zane's nanos kept reproducing, kept eating away at him. Mom said they stopped at some point, but not before they did a . . . certain amount of damage."

The sickening feeling in Tally's stomach redoubled as the realization sunk home: This was *her* fault. She had swallowed the pill that would have kept Zane from this, the cure for the cure. "How much damage?"

"We don't know yet," Maddy said. "I had enough stem tissue to regenerate the destroyed areas of his brain, but the connections that Zane had built up among those cells are gone. Those connections are where memories and motor skills are stored, and where cognition happens. Some parts of his mind are almost a blank slate."

"A blank slate? You mean . . . he's *gone*?"

"No, just a few places are damaged," Fausto spoke up. "And his brain can rewire itself, Tally. His neurons are making new connections. That's what he's doing right now. Zane had been doing it all along; he hoverboarded all the way here on his own before he collapsed."

"Rather amazing that he lasted so long," Maddy said, shaking her head slowly. "I think not eating is what saved him. By starving himself, he eventually starved the nanos. They appear to be gone."

"He can still talk and everything," Fausto said. He looked down at Zane. "He's just a little . . . tired right now."

"It could have been you in that bed, Tally." Maddy shook her head. "A fifty-fifty chance. You just got lucky."

"That's me. Little Miss Lucky," Tally said softly.

Of course, she had to admit to herself that it was true. They'd split the two pills randomly, assuming they were the same. The nanos could have been eating away at Tally's brain all this time instead of Zane's. Lucky her.

She let her eyes close, realizing at last how hard Zane must have worked to hide what was happening to him. All those long silences when they'd been wearing the cuffs, he'd been fighting, struggling to keep his mind together, unsure of exactly what was happening, but risking everything to escape becoming pretty-minded again.

Tally gazed down at him, wishing for a moment it had been the other way around. Anything was better than seeing him like this. If only she'd taken the nano pill, and he had taken the one that . . . had done *what*? "Wait a second. If Zane got the nanos, how did my pill cure me?"

"It didn't," Maddy said. "Without the other pill, the anti-nanos you took would have no effect whatsoever."

"But . . ."

"It was *you,* Tally," came a soft voice from the bed. Zane's eyes had opened a slit, catching the sunlight like the edges of gold coins. He gave her a weary smile. "You got bubbly on your own."

"But I felt so different after we . . ." She fell silent, remembering that day—their kiss, sneaking into Valentino Mansion, climbing the tower. But, of course, all those things had happened *before* they'd taken the pills. Being with Zane had changed her from the beginning, from that first kiss.

Tally remembered how her "cure" always seemed to come and go. She'd had to work to stay bubbly, more like the other Crims than Zane.

"He's right, Tally," Maddy said. "Somehow, you cured yourself."

COLD WATER

Tally stayed at Zane's bedside. He was awake and talking now, and it was easier to be here than dealing with everything that she and David still had to work out. The others left them alone.

"Did you know what was happening to you?"

Zane took a moment before answering. His speech was full of long silences now, almost like Andrew's epic pauses. "I knew that everything was getting harder. Sometimes I had to concentrate just to walk. But I hadn't felt so alive since I'd turned pretty; it was worth it, being bubbly with you. I figured once we found the New Smoke, they could help me."

"They *are* helping. Maddy said that she put in some new . . ." Tally swallowed.

"Brain tissue?" he supplied, and smiled. "Sure, blank neurons fresh out of the oven. Just got to fill them up now."

"We will. We'll do bubbly-making things," Tally said, but the promise felt strange in her mouth—"we" meant she and Zane, as if David didn't exist.

"If there's enough left of me to be bubbly," he said tiredly. "It's not like all my memories are gone. It was mostly my cognition centers that were affected, and some motor skills."

"Cognition? You mean like *thinking*?" Tally said.

"Yeah, and motor skills, like walking." He shrugged. "But the brain's built to take damage, Tally. It's wired so that everything is stored everywhere, sort of. When a part of it gets damaged, things don't get lost, just fuzzier. Like a hangover." He laughed. "A really bad one. On top of which, I'm sore from lying in bed all day. And it feels like I've got a toothache from all this Smokey food. It's just phantom pains from brain damage, Maddy says." He rubbed one cheek with a scowl.

She took his hand. "I can't believe you're so brave about this. It's incredible."

"You should talk, Tally." He struggled to sit up, his movements shaky and infirm. "You managed to cure yourself *without* getting your brain chewed up. That's what I'd call incredible."

Tally looked down at their clasped hands. She didn't feel very incredible. She felt smelly and dirty, and *horrible* that she hadn't had the guts to take both pills, which would have prevented all of this from happening. She didn't even have the guts to talk to Zane about David, or vice versa. Which was just pathetic.

"Is it strange, seeing him?" he asked.

She looked at Zane, and he chuckled at her surprise. "Come on, Tally. It's not like I'm reading your mind. I had plenty of warning about this. You told me about the guy the first time we kissed, remember?"

"Oh, yeah." So Zane had been expecting this all along. Tally should have foreseen it herself. Maybe she simply hadn't wanted to face the obvious. "Yeah, it *is* strange seeing him. I definitely didn't expect to find him waiting for me in the ruins. Just me and him alone."

Zane nodded. "It was interesting, waiting for you. His mother said you wouldn't come at all. That you must have chickened out, because you hadn't really been cured. Like you were just playing along with me, imitating my bubbliness."

Tally rolled her eyes. "She doesn't much like me."

"You don't say?" He grinned. "But David and me figured you'd show up sooner or later. We figured that—"

Tally groaned. "So are you guys like *friends* now?"

Zane took one of his excruciatingly long pauses. "I guess so. He asked me a lot about you when we first got here. I think he wanted to know how being pretty has changed you."

"Really?"

"Really. He was the one who met us when we arrived in the ruins. Him and Croy, camping out and watching for flares. It turns out that those two left the magazines for the city uglies to find, so they'd know the ruins were being visited again." Zane's voice had gotten dreamy, as if he was falling asleep. "At least I finally got to see him again, after chickening out all those months ago." He turned to her. "David really missed you, you know."

"I ruined his life," Tally said softly.

"You didn't do anything on purpose; David understands that now. I told him how when you'd planned to betray the Smoke, it was because the Specials threatened to keep you ugly for life."

"You told him that?" Tally let out a slow breath. "Thanks. I never really had a chance to explain why I'd come to the Smoke, how they'd forced me. Maddy made me leave the same night I confessed everything."

"Yeah. David wasn't happy with her about that. He wanted to talk to you again."

"Oh," she said. There was so much that she and David hadn't gotten straight between them. Of course, the thought of Zane and him discussing her history in great detail didn't exactly thrill Tally, but at least David knew the whole story now. She sighed. "Thanks for telling me all this. It must be weird."

"A little. But you shouldn't feel so bad. About what happened back then."

"Why not? I destroyed the Smoke, and David's father died because of me."

"Tally, everyone in the city is manipulated. The purpose of everything we're taught is to make us afraid of change. I've been trying to explain it to David, how from the day we're born, the whole place is a machine for keeping us under control."

She shook her head. "That doesn't make it right to betray your friends."

"Yeah, well, I did, long before you even met Shay. When it comes to the Smoke, I'm just as much at fault as you."

She looked at him in disbelief. "You? How?"

"Did I ever tell you how I met Dr. Cable?"

Tally looked at him, realizing that this was one conversation they'd never had a chance to finish. "No. You didn't."

"After the night that Shay and I chickened out, most of my friends were gone away to the Smoke. The dorm minders knew I was the leader, so they asked me where everyone had run off to. I played tough, and didn't say a word. So Special Circumstances came for me." His voice grew softer, as if the cuff were still around his wrist. "They took me to that headquarters of theirs out in the factory belt, same as you. I tried to be strong, but they threatened me. Said they'd make me into one of them."

"One of them? A *Special*?" Tally swallowed.

"Yeah. After that, being a pretty-head didn't seem so bad anymore. So I told them everything I knew. I told them that Shay had planned to run away, but also chickened out, and that's why they knew about her. And that's probably why they started watching . . ." His voice trailed off.

Tally blinked. "Watching *me,* when she and I became friends."

He nodded tiredly. "So, you see? I started the whole thing, by not leaving when I was supposed to. I'll never judge you for what happened to the Smoke, Tally. It was my fault as much as yours."

She took his hand, shaking her head. He couldn't accept blame, not after everything he'd gone through. "Zane, no. It can't be your fault. That was a long time ago." She sighed. "Maybe neither of us is to blame."

They were silent for a while, Tally's own words echoing in her head. With Zane lying here in front of her, his mind half-missing, what was the point of wallowing in old guilt—his, or hers, or anyone's? Maybe the bad blood between her and Maddy was as meaningless as the feud between Andrew's village and the outsiders. If they were all going to live together here in the New Smoke, they would have to let the past go.

Of course, things were still complicated.

Tally took a slow breath, then said, "So what do you think of David?"

Zane looked at the arched ceiling dreamily. "He's very intense. Really serious. Not as bubbly as us. You know?"

Tally smiled, and squeezed his hand. "Yeah, I do."

"And kind of . . . ugly."

She nodded, remembering how back in the Smoke, David had always looked at her as if she was pretty. And at times, looking at him had felt the same as looking into a pretty's face. Maybe when she'd had the real cure, those feelings would come back. Or maybe they were really gone for good, not because of any operation, but just because time had passed, and because of what she'd had with Zane.

When Zane had finally fallen asleep, Tally decided to take a bath. Fausto told her how to get to a spring on the far side of the mountain, choked with icicles at this time of year, but deep enough to submerge your whole body. "Just take a heated jacket," he said. "Or you'll freeze to death before you make it back."

Tally figured death was better than being this filthy, and she needed more than a rubdown with a wet cloth to feel clean again. She also wanted to be alone for a while, and maybe the shock from some freezing water would help her get up the nerve to talk to David.

Hoverboarding down the mountain in the crisp, late afternoon air, Tally was amazed at how clear and bright everything looked. She still found it hard to believe that she hadn't really taken the cure; she felt as bubbly as ever. Maddy had muttered something about a "placebo effect," as if believing you were cured would be enough to fix your brain. But Tally knew it was more than that.

Zane had changed her. From their very first kiss, even before he'd had the cure himself, being with him had made her bubbly. Tally wondered if she even needed the cure now, or if she could stay this way forever on her own. The thought of swallowing the same pill that had eaten away Zane's brain didn't thrill her, even with the anti-nanos as a chaser. Maybe she could skip it altogether, and rely on Zane's magic. They could help each other now, rewiring his brain at the same time Tally fought becoming pretty-minded.

They had come this far together, after all. Even before the pills, they had changed each other.

Of course, David had changed Tally too. Back in the Smoke, he'd been the one who'd convinced her to stay in the wild, even to stay ugly, giving up her future in the city. Her reality had been transformed by those two weeks in the Smoke, starting . . . when? That first time David and she had kissed.

"How lucky is that?" Tally muttered to herself. "Sleeping Beauty with two princes."

What was she supposed to do? *Choose* between David and Zane? Especially now that all three of them were living together here at Fort Smokey? Somehow it didn't seem fair that she found herself in this position. Tally had barely remembered David when she'd met Zane—but she hadn't *wanted* to have her memories erased, after all.

"Thanks again, Dr. Cable," she said.

The water looked really cold.

Tally had easily kicked through the layer of ice on top, and was now staring down with dread into the gurgling spring. Maybe smelling bad wasn't the worst thing in the world. Spring would come in only three or four months, after all. . . .

She shivered, turning the heat up in her borrowed jacket, then sighed and started to take off her clothes. This little bath would be very bubbly-making, at least.

Tally smeared a soap packet onto herself before jumping in, rubbing some into her hair, guessing she would last about ten seconds in the half-frozen spring. She knew she'd have to jump—no dangling of the foot or lowering herself in slowly. Only the laws of gravity would keep her going once her naked flesh hit cold water.

Tally took a breath, held it . . . and leaped into the spring.

The icy water crushed her like a vice, forcing the breath from her lungs, locking every muscle tight. She hugged herself with her arms, rolling into a ball in the shallow pool, but the cold seemed to cut through her flesh and straight into her bones.

Tally fought to take a breath, but managed only shallow little gasps of air, her entire body shaking as if it would break apart. With a titanic act of will she dunked her head in, erasing all sound, the rasp of her breath and gurgle of the spring replaced by the rumble of roiling water. She rubbed furiously at her hair with trembling hands.

When her head burst into the air again, Tally drew in great breaths and found herself laughing—everything had turned strangely clear, the world more bubbly than a cup of coffee or a glass of champagne could make it, the sensation more intense than falling toward the earth on her hoverboard. She lay there for a moment in the water, amazed at it all—the clarity of the sky and the perfection of a leafless tree nearby.

Tally remembered her first bath in a cold stream on the way to the Smoke, all those months ago. How it had shifted the way she saw the world—even before the operation had put the lesions on her brain, before she'd met David, much less Zane. Even then, her mind had started to change, realizing that nature didn't need an operation to make it beautiful, it just was.

Maybe she didn't need a handsome prince to stay awake—or an ugly one, for that matter. After all, Tally had cured herself without the pill and had made it all the way here on her own. No one else she'd ever heard of had escaped the city *twice.*

Maybe she'd always been bubbly, somewhere inside. It only took loving someone—or being in the wild, or maybe just a plunge into freezing water—to bring it out.

* * *

Tally was still in the pond when she heard the cry: a hoarse shout that came from the air.

She climbed out hurriedly, and the wind cutting through her felt colder than the water. The towels Tally had brought were brittle in the chill air, and she was still drying herself when a hoverboard streaked into view, banking to a halt a few meters away.

David hardly seemed to register that she was naked. He jumped from the board and ran toward her, clutching something in his hand. Skidding to a halt by her pack, he waved the device across it—scanning it for bugs, she realized.

"It's not you," he said. "I knew it wasn't."

Tally was pulling on her clothes. "But you already—"

"A signal just started up out of nowhere, broadcasting our location. We picked it up on the radio, but haven't localized it yet." He looked down at her pack, the relieved expression still on his face. "But you didn't bring it."

"Of course I didn't." Tally sat down to yank on her boots. Her pounding heart began to drive the cold from her body. "Don't you scan everyone who joins you?"

"Yeah. But the bug must have been dormant—it only started sending when someone activated it, or maybe it was set to go off at a certain time." His eyes scanned the horizon. "The Specials will be here soon."

She stood. "So we run."

He shook his head. "We can't go anywhere until we find it."

"Why not?" She pulled on crash bracelets.

"It's taken us months to build up the supplies we've got, Tally. We can't leave them all behind, not with all you Crims having just joined us. But we won't know what's safe to take until we figure out where the signal's coming from. It's not showing up *anywhere*."

Tally hoisted her pack and snapped her fingers, her board rising into the air. As she stepped on, her mind still racing from the freezing bath, she recalled something from earlier that day. "Toothache," she said.

"What?"

"Zane was in the hospital two weeks ago. It's inside him."

TRACKER

They swept back up the mountain, banking hard against the high gravities of their turns. Tally stayed in the lead, positive that she was right. The doctors had made Zane unconscious for a few minutes in the hospital while they'd repaired his broken hand. They must have hidden a tracker in his teeth at the same time. Of course, regular city doctors wouldn't have done something like that on their own—it had to be the work of Special Circumstances.

The camp was bedlam when they arrived. New Smokies and Crims ran in and out of the observatory door with equipment, clothing, and food, making two piles beside Croy and Maddy, who stood waving scanners over everything wildly. Others hurriedly repacked the scanned gear, getting ready to flee once the bug was found.

Tally tipped back her hoverboard and forced it up as high as it would go, launching herself over the chaos, directly at the broken dome. When the board reached its maximum height the lifters shuddered, then firmed up as the magnets found the steel frame of the observatory. The crack in the dome was wide enough to glide through, and Tally dropped straight down through the rising smoke, jumping off next to Zane's makeshift bed.

He looked up at her with a soft smile. "Nice entrance, Tally."

She knelt beside him. "Which tooth hurts?"

"What's going on? Everyone's freaking out."

"*Which tooth hurts, Zane?* You have to show me."

He frowned, but stuck a trembling finger into his mouth, tenderly probing the right side. Tally pulled his hand away and opened his mouth wider, and he made a whimper of protest.

"Shush. I'll explain in a second."

Even in the dim firelight, she could see it: One tooth stood out from the others, its shade of white imperfectly matched—a rushed bit of dentistry, of course.

The signal was coming from Zane.

The *wheep* of a scanner booting up sounded beside her ear; David had followed her down the hole into the dome. He waved the scanner past Zane's face, and it buzzed angrily. "It's in his mouth?" David asked.

"In his *tooth*! Get your mother."

"But, Tally—"

"Get her! You and I can't take out a tooth!"

He put a hand on her shoulder. "Neither can she. Not in a few minutes."

She stood, staring into his ugly face. "What are you saying, David?"

"We'll have to leave him behind. They'll be here soon."

"No!" she shouted. "Go get her!"

David swore and turned away, running toward the door of the observatory. Tally looked down at Zane again.

"What's happening?" he asked.

"They put a tracker in you, Zane. At the hospital."

"Oh," he said, rubbing his face. "I didn't know, Tally, honest. I thought my toothache was from all this wild food."

"Of course you didn't know. You were unconscious for those minutes at the hospital, remember?"

"Are they really going to leave me?"

"I won't let them. I promise."

"I can't go back," he said weakly. "I don't want to be pretty-minded again."

Tally swallowed. If Zane was returned to the city now, the doctors would put the lesions back in, right on top of his blank new tissue. His brain would rewire around them. . . . What chance would he have of staying bubbly?

She couldn't let this happen.

"I'll take you on my hoverboard, Zane—we'll escape on our own if we have to." Her mind raced. She'd still have to get rid of the tracker somehow. She couldn't just bash it out with a rock. . . . Tally looked around for some sort of tool, but the New Smokies had taken everything useful outside to be scanned.

Voices came from the darkness. It was Maddy, David, and Croy. Tally saw that Maddy was carrying some sort of forceps in her hand, and her heart skipped a beat.

Maddy knelt beside Zane and forced open his mouth. He whimpered in pain again as the metal tool probed his teeth.

"Be careful," Tally pleaded softly.

"Hold this." Maddy handed her a flashlight. When Tally pointed it into Zane's mouth, the discolored tooth was obvious.

After a moment, Maddy said, "This isn't good." She released Zane's head, and he fell back onto the blankets with a groan, his eyes closing.

"Just take it out!"

"They've rooted it to the bone." She turned to Croy. "Finish packing up. We have to run."

"Do something for him!" Tally cried.

Maddy took the light from her. "Tally, it's bonded to the bone. I'd have to shatter his jaw to remove it."

"So don't take it out, just make it stop sending! Smash the tooth! He can take it!"

Maddy shook her head. "Pretty teeth are made of the same stuff they use in aircraft wings. You can't just smash them. I'd need special dental nanos to break it down." She turned the flashlight on Tally, reaching for her mouth.

Tally twisted away. "What are you doing?"

"Just making sure about you."

"But I didn't go into the hos—," Tally began, but Maddy wrenched open her mouth. Tally growled at the back of her throat, but let the woman poke around for a moment; it was quicker than arguing. When she grunted and let go, Tally said, "Satisfied?"

"For now. But we have to leave Zane behind."

"Forget it!" Tally shouted.

"They'll be here in another ten minutes," David said.

"Less." Maddy stood.

Tally's vision swam with spots from the little flashlight. She could hardly see their faces in the firelight. Didn't they understand what Zane had gone through to get here, what he had sacrificed for the cure? "I won't leave him."

"Tally—," David began.

"It doesn't matter," Maddy interrupted. "Technically, she's still a pretty-head."

"I am not!"

"You didn't even take the right pill." Maddy put a hand on David's shoulder. "Tally's still got the lesions. Once they scan her brain, they won't even put her under the knife. They'll think she just came along for the ride."

"Mom!" David shouted. "We are not leaving her!"

"And I'm not coming," Tally said.

Maddy shook her head. "Perhaps the lesions aren't as important as we thought. Your father always suspected that being pretty-minded is simply the natural state for most people. They *want* to be vapid and lazy and vain"—Maddy glanced at Tally—"and selfish. It only takes a twist to lock in that part of their personalities. He always thought that some people could think their way out of it."

"Az was right," Tally said softly. "I'm cured now."

David let out a pained growl. "Cured or not, Tally, you can't stay here. I don't want to lose you again! Mom! Do something!"

"You want to argue with her? Go ahead." Maddy spun on one heel and strode toward the observatory entrance. "We're leaving in two minutes," she said without turning around. "With or without you."

David and Tally were silent for a few moments. It was like when they'd first seen each other in the ruins that morning, neither knowing what to say. Though now, Tally realized, David's face no longer shocked her. Maybe the panic of the moment or the freezing bath had stripped her remaining pretty thoughts away. Or maybe it had simply taken a few hours to align her memories and dreams with the truth. . . .

David wasn't a prince—handsome or otherwise. He was the first boy she'd fallen in love with, but not the last. Time and experiences apart had changed what had been between them.

More important, she had someone else now. However unfair it was that her memories of David had been erased, Tally had built a whole new set of memories, and she couldn't just trade them in for the old ones. Zane and she had helped each other become bubbly, had been imprisoned by the cuffs together, and escaped the city together. She couldn't abandon him now, just because he had been robbed of part of his mind.

Tally knew too well what that was like, being handed over to the city all alone.

Zane was the one person in her life she had never betrayed, and she wasn't about to start now. She took his hand. "I'm not leaving him."

"Think logically, Tally." David spoke slowly, talking to her like she was a littlie. "You can't help Zane if you stay here. You'll both be captured."

"Your mother's right. They won't do anything more to my brain, and I can help him from inside the city."

"We can smuggle Zane the cure, like we did for you."

"I didn't *need* the cure, David. Maybe Zane won't either. I'll keep him bubbly, I can help him rewire his brain. But he won't stand a chance without me."

David started to speak, but froze for a moment. Then his voice changed, his eyes narrowing. "You're just staying with him because he's pretty."

Tally's eyes widened. *"I'm what?"*

"Don't you see it? It's like you always used to say: It's evolution. Since your Crim friends got here, Mom's been explaining to me how prettiness works." He pointed at Zane. "He's got those big, vulnerable eyes, that childlike perfect skin. He looks like a baby to you, a needy child, which makes you want to help him. You're not thinking rationally. You're giving yourself up just because he's pretty!"

Tally stared back at David in disbelief. How dare he say this to *her*? The mere fact that she was standing here proved that Tally could think for herself.

Then she realized what was going on: David was only repeating Maddy's words. She must have warned him not to trust his feelings when he saw the new Tally. Maddy didn't want her son turning into some awestruck ugly, worshipping the ground Tally walked on. So now David thought that all that Tally could see was Zane's pretty face.

David still thought she was just some city kid. Maybe he didn't even really believe that she was cured. Maybe he'd never really forgiven her.

"It's not the way Zane looks, David," she said, her voice trembling with anger. "It's because he makes me bubbly, and because we took a lot of risks together. It could just as easily be me lying there, and he would stay with me if it was."

"It's just programming!"

"No. It's because I love him."

David started to speak again, but the sound choked off.

She sighed. "Go on, David. Whatever your mother said a second ago, she won't really leave without you. They'll all get caught if you don't start moving now."

"Tally—"

"Go!" she cried. David had to start running, or the New Smoke would die, and it would be her fault again.

"But you can—"

"Get your ugly face *out of here*!" Tally screamed.

The echoes shuddered back at her from the observatory walls for a moment, and Tally tore her gaze away from David. She cradled Zane's face in one hand and kissed him. The shouted insult had the effect she'd wanted, but Tally couldn't bring herself to look up as she heard David's footsteps retreating into the darkness, first walking, then at a run.

She saw shapes pulsing in the corners of her vision. It wasn't shadows cast by the flickering fire—it was her heart, pounding so hard that she could see the rushing blood beating against her eyes, like something trying to escape.

She had called David ugly. He would never forget that, nor would she.

But she'd *had* to use that word, Tally told herself. Every second counted, and nothing else would have pushed him away so powerfully. She'd made her choice.

"I'll take care of you, Zane," she said.

He opened his eyes into slits and smiled weakly. "Um, I hope you don't mind if I pretended to pass out for that."

Tally let out a strangled laugh. "Good idea."

"We really can't run? I think I can stand up."

"No. They'd just find us."

He probed at his tooth with his tongue. "Oh, yeah. That sucks. And I almost got everyone else caught too."

She shrugged. "Been there. Done that."

"Are you sure you want to stay with me?"

"I can escape the city again, Zane, anytime I want. I can save you and Shay, and everyone else we left behind. I'm cured for good now." Tally looked at the entrance, saw hoverboards lifting into the air. They were leaving, all of them. She shrugged again. "Besides, I think it's pretty much a done deal. Running after David now would kind of spoil my brilliant breakup line."

"Yeah, I suppose that's true." Zane chuckled softly. "Do me a favor, Tally? If you ever break up with me, just leave a note."

She smiled back at him. "Okay. As long as you promise never to put your hand in a crusher again."

"Agreed." Zane looked at his fingers, then made a fist. "I'm scared. I want to stay bubbly."

"You'll be bubbly again. I'll help you."

He nodded, grasping her hand. His voice shook as he said, "Do you think David was right? My big beautiful eyes are why you chose me?"

"No. I think it was . . . what I said. And what you said, before you jumped off the balloon." She swallowed. "What's your opinion?"

Zane lay back and closed his eyes, and was silent so long that Tally thought he had fallen asleep again. But then he said softly, "You and David could both be right. Maybe humans beings *are* programmed . . . to help one another, even to fall in love. But just because it's human nature doesn't make it bad, Tally. Besides, we had a whole city of pretties to choose from, and we chose each other."

She took his hand and murmured, "I'm glad we did."

Zane smiled, then closed his eyes again. A moment later, she saw his breathing slow, and realized that he had managed to pass out again. At least brain damage had some advantages.

Tally felt the last scraps of energy leave her body, and wished she could sleep too, just spend the next few hours unconscious and wake up in the city—an imprisoned princess again, as if this had all been a dream. She laid her head onto Zane's chest and closed her eyes.

Five minutes later, Special Circumstances arrived.

SPECIALS

The scream of hovercars filled the observatory, echoing like the cries of predatory birds. Whirlwinds from their rotors swept through the crack in the dome, sending the fire into a sudden blaze. Dust choked the air, and gray forms charged through the entrance, taking up positions in the shadows.

"I need a doctor here," Tally announced in a tentative, pretty voice. "Something's wrong with my friend."

A Special appeared beside her out of the darkness. He held a weapon. "Don't move. We don't want to hurt you, but we will if we have to."

"Just help my friend," she said. "He's sick." The sooner city doctors looked at Zane, the better. Maybe they could do more than Maddy had.

The Special said something into a handphone, and Tally glanced down at Zane. Fear showed through his slitted eyes.

"It's okay," she said. "They'll help you."

Zane swallowed, and Tally saw his hands trembling, the last of his brave front crumbling now that their captors had arrived.

"I'll make sure you're cured, one way or another," she said.

"A medical team is coming," the Special said, and Tally smiled prettily at him. The city doctors might mistake Zane's condition for some kind of brain disease, or maybe they would figure out that someone had attempted a cure for the lesions, but they would never recognize how Tally had transformed herself. She could pretend that she'd just come along for the ride, as Maddy had put it. Tally was safe from the operation now.

Maybe Zane could be cured again without more pills. Maybe everyone in the city could be changed. After their balloon escape and another "rescue" by the Specials, Tally and Zane would be even more famous. They could start something huge, something the Specials couldn't stop.

A razor-edged voice came through the shadows, and Tally flinched.

"I thought I might find you here, Tally." Dr. Cable came into the light, stretching her fingers toward the fire as though she'd stepped inside to get warm.

"Hi, Dr. Cable. Can you help my friend?"

The woman's wolflike smile gleamed in the dark. "Toothache?"

"Something worse." Tally shook her head. "He can't move, can hardly talk. Something's wrong with him."

More Specials streamed into the observatory, including three carrying a stretcher, wearing blue silk instead of gray. They pushed Tally out of the way and laid the litter down next to Zane. He closed his eyes.

"Don't worry," Dr. Cable said. "He'll be fine. We know all about his condition from your little trip to the hospital. It seems that someone slipped Zane some brain nanos. Very bad for his pretty head."

"You knew he was sick?" Tally stood up. "Why didn't you fix him?"

Dr. Cable patted her shoulder. "We brought the nanos to a halt. But the little implant in his tooth was programmed to give him headaches—false symptoms to keep you motivated."

"You were playing with us . . . ," Tally said, watching as the Specials took Zane away.

Dr. Cable was looking around the observatory. "I wanted to see what you were up to and where you would go. I thought you might lead us to those responsible for young Zane's illness." She frowned. "I was going to wait a bit longer to activate the tracker, but after you were so rude to my good friend Dr. Valen this morning, I thought we should come out and bring you home. You certainly know how to cause trouble."

Tally stayed silent, her mind racing. The tracker in Zane's tooth had been activated remotely, but not until the other scientists had discovered Dr. Valen. Once again, Tally had brought Specials along with her.

"We wanted a car to get away," she said, trying to sound pretty. "But we got lost."

"Yes, we found it in the ruins. But I don't think you made it all the way here on foot. Who helped you, Tally?"

She shook her head. "No one."

A Special in gray silk appeared beside Cable and gave a quick report. His razored voice made Tally's flesh crawl, but she couldn't make out any of the muttered words.

"Send the youngsters after them," Dr. Cable ordered, then turned to Tally. "No one, you say? What about the cooking fires and hunting snares and latrines? Quite a few people were camped here, it seems, and they left not long ago." She shook her head. "Pity we didn't get here quicker."

"You won't catch them," Tally said with a pretty smile.

"Won't we?" Dr. Cable's teeth gleamed red in the firelight. "We've got a few new tricks ourselves, Tally."

The doctor turned and strode toward the entrance. When Tally tried to follow, a Special took her shoulder in a grip of iron and sat her down by the fire. Shouted orders and the sounds of more hovercars landing filtered into the dome, but Tally gave up trying to see what was going on through the entrance, and stared at the flames unhappily.

Now that Zane had been taken away, Tally only felt defeated. She'd been played perfectly by Dr. Cable again, tricked into finding the New Smoke, almost betraying everyone one more time. And after her last words, David probably hated her now.

But at least Fausto and the other Crims had escaped the city, hopefully for good. They and the New Smokies had the benefit of a few minutes' head start. They couldn't outrun the Specials' cars in a straight line, but their hoverboards were more nimble. Without Zane's tracker to give them away, they could simply disappear into the surrounding forest. Tally and Zane's rebellion had swelled the ranks of the New Smokies by a couple of dozen members. And now that the cure had been tested, they could bring it to the city, and to other cities, and eventually everyone would be free.

Maybe the city hadn't won, this time.

And being caught might be the best thing for Zane. The city doctors would be better able to treat him than a band of outlaws on the run. Tally focused her mind on how she would help him recover, making him bubbly all over again if she had to.

Maybe she would start with a kiss. . . .

An hour or so after the Specials had first arrived, the fire had burned low, and Tally began to feel the cold again. As she turned up her jacket's heater, a shadow moved in the red shaft of sunset that slanted through the dome's opening.

Tally started. It was someone coming down on a hoverboard. Was it David returning to save her? She shook her head. Maddy would never let him.

"We got a couple of them," a harsh voice called from the board. The gray silk of Special uniforms fluttered in the gloom—two more figures descending through the crack in the dome. The hover-boards were longer than normal, with lifting fans built into their front and back ends. Their rotors stirred the embers of the fire.

So this was their new trick, Tally thought. Specials on hoverboards, perfect for tracking the New Smokies. She wondered who they'd caught.

"Uglies or pretties?" Dr. Cable called. Tally looked up and saw that the doctor had rejoined her by the fire.

"Just a couple of the Crims. The uglies all got away," came the answer. Tally realized that beneath its razor sharpness, she recognized the sound of the Special's voice.

"Oh, no," she said softly.

"Oh, yes, Tally-wa." The figure hopped off her board and strode into the firelight. "New surge! Do you like it?"

It was Shay. She was Special.

"Dr. C let me get more tattoos. Aren't they totally dizzying?"

Tally looked at her old friend, awestruck by the transformation. The spinning lines of flash tattoos covered her, as if Shay's skin were wrapped in a pulsing black net. Her face was lean and cruel, her upper teeth filed down to sharp, triangular points. She was taller, with hard new muscles in her bare arms. The line of the scars where she had cut herself stood out prominently, outlined with swirling tattoos. Shay's eyes flashed in the firelight like a predator's, shifting between red and violet as the flames danced.

She was still pretty, of course, but her cruel, inhuman grace sent shivers through Tally, like watching a colorful spider traverse its web.

Behind her, the other hoverboards descended. Ho and Tachs, Shay's fellow Cutters, each held a limp form. Tally grimaced when she saw that they'd caught Fausto, who'd never been on a hoverboard in his life before a few days ago. But most of the others had escaped, at least . . . and David had made it to safety.

The New Smoke still lived.

"Think my new surge is pretty-making, Tally-wa?" Shay said. "Not too much for you?"

Tally shook her head tiredly. "No. It's bubbly, Shay-la."

A broad, cruel smile filled Shay's face. "About a zillion milli-Helens, huh?"

"At least." Tally turned from her old friend and stared into the fire.

Shay sat down beside her. "Being Special is more bubbly than you can imagine, Tally-wa. Every second is totally spinning. Like, I can hear your heartbeat, can feel the electric buzz of that jacket trying to keep you warm. I can *smell* your fear."

"I'm not afraid of you, Shay."

"You are a little bit, Tally-wa. You can't lie to me anymore." Shay put her arm around Tally. "Hey, remember the crazy faces I used to design back when we were uglies? Dr. C will let me do them now. Cutters can surge however we want. Even the Pretty Committee can't tell us what we can and can't look like."

"That must be great for you, Shay-la."

"Me and my Cutters are the bubbly new thing in Circumstances. Like *special* Specials. Isn't that totally happy-making?"

Tally turned to face her, trying to see what was behind the flashing violet-red eyes. Despite the pretty-talk, she heard a cold, serene intelligence in Shay's voice, a pitiless joy in having snared her old betrayer.

Shay was a new kind of cruel pretty, Tally could see. Something even worse than Dr. Cable. Less human.

"Are you really happy, Shay?"

Shay's mouth quivered, her sharp teeth running along her lower lip for a moment, and she nodded. "I am, now that I've got you back, Tally-wa. It wasn't very nice, all of you running off like that without me. Totally sad-making."

"We wanted you along, Shay, I swear. I left you all those pings."

"I was *busy.*" Shay kicked at the dying fire with one boot. "Cutting myself. Searching for a cure." She snorted. "Besides, I've had enough of the camping thing. And, anyway, we're together now, you and me."

"We're against each other." Tally barely whispered the words.

"No way, Tally-wa." Shay's hand squeezed her shoulder roughly. "I'm sick of all the mix-ups and bad blood between us. From now on, you and I are going to be *best friends forever.*"

Tally closed her eyes; so this was Shay's revenge.

"I need you in the Cutters, Tally. It's so bubbly-making!"

"You can't do this to me," Tally whispered, trying to pull away.

Shay held her firmly. "That's the thing, Tally-wa. I can."

"No!" Tally cried, lashing out and trying to struggle to her feet.

Quick as lightning, Shay's hand shot forward, and Tally felt a sharp sting on her neck. Seconds later, a thick fog began to settle over her. She managed to pull away and take a few stumbling steps, but her limbs seemed to fill with liquid lead, and she fell to the ground. A shroud of gray descended across the fire in front of her, the world growing dark.

Words tumbled at her through the void, carried on a razor voice: "Face it, Tally-wa, you're . . ."

BOGUS DREAMS

Over the next few weeks, Tally never quite awoke. She would stir sometimes, and realize from the feel of sheets and pillows that she was in bed, but mostly her mind floated free of her body, drifting in and out of disjointed versions of the same dream. . . .

There was this beautiful princess locked in a high tower, one with mirrored walls that wouldn't shut up. There was no elevator or any other way down, but when the princess grew bored of staring at her own pretty face in the mirrors, she decided to jump. She invited all her friends to come along, and they all followed her down—except her best friend, whose invitation had been lost.

The tower was guarded by a gray dragon with jeweled eyes and a hungry maw. It had many legs and moved almost too fast to see, but it pretended to be asleep, and let the princess and her friends sneak past.

And you couldn't have this dream without a prince.

He was both handsome and ugly, bubbly and serious, cautious and brave. In the beginning he lived with the princess in the tower, but later in the dream he seemed to have been outside all along, waiting for her. And in a dream-logic way he was often two princes, which she had to choose between. Sometimes the princess chose the handsome prince, and sometimes the ugly one. Either way, her heart was broken.

And whomever she picked, the dream's ending never changed. The best friend, the one whose invitation had been lost, always tried to follow the princess. But the gray dragon woke up and swallowed her, and liked her taste so much that it came after the rest of them, hungry for more. From inside its stomach, the best friend looked out through the dragon's eyes, and spoke with its mouth, swearing it would find the princess and punish her for leaving a friend behind.

And over all those sleepy weeks, the dream always ended the same way, with the dragon coming for the princess, saying the same words every time. . . .

"Face it, Tally-wa, you're Special."

Read on for a look at Scott Westerfeld's newest series, Zeroes, co-written by Margo Lanagan and Deborah Biancotti.

"MORE COFFEE?"

Ethan jumped. It'd been a long night. "Okay."

The waitress wasn't even listening, the coffee pot dipping toward Ethan's cup. Which was fine. The coffee was crap and he was already wired, but it gave him an excuse to keep sitting there.

He'd spent the last two hours hunched in a back booth of the Moonstruck Diner, staring out the window at the Cambria Central Bank. It was right across the street, and it opened at eight.

"Want anything else?" the waitress asked.

"I'm good. Thanks."

He drank some more coffee. Still crap.

At least the bitter java gave him a reason to seem jumpy.

Nobody would look at him and say, "Hey, that kid is real jumpy. Must have something to do with the army-green duffel bag under his feet."

Nope. Nobody would blame the bag.

He glanced around the diner. Everyone was wrapped up in their own six a.m. thoughts. Nobody was even looking at him. Okay, one girl was looking at him. But she glanced away like she'd been caught staring. So apart from that one cute girl at the front of the diner, nobody was looking at him.

Besides, this was the middle of Main Street. Nobody would come rolling in to seize Ethan and his bag and haul them both out into the dawn. Nothing bad ever happened here in Cambria, California, population half a million during a college term.

The diner was filling up with delivery guys on breaks, respectable citizens in suits, and the occasional group of clubbers winding down. All Ethan had to do was watch the bank and wait for the doors to open.

Easy. As long as the waiting didn't kill him.

"More coffee?"

"Seriously, it's been five minutes. Can you stop with the coffee?"

The waitress looked stung.

"Sorry," Ethan said. But she was already gone.

He pulled the duffel bag up and wedged it into a corner of the booth like a makeshift pillow. Which was pretty funny, given what was *in* the bag. It was the stuff *in* the bag that was keeping him awake. That, and the people looking for it.

He'd always known the voice would do this one day—get him into serious trouble. The voice didn't care about consequences. The voice didn't weigh up the pros and cons and then say, "Hey, Ethan, this is how you can get what you want." The voice wasn't sentient like that; it wasn't smart. It didn't negotiate. The voice just went for it. It lied and lied, and most of the time Ethan didn't even know where the lies came from when they poured out of his mouth. How did the voice know half that stuff?

But Ethan had always known that one day he'd pay for all those lies.

Right now he was hoping today was not that day.

THE EVENING BEFORE HAD STARTED WELL.

A date with a beautiful woman, a premed student from the north side. Ethan put on his best shirt, a pin-striped button-up his sister had bought him last year, promising it would drive girls crazy.

The premed girl was way out of his league, even with the shirt, but the voice had talked her into it. He could see her trying to understand it herself. She was at least four years older than him, way more sophisticated and much hotter. But every time she seemed uncertain, Ethan would draw her back in.

Or, rather, the voice would.

It would say just the right thing about the midnight art-house film they'd seen, or the obscure premed stuff she was into, or Ethan's plan to study at the Sorbonne one day. Whatever the hell the Sorbonne was.

But then it got late and exhausting and frankly kind of expensive. He'd used up all his cash buying movie tickets and caramel popcorn and drinks from a wine bar so divey that Indira had called it "quaint." The wine was fifteen bucks a glass. Ethan didn't even like wine.

If it'd been up to him, he would have scammed his way through the night. The voice was great at getting stuff for free. But Indira clung to Ethan's side, watching his every move like he was some exotic breed she'd never seen before. A teenage kid from the wrong side of town. She probably thought he was quaint too, in a divey way.

It was pretty clear that the voice could never convince Indira to do anything more than talk and smile and cling. A nice girl from the north side, she probably wouldn't even make out on a first date.

So the voice switched itself to mute while Ethan worked out what he wanted to do next. When he decided all he wanted was to go home, the voice sorted that out too.

He left Indira standing by her car in front of the art-house cinema. She seemed to glow, lit by the marquee lights announcing a lineup of classic films. Her long summer dress billowed in the night sea breeze. She looked confused by his sudden departure. Maybe a little hurt.

"This blows," Ethan muttered to himself. In his real voice.

He hated how sad she looked. But he didn't have the energy to turn around. It was all the fault of that stupid art-house film. Who knew it could be *that* boring? Watching it had sucked the life out of him.

As Ethan walked away, he rubbed his jaw with the palms of both hands. His muscles always felt weird after a long night of letting the voice talk for him. Like he'd been speaking a foreign language. It left a taste in his mouth too. Oily charm with notes of bullshit.

The worst part was, he had no way home. He was totally out of cash, so a cab was out of the question, and buses didn't run this late. Indira would've given him a ride, but of course the voice had spun some crap about his vintage Jaguar parked a few streets away, just to get rid of her.

The voice sucked at planning ahead. The voice just knew when Ethan wanted out.

It also liked to twist the knife sometimes. It had claimed the Jaguar was a present from his dad. Yeah, right.

Luckily, it was summer and Cambria's nightclub strip was still in full swing. There were plenty of people to hitch a ride with on Ivy Street. Ethan followed the thudding drumbeat until he reached the crowd. Light spilled from canopied doorways, and people shouted at each other, deafened by music that rebounded from the pavement and warehouse walls.

The voice could talk Ethan's way into one of the clubs. But once inside, no one would hear him over the music. He'd be just another gawky seventeen-year-old with a mousy buzz cut and too many freckles.

No, what he needed was somebody here outside.

A muddle of tribes skirted each other on Ivy. Hipsters and scene kids, crumpled coked-up suits from the stripper bar, a few raver wannabes in summer outfits showing lots of skin. They were mostly older than Ethan, which meant they mostly had cars. Somebody could be talked into giving him a lift home.

Just ahead of him, a guy exited one of the clubs from a side door. Which probably meant he was staff and sober enough to drive.

Ethan sped up.

The guy walked with a steady purpose. He had an army-green duffel bag over one shoulder. Ethan let himself drift into the guy's way until the bag slapped against him.

"Hey, watch it!" he said in his own voice.

The guy spun to face him. He was a few inches shorter than Ethan, but twice as big across the shoulders. And he had no neck. The sort of guy who could crush you with an annoyed glare. His right hand dropped into a jacket pocket, like he was ready to pull a knife.

"Whoa." Ethan backed away. "My mistake. Sorry about that."

The guy scanned Ethan. His eyes were piercing, way too blue. Almost electric. But a moment later he smiled, eased his hand out of his pocket, and gripped Ethan's shoulder. It was like being held up by a wall.

"Sorry, man," the guy said. His voice was calm and low. "Did I hit you?"

"No problem. You missed, actually," Ethan sputtered, fear beating in his chest. All he wanted was to be on the same side as this guy in his next fight. He let the voice take over. "Taylor sent me over to help you out."

That was one of the voice's specialties. Names.

The big guy paused, looking him up and down. Not smiling anymore.

"Taylor sent you?" An edge of disbelief in the low rumble of his voice. "How's a squirt like you gonna help?"

Ethan hated when this happened. The voice would get him into situations that only the voice could get him out of. Then he was stuck, listening and waiting. Letting it talk.

"Taylor said you were bad off last night. Wasn't sure you'd remember the way to his house." The voice sounded like it was making a joke, so Ethan tried to smile.

The guy stared at him another moment, then laughed. Abruptly, like that was the stupidest thing he'd ever heard. "What a dickhead. I worked off that hangover in the gym this morning. How do you know Taylor?"

"My sister's in his old army unit," Ethan heard himself say, and cringed.

Thing was, his sister really was in the army. Stuff could go really wrong when the voice told the truth. What if the guy asked for his sister's name? What would the voice say then?

But the guy relaxed, like he understood everything now. "So you're family. Taylor wants you to join the team."

Ethan nodded, because it seemed like the right thing to do. "He said I should learn from the best." The voice twisted his throat, like it was imitating someone. "'Nobody better than the Craig.'"

A low thunder of laughter spilled out of the Craig, who reached over and took Ethan's shoulder again. The weight of his hand almost buckled Ethan's knees.

"He tell you to say that? What a dickhead." He shoved Ethan, sending him stumbling a few steps backward. "Come on. Car's this way."

The Craig headed for a side street. Ethan took a breath and followed.

Hell, maybe he could still get a ride home out of this.

THE CRAIG OWNED JUST ABOUT THE CRAPPIEST car Ethan had ever seen. It was an old beat-up Ford sedan. Either it was brown or it was covered in enough dirt to make it look that way. It was hard to tell.

The Craig saw his expression and laughed that sharp, abrupt laugh again.

"Lesson one, kid: Skip the fancy cars. Too easy to spot. Don't let your ride make you an easy mark. Someone sets up on you, they'll be looking for a fancy car."

Ethan shrugged. There was a kind of paranoid logic to what the Craig was saying. Plus, his right hand had sunk into his pocket again, and Ethan still couldn't decide what was in there. A gun? A knife? Even at four a.m., it was way too hot to be wearing a jacket.

Craig noticed the direction of his gaze. "You're not carrying, are you?"

Ethan clenched his jaw, not trusting the voice. He shook his head.

"Good." Craig looked both ways up and down the street, then opened the Ford's back door and slung the duffel bag across the seats. "For now, your job is to keep your eyes open."

Ethan nodded mutely. A trickle of cold ran down his spine. He was about to get into a car with a strange man—a *really* strange man—who was armed and probably a criminal, with a duffel bag full of who-knew-what, and head for someplace unknown.

He opened his mouth to let the voice take over. It could say whatever it wanted—lie, plead, beg—as long as the Craig let Ethan walk away, back to Ivy Street, where he could charm some clueless raver into a ride home instead.

But the voice didn't say anything. Which meant there was nothing to say and no way out of this, not without raising Craig's suspicions. Ethan wasn't sure what would happen if Craig called Taylor and found out that everything he'd said was a lie. But nothing good, that was for sure.

So Ethan shut his mouth and got into the car.

Read on for an exclusive UGLIES short story.

HOW DAVID GOT HIS SCAR

The three hoverboards approached the unfamiliar city at low speed, gliding just above the rocks and dirt of the dried-out streambed. The riders knelt or crouched, wearing camo jackets and night-vision goggles. The valley below glittered with city lights and safety fireworks, but up here only slivers of starlight cut through the trees.

"Picking up some broadcast feeds now," one of the riders said into his headset mike. He was riding last, his board obediently following the others' as he stared into a handheld screen. Woven through his camo jacket were antennae that flowed out behind him like wings, their smart fibers twisting gracefully to avoid the tangling branches in the dark.

"Anything unusual?" asked the rider in the lead. Of the three, he crouched the lowest on his board, always wary and nervous this close to a new city.

"The usual blather," came Croy's voice from the back. "Fifty channels for the bubble-heads and exactly one for a city council meeting."

"Just like home," the middle rider said. "Cities are all the same."

The leader of the group only grunted at this. It was Astrix's first contact mission; she would learn.

The cities always seemed alike at first, with their spires held aloft against the law of gravity, their hide-bound leaders, their spoiled and clueless kids. But quite often the differences would surprise you, and growing up in the wild had taught David to dislike surprises.

"Hang on," Croy said. "Something funny up ahead."

David banked to a stop, the others gliding up behind him. They huddled around Croy's handheld screen, close enough to turn off their headsets and whisper.

The tendrils of antennae in Croy's jacket drifted up into the air, snaking through the tree branches, greedy for a signal. David tried not to watch them. Smart fibers were useful, but creepy, so he always let Croy do the scanning. Tech was something city kids were good at.

Croy gestured at a dozen little thumbnail images across the top of his screen, singers and fashion shows and costume dramas.

"That's everything from the city's main transmitter, the usual crap. But check these out." His finger moved to three tiny lights in the center of the screen, pulsing with gentle hieroglyphics. "They're just ahead of us, sending out low-powered pings every few seconds. Some kind of device checking in with the city network."

"Motion sensors," David whispered. "Somebody doesn't want us sneaking in."

"Really? No city's *that* paranoid." Astrix bent closer to the screen. "It's probably just some kind of tracking system, in case a hiker gets lost."

David almost laughed. "But you can *see* the buildings from here. And isn't that music I hear? Even a city kid couldn't get lost this close to home!"

Astrix and Croy both gave him a look. They'd been city kids not that long ago, of course. Pretty much everyone back in the Smoke had started out life as a city kid, except for David.

"You know what I mean," he added. "We'll go around them, just in case."

"Whatever you say, boss," Astrix said, and angled her hoverboard away.

They were at the edge of the city's metal grid, so as the minerals of the dried streambed were left behind, the hoverboards began to sputter a little, drifting toward the ground. Soon the boards had to be carried, leaving the three Smokies struggling through the branches in total darkness.

It was always tricky, approaching a new city for the first time to find rebellious uglies and teach them about the Smoke. Some authorities were totally open to the idea of letting their uglies head off into the wild to live, like it was nothing more than an outdoor education project. Some didn't encourage it but turned a blind eye, trusting that their spoiled brats would come crawling back. Most of the time, they were right.

But a few cities were like fortresses, or prisons, depending on whether you wanted in or out. They jealously guarded their citizens from outsiders, and from new and unexpected ideas. Over his years of helping runaways to find the Smoke, David had encountered wild animals, forest fires, and bio-engineered poisonous plants. But nothing was more dangerous than a city afraid of change.

Astrix and Croy had escaped from a very paranoid and controlling city only months ago, but even their home wasn't protected by motion sensors. David looked into the valley again. For whoever was in charge down there, even brain-addling surgery wasn't enough control. They needed electronic surveillance as well.

"More sensors ahead, strung out in a line at the edge of the grid," Croy said after ten minutes' struggle through the trees. "Looks like they've got the whole city ringed."

"Okay." David turned back toward the streambed. "If we can't go around, we have to go through them. Either of you ever cloned a sensor before?"

The other two both stared at him, and he smiled. It was always fun to teach new Smokies the tricks of the trade.

David let Astrix take the lead. She'd been a competitive hoverboarder back in her home city, and a dancer as well. She could move very gracefully when she wanted to.

She and David were crawling toward the nearest motion sensor to the streambed, taking their time. They froze whenever the air grew still, only moving when the leaves around them were dancing in the wind, hopefully distracting the sensors.

The descent into the valley was steep here, the stones loose underfoot. David stayed ready to call for their boards if either of them slipped, or if the motion sensors made even half a squeak.

City tech was unpredictable. Sometimes it was easy to fool, built so that tricky uglies could discover ways around it. But other times it turned out to be deadly serious, especially here on the borders of a city like this, so clearly afraid of intruders.

"Those sensors still quiet?" David asked during a long pause in their descent.

Staring into his screen twenty meters behind them, Croy muttered, "Like I wouldn't *tell* you?"

Astrix's soft laughter came through David's headset. "Don't worry, nature boy. I was sneaking out of my dorm room back when you were learning how to start a campfire. I got this."

David rolled his eyes. Whenever he took them on contact missions, city kids would spout dialog from old flat-screen thrillers that he'd never seen. It was best to just ignore them.

But he couldn't resist saying, "Just remember, Astrix, snakes are cold-blooded, so they're invisible in these thermal goggles."

"Cute," she said.

The wind picked up, the leaf shadows fluttering around him, and David crawled forward again.

Something loose shifted beneath his left elbow, and a rain of pebbles tumbled down, skittering and dancing as they went. David swore. This part of the streambed was steep enough that it would bloom into a waterfall later in spring, but now the dirt was dry and crumbly. He felt the ground slowly shifting under him and tried to brace himself. . . .

But something big was giving way.

David began to slide forward, for a moment riding the crumbling chunk of ground beneath him. Then he was tumbling, and he curled himself into a ball, dirt spraying against his goggles, rocks jabbing at his spine and sides. The shoulder of his jacket hung on something, and he was yanked to a skidding halt.

"You're welcome," Astrix said.

David opened his eyes. She was grinning down at him, her gloved hand grasping him by the shoulder. Beneath him was a torn packet of SpagBol. His favorite flavor of camping rations spilled out across the rocks.

But an even worse sight was the motion sensor ten meters ahead, camo-brown and spiky and hovering a few meters in the air, like a pinecone halfway fallen from a tree. There was no way it hadn't spotted his humiliating tumble.

"We have to get out of here!" He reached for his crash bracelet to call the hoverboards.

"Wait!" came Croy's harsh whisper in his headset.

David and Astrix froze, staring at the motion sensor. It didn't *seem* to be doing anything, but surely it was signaling the city's wardens or Special Circumstances, or whatever they called the enforcers here.

"Huh," Croy said an endless moment later. "Not a peep."

"My fingers are . . . unhappy," Astrix said through gritted teeth. Her hand was still wrapped around the shoulder of his jacket.

David moved carefully, digging his boots into the crumbly ground beneath him, reaching for a branch to his right. "Okay, Trix. Let go."

She did, and David felt his weight settle.

"Ow." She wriggled her fingers.

"Stay still," he warned.

"Are you kidding? That thing is obviously busted."

David stared at the hovering sensor. Maybe it was defective, or maybe it was being very clever, sending some sort of signal that Croy's equipment couldn't detect, like a dog whistle.

"We stick to the plan," he said. "We grab it, clone it, and leave a fake one sending out the same signals."

"Why bother," Astrix said, "when we can just crawl past?"

"Because when we come back, we might be in too big a hurry to crawl. And this leaves a permanent hole in their perimeter. Stick to the plan."

She let out a sigh. "Whatever you say, boss."

Half an hour later they were back on their boards and riding down into the valley, the cloned sensor in place behind them, dutifully updating the network every few seconds. The real one was in David's backpack, disabled. He could take a proper look at it back at the Smoke to figure out why it hadn't spotted him.

About a kilometer below the ring of sensors was a large open field. It was clear of trees, and the ground was level in a way that suggested earth-moving machines. The cities always professed to love nature, but the natural world was never quite good enough for them to leave alone.

The field was strewn with plastic cups and other rubbish, and the grass was beaten down. There'd been a party here not long ago. David had even heard the music from above.

He surveyed the wreckage from his board, sighing. Dealing with the sensors had put the Smokies behind schedule, and it was getting close to dawn. Probably too late for even the trickiest uglies to be out making mischief. And any party this big was probably for pretties only. Anyone who'd had the surgery wouldn't dream of leaving their luxurious life to live in the Smoke.

But now that the ring of sensors was breached, the three Smokes could always sneak back again tomorrow night.

Then David saw a flicker of heat in his goggles, two forms shimmering in the trees at the edge of the field. They seemed to be hiding, which was a good sign. Pretties never hid. Uglies often did.

David signaled to Astrix and Croy to wait, then angled his board toward the hidden figures, skimming just above the grass. As he drifted to a halt, he pulled off the night-vision goggles, revealing his unprettified features.

"Hello?" he called into the trees. After three years of making contact with tricky uglies, this was still the best greeting he'd come up with. It seemed to work better than *I'm here to start a rebellion. Want to run away from everything you've ever known?*

No answer came at first, but after a moment a short, slight girl stepped from the shadow into starlight.

"Hello, yourself," she said.

David smiled. It was dark, but with her lopsided grin and the wary, intelligent look in her eyes, this girl definitely hadn't had the pretty operation.

"My name's David."

She frowned. David was an old-fashioned Rusty name from centuries back, the perfect way to alienate city kids. Nice work, parents.

"Zada." She turned toward the trees. "And this is my scaredy-cat friend Ardy."

A tall, reedy boy stepped from the shadows, looking sheepish.

"Sorry," Ardy said. "Thought you were a warden."

"We were recording the party," Zada explained. "For this civics project we're doing, about exclusionary practices."

"Sounds interesting," David said, smiling. Any uglies willing to spy on a pretties-only party were prime candidates for the Smoke.

"Nice hoverboard," Ardy said.

"It's built for cross-country," David explained as he stepped off. "Stronger lifters, recharging flaps." Talking about the board was sometimes the most natural way to get a conversation about the wild started.

"Where the hell are you from?" Zada asked.

Of course, sometimes the direct route was easiest.

"I'm from the Smoke," David said. "Have you heard of it?"

Zada's mouth fell halfway open. Clearly she'd heard rumors. Most tricky uglies had.

Her eyes were scanning David now—his handmade leather

jacket and boots, the survival-hardened tech of his goggles and hoverboard. All those rich, serious textures that the city's holes in the wall would never create.

She took another step closer and reached out to him. "Can I just check something?"

"Um, sure?" David said.

Zada took his hand in hers, staring down at his calluses and the dirt ground into the whorls of his palm. City kids' hands were always so clean and soft, as if they'd never touched raw earth in their lives. Zada's hair might be tangled and she might look a little tired, like someone who'd been spying on a party all night, but David and the others had been camping for two weeks straight, bathing sparingly in freezing streams. There was no comparison.

She looked up and caught David watching her, but she didn't flinch.

"So the Smoke is real," she said.

"Realer than anything you've ever seen." He pulled his hand from hers and started his standard speech. "You don't have to get the operation. You don't have to look like everyone else and think like everyone else. There's a place you can live in the wild, following your own rules. It isn't easy, but it's real."

"Whoa," Ardy said. "I thought Leland was just making that stuff up!"

David turned to him. "Who's Leland?"

"Our civics teacher," Zada broke in. "He's always talking about how any system as ordered as the pretty regime creates revolutionary opposition. The Smoke is a typical example."

David blinked. "Um . . . they actually call it the 'pretty regime' here?"

"Yeah, but only in civics class," Zada said. "Hey, it would be awesome if we could do a project on you guys! Can we do an interview?"

David stared at the two kids in front of him, so full of energy and enthusiasm, so ready to question authority—as long as they got a good grade for it.

It made sense in a way. Some cities, like Diego, controlled rebellion by turning it into fashion, allowing their citizens to get weird surgeries or shocking colors of hair and skin. In other places, uglies were allowed to play all the tricks they wanted, but ultimately the most talented were turned into enforcers with bribes or brain surgery. In this city, apparently, the authorities crushed revolutions before they started, by turning them into homework.

"Sure, we could do an interview," David said. "Let's say we meet back here tonight."

"Fantastic!" Zada said.

"But I've got two conditions. The first is, if any of your classmates—or friends—want to come, you have to bring them along."

Ardy frowned. "But how are we supposed to get extra credit if everyone else gets to meet you?"

"This isn't about getting extra credit," David said. "It's about spreading the word that the Smoke is real. Bring at least five more uglies with you tonight, or the interview's off. Understand?"

"Understood," Zada grumbled.

"The second condition is, you can't tell your civics teacher about us until *after* your project is done. In fact, don't tell anyone who's had the surgery that you met us."

"Duh," Zada said.

"Anyway," Ardy added, "it'll be way better as a surprise project!"

David sighed. Every group of city kids had their own motivations for wanting to come to the Smoke, he supposed. Whether it was rebellion, a hunger for adventure, or just plain boredom didn't really matter. The main thing was that they could imagine a future other than surgery, perfect beauty, and lifelong compliance.

This was a start, at least.

As dawn began to break, the three Smokies headed back up into the mountains. The sky was turning slowly pink, and the scudding clouds were high and thin. No rain anytime soon.

"Isn't that kind of weird?" Astrix was saying. "Letting their uglies study us, but keeping them pinned in with all those motion sensors?"

David only shrugged, dipping his board around a tree. Zada and Ardy's first round of questions had worn him out, and the crazy logic of city authorities was always exhausting. It was as if the cities *knew* that the pretty regime couldn't last forever, and were just improvising until it fell apart.

"Maybe they don't stop runaways from leaving," Croy said, "but they want to keep a close eye on them. Those sensors could shoot out a tracker of some kind as you walk past."

"Hell, maybe it's someone's civics project!" Astrix added, and the two of them had a good laugh.

David ignored them and pulled on his night-vision goggles again. Even with dawn breaking, it was dark here beneath the canopy of trees, and they were getting close to the sensors again. They had to fly past the sensor they'd cloned, careful not to set off the ones on either—

What the hell was that?

A huge form loomed just ahead, pulsing in David's thermal vision. Something alive but insulated with a layer of fat, the colors only slightly hotter than the surrounding landscape.

Strangely, it was waiting at the exact spot where he'd fallen on the way in.

He held up his hand for a halt. "Guys . . ."

Suddenly the huge form turned, and a distinct face was staring at David. Sharp eyes and a long snout, bright with body heat.

A rumbling growl reached David's ears.

"Straight up! Straight up! Straight up!" he cried, tipping the nose of his board back as hard as he could.

As it rose, he turned to see Astrix and Croy looking up at him with dumb expressions.

"Now!" David tried to yell, but something struck him with a hard blow to the face, cracking his forehead. The crunch of a tree branch snapping filled his ears, along with the sound of leaves showering down around him.

He opened his eyes, and the world was a riot of random colors and glittering stars. His goggles were knocked askew.

As he pulled them off, a roar came from beneath him, sending thunder through his bones.

The huge sound broke the spell on Astrix and Croy, and the two of them shot up into the air on their boards. A quarter-ton of teeth and claws and fur went charging through the spot where they'd been hovering, another roar making the trees around David shimmer.

"Holy crap!" Astrix cried, looking at the ground in astonishment. "What is that thing?"

"Grizzly bear," David managed to say. He sank to his knees, gripping the hoverboard with both hands. He was dizzy, and blood was running into his eyes. If he fell off now, crash bracelets wouldn't save him from being eaten.

The three of them stared down at the bear from five meters up, as high as the hoverboards would take them here, at the city's edge. The bear stared back at them, pacing and snarling, even testing a couple of the nearby trees for climbing, but they were too young to hold its weight. Eventually, the grizzly ambled back to where David had first seen it—the spot he'd fallen on the way in—and began snarfling in the dirt.

Of course.

"My SpagBol," he said, and the other two just stared at him.

David shook his head, too light-headed to continue. Here in the final throes of winter, the hungry bear had smelled the spilled food and headed down into the valley.

"Oops," Croy said, apparently having the same thought at the same time.

Astrix spun in the air to face him. "What?"

"The motion sensors," Croy said. "They weren't about us at all. Or runaways, either. That's why they didn't notice David's little tumble."

"They were set for bear," David said. "Calibrated to ignore anything smaller than a grizzly. We could've walked right past them."

"You mean, like that bear is doing now?" Astrix asked.

True enough, the grizzly was descending down the dried streambed and into the valley, ignoring the cloned motion sensor. No doubt he could smell the leftovers from the party the night before.

"Yep," Croy said. "And by pulling that sensor out of the ring and replacing it with a fake, we let him in."

"Or her," Astrix said.

David pulled the real motion sensor from his pack. "Put this one back in place, Croy. I'll go set off the next one over so the wardens come and deal with this bear."

"I'll do it, boss. You aren't going anywhere." Astrix pointed at his jacket, and David looked down. He was covered in blood that glistened dully in the dawn light.

"Oh. Right," he said. "Tree branch."

An hour later they were back at their base camp high in the mountains. The sun was fully up, and now that the adrenaline of the bear attack had worn off, David's head was throbbing. The tree branch had cracked the goggles against his eyebrow, splitting the skin.

"In a way, I'm almost sorry those were bear sensors," Astrix was saying. "That would have been so ingenious! A city teaching their kids about rebellion and freedom, and then using surveillance tech to make sure they never acted on it."

"Sounds like a Rusty idea," Croy said.

"Ouch," David said. His fingers had slipped a little.

Astrix looked at him in horror. "Speaking of Rusty ideas, I still can't believe you're *sewing your face back together.*"

"It's pre-Rusty, actually," David said. He had decided on putting stitches in where the goggles had cut his eyebrow. It was an ancient technique for closing wounds, one that his father had shown him in case he was ever stuck without medspray.

The needle and thread had come from David's kit for repairing his jacket and boots, and Croy's handheld screen had a front camera, so it was a pretty decent mirror. With the sun up, there was plenty of light.

David had used just enough medspray to kill the pain and prevent infection, but not enough to close the wound. But even with the nerves switched off, it was pretty weird sticking a needle into his own face.

But he wanted a record of this accident.

In one sense, the cut through his eyebrow had been caused by the tree branch, but that would make a pretty boring story. He could also blame it on a hasty ascent on a hoverboard, one of the most modern and sophisticated pieces of tech around. But really, it was something much more basic and natural that had caused this scar—the vital hunger of a beast, the primal desire of a human being to not be eaten.

Stitches weren't as easy as slathering on more medspray, but his father had said they always left a better scar. So David had decided that old-fashioned was the way to go.

This was a story he would want to tell someday.

ABOUT THE AUTHOR

Scott Westerfeld is the author of the worldwide bestselling Uglies series, and the Leviathan series, the first book of which was the winner of the 2010 Locus Award for Best Young Adult Fiction. His other novels include the *New York Times* bestseller *Afterworlds, The Last Days*, *Peeps*, *So Yesterday*, and the Midnighters trilogy. Visit him at ScottWesterfeld.com or follow him on Twitter at @ScottWesterfeld.